TURN OF THE

KURT ANDERSEN

TURN

RANDOM HOUSE · NEW YORK

TURN OF THE
CEN

Copyright © 1999 by Kurt Andersen

All rights reserved under International and Pan-American Copyright Conventions. Published in the United States by Random House, Inc., New York, and simultaneously in Canada by Random House of Canada Limited, Toronto.

Random House and colophon are registered trademarks of Random House, Inc.

Library of Congress Cataloging-in-Publication Data

Andersen, Kurt
    Turn of the century: a novel / Kurt Andersen.
       p.   cm.
    ISBN 0-375-50008-1
    I. Title.
  PS3551.N34554T87   1999
  813'.54—dc21   99-18954

Random House website address: www.atrandom.com
Printed in the United States of America on acid-free paper

9 8 7 6 5 4 3 2

First Edition

For Anne Kreamer

TURN OF THE

PART ONE

February

March

1

He has just left an early breakfast meeting—very early—with three men he's never met before. He's never heard of the men, in fact, and he planned to blow off breakfast until his partner told him he should go, because the men are important and potentially useful. He trusts his partner, who used to work for their agency. They are agents, all three of the men at breakfast, but agents who made it very clear that they prefer never to be called agents. He is already confusing and forgetting their names, even though the men's main purpose in coming to town, they strongly suggested, was to meet him and tell him they would love to be in business with him. That's the phrase these people always use: "We would love to be in business with you," said in a breathy, solemn, confidential way that makes it sound profound and salacious. He is walking up the Avenue of the Americas, just south of Forty-seventh Street, now thinking of almost nothing but the morning sunlight pouring over from the right, making the line of proud, gray, dumb, boxy giants on the left—Smith Barney, Time-Life, McGraw-Hill, News Corporation—prettier than they deserve to be.

A pair of mounted police walking past him, about to make the turn onto Forty-seventh Street, snags his attention for an instant, the very instant a signal reaches the tiny device wedged in his left inside jacket pocket. It is forty-two minutes and forty seconds past eight on the twenty-eighth of February.

Between his right thumb and forefinger he grips a huge paper coffee cup, and, with the other three fingers, the handle of his briefcase. As the device's programmed sequence proceeds, there is no noise, not even a click, only a tiny, continuous, hysterical vibration. In the first quarter second, the muscles in his chest tense and his left nipple goes erect. He takes a short, sharp, surprised breath and, without thinking, flings the coffee toward the gutter, then grabs at his left pocket with his right hand. But already the first instant of dumb panic has congealed to dread—*two seconds*—as he claws to find the device, to punch the button, to shut the thing down before the sound—*three seconds . . . four seconds*—before it is too late.

It is too late.

"Hey, *man,*" says the young man kneeling and looking up at George Mactier. His eyebrows, George sees, are sculpted into what look like Morse code dots and dashes, each eyebrow a different letter. "What the *fuck* you, man, you fucking clumsy *dick,* man! Shit."

The messenger's electronic signature-slate clipboard and his Day-Glo green nylon satchel of envelopes are drenched now in steaming ultra-venti latte, skim milk, extra shot of espresso. His helmet—a glossy magenta with built-in radio mouthpiece, like a fighter pilot's—has been knocked off the handlebars and into the street by George's briefcase. The helmet is now skittering up Sixth like a pinball between the tires of an accelerating Harlem-bound M5—one of the dozen new, clear, vodka-bottle-shaped Absolut Transit buses the city has been given for Christmas. The two men each survey the wreckage. If only the restaurant's espresso machine hadn't been broken, George knows, he wouldn't have stopped at Starbucks; if the espresso machine at the Millennium hadn't been broken and he hadn't stopped at Starbucks, this poor groovy schmo wouldn't despise him, and the chasm between the races and the classes and the generations wouldn't now gape a nanometer wider. Perhaps it was the fluttering of a satyrid's wings in Bhutan that had roiled into a breeze in the South China Sea that blew across the Pacific and became a thunderstorm last week in Oakland, and that delayed the shipment of an espresso-machine valve to the Millennium.

"Maybe the helmet, maybe you can—"

"Maybe I can *what,* man? My boss is gonna motherfucking criticize my ass so bad, man," the messenger says, looking up at George. "You know that? He's *Soviet,* man!"

"I'm really—oh, jeez, look at your pants, too. I'm *sorry.*" George leans in to help him up, but then remembers the kid hasn't been knocked down. He was kneeling when George flung the coffee, fiddling with his bike, and so instead, George just quickly touches his sweaty green-and-pink-spandexed shoulder and says again, "Sorry."

"The thing was brand-*new,* like three *hundred* dollars, I think. *Man.*" They stare together across the street at the bashed, cracked pink helmet still wobbling crazily. (Stenciled on its side in big teal letters is a phrase George reads as !MOM !69. A rap group? A brand of heroin? A lifestyle choice?)

"The coffee cup sort of like . . . *collapsed.*" Sort of.

The silent, five-second-long vibrating alert on the tiny device in George's pocket has given way to the up-and-down *do-re-mi-fa-mi-re-do* chromatic tweet of the audible alert. His wife, Lizzie, has said it sounds like reveille for pixies, and his stepdaughter, Sarah, has asked him if he cares if it makes strangers think he is gay. But George has stuck with the little tune rather than any standard beeeeeep choice, because it subverts the display of self-importance, he hopes, of getting a cell-phone call on the sidewalk, in an elevator, at a restaurant table. It has finally become possible, for about three years now, to carry on a phone conversation walking down the street and not look like an asshole. It's still not possible in a restaurant, he and Lizzie agree. Yet is consistently *looking* like an asshole really any different from *being* an asshole? This they are less sure about.

"My phone," George says to the messenger with a lame, bashful smile. He nods toward the silly electronic noise *deedle-de-deeing* from his chest and starts to move away. "Sorry." Shrug, step. "Sorry." Five paces later, crucially beyond the latte blast radius, freed again to be just another pedestrian, George puts his briefcase on the sidewalk and finally pulls out the phone.

"Hello?"

"George? Honey—"

"Yeah?" He hears nothing. "Lizzie?" Nothing. "Hello?" He punches END. He will wait for her to call back. Holding the phone a foot from his face, he leans against the sandstone of Rockefeller Center, the *real* Rockefeller Center, staring distractedly through the mists of his own winter breath at new Rockefeller Center, the stolid late-fifties and early-sixties addendum across the avenue. The sunlight has diffused now. But the buildings still look strangely, unaccountably handsome. Have they been steam-cleaned? Is it the new outdoor sculpture (*Torqued Mousetrap with Logo,* three blocks long, by Richard Serra) that Disney installed on the sidewalk? Or is it because Lizzie announced this morning as he said goodbye and she spat out toothpaste that she is desperate for him to fuck her? Where has his contempt gone? Then he realizes: the skyscrapers that looked atrocious in 1980 and 1990 now, in 2000, look quaint, elegant, swingy. He isn't aware of having revised his opinion; his opinion has been changed for him, updated automatically, gradually, by sensibility osmosis, leeching from glossy magazines and newspaper style sections into George's brain. First Frank Sinatra, cocktails, Palm Springs, rayon garments, plastic furniture, and all kinds of Cold War bibelots were resuscitated, even the words *VIP* and *chick*—and now, *as of this morning,* these buildings, which George has spent a few seconds every week of his adulthood loathing actively, are looking kind of cool. He doesn't know whether to feel pathetic or liberated by the insight.

The phone jiggles.

"Yeeeesss?" he says joshingly.

"Oh, George."

"What is it?"

"Your mother died last night."

"Ohhhhh . . ." He feels like he's been shot in the face at close range. With blanks, but it's still loud and sickening. "Oh, Christ."

"I'm so sorry, darling."

"How? I mean . . ."

"Honey?"

"She told me a couple of weeks ago her doctor said she probably has years."

"It wasn't the cancer. She was in a car accident, honey. She was driving home on the interstate from her line-dancing class, and she slowed way down for some animal, a weasel, and a giant semi rammed into her."

"Which car?"

"Which car? The Yugo."

"Christ."

"Your sister says she, you know, she didn't—it all happened so fast, she died instantly."

George watches the messenger he victimized pedal west toward Times Square. With the helmet now right side up, he sees that the odd legend, on the satchel as well as the helmet, isn't !MOM !69, but GO! NOW! It's the name of a messenger service; the same company operates the car service Lizzie uses at work.

"So," Lizzie says, "I'll go home and pack."

"You don't have to. We can fly out in the morning."

"Why not tonight?"

"We're presenting the shows to Mose at six-thirty, which means I'm out of here at seven. At the earliest. This is *the* meeting, Lizzie. I guess we could try to reschedule, but Emily's flying in from L.A. for it, and she needs to be in Washington at some Kennedy Center Al Gore thing tomorrow." He knows he's babbling. "But, I guess, if we could maybe get in to Mose tomorrow . . . No, shit, tomorrow is, he's—Mose and the rest of them are going—are in, uh, Washington State? . . . Maybe Vancouver. Someplace out there, I'm not sure, for something." He coughs; so lame. "I think I really ought to be here this afternoon."

His mother was killed hours earlier; he and his partner are to have an audience with the chairman of the network to pitch two new shows; now he's concealing a business secret probably not worth concealing from his wife, and doing it clumsily. He isn't even sure what he's dissembling about. He's only heard snippets, glancing references, roundabout allusions, all equally plausible and implausible, all equally reliable and unreliable. Asian video-game programming? An agreement to earmark MBC's extra digital channels for data transmission in return for putting the network's two-A.M.-to-five-A.M. home-shopping show *Booty!* on Microsoft's WebTV? Some grander plot to ally with Microsoft against Intel, or to make life a little unpleasant for NBC vis-à-vis MSNBC? Computers and the internet, so radiant with revolutionary promise and terror, change everyone's business strategy every other month, so the gossip changes every week to keep up. All he knows definitely is that he shouldn't be frank with Lizzie. The strands of anxiety are too much, each exacerbating the other and making George feel guilty and stupid.

Lizzie saves him. "We'll go to St. Paul in the morning. Sarah's got a sleepover at our house with Penelope tonight, anyway, to work on their video. We can go tomorrow."

"Did you tell the kids?"

She doesn't answer.

"Lizzie, do the kids know about my mom?"

The connection is lost. Taking full advantage of the convenience of the wired era, George finds, can be very difficult.

He dials home, using his thumb, and the voice mail picks up ("Hello—we're not here," his own voice says to him, which always gives him the willies), then calls her office ("This is the office of Elizabeth Zimbalist at Fine Technologies," the recording of Lizzie's assistant Alexi says. "Please leave—"), and finally the phone in the Land Cruiser, which generates a sort of Disney World PA-system announcer: "Welcome to AT&T Wireless Services. The cellular customer you have called is unavailable, or has traveled outside the coverage area." George specifically hates this passive-aggressive record-o-man. The prissy, vague excuse—"unavailable"?—always strikes him as a prevarication meant to keep him from speaking to Lizzie, or his colleagues, or other cellular customers. (Nothing like America Online's digital butler, with his fake-enthusiastic utopian-zombie voice. George continues to find "You've got mail!" entertaining enough, even ten thousand repetitions later, so that he didn't finally deactivate it until around the time the movie came out and he read that the AOL man, whose first name is Elwood, has his own web site.)

"U.S. West!" a female electronic voice says over the opening chords to the overture from John Williams's new *U.S. West Symphony,* "Directory assistance . . . for which community in the . . . 6-5-1 . . . area code?"

"St. Paul," George says.

"Which customer listing?" the robot operator asks.

"Edith Hope Mactier." He figures his sister is at his mother's house. He can never recall his mother's new phone number, which she changed a few years ago to dodge telemarketers; from now on, he won't have to try to remember it.

"One moment," the robot operator replies.

John Williams, "Fanfare for the New Economy," the same four chords, once again. "Northwest Airlines flies . . . *five* . . . convenient, comfortable nonstops to the Twin Cities from . . . *New York/Newark* . . . every day! The number you requested . . . can be automatically dialed by pressing the star or dollar keys, or by saying the word *please*."

Dollar key? The star key on his cell phone has not worked for a year. George, walking past Radio City, says, *"Please."*

His sister answers.

"We'll do the modified fondue option," she is saying, "but we do *not* need *Smithfield* ham," and then, into the phone, "Hello?"

"Alice? Hi, it's me."

"Hello, George."

He sighs. "You okay?"

"Yeah," she says, sniffling violently. "When are you coming?"

"Tomorrow."

"Tomorrow, huh."

"Sarah has to finish some important school project tonight."

His sister doesn't reply.

"I mean," George continues, filling the space, not quite lying, not quite being honest, "I guess I could fly out with Max tonight and then she and Lizzie and Louisa could come tomorrow."

Still no response.

"Tomorrow, I—we'll all be there before lunch. Alice?"

The connection is lost. Maybe, he thinks as he lurches into the revolving door of the tower on Fifty-seventh Street, he really ought to get a new phone, a smaller, digital one. This phone cost a fortune when he had ABC News pay for it four years ago; the same model now sells for twenty-nine dollars. Did the thing really work better in 1996, he wonders, or did it just feel more reliable and powerful when it was selling for seven hundred dollars? It was the smallest one available back then, but now it seems as clunky and enormous as an eight-track tape cartridge. On the other hand, George, six foot three and one-ninety, feels out of scale using the new three-inch-long, 1.9-ounce models, like he's handling a piece of fragile dollhouse furniture or someone else's newborn.

Which leads George to an idea for *NARCS*, a B-story for an episode this spring: the new deputy commissioner wants the detectives to start using tiny pocket-size computers, a vice-cop intranet, and Jennie has to get the old guys cyberready . . . No, he thinks, no . . . make Jennie *resist* the computers as trendy bullshit.

"Hello, *NARCS*." Daisy Moore, the twenty-six-year-old English receptionist, looks up, punches a button—not a button, really, but a picture of a button printed on the flat plastic plane of her black telephone console—and says, parodying deference, "Good morning, Mr. Mactier, sir," taps the little picture of a button again and says into her headset, "Hello, *NARCS*." Being black as well as English, Daisy said to George when she was interviewing for the job, she would give him two for the price of one—convenient not only in the routine way that black receptionists are convenient in America, but also in pandering to Americans' Anglophilia. Her second week, in a conversation with Daisy about her family, George used the term African-American. "Crikey, George!" she had said, "I'm *English!*"

George loves coming to work, the arrival and the settling in, the wakeful, hopeful, testing one-two-three-four sameness of that first hour. Each morning he all but marches through the reception area and down the corridor that bisects the open space, his hair still wet, his eleven-year-old Armani overcoat unbuttoned and flapping, and makes the ritual heartfelt exchanges of hellos with Daisy, with the story editors, Paul and Phoebe, with Jerry the line producer and Gordon the director, with the odd writer or production designer, with Iris Randall, his assistant. He likes the sight of Iris making the fresh pots of freshly ground, freshly roasted coffee, and of his in-baskets filling tidily with fresh Nielsen packets, fresh *Daily Varietys* and *Hollywood Reporters,* fresh network memos, fresh drafts of scripts. He gets a little high on the sense of readiness, even if that readiness is almost always also the imminence of frenzy, of third-act scenes that weren't ever fresh and aren't working now, of MBC executives quibbling knowingly and meaninglessly about "beats" and "arcs" and "laying pipe" in scripts they haven't read, of sulky guest stars, incremental ticks in the ratings, negotiations with the network standards-and-practices woman (she didn't want a character's seven-year-old son to call him a bung-hole, and she didn't want the star to refer to Pat Robertson as "a born-again Nazi" or to a colleague as "white trash"), of leased camera cranes that won't swivel or a fake-bullet squib that burns an actor, of do-or-die presentations to the chairman. ("Do *and* die," as Emily Kalman, his L.A. partner, says at every opportunity about every important task.) The beginning of the workday, from the moment he steps into the lobby until the ten A.M. phone call with Emily, is a consistently fine, bright swath of life: hopeful, purposeful, organized. George takes pleasure in the anticipation of familiar problems. All problems are either soluble, in which case he promptly solves them, or else insoluble, which is rare, and these he ignores.

As he checks his e-mail, he realizes that his mother's death has completely slipped his mind.

He has never assigned his sister a programmed speed-dial number on his office phone, so he has to punch in nine for an outside line, zero, all eleven digits of her phone number, and then the fourteen digits of his calling-card number, since it's a personal call. (He has become scrupulous about that kind of fiscal niggle, almost obsessively so. Since he is now making $16,575 a week—an astonishing figure that occurs to him often, daily—he can afford it.) Twenty-seven digits, all from memory! Given the proliferation of number-dialing automation and number-dialing assistants in his life, it seems to George a sweet, old-fashioned task, like subway riding, that he seldom performs anymore.

When her machine picks up, he remembers that he just spoke to Alice at their mother's house. He has only a few seconds to decide whether to hang up; to leave a message admitting he dialed the wrong number—which Alice might attribute to grief-stricken insensibility or (more likely) heartlessness—or to leave a message pretending that it's earlier in the day and that he hasn't, in fact, spoken to her already. But what if her phone machine registers the times of incoming calls?

At the beep, he finesses a not-quite-lie that straddles options two and three.

"Hi, Alice, it's George. You're over at Mom's? I'll try there. If I don't get you this morning, we'll see you tomorrow around lunchtime. Okay. Bye."

Iris has entered, shiny brass watering can in hand, to water the huge flowering plants that don't annoy him quite enough to make her remove them.

"You know the author Dr. John Gray? *Guys Are from Mars . . .* Men . . . whatever? Last night in my book group we discussed his new one, *Children Are from Pluto.* You and Lizzie would *love* it, and there was this new woman there I kind of know from Harold Mose's office— You don't care. I'm droning, sorry, let me spritz your orchids, bye."

"My mom died last night, Iris."

"What?"

"In a car accident."

"Oh, *George!* Oh, my *God.*"

"Yeah, it's pretty . . . shocking. Lizzie is going to be really upset."

"Of *course.* That is *terrible.* Oh, my *God.* . . ."

"We need to fly to St. Paul for the funeral—"

"Whatever I can do—"

"—so we'll need reservations for tomorrow morning for the two of us and all three kids. Nonstop. To Minneapolis."

A pause. *"Business class* for the *baby?"*

"She's six, Iris. That's a little large for laps." The price sensitivity mooted by earning $16,575 a week sometimes needs to be supplied artificially by Iris or Lizzie. Sometimes, coming from Iris, there's more point of view than necessary.

"George, I am *so* sorry, how old *was* she? I *loved* your mom. May she rest in peace."

"Uh . . ." This year, 2000, minus 1918 equals eighty-two, but Armistice Day is months away. "Eight-one. She's eighty-one. Was."

Iris starts to cry, and leaves her extremely shiny watering can on his desk, dripping onto the tiger maple, as she rushes out.

Almost immediately, she is back, now wearing a black sweater and sunglasses. "George," she says, holding back sobs, "I know it's only nine, but pick up for your ten o'clock."

"Hiya, Emmy."

"Hi, George, it's Becky. I have Emily for you. Go ahead, Emily, it's George."

"Morning." She's on a speakerphone.

"Emily, the next time I get the assistant when it's supposed to be you, I hang up. And if you stay on the speakerphone, I'm hanging up right now." He's kidding, sort of, and she knows it, sort of. "And why aren't you on the plane?"

"Tranh's doing me. I'm coming—*ahh!*—as soon as I finish here."

"Emily, I'm not sure I want to have a serious business discussion with one of us naked and greasy."

"So: nasty numbers." She means the instant overnight ratings, derived every night from a sample of TV viewers in big cities. "The nationals'll drop." One of the reasons George enjoys being in business with Emily (in addition to the fact that she's an experienced showrunner, and has actually created and produced her own network entertainment series—*Girlie,* a 1996 Fox show about a hooker turned feminist lawyer) is her extreme economy of speech. Except when she gets excited, she speaks as though she's being charged by the word, double for verbs.

"Yeah," he says, "the numbers are not what one would hope for." Since *NARCS* went on the air in October, five months ago, its average rating has been 7.2, and its average share 14—which means, as every American knows, that the show is watched in about 7 million households, which, at ten o'clock on Saturday nights, amounts to 14 percent of the houses in which TVs are on. This past Saturday night the rating was 7 and the share 12, down .4 and 2 respectively, from last week's rating and share. George and Emily vowed, the day the *NARCS* pilot was picked up by Mose for thirteen episodes the previous May, never to obsess over ratings, certainly not the weekly overnights. But of course they can't help themselves. And their success has made them stew more.

"*Dharma Minus Greg* only got a six, nine," George says hopefully. "And we were up against the Rosie O'Donnell special with Tom Cruise, and all the septuplets and octuplets on NBC, and the big NBA game, at least in the West—"

"And Ken Burns's show about Des Moines in the fifties was on PBS. Stop. No excuses."

"Do we think doing 'The Real Deal' so early on was a strategic mistake? You know, maybe we raised the bar too high too soon."

"No. We got a *fourteen,* George. Ted Koppel said it transformed the face of television."

"It wasn't praise."

"It wasn't not. But you do have to top it for May sweeps."

"*Emily,*" he says, mock sternly, fondly, as he might say "*Max*" to his son after a loud fart at the dinner table.

Ordinarily, each forty-four-minute-long episode of *NARCS* is filmed and edited a few weeks before it airs. Eight weeks ago, on the first night of the year (and of the decade, the century, the millennium), they broadcast an episode of *NARCS* called "The Real Deal" live, from four locations in Queens, the Bronx, and Manhattan, and on three sets on their soundstage. Doing a dramatic show live is not an original stunt, but it is still rare, and none had ever been so . . . *ambitious* is the word George and Emily used in interviews. The episode's B-story was its unannounced climax, an actual bust of an actual Ecstasy dealer on Ludlow Street who had been celebrating the New Year for twenty-four hours straight. Actual New York police detectives made the arrest, but the *NARCS* stars were in the shots with them, physically handling and delivering scripted lines to the bewildered suspect, who was in handcuffs and bleeding from a small, telegenic cut on his forehead. The dealer's actual girlfriend, a pale, very pretty young blonde wearing only underwear and an unbuttoned leather coat, stood sobbing in the doorway; one camera was isolated on her during nearly the whole arrest, and the director, with George's encouragement from inside the motor-home control room on Houston Street, had cut to her repeatedly, including a long fade-out to the final commercial break.

It was extremely cool television. That's really all George was trying for. Didn't the fact that they wrote the sensational cinema verité scene as the finale of the B-story, not even of the main story line, demonstrate their restraint? Editorial writers and legal scholars were unanimously appalled. Nearly everyone else was fascinated and amused and thrilled as well as a tiny bit appalled. The dealer, it turned out, had appeared briefly in *Rent* in 1998, and belonged to Actors' Equity; his lawyer asked for and got scale plus 10 percent for his client's "involuntary performing services" during the arrest. It was Emily's idea to sign the boy to the series for a possible recurring role, which provoked a small second wave of news coverage, all of which contained a lead sentence containing the word *ironically.* Stories about the show appeared everywhere, including the cover of *Entertainment Weekly* and even page A-1 of the *Times. Nightline* devoted a whole program to the episode. Ted Koppel mentioned in his introduction that George was "a respected former television journalist who used to work with us here at ABC News." It felt odd, being splashed with drops of Ted Koppel's disapproval, but not awful. When the episode was rebroadcast the following week, it got a 16 rating and a 29 share, twice the highest rating Mose Broadcasting has gotten for any show ever.

"So. (Thanks, Tranh.)" The fuzzy ambient sound of her office disappears as she picks up the receiver at last. "Why are you so . . . wormy?"

"My mom died last night." He swivels away from the desk and puts his feet on the maple credenza, and stares up toward the park, the snowy, astounding park. Why doesn't he adore Central Park as much as everyone else? Maybe because it's uptown, and uptown still disconcerts him slightly, even though he's making $16,575 a week. (Twenty years ago, his annual salary was $16,000. Five years ago, his and Lizzie's combined salaries were still only—only—$16,000 a month. They are discovering that they like making plenty of money, particularly George, even though it reinforces their disapproval of people who seem motivated by money.)

"Why didn't you say?"

"I guess I'm sort of numb."

"She was sick?"

"She was. But it was a car accident. She was, you know, boom, it was instant. We're flying out in the morning."

"Anything I can do . . ."

"Thanks. I know. Thanks."

"You're okay?"

"Yeah. I am."

"Well . . ." Seconds pass. "So, Mose, six-thirty?" Emily asks. "Ready?"

"I think."

"Yesterday Timothy said to me on the phone, and I quote, 'Let's literally lock and load, my mad dude.' "

"No."

"Uh-huh." Whenever George mentions Timothy Featherstone, Mose's head of programming, it briefly sets Emily off, which both of them enjoy. Provoked by the idea of Featherstone, her language becomes practically expansive.

"I ran *into* the second-dumbest man in TV at the Getty just last night. He had both kids—it was a Flemish seventeenth-century circus, a fund-raiser for Yucatán war orphans—*and* the pregnant twenty-one-year-old Chinese girlfriend."

"Vietnamese, I think," George says.

"Whatever. The girlfriend and the older daughter—bare-bellied, and pierced, both of them. Matching belly rings, I think. They sang the *Melrose Place* theme song together."

"Wow. It had words?"

"No, you know, humming it. And *Timothy* knew the tune too. And sang it. *On* the Getty plaza, in front of *everyone, arm in arm* with his daughter and his mistress. It was just . . . stupendous. I cannot believe he still has that job."

"He doesn't, really. Mose does."

"Yeah, yeah."

"So I'll see you. Safe trip."

"Live *here,* George," Emily says. For five months last summer and fall, Emily decamped to New York to get *NARCS* on its feet, with George as her apprentice show-runner. "Seriously."

Iris's head is suddenly in his office. "George! Your ten-thirty!"

"Bye, Em," he says, "see you this afternoon." He turns to Iris. "My ten-thirty?"

"*Caroline Osborne,*" she whispers loudly, surely loud enough for Caroline Osborne to hear.

"Ah." Caroline Osborne is Gloria Mose's twenty-five-year-old daughter by a previous billionaire. Featherstone, when he asked George last week to meet with her, called her "the viscountess," which may or may not have been a joke. She isn't, technically, Harold Mose's stepdaughter, but here she is, come to talk to George about working for *NARCS* as an associate producer. As soon as George sees her stepping up quickly, bobbling a little on her high heels, to shake his hand—even before he makes a point of pronouncing Magdalen College correctly and asks her about her job at Channel 4 in London—he knows this interview is just a courtesy, a formality. He will not hire Caroline Osborne to work in this office. It's not just that she's English ("Scottish, actually"), although that is part of his problem. It's the way she looks and acts. His state of mind may now be in violation of city, state, and federal antidiscrimination laws. It's unfair, he knows, even piggish in some convoluted way. But she is unacceptable. She's too pretty, too bosomy, too beautifully dressed, too ripe, too smart, too funny, too flirty, and too tempting to have around all day, every day.

2

"Sorry, what?"

"I said, how are your direct reports incented?" The tan ectomorph in his late twenties—Chad? Chas?—is sitting in Lizzie's office questioning her. He is, he has said twice in the last twenty minutes, "the senior relationship manager, business interface, and technology liaison" at a software company outside Boston.

Huh? "Incented?" What in tarnation do you mean by that, young fella? Lizzie is tempted to reply, but instead talks his talk, figuring that if the interview proceeds with maximum efficiency, Chad, or Chas, who has an MBA, will go away sooner. She says, "Bonuses, based on meeting revenue goals, maxing out at a hundred and fifty percent of base salary, plus equity, with two-year vesting that's IPO-accelerated."

She dislikes the part of her work that requires conversations like this. During the second of her two brief periods of employment by big companies (ages ago, Procter & Gamble for nine strange months in 1987 and Rupert Murdoch's News Corporation in 1994) she always complained that dealing with the human resources department was the worst part of the job. Now she realizes that having a human resources department, so she never had to discuss vesting and bonus targets and inpatient mental health benefits with employees and potential employees, was actually the best thing about the Murdoch job.

Lizzie wants to hire someone to open and run a Fine Technologies office on the West Coast, because it's halfway to Asia, where business is picking up again, and because the rest of her industry is there. She has been interviewing people for two weeks. According to Chas/Chad's résumé, before he moved east (*"back* east," as they say in Seattle) he worked at Microsoft and Starwave. And Chas/Chad is not the worst. Out in Seattle or San Jose, Lizzie knows, she could have seen half a dozen qualified people the first day. In New York, the candidates are ad agency account jerks looking for any way out, the hustler marketing partners from bankrupt web-site design shops, bullshitters (*uninteresting* bullshitters) and losers. George doesn't like it when she uses the word *loser,* and neither does she, really—it's so categorically harsh. But in her world, the losers seem to be multiplying. Partly this is a classic Ponzi-scheme latecomer phenomenon, where the logic of a mania finally requires a big crowd of failed contenders—the thirty-eight-year-olds who decided in 1998 that this online web thing looked like it was going to be *big.*

The very worst, no contest, was the self-satisfied, hard-sell fat boy who came in just last Friday to show her the "A Is for Alzheimer's" multimedia video wall that he "conceived, conceptualized, designed, and created" for the marketing department of a drug company. "Have you ever seen PET scans, MRI scans, 3D models, and CGI combined like this?" the fat boy said to her. "You have not, I guarantee you. Have you ever seen memory loss, disorientation, mood swings, and dementia depicted so intensely or so interactively? You have not."

By comparison, Chas/Chad is a charmer. Chas/Chad has said nothing for a few seconds, Lizzie suddenly realizes, so it must be her turn to speak. She stands up. "Well, thank you," she says, smiling for the first time in the interview, as she walks around her particleboard desk, ostentatiously unostentatious like everything in the office, to shake his hand. "We want to have this figured out in a couple of weeks, so we will let you know." In the first usage, *we* means *I;* the second *we* means Alexi, her assistant.

"So on my end," he says, rising, "there's no action point?"

An intelligent kid, Lizzie thinks, maybe the right person for the job. *Asshole,* she also thinks—

"Because," he says, "I'm leaving Sunday A.M. for Singapore—"

Go.

"—trying to jump-start a little fast-track consulting project for their CyberMart. I mentioned, didn't I, that I was in K-L back in '97, consulting on their Multimedia Supercorridor? RIP. This trip I'm swinging through Vietnam—"

Leave, she thinks, willing him to turn away, past Alexi, past the programmers' sector of the office, past the huge SPARC workstations of the game designers, out. "A little consulting project. Multimedia Supercorridor. Fast-track. Jump-start. K-L. Vietnam." *Go now.*

"—but your guy has my e-mail. And I'll be back in the States ASAP—no later than four-three or four-four. FYI."

Finally he is leaving. "Alexi?" she says as Chas/Chad walks out of earshot, looking over at the programmers' whiteboards covered with rough-draft notions, half math, half German and English, scrawled in purple and red marker. "*You*"—she snaps her right forefinger and thumb into a pistol pointing at Alexi and winks—"are *my guy.*"

Alexi is in the middle of a phone conversation in Spanish with a Mexican mouse-pad manufacturer. (Lizzie covets his new wireless headset, but knows she would never wear one.) Glancing at Chas/Chad, he rolls his eyes and, one hand to his mouth, daintily mimes vomiting.

She heads toward the back of the loft for her daily midmorning encounter with Bruce Helms, who dresses every day in identical charcoal-gray Brooks Brothers suits and white button-down shirts. He isn't a square—he's a former morphine addict with a trust fund; he dresses like a square, a perfect 1965 WASP square, not exactly in a spirit of parody but as a function of his deep native sense of decorum, expressed . . . was it ironically? "No, um—maybe allusively," Bruce said, obviously embarrassed, during Lizzie's one conversation with him about his clothes. His business card calls him Chief Technology Officer. A few times, exhausted and in high spirits, Lizzie has introduced Bruce to outsiders as "Mr. Helms, our senior executive vice president, quality" or "Bruce Helms, our deputy chairman and president of pure research and advanced software engineering." (The only time she felt guilty was when a pair of middle-aged executives from Japan bowed furiously, made notes, and insisted on arranging a conference call with *their* deputy chairman and president of pure research and advanced software engineering in Osaka for eleven P.M. Japanese time.) She plops into his bright green AstroTurf-covered armchair, the only piece of upholstered furniture at Fine Technologies, and leans back.

"Man," she says, shaking her head, "I don't know, finding anyone here who can do the West Coast job is a nightmare."

"I hope you didn't hire the Mormon."

"*Shush.* They'll arrest us for discrimination. That's 'creed.' "

"And race. Ultrawhiteness."

"I have seen nobody close to perfect."

"So interview out in Seattle. The job is vice president for Microsoft, right?" As he speaks, his right hand remains on his mouse, and only between sentences does he glance away from his twenty-five-inch monitor and look at Lizzie. His speaking manner, almost monotonic but essentially sunny, is the way people their age and younger tend to talk. *Whateverese,* she calls it, and it reminds her of Huckleberry Hound's voice or, as George said, Eeyore on antidepressants. "Go west," Bruce says. "Get somebody predigested."

"I know, I know."

"And go see my friend Buster when you're in Seattle. And hire him too. I've always said we should."

"Maybe so."

Bruce lifts his hand from the mouse and swivels finally to face Lizzie. "Your problem—if I may . . . ?"

"Please. . . ."

"Why would the right person still be *in* New York?"

"You're in New York. I'm in New York. Willibald and Humfried and Markus and—"

"You're here because of George and the kids. I'm here because my act would seem too much like an act out there."

Lizzie smiles and shakes her head.

"The Germans don't know any better. They love nicotine and decay too much to leave New York—plus, since they're communists, or anarchosyndicalists, or whatever, they would never work for Morgan Stanley or Goldman Sachs even for twice what you're paying them. Madeline obviously can't leave." Madeline, who runs sales and marketing, is married to a city councilman. "Alexi is gay—"

"He *is*?" Alexi's lover, Tony, is the building's landlord, and Alexi wears a baseball cap imprinted with the words GO HOMOS in bright orange letters.

"—and he thinks he's in some kind of Preston Sturges movie—"

"I think it's more like *The Brady Bunch*—"

"And you're Rosalind Russell and he's—"

"Ann B. Davis?"

"Thelma Ritter."

"Same thing. But I am *not* Rosalind Russell. Katharine Hepburn. Maybe Barbara Stanwyck."

"Lance has his mother on the island. Boogie . . ." he says about their chief game designer, "Boogie I don't really understand. Maybe his incubus overlord assigned him to Manhattan for a tour of duty. And Karen, well, to Karen this is some kind of digital *Real World,* turn-of-the-new-century thing. Spice Women. Vulva power. You're her hero."

Lizzie almost blushes at the workstation intimacy with Bruce, her first employee and de facto partner.

"So you're saying that the only reason everyone here isn't in Red-mond or Mountain View or Los Altos or somewhere is that we're each occupying our own little black-and-white Manhattan fantasy realm?"

"Well . . ." he says, chuckling in that not-quite-jaded way of smart young men, "*yes.* We're optimizing instead of maximizing. It's Twee-ville. Why do you think we only have twenty-percent turnover? The Germans and Datuk and Chairyawat and the rest of those guys are also here because you're paying for the green-card lawyers."

"Who's Chairyawat?"

"Gaz. That's his name. Plus, I don't like to drive. And also, speaking for myself, but maybe also for you, because we don't want to live in a company town. We like being fish a little bit out of water. Optimizing versus maximizing."

"Yeah, well," she says, "sometimes I think I could get used to being a fish *in* water. You know?"

Lizzie swings her legs down off the arm of the chair, and as she sits forward both feet fly—*thwack!*—onto the grubby yellow pine floor, a hundred-square-foot patch of which remains exposed, like an archaeological exhibit, only in Bruce's office, at Bruce's insistence. Her stomp is a half-conscious device to help her change the subject to the business of the day. It's what George calls her jump-cut, and Bruce her double-click, the segueless conversational shorthand among colleagues in twitchy new businesses, the kind of cheerful-hysterical brusquerie endemic to the digital Northwest, but still uncommon in New York and nonexistent in old Hollywood. "Excellent news," she says. "We shipped thirty-six thousand four hundred YAKety-rex"—this is how she pronounces Y2KRx—"in the fourth quarter—nineteen thousand of those downloaded at fifty percent above wholesale. *Thirty-six thousand copies,* Bruce. The budget was twenty-nine."

Lizzie's company made most of its early money from something called automatic speech recognition. They perfected and licensed to a bigger company a piece of software Lizzie called Speak Memory, which was permitting strangers—young and old strangers, stupid strangers, strangers with funny accents—to call a corporate phone number, ask a talking computer for any one of the corporation's hundred or hundred thousand employees by name, and be connected to the employee's extension automatically. (Lizzie's friend Pollyanna Chang once asked her if she felt guilty about putting thousands of operators and receptionists out of work. No, Lizzie said, for three summers she worked the fucking switchboard at Chiat/Day in L.A., and she is proud to help make *that* fucking job disappear.)

As for Y2KRx, Lizzie first conceived of it years ago, when Louisa was a baby, before Y2K was a buzzword, before anyone but a few cranks and information-technology nerds was worried about the inability of certain computers to tell the difference between 1900 and 2000, or 1901 and 2001.

"Do-it-yourself millennial hysteria," George called the two years of anticipatory Y2K fuss. Bruce's first idea was to write a piece of software that would turn any computer's serious Year 2000 problem into a negligible Year 1900 problem. That is, his software would instruct a computer to interpret every aught year as a twenty-first century date. Under this scheme, the first decade of the twentieth century would become digitally unrecognizable on January 1, 2000. Everyone would agree simply to ignore the years from 1900 to 1909. For at least the first decade of the twenty-first century, the Y2K problem would disappear by means of an act of collective will, to be addressed again in 1910. "When they changed to the Gregorian calendar in 1582," Bruce said, "they dumped fifteen days to make everything align properly. This is the same principle." "But I'm not the pope," Lizzie replied.

Bruce refused to admit he was joking, or that his idea was unworkable. But one morning, as she stooped to sponge Louisa's carrot puree off the cat's head, she realized that her wiping was making the cat a lot unhappier than the baby's spilling. It started Lizzie thinking about the messes that would inevitably result from half-baked Y2K solutions. Thus their product: it diagnoses and attempts to fix any new software problems unintentionally created by software meant to fix the core problem. Bruce wanted to call it the Root Doctor, as a joint allusion to the Mississippi blues (his hero, the singer Robert Johnson, had consulted an herbalist "root doctor") and the deep code in computer programs. The medical reference led Lizzie to Y2KRx, which she sometimes describes in sales presentations (to buyers who don't really understand technology) as "good medicine to protect against bad medicines." She also calls it "disposable enterprise software" (to buyers who fancy themselves tech-savvy) or "retro-remediation" (to the information-systems geeks) or "the Y2K metasolution" (to the press).

When Al Gore's presidential campaign adopted Y2KRx for its computer systems last summer (George's partner, Emily, gave a copy to the campaign director) and the candidate mentioned it in an important stump speech, making it a symbol of pragmatic, nothing-to-fear-but-fear-of-the-twenty-first-century-itself optimism, sales increased by 300 percent in a month.

"So as our official Year 2000 professional services regional support and project manager," Bruce says, "you have determined that we're happy?"

"We are happy," Lizzie says. "Optimally and maximally. That's more than enough over budget to float us through the middle of the second quarter. By which time we'll have the Range Daze alpha—"

"No."

"—when I hope we'll have the Range Daze prototype. And in any case the Microsoft deal should be closed by the end of this quarter, God willing, and we can all relax a little." Lizzie has been talking with Microsoft about selling them a piece of Fine Technologies, 20 percent, plus warrants giving them the right to buy another 20 percent. War-rants! The deal makes her feel as if she has finally crossed to some other side. During her time as a not-for-profit fund-raiser she used to look down on her business school classmates who went straight to Wall Street and into M & A, the jerks who practically couldn't let a conver-sation pass without mentioning roll-ups and debt tranches and mezza-nine rounds and secondaries and warrants. (Particularly the women, she hated realizing. Particularly Nancy McNabb, who, she knew, looked down on her, reciprocally, during the entire four years Lizzie worked for the children's foundation. Nancy used to call Lizzie once a year to solicit a donation to Harvard. Now she calls every month or so on one pretext or another, which Lizzie knows is silly to find flattering.)

"Shouldn't Microsoft, of all people, be sympathetic to an, uh, over-ambitious production schedule? Their test phase on this would be longer than our whole development time. But, yes, we'll have some-thing. Boogie's pretty sanguine." Sheldon "Boogie" Boffin, their game-design auteur, is a twenty-seven-year-old with shoulder-length red pigtails and prosthetic horns made of barnacles implanted under the skin of his forehead. "And listen to the Germans," Bruce adds, nodding toward the center area where the thirty-two full-time pro-grammers and game designers sit, three million dollars' worth of salary—almost three and a half including Boogie. Four of the pro-grammers were classmates at the Technische Universität in Berlin. "Lately it's all '*Achtung ich bin ein* Range Daze *Fassbinder kunstwerk.*' They've abandoned English. We're cranking."

Seven of the programmers are from Asia. Every two weeks, when Lizzie signs the payroll, she marvels at the alien names of so many of her employees, among them Djiwandono Ahmad, Jaikumar Wibul-swasram, Rangaswami Chairyawat, Soedradjad Khosla, Datuk Chan-drashekaran, Sudeshna Vangarha, Goyigit Madhavan. Since all of them except Ahmad use Americanized nicknames in the office—Jake, Gaz, Soho, Date, Suds, and Goy—she has no idea how to pronounce most of their real names, and is never clear about which are first names and which are last. Occasionally, when the Asians and the Germans have one of their noisy, emotional group debates about an engineering problem, none of them speaking in their native tongues—

"The transition vector is totally in the application heap!"

"And quitting the first application but leaving the second running will cause a crash, big time!"

"If the gestalt function was in detached classic 68K code, then the problem might not recur!"

—Bruce will, for Lizzie's benefit, put on a David Niven accent or start whistling the "Colonel Bogey March" from *The Bridge on the River Kwai.*

Range Daze is to be Fine Technologies' next major product, a gedanken time-travel video game. Lizzie really stumbled onto game making as a result of subcontracted work they did in 1997 on a piece of animation software. Range Daze also incorporates a version of Speak Memory, their speech-recognition software. It should have been finished months ago. Players can "range" at will from country to country and historical moment to historical moment by speaking travel commands out loud. Optional skin sensors (a kind of Velcro wristband Lizzie found last summer during a trip to Russia) make the game action less or more anxiety provoking according to the player's real-time reactions. If you travel to 1792 Paris, for instance, you are designated a besotted peasant or a frightened aristocrat or an angry sansculotte according to your heart rate, blood pressure, and skin conductance; too many twitches, the wrong sort of palpitation, and you're a marquess (or marchioness) headed for the guillotine.

Lizzie first got the idea for the game a few Christmases ago watching *It's a Wonderful Life,* and so she has insisted that anything players do to change the past should affect the future within the game. As a piece of programming, this has proven exceedingly difficult to accomplish. If a player manages to assassinate Hitler in 1944, then for the remainder of that game, the war ends sooner, there is no atom bombing of Hiroshima or Nagasaki, and the Soviets begin the Cold War at a disadvantage. But after days of debate, for example, it was deemed impossibly complicating to give "Nazi" players the option of making their 1923 putsch a success. The alternative histories in the game cannot be unlimited.

Range Daze will come out simultaneously both as a CD for PCs and Macs and as a cartridge for the new Sega. People in the business are always asking Lizzie, "Which platform are you optimizing for?" and she always answers, dissembling a little, "We're completely agnostic." Lizzie, a yoga-practicing Jew married to a lapsed Unitarian, whose children attend a nonreligious Episcopal school, alternates between confidence that all her bets are covered and fear that she has no coherent strategy.

The working title "Range Daze" is the staff's, a play on *Strange Days,* a cybernovel that Lizzie hasn't read; they sometimes call it "Matrix," from *Neuromancer,* another cybernovel that Lizzie hasn't read. Lizzie doesn't love the puns and in-group references that pass for wit in the digital world, but she's a thirty-six-year-old woman with two houses, a husband, and three children, not a twenty-two-year-old Beavis with an 800 math SAT, a Cooper Union degree, a goatee, and a pet ermine on his shoulder.

A husband, three children, and a trip to Minnesota the next morning for her mother-in-law's funeral. Lizzie stands and begins rebending a crudely straightened paper clip she has picked up from Bruce's desk.

"George's mother died last night—"

"Lizzie!" Alexi shouts from across the loft. "A call!"

She drops the paper clip, which now looks like half a swastika.

"Sorry," Bruce says, picking up the silver half swastika and restraightening it. "Tell George I'm sorry."

"*Li*zzie!" Alexi shouts again, this time as if to a headstrong child. He must think the call is important.

"—so I'll be gone tomorrow and probably Wednesday." She is walking fast now, backward. "E-mail me," she says.

"It's Moorhead, the business affairs guy at Microsoft," Alexi says.

" 'Business affairs' is Hollywood."

"Whatever. The Microsoft talk-to guy." Since Lizzie began her deal conversations with Microsoft six months ago, the company has undergone three corporate reorganizations, three that she knows about, and Moorhead is her fourth handler.

Deep breath, and she kicks her door shut, the only door in the place, and grabs the phone. "Hello, this is Lizzie Zimbalist."

"*Ms.* Zimbalist, this is Howard Moorhead in Redmond, how are *you* today?"

The carefully fondled *Ms.* and the stranger's unction make Lizzie recoil. "Sorry I kept you waiting. I was just in a meeting about our speech-recognition and force-feedback software. The game."

"That's super. I know our people down at WebTV are very anxious to hear about your deliverability issues on that? I'm sure we'll all be excited to see the product?" Like many men raised in the South, Moorhead turns his sentences up at the end, transforming statements into acknowledgment-seeking quasi-questions. Growing up in Los Angeles in the seventies, Lizzie trained herself out of the same verbal tic in the sixth grade. "And your Mr. Haft seemed to think our proposed time frame on the warrant expirations is no problem?" Lance Haft is her controller. "Is 2005 acceptable to you?"

Lizzie still cannot quite take years like 2005 seriously, even now, two months into the new year. Plans and deals involving dates in the aughts and the teens inflame her chronic, secret sense of work as a big make-believe game, dress-up Monopoly. *Sure, Moorhead,* she thinks, *as long as you pay me in fresh, crisp twenty-million-dollar bills—the bright pink ones.*

"Sure," she says, "2005 sounds fine."

"Ms. Zimbalist, I do want to let you know that based on the data you've supplied, we've done some new calculations? Of the projected earnings-multiples for your out years?"

"Uh-huh."

"And we think right now we're looking at a somewhat adjusted acquisition benchmark number for our investment?"

A pause. "What are you saying?"

"Well, we're now prepared to offer two-point-nine million dollars for ten percent equity in the company."

Lizzie stares for an extra, calming beat at the photograph on her desk, all three kids laughing by the Neva River last summer in St. Petersburg, Max and Sarah holding hands with Louisa, airborne and blurry, between them. Sarah still had her long hair.

"For *ten* percent of the company?"

"Exactly," Moorhead says, his smile audible, as if Lizzie had just agreed to the new terms. "Exactly right."

"Two-point-nine million dollars? You are fucking kidding me."

For three full seconds, Moorhead says nothing.

"Ms. Zimbalist," he finally manages, "I—I—that type of language—"

"Two-point-nine implies a valuation for this company of twenty-nine million. In *every* discussion I've had with Microsoft, the valuation

range has been thirty-five to forty million. Two-point-nine is bullshit."
Lizzie is almost screaming. She curses often, but she seldom screams.

"I do not appreciate that type of language, Ms. Zimbalist."

This jerk, this geek—not even a geek, this oily *lawyer*—is upset! About a girl swearing! She needs to get off the phone before she's overcome. Her . . . *language*!

"I don't appreciate the bait and switch," she says, scribbling Bennett Gould's initials, *BG,* and "2/28/00 BG—*NO $!*" on a Post-it. Ben Gould is a member of her board, and she needs to discuss this with him. "You and Lance Haft can try to resolve the numbers. Goodbye." She bangs the phone down on its cradle. *"Fuck."*

Bruce pokes his head in, smiling, with Alexi hovering avidly just behind.

She shoots to her feet, sending the Aeron chair wheeling into her CD tower, which totters. Three discs (Beth Orton, Morcheeba, and Stravinsky's *Apollon Musagète*) fall to the floor, and Lizzie steps on them, cracking the plastic cases—"Shit!"—as she comes out from behind her desk. "I do not believe those duplicitous shits. Two-point-nine million. Christ. And my 'language.' My *language*! Give me a fucking break." She sighs so violently she roars.

Alexi points to the phone. "It's *Louisa,*" he says, enunciating extra crisply, "on line three."

"Hello, my baby-duck!" Lizzie says, with her free hand pulling her curly hair, which is brown verging on red, behind her extremely red ears. Bruce and Alexi wander off. "Yes, it *is* Mommy, LuLu. I am not a robot mommy. It's *Mommy.*" Her brain is still hot. "No, I am not an alien. Okay . . . Who's there? Ahtch? Ahtch *who*?"

3

He hangs up the phone. *Yes.* A canceled lunch.

When New Yorkers call friends or acquaintances at the office, it's always for a particular reason—to get advice on how to handle this newspaper reporter or that magazine editor, to sell a pair of five-hundred-dollar tickets to a black-tie fund-raiser ("Pediatric Epstein-Barr is no joke, George"), to get credit for being the first to deliver news of a mutual friend's firing, to make a lunch date for next month or to break one for today. The opening small talk is brief. And computer people have taken New York curtness one step further and sideways, with a technology that tends to screen out schmooze: e-mail is not a natural small-talk medium. Los Angelenos are still reluctant e-mailers, George has discovered, apparently because they love the telephone itself. They make phone calls without any agenda, just to check in, to say, *Hi,* great to hear your voice, how goes it, *fantastic*—no matter how tenuous the relationship. The first few times a Hollywood manager or studio executive phoned George with no particular purpose, George kept waiting for the point, and waiting. It still weirds him out a little, as do certain effusive L.A. forms of telephone farewell. "Perfect!" they say in response to closing statements about

FedEx tracking numbers and brunch logistics. "*Perfect!* Thanks much! Take care!" Maybe show business people say yes so emphatically about banal matters because they hear no so often about consequential ones.

Today's lunch has just called to cancel, which delights George. It's not because the young man, who wants work, is a director of jumpy black-and-white TV commercials and "some, like, Franz Werfel–type mixed-media pieces down at P.S. 122." Lunches canceling at the last minute always please him. Because the allotted lunch period is a sunken cost, already written off as time when real work won't get done, cancellations make George feel free to lose focus a little and screw off. An instant miniature vacation! Even when he spends canceled lunch hours working, the work feels sweeter. But today, because of his mother, he hasn't been able to concentrate. And the sympathy from his colleagues is relentless. Each time Iris or Phoebe stares hard at him, for a beat, and asks, "Are you *okay*, George?" it depresses him, since until that instant he has been feeling fine.

So he riffles through the mess of naked CDs on his desk, decides against Gershwin (*An American in Paris,* not *Rhapsody in Blue,* but still too themed), clicks Bix Beiderbecke into his antique Discman, and lights out, walking to walk, thrilled to wander pointlessly in the middle of a day that's chockablock with points. He decides on a southerly zigzag down through Infotainment Zone. Infotainment Zone is what Sarah started calling midtown Manhattan last summer, intending to bug him a little with smart eighth-grader contempt. But instead he's started using the phrase himself, just as he started borrowing her Jakob Dylan and They Might Be Giants CDs to play in the Land Cruiser. So now Sarah calls it midtown again.

He turns down Broadway, thinking how little his mother liked the city.

George himself isn't particularly crazy about midtown. It has St. Patrick's, the library, Times Square, and four great office buildings (the Chrysler, 30 Rockefeller Plaza, Lever House, the Ford Foundation), but so much of the rest is mid- and late-twentieth-century scrub, a thicket of chain-store pharmacies (all operated by South Asians now), banks (Caribbeans), tchotchke shops (Israelis and Arabs), and espresso outlets (kids). Midtown, for all the crowds of women, is also pretty sexless. *No; no; no; no; no; no; no; yes; no; no; maybe; no; no; no.* As he does every month or two on a random stretch of Manhattan sidewalk, George is mentally conducting a census: *With how many of the next one hundred women can I imagine having sex?* On upper Madison and downtown, he regularly hits one in nine. One June Friday a few years ago in TriBeCa, he hit one in five, the all-time record, but with an asterisk—Lizzie had been out of town on business for a week and he had had two glasses of wine at lunch. In midtown, one in twelve is the highest ever. Today—*yes; no; no; no; no; no; no*—the tally is five or six out of a hundred, about average for the neighborhood.

Midtown ought to be an astonishing place, given the irrational concentration of big newspapers, big magazines, big book publishers, big TV networks, big record companies, big art galleries, big theaters, and big advertising agencies in one tiny plot—the show-and-tell orgy. If it's possible to feel the mad shiver and hum anywhere, the ecstasy of communication, it ought to be possible here. Here is an absolute majority of the big owner-operators of American culture, recruiting and promoting new regiments of good-looking twenty-seven-year-olds for prime time, confecting and promoting the hits and the bestsellers, tallying and promoting this year's Men of the Year and the Sexiest Men Alive and the Biggest Corporations and the Most Powerful People, making lesbianism *and* monogamy, five-foot-tall digital TVs *and* Shaker austerity, fiscal conservatism *and* stock speculation simultaneously fashionable. And the executive confectioners of Infotainment Zone, including George and the other marketers and editors and publishers and designers and producers and creative directors, all practice their rarefied craft, sublime as well as ridiculous, on these jam-packed five hundred island acres, a piece of land—he can't get over this, not even after twenty years—smaller than his grandparents' alfalfa farm.

In fact, everyone in Verve, South Dakota, his grandparents' hometown, could fit on one floor of any one of these buildings. And although by reputation New York is smelly, midtown doesn't have much of a scent. All of George's favorite places possess a special, ripe stench: the warm, fulsome reek of dehydrating alfalfa in Verve; tobacco smoke and diesel fuel in Paris; the herbal-cream-rinse breezes of the Hollywood Hills; the animal rot of old Manhattan (fish entrails on South Street and beef fat on Washington Street at dawn, human urine everywhere in August).

Out on the 20th Century Fox lot in Century City or even the Microsoft campuses in Redmond, one is aware, thrillingly and disconcertingly, of being on the reservation, an inhabitant of a particular dreamed-up place somewhere between Toontown and Alphaville. Infotainment Zone, however, to George's regret, is mostly an abstraction. Midtown: so much power, so little fun.

But then, for the first time ever—passing Forty-fifth Street, Forty-fourth Street, the Gershwin Theatre, Viacom, the *Times,* the new Reuters and Condé Nast towers—George thinks: Infotainment Zone is actual at last. It's as if the neighborhood has just achieved full self-consciousness. The renovation of the Viacom headquarters was the tipping point. At the end of last year the building was entirely reclad in a new type of quarter-inch-thick video-screen polymer that can be programmed to display hundreds of different moving pictures or—what George and Lizzie and the kids adore—a single continuous image bending and wrapping around the whole building, a kinetic cubist wonder of the world. Sometimes Viacom's "image administrators" display a single phrase on the tower, such as a sideways fifty-three-story-tall SOUTH PARK ON ICE AT MADISON SQUARE GARDEN DOESN'T SUCK, with SUCK exploding into animated ice chips, or YOU WILL NOT BELIEVE THE NEW MTV, with BELIEVE morphing at high speed into dozens of different musicians' eyes. At this moment, the building is covered by a moving image of Howard Stern, five hundred feet tall, walking in place against an impossibly meteoric Manhattan night sky, his head stretching from the forty-fourth to the fifty-third floors, his hair hanging down to the thirty-ninth, his boot tips almost touching the sidewalk. It's only a billboard, a monstrosity, genius technical means applied to squalid, stupid ends; yeah, right, sure. But it is also quite beautiful. It is awesome the way new train stations and skyscrapers were a century ago.

Where has all the porno gone? George wonders. Gone to online, every one, he figures. He had always enjoyed Times Square's cluster of pornography shops and live-nude-junkie nickelodeons. The Giuliani law limiting smut stores to one every two blocks is antithetical to the deepest commercial traditions of New York, of course. The city has always been about specialization run rampant, cuckoo geographical overconcentration—not just the flower and fur and theater districts but the electrical-pump district, the coffee-machine district, the feathers-and-velvet-trim district. Suddenly the pornography district is no more.

George sees there's a Steve Buscemi film festival playing this weekend at one of the old porno theaters.

He walks east on the downtown side of Forty-second, looking across the street and up, casually searching for the drone video cameras his friend Zip Ingram told him are up there somewhere, aimed down at Bryant Park and feeding the images twenty-four hours a day to web sites—yet one more amusingly profitless, vaguely Dada internet project. He sees one of the new postmodern brushed-steel Bell Atlantic kiosks and notices that displayed in its glass sides are giant black-and-white photos from the 1950s of earnest, crew-cut, gray-flannel white men talking on the phone and looking silly—the telephone company thereby satirizing what was until the day before yesterday its very ethos. Past Grand Central, where midtown gets tired—all postwar warp and woof—the lesser UN missions, the lesser media, the crummy simulations of crummy Irish bars, the immigrant coffee shops and boutiques too glossed-up to be interesting yet not actually classy. He is in the forgettable Manhattan of his first years as a New Yorker, his time as a reporter for the *Daily News.* When he phoned his mother after he decided to drop out of Columbia architecture school, to tell her about his job, she was not effusive. "It's one of those . . . *vertical* newspapers, is it, that you'll be writing for?" she said. Edith Hope Cranston Mactier, whom everyone called Edith Hope, wouldn't use the word *tabloid,* which in 1978 she thought was somehow vulgar, just as she wouldn't use the word *stink.*

Zigzagging uptown again, west on Forty-fifth, north up Madison, George looks up at the old *Newsweek* building—3:03, the Microsoft/Time Out New York/New York digital clock on top says; he should get back to the office—and experiences a moment of eighties nostalgia. The magazine was his second employer. ("*Newsweek?*" his mother said when he called to tell her he was leaving the *Daily News.* "That's the one that imitates *Time,* is it?") In his twenties, in the 1980s, *Newsweek* seemed glamorous—the year in Bonn at the twilight of the Cold War, Gary Hart up for coffee, the hipsters snorting lines of coke off art-department light boxes, a day trip to Washington to chat with Ronald Reagan about the ivy plant on his Oval Office mantelpiece, chauffeured Town Cars caravanning from Madison Avenue out the Long Island Expressway at four A.M. on summer Saturday mornings at $160 a commute. To a twenty-six-year-old, the expense account itself was a druglike thrill.

George produced one very fine piece of work at *Newsweek*. In 1984 he spent a month and a half driving a station wagon down the Pan-American Highway from Texas to Guatemala, then through El Salvador, Honduras, and Nicaragua to Panama. The magazine sent along a British photographer, Edward Ingram, a jittery son of a thief who called himself Zip, and their big cover package on the several ongoing civil wars won magazine awards and then, reconstituted as an eight-hour PBS documentary miniseries that George took a sabbatical to help produce, won Peabody and Polk awards. So George found himself a TV producer. ("*Television,* George?" his mother said, as if she thought he was joking about the new ABC News job. "So you'll write the . . . *scripts* those anchormen read?") As it happens, he is now eating a Sabrett sausage bought from a vendor outside the old ABC tower on Sixth Avenue. Swallowing the hot dog too fast, tossing the mustardy napkin wad in the garbage, he fixes on his new building's six-foot-tall letters, in platinum italics—THE MBC. Already the sign seems dated, a little vestigial. Almost everyone calls the network MBC, although it is still officially *The* MBC. Since England has the BBC and Canada has the CBC, why shouldn't America have the MBC, the founder and chairman asked his first executive team. "Because Warner's beat us to it with the WB," the former president of his Entertainment Group told him. *And because Mose, unlike Britain, is not the name of a sovereign nation,* no one said.

George pulls the Discman earplugs out just before he takes that final jump-step into the revolving door, and thinks, *As we approach the New York headquarters of the Mose Broadcasting Company and Mose Media Holdings, we have come to the end of "George Mactier, Infotainer: A Walking Tour." Thank you. Please return your audio devices.* And now he realizes for the first time, connecting the dots, that each successive job has taken him farther northwest. (Thus, extrapolating: Lincoln Center in 2003, New Jersey around 2008?) And he also realizes, thinking again without grief or anger of Edith Hope Cranston Mactier, born 1918, died 2000, that in his own career, ontogeny has absolutely recapitulated phylogeny—from newspapers to slick magazines to TV news to docudramatic entertainment, the whole media century compressed into his last twenty years. *Jesus,* George thinks, stepping off the thirty-eighth-floor elevator toward Daisy's sweet, skeptical smile, *that is so pat.*

4

"Hey, buddy! What up!" Timothy Featherstone has arrived. He walks straight into George's office as if he owns it. Which he does, more or less, since the MBC owns half the assets of Well-Armed Productions, George and Emily's company, and the *NARCS* offices are in the MBC Building, and Featherstone is the acting president of the Entertainment Group. "T minus . . ."—he checks and taps his gigantic platinum Rolex, which he has customized to receive alphanumeric pages— ". . . one hour forty-seven, and counting. Are we ready to rock? Are we ready to roll?" His left hand springs up, a high-five receptor. George never liked any of the elaborate cool-cat handshakes in the sixties and seventies, and his timing at high fives is inevitably half a beat late. But what choice does he have? He slaps Featherstone's hand. "Mac Man!" Featherstone says—sings, really, to the tune of the theme song of the old Batman TV show—as their palms make contact. Although the over-amped bonhomie is that of a big guy, Featherstone is small and almost prissy, with facial hair like Beverly Hills shrubbery, insubstantial but in-tensively manicured. Since the last time George saw him, just after the first of the year, his long sideburns and goatee have been replaced by a kind of Philippe Starck handlebar mustache, with swoops that are slightly, deliberately asymmetrical. He's wearing a brand-new charcoal-gray cashmere Nehru jacket so beautifully made that it almost doesn't look foolish. George is never sure whether Featherstone is a dork or affecting a version of dorkiness-passing-for-hip. He just turned fifty.

"Hey, Timothy." He punches the remote control to mute the Coleman Hawkins on his stereo. MSNBC, already muted, is on the TV. "How was the flight?"

"Not too shabby. I ran into your partner getting off the plane—*business* class! Frugality! Love that! *Love* it. Where *is* Emiliana?" Featherstone calls practically everyone by special nicknames, often several different special nicknames, particularly people who have no nicknames, who've never had a nickname. No one else calls George Mac or Mac Man, and no one calls Emily Emiliana.

"She's in a meeting." She's napping on a couch in an editing bay. "She'll be back by quarter of." He plans to wake her up as soon as Featherstone leaves. "Do you want to talk before we meet with Mose?"

"A quick huddle never hurts. Why don't you and Emmy Lou drift up to my place on Five-Nine at"—he exposes and taps the Rolex, its face as big as an Oreo cookie—"six-fifteen? Yeah? Groovy." He finally turns to go. Is that a retro, semi-ironic "groovy," or an earnest, unthinking, post-retro "groovy"? "Hey," he says, inspecting George's computer monitor, "where's your camera? No videocam? Get digital, bro! Official MBC policy! V-mail is the coolest, man, completely mad. I just got one from Ng this morning. Even Harold's started sending them."

"Yeah, I should get hooked up."

"Hey," Featherstone says, reminded, "you know the conversation we had in Vegas with Sandi?"

"Sandy Flandy, from William Morris?" Flandy is a Hollywood agent who represents two of the stars of *NARCS*. (Everyone repeats his full name—*Sandy Flandy?*—with a smile and a question mark the first time they hear it. Saying Sandy Flandy's name absolutely straight-faced, George realized last fall, is one tiny measure of show business insider-dom.) George has no memory of encountering Flandy in Las Vegas. George and Featherstone did spend an evening together there in January at NATPE, the annual convention of the National Association of Television Programming Executives. It was George's second NATPE, and one of those rich, ghastly contemporary spectacles—cigar aficionados, Scotch breath, extreme tans, *winking*—that are highly entertaining once, tolerable another time or two, pretty much unendurable thereafter.

"Nooooo, *Sandi,* my *friend,* Sandi Bemis, the therapist." Now George remembers. After dinner in Las Vegas, he consented to go to the Hard Rock with Timothy and Sandi, a woman who looked like a fortyish Cameron Diaz, and whom Featherstone introduced—seriously? jokingly? both?—as "the aromatherapist to the stars." George figured she was somewhere in that fuzzy Hollywood sector between executive girlfriend and call girl, particularly after he learned that she was the aromatherapist to the stars' pets, pet aromatherapy seeming like a plausible exit strategy out of high-end prostitution—*Wow, Sandi, your Shalimar really seems to calm down the border collies.* George's attempt at conversation consisted of asking if she knew Buddy Ramo, his step-daughter's father, who made his living therapeutically massaging horses around Malibu; she didn't. At the Hard Rock, Featherstone ordered her a nine-dollar-a-bottle granite-filtered, sorghum-infused microbrew lager from Montana, because he thought it was more her style than his other possible choice, a Washington State ale—which, he had added, wasn't "really a craft brew, since the company produces, I think, like, *twenty-five thousand* barrels a year." In the old days, prostitutes were obliged only to pretend to enjoy sex; now they have to pretend to be impressed by beer connoisseurship.

"You know, the girl who looked like the young Michelle Pfeiffer . . . the one *you,*" Featherstone adds with a smirk, "copped a Miata for. Back in the day, Jo-Jo, back in the day." Now George remembers why he recalled her as a version of whore: Featherstone asked him, literally with a nudge and a wink, to charge Sandi Bemis's car rental and room at the Venetian to the *NARCS* T & E budget. At first George had thought he was kidding, some kind of Rat Pack revival joke. But he was serious, and George handed over the Well-Armed Productions corporate Amex card when asked a second time. George's problem with being an accomplice wasn't so much ethical as aesthetic. Putting the girlfriend on his expense account—in Las Vegas!—is the cheesiest act he's committed during his first full-time year in show business. Featherstone's show of male bonding, the dirty grin four inches from George's face, the mingled scents of Stephen Sprouse pour Homme and Tic Tac, made it even worse.

"Remind me about the conversation in Las Vegas?"

"You promised Sandi you'd talk to Angela about enrolling her pooch in one of Sandi's seminars, which are literally fantastic. Aroma *and* meditation, one price. It rocks. The other dogs are A–list."

Dogs can be trained to meditate? He has erased the conversation entirely, and now he sees an even more mortifying show business moment rushing toward him: he will have to ask Angela Janeway (his Yale School of Drama star, his Creative Coalition board of directors star, his star who's insisting that he figure out a way to get Nelson Mandela to guest-star on an episode of *NARCS*) if she'll let the network president's girl-friend—the acting president, and not even his main girlfriend—perform some quack regimen on her German shepherd, Peacemaker. The dog, which Angela adopted during a visit to Sarajevo in 1996, appeared with her on the cover of *People* last month. (Sixteen thousand, five hundred and seventy-five dollars a week sounds like a lot, sure, but it amounts, after taxes, to not even $200 an hour—less than lawyers make.)

"Right," George replies, standing up, in an aggressively noncommittal attempt to change the subject. "Right."

"The sessions are at Trump's hotel on Columbus Circle. Sandi's there for a week in April. Mega-exclusive. Sandi would comp Angela, needless to say. It's a total win–win."

"Right."

"The new Mrs. Ron Perelman has already signed up all three of her whippets, and Puffy Combs's two shar-pei bitches will be there."

"The actors are on hiatus this week, but I'll have Iris let Angela know all about it."

"My *man!*" Featherstone says, giving a double thumbs–up as he steps toward the door. "See you and Emmarooni upstairs."

The *NARCS* production meetings take place at a long, cheap, paint-spattered table right on the soundstage, in the basement of the MBC Building (or "the The MBC Building," as the office clowns call it). This is partly for expediency, since most of the principals—the directors of photography and sound, the designers of costumes and sets, and the gatherers of props—spend so many of their hours in the adjacent offices and nooks. But George also prefers having the meetings down here because he likes the glamorously unglamorous industrial space, the Masonite slabs covering wood beams and tons of sand (to keep the floor level and vibration-free), the trusses and lights overhead, the cozy pool of light at the center of the dark factory cavern. Down here, George is the master among his trusty craftsmen. The questions and answers are precise and straightforward. The chain of command is clear. Shooting on West Fifty-seventh Street, an elevator ride away from the production offices, is more convenient than schlepping out to Astoria, Queens, or down to a pier in Chelsea. But the numbers are not what justify spending nine million dollars on a new soundstage in midtown Manhattan—Harold Mose enjoys having a studio underfoot because it's a palpable reminder that he's in show business. Just as the MBC soundstage makes George feel like Preston Sturges, it makes Mose feel like Irving Thalberg.

The below-the-line production staff, unlike the writers, convey by their very demeanor a kind of proletarian deference: George is the show-runner, the boss. Lizzie says she dislikes the sense of always scaring her employees slightly, but George finds it pleasurable. He tries never to abuse it, but that special combination of overeager friendliness and fear, as if he's walking around with a loaded weapon or a live grenade, is just old-fashioned respect.

Two people, Mary Ann the makeup artist and Marjorie the director of photography, both tell him they're sorry about his mother. Gordon Downey, the director, has already sent him flowers.

"Really excellent sound, the footsteps crunching on the cocaine, on Saturday night's show," George says to Fred, the long-haired sound designer whose job it is to enhance natural noises—to intensify audio reality, sweeten it.

"You liked it? Cool."

And the production meeting begins, calm and orderly, with each department head posing problems and solutions as they move through the script scene by scene. George will make dozens of choices in the next half hour that will aggregate into the look and sound and feel of the episode. He doesn't have to *do,* he must only decide. It's grand.

"I don't mind white at all," he's telling the production designer about the proposed color for a fake airport interrogation room.

"White won't give you any trouble in post. We'll have to rebuild that wall."

"Can we just attach the RPG to that header?" asks Gordon about a rocket-propelled grenade launcher in another scene. "It only has to be functional from this side, and we can have a plug on that side."

"We don't have to build it, do we?" George asks. "Isn't there a boneyard where we can get one?" A boneyard, he has learned, is a warehouse where props from old shows and movies are stored for reuse. It's one of the antique, below-the-line show business words he gets a kick out of saying.

"They won't let it out," the prop woman tells him.

"We can sell it with effects in post," Fred the sound guy says about the big-machine-gun sound.

"Marjorie," Gordon says, "you have to be able to light the thing."

"We can fix that in post too," she replies.

The discussion moves onto another scene, in which one of the stars, DEA agent "Cowboy" Quesada, is at home watching TV, and the camera moves around a wall of his apartment to find his girlfriend snorting heroin in the bathroom. The script specifies that Quesada is watching a video of *77 Sunset Strip,* the fifties TV show.

"How much is the clip?" George asks.

"Eight grand," Jerry, the line producer, tells him.

"You're thinking of a Foy track here?" Gordon asks the director of photography, who nods.

"In scene twenty-five," George says, "in Cuba, have we figured out how to make the hurricane look real? It needs to look like Jennie is about to be blown into the sea."

"A big Ritter fan won't do what we want," the production designer says. "You're going to need an air mover—you hook it up to a compressor."

"Expensive," the line producer tells George.

"I'm not worried about cost," George says, "as much as I am about the time it's going to take to shoot it."

"We can sell the wind in post," Jerry says.

"Let's do an overcranked master on that," Gordon says, and his first assistant director makes a note.

"Gordon," George asks, "is it undercranking or overcranking that makes things look slow-motion?" George can never remember this. And by occasionally exposing his own ignorance, he figures he appears secure in his new-boyhood, an unembarrassed mensch.

"Overcranking. And George, we'll use a little person, not a real child, for the smuggler's kid, right? I got a time problem with kids."

"As long as he looks like a kid," George says. "I mean, we're going to be pretty close. And he's got a line."

"It's just 'Por favor, Papi!' which we'll put in in post. And just his body is in the shot, not his head," Gordon says. "It's the head with the body that makes little people look like little people."

"In the next scene," one of the prop people says to George, sounding excited and proud, "when the bad guy gets sliced to ribbons in the sugar-cane harvester? We're getting a yard of actual bioengineered skin, this new stuff called Apligraf that surgeons use. It looks really real. Even feels real."

There are a few smiling *ewwws* around the table. "Nice," George says, pleased as well as disgusted.

Over the next hour, George and his staff say another dozen times, "You can do that in post" or "Can we put that in in post?" or "We'll fix that in post." And before the meeting is over, George finds himself thinking about his mother, how his equanimity over Edith Hope's death is causing him more pain than her death, how he's like the awful Jonathan Pryce character in *The Ploughman's Lunch*. He hasn't yet cried, not a tear in eight hours. He thinks, *Can we put that in in post?*

————

At the MBC, the Fifty-ninth Floor and Fifty-nine and (as Featherstone calls it) Five-Nine are proper nouns. Even though Mose himself is only intermittently in the city, the synecdoche is total. It is the floor where Harold Mose and all his senior New York executives have offices—Featherstone; Arnold Vlig, the chief operating officer; Hank Saddler, the head of corporate communications; and a dozen men whose names George doesn't know. Depending on context and vocal inflection, "Fifty-nine" can be portentous, menacing, flip, or contemptuous.

The Fifty-ninth Floor wants to lose the question mark in Janeane Garofalo Live? *as soon as possible.*

Fifty-nine wants to try selling coffee break sponsorships company-wide.

No, she's too skinny for daytime talk. Fifty-nine wants a host for Day-O! *who's more than thirty pounds and fewer than fifty pounds overweight.*

The Fifty-ninth Floor just doesn't understand why Mr. McCourt *is cleared on only sixty-one percent of the affiliates.*

News will definitely have to get a sign-off from Fifty-nine to start announc-ing exit-poll numbers at eight Eastern Time.

"I'm frankly amazed Fifty-nine is cool with your going so urban," Laura Welles, Featherstone's smart deputy, told George a few days ago. "I've been telling Timothy for a year that part of the show's genetic code is definitely urban."

In the entertainment business, "urban" is the euphemism for black. George and Emily decided, starting with the January fifteenth show, to lay bits of rap into the *NARCS* soundtrack—what the show's musical director calls their Spackle of Sound, a maximum of six seconds at a stretch, three times per episode. A week of audience testing in Omaha determined that was optimal: any less and the young, rap-friendly audi-ence segment didn't respond, any more than eighteen seconds an hour and the antirap audience majority became, as the research firm de-scribed it, "assertively intolerant." Testing over the last month has dis-covered a substantial audience segment, mostly whites in their thirties, who find the rap interludes on *NARCS* "energizing" and "stylish," but only in the precise, small doses the show is giving them. The research firm calls this middle group the Hip Urban Ambivalents, or HUAs. It is all such a delicate balance—fascinatingly so, like constituency politics, like trying to keep soccer moms and Social Security recipients all vot-ing Democratic, or Christian fundamentalists and libertarians in the Republican party. No, not *like* politics, George realized the day after the New Hampshire primary: getting an audience for a TV show (or a movie or a magazine) *is* politics, what America has now in lieu of real politics. Being a *Saturday Night Live* viewer or a *Touched by an Angel* viewer or a *NARCS* viewer is at least as meaningful for most people as being a Democrat or a Republican. Sure, the Democratic party "has mismanaged its brand image and brand equity for a generation," as Bill Bradley said at Ben Gould's cocktail party last month, pandering smartly to the Manhattan crowd, but Republicanism is a dying brand too; national politics is a dying brand category, like organ meats and typewriters. When Fifty-nine wants their disinclination to cover cam-paigns affirmed, George knows they have more than once cited "Mac-tier's end-of-politics paradigm." It's easier for them to make a zeitgeist argument than a lost-ad-revenue argument. George has become their pet intellectual. It both embarrasses and pleases him.

"Iris, we'll be—"

"I *know*," she says in her perpetual stage whisper. *"Fifty-nine."* From Iris's mouth, it always sounds like "the *principal's office*" or "the *oncologist*."

George carries the notes, as he always does when he and Emily are in meetings together. That way, she doesn't have to be the girl. With her expensively blond, not-quite-short hair, Emily looks ten years younger than she is. She acts ten years older, George thinks.

"So I understand you flew back with Timothy."

She gives George a look and an elaborate sigh.

"You *downgraded* yourself to business class just to avoid sitting in the same compartment?"

"Same *row.*"

"I don't know, Emily," he says, smiling, "I thought you were supposed to be the plugged-in Hollywood partner."

Emily doesn't respond. "The gay PR guy, the hairplugs, the smile . . ." Emily is changing the subject, George realizes after a beat. She is making a quick index finger loop-de-loop to indicate that George is supposed to fill in the blank.

"Hank Saddler. He's supposedly married, by the way."

"He said downstairs, 'Fifty-nine is convinced you guys can walk on water.' "

"I don't trust Hank."

"Factually? Or ethically?"

"He's a creep."

"He's a PR guy."

"He's also a basically stupid person who sincerely believes he's smart. It's a dangerous combination. Dumb schemers frighten me. Hi," George says, smiling big to the main receptionist on Fifty-nine. George is friendly and respectful to the assistant class. He is a natural at endearing himself to them and at impressing the top people; it is the middle people, like Saddler, he tends to ignore or dislike, and vice versa. "We're here to see Timothy."

There are two basic show-business personality types, the Merry Chatterer (Steve Ross, most of the DreamWorks principals, a majority of record executives, almost every agent and TV executive) and the Inscrutable Hardass (Michael Ovitz, Barry Diller, John Malone). George finds virtues in both. A majority of Merry Chatterers may be silly people, but what's the point of show business if it doesn't occasionally transmute work into a fiesta? He enjoys even insincere Hollywood gaiety if it's energetic enough. Some Inscrutable Hardasses are brilliant, but every one is dead-set on *appearing* to be brilliant—if you doubt that their still waters run deep, well, they might drown you just to prove the point. Inscrutable Hardasses often form good-cop/bad-cop partnerships with Merry Chatterers—Ovitz with Ron Meyer at the old CAA, Jon Dolgens with Sherry Lansing at Paramount, and at Microsoft, as Lizzie once pointed out, Bill Gates with Nathan Myhrvold. But George's preferred executive type is an old-fashioned mogul hybrid, the Merry Hardass, who he's discovered is surprisingly rare, especially in Los Angeles. Merry Hardasses are scary but fun, like fairytale creatures. Harvey Weinstein of Miramax, who talked to George and Emily about coproducing *NARCS* with Harvey Keitel as the star, is one. (George half expected him to shout "Fee! Fi! Fo! Fum!" when he rumbled in for meetings.) Sumner Redstone of Viacom (Rumplestiltskin as Lear) and the movie producer Scott Rudin (Popeye crossed with Bluto) are also Merry Hardasses. Harold Mose, who arrived from Toronto a year and a half ago to patch together MBC, is another.

Featherstone is pure Merry Chatterer. "Yabba *dabba* doo!" he says when he spots George and Emily, instead of *hello.* "Long time no see, Emmy Lou!" He kisses Emily on both cheeks.

"Timothy," she says.

Featherstone winks at George, and says as he leads them into a conference room, "Let me take you into my la-*bor*-a-tory." The walls are covered in magnesium panels, expensively riveted. A line of several dozen TV screens wrap around the room like a belt.

Emily smiles by reflex, hating herself for pretending to enjoy the pointless Bela Lugosi impression. "Good Grandpa Munster," she says, inching back into her own good graces.

"No—*George Hamilton,*" Featherstone says. "He taught me. I worked with him, you know, right after I ankled Woody." Timothy Featherstone was fired as a second assistant coffee boy on *Interiors,* and his father, who was a huge Jack and Bobby Kennedy contributor, had asked Jack Valenti to get young Timothy a gofer job on *Love at First Bite.* That was his career in feature films. While he was on "sabbatical" he totaled his Porsche in an accident on the Pacific Coast Highway, killing his twin brother, then produced a highly rated movie of the week based on the accident, which led to a successful career phase as a "long-form" TV producer. (He claims he was the first producer to show "female butt cleavage," as he calls it, in network prime time.) Then he worked as a programming executive under both Howard Stringer (smart Merry Chatterer) at CBS and Brandon Tartikoff (an exotic hybrid: Inscrutable Chatterer) at NBC, then briefly at Fox and VH1, and now here he is at the MBC, practically in charge. "So, I don't want you guys to be blindsided in there. I want to set the table for you on Harold's state of mind, okay?"

"Is there a problem?" George asks.

"No. Absolutely uh-uh. *Niènte.* But ownership's back on the table, comrades."

MBC owns half of *NARCS,* and although it's successful, which gives George and Emily some leverage, they have already agreed to give the network half ownership of any future MBC series they create.

"A longer license term?" Emily asks, all nice disingenuous calm. "He wants five years instead of four?"

"No," Timothy says, "we're going to want one hundred percent ownership on the new shows, but with a guaranteed back end for you guys, as well as—"

"Timothy," Emily shouts, "we're not . . . *employees.* We're not—"

"Emmo, Emmo, Emmo," Featherstone says. "Don't go there, Emi-line."

"Full ownership?" she says. "No. Unacceptable."

George had been surprised that MBC hadn't demanded more ownership earlier. He's always quietly preparing for the worst, ready for the secret trapdoor to swing open directly under hiiiiiiiiiim. It is automatic. Anytime any boss asks to meet with him, he steels himself, ready to be fired. If Lizzie is more than a half hour late coming home, he starts imagining her raped, then murdered, the phone call to her father, life as a widower. Since things usually turn out much better than awful, George feels lucky most of the time. And if they don't, he's ready.

For several seconds, no one makes a sound.

"Em," George finally says, "we've said ourselves that *Reality* is not going to have a billion-dollar syndication life. This isn't exactly *ER.* Back-end ownership—"

"Or *Baywatch,*" Featherstone adds, a beat late.

"—is really kind of a theoretical deal point here."

She gives George a hard look. George is not just caving in, but ganging up with the second-dumbest man in television to humiliate her with a smile, in the name of reason and easy compromise. This was why she had come to despise the president of the United States long before impeachment. Not because he was a liar, or a sex addict (Emily, as it happened, went down on him once, in a limousine outside the Hotel Inter-Continental during the 1992 convention in New York), but because he's just a high-end New Man gone pathological, slipping and slithering on a dime.

"For *Reality,* maybe," she says, playing along against her instincts. "It's different. But everything else is straight-ahead entertainment. Long shelf lives."

"Riiiight . . . ?" Featherstone says.

"Right, *what?*" she spits.

"But Timothy," George asks, "what is the argument for the network owning shows like *My People, Your People* or *The Odds* or *Actually Bizarre?*" These are the three other series George and Emily have in development. They are, respectively, an hour-long "sitcom of manners" about husband and wife executives; a zany "alternative" comedy set in Las Vegas; and a cross between *The Twilight Zone* and *Candid Camera* in which unwitting "contestants" would secretly be taped as apparently supernatural tricks (UFOs, phantasms, emptied offices) are played on them.

"Well, we're prepared to give *Reality* a thirty-nine-week commitment. Rock solid."

This is news. George and Emily have asked for twenty-six weeks, were hoping for thirteen, and prepared for six. (George has been prepared for a pilot order, period.) Now the network is going to hand them $50 million and eighty hours of prime time to execute his weird, untried idea.

"*Timothy,*" George says, smiling as big as he ever smiles. He is almost dizzy. Is this what crack feels like? "You buried the lead."

"What do you mean?"

"He means that a firm thirty-nine-week commitment sounds absolutely fantastic as far as we're concerned, Timothy," Emily says. She's grinning for real now, using adjectives, verbs, and adverbs. But she won't let the astonishing good turn make her irresponsible. "And you mentioned back-end guarantees? On the other shows?"

"Business affairs, Emma Bovary, business affairs! Good-faith negotiation, et cetera, et ceterama."

Emma Bovary? Ridiculous as ever, but George is impressed by the erudition.

"Harold will buy and air thirty-nine weeks of *Reality?*" Emily says to Featherstone. "One-point-six million a week?"

"*D'accord,* darlin'."

"No speaking French. That's why I defected from Canada." Mose is in the room. Featherstone swivels his chair and bolts upright. George and Emily stand.

"George! Emily."

"Superb," Emily says, and George, dumbstruck, manages only a robust, "Hi!"

"How are you?" Mose asks.

Having already answered, Emily offers her cheek for a kiss.

"Great!" George pipes up, suddenly as taut and overwrought as a teenager. He always notices the aroma of Harold Mose. Why hasn't Ralph Lauren bottled this fragrance? Maybe he has. It must be the daily haircut plus fresh flowers plus cashmere plus BMW leather plus the executive-jet oxygen mix plus a dash of citrus. That is, Mose smells luscious. He smells rich.

"Pellegrino?" It is Mose's secretary, Dora, who looks uncannily like Queen Elizabeth II would, if the queen cut her hair very short, dyed it platinum, lost forty pounds, and wore Anne Klein suits. (The queen in Diana's dreams.) Dora's beautiful assistant, Lucy, has just set down the boss's Pellegrino with Rose's lime juice.

"Your pilot was perfect for my attention span," Mose says. "Have you considered making the actual show only fifteen minutes a week?" George and Emily grin. Featherstone chuckles. They have produced a fifteen-minute minipilot for the show—a five-minute newscast and ten minutes of behind-the-scenes fiction. "I expect that Timothy has, in every important respect, badly misrepresented the program to me," Mose continues, not quite smiling, in his happy-gangster baritone. Are there Canadian gangsters? "So: is this a mutant news program that all people of substance and seriousness will despise, or a bizarre entertainment program that half the audience won't understand even if they watch it, which they won't?" He plucks the lime slice from his drink and bites the flesh.

"Well," George says, "a lot of people in news are going to go nuts, that's true, unquestionably. The op-ed pages and the journalism professors will kill us."

Featherstone glances anxiously at Mose. The chairman is expressionless.

"Oh, *dear*," Mose says, pulling the desiccated lime from his mouth. "Oh gosh, oh my. And the *down*side is?" It takes Featherstone a second to realize he should chuckle, and he does.

"We figure it'll be similar to the fallout from the *NARCS* New Year's show," George says, "times ten—a fuss that (a) makes people look at the show, like with the Donna and Rudy Giuliani thing on Fox or the Dan Rather nipple episode on the Farrellys' show. And (b) as a marketing position, I think we could do worse than 'The Groundbreaking Program the Media Elite Doesn't Trust You to Watch.' "

Finally Mose smiles. "Correct," he says. "Exactly."

"When the noise clears," Emily says, "this is smart, tough, good TV. First-class news. First-class drama."

"Dramedy," Featherstone amends, then turns to Mose. "It's dramedy, Harold. That's my top-line note. There's got to be fun elements. A little *Mary Tyler Moore*, right? *Murphy Brown* when it had an eighteen-point-six rating. *Larry Sanders* with heart and a high-Q star. We want it zoomy."

Emily glances at Featherstone and George nods too, just long enough, just, to indicate acknowledgment.

"Explain to me exactly why we need *two* half hours every week before we get to the actual news program on Friday," Mose says to Emily and George. "Timothy gave me the amortization argument. But *creatively,* what?"

It is unclear to George if Mose's emphasis on the word *creatively* implies curiosity or skepticism.

"The basic idea," George says, "is we can roll with events, evolve the story lines during the week. As news unfolds, we slip in references on the Thursday show, adjust the tenor, fix it as we go."

"Maintain the *arc,* Harold," Featherstone says.

"If the week starts off early as fun and games," George continues, "a story like Clinton in Sausalito with his English actresses, but then, you know, a bunch of people are massacred in Mexico on Wednesday afternoon, we can adjust the trajectory for that before the Friday program. And the second episode midweek reminds the audience that we've got a real, functioning news operation here. It's also," he says, glancing over at Emily, "the three-act principle. We need a middle episode to make the transition from the docudrama of the Tuesday show—"

"Docu*dramedy,*" Featherstone says.

"—to the straight news hour on Friday. We can't just go slam-bang from *Murphy Brown* to *60 Minutes.* Thursday's the hinge."

"Thursday, nine-thirty," Emily says, referring to the time slot Featherstone has broached. "Yes?"

"Whoa there, little lady," Featherstone says now in an Elvis Presley voice.

"But you're confident," Mose says, "that you'll find actors who can cry and argue and laugh and kiss on Tuesday and Thursday and then deliver the actual news on Friday? Credibly? They need to seem genuinely . . . knowledgeable."

"Compared with the people who do news now?" Emily says. "Yes. Compared with Connie Chung. Compared with blondes on MSNBC."

"Brian Williams is actually a very bright guy," Featherstone says.

"The turnaround time won't be murder?" Mose asks. "To stay topical?"

"Writing off the news will be the big challenge," George says, "no question. But half of the Tuesday-Thursday shows will be non-timely evergreen stuff, relationship stories. Maybe more than half. And a lot of Tuesday-Thursday will be real, our process stuff— footage of camera setups, footage of staff meetings. Which will be about editing, not writing."

"Postproduction Tuesday-Thursday will be a killer," says Emily. "But we want it rough, real—"

Featherstone leaps in. "Like *Homicide,* Harold, but sexy and fun and *up.* Or the MTV shows—you know, the black-and-white, the hotties in the lofts, vacationing, et cetera. If the kids were grownups with jobs."

"I get it," Mose says.

"Talk about how we leverage in the interactive piece," Featherstone says. "Reality-dot-com." Featherstone still welcomes any excuse to say "dot-com."

Harold Mose has become very alert.

George doesn't want to get into the bells and whistles. "It's just a notion," he says. "It's not a major thing."

"Tell me," says Mose.

"Well, we could let viewers access the news show in progress during the week on a web site. Give them bits of raw footage and wire copy and real e-mails and story lists and draft scripts, as if they're hooking directly into our intranet . . ."

"Extranet, you mean," Mose says.

"Right," Featherstone says.

"I guess so," George says.

"You'd put up all the in-house material for anyone on the net to see?" Mose asks. "That's taking transparency a bit far, isn't it? Sounds dodgy."

"No, we give them access to kind of a core sample, a *selection* of real material," George says, making it up as he goes along. "Everything vetted, nothing confidential. Just enough to give an authentic insider's feel. Not transparency. More like translucency."

"Clever," Mose says.

"Multiplatform it," Featherstone says, winking, verging on meaninglessness. Then he chants, pumping one arm, "Convergence, convergence, convergence."

"It's Lizzie's idea," George says. "My wife."

"I know Lizzie," Mose says. He doesn't wear a watch, so he checks Featherstone's and looks up at George and Emily. "I need to be at Teterboro by seven-thirty if I'm going to have a nightcap in *Seattle* tonight." Here the overenunciation is clearly derogatory, the way James Mason might have said *Cucamonga* or *tuna casserole*.

Emily leans toward Mose. "Timothy told you about *My People, Your People*? Our other . . . dramedy?"

Featherstone nods quickly.

"He called it 'a twenty-first-century *Upstairs, Downstairs* meets *thirtysomething*.'" Mose pauses like a pro. "Haven't we seen that? Wasn't that *The Jetsons*?"

"Romantic comedy," Emily says.

"The guy is the commissioner of the NBA," George explains. "His wife is an architect, he's white, she's black, the kids are punky Vietnamese twins, her assistant's a gay guy. The housekeeper is Bosnian."

"Very Norman Lear," Mose says.

"Right," Featherstone says enthusiastically, "exactly. . . ." And then, getting Mose's drift, he catches himself and repeats, *"Right,"* this time with a sneer, barely missing a beat.

"No, no," George says, "*anti-*P.C., quirky, a little dark. We'll spend as much time on the assistants' lives as we do on the leads'."

"It's about class. Complicated class differences," Emily says.

"Which nobody else is doing," George adds.

"Correct, but maybe for good reason," Mose says. "You want to do *A Very Upstairs, Downstairs Millennium*—Roseanne as Seinfeld's nanny, the guy from *Cabaret* as Bebe Neuwirth's secretary. *Married with Staff.* Oh, for all I know it'll be the breakout smash hit. I'm just a birthday-card salesman. Picking pilots is Timothy's job. But you know, when we call this the New Network for the New Century, I want us to *mean* it." Mose is now an American citizen, but he has spent most of his life and made most of his fortune in real estate in Canada. He also has stakes in East Asian telephone companies and owns the world's third-largest greeting-card company—it is, George has heard him say more than once, "the Hallmark of the Pacific Rim." Before he conjured MBC into existence, Mose Media Holdings' only media holding was his half interest in the Winter Channel, the faintly conservative sports-weather-and-holiday-themed channel carried on cable systems in Canada, the upper Midwest, and the Great Plains. Mose also operates two hundred movie theaters in Saskatchewan and Alberta, which, like greeting cards, apparently qualify as "media" under the loose modern definition.

"That was my big note on this too," Featherstone pipes in. "I mean, raise the stakes, guys! *Raise the frigging stakes.*"

At this moment, George wouldn't be unhappy if Featherstone died.

"It seems to me you guys have an awful lot on your plate, with *NARCS* and this new monster of yours, your—"

"Reality," George says.

"Correct. *Reality,*" Mose says, and pauses. "You know, I don't know about *Reality*. . . ."

George and Emily exchange a panicky glance. He's already changed his mind? They are suddenly zero for two?

"It's so . . . arty. Like a scriptwriter's idea of a newsmagazine."

"Fantastic note," Featherstone says.

George and Emily exchange another fast glance.

"You have a problem with *Reality*, Harold?" George asks, wanting the end to come quickly now that he knows he's doomed.

"Now you may absolutely hate this," Mose says, "but what about *Real Time*? Is that a horrible name for this show?"

It's only the *name* Mose doesn't like.

"No, that's just fabulous. I mean it. It's superb," George says. Emily looks at George; she figures it's the adrenaline talking. "Don't you think so, Emily?"

"*Real Time* could be perfect," she says.

"Yessss!" Featherstone says, clenching a fist, pumping his arm. "Out of the park! Homer alert!"

"And besides, Timothy," Mose says, "aren't we calling that other project RealityVision? The Reality Network? The Reality Channel?"

"Reality Channel. No 'The.' " Keeping his body facing Mose, he turns his head a good 120 degrees toward George and Emily. "Possible concept shift for the Winter Channel. A New Age cable channel, although 'New Age' is a no-no. Demi, Deepak, Marianne Williamson, Mars and Venus, Mayans and the Sphinx, gyroscopes, high colonics, homeopathics, chiropractic, yoga, Enya, John Tesh, Dr. Weil, Kenny G, vitamin E, herbs, Travolta, Cruise, lifestyle, feng shui, ginseng, ginkgo, tofu, emu oil, psychics, ESP, E.T., et cetera, et cetera. Aromatherapy. VH1 meets Lifetime meets the PBS fund-raising specials meets those good-looking morning-show doctors meets QVC meets the Food Network. You know? And in the late-night daypart, tantric sex."

"I do know," George says to Featherstone, who has already turned toward Mose, grinning, preparing himself to appreciate the imminent bon mot.

"Or, as I like to call it," Mose says, "the Lunatic Network—all credulity, all the time." Everyone smiles. He stands. "I'm not completely convinced it's scalable. I don't know how it will scale." Mose salutes the room—"Gentlemen. Lady."—and starts out, Featherstone at his heels. But Mose stops. "George," he says, "I was terribly sorry to hear about your mother. Anything we can do. Do you understand? Anything you need, ask Dora." Then, to Featherstone—"We've got to lance the boil now, Timothy. I want both versions of the broadband presentation in Redmond, in case they have some idea that they can"—and then they're gone. In the conference room, it's as if a violent afternoon storm has suddenly passed. George and Emily are drenched, but now the sun is shining.

" 'Scalable'?" Emily asks. "Canadian union-buster talk?"

"No. The internet. It means, can the thing be rolled out wide? So I guess we have a show, Em." George hasn't felt quite so jazzed, so supremely confident, in months.

"I guess," she says, nodding. "*A* show. It's do-and-die time now." Of the two ideas they were here to pitch, *My People, Your People* is the series Emily has been most eager to make. *Real Time* will be difficult to produce. And while she likes imagining the seriousness it will confer on her in Los Angeles, the prospect of actually doing it—*news?*—is frightening.

"I actually do think the name *Real Time* works," George says. "It's good."

"Only *good?* Not"—she takes a sharp breath, and squeals—"*fabulously superb?*"

"Fuck you. Did you notice our New Age joke has been stolen? The channel we invented that night at Nobu?"

"I did. Fine. Let Timothy know we know it's ours. Let Harold know we know. It's leverage on series ownership. Plus we may not have to go to hell."

George smiles, and stands to leave. "Really? Passive beneficiaries of evil ideas are hell-exempt?"

"Well, *you'll* probably be going to hell, anyway. Journalist hell. On account of *Reality.*"

"*Real Time.*"

5

Lizzie left the office a few minutes after five. It's the first time this winter she's left before dark. Entirely apart from Edith Hope's death, it's been a lousy day, ten hours at work without even a whiff of science. The whiffs of science are what draw her into this business, real business, in the first place. But today she has accomplished nothing. She signed expense accounts, extended supplier contracts, agreed to pay $940 a month extra to insure her employees against carpal tunnel syndrome (which she secretly considers a half-phony fad disability), interviewed prospective employees, and screamed about hypothetical seven- and eight-figure sums of money to a man in Redmond she has never met. Today has been one of those days when she feels like America's most overeducated, overinvested postal clerk. Since making breakfast for the kids and handing them their backpacks, she has done nothing gratifying or important, even though she's exhausted, as drained as if she'd spent the day overseeing the invention of a disposable solar-powered twenty-five-cent supercomputer the size of a cricket.

She was too tired to go to yoga, so she's been wandering for an hour and a half toward home, around Chelsea and the Village and the neighborhoods she refuses to call NoHo and NoLIta, through Chinatown

and the Lower East Side, looking in shop windows, looking at her reflection in shop windows, wondering if she looks thirty-five, stepping
into shops, not shopping. Now, in a store on Grand Street, an 1891
map of Minnesota decorated with a border of old paper strings from
dozens of Hershey's Kisses (folk art: $300) has started her quietly sob-
bing. Edith Hope's death is discombobulating her. It isn't because she
is reminded of her own mother's death, Lizzie feels certain. Her own
mother's death was depressing, because it made her face up to just how
little they loved each other, but this is different. Edith Hope's death has
made Lizzie sad, surprisingly sad. The surprise makes her even sadder.

They were never soulmates. "Honey, will the offspring be Jewish,
too?" Edith Hope said to Lizzie with a big smile over coffee an hour
after they met, during the 1988 Republican Convention in New Orleans, which George was covering for ABC and where Edith Hope
was a Minnesota alternate delegate pledged to Jack Kemp. "Yes, Mom,
they will," George said. "But if they're boys they won't be circum-
cised, so no one will know." His mother just nodded.

Edith Hope and Lizzie spoke every few months at most, and saw
each other only once a year. But her mother-in-law finally seemed to
love her more easily than her own mother ever did—not love her more,
maybe, but enjoy her company, cut her some slack, get a little drunk
with her on Thanksgiving after the dishes were done and everyone else
was sprawled on the davenport in the family room (the davenport! the
family room!) staring at football. Six or seven Thanksgivings ago—six;
she wasn't pregnant—after Alice and the twins had gone home with all
the leftovers, LuLu must have been asleep, George and Sarah and Sir
were half watching *The Philadelphia Story,* one of the three videotapes
Edith Hope owned. The two women were leafing through George's
old school pictures. Lizzie said that when George was in junior high he
looked like the singer Beck. Edith Hope said that people always
thought George's father looked like Jimmy Stewart. She asked Lizzie
when she realized she was in love with George. Lizzie grinned. "On his
couch during our first real date, about ninety seconds before we
fucked," she said. Edith Hope looked as if she'd been slugged. Lizzie
lurched protectively an inch in her direction, feeling she was watching
some dear old vase fall to the floor. Then her mother-in-law said,
"Goodness! I don't think I've heard anyone use that word since

George's uncle Vance died." Then she smiled. "The way you just . . . *say* it sounds so"—Edith Hope wiggled her shoulders and moved her eyebrows up and down, Donna Reed doing Mae West— "It's like . . . a movie." Edith Hope finished her third vodka and cranberry juice, and the ice dregs with it. "Good for you, dear. I'm glad you were in love. *Before.*"

Lizzie is so glad to be living in the city again. She is so glad they can afford to admit that their two-year country-squire experiment in Sneden's Landing was a disaster. Walking down Delancey Street, she passes a store that sells wigs and knives and bootleg videos. There seem to be a lot of wig stores in New York, more than necessary. Lizzie enjoys their presence the way she enjoys the storefront psychics and the Dominican flavored-shaved-ice vendors, all the unsanitary but unthreatening alien city bits. Wig stores (like psychics) strike her as implicitly pornographic—the hubba-hubba cartoon *volume* of the hairdos, the insane Slurpee colors, the fibers that make no human-hair pretense, the smudged-shop-window intimacy that seems more charged than the stores selling penis-shaped loaves of pumpernickel and multizippered black vinyl panties.

Crossing a quiet stretch of Kenmare Street at sunset, a backlit old wino comes toward her through the gloaming, pushing a packed, smoky shopping cart and chanting, in a turn-of-the-last-century oystermonger singsong, "*Flaming* potatoes! Now. *Flaming* potatoes! Now." From a good four feet away, Lizzie reaches into her pocket and tosses all her change at the box hanging from his cart handle. (Performance folk art: only $1.37.)

On Broadway, she stops in a Korean deli to buy milk, and notices that the rack of produce is oddly speckled. Looking closer, she picks up an avocado and sees that the speckle is a tiny red, star-shaped sticker that says GORE 2000. It's a campaign ad. She looks around and sees now that almost every piece of fruit and every vegetable in the place has one of the little stickers. On the apples, the GORE 2000 stars are embossed directly into the skins. (Pop art: $2.50 a pound.)

As she gets closer to home, Lizzie automatically turns to glance up at St. Andrew's School, thinks of LuLu and Max, and feels relief. Heading east toward Water Street, she breathes deeper, as usual, and feels calmer, even cheery, as if she's had half a beer. Two buildings down from theirs, she glances in at the rococo parlor and sees something new—filling the room is a giant television screen, on it an intense electronic cyan background with foot-high letters that say NINETEENTH-CENTURY EUROPEAN LEADERS. She is bewildered and delighted (Installation art: free), but a moment later, as she pulls her keys out, she realizes what she's seen, and thinks that if she were the *Jeopardy!* contestant she definitely would have picked a different category for $300, Alex.

She tosses her leather backpack on the kitchen table, and the scrape of the metal Prada tag across the zinc surface scares the cat off its window seat. "Hello, Johnny," Lizzie says to the cat. "Where is everybody?" She sees that Max has brought home this year's school pictures, twelve unsmiling Maxes on one sheet, plus two big five-by-seven unsmiling Maxes. The cheap generic portraits always give Lizzie a chill. The pictures make her children look like any children, like pathetic children in the newspaper or on milk cartons, like victims. She turns away.

She scans the mail. Do other people get real letters? The only personal correspondence George and Lizzie receive regularly are invitations (three today: a Roger Baird and Nancy McNabb "Remember the 1980s?" costume party at the Frick Museum to raise money to supply T1 internet hookups for the fifty poorest schools in New York, a party celebrating the Philip Morris Corporation's sponsorship of the upcoming Jean-Genet-and-Jim-Morrison season at Brooklyn Academy of Music, one addressed to "Mr. and Mrs. Zimbalist" from Bennett Gould reminding them about the grand-opening party at BarbieWorld in Las Vegas next week); thank-you notes (one today from her friend Beverly for a Tiffany's silver teething ring); and those quasi-celebrity chain letters (the last one from Angela Janeway, soliciting ten dollars for clinics in southern Mexico—copies of which also were sent by Danny Goldberg to Courtney Love, to Pete Hamill by Ken Kesey, to Bianca Jagger by Arthur Schlesinger, Jr., by Mort Zuckerman to Tony Blair, by Patricia Duff to Harold Mose, and by a hundred other quasi-celebrities to five hundred other quasi-celebrities who are all pleased, in the name of a good cause, to make you aware that they know one another). Nowadays even thank-you notes and Christmas cards have addresses laser-printed on an adhesive label. The last piece of absolutely bona fide personal mail Lizzie received was a note in December from George's mother that included a recipe for Szechwan Christmas succotash (*"Very zippy!!"*) and a Minneapolis *Star Tribune* clip about a coven of suburban teenage computer hackers, all girls. ("Thought you'd be interested regarding female computer 'progress' out in these parts! Tell George one of these gals from Edina is the daughter of his high school friend Jodie—small world!") The note, the recipe, and the newspaper clipping were all included with their 1999 Christmas present, a "media-storing ottoman," which had an upholstered plaid hinged top and a drawer. It could hold three hundred compact discs or a hundred videos. Max said LuLu could use it as a mausoleum for her Barbies. Lizzie gave it to the cleaning lady the Monday after Christmas.

Louisa, sounding like a dropped piece of carry-on luggage, comes tumbling down the three flights of stairs. During the brief pause at each landing Lizzie hears the slow, even footsteps of Rafaela, their new baby-sitter. (Lizzie won't use the word *nanny.*)

"Hello, baby-duck!" Lizzie says, mail in hand, as Louisa finally stands before her.

The six-year-old, zipped into her snowsuit, looks past her mother, bows her head, frowns, and says, "Hello, Missus."

"What?" Lizzie says, startled, smiling, staring at LuLu, who runs out to the tiny backyard. (Lizzie won't use *garden* as a synonym for yard, even though it would be more accurate.)

Rafaela arrives in the kitchen. She is wrapped in an old Missoni cardigan of George's and a prop DEA jacket from *NARCS,* with a WIRED watchcap pulled way down.

"Hi, Rafaela."

"Hello, Missus," she says, not quite making eye contact, following Louisa outdoors. She turns. "Missus, the store don't have whole-wheat Mega-Cheerios you want. Store brand only."

"The children will survive, Rafaela. That's fine."

"Okay," Rafaela says, and pulls the back door shut.

With Margaret, the previous and perfect baby-sitter, who went home to St. Kitts at Christmas and decided to remain there with the husband she'd abandoned eleven years earlier, George and even Lizzie enjoyed the Anglo-Caribbean bits Louisa and Max had picked up—saying "straightaway" instead of "immediately," pronouncing the first syllable of "radiator" with a broad *a*. A few years back, however, Max required heavy persuasion to stop referring to black people as "colored," even though Margaret, who was black, would continue to do so. "Is Margaret bad for saying 'colored'?" LuLu asked then. Now she will need to be told why she shouldn't call her mother "Missus," even though Rafaela does.

"Mommy?" comes a voice from all the way upstairs.

"Hello, Sarah."

"Hi," Sarah yells down. "Sir spilled the perfume, not me. Penelope and I already had dinner. Can you get *firm* tofu next time? Can we use one of your old cigarette lighters for our video?" Max changed his name to Sir almost two years ago, in second grade, after seeing some old war movie on television. At about the same time, it seemed to Lizzie that half the boys in school were named Max, and she felt some regret that they had given their son the name: too trendy too late in the wave. So she and George decided to let Max call himself Sir. Everyone but his parents and grandparents now called him Sir, and even Lizzie sometimes does, for fun. "And, Mom?" Sarah yells. "What time are we leaving for Minneapolis tomorrow?"

"Eleven. What's the lighter for? Sarah, I don't want to shout." She and her classmate thunder down the stairs like a 1970 drum solo, recklessly fast and loud, almost virtuosic.

Sarah and Lizzie hug. "Is he okay?" Sarah says softly into her mother's neck.

Lizzie feels her sinuses sting. Her eyes water. "Yes, I think. Yeah." They decouple. "What do you want to burn?"

"Well, in the southern part, the sheriff is going to torture Penelope while she's in jail? Put a cigarette near her face and burn her hair."

"Really just *singe* it, more," Penelope says, looking from Sarah to Lizzie. Penelope has magnificent hair, tiny glistening labor-intensive coils that Sarah has informed Lizzie are *not* to be called dreadlocks, but simply 'locks or microbraids. "I promised my mom. *And* my locktician," she adds with a smile that could indicate either embarrassment or pride.

"Be very careful. Who plays the trooper?"

"Sir," Sarah says.

"Interesting casting," Lizzie says. "Make sure he's *really careful* with the flame."

"We're not, like, cretins."

"Where did you get the cigarette?"

"Penelope's brother. I was going to ask George to play the trooper, but—"

"No," Lizzie said.

"I know." Lizzie feels a pang whenever Sarah calls her stepfather "George," which she is doing more and more. It seems to be one of those small adolescent cruelties passing as grownup sophistication. Sarah's biological father is a man named Buddy Ramo, whom she and Lizzie haven't seen in years, and who lives somewhere north of Malibu. Buddy Ramo was a child actor managed by Lizzie's father, Mike. His biggest break was the title role on *Li'l Gilligan,* a *Gilligan's Island* prequel series that was canceled after two episodes. He was a crush that lasted fifteen years and ended only after he and Lizzie finally slept together a few times the summer before her last year of college. Buddy is the stupidest man with whom she has ever had sex. Once, when she heard Emily call Timothy Featherstone "the second-stupidest man in television," Lizzie actually wondered for an instant if Buddy Ramo was well enough known to be considered the stupidest.

"Your brother's on the computer?"

"Yeah. I have to go force him to stop."

Without another word, Sarah, wearing a blood-red U.S. OUT OF MEXICO NOW T-shirt, and Penelope, wearing a lavender Ralph Lauren alpaca turtleneck, start back upstairs, two steps at a time, to continue shooting their Unfortunate American History docudrama.

Lizzie turns on the computer in the kitchen—the musical chord that Macs play as they boot up pleases her, as always, like a little electronic dawn—and she sends a message to her son, who is upstairs. As a surprise housewarming present last year, Bruce, from the office, wired the family's five computers together into a local-area network, which George and Lizzie at first regarded as a joke conversation piece but now find themselves using.

HI. DINNER IN 20 MINUTES WHEN DADDY GETS HOME.

Max replies instantly.

I ATE WITH SARAH AND PENELOPE ALL READY. BYE.

When George walks in, Lizzie is sitting in the big, ratty old leather armchair in their bedroom looking at pictures of their wedding, of George dancing with his mother, of his mother dancing with her father, of the Laura Ashleyed toddler Sarah on George's shoulders.

"Did you just sneeze?" he asks from the hallway. "I thought I heard you sneezing from out on the street." Lizzie always sneezes violently, without restraint. George finds it sexy. He reaches their room and sees her. Her eyes are red. Her cheeks are wet. She hasn't been sneezing.

"Aw, sweetie," he says.

"I miss your mom."

"Sweetie."

"I hate people dying. I know that's stupid to say. But I hate it."

Lizzie continues crying. Kneeling in front of the chair, George puts his arm around her. He doesn't cry.

"I know," he says. "I know."

From upstairs they hear Max shout, "We got ways of making you show a little respect, you uppity nigger girl!"

George pushes Lizzie back from his shoulder and looks at her.

They hear the girls laugh and Sarah says, "Great! That was awesome, Sir."

"Sarah's video. About civil rights," Lizzie says, and then gives a long, loud, sinus-clearing snort. "God." She chuckles through her final sob. "How was your meeting with Mose?"

"I think we sold the *Reality* show."

"I think I queered my Microsoft deal."

"Mose didn't like *My People, Your People*."

"Good. I'm sorry. But I didn't want our life to be a sitcom."

George smiles. "It's not a sitcom, it's a"—George makes quick little midair quotation marks with his hands—" 'dramedy.' Emily wants to take it to ABC. What happened with Microsoft?"

"I say *fuck* too much." George smiles. "According to some anti-Semitic sexist asshole in Seattle. But I do swear too much. I'll tell you about it later." She stands up. "I need a big drink. The kids have eaten. You want to order sushi in? Hiroshima Boy?"

They had martinis on their first date, almost twelve years ago. She was twenty-four and he was just thirty-two and drinking martinis was still, for people their age, a self-conscious, tongue-in-cheek act, playing grownup. They'd met at a Dukakis fund-raiser at Bennett Gould's triplex on East Thirteenth Street, and they left together for a drink at a noir-in-outer-space-themed bar in the East Village called Blue Velveteen. The olives were plastic. Sometime after their second martinis,

Lizzie did a Kitty Dukakis impersonation that made George laugh so suddenly he sprayed gin out his nose all over baby Sarah, sleeping next to him on the tatty velvet banquette.

Twelve years later, the martinis in Manhattan are sipped without olives or irony. Martinis for two remains a residual romantic ritual. George has punched on the television, and it plays its turn-on music, the five-note Intel-inside jingle. That started when they installed the cable modem. He sits next to Lizzie on the couch in the living room, looking down on Rafaela playing with Louisa outside in the dark.

"... the actress denied the allegations, and spokespeople for both Senator Kennedy and the White House declined to comment." One, one thousand. "Are humans about to become bionic?"

"Oh, lose the smirk, asshole," George says. "I still can't figure where they all learn to smirk." He turns to Lizzie. "Does any actual person switch between a frown and a smirk all the time like that?"

"... at the University of Washington, where a controversial scientist reported today that he has succeeded in establishing a direct communications link between two living mammals' brains by means of computer chips."

"As opposed to dead mammals' brains," George says.

"Although computer industry observers agreed the feat was exciting, they—"

" 'Industry observers agreed,' " George says. "God, TV news sucks."

"Shhh," Lizzie says, waving the remote toward him like a giant black index finger.

"—that the practical applications of the so-called mental modem are years away. In Mexico, a spokesman for the American embassy denied allegations that an American military attaché had participated in the torture of civilians in the Chiapas village of Taniperla. Calling the charges—"

She mutes the TV.

"Bruce knows that guy."

George is interested. "Bruce knows the CIA torturer?"

"No."

"Brian Williams? So does Featherstone."

"No, no, the person at U-Dub who did those animal-chip experiments."

"U-Dub?"

"U of W, University of Washington," Lizzie says. "Bruce worked with the guy in Oregon writing bioinformatics code."

"Ah," George says, feigning comprehension. "So who at Microsoft did you say *fuck* to that you shouldn't have?"

"Some lawyer. A bean counter. They're suddenly offering two-point-nine million. They're not taking me seriously. They're trying to gyp us."

"Jesus, three million for a fifth of the company is an insult? *Gyp* is an ethnic slur, you know."

"Two-point-nine is for a tenth—they say they only want ten per-cent of the company now."

"It's still free money, isn't it? I mean, it's not like you won't be in control."

Lizzie sighs again. "George, that would value Fine Technologies at *twenty-nine million dollars.*"

"Sounds okay to me."

Lizzie is often charmed by George's vagueness about business mat-ters. But not right now. "We have earnings, George! Almost a half mil-lion dollars last year! When fucking TK Corporation, with two million in revenues and not a dime in earnings, gets a market cap of two hun-dred thirty million the day of their IPO? No way! Plus it's *Microsoft,* George." After she left the News Corporation online debacle, she joined a little company called Virtual Fortress that made firewall secu-rity software for web sites, just as prices for firewall security software started dropping; when Microsoft entered the business, her company immediately went belly up.

"TK Corporation is Nancy McNabb's brother Penn's company? So go public."

"Why should I go public? This is a real business, with real products. The company doesn't need the capital."

"Then don't go public."

"And you and I don't need the money. We can't find any stuff for this place that we like enough to buy anyway," she says, gesturing toward the dark, naked dining room and the dark, naked room with books and the piano but no name. "And not counting Russia, we haven't taken a real vacation since about 1996."

"You know, it's funny. My mother used to say to my dad, after he bought some big wind-powered composting unit or gone on a sailplane fishing trip to Alaska or something, 'Perry, you just can't

spend money *fast* enough.' We've actually reached the point now
where we can't spend it fast enough. You know? Literally. This couch
is really not comfortable, you know."

"With Microsoft it's the *principle* of it, George. They said eight million for a fifth. It was a handshake deal."

"Whose hand did you shake?"

"Figuratively."

"Well, there you go."

"You're not taking this seriously." Lizzie sips her martini, then puts
her glass on the red coffee table that looks like scuffed, circa-1960
Formica but is, in fact, 1924 Le Corbusier—the single really expensive
object they own. "Honey?" she says, her face softening. She puts her
hands on his crossed knees. "How're you feeling about your mom?"

He looks at Lizzie and shrugs. After a moment, he says, "I was all set
for the ordeal. Months, years. 'Is it better to have someone you love die
suddenly or after a long illness?' And now I get both. Bang *and* whimper." He sticks his tongue into the apex of his glass, lapping the last,
vermouthy drops of gin. "Two mints in one." He looks up from the
glass. "I haven't talked to her in like . . . three weeks." For several long
minutes, they sit in silence, both looking out the six-foot-high back
windows as Louisa dances with her shoulders hunched up around her
ears and her arms turned inside out. She is doing one of her im-
promptu rap performances for Rafaela.

"I really should be doing this somewhere out West," Lizzie suddenly
says, sliding down and crossing her own legs so they are knee to knee.

"Fine. We'll move. Make sure Rafaela tells the kids."

"I can't do this business here the way it should be done. I feel like
I'm overseas, in some island outpost where I never quite know what's
going on back at headquarters. And everything needs translating, and
the phones don't work. It's so hard."

"Your phones don't work?"

"Figuratively. So they bought *Reality*? That's so excellent."

George smiles. "He's committed to thirty-nine weeks."

"No! George!"

"I know. It's crazy." He's still smiling. "I told him your fake-real
web-site idea for the show. 'Clever,' he said."

"So Mose gets it?" she asks.

"The show? I think so. Yeah. He wants to call it *Real Time*."

"Mose must be smart."

"I can't tell for sure. He's witty and articulate, which non-smart people never are nowadays. Not Americans, anyway. Although now that I think about it, there are a lot of articulate dumb people in TV. This afternoon Mose said, 'You know "The New Network for the New Century"? I want all of us to *mean* it.' I don't know if he's brilliant, or just unafraid of sounding superficial."

"What's the difference? At his level. That's what makes a good leader. Not being afraid of sounding superficial. Really believing your own bullshit. 'Men believe in the truth of all that is *seen* to be strongly believed.' "

"You remember you said that to me when they first brought up executive producer at ABC? My little Nietzsche."

"That was so long ago."

"Nineteen ninety-five, only."

"Exactly," Lizzie says. "I think the guy from Hiroshima Boy's here. *Rafaela?*" she shouts.

He stands, grabbing both of Lizzie's hands with his right, and as he slides her off the couch, which they've reupholstered in black leather, her jeans squeak. "I'm fat as a pig," she says. As he uses his teeth to pull the cork from a half-full bottle of Chardonnay, it squeaks, and squeaks again as he jams it back in. As they pop open their dinners, the Styrofoam sushi containers squeak. In the bedroom, as Lizzie reads and deletes each e-mail, the computer makes its *eep* sound, its electronic squeak. In his office on the top floor, his rubber-soled Ferragamos squeak across the bare white wood. On the table is the photograph of his parents, smiling fifties newlyweds, his father making it appear as though a giant Paul Bunyan statue way behind them is between his fingers and on top of his mother's head. His father died of a stroke just after George and Lizzie's wedding. George, his throat tightening, squeaks.

"What?" Lizzie shouts up from the bedroom.

He exhales. "Nothing."

Back down on the third floor, he sits on the bed. "I feel awful that I don't feel like—how I'm feeling about my mother."

She comes out of the bathroom, wearing only black panties and holding a piece of floss in one hand. He holds her around the waist, and she, standing in front of him, presses his head to her chest, stroking his hair.

Down in the basement, the furnace ignites. "We have liftoff," George does not say, as he often does when they're alone together and hear that sound—the muffled bang, the deep rumble resolving into a continuous, quiet thunder. It reminds him of the space launches he never missed as a kid. Lizzie, born a year after the JFK assassination, doesn't remember watching a space launch live until the one after *Challenger* exploded.

George sighs. "I mean, I was a wreck when my dad died. I could hardly function."

"I know." She rubs his temples. "With your mom, I think you've maybe already gotten kind of adjusted to the idea, you know? Because of the cancer."

He looks up into her face. "And I hated it this morning when I tried to lie to you about Mose going to Seattle to meet with Microsoft. I mean, why did I do that?"

"Long day," she says.

"Christ. Fuck."

"I know."

"I hate keeping secrets," he says.

"Being a grownup," she replies.

He kisses her belly and cups her left breast with his hand. She looks to see that the door is shut, kneels on the bed, and he pushes her over backward, deep into the comforter under her. As they squirm and pull and rub, squeeze and breathe and lick, and finally kiss, his sweater stays on. (It isn't self-consciousness about the stump, he told her when she finally asked one night, right after they were married. But with only one hand, a demi-arm, he said, you sometimes have to do triage, make a choice between romantic momentum and romantic etiquette—and pants off trumps shirt off.)

Whimpering is so basic: whimpering is a sound of fear or grief, a starving man whimpers when he finally eats, marathon runners whimper at the point of exhaustion, and sex is an absolute racket of whimpering delirium. As always, very nearly always, George and Lizzie's minutes of whimpers seem both perfectly endless and instant, like a dream with shape and weight and consequence, a dream dreamed miraculously by both of them together. The whimpering grows louder, turns to rugged, rhythmic, loud syncopated whimpering, a ferocious duet of syncopated whimpering with the other's hot breath on one's neck and face until the sounds of the breaths rise together into a splendid aching crescendo of release and arrival.

A little later, Lizzie sits on the floor next to the wall, her panties back on, legs and arms both crossed in front of her, smoking a Marlboro Light. She has opened the window a crack, two inches—just enough to lean down and blow smoke out, not so wide to set off the burglar alarm, which is programmed to switch on automatically at midnight. She is back up to three or four cigarettes a day, a pack a week. She hides her smoking from the children.

"How much are you smoking?" he asks from the bed, propped on his left side, watching her looking out the window.

"A couple a day."

"You know, if we lived out in Kirkland or Palo Alto or somewhere like that, you wouldn't be able to smoke *anywhere*. I mean, I think you can literally be arrested."

She smiles. "Another reason to move. Protect me from myself."

She takes another drag.

"Whoa!" she says. "When did they start doing those pulsing Day-Glo lights on the Empire State Building? Have you seen this? It's kind of cool. Why have I never noticed that?"

"I do love you, Lizzie Zimbalist."

The phone rings, and when George answers it, Lizzie sees the squirt of adrenaline make him over instantly.

"Hello," and then, "Hi, Timothy Featherstone."

"Porgy! Not calling too late, am I?"

"Are you in Seattle, Timothy?" Snuffing out her cigarette in a Pellegrino cap, Lizzie exchanges a look with George. She closes the window.

"Nope. Meet-and-greet with the geeks got moved. We're flying out tomorrow. Harold asked me to ask if you and the family want a lift out to Manitoba on the jet. We can drop you."

"It's Minnesota. But, that's, we're—" He looks at Lizzie, who frowns and mouths, *What?* "Timothy, that would be great. That's really nice. You know there's, there'll be five of us."

"No problemo. It's just three of us from Five-Nine. The rest of our people are cruising up from L.A. You'll need to be at Teterboro at eight o'clock. Wheels up at eight-fifteen."

"Great. Thanks."

"Hey, George-o? You see the news about the ESP computers?"

"Yeah. Lizzie knows the guy."

"It wasn't a *guy*. It was a cat, a cat's soul they wired up."

"She knows the scientist who's doing it."

"Cool. Well, I was thinking it would be a great arc for the show—high-tech dope dealers who can't be caught because they only *think* about their drug deals, and never actually talk out loud about them. Could be scaled up into a series of its own."

"That's an interesting idea, Timothy. We'll kick it around."

"Cool! See you locked and loaded at dawn in Joisey."

George flips over so that his right arm is next to the phone, and hangs up. Lizzie is back on the bed now.

"Mose is flying us to St. Paul."

For a long time, they stare at each other, their minds too jammed to speak.

From upstairs, where Sarah and Penelope are still working on their school project, George and Lizzie hear John Lennon singing "Imagine."

"Their video," Lizzie says, nodding upward.

"I thought it was set in '63 and '64?"

Lizzie shrugs.

Then they hear Max logging off his computer. "Goodbye!" says the online voice, exactly as chipper as ever.

6

George sits in the front passenger seat of the car next to the driver (a Russian in a black suit), Lizzie in back with the kids, Louisa on her lap. Up ahead is a perfect, black BMW 750 with one door open, and right in front is Mose's hunter-green Bombardier Global Express, idling, with its door open. A pilot in dark glasses stands at the foot of the stairs beside the jet. In the distance, George and Lizzie and the kids see Manhattan, the sun ridiculously huge and pink just above the World Trade towers. As their car-service Lincoln glides past a security guard directly onto the runway, George starts *ding-de-de-ding-ding*ing the opening electric-guitar riff from *Goldfinger*. They come to a stop just behind the big BMW.

George turns and looks at the children sternly. "Sarah. And Sir," he says in a grave, exaggerated bass, "it is now . . . zero eight hundred hours. Do not activate your weapons until I give the signal."

Sarah has grown up understanding that, a lot of the time, George is joking. When something he says doesn't make sense, she knows to assume he's kidding. On another day she might ignore it or roll her eyes. Today, because they are on their way to his mother's funeral, she looks at him and smiles.

"Whoa! Coo-*ool!*" says Max, snapping pictures of the jet, desperate to get aboard.

"*Hey* there, little man!" It's Hank Saddler, Mose Broadcasting Company's president of corporate communications, standing just inside the door of the jet. He tousles a handful of Max's hair overenergetically, clumsily, like someone who has read about avuncular hair tousling in a manual but never actually seen it done. "Elizabeth. And George. *George.*" The ooze has instantly changed flavor, from Coach Hank to the Most Reverend Saddler. Frowning sympathetically, he seems to be shaking his own hand, or resisting the urge to kneel down on the tarmac and pray. "I'm *so* pleased we could grant this . . . token of the company's condolences to you and yours at your moment of personal grief."

"My man! Macaroon!" It is, of course, Featherstone. He shoves aside the little built-in flat-screen TV on which he was watching *Up & At 'Em,* MBC's "morning show with attitude," and pops toward George and Lizzie. "Betty!" He kisses Lizzie on both cheeks. "Top of the morning, Mactier-Zimbalists. Happy leap day."

Leap years are a subject Max has studied exhaustively. "This is only the second time ever," he says, for approximately the tenth time this month, "that a hundred-year year has been a leap year."

"Trippy," Featherstone says, a little confused but, like lots of Angelenos, not uncomfortable being a little confused. "Your brainiac here reminds me of my pal Goldblum." The movie star Jeff Goldblum, George assumes Featherstone means, not Goldbloom his college roommate or Goldbloom his accountant. Absent any clear contextual clues, George has learned that a name mentioned by Timothy is a name being dropped.

"Where's the boss?" George asks.

"Harold is aft," Saddler explains.

"The private office," Featherstone says, nodding to the back of the plane as he returns to his seat. "Working the phones."

A Cindy Crawford doppelgänger stows their two L. L. Bean tote bags and their five coats; the other flight attendant, a sort of black Pamela Anderson, guides the children to seats equipped with video-game joysticks and brings out a silver platter of hot croissants. Both women are like first-class stewardesses from the cha-cha-cha days, before age discrimination and sexual harassment were crimes, when serving cocktails on jets passed for a glamorous profession. The piped-in instrumental music is New Agey, but just repetitious and somber enough to be tasteful; Brian Eno or School of. The cabinetry is bright yellow. Above the cockpit door is an LCD display that alternately flashes the current time, the ETA, and Mose Media Holdings' stock price, delayed fifteen minutes.

"Sheesh," Lizzie says softly once they're seated. "Very glam."

Before George can reply, Saddler is suddenly in front of them, crouching. "Ettore Sottsass," he says, his voice verging on a whisper like a TV golf announcer. "The legendary Italian designer. It's the only aircraft he's done. Personal friend of Harold's."

"We really appreciate this, Hank," Lizzie says. "It makes everything . . . so much easier. It's fantastic."

"Henry. At Mach 0.88 and FL 510—that's fifty-one thousand feet, *completely* above the commercials—you'll be at your mom's home by brunchtime, George, God rest her soul."

"Ordinarily you'd just fly all the way straight to Seattle?"

"Elizabeth," Saddler says, smiling, "Harold and I flew back from Davos last week on half a tank of fuel."

"Does Bombardier have you on commission, Hank?" Mose has appeared. Everything but his shirt is velvety, the blue-green Zegna suit, the purple tie, the black suede loafers. He leans down to kiss Lizzie, but remains standing. Saddler continues to crouch.

"They don't have to—I just *adore* this aircraft. By the way, Harold, I found out that our cabin air actually *is* fresher, just like you were saying the other day at Stanstead." Saddler flares his huge nostrils and takes a deep breath through his nose. "The fellas," he says, meaning the pilots, "told me they keep the oxygen level at the equivalent of six thousand feet altitude, instead of the customary eight thousand."

"Denver air instead of Mexico City air," Mose says, winking at Lizzie and George, but mostly Lizzie. "That's certainly worth forty million to the shareholders, don't you think?" Saddler forces a big, anxious guffaw that sounds like a seal's muffled bark.

Max has wandered into the cockpit, and is now returning to his seat. "It's so awesome," he says when he reaches his parents. "The pilots let me move their power handles back and forth."

"Max," Lizzie instructs, "can you say hello to Mr. Mose?"

Max makes momentary eye contact with Mose, and waves once at his wrist. "Hi." George and Lizzie are aware of their children's indifferent, inconsistent manners, which they attempt to improve. Somewhat indifferently and inconsistently.

"Hello! Did they show you their computer?" Mose glances at Lizzie. "It pilots the thing, as near as I can tell. Like HAL, in *2001*."

"No, uh-uh," Max says, now a little interested in Mose.

Saddler, still crouching, yanks on Max's hair again and says, "The flight plan is digitized—the guys load it in on a disk. It can even be done wirelessly, from a remote location."

Max is excited. "To take off, you just like slide the power levers to the words TAKE OFF. Then you slide them to where it says CLIMB, then CRUISE. I mean, it's really like . . . on TV or in a cartoon or something. You know? It doesn't seem real."

"It *isn't* real," says Mose, smiling. "The throttle levers"—*leevers*—"are vestigial. Completely unnecessary. They're just a sop to the pilots. Pure nostalgia. Welcome to the twenty-first century."

"The twenty-first century doesn't start until *next* year," Max says seriously. "January first, two thousand *one*."

As the jet begins to taxi, Louisa runs over and takes the seat across from her mother and father. George helps her fasten her seat belt.

"If we crash," she asks cheerfully, "will I die because of burning or because of drowning or because of getting ripped up?"

"We won't crash," Lizzie answers.

"I have another question."

"Shoot," Lizzie says.

"If the plane blows up—"

"LuLu, *stop*," George says.

"This is a *good* thing, Daddy. If the plane blows up in the air, we'll be closer to heaven than if we just got murdered on the ground, right?"

Saddler turns his head, tilts it fifteen degrees, and smiles. *"Precious."*

"Do your puzzle, LuLu," George tells her.

She stares hard at Saddler a couple of seconds, then says brightly, "Your hair is like my Mufasa's mane." She holds up her stuffed lion, a hand-me-down from Sarah. "Except less orange."

For the same instant, Lizzie and George glance at Saddler's red hairplugs, then return quickly with studied obliviousness to their newspapers. Saddler struggles to remake his pastoral grin as he stands and slides into the seat across from Mose, whose eyes are closed.

"Mufasa dies. When the wildebeests stampede," LuLu calls over to Saddler. "But Simba thinks *he* killed him."

"*Louisa,*" Lizzie says.

"What?"

Their happy youngest child has been fascinated by death and dying ever since the concept was explained to her. At the preschool she attended the first year they lived in the suburbs, LuLu one morning decided to play dead. The playrooms at the school (the Total Child Institute, chosen by default over Wee Winners and the Hudson River Christian Academy) were equipped with digital cameras that fed still images of the classroom to the TotalChild.com web site, so that parents could monitor their children from their offices and homes. Lizzie happened to be online the morning that LuLu lay perfectly still in a corner, face down, her head under a toy chest. A new picture was downloaded every thirty seconds. Lizzie noticed only the third or fourth LuLu-playing-dead image, and she instantly recognized the red-striped Hanna Andersson pants and Edith Hope sweater. As she stared at two adults trying to resuscitate her, and the dozen other Total Child children standing in a semicircle around their motionless classmate, Lizzie dialed the phone. As the next image Levolored onto her computer screen, she saw there were now three adults around the immobile LuLu, all clearly hysterical. By the time Total Child answered Lizzie's phone call, LuLu had abandoned her game.

Why does George always feel safer flying on a private jet than on any commercial airliner? If not precisely safer, certainly less fretful. Is it the intimacy? Part of his dread of plane crashes is the prospect of mass hysteria, sitting among hundreds of screaming, incontinent strangers who all know they are about to die.

They are up through the clouds before George even has a chance to entertain morbid takeoff thoughts. As the plane banks steeply, parallel shafts of morning sun trace up the curved wall of the cabin, then down again as the plane levels off, heading west. George and Lizzie both look out his window. They are a little astonished, as always, by the way it looks at thirty or forty thousand feet, fifty degrees below zero, the impossibly pure blue sky and perfect rippling pink-and-gray cumulus tops, a Maxfield Parrish mural in ultra-Imax 3D. Off to the left and below them, lightning flashes, diffused by a dull gray cloud wall.

"Whoa," George says quietly. "Good effect."

They watch as the center of a fat white cloud just ahead disintegrates, and the sun, now behind them, bursts through that hole, shining like a spotlight on a darker cloud beyond. And at the center of that bright spot they see the jet's shadow.

"*Great* effect," she says, still staring at the sky. "It's funny, you know—if we saw a painting like this, this over the top, we'd absolutely hate it. So cheesy."

George smiles, at her and himself. He had been thinking how much it looked like heaven.

"I'd put it in the red-flag category. Fourth quarter we had seventeen versus the previous fourth quarter, 1998, when we had . . ." Hank Saddler consults a multicolored graph. "Yup—*thirty-three*. And the line is definitely slightly trending down, Harold, even seasonally adjusted."

"Didn't the *NARCS* live show get us some vision points?" Mose asks.

"The MBC and MMH, yes. You personally, not really." MMH is how Saddler refers to Mose Media Holdings.

"I'm the one who got Giuliani to get the cops to play along."

"Which the press doesn't know. So . . ."

"Ah. Correct. And so now you need to script me. Like Ronald Reagan."

"This is just one piece of one strategy to preempt any further erosion in your numbers."

"What have I done lately, eh? I guess I have to launch a new network every eighteen months to maintain credibility."

Saddler nods.

"Where's Rupert on your chart?"

Saddler turns a page on his printout. "Murdoch is steady at forty-two, give or take. He also has nine 'genius'es last quarter."

"How many of those were '*evil* genius'?" Mose asks.

"What we want to prevent, Harold, is a John Malone–type syndrome. In 1994, Malone was in first place by a huge margin—"

"Really? Ahead of Diller? Of Eisner?"

"Oh, absolutely. Far ahead. Michael Eisner scores consistently high on 'brilliant,' but never 'visionary.' But Malone, by 1997, was pretty deep in the tank."

George opens his eyes.

"Not a single 'visionary,' " Saddler says to Mose, "the whole darned calendar year. In any publication or broadcast. And except for some upticks in 1998 after the AT&T deal, he's been in the single digits ever since. Barry Diller has stayed high on 'visionary.' And he's currently number one on 'legendary.' Which correlates with age, of course. Particularly in TV news and the newsmagazines."

George doesn't think he's dreaming, but as he awakes he is conflating this conversation with conversations from seventeen years ago about Bennett Gould's Saturday cliché tally. Ben wrote for the business section at *Newsweek*. They had only recently started working on computers, and just for fun Ben created a program that, at the end of each week, searched every story in the magazine for clichés of the moment—phrases like *jet-setting powerbroker* and *street-savvy mogul* and *postmodern sleight-of-hand*—and ranked them by frequency of appearance. Then on Saturday he distributed the cliché tally to George and their friend Greg Dunn. One Saturday, because he had been up all night figuring out how to do it, Bennett programmed the system to *replace* each of the designated clichés in the live, computerized texts with the phrase NEW CLICHÉ TO COME. He assumed each of his little jokes would be caught and deleted by some responsible person poised along the assembly line—fact checker, writer, senior editor, lawyer, top editor, *top* top editor, copy editor, someone. And most were, but the first 150,000 issues of the magazine that week contained fifteen printed instances of NEW CLICHÉ TO COME, fourteen of them in a single article, and six of those in one sentence. ("Ronald Reagan, although accused by critics of both NEW CLICHÉ TO COME and an old-fashioned NEW CLICHÉ TO COME, was uncertain as he strode out to the dusty front porch of Rancho del Cielo, where the NEW CLICHÉ TO COME Stockman and NEW CLICHÉ TO COME Darman, both NEW CLICHÉ TO COME, waited to hear the president's NEW CLICHÉ TO COME.") Bennett quit before he could be fired, and became a stock trader.

Mose looks across the aisle and catches George staring.

"You're the journalist," Mose says. "Explain to us why your former colleagues no longer consider me a genius."

" 'Visionary,' " Saddler says, looking at George. "That and 'brilliant' are the key phrases."

"I don't—I was asleep. The key phrases?"

"My Media Perception Index. MPI. We track Nexis and a few other databases to measure how frequently Harold and our competitive peer group are described in the press as 'visionary,' 'brilliant,' and so forth."

"With Hank's help, I'm 'voracious' and 'mercurial' forty percent less often than I was in early 1999. And I'm holding firm on both 'shrewd-slash-savvy' and 'contrarian-slash-maverick-slash-pirate-slash-asshole.' "

" '*Buccaneer,*' not pirate," Saddler says, and then adds, "We do *not* monitor the *a*-word. Harold is joking."

"I'm still up in the stratosphere on 'vanity,' higher than Mort Zuckerman ever got in the early nineties. Buying into the network television business at the turn of this century remains, according to journalists, an insane, egomaniacal act."

"Most of the numbers are where we want them," Saddler says, "but 'visionary' is lagging a bit. Over the last decade in the entertainment and communications sectors, 'visionary' has correlated with market valuation. And, anecdotally, with deal leverage."

"Your formula can actually predict how many times Larry King and *Fortune* need to call Harold a genius in order to push up the stock price?"

Saddler nods emphatically, as proud and smug as a fugitive Serbian army officer. "Something like that."

"Disgusting, isn't it, George?" Mose says. "It's no longer about my ego! Well, it isn't *just* about my ego. Hank has discovered the wire that connects my reputation to the stockholders' interests. He's the PR Einstein. Earnings equals spin squared." Mose looks down at a sheet on which a half dozen sentences are printed, each in big, sixteen-point type. "Now who am I supposed to *say* these things to, Hank? People in elevators? Random pedestrians?"

"Media interviews. Analyst presentations. Staff memos. All the public-perception crucibles."

"All the PPCs, you mean?" Mose says, deadpan, a joke in code for George's benefit, George figures, flattered.

Saddler nods. "Right. And each nugget represents a piece of your current on-the-record thinking. Distilled by our guys. All of them are between five and fifteen words apiece. Every one has been focus-grouped."

Mose looks up at Saddler, either aghast or impressed. "A focus group? Composed of whom?"

"Focus *groups.* Journalism graduate students. Geographically, demographically, and ideologically balanced to reflect—"

" 'Euphoria is not a business strategy.' That's nice and simple. Did I say that?"

"No. Not originally. But it struck me as *so* Harold Mose. Tested well, too."

" 'Market research is bad navigation.' Good. 'We don't just make TV programs—we create broadband content franchises.' No. That one's horrible, Hank. 'We're not technology bigots. The technology is irrelevant.' Okay. 'Television is the ultimate high-volume end-user delivery business.' That'll be easy to drop casually over Diet Cokes with Gates. Although it is the sort of thing *he'd* say. 'Managing change and not being completely in control of that change—*that's* the adventure.' Christ, Hank, I'll sound like goddamn Obi-Wan Kenobi."

"Hey!" It's Featherstone, suddenly hovering. "The force be with us!"

"Where's 'consensual marketing'?" Mose asks Saddler.

"Tested badly. Sex connotations. And we couldn't register the trademark."

"And 'transparency'? I love 'transparency.' "

Saddler shrugs, and Featherstone fills the space. "George, your kids are keeping it real back there, watching the *Episode I* DVD. Sir is unbelievable, by the way—he knows the *day* of the *week* that the original *Star Wars* was released."

"Yeah, he can do that mental trick with dates," George tells him.

"*Rain Boy!*" Featherstone says, and then snatches his inspiration before it flies off. "Series concept, do you think? Kooky kid superhero? Anyhow, he and I agree: Liam Neeson ain't no Harrison Ford. And Sarah Smile agrees with me that Ewan McGregor is much, much hotter than Luke—what's his name? The kid, you know, who smashed his face up."

Lizzie, returning from the back, slips past Featherstone. As she sits, the poof of her seat cushion sends a sugary disinfectant gust past George.

" 'Hotter,' Timothy?" Mose turns to George and Lizzie. "If I were you, I wouldn't let this man anywhere near my daughter."

Everyone smiles except Featherstone, who draws a hash mark in the air with an index finger, makes a quick frying sound with his tongue, then laughs loudly, actually slapping his thighs with both hands like Sammy Davis, Jr., used to do.

"Speaking of *Star Wars,* boss, we're a bitsometer away from closing the *Shampoo* sequel in time for November sweeps. Carrie script, Drew signed to play *her* daughter." Saddler scribbles a note. "We're begging Warren to do a cameo."

George catches Lizzie's puzzled look: Warren (Beatty) and Drew (Barrymore) she gets, but *Carrie?* she mouths to him. "Fisher," he whispers quickly.

"Beg away," says Mose, looking straight ahead at his *Wall Street Journal.* "By the way, *not* Ethan Hawke for the hairdresser role, please, even if he'll do it; Robert Downey, maybe." Mose glances down the aisle to where the three children sit, then lowers his voice a symbolic notch. "Do you really intend to use the word *blowjob*? Can we?"

"Standards and Practices says no problemo if it's after ten. It's an overall tonnage issue, too. We can use *blowjob* once. Plus one use of the verb *suck.*" Featherstone turns to George. "*Suck*'s a verb, right?"

"It certainly can be, Timothy," George says.

"So," Featherstone continues, "we just slip that scene to the end of the second act, and bingo, we're cool." Saddler scribbles another note.

Still holding the *Journal* in front of him, Mose folds down a corner of the paper with his index finger so he can see Saddler, and says, "I introduce fellatio to network television. Shouldn't that qualify as 'visionary,' Hank?" Saddler blushes.

The black flight attendant brings Mose a fresh Pellegrino with Rose's lime juice, a Virgin Mary for Featherstone, Diet Pepsis for the other adults, and asks Lizzie's permission to serve the children root beer floats.

"Of course," she says. "Sure."

Mose puts down the paper and shifts in his seat to face George and Lizzie again.

"A woman of the modern age who lets her children watch violent movies *and* gobble sugar. Bravo."

Lizzie smiles and shrugs. "They're Americans," she says. "I figure they need to develop their own immunities."

"Yes!" Mose replies. "Just so." George glances at her. The idea of cultural inoculation, letting the kids buy plastic toys and eat occasional Whoppers so that they develop a kind of robust autoimmune response to mass culture—that is his theory, which Lizzie derided and resisted when they were first married. Lizzie didn't let Sarah watch TV at all until she was four, when a preschool classmate told her she was a retard if she didn't know who the Power Rangers were.

"How's business, Elizabeth? Timothy tells me your company is involved in this mental-modem breakthrough."

"Business is just great, but, no, the thing in the papers—my chief technology officer knows the researcher working on it." She pauses, sensing the disappointment. "But we are developing biofeedback software, where the computer responds automatically to input from skin sensors—pulse, skin moisture, that kind of thing."

"Cool," Featherstone says.

"It really is," Lizzie replies.

"By the by, Georgie, while I'm thinking—on *NARCS*, my ESP idea, I thought you could have our team wiretap the drug dealers' *brains*."

George does not respond immediately. "That sounds pretty far over into sci-fi territory, Timothy. You know?"

"You mean like the season of cloning on—" Mose grins. "What was that disaster you had on Fox, Timothy? The sitcom you turned into science fiction in the middle of its first season?"

"*Whoa! That's Awesome!*, you mean. Actually, the first cloning show with the Barbi Twins and the two Sheen brothers was the biggest number that *Whoa! That's Awesome!* ever got. And with *NARCS*, there could be some interesting synergy. You know," he says to Mose, eyebrows arched meaningfully, "computer-wise. Digital-wise."

Mose nods with a kind of diagonal sweep, once, which indicates provisional agreement.

"All I'm saying, George," Featherstone continues, "is don't forget to leverage it up. Leverage it up."

"Right." George has no idea what he means.

Mose leans toward Lizzie. "We have an online business. That is, 'business,' in quotes."

"R and D," Featherstone says. "You've got to pay to keep your plug in the port."

George feels small about feeling anxious that Lizzie is having a conversation with Mose. He doesn't know if it's because Mose pays his salary, or because Lizzie can be conversationally rash, or because he's a sexist, or what.

"I know," Lizzie says to Mose, her smile a little tight. "I've seen the web site." She pauses. "How big is the MBC-dot-com staff?"

"A hundred people, give or take," Mose answers. "Almost all of them in News." He's looking straight at her.

"If I were you?" she says sweetly, reminding herself for an awful moment of the lawyer from Microsoft, "I'd get rid of about ninety of them. Keep the web site up, but if you're not committed to it as a business, why spend what you're spending? I mean, either be in the online business or stay out if it, but *kind* of, *sort* of being in it is a waste of money. And focus. In my opinion. I'll bet you don't even get any credit on Wall Street for it, not this late in the game." Her smile has loosened. "All the money you'll save you can spend on George's new show."

"Hey, girlfriend!" Featherstone says.

"So," Mose says, "it's fish or cut bait, you think?"

"I do."

"I do, too," he says. "I do, too."

The engines are whining down. The flight attendants are at the door, smiling, with Max and, in her oversize satin *NARCS* crew jacket, Sarah.

George holds the sleeping LuLu toward Lizzie. "Can you take her?" He needs his good arm free to get up. Lizzie takes her, and as George pushes himself up and out of the seat one-handed, he puts his weight on the swiveling video screen in the armrest. The TV snaps off and drops into the aisle, dangling stupidly from a cable. George has slipped and slammed with a loud thud back into his seat. The Cindy Crawford stewardess rushes back.

"Can I help—"

"Hell. Sorry," George grunts, and is already up and walking when Saddler puts a hand on his left arm as if to help.

"You know, George," he says, "I always forget that you are a disabled person." Saddler squeezes George's elbow and smiles. "I really do." George nods. "God bless."

George says nothing until they are all loaded into the rented Volvo wagon, Lizzie driving. "You know that scumbag Saddler has hair-plugs *and* wears a rug?"

"George," Lizzie says.

"Smarmy little fuck."

"George," Lizzie says.

"No cursing, Daddy," LuLu says from the backseat.

"What's 'smarmy'?" Max asks, eyes fixed on the screen of his new Touch Terror Game Boy, which shudders, and grows physically cold and hot as it's played.

"Oh, excuse me—*you* find *my* language offensive? That's funny."

For a couple of minutes, the electronic growls and hip-hop whinnies from the Game Boy are the only sounds in the car. Finally Lizzie turns on the radio, an Ani DiFranco song. Sarah and her mother sing along. The temperature inside the car is returning to normal.

Then George speaks. "By the way, I'm sure your advice to Harold to stay focused is right." Lizzie gives a small conciliatory nod. "It's ironic, though, since whenever I suggest that you might think about focusing your business, you yell at me."

"I'm sorry you slipped on the plane."

"That is not it, that's not—"

"And I know your mother just died, but I'm not your rival, George. I'm not competing with you."

"I know." Then, "You realize you probably just got people fired?"

"What are you talking about?"

" 'If I were you, I'd dump the news online service.' He'll do it, you know."

"Come on."

"I'm serious. You can't do that casual la-di-da shit with someone like Mose. There are consequences. These are people's lives."

"Oh, fuck you, George."

"Mommy!" LuLu scolds.

But Lizzie can't stop. "Like Henry Grisham, Harvey Grisham, that sixty-year-old writer you fired. Don't get righteous with me."

"Herb Griscom is fifty-eight. And he hadn't produced a usable line of dialogue in nine months. It was *a* person. And at least I didn't have Harold Mose do my dirty work for me."

"You apparently had Harold slime the mayor to let you use the fucking NYPD as extras. *That* was interesting to find out about."

"Stop it," Max orders.

"Really," adds Sarah.

"Fine," says George. As he turns to fix his gaze out the side window: "You're going eighty-five, you know." Then, after a few pouty seconds, he says as if musing, "You can take the girl out of Harvard Business School . . ."

"Fuck *you*."

7

"**Greetings!**" **The Unitarian** minister, a husky, scrubbed, red-faced
Minnesota woman with both palms open and raised toward the mourners, has never met George's mother. "Greetings! Peace!" Smiling
fiercely, head back, she takes a deep breath, field-mare nostrils aimed at
her audience. "We gather today to celebrate a being of peace, a being
who lived her life in a century of violence. Born the very day the War
to End All Wars ended, Edith Hope Cranston Mactier represents, I
think, for all of her friends and loved ones, something very special. She
was, like her name, a creature brimming with hope. . . ."

George sighs, then swallows back a sob and wipes his right eye. At
last! He's not crying because his mother has died, exactly, but because
his dead mother is being depicted generically, conveniently, a name
scribbled into a fill-in-the-blanks, goodie-goodie Unitarian garble.
"You know, George, the day you were born," he remembers his
mother saying to him on the phone on the day Max was born, "I didn't
even realize I was in labor. Not until the doctor came. I thought it was
just, you know, a little hangover. From all the Manhattans we'd had the
evening before." He can't remember if she told this story before or
after she said, "*Max*. That's a Jewish baby name, is it?"

George feels the electric tremble in his pants pocket. Mashing his hand against his pocket as if he's taking a palmprint, he makes the phone stop vibrating.

Lizzie's thoughts have already drifted away, away from her mother-in-law, away from the service, from the Twin Cities, from winter. How much attention does anyone pay in church? She is thinking about hydrangea and the Adirondacks. But the minister is suddenly shouting. "*Bless* the new millennium! *Bless* this year 2000! Bless the United Nations resolutions on Mexico! And," she shouts, raising both arms, "*viva* Edith Hope Mactier! May she rest . . ." and here she pauses for a couple of seconds once again to pan the room meaningfully—"in *peace*." Smiling, she balls her hands into fists and brings them together against her breasts, as if in prayer, or handcuffs.

Again the phone does its frantic wiggle in George's pants. This time the vibration is different, slow ticks accelerating to rapid in repeating five-second cycles—the silent code Iris has programmed to signify urgency, and which she triggers at least once a day. Every couple of weeks, she really does have an important call to patch through.

A quartet—piano, Irish pennywhistle, bow-hammered dulcimer, and didgeridoo—begins performing "I'd Like to Teach the World to Sing," which was one of Edith Hope's favorites.

"Iris is buzzing me," George says to Lizzie, standing and pointing toward his crotch. "Let me go take it, and I'll see you all downstairs in two minutes."

As his family shuffles out of the pew and turns toward the back of the church, everyone eyeing them sympathetically, George darts in the opposite direction. A few people glance at his odd, hasty exit and have the Minnesotan thought: *Look, poor George doesn't want us to see him crying, he's gone back somewhere to compose himself.* Although the fundamental insight is almost correct—George despises pity of any kind—right now he's simply trying to find a private place to take a phone call from New York. Circling behind the altar (or do Unitarians just call it the podium?), passing into the short hallway to the "new wing," as he still thinks of it, George, now safely out of view, flips open his phone.

"Iris?"

No answer, but he hears her chatting with someone.

"Iris?" *Fuck,* Iris. Waiting, staring at the handcrafted yellow china light switch, which is marked TURNED ON! and NOT TURNED ON YET! in painted purple letters, George realizes where he is: it's the Rap Room. The Rap Room is where, in 1970 at age fourteen, he helped organize counseling sessions for prospective seventeen- and eighteen-year-old draft dodgers. It was also where, late one Friday night in 1971 after a Free University group discussion of Alan Watts, as he first cupped Jodie Eliason's breast—the first time he got to second base with any girl—she whispered, unimaginably, "Pinch it, George."

"George Mactier's office."

"It's me. You called me. What is it, Iris?"

"George!" For Iris, every long-distance call demands emotion, as if it were a special occasion, a surprise reunion. She is only a few years older than George, but she is wired like a woman of his mother's generation, always overexcited and killingly sincere. And thus happy to be his secretary.

"I'm at my mom's funeral. What is it?"

"Timothy Featherstone! Calling from Seattle!"

"Okay."

Silence—the soft, random, hum-click-static ghost-voice pseudo-silence of modern telecommunications. George wonders, looking around, if this place is still a social center for Unitarian teenagers. (Or has the whole culture gone so Unitarian—so relativistic, so empathetic, so concerned about teen suicide and teen pregnancy—that the real thing has become moot?) There are three cots. And a wicker basket filled with dirty laundry. And—*no;* phone to his ear, he walks over to the slick cardboard dispenser on a counter; *yes*—condoms! The Unitarian Church provides a room for teenagers *to fuck*! His instant hybrid reaction, envy plus disapproval, surprises him, interests and disappoints him.

"Mac the Knife!"

"Hi, Timothy. What's up?"

"Just a great big gabfest up here in Geekopolis. Very strange place, man. It's like a bunch of writers and DPs and grips took over the world. Is your smarter half around?"

"Lizzie?"

"Yeah, Harold has something he wants to run past her. A question on some streaming bandwidth thingamajig. If she wouldn't mind. Before Harold and Bill G. talk this afternoon."

"No. No, she's—she's at the event, the reception. For my mother. Harold wants to speak to Lizzie?"

"Just a quick hey-ho, ninety seconds—before four our time, six yours. Probably easiest to have her call my Iridium number. Okay? Thanks, Mackinac. *Adiós.*"

Mose has never called George for a quick hey-ho. He evidently thinks he can use Lizzie as some kind of free computer consultant just because he happens to be in business with her husband. Presumptuous bastard.

George considers calling Emily. In case she's had any second thoughts about *Real Time,* or about back-end ownership. He should be abreast of any fresh tremors in the deal force field before Lizzie calls Harold back and sends the energies rippling off along some new vector.

He's about to dial, but there's a voice coming from the phone.

"—and, Faith? After I talk to Barry, I want you to get me Ng at her studio."

George holds his breath. It's Featherstone, speaking to one of his Los Angeles secretaries. They're still patched through to George's phone.

"No, she isn't," Featherstone says to someone else in the room with him. "I told him to have her ring us back after the service."

George is "him," and Lizzie is "her"; Featherstone must be with Mose. Can anyone tell he's listening? Does a switchboard diode in L.A. flash a warning? Will he leave some kind of Caller ID fingerprint? But he stays on, guilty and a little frightened by what he might hear and too thrilled not to listen, the mouthpiece now at his forehead. (He hasn't planned to eavesdrop. It's serendipity.) Featherstone's next call is ringing through.

"Hello?"

"Gooseberry! It's Timothy Featherstone."

"We're not really calling the show *Night of the Living Dead,* Timothy. I don't know how the putz at the *Times* got that, but it was just an internal joke—"

George recognizes the voice of Barry Stengel, the president of MBC News.

"I know, I know," Featherstone says, "and on Five-Nine we thought it was pretty funny." (One morning last winter, after some B-list celebrity's murder by her children's nanny dominated news coverage for half a week, George cracked to Featherstone, *You ought to do a whole weekly prime-time show—nothing but the deaths and funerals of famous people.* The obit series, which will also cover the illnesses and recoveries of celebrities, is now in preproduction, scheduled to go on the air next month.)

"Speaking of the obit show, Barry," Featherstone says, "I think we may have figured out a way to get you all the staff you need for it. Shifting some heads around."

"From where?" Stengel asks. "You know we don't have bodies to spare in News. And we cannot use infotainment jokers on a real news program. Those banana-brains at *Freaky,* or from that game show—"

"One Heck of a Week."

"Those people are not journalists. We'd be laughingstocks."

"I'll let you know. But Harold wants me to give you a heads-up right away about a show we've got going. It's very edge-of-the-envelope. And we don't want you to hear about it from some reporter."

"I think I already have. Is this the fake news show George Mactier's trying to sell you? Because if what I hear is true, then we've got a problem."

Until this instant, George has felt, at worst, neutral toward Stengel, even inclined to like him. The pernicious fucker.

"Whoa! Hold on, Stingo."

"I told the nigger he be sipping dialysis fluid," shouts an old black woman coming through the glass door twenty feet from George to a young black woman following her. "But he say, 'Hey! Cocktail's a cocktail'!"

"Shiiiit!" the younger woman screams happily.

The women spot George and freeze.

"Barry?" he hears Featherstone saying on the phone, "what the hell is—" George punches the power button.

"My mother died," he says to the women, who stare at the one-handed white stranger in the blue Brioni suit holding a cellular phone.

"Well, this is the shelter, you know," the old woman finally says to him. "The women's shelter?"

"Ah," George says. "I'm here for my mother's funeral."

"Uh-huh," the woman says.

George forces an awkward, cheerless smile, pockets his phone, and starts to leave. He feels like a jerk.

"Condolences," the younger woman says.

"Thanks," George says, turning back for a moment, blushing. "Thank you."

The old woman is not, in fact, old. Doreen Wiggins graduated in the class of 1975 from Henry Wallace High School, a year behind George.

———

"Would you like some sangria, Dad?"

George smiles at his son, who he realizes has never before worn a necktie. "Yes, I will have some sangria, Sir, thanks." George takes the plastic Dixie cup, pleased and amused by the outburst of etiquette.

George always loved coming to this room as a child, the smell of varnish and candles and (he realizes now) mildew, the fussy oak panel-ing and Tiffany lamps. It was for George an oasis of northeasternism, where men in cardigans smoked pipes and pronounced aunt "ahnt" instead of "ant." One Sunday morning here, when he was eleven, the Sunday school class was divided randomly into teams for a four-way debate in front of all the parents. His big sister, Alice, was on the Chris-tian side, and George, as the Buddhist team's leader, humiliated her over the issue of transubstantiation.

"Hi," Lizzie says. "That took a long time. What was the problem?"

"It was Featherstone, from Redmond. Harold Mose wants you to call him." He sips some sangria, and instantly spits it back into his plas-tic Dixie cup. "What *is* this shit?"

"*What?* Why did he call? You're dribbling, George. Sugar-free Hawai-ian Punch and St. John's wort. Why does Harold want to talk to me?"

"I guess he wants some advice about computers." *Maybe he wants you to fire his whole online staff personally. . . . Don't.* "Whatever it is, you're supposed to call him back before six."

"Huh." Lizzie fights back a smile. "How odd."

"Kind of sexist."

"How do you mean?" Then, as George tries to work out what he does mean, Lizzie almost imperceptibly flicks her chin toward George's right and says: "Cubby's about to come over. He has a business idea he wants to run past you. I'm going to the bathroom. Watch the kids." Cubby Koplowitz is Alice's second husband, a man brimming with ideas. Cubby owns two big arts-and-crafts-and-collectibles stores, Cubby's Holes. At his own wedding nine years ago, he asked George if

Nightline might do a story about To Hell 'n' Back Booby Babies, his line of humanoid plush toys. The packaging calls them "fuzzy li'l devils who escaped Satan and now need your love!" To Hell 'n' Back Booby Babies were advertised on the Winter Channel and became a hit in the upper Midwest. When Beanie Babies appeared two years later, George and Lizzie decided that Cubby did indeed possess some kind of awful genius. Alice said last fall that they sold To Hell 'n' Back Booby Babies to some big company that was going to manufacture them offshore for a national relaunch this year, and George dreads that he's about to be begged for help with a fresh round of motorized plush toy promotion.

"Harold Mose wants your advice. Cubby Koplowitz wants my advice."

"*George,*" Cubby says, grabbing his brother-in-law with both arms, beard pressing George's cheek, hugging harder, shaking him. "*Geooooorrrge.*" Heterosexual men have been bear-hugging heterosexual male acquaintances for a quarter century, but George still can't do it gracefully. George's unhugginess, he knows, is essentially why he was an unconvincing hippie in the early seventies, his three years of long hair, intensive drug use, and Fabian socialism notwithstanding.

"Hi, Cubby."

Cubby's shirt cuffs are unbuttoned and rolled with his jacket sleeves up past his wrists. He's wearing an M. C. Escher necktie, and his argyle V-neck sweater vest is tucked into his Dockers.

"I'm sorry you guys can't stay over. We'd love to have the twins and your little ones interact."

"No, I know, so would we, Cubby. But Lizzie really needs to get back." They're booked on a nine o'clock return flight. The desire to avoid a dinner with his sister and brother-in-law and their children is unspoken.

"I know you guys are crazy busy. Did Lizzie happen to mention Families Together Forever?"

George, figuring Families Together Forever is some religious group, smiles and shakes his head gently. Cubby was a Scientologist in the seventies. (In fact, he claimed to have invented a crucial technical innovation for the Scientologists' "E-meter," the device the church uses to measure adherents' progress toward enlightenment. But his lawsuit against Scientology in the late eighties—in which he named John Travolta and Tom Cruise as codefendants—was dismissed.)

"Okay. Final resting locations. A totally fragmented, totally localized business, right? No economies of scale. No national marketing. And just no darned *fun*. Right? Okay, we acquire parcels of a hundred acres or more. That is, the franchisees acquire the acreage, mall-adjacent, which gives you visibility, which gives you convenience, which makes it easy and natural to visit Mom or Granddad frequently. Families. Together. Forever." Cubby quickly looks around the room, nodding and making a sort of papal-blessing gesture with his hands.

"Huh." George has no idea what Cubby is talking about.

"Right? You have a water feature, and a café facility—indoor-outdoor depending on season and climatic zone. You have a putting green, maybe even minigolf, we're not sure—but you definitely use the grass motif, make it part of *life*. Tasteful minigolf, with traditional structures. Everything tasteful. The point is, we turn the cemetery experience into a *park* experience."

"You're starting a cemetery?"

"The business concept is cemeterial, but it's really so much more than that, George. It's location-based entertainment that's nature-themed, spirit-themed, love-themed. And with a major personal video component. That's my question for you, George."

"What is?"

"Our memorial marker is a video concept. We're developing a weatherproof monitor, polymer casing, approximate shape and size of a conventional headstone. Right? So instead of just a chunk of granite—'Edith Hope Cranston Mactier, born 1918, died 2000, RIP,' end of story—we'd have a loop of beautiful video scenes of your mom in life, dissolving, fading in, fading out—well, *you* know, George, better than I do, the show business possibilities. It's mass customization. Right?"

In fact, George's mother was cremated the night before. There will be no grave, no stone. "Every gravestone in the cemetery is a TV set?"

Cubby, nodding, gets to his point. "And what we need is a world-class anchor."

"An *anchor*?" George is fascinated. He knows he ought to be appalled, and a year ago, before they sold *NARCS* to MBC, before he was running a business, when he was a journalist, he might have been. Journalists appall easily, for all their supposed impassivity.

"A host. Someone with real brand equity—serious, prestigious, likable, loving, caring. Someone who can be the Families Together Forever Colonel Sanders, okay? Billy Graham without the religious baggage. Who we'd use in the marketing, but also integrate into every single headstone video package. He'd welcome the visitor, and segue into scenes of the loved one."

Lizzie has returned, which lets George relax.

"You are one brilliant man, Cubby Koplowitz," he says, meaning it, but also, since Lizzie is back, being a little arch. Sincerity plus irony simultaneously equals . . . what? Nuance. Cosmopolitanism. Weaseliness. Cosmopolitan weaseliness.

"Do you think," Cubby asks, "that you could put me together with your boys Phil Donahue and Bill Moyers? They're both on our very short list for spokespeople. You'd be doing them a favor, George. I mean, when the IPO goes—look out, ladies! Speaking of which, I'd love to talk to your Wall Street friend Benjy Gold about possibly getting involved. He's into start-ups, isn't he? Venture capital kinds of . . . ventures?"

Lizzie feels sorry for George, and for Cubby. George has met Donahue twice, and talked once with Moyers, sixteen years ago about the PBS Central America show.

"I don't know, Cubby. I could mention it to Bennett. But I don't really know Donahue or Moyers. I can find out for you who their agents are. . . ."

"And I can use your name?"

"Well . . . I guess, sure. Okay."

"Okay, *super!*" Cubby hugs George again. "Super. Now don't sneak out of here without telling your brother-in-law goodbye. Bye-bye, Lizzie."

George and Lizzie glance at each other, happy to be married, happy to live elsewhere, ready to leave.

"Hello, George Mactier."

He turns. "Jodie Eliason." He hasn't seen her in twenty-five years, not since the disastrous Thanksgiving weekend she spent with him in his freshman room at Wesleyan, after taking the bus fourteen hundred miles from St. Paul. He leans in to kiss both cheeks, which startles Jodie, as it would most Minnesotans.

"I did love your mom a lot," Jodie tells George, sandwiching his hand between hers. Releasing George, she turns to Lizzie, extending her right hand. "Hi. You must be Elizabeth. I'm Jodie Eliason Taft." A skinny, pale teenage girl in tattered tights and a short denim skirt, with very short, very black hair and one blue eyebrow, lurks nearby. "And this," Jodie says, "is my daughter Fanny."

"Hi," Fanny says, her eyes fixing on Lizzie. "Good to meet you." Fanny looks uncannily like Jodie did as a teenager, except cool and angry, more like George wished Jodie had looked in 1973.

"Well, I just wanted to, like, stop by and say a quick hi," Jodie says. "*NARCS* is just the best, by the way." Not great, not her favorite on Saturday night, not the best new hour-long dramatic series in several seasons, but just "the best." She still talks like she did in tenth grade, when she told George that "Thoreau is just the best."

"Thanks a lot for coming. How's . . ."

"Billy? We split up in '97."

"Ah," George says, recalling the time Billy Taft slugged him in the face, without warning and for no apparent reason, at a church dance in the seventh grade.

"There's a bug in Y2KRx," Fanny abruptly announces to Lizzie. "It doesn't recognize January first, 2001, at all. At least not running on Pentium III it doesn't."

Lizzie is dumbstruck. Jodie shakes her head, putting on a who-can-understand-these-kids-today smile. "Fanny is our computer genius. Loves the computers and the software and whatnot. When I told her I knew you, kind of, she was mighty impressed, let me tell you."

God, she's middle-aged, George thinks. Outside big cities, people seem to age faster, become fatter and balder sooner, even though they also tend to dress and talk and eat like adolescents at thirty and forty and fifty. They're teenagers with mortgages and multiple marriages and forty extra pounds.

Fanny asks Lizzie, "Um . . . when does Range Daze ship?"

"You don't work for Microsoft, do you?" Lizzie says, quietly thrilled by this encounter with a bona fide fan—her first fan, Fanny.

Shaking her head quickly and looking away, Fanny smiles despite herself, then giggles.

"End of the year, I hope," Lizzie says. "You know, the bug in Yack-ety-rex was in the beta version only. We fixed it before it shipped."

"Cool," Fanny says, "but I have a question? About Range Daze?" Fanny asks. "In terms of multiplayer functionality? Are you going to optimize for copper wire fifty-six-six or SDL or cable modem or what?"

"We're completely agnostic," Lizzie says, oblivious to where she is.

Jodie, grinning, frowning, and shaking her head, turns to George and asks, "Do you understand all this crazy stuff, George? Or are you in the wrong generation, like me?"

He shrugs, just like his father used to do when he didn't want to answer a question, and starts jollying his wife away. Lizzie notices that Fanny is wearing a ridged, purple plastic ankle bracelet a half inch wide. It looks cool, she thinks, and wonders if she could get away with wearing a plastic ankle bracelet. Probably not, she decides, at least not in New York.

––––––––

Alice has just left, but Lizzie hears George still upstairs, wandering, inspecting. Max is in the living room watching a forty-year-old episode of *The Twilight Zone* in which a pioneer travels eighty years forward through time in a Conestoga, to 1960, to get medicine for his sick child back in the nineteenth century. Louisa has refused to watch ("*Mom!* Grandma has only a *white-and-black* TV! The commercials are white-and-black, too!"), even though Max explained to her that the show itself would be black-and-white on the TV at home, too. She finally got bored using Edith Hope's Clapper to turn lamps on and off, and couldn't understand the jokes in the old *Reader's Digest*s, so she consented to go with Aunt Alice to play with the twins. Sarah, wearing a T-shirt Lizzie has never seen (FORGET THE ALAMO. STOP THE WAR.), is in the kitchen, eating prepeeled baby carrots out of the bag, dipping them into a jar of Cheez Whiz the size of a beach bucket, and giggling at her mother.

"It wasn't *jewelry*, Mom, it was a *device*. That's so funny you thought it was jewelry. It's so some police guy knows where she is all the time. Because of getting arrested for computer hacking. An arf ID, she said it was."

"RFID," Lizzie says. "A radio-frequency ID tag. We've fooled around with them at the office for the time-travel game."

"Whatever. I think it's kind of sick. She has to wear it for nine more months. I feel sorry for her." Sarah sucks and licks off the synthetic cheese, orange on orange, and dips the same wet, uneaten carrot back in for more. Her mother frowns and starts to open her mouth, but then lets it go; it's been a long day, and anyway, no one else is going to be eating Edith Hope's Cheez Whiz.

"Mom? Is it weird for you to meet a woman George has fucked? Fanny's mom?"

"You don't have to use that word, Sarah."

"But—"

"And don't say 'but *you* use it,' because I do not use it to mean making love. It's ugly." She thinks better of adding, *Even for a super-sophisticated eighth grader,* and says instead, in a higher-pitched, what-time-is-it tone of voice, "Did Fanny tell you that?"

"Uh-huh." Sarah licks the same carrot a third time. "She was really nice to me. But also strange," she decides, slurping the last of this Cheez Whiz load. "In a pretty cool way." The slick little carrot plunges back into the jar. "So? *Is* it weird for you? Were you jealous at the church this afternoon?"

"No," Lizzie says. "Oh, maybe. You think about it for a second. But it's so stupid. I mean, they were children at the time. *Eat* the carrot, Sarah."

"Children?"

Unfortunate word choice. "They were young." *No.* "Eighteen, I think." *Fifteen, liar.*

"Has George told you about every woman he ever, you know . . . made love to?"

"No. And I haven't gone into detail about every old boyfriend, either. But we haven't *not.* I'm surprised Edith Hope would have baby carrots. They're expensive."

"She doesn't. I brought them from New York."

In the attic, George, relieved that his sister has gone, is reminded of the two dozen afternoons he spent here as a kid. Once or twice a year he'd wander up to search through his parents' stuff. He never went looking for anything in particular, but to wallow in the heavenly, mote-filled dormer light, the TV- and chatter- and Formica-free aus-terity. Downstairs, almost everything was useful and unimportant; up here, jammed into raw utilitarian space, was only meaningful residue, all the useless and important things. Suddenly his dreamy childhood hours take on the tang of precognition: Did he sit here, on a Saturday afternoon in 1963 or a Sunday morning in 1967, somehow anticipating this Tuesday afternoon in 2000? Now, for once, this one last time, he is *supposed* to be snooping through his parents' private papers and precious castoffs. Is there a word for the converse of déjà vu?

Then the sun moves just under the eaves, spraying the room with a gorgeous honey glow. For ten seconds, George stares toward the piles of artifacts, in a trance, as sunlight floods in. The attic, George notices now, seeing the exposed joists, the unfinished planks, the pure, uninterrupted space and sheet-metal ductwork bursting out of and into walls and floors exactly like a sculpture George saw at the Dia Foundation in the early eighties, is a loft—a nice raw loft, a couple of thousand square feet, light on three sides, river view. Like those white corporate monoliths along Sixth Avenue, the attic (of all rooms) in his parents' house (of all places) has become accidentally stylish, innocently, unwittingly, posthumously cool. Snapping to, George sees the scene, and himself backlit in it, as a shot from a very expensive television ad, the inspirational kind for Cotton Incorporated or General Electric that make Lizzie tear up against her will. But George doesn't let knowing TV-commercial reverb spoil the moment. Conventional beauty does not equal kitsch. Not all sentiment is sentimentalism.

Down in her late mother-in-law's kitchen, Lizzie is improvising a chef's salad from Safeway cold cuts—"Luncheon Meat" is the name of the product, not salami or bologna or olive loaf—Safeway-brand cottage cheese, and water chestnuts, and heating up quarts of Campbell's tomato soup. As George passes through on his way to the basement, she says, "It's like a time warp. I really thought canned green beans and canned carrots had sort of been phased out. How was the attic? It must stir up memories."

"Memories of memories, more like. Nostalgia for nostalgia. I used to sit up there as a kid for hours, rifling through Mom and Dad's stuff. What a snoopy little fuck I was."

She smiles. "You were curious. You are curious."

Lizzie chops. George stares. He feels vague and stupefied. Is it his mother's death? Is it being away from work, being in St. Paul, in his parents' house? George sees that it's 5:22 on the digital clock—the original kind of digital clock, circa 1970, with the sequential black-and-white metal numerals that flip down as each minute and hour pass, like the scoring mechanism on *What's My Line* that the sly host had to flip by hand, which even in 1962 seemed strangely, unnecessarily primitive to six-year-old George. In retrospect, of course, that also seems charming now, like everything from the middle of the last century. Lizzie is too young, just, to remember the original *What's My Line.* John Daly: that was the host's name. Harold Mose is John Dalyesque, except manlier, more North American. And richer.

"What'd Mose want? Did you call him back?"

Lizzie is trying and failing to twist off the encrusted top from an elderly bottle of soy sauce—not soy sauce, in fact, but Safeway-brand "Super-Oriental Sauce." She stops, and holds the bottle toward George. It is so old it has no nutritional information chart on the label.

"Oh, he doesn't understand streaming video, exactly. What the proprietary technology is. I don't really, either, but I know enough to make him think he could have a conversation with Gates and not seem like a moron."

"How long did you talk?"

"Not long. Five minutes. Ten."

Ten minutes? George can't help himself. "What else did you talk about?"

"Nothing. He asked me about people at Microsoft. It was small talk. Boring computer business small talk."

Using his teeth, the right molars, George finally gets the soy sauce bottle open and hands it back to his wife, who takes it with two hands. He stretches his jaw open wide, clicks it from side to side, and heads for the basement.

At the foot of the stairs are two pairs of sneakers. The white P F Flyers with blue trim are the kind George wore almost every day of his life until junior high; the blue Nikes, which he sent his father for his sixty-fifth birthday, look like they've never been worn. All four shoes are carefully placed on the bottom step, as though they're about to walk up. His mother wouldn't have put them there like that. This must be some cryptic unconscious sign from Alice. She spent last night and this morning going through the house, unplugging, stacking, organizing. The basement, it looks like, is the depot for mint-condition footwear and small appliances.

So many gadgets! So much hundred-dollar-a-pop uselessness masquerading as usefulness! Her old weather station. "George," she would say in the course of several phone conversations a year, "is the barometric pressure there in New York City still as *terrible* as it was last time I visited?" Here's a newer weather machine, which she must have bought after Uncle Vance died and melanoma anxiety became one of her hobbies. The Health EnviroMonitor, George sees, displays the levels of ultraviolet intensity, solar radiation, heat stress, wind chill, and *seventy-five* other measurements of climate-derived dangers. It let her know on any day precisely how many minutes it would take her to get a sunburn. "I'm so fair, you know," she said. "You're lucky—oh, and Lizzie, with *her* skin, she's *so* lucky. . . ." "Them Jews sure do tan up real good, don't they, Mama?" he teased. She hated it when he did that.

Alice has piled all the emergency equipment together in one corner. The carbon monoxide detector—which Edith Hope had owned for years and years, she called to tell George the day after Vitas Gerulaitis died from carbon monoxide poisoning. And something called a Beep Seat. With which prospective emergency situation does it cope? George reaches down for a closer look. The Beep Seat, he reads, is an alarm that goes off if the toilet seat is raised for more than sixty seconds. The Beep Seat box is unopened, shrink-wrapped, and dusty. She must have bought it just before his father died, and never needed to install it. George wonders if the prospect of electronic toilet-seat monitoring contributed to his stroke.

"Well," he says, flipping off the basement light, climbing the stairs slowly back to the kitchen, reminding himself of his father, "that was depressing."

Lizzie tastes her salad. "Did you know she doesn't have any herbs? No spices whatsoever. Except for salt and pepper and something called 'Not-Too-Spicy South of the Border Flavoring.' "

"No! No, no." George goes to an out-of-the-way cabinet and opens the door, revealing a complicated yellow plastic device that looks like a scale-model grain elevator. He gestures in the manner of a magician's assistant. "It's the *Spice Carousel,* dear. *Fourteen* different herbs and spices. Just dial the particular herb or spice you want, and press the button."

"Don't be mean about your mother, George."

"I think the *ethnic* spices are probably somewhere back here," he says, reaching in and twirling the thing. "In this flavor sector."

"*Stop* it," she says, laughing, her eyes still red from crying. Behind the Spice Carousel, he spots something that, Lizzie sees, sucks the levity out of him. "What is it?" she asks.

He pulls out a clear plastic cylinder, fatter than a tennis-ball can, with slits in the lid. At the bottom is a fresh-looking poppy-seed bagel. On the side is a big purple Star of David and purple letters: 1946–1996 MAZEL TOV! FRIENDS OF TEMPLE BETH ISRAEL, ST. PAUL. It's a commemorative bagel canister. George and Lizzie look at each other.

"She wasn't a bad person, George."

As George puts it back, Sarah shuffles in and looks at the salad skeptically. "When's dinner?"

"I know she wasn't," George says. "I know."

"*Daddy!*" Sarah says suddenly. She has not called him Dad in weeks, maybe months. She has not called him Daddy for a year. "*Where* did you get *those?*"

George holds up his old P F Flyers and the Nikes his father never wore. "Which?"

Sarah's mouth is agape. She looks at the size eight P F Flyers, then takes a Nike in both hands and inspects it as gently and carefully as George and Lizzie have ever seen her do anything.

"These are first-edition Nike Air Jordans! *1985!* Mint! In *Carolina blue*! Heather Harper's father paid *sixteen hundred dollars* for a pair last year. I'm serious! He buys and sells to all the big Japanese collectors in Scarsdale. And I know he's got a pair of those," she says, pointing to the P F Flyers. "Was Grandma a collector?"

———

Shit. He missed the turn onto the Eugene McCarthy Parkway. As Lizzie says, daydreaming is his true disability. He'll have to do a U-turn, which means he'll have to grip the wheel with the prosthetic left hand, which he wears only for driving. He calls it "the hook," although it is not a hook at all, or handlike. It looks like a very high-tech titanium bicycle part. George has been stopped for making illegal U-turns three times in the last fifteen years, twice in New York and once in L.A., and each time, when the cops saw his prosthesis, they let him go without a ticket.

George has never been to Alice's new house. Her "new" house: she married Cubby in 1991, and they moved here right after the wedding.

It looks as if it was once handsome, a Prairie-style bungalow, but a second story added in the seventies has turned it into a freakish raised ranch, like an old man with a huge blond toupee. As George gets out of the car, he sees that the original detached garage has a new addition too, doubling its depth into Alice and Cubby's backyard. Knowing his sister, George figures they probably keep freezers filled with discount sides of beef back there, pallets of generic toilet paper and paper towels, hundred-pound bags of fertilizer and salt pellets stacked to the rafters, God knows what dreary and prudent stores.

"Hello, Daddy!" Louisa says, jumping into his good arm the moment he steps into the Koplowitzes' family room.

The eight-year-old Koplowitz twins are sprawled on a *Losers* beach towel in front of a thirty-five-inch TV, watching *Entertainment Tonight,* both chewing on Slim Jims and sharing the same large, realistic-looking stuffed opossum as a pillow.

"Hi, Roddy and Rance!" George shouts to the twins, who wave but do not look over or get up.

"Hi, Alice."

"Hello, George."

"You did a terrific job at Mom's house. Organizing. You'll have the lawyer call me. Okay? At the office."

"I will."

Cubby puts his hand on George's shoulder. "You're not getting out of here without seeing my layout, George. The Project."

"Your layout?"

"Uncle Cubby's got the fanciest toy train set in the *world,* Daddy! It's like a real city!"

It's in the garage.

As they go in, entering a little foyer, Cubby presses a lighted button—one of a column of tiny rectangular plastic light-switch buttons, each like a cherry Pez candy split in half lengthwise. Dozens of different lights inside the garage power up slowly, smoothly.

"Ta-dahhh," Cubby says, proud but not too proud. "I've been working on it since I was eighteen." Cubby is forty-seven. "No wonder the first marriage flopped, right? Let me go switch on the breeze." He walks toward a darkened, closet-size control room, turning back to tell George, "Everything else cycles on automatically."

The space is twenty feet by forty feet. The smooth walls and domed ceiling (fiberglass? plastic?) are blue—a startling, complicated, authentic-looking sunny sky blue. The bottom couple of feet of the room are a lightless pool, so dim that George can't see his feet. A narrow walkway, thick rubber from the feel of it, apparently extends in an oval around the perimeter. The rest of the room, from two feet off the floor to well over George's head, is a perfect downtown, a city of dramatic topography and streets and alleys, and complex, meticulous architecture. His gaze fibrillates back and forth, back and forth between the whole city and its thousands of details—the inch of pink steam wafting up from a pinhole in a cobbled street, the fingernail-size LCD billboard flashing its message (*QUATRO MINUTOS* . . . FOUR MINUTES . . . *QUATRO MINUTOS*) inside a mass-transit station, a TV set the size of a corn kernel, illuminating its tiny room with a blue-gray video light that changes its hue and intensity every few seconds, simulating the rhythm of TV cuts. It is a city evidently some hundreds of years in the future, apparently semitropical but not Miami or Rio or any particular city, as nearly as George can tell.

It is a place concocted entirely out of Cubby Koplowitz's imagination. Bits of the architecture are familiar. In the "old" neighborhood, a pseudo-mid-twentieth-century skyscraper, a clunky imitation Empire State Building that Philip Johnson might have designed in Houston in 1985, is half demolished, in the process of being torn apart by a little robot wrecking crew. But mostly the buildings are of two or three distinct new styles, glassy or metallic, and all "futuristic" enough to sell the idea but unlike any depiction of the future George has ever seen in books or movies. The largest building, about the size of a small air conditioner and decorated like a circus tent or a painting by Howard Hodgkin, is apparently some kind of cathedral or temple. It's lit by a circle of pivoting, thimble-size searchlights, and seems to emit a kind of warbling hum, as if a chanting chorus were inside. The cathedral is in a neighborhood that could be religious or industrial, with buildings that resemble both power-plant cooling towers and temples at Angkor Wat. The city looks as if it's grown over many years (and so it has, George remembers) but also as if it's been designed by different hands—like a real city. All but a few of the individual streets and parks and skyscrapers are unheroic—exotic certainly, but regular, disparate, plausible. Some of the oddest and newest buildings have gridded skins in an opalescent gray-turquoise that looks like no color George has ever seen. The mood is neither *Blade Runner* scary nor World's Fair perky. It seems like the center of a very specific metropolis, an actual place that's quirky and a little dreamlike but not intending to be quirky or dreamlike, a city that's surreal by accident, only to viewers from a different century. It is magnificent. It is an unimaginably beautiful creation. George doesn't know what to say to Cubby. He feels like crying.

"Isn't it neat, Daddy? Look! In that tunnel behind the little waterfall! Here comes the neatest train!"

The nose of a tiny, sleek, bronze-colored bullet train, practically noiseless, shoots out of a translucent, sandblasted glass tube under a two-inch-wide gush of water, toward them, then sharply turns away, rising toward some kind of randomly throbbing orange glow behind a rocky hill in the back of his brother-in-law's garage. The train doesn't seem to be riding on a track. It seems to float. George looks at Cubby.

"My new mag-lev loco."

When he's in here, does Cubby speak some sci-fi lingo that he's also invented? George feels drugged. "It's what?" George asks in a surprisingly tiny voice. His throat is dry.

"Mag lev. The locomotive runs by magnetic levitation. It's a real, real nifty little item. It actually floats, just barely—see?—right over the track. Five hundredths of a millimeter. Just got it a couple of weeks ago off the web from a guy in Dresden who makes them. That is the future right there, George. They're constructing a mag-lev line from Hamburg to Berlin as we speak. Japan's got it, too. The real ones go two hundred miles an hour. And they're capable of going double or triple that."

"You designed all this, Cubby? The buildings? And those—those gardens?"

"Eco-malls, they call them. Well, *I* call them. And that one way over there, behind the mercury ponds? Is a Families Together Forever facility." A hundred little simulated-video tombstones flicker in a trees-of-paradise grove.

"The parallel lines of light over there are lasers?"

"Actually not parallel, George—just off. The idea is they're power lines, and meet up a hundred miles away. You know, in another city. If there were another city. So, uh-huh, mostly, I guess you could say I designed it all. I mean, a lot of the operating equipment, like the mag lev, I got from vendors, but otherwise . . . yeah."

"Like those towers over there," George says, pointing to the cathedral neighborhood. "Did you base them on particular models? Angkor Wat? Or Gaudí?"

"Who?" Cubby regards George with the kind of wounded look Alice perpetually gives her little brother from New York. "This is all my design, George. A hundred percent."

"Oh, I *know*, no, it's *amazing*, I just . . . Does it have a name?"

"Well, I sometimes used to call it my Mini-Epcot, you know, just to myself and my wife and friends and, you know. Ex-wife, I mean. Look! Did you see the old N-scale diesel loco go into the wooden sports dome? I love this. Listen!" An unseen crowd inside the stadium boos. "For a while after that I called it Kennedy. The city of Kennedy. I had this whole story behind that, which is some Chinese terrorists shot down President John F. Kennedy, Jr., and his family and Caroline in 2016, and the United States established a new city called Kennedy in their honor outside San Juan, Puerto Rico, and so forth, and this is the city a hundred eighty-four years after that. It's set two hundred years in the future. Your sister hated my calling it Kennedy. I guess because your mom and dad hated the Kennedys so much. So anyway, now I just call it the Project."

"Can we go, Daddy?" Louisa has grabbed onto George's belt with both hands, and is propelling herself off the ground, up his leg.

"In one second, honey," he says, putting a foot forward and leaning back to let her climb. "It's always two hundred years in the future?"

"Right," Cubby says, looking over his creation. "When I started, it was 2171. Now it's the year 2200—that orange light over behind Mount Diana would be, like, some turn-of-the-century commemoration. And next year it'll be 2201. And so on." He looks at his brother-in-law. "So do you like it?"

"I've never seen anything so incredible. You should be very proud. It's spectacular. It's wonderful."

"Hey, thanks, man," says Cubby, grabbing his brother-in-law for a hug, making George regret his effusiveness a little.

"We'll see you," he says, decoupling. "Tell Alice goodbye again for me."

"Will do. Hey! That's a new model, isn't it?" He's grabbed George's prosthetic driving hand.

"No, I've had it a few years."

"Hmmm," says Cubby, examining the wrist mechanism. "This servomotor here looks exactly like what I've just started using on the retractable roofs on some of the newer buildings. On the Project," he says, nodding sideways. "Who's the vendor on this? Dutch? I'll bet it's Dutch. Benelux for sure."

"I don't have any idea, Cubby," he says, pulling his hand away.

It has started snowing outside, and the sun is down. As he drives back to his mother's house, George can't stop thinking about Cubby's imaginary city. After his initial astonishment, he looked for some unintentional flaw, some sign of amateurishness or stupidity. But even the Koplowitzian turns of phrase—Eco-malls, Families Together Forever—are perfect. The difference between a piece of art and a piece of folk art is a matter of schooled versus self-taught, knowing versus innocent, slick versus raw (or willfully raw versus authentically raw). Where does that put Cubby? Slick folk art? Kitsch profundity? A web-empowered naïf? Genius dimwit? Maybe Cubby Koplowitz is the first twenty-first-century man.

George glances at the sign announcing the next several interstate exits. Harold Stassen Drive is closed for repairs.

"Daddy, are you happy?" LuLu says from the passenger seat. "Why are you smiling?"

"Oh, I was thinking about Uncle Cubby. And Grandpa."

"Do you know why I'm holding the pen like this?"

George looks over at Louisa, who is holding a Bic with both hands against her forehead, ball point facing forward.

"No, LuLu. Put it down. Why are you?"

"Because in case we crash? And the air bag goes off? The pen will pop it so it can't smother me." Louisa's morbidity is never overtly fearful. She is simply fascinated by the physiology of death, the psychology, the sociology (thus her stunt in preschool), the theology, actuarial issues, all of it.

As George gets out of the car and heads for the side door, he sees Sarah sitting on the front porch, coatless, staring at a yew twig, stripping it of needles one by one. "Sir?" LuLu yells, shooting inside ahead of George. "The cousins have a stuffed pet possum they shot themselves!"

"Do we want half of Mom's ashes?" George asks Lizzie, more jovially than he intends, as he comes into the warm kitchen. She's crouching at a cabinet, reaching way into the back. "Alice offered to FedEx my half to us."

Lizzie withdraws her head from the cabinet and turns to face him. She sighs. "Mike's in the hospital."

"Come on. No. Your dad?"

She stands, nodding. "He's in the ICU. His liver. I made reservations for all of us. We leave at six-something tomorrow morning, and get to L.A. at ten. Sorry about this."

The sob starts as a cycle of several quick, violent exhalations alternating with deep, ravenous gulps. It looks like a seizure. Now, fifteen seconds later, instead of the breathy gasp for air comes a real sound, a high-pitched, unsteady screech, like a violin string bowed wrong. Lizzie feels terrible for him. "Shhhhhhhh," she says, gently reaching up to stroke his face, and keeps her arms tight around him as he falls into a chair, crying and crying.

8

"**A convertible?**" **Lizzie** says when they find their parking space in the Hertz lot.

"I always ask for a convertible in L.A."

Lizzie thinks of saying, *That's like if I insisted on canoeing every time we go to Minnesota,* or even, *That's like the time Cubby and Alice came to New York and made us ride with them in the hansom cab to dinner at Tavern on the Green—and when you spotted Roone Arledge walking along Central Park South, you crouched down so he wouldn't see you.* But she finds his L.A. out-of-townerism sweet, says nothing, and lifts her luggage, LAX tags dangling, into the trunk of the Saab.

Some well-to-do young people born during the era of Lizzie's girlhood (temporarily) despised the comfortable lives provided by their parents as bland and phony. But what Lizzie disliked about Los Angeles, still dislikes, is not so much the phoniness as the lack of rigor. She doesn't think that people in Los Angeles are lazier than people elsewhere—in high school, a Chicano boy in Lizzie's urban history class accused her of being a racist on just this count. But their minds do tend to waft from place to place and from notion to notion uncritically, childishly, almost randomly, like colored tissue paper and strands of cotton candy drifting along on breezes. For Lizzie, it all became clear in a series of blazing revelations in her seventh-grade Peoples of Earth class at Oakwood. (Learning has never since been quite so ecstatic for her.) Los Angeles, she realized at age twelve, is a hunter-gatherer society, a city of believers in the permanent cornucopia, cargo cultists. Natural Angelenos are people inclined, when they feel hungry, to pick the nearest ripe papaya or accept any old sitcom role, to go with the flow, live off the land. Lizzie announced to her parents that she was more of a Mesopotamian, attracted to tilling, planting, and harvesting. "You mean," Mike Zimbalist said to her at the breakfast table as he cocked his head back and slid a girder of reheated tofu tempura into his mouth like a giant French fry, "you're a Jew." Until that moment in 1976, Lizzie believes, she had never heard anyone say the word *Jew*.

At age ten, this world-historical revelation—Lizzie Zimbalist as an agrarian among nomads—transformed her personality, liberated her from the tyranny of the mellow. As soon as she realized that she didn't need to be a feckless hunter-gatherer like her parents, she lightened up dramatically. In the middle of seventh grade she had been a glum, chunky, lonely Wednesday Addams junior beatnik who neglected her homework; by eighth grade she was a geography-loving, cello-playing, field-hockey-starring A student, cheerful and thin and full of grace, with goody-goody friends, nerd friends, punk friends. It was like puberty in reverse. Her mother, alarmed by the sudden mysterious transformation, hired an Orange County cult deprogrammer to examine Lizzie secretly; the deprogrammer, at Serene Zimbalist's direction, posed as her fill-in sailing instructor, but when during her second lesson he pronounced jib "jibe" and Lizzie had to tell him what a keel was, he admitted the ruse to her. "Mother?" Lizzie said coolly that evening as Serene walked in from a Sargent Shriver for President fundraiser at Ma Maison, "I just want you to know that I will never, ever trust you again." She didn't speak to her mother for two weeks. Although her parents separated a few months after this incident, Lizzie never blamed herself for their divorce.

The new self-knowledge was why Lizzie left her excruciatingly hip Hollywood private school and enrolled in Palisades High, and why she understood that she would go to college in the east and settle there. ("In a sophisticated urban center the other side of 38° latitude and 88°

longitude," according to her eighth-grade diary.) It's why at Harvard she studied biological anthropology, disappointing her father (he wanted her to major in visual and environmental studies), her mother (French), and her stepmother (social work, which Harvard didn't offer). It's why she married George, why she got her MBA, why she got into the software business. Although programmers are odd, they think and speak precisely. Their insufferability, Lizzie thinks, is just an extreme, involuted version of her own.

But this *weather,* she has to admit, zooming up the 405 at eighty with the convertible top down in the middle of winter, hair whipping her neck, shades on, wind too loud to chat, is delicious. And she does like driving. It's short-term mindlessness, mindlessness with a definite and necessary purpose, like pulling weeds. Back in her teenage know-it-all days, she regarded southern California's wiffiness and its happy weather as flip sides of the same coin—she used to tell Californians she loved the *real seasons* of the Northeast, bittersweet autumn, unmitigated February. The L.A. climate, she enjoyed saying to her parents when she was home from college on winter break, was a smiley-face climate, the weather of stasis, of denial, of death itself. But lately she's realized she likes sunny skies, and no longer disapproves of endless dry days in the seventies. Maybe life is changeable and tough and interesting enough, she thinks, pulling into the Westwood exit lane; maybe the weather doesn't have to be, too.

George, twisting around to stroke Lizzie's neck and shoulder with his right hand, asks in a loud voice, "You okay?"

"*Fine!*" she screams back. She's afraid the scream, necessitated by the wind and the freeway noise, misrepresents her emotional state. "Really, I'm good," she says to George at normal volume, now that they're off the freeway, on Wilshire, heading for Beverly Hills. She is. In fact, Mike Zimbalist has come so close to dying so many times—the mysterious beating outside Slapsy Maxie's nightclub by "a couple of Eye-tie savages," the melanoma, the midnight stumble with a young Czech actress off the cantilevered deck on Mulholland Drive ("the Mariel Hemingway of the Warsaw Pact," he told her and Serene in the emergency room at three A.M.), the second melanoma, the seaplane accident in Central America, the quadruple bypass, the tequila-related snorkeling emergency in Tahoe—she realizes she has already fully discounted for her father's demise. It's like in the stock market, when investors expect some specific piece of bad news—higher interest rates, lower earnings, a dying CEO, whatever—and when the bad news actually arrives it has no effect on share prices.

"Elizabeth Zimbalist, sometimes I think you're half adding machine!" her father would say if he knew what she was thinking right now, as he says whenever she acts a little too candidly or sensibly for his tastes. He said it when she dumped Buddy Ramo. ("Buddy's a *client!*" he said the night she announced she was breaking up with him. "There've been a gazillion times I've wanted to dump Buddy myself, you know, but I didn't, you know why? Because the beautiful little dumbbell needs me." "All right, Daddy," Lizzie replied, "from now on *I'll* book Buddy into dinner theaters and *you* have sex with him.") He said it when she cashed in his college graduation present to her, a ninety-nine-day-long round-the-world "cruise to the grand past" ("Constantinople," "Ceylon," "Siam," "Saigon"), and instead invested the money in Compaq stock. ("Why would I want to spend the entire summer on a stupid ship with a bunch of strangers living some good-old-days hallucination?" "Because, Ms. Wet Blanket, it's *romantic,* that's why! My God: did your mother have intercourse with an adding machine at some orgy back in the sixties? Is that what happened?") He said it when she declined to take a week off from work to attend his wedding to Tammy, his third wife, in Australia five years ago. ("Dad, I'm trying to start a business." "Yeah? And? So? Do you know how many businesses your old man has started, Ms. CEO? *Every* engagement for *every* client is a separate business!" At the time, she figured this was a piece of Mike Zimbalist hyperbole. But a year later, George brought home a clipping from *Daily Variety* reporting that her father, doing business as Major Show Business Attractions LLC, had signed a consent decree with the California State Attorney General in which he agreed to dissolve the 1,278 shell corporations he had established during the previous six years.) And Mike Zimbalist said it the last time she was with him, late the Saturday night after Passover last year in Palm Springs. Tammy had gone to bed and Lizzie had presumed to ask how her four stepsiblings would be treated in his will. (Lizzie and her father had finished two one-liter buckets of frozen margaritas from the built-in frozen-margarita machine.) The single major irrational act of her life, deciding at age twenty-one to carry Buddy Ramo's baby to term and to raise her alone, made Mike Zimbalist weepy with pride.

With Sarah tutored in the use of the Beverly Hills Hotel digital key card and installed at the Polo Lounge with the little kids for brunch, George and Lizzie head to the hospital. Even before they reach the ICU waiting room they hear Tammy, who is evidently talking on the phone. They see her before she sees them, dressed in a black T-shirt imprinted with a huge close-up of the singer Yanni, black yoga pants, black high heels, and sunglasses with dark green lenses the size of hockey pucks. Tammy was some kind of Adelaide music-hall gal turned television performer. To Mike's credit, he married Rachel, his second wife, and Tammy, his third, when they were the same age as Lizzie's mother would have been if she were alive. Tammy is extremely tan, almost bluish, tan in the way women tanned back in the days before SPFs and Nicorette and Evian.

"Elizabeth!" she says, hanging up the phone and springing toward them, her loose breasts swinging ahead of her as she moves in for the hug. "George! Darling hearts!" Women, George has no problem hugging. He and Lizzie both prefer Tammy to Rachel, who started calling George "my right-wing Reaganite son-in-law" after George admitted to her one night that he had voted for Rudy Giuliani for mayor.

"Are you exhausted? You just missed your brother, Elizabeth. Are you both about to collapse? I'm so sorry about your mom, George. What a week! I mean your brother Ronnie. George, you skinny boy! What a time! How was your flight? I'd kill for a cigarette, Elizabeth! Congratulations on the show, George! Where are you staying? When can I see the kids? The gray looks nice on you, George, it really does!"

"How is Daddy doing?" Lizzie asks.

"Good news! They're taking him into surgery! A brilliant new procedure! Transplant! The 'OR' means surgery up here, doesn't it? By the way, I was at Fred Segal and the Gap all morning—bought you and the kids *everything!*"

"They decided—they're giving him a new liver?" George asks. "But I thought that wasn't . . . available. Advisable. Possible. At his age. Right?"

"Right! That's the genius part! Exactly! Only one liver for every three people who need one! Mike's too old! That's why he's eligible

for this! You know, Elizabeth, Buddy Ramo called last night and offered to donate one of his livers. '*One* of his!' Sweet, sweet Buddy."

Lizzie puts her hands on Tammy's shoulders. "Tammy? Tell us
what's going on here. Why is Daddy suddenly getting a liver transplant?" Then, lowering her voice: "Did he pull strings? Who did he
hondle to arrange this?" Lizzie is surprised at her "hondle"; she never
uses Yiddish phrases.

"No, Elizabeth! Mikey is a hero! A scientific hero! They offered! He
didn't ask! Xenotransplantation! He woke up early this morning for a
sec and said, 'Tam, I want to go for it!' He wrote a note to you, signed
the form, and went! History in the making! Do you believe it? Transgenic swine!"

"Tammy!" Lizzie says. "What the *fuck* are you talking about?"

It is always this way with Tammy. She has a funny kind of zero-sum
relationship with the rest of humanity. The moment she succeeds in
making someone else slightly cuckoo, she is grounded and becomes
calm and linear. "Aw, poor darling. You're upset. You're upset about
your dear old dad, aren't you? Ohhhh. Poor tired babies, both of you.
George, Elizabeth, over here. Sit. Eat some animal crackers. I brought
them for the children. I'll run and find Dr. Bob." And she is off, down
a corridor, heels clacking, big boobs swaying.

A few minutes later, Tammy returns, pulling an East Asian man
about George's age by his white coat. His name tag reads BAMBANG
S.H.H. "BOB" HARDIYANTI, M.D.

"Good morning. Your mother says you have several questions about
our xenotransplantation protocols."

She is not my mother, Lizzie thinks. "I'd like to know what we're
doing to my father, yes." *And by the way, Tammy, just for the record, Ronnie isn't my brother, he's my ex-stepmother's sleazeball son.*

"Of course," the doctor says. "We will be grafting a genetically enhanced organ from a special ungulate herd. The procedure is highly
experimental, of course. As I explained to your father last evening."

"What's an ungulate herd?" Lizzie asks.

"Swine," the doctor says, smiling. "The liver was harvested from
our own transgenic swine."

"You're giving my father a pig's liver?" Lizzie asks, not shocked, not
horrified, just impatient at having to wade through so much eu-
phemistic politesse.

Dr. Hardiyanti smiles a little too broadly, takes a deep breath, and nods. "Quite right. Yes. From a special herd we cosponsor. The . . . 'pigs' are genetically altered. We redesign their cells especially, you see, to trick the human immune system—your father's immune system—into accepting the liver, into letting it become *his* liver. And the liver cells are tricked, as I say, so to speak, into believing they are still living in the pig. You see? We fool the flesh, I like to say. With the goal of making each side able to live together."

Lizzie doesn't know if it's jet lag or Dr. Hardiyanti's pseudo-Etonian Singapore singsong, but she realizes she's taking in his explanation on two channels, like simultaneous translation. On one channel he's describing a liver transplant, but on the other he's speaking metaphorically, about some noble and terrifying scheme to engineer a global solution to racial and ethnic hate. She says nothing.

George asks, "And he won't be at risk for catching some kind of . . . pig illness?"

Dr. Hardiyanti is loving this. "These are sterile livers, I assure you. Exceptionally sterile. The piglets are removed from the womb by cesarean section. They don't suckle, they don't have any contact at all with their mothers. So they are disease free. And in a sense, they don't even know they are swine."

Lizzie is still a little spooked. When will the doctor say something that isn't ripe with *Brave New World* double meaning?

"Isn't it fantastic!" Tammy says. "Is this the twenty-first century or what? And you know, this would cost five hundred thousand dollars! At least! But they're doing it for us for free! I'm so proud of Mikey. He said, 'Maybe I'll be a celebrity, the next Christopher . . . Bernard.' What's the name? That first guy to get a heart transplant? The South African?"

"Christiaan Barnard," George says, "*performed* the transplant."

"See, you still remember his name!"

"We do appreciate your mother's enthusiasm," Dr. Hardiyanti says. "But I want to be quite candid. The chances of survival are, you must understand, small."

"How small?" asks George.

"Quite small."

"Like one in ten?" George asks. "One in twenty?"

The doctor says nothing.

"One in a hundred?"

"We are having real success with skin grafts from swine. And routinely for heart valves. And islets—the bits in the pancreas? At our research facility in Ventura we have a baboon that is living very successfully with a transplanted swine liver. His postop survival is now at"—Dr. Hardiyanti checks his watch—"one hundred sixty-seven days."

George chews a fleck of flesh from the inside of his lower lip. Lizzie looks over at Tammy, who's nodding excitedly.

"This is a wholly experimental procedure," Dr. Hardiyanti says, smiling more broadly than ever. "Wholly new. With human recipients, the success rate remains approximately zero." His beeper goes off.

"*Approximately* zero?" George and Lizzie say together in a mixture of incredulity and curiosity that sound unpleasantly to Dr. Hardiyanti like a peer review.

Slightly taken aback, he checks his beeper message and stands. "Approaching zero, yes. In Ukraine, they claim to have a girl living for the last five months with a baby gorilla's liver. But we are, quite frankly, skeptical."

George swallows hard against a sob. Lizzie thinks of Mike Zimbalist: irrational optimist, freeloading ham, a man who claims he wrote the line "You ain't seen nothin' yet!" for Jimmy Durante, now betting everything on an expensive, untried, inherently ridiculous procedure with no chance of success. What a surprise.

Dr. Hardiyanti shifts his weight to leave. But then the doctor can't resist mocking Ukrainian medicine a little more. "The same researchers in Ukraine, by the way, announced in January that they had transplanted the entire head of a weasel onto the body of a codger." He clucks. They stare. "A *badger*, I mean a badger, of course. Can you imagine? It's been a pleasure to meet you both."

Tammy grabs the doctor's right hand with both of hers, and snuggles it. "Thanks so much, Dr. Hearty Yenta. *Thank you*, Doctor!"

Another weasel, George and Lizzie both think. What is it with *weasels*? George and Lizzie each have just enough embers of spiritual impulse that any curious coincidence always catches their attention for a breathless second or two as it bursts prettily into flame. (*Synchronicity.*) And then disappears.

It's intense, the sun, for the first of March. Lizzie feels as anxious about work (back in the room just now, she played her controller's voice mail: *Microsoft isn't showing any flexibility, and they want an answer soon*) as she does about her father's operation. Which is natural, she told herself on the way down to the pool, since Mike Zimbalist's survival, unlike Fine Technologies', lies entirely beyond her control. Is that Zen? Or cold?

George, Lizzie, and Sarah are lying on adjacent chaises. Lizzie picks up Sarah's paperback translation of *The Aeneid* and reads at random.

> *So easily one slithers down to hell—*
> *By night or day, no matter, one gets in.*

Microsoft, Lizzie thinks. *And Mose,* for all she knows. For a few years after college, as she abandoned her absolute adolescent rejection of fuzzyheaded mysticism, she occasionally used an I Ching computer program for advice. But she found the hexagrams a little arcane ("The new roofbeam warps upward. A withered willow sprouting leaves at the foot of its trunk") to be useful for evaluating jobs or boyfriends. Western directness—*So easily one slithers down to hell*—is more her oracular speed.

> *But grappling one's way up again to light,*
> *That is the task, the toil.*

She looks up from the paperback. "You know, Daddy looked good. It isn't depressing to me."

"He did. It isn't. To me either."

"*Warn* me first if you drown me!" Louisa says happily to Max, who's carrying her piggyback in the pool ten feet away. George is looking at Sarah's premiere issue of *Teen Nation, The Nation* magazine's "Super-Rad Journal of Politics & the Environment for a New Generation." (The cover story is "Jimmy Smits and Jennifer Lopez in Mexico: This Revolution *Will* Be Televised." George wonders what Sarah thinks of the articles, such as "Girls 2 Grrrls," a column by Morgan Fairchild and Susan Sarandon on "reproductive choice and other teen issues," and the journalist Bill McKibben's anti-fast-food, anti-TV, anti-sport-utility-vehicle jeremiad "Wasted!" There are also comic strips that make fun of Bruce Willis, Ken Starr, Dan Quayle, William Rehnquist, and Ted Nugent.

"Are you sure," asks Sarah, reading a hospital booklet called *To Life! To Livers! A Hepatology Primer,* "if Grandpa was, you know, mentally *there* when he signed the consent form? According to this, 'End-stage liver patients frequently experience delirium.' "

"Tammy was with him," Lizzie says. "I'm sure he knew exactly what he was doing. Besides, when isn't my father delirious?"

"God!" Sarah says. " 'Hopefully, the national five-year nonsurvival rate for liver-involved oncology patients, which remains at an unsatisfactory ninety-four percent level, will improve with increased research resources.' "

"Sarah," her mother says, "we can do without the fun facts."

" 'This service is hygienized automatically at every use,' " George says. He saw that phrase on a sign above a urinal in Savannah during their honeymoon, and they have both used it ever since as a private shorthand whenever they encounter especially egregious English written by native speakers.

Reminded of their honeymoon, Lizzie strokes George's hand. "Can I look at this?" he says, touching the envelope Lizzie has stuck in the hepatology pamphlet. She nods. It's a note to Lizzie from her father that Tammy gave her at the hospital, written on stationery from the Ingleside Inn in Palm Springs. Everything Mike Zimbalist has ever written by hand, as far as Lizzie knows, is written on hotel stationery. He keeps drawers full of it. As with so much her father does, this mortified Lizzie as a teenager. The first time he sent George one of his notes, on a sheet from the Astor Hotel with the phone exchange ROosevelt 7 (and the slogan: "Air-Conditioned Elegance in the Cosmopolitan Heart of Gotham"), George was so thoroughly charmed that Lizzie felt embarrassed that she'd ever been embarrassed by her father's stationery cache. " 'My Dearest Darling Lizzie,' " George reads. " 'Welcome to LA! You don't have to love Ronnie and the stepsiblings, but please call them?' " That Zimbalist family phrase, Ronnie and the stepsiblings, always makes George smile. It sounds to him like a fifties singing group.

Just in case whatever, may I rest in peace, a few details:

• You can sell the Palm Springs place if you want (you & I still each own 1/3, the stepsiblings own 1/3 and in the event of blah-blah-blah my 1/3 goes to you), but I remember how much you loved it there, and I dig the idea of my grandchildren in that pool, etc.! Up to you. (If you sell, please, please, PLEASE give Gennifer the listing. Family is family, etc.) The Dalí oil feel free to get rid of. (Tammy hates it also.)

• I've been to a marvelous party—i.e., since the whole medical enchilada is comped (!!!), feel free to go crazy on a service—caterers, music (Duchin? Sedaka?), so forth. Invite Rachel (and pls *do not* tell her about my new you-know-what liver; you know her, why get her upset, etc.).

• I came out 180° different than my folks. You came out 180° different than me. But you're nothing like my folks, either. So? *Life ain't geometry!* Remember it.

• Love & xxxxxx to the world's most wonderful WASP. And beautiful Sarah and Max and Louisa.

Hasta Dan Tana's,

Pop

"Extremely Daddy, isn't it?" Lizzie says.

George, holding the note but looking away, doesn't answer. Like his wife and eldest daughter, George is wearing dark glasses. Small children's delusion that they become invisible by shutting their eyes tight is halfway to the truth—by wearing dark glasses adults can become semi-invisible, invisible enough to stare at strangers on the subway, or to privately cry in public.

"Baby?" Lizzie asks, touching his arm. "Are you okay?" George nods his head, holding his breath for a second, swallowing hard, and hands the envelope back to her.

David Spade, on the opposite side of the pool in tiny red trunks, laughs explosively and mulishly into a phone, sounding like Burt Reynolds circa 1975. Only in the Talk Show Age, George thinks, can we recognize and cross-reference the guffaws of the celebrated.

"By the way," Lizzie says, "just for the record, I *never* enjoyed going to Palm Springs as a kid. It always felt like that Dalí painting he has. Surreal in a really tawdry, boring, obvious, sucky, *duh* way."

"Can we go to Palm Springs?" Sarah says, grabbing her *Teen Nation*, open to an article called "PCBs: Why Leonardo DiCaprio Says N-O to NBC and GE," off George's chaise. "We could see the wind-generator fields they have there. Isn't Palm Springs where Quentin Tarantino jumped that movie critic guy you know?"

"Mommy! Daddy!" Louisa yells from the pool, smiling. "Look! Sir is dead!" Max is floating face down, arms and legs limp.

"No, we're not going to Palm Springs. Stop that, Max! LuLu, time to get out of the pool! You too, buster. It's almost four. Now!"

In the west, the sky had turned faintly violet, the color of a sigh.

As they pack up their lotions, reading material, and children, Sarah urgently whispers, "Sinbad."

Her parents look where she's looking. Across the pool, just behind David Spade, the comedian Sinbad, holding a copy of *The Economist* with a giant flaming question mark on the cover, has come lumbering out of a cabana, accompanied by a perfect, tiny blonde.

"She's practically your age, Sarah," Lizzie teases.

"Right," replies Sarah, dubious, embarrassed, and flattered all at once.

"Could be an assistant," George suggests halfheartedly as the five of them shuffle toward the looming pinkness of the hotel. "Remember when they formally forbade us from doing that piece at ABC?"

"What piece?"

"Black celebrities, white chicks."

"Racist," Lizzie says good-naturedly as George holds open the door for her and Sarah and the sopping children.

———

He has said nothing so far. Dr. Hardiyanti and a female colleague stand at the foot of the bed. Tammy is between them, squeezing both doctors' hands. Mike Zimbalist opened his eyes ten seconds ago, but now he's laboriously, twitchily shutting the left one tight. George, wondering if there's some neurological problem, glances at the doctors, who are still beaming. Lizzie, holding her father's left hand, idly rubbing the big gold pinky ring, realizes the eye shutting is a wink—a slow-motion, postanesthesia wink. Her father is a big winker, and he always winks before he makes a wisecrack. Lizzie prepares to cringe. (A couple of days before his parent-teacher conference with Lizzie's seventh-grade teacher, he had one of his comedian clients write him a half dozen jokes about the New Math, Jimmy Carter, and disco, "just in case things get slow." Lizzie was aghast. The teacher, of course, was smitten.) Mike Zimbalist lets his winked left eye pop open, and purses his lips. He's going to speak. "Oink!" he says. "Oink! Oink! *Oink!*" Everyone chuckles—even Lizzie.

———

Three days later, he's still alive, still in critical condition, still beguiling the medical staff with pig jokes. "Hey, I guess now I'm *really* a male chauvinist pig." Interspecies transplantation "isn't just chopped liver." He could do an endorsement for the hospital, touting "the other white meat."

This morning, Tammy invited the whole family to move in to her and Mike's house "for the duration." And what is the duration? This morning, Lizzie dared to broach the topic for the first time with George. They were still in bed, and Lizzie was watching TV. On the KABC local news a man with a chirpy, nasal voice was delivering almost telegraphic reviews of forthcoming movies, ten in a minute. "Can a woman from the year 2000 save the world and get a boyfriend when she finds herself in the year 2125? Julia Roberts stars in *The Good Old Days,* B-plus! Opening Friday!"

"This asshole sounds like a recorded message," Lizzie said. "You know? He sounds like the 'Welcome to MovieFone, press one *now* for a theater near you' guy."

George, face down with his eyes still closed, said into his pillow, "It *is* the MovieFone guy."

"No! It isn't."

"Uh-huh. He's become a critic."

"Amazing."

"You're suggesting he's not qualified?"

"*Just* amazing." She punches MUTE on the remote. "The kids have missed four days of school already." She poked at George's nearest buttock with an index finger. "George? Are you going to fly home with the kids tomorrow?"

George turned over and sat up. He had an extremely sincere expression that took Lizzie aback.

"They could go without us," he said. "Sarah would be in charge. With Rafaela. And both of us stay here for a while, playing it by ear with your dad."

As she had feared: empathy one-upsmanship. "Until when? Tammy says they're not going to let him go home for at least four weeks, best case. If and when we need to come back, well, you know, we will." If and when her father's immune system finally wakes up and realizes that the liver isn't just new, *it's from a pig,* and does what it is designed to do—attack the pig liver, kill the pig liver, fight to keep Mike Zimbalist pure and (his native cells believe) healthy . . . the dumb, tragic loyalty of antibodies. If and when they need to attend the Neil Sedaka funeral gala at Merv Griffin's Beverly Hilton.

The family has just arrived for Saturday dinner at a big, dark, sleek Chinese restaurant called Powerful on Sunset, at the Beverly Hills end of West Hollywood on Sunset Boulevard. On one wall hangs a life-size, photorealistic black-and-white portrait of the Gang of Four, overprinted in pink with the Courier typeface line INT. SECRET LAB, SAN BERNARDINO, NIGHT. On the matches and menus is the restaurant's subtitle: CHINESE CUISINE FOR THE THIRD MILLENNIUM. The giveaway that they are in a West Los Angeles restaurant is the background music: in a restaurant this smart in Manhattan, there would be no Lite FM instrumental medley.

The male half of the restaurant's clientele can be divided just about evenly into thirds, the standard West L.A. cut. There are those wearing mint-condition blue jeans or chinos, perfectly white sneakers, and freshly laundered casual shirts—the Spic-and-Span Super-Casuals, tanned and aggressively cheerful Maliboomers (Emily Kalman's phrase) who would prefer that you envy their happiness and serenity more than their money and power. The Sullen Seven-Figure Scruffs, about a decade younger and dressed in well-worn jeans and dirty sneakers and shirts that do not look lemony fresh, are happening nerds and young dudes—wan, chubby sitcom creators, and actors with 1870s-by-way-of-the-1970s first names like Ethan, Billy, Christian, Vince, Ben, Skeet, and Stash. The nameless third group of men, lawyers and lawyerlike executives and older agents, are in jackets and dress shirts—they'd be more comfortable wearing suits and ties, but can't because it's the weekend; it would make them seem uptight to the Spic-and-Span Casuals, the Seven-Figure Scruffs, and their own wives. The female half does not divide so neatly. Most (but not all) of the classic southern Californians, the genetically and surgically awesome Nicole Simpsons, are at tables with group-three men.

George hasn't shaved today. But with his short new haircut he thinks the stubble might pass for rugged instead of slovenly. ("A grayer Mel Gibson?" he asked Lizzie the night he walked in with it. "A taller Rowan Atkinson?" she replied.) In his khaki pants, the peach-colored polo shirt he bought yesterday at the Gap, and an old blue Armani blazer, and with his fresh tan, George might pass for a Spic-and-Span Super-Casual. Which is fine with him. It seems the lesser evil, or anyway the less unattractive evil. Spic-and-Span Super-Casuals are, in effect, a youngish subset of Merry Hardasses and Merry Chatterers; David Geffen, a Merry Hardass, is paradigmatic, the Cary Grant of Hollywood's underdressed generation.

Lizzie, wearing her Helmut Lang pants and black silk Cynthia Rowley shirt, looks like the friend of a Spic-and-Span Casual visiting from New York, or an agent. In New York, Lizzie sometimes wonders if wearing her hair loose makes her look too girlish and foofy. In L.A., as long as she's not wearing very short shorts or Lycra, or exposing belly flesh, she won't be considered frivolous, which is a relief. On the other hand, nothing she can wear or do will ever get her or any other woman taken entirely seriously in Los Angeles. The category, woman-taken-entirely-seriously, does not quite exist here, does it, still? As always when she returns to L.A., she thinks of Barbra Streisand: for all the crappy movies, the sunstroke spiritualism, the pussycat feminism, the angry insecure art-collecting autodidacticism, the diehard paleoliberalism, despite attaching herself to Bill Clinton and James Brolin, as ridiculous and annoying as Barbra Streisand is, in the southern California context, you start feeling sympathetic. Lizzie does, at least.

"Your dad was certainly chipper," George says.

"Of course. He feels important. Some reporter from *USA Today* who heard something called the hospital. Daddy told Dr. Hardiyanti to hold out for *The New York Times,* and offered to get him a TV agent for 'the MOW deal.' Remind me what MOW is?"

"Movie of the week," Max says, standing up along with his little sister. "LuLu needs to go to the WC," he announces over his shoulder as he walks away, using one of their former nanny's phrases.

"Sarah?" Lizzie says.

"I'm reading my book," says Sarah, who's now deep into *Kissing for Dummies.* "He's almost ten, Mom. They'll be okay."

"I hadn't thought about that part," George says. "The press. This is a story, isn't it? This could be a big story. *Jesus.*" For a fleeting, terrible moment they both think: *And next week we're going to be the smiling freak-show loved-ones sidebar if he actually survives.*

"Dr. Hardiyanti also asked me this afternoon who Ben Kingsley is. Daddy, of course, is already casting the movie."

"Ben Kingsley in a TV movie? Maybe a feature—*The Island of Dr. Moreau,* but contemporary and comedic. And," he adds, shifting down to an announcer's bass, "*inspirational.* Possibly HBO."

"My God: no wonder you and my father get along so well."

"You had a whole childhood to get nauseated by show biz. I was vulgarity-deprived. I'm still gorging." George glances at Sarah, who's slouched down in her chair reading. "Cubby told me in St. Paul that Alice, quote, 'has a few envy issues with her little brother.' "

"*Duh.*"

"He said she always feels like she's my 'spacer car.' "

"Spacer car?"

"I had no idea either. It's a train thing—they attach an empty car to each end of a full car carrying a heavy load, to spread out the weight for when the train crosses bridges. So the bridge won't collapse."

"Who's my spacer car?"

"We take turns?"

"What are you guys talking about?" Sarah asks, using her middle-of-the-conversation confusion as an opportunity to be annoyed.

"Trains," George tells her.

"Fuck!" Lizzie says. Sarah looks up. "George, I just remembered, while you were in the shower, Iris called. I'm really sorry. . . ."

George hasn't brought his phone to dinner. "On Saturday night? What'd she want?"

"She didn't say. She wouldn't. That's why I forgot. I'm sorry. She said it's confidential."

No one else would notice, but Lizzie watches George go a little tense, disengage, and look away a few degrees, deciding whether to resist his urge to call Iris now, thinking, *Mose has decided Real Time is too expensive, or too complicated, and backed out; or, they're moving NARCS to Sunday to go against 60 Minutes; or, Angela Janeway is refusing to go back to work until I book Vaclav Havel as well as Mandela for guest shots.*

Max and his sister have returned. "LuLu saw the actress who plays Clarissa taking a dump downstairs," he announces.

"How charming, Sir," Lizzie says. Since she is still fighting a holding action against *butt*, she decides to let *dump* pass this time. She capitulated on *sucks* two years ago.

"No, it was Sabrina!" Louisa corrects. *"Sabrina!"*

"Same actress," Max explains to the table.

Yesterday the whole family debated whether they had watched Halle Berry or Jada Pinkett or Jasmine Guy waiting to get her BMW at the hotel. The day before, the confusion was over a man standing near them in one of the seventeenth-century rooms at the Getty Museum: was it Alex Trebek (Max and LuLu) or Tom Selleck (Sarah and George) or Kevin Kline (Lizzie)?

"This is like license-plate bingo," George says.

"What's license-plate bingo?" Sarah asks.

"Yes, Opie," Lizzie asks, interested as ever by the residual oddments of middle Americana that cling to her husband, "what *is* license-plate bingo?"

After how many generations of upward social mobility and whizbang novelty is a plateau finally reached, George wonders, and children once again live the childhoods their parents lived? "Nobody else at this table has ever taken a cross-country car trip, have they?" George says, shaking his head and doing a sort of parody of a tough-old-fogey dad. "Private schools, nannies, computers . . . no firecrackers. License-plate bingo is where you spot car license plates from as many different states as you can."

"Why?" Sarah asks.

"Were license plates white-and-black when you were a boy?"

"Yes, Louisa, whittled by hand out of wood by hillbilly slaves."

"Really?" she asks hopefully.

"Dad," Max says, "you should have your network make a TV show out of TV-star bingo. With kids and adults competing against each other to search for the celebrities. Like a giant scavenger hunt, but for human beings."

George doesn't know exactly how that would work, and he has no desire to go into the game-show business, but he knows that his little boy has had a cunning commercial inspiration.

A Chinese woman in her early twenties has appeared to take their order. She's wearing a translucent Day-Glo yellow Bao Dai dress and has a tiny 1950s orbiting-atom tattoo on her neck just behind her right ear. George and Lizzie both wonder if her breasts, implausibly large, are real. Lizzie also thinks, *Ten years ago, you saw stylish, sexy Japanese women, but almost never Chinese (except for Pollyanna), and now suddenly they're everywhere.* And George thinks, *Why aren't there any Asian-American stars?*

"Dad," Max suddenly asks as George stands, "how famous are you, exactly?"

"Exactly?" he says with a smile. "I don't know. Not very. But give me a few minutes to calculate."

When he finds the phone, he pushes the VOICE button on his new PalmPilot and says, "Contacts . . . Iris Randall . . . home" toward a tiny slot. Then on the pay phone he pushes the correct twenty-five-digit sequence necessary to reach his secretary in New York.

"Thank you very much for using Pacific Telesis," a recorded female voice says before putting him through. "This evening. We really hope you have a super. Dinner at. Powerful on Sunset. Mr. Mac Tire."

"It's. Pronounced. Mc*Teer,*" George says, fooling around.

"Hello?"

"Hi, Iris, it's me. You called?"

"You didn't tell me about *Reality* getting picked up by the network! I'm brimming with pride for you!"

"Ah. Thanks. I guess I assume you know everything."

"George! *Michael Milken* called you," she says in the same insistent whisper that she says *Fifty-nine.* "His executive assistant. It was yesterday at, um, wait a second, let me find it." And she's gone. He hears her rustling; he hears her TV. *Mike Milken?* How would the richest and most respected criminal in America chart out these days on Saddler's Media Perception Index? Now there's a true visionary, like Jay Gould and Lex Luthor and Dr. No were visionaries. Barry Diller, whom George knows slightly, introduced him to Milken at a party for the media watchdog magazine *Brill's Content,* in which Diller was an investor. (George is embarrassed to admit, even to Lizzie, even to himself, that he had wished for the magazine's demise—not out of idle Manhattan malice, but because he knew the magazine would wage a righteous and annoying crusade against *Real Time.*)

"Hello? Iris?" Nothing, just the noise of distant rummaging and the infamous TV ad for an advertising agency that has been running all winter on New York stations. (The commercial consists of magnificent stock shots of forests and American cities, run under a Satie piano étude and a vocal track of a woman moaning orgasmically.) George watches a young woman step out of the bathroom a few yards from the phone. She smiles as she passes. Women outside New York smile at strangers. He thinks she may be Dominique Swain—excellent memory, George!—who had the title role in the *Lolita* remake. Or is it Britney Spears? Is this who LuLu mistook for the girl who plays Clarissa and Sabrina? Do all blond twenty-two-year-old actresses look more or less the same to six-year-olds, the same way they do to forty-four-year-olds?

Where in God's name have you gone, Iris? He considers hanging up. Then he hears, as if out of his own brain, the opening bars of the *NARCS* theme music, the Wagner played on electric guitar and the strings-and-percussion stew (cellos, digital congas, timpani, automatic weapons cocking), which gives him goose bumps even now. It's ten o'clock in New York, *NARCS* is just starting, and Iris is at home alone, on Saturday night, settling in to watch his show as it's broadcast. This is why she keeps her job.

"At seven-fourteen," she says.

"What?"

"The call from Michael Milken's office. Last night. Well, yesterday afternoon, I guess, his time. No, it's a Miami number, 305—so it was last night. I have the number. You want it? Shall I try patching you through? But it's Saturday. And it's late."

"What did he want, Iris?"

"I don't *know.* I asked. The assistant wouldn't say."

"Then why did you tell Lizzie that you were calling about something confidential?"

"Because you told me on Monday to be sure never to tell anyone anything, nothing, including Lizzie, because of fiduciary whatever, and church and state and competition we may not even be aware is competition, blah-blah-blah. Don't you remember? On Monday you told me."

"Can the Milken call wait until Monday?"

"Do you think I should try to get him now and find out?"

"Let's return the call Monday morning. And Iris, we need a flight back home tomorrow, all five of us. After lunch.

"Also, Iris? Can you find out if Angela wants a free, um, therapy session for her dog?"

"Of course! George? How's Mr. Zimbalist doing? Is he . . . copacetic?" She pauses just long enough for George to start to take a breath. "No, I apologize, it's none of my beeswax. So I hope he's fine. See you Monday. Bye." Does she mean copacetic or comatose?

9

How I hate running, George thinks as he runs east up Sunset past gardeners' pickups arriving for work, his lungs burning, mouth wide open, slurping air, blinded by the rising sun, on each left stride the brand-new nylon shorts tugging scrotum flesh. Dropping dead while running: George dreads the prospect of an ironic death. As interesting-story deaths go, being killed by the contra mortar shell in 1984 would have had its virtues. The line-of-duty nobility; the youthful and politically correct martyrdom (although it could have been a Sandinista round just as easily); the clips from the movie *Under Fire* that the TV news shows would have run to sex up their reports; the tacit rebuke to all the baby-boom pussies who will wind up dying on the StairMaster or some rusty nursing-home gurney.

"My God! Gordon *Mac*Rae!" yells a man enthusiastically a half block down Santa Monica.

Where? George wonders, running. Is Gordon MacRae still alive? Movie-star bingo, live.

"*Hey,* Gorgeous George!" the man yells.

A nut. An interesting nut. In fact, the perfect Beverly Hills lunatic. He's walking several extremely tiny dogs. George veers right, giving the guy room, and averts his glance.

"Whoa! One-armed man! David Janssen chasing you or what?"

It's Featherstone, of course. He has on yellow leather pants, a complicated white collarless shirt, and dark glasses with frames so fine and wirelike that at first George thinks he's wearing a pair of smoked-glass monocles. Which, someday, Timothy Featherstone might very well do, depending on the caprices of twenty-first-century fashion.

"Timothy!" George huffs. "Great to see you!" He holds up his index finger as he tries to catch his breath. "One sec." At first George thinks his discombobulation is due to the unexpectedness of the encounter, or because he's dressed in embarrassing ad-wear (a Y2KRx T-shirt, shorts with the Gap logo). Ordinarily, around Featherstone, George feels a kind of beneficent superiority—certainly not nervousness or deference. But this, George realizes, is their first face-to-face encounter since the network pickup of *Real Time* has had time to sink in. Last week, before they had the deal, George could be pessimistic and carefree. Not anymore. His long shot has come in, and his reflexive grovel is part of the price, the agony of victory. It must run deep, this ancient human impulse to suck up.

"My main dude!" Featherstone holds a hand near George's crotch, palm up. George, sweaty and out of breath in his running clothes, for once feels butch enough to slap five.

"Cute poodle."

"Bichon frise."

"What?"

"Peter is a bichon frise."

"Ah. Right." All four dogs are odd-looking, but the weirdest seems literally extraterrestrial: eight inches high, cartoonishly fluffy, and all white except for a perfect black triangle around each of its huge surprised eyes. It could be a canine-feline crossbreed, combining the least endearing aspects of each species. "That's a really interesting one."

"Paul? Paul's a Japanese chin. Fabulous breed. Johnny Depp has a chin. I'm told that Jennifer Aniston is into chins. Paul"—he tugged on the leash of what looked like a shrunken, hairless German shepherd—"is a xoloitzcuintili. And Ringo, here, is a schipperke pup."

A "zuh loytz-queen-teeley" and a "shkeep-ur-kuh." The breeds sound like extemporaneous nonsense, the kind of words Max makes up when he tries to scare LuLu. Featherstone's xoloitzcuintili is yap-ping angrily at George, which makes the schipperke start yipping at the xoloitzcuintili.

"So what're you doin' out here in my hood, man? *Prago!* No! *Prago!*" he says sharply to the dogs, which instantly stop barking. "The trainer is from Umbria."

"Lizzie's father went into the hospital on Monday."

"Ay-yai-yai! Rough week for the Mactier-Zimbalists. Ringo! *Sedersi giù, cane! Sedersi.* Where you staying?"

"The Beverly Hills." The A-list hotels are the Bel Air and the Peninsula. The Beverly Hills is a bit A-minus, especially since the renovation in the nineties polished away the singed, mildewy, Dewar's-and-soda patina of old Hollywood.

"Really? Hmmm. Why don't you pop over with me and have a mochaccino and a scone, whatever. *Mi* crib *es tu* crib."

"Lizzie will wonder where I am. She's alone with all three kids."

"Hey, man, it's century twenty-one. Telecom!" Featherstone pulls from his pocket a black plastic object the size and shape of half a Ping-Pong ball, and twists its rim. Two rubbery, wormlike appendages unfurl and stiffen in opposite directions. He puts the flat side of the Ping-Pong hemisphere to his ear. The stubby neoprene worm pointing up must be an antenna, the head of the worm near Featherstone's lips a mouthpiece. "Beverly. Hills. Hotel," he says into it, then hands the phone to George. "Mad flossin', *n'est-ce pas?* You can't even buy it in this country yet."

"I'm calling George Mactier, please," George says.

Lizzie answers. "Buddy?"

"*Buddy?* No, this is your actual husband."

She giggles. "Hi, darling." Spouses can turn so nice, all flattered and patronizing, when they detect a little jealousy. "Buddy wants to meet us for early brunch at someplace in Sullivan Canyon, and I told him we would. He's on his way to Mandeville Canyon to work on a horse, and I'm waiting for him to call back with directions. So we can drive to the restaurant." So nice, and so forthcoming with babbly, excessive detail.

"Who's 'we'?"

"Whoever. You, me. All of us. You're being silly. Buddy wants to see Sarah. It's been five years."

Buddy Ramo, child star turned equine massage therapist, unwittingly suicidal would-be liver donor, biological father of Sarah. George knows if he joins them he will be overcome by an L.A. cocktail of unworthy emotions—three parts amused pity at Buddy's ridiculous profession and surfer-dude manner, one part envy of Buddy's buff good looks and surfer-dude manner, a dash of unjustifiable rage at the blood connection to his eldest daughter. "I'm here with Timothy on the street. We just bumped into each other."

"Lucky you. God, the man is everywhere."

"Timothy invited me to stop by his house for a bite to eat."

"Okay, see you," she says, maybe a hair too eagerly. "Enjoy yourself with your friend Timothy. I'll see you back at the hotel by . . . noon?"

"Give my best to Li'l Gilligan. Hold on."

Featherstone has raised his eyebrows and is pointing at his own sternum with his index finger. George hands the phone over and, inhaling a big warm lungful of tuberose, luxuriating in the endorphin flood—how he loves *the end* of a run!—and watches, half naked, as Timothy schmoozes his wife wirelessly from the corner of Sunset Boulevard and Benedict Canyon Drive.

"Queen Elizabeth! The sister with the *flow*! I just want you to know you saved Harold's tushie the other day in Seattle. You really hipped us to it. I mean that. Gratitude squared. Absolutely! We were hoping for sixty/forty, but I'd say it went eighty/forty our favor, net/net, thanks to you. Now we know who wears the brains in the family." Featherstone turns an inch toward George for a second and, George assumes, winks behind his very dark glasses. "No, I won't breathe a word to George, I swear." He turns and presumably winks again. "And by the way? Harold really meant what he said. That's the God's honest four-one-one. Okay, Zimbalista. See you around campus." Featherstone gives the rim of the earpiece a quick hard squeeze and, as both appendages go limp and retract with a hurry-up snap, stuffs the phone in his pocket. Bulging the yellow pant leather, it looks like the head of a gargantuan penis. Maybe unintentionally.

"Let's boogie," Featherstone says to George, and then to the dogs, *"Avanti!"*

" 'Sort of'?"

Lizzie turns down La Cienega toward the airport. George has asked if they had a good time with Buddy.

"Yeah. It's always vaguely depressing for me to talk to him."

Yes! George thinks. *Okay!*

"Maybe we should've taken the freeway," she says, slowing down for traffic. "I do think Max and LuLu had fun with Buddy. They got to sit on his client's horse."

"Daddy," Louisa says, "did you know that if a horse gets sick? They just *kill* it."

"And," Lizzie continues, "I think it was interesting for Sarah to see Buddy."

"He's kind of a cretin," says Sarah from the backseat.

"She's saying that," Max explains to George, "because when Buddy asked when I'll turn ten and I said 'Saturday, April eighth,' he said, 'Wow, I couldn't tell you what date *next* Saturday is.'"

George is glad his children have visited Buddy Ramo.

"Timothy's house is in Bel Air?" Lizzie says. "I thought he said something on Mose's jet about Los Feliz."

"His girlfriend Ng's *studio* is in Los Feliz," George says.

"And what does Ng *do* in her studio?"

"Keeps a pet gibbon and 'makes dance pieces.' And does her homework, I guess." But George wants to get back to the very promising Buddy Ramo discussion. "What was so depressing about Buddy?" he asks carefully, evenly, not quite fake-sensitively—as if he really cares about the well-being of the has-been pretty-boy who impregnated his wife fifteen years ago—but definitely glee-free.

"Nothing. *He's* not depressing. His life is so simple. He's so happy. It's really kind of . . . I don't know. Beautiful. He lives in some two-room cedar pavilion he designed and built himself up near Point Dume. He makes me feel like we're doing something wrong."

Oh, hell. On a bad day, Buddy has always looked like Jeff Bridges or Kurt Russell on a good day, and now he's achieved some kind of Zen mastery as well. Making no-account stupidity look like bliss: impressive. Even when George feels blissful, he never radiates a glow of inner peace or smiles infectiously—another reason he was not a very good hippie in the seventies.

"Oh, *wow.*"

"I'm serious."

"Oh, honey," George says, "come on. It's just so California. He's a caricature."

"Mommy, why did he call you 'my Pally gally'?" Louisa asks. "And is that good or bad?"

George waits for the answer, too.

"The high school I went to was called Pally," Lizzie tells her, and then says to George, "You don't have to tell me about California caricatures. I'm just telling you, I felt jealous. It tasted awfully real to me. And I've got to say, it tasted pretty good."

George doesn't reply. It tasted good? That's an intimate verb, *tasted*. Suddenly a knot of ethical anxiety relaxes: Featherstone told him, over whipped mochaccinos *brûlée* in his rock garden this morning, that Mose is "seriously kicking the tires" of TK Corporation, Penn McNabb's internet video software company, as a possible acquisition. "Still a ways to go before we open our kimono, but Harold's definitely aroused." George knows, strictly speaking, that he shouldn't pass this news along to Lizzie, but he has assumed this morning that he will tell her anyway, because she is his wife and it's good gossip. Right at this moment, however, George feels rigorously committed to the rules of fiduciary confidentiality.

"Buddy has the whole first sentence of *The Hobbit* tattooed on his chest," Max says. "In big fairy-tale-book letters. It's awesome."

"So I've heard," George says. Seconds pass. "I'm surprised he hasn't updated himself, and tattooed *The Celestine Prophecy* on his butt."

LuLu giggles. "*Daddy* said 'butt'!"

"Uneducated people can have deep feelings," Lizzie says.

George's phone vibrates in his shirt pocket.

"You're right." He grabs his phone. "Maybe you could have that needlepointed on a saddle blanket for him," George says, regretting the line even as he utters it. "Hello? Hi, Em. On the way to the airport. Uh-huh. Why? Really? You really think *I* need to be there? I mean, we're five minutes from LAX right now, on our way out." He's looking at Lizzie, who now looks over at him. "Oh, sheesh. Whose idea was that? Yeah, *sure.* Yeah. What, so he can personally manage the California primary coverage? Bullshit. According to whom? Well, Harold is probably right about that. Yeah. Okay. Okay. Bye, Em."

"What?"

"Mose wants Emily and me to spend Tuesday explaining *Real Time* to everyone out here. Timothy's people, the ad sales guys. According to Emily, according to Timothy, Harold said, 'If you want to go out of the box, first you have to sell it in-house.' "

"And Emily can't do that alone?"

"Barry Stengel from News just happens to be flying out here to-morrow. For the primary. He's already trying to poison the well against us." George realizes he's never told Lizzie about eavesdropping on the phone conversation between Featherstone and Stengel the other day. And he's not going to tell her now, in front of the kids. "Emily can't go up against Stengel by herself. I've got to be there."

Lizzie sighs. "Whatever."

"So," George says, "I guess I'll drop you guys off at the airport and fly home Tuesday night."

"This sort of sucks," Lizzie says.

"You're telling me. We go back into production this week."

"You're not coming on the airplane with us, Daddy?"

He turns around. "No, honey, I guess not."

"That's bad, but it's also good," Louisa says. "Because if our plane crashes? You can be alive to hunt for the pieces of us."

Beverly Hills, Sunday afternoon, family eight miles over Iowa, nowhere he has to go, nothing he must do. Such scrumptious sloth! The TV is, of course, on. He's lying on the half-made king-size bed, naked. He has already finished a little six-dollar bag of minibar blue corn chips, half a five-dollar eight-ounce Evian, and six minutes of Spectravision. (Just as video pornography is more pornographic than filmed pornography ever could be, pornography watched in daylight is almost too porno-graphic to enjoy. Almost. But maybe, it occurs to George, he's just old-fashioned.) He has dumped a fourteen-dollar jar of minibar macadamias onto one of the four huge, plump pillows, and he swigs a nine-dollar minibar Heineken. He's discovered Channel 53, something called the Chopper Channel. It runs nothing but news shot from helicopters, all aerial panning all the time—a high-speed police chase in Orange County and a five-alarm fire in downtown San Diego and an over-turned tractor-trailer on the 10, but also the Dublin Marathon, a herd of wild mustangs in Montana, a five-hundred-acre oil spill in the North Sea, surprised rock climbers in Yosemite, guerillas cowering in the heli-copter's backdraft somewhere south of Oaxaca, live and taped, from southern California and the world. The Chopper Channel! George isn't sure if it's insane, or brilliant, or both. So many things today are both. The Americas Cup training race off Catalina is losing him, though, and the third time he hears Morgan Freeman giving the channel ID slogan—"The big picture, from the air, on the air, for you"—he flicks off the TV. This set, however, is a kind he's read about: push TV. It can't be turned off. Pressing the off button only switches the set into a low-power mode, during which advertising copy appears noiselessly on the screen. George hops out of bed, idly fluffs his pubic hair and ruffles his testicles, and, wandering toward the desk, shoves the door of the TV cabinet shut with his elbow so he won't have to look at the flashing words WOULDN'T YOU LIKE TO SEE YOUR MESSAGE HERE? YOU CAN! alternating every ten seconds with NOT JUST THE FINEST HOTEL IN LAS VEGAS. THE MOST SPLENDID EXPERIENCE ON EARTH. THE VENETIAN.

He phones Iris at home and, blessedly, gets her machine. "Hi, Iris, it's George. Lizzie and the kids are flying back, but I'm staying in L.A. for meetings in Burbank on Tuesday. First, I need a reservation Tuesday on an afternoon flight back to JFK. Or Newark. Second, I need to fly to Las Vegas tomorrow afternoon, returning to LAX first thing Tuesday morning. And a room in Vegas tomorrow night. At the, um, the Venetian, I guess. Third, you need to get all my *Real Time* files there, in Las Vegas, by tomorrow night. Okay? By courier or whatever. Tomorrow. Thanks. Bye."

This morning the room had been theirs, George and Lizzie's, a comforting fifty-fifty mingle of his scent (espresso) and hers (lavender), her detritus (Chinese vitamins, jade earrings, a fax from Nancy McNabb, loose tampons that inevitably remind George of the rubber bullets he picked up off the street one night in Bethlehem as souvenirs of the intifada) and his detritus (paragraphs torn from newspapers and magazines, *NARCS* faxes, spare lithium ion batteries for the fake driving hand, inside-out black socks on the floor, which always look like husks left to rot after the fruits have been extracted). Now it's just his—his Post-it stuck to the lamp, his wads of fives and ones in the armchair, his room-service tray and salad leavings, his damp towel on the couch, his warm PowerBook G3 on the desk.

Their PowerBook, technically, but he uses it more. Given her profession, Lizzie is only desultorily wired, aside from e-mail indifferent to computers in her personal life. George finds this charming. Neither of them fully embraces the web lifestyle. If you're a reporter who requires many disparate bits of information quickly, fine. Or a trader in stocks or bonds or currencies who really does need prices and news this very instant. Or if you're a person in the thrall of a cult or pathology or hobby, or some lonely loser who can't make friends the ordinary ways. Or a curious child. But otherwise, what is so compelling about the web? Instant access, at any time of day or night, to ten million corporate brochures, card catalogues, and strangers' queer obsessions?

"But you just said it, sweetheart," George told her the night in 1994 she was trying to convince herself not to go to work for Rupert Murdoch's new online service. "You just hit on *exactly* why this World Wide Web"—the phrase *World Wide Web* already sounds as antique as motorcar or aeroplane—"really *will* work."

"Because it's a tewwible tongue twister?" Lizzie said.

"Because most Americans are in the thrall of some cult or pathology or hobby. Or don't have any friends because they live in some ten-minute-old suburb in the middle of a cornfield or desert and spend all their spare time commuting and watching TV and looking at catalogues. Highways made the suburbs happen. The suburbs will make your World Wide Web happen." She took the Murdoch job the next day. (And lost it a year later when the business had its plug pulled.)

Similarly, George has very little personal interest in prime-time television. Except for shows he produces and shows that compete directly with shows he produces, he literally has to force himself to watch TV at home. As a child, he watched his full American ration and then some, thirty-five or forty hours a week. Eating thickly frosted cookies, reading *Tom Swift,* doing homework, talking by walkie-talkie to his friend Tuggy Masterson two houses down or by phone to Jodie Eliason, building plastic models of military vehicles from the past and the distant future, jerking off—almost nothing George did as a child wasn't done while watching TV. ("That's why men multitask so much better than women," Lizzie concluded from George's description of his all-TV childhood. "That's why they like looking at Bloomberg screens with seventeen different data streams. You've all been in training for this since you were boys.") But in adolescence his TV gluttony was slaked, or suppressed, or desublimated. As an adult, George hasn't watched more than a minute of most series on television—a disengagement that would have been simply unimaginable when he was young. He's never admitted to anyone at work that the final episode of

Seinfeld was the first time he watched the show. The night he had the idea for *NARCS,* half drunk, inventing on the spur of the moment, seated next to Emily at a dinner party, he had to ask Lizzie on the way home if his idea for *Drug War* (as he called it then) sounded too similar to *NYPD Blue* or *Homicide,* since he had never seen either show.

"What do you mean, 'too similar'?" George remembers Lizzie saying in a taxi hurtling in the rain down Fifth Avenue. "All TV shows are like other TV shows. Fuck, George, just for having a police show with cool music and a woman commander and a virtuous cop who smokes pot you'll get credit for being revolutionary. Make it good too, and you'll be home free."

George catches himself, and smiles: he has been standing for two minutes in front of his big window overlooking the hotel's parking area, naked, combing through his pubic hair with his hand, staring at the top of a browned palm tree on Sunset, in full view of a pair of parking attendants sharing a cigarette. He grabs the curtain closed. Emily won't be here for two hours to pick him up for Hank Saddler's charity cocktail party. He'll read the new script they e-mailed him from New York yesterday. The PowerBook is in sleep mode, which is more properly eyes-closed-pretending-to-sleep mode, since the computer springs instantly to full wakefulness the moment he touches it. Barely but precisely tickling a rectangular indentation near the keyboard, the body heat of his index finger moves the cursor (that is, the tiny drawing of an arrow) over the ragged mob of icons (that is, the little pictures of file folders) to the one labeled NARCS 99–00, and he clicks, bursting open a sublist of file folders. Then, tickling the cursor down an alphabetical stack of other little file folder pictures, past BUDGETS, CASTING, DIRECTORS, MEMOS, and KALMAN, toward SCRIPTS, he comes across a file he doesn't remember creating, tucked between LINE PRODUCERS and NETWORK. It's called MOSE. He clicks it open without thinking, like swatting a gnat away.

Filling half the screen is a catalogue of three documents: HAROLD MEMO, WEBTV-REALVIDEO RESEARCH, and BLAH-BLAH-BLAH NOTES.

It's a folder of Lizzie's, stored automatically and inadvertently in his NARCS folder.

HAROLD MEMO? Not MOSE MEMO. Not MBC MEMO. HAROLD.

He looks at the names of each of the files again, taking refuge in the mechanical act of reading and rereading. Suddenly the quiet in the room seems noisy: the soft but audible electronic gear shifting inside the idling computer, the breeze jostling the plastic wand hanging from the drape rod, the burble of valet Spanish from the asphalt outside.

George pulls the MOSE window open wider. He looks at the column of three dates. She last worked on HAROLD MEMO and WEBTV-REALVIDEO RESEARCH this morning, SUN, MAR. 5, 2000, 8:05 AM. While he was out running. She must have stopped when he called from the street. The last time she worked on BLAH-BLAH-BLAH NOTES was SUN, MAR. 5, 2000, 12:05 AM. Which was last night, after they turned off *Saturday Night Live*. (Paul Simon was guest host and the Rolling Stones were the band, the announcer said, for the first of twenty-five twenty-fifth-anniversary shows; Lizzie thought it was a joke; George wasn't sure.) It was after she declined to make love, after he turned his light back on to read and mope and punish her for a few minutes, after he fell asleep.

He wiggles the cursor over HAROLD MEMO hesitantly. He presses the execute button once, blackening the name of the file. And then with a flick of his index finger he shoots the cursor up to the top of the screen, slides it to SPECIAL and SHUT DOWN, then in one quick motion pushes himself away from the desk and stands up, moving away, into the bathroom to get clean for Saddler's party.

"I've never been to an apartment in Los Angeles."

The elevator door opens. "Tasteful," Emily says as they step into a car covered in a LeRoy Neiman mural of snowboarders, except for the floor, which is a spiral of throbbing green neon tubing beneath a translucent plastic sheet.

"Which level do you desire?" says a deep, young male voice from out of nowhere. It sounds like a soap opera actor playing a butler.

"*What* is *that*?" Emily says, looking up.

"Penthouse," George tells the elevator, his chuckle turning the word into several syllables.

"I didn't understand," the elevator says, now a little put out. "Please repeat your request for me."

"Pent-house," George says, this time unconsciously imitating the machine intonation, the same way he puts on a slight French accent whenever a maître d' answers the phone, *"Bon soir!"*

"Tell me again, what's this for?"

"Just Get Along."

"What?"

"Just Get Along is the charity. Pro bono anger management counseling for the poor of Los Angeles."

"Have a splendid time at The Wellingtons on Wilshire!" the elevator says, its tone once again deferential as George and Emily step out, and then, after the door is almost closed and they're too far into the apartment to hear, adds softly, even a little wistfully, "It's five thirty-five P.M."

They see Saddler before he sees them. He stands in a semicircular white-shag-carpeted depression—what used to be called a conversation pit—shirt unbuttoned, left hand on his hip and right hand hanging on to his right nipple the way another man might park a thumb in a belt loop. He's looking down at two young Latino men, both in turquoise-colored shirts and pants, on their hands and knees just in front of him, scrubbing furiously with toothbrushes. Two other turquoised Hispanics stand precariously on the arms of chairs set on the rim of the pit, wearing oven mitts as they reach up toward the blazing halogen track lights bolted to the ceiling. The lights are all pointing toward a single patch of floor.

"I still see a smidge of green," Saddler says, indicating with his bare foot the intensely illuminated spot of carpet. *"¡Verde! ¡Aquí! ¡Verde!"*

"¡Ay! ¡Chinga!" says one of the glove wearers as he touches his wrist to the hot light and nearly falls from his chair. As he steps for a moment onto the stone coffee table to steady himself, the tremor causes dozens of black, skyscraper-shaped candies set up like dominoes to fall. The domino candies, hundreds of them, had formed eight cursive letters—*EVPCCSSP.*

"*My God,* you clumsy twat!" Saddler says.

Emily gives George a look. It's too late to sneak out. He shrugs. How ghastly. How unfortunate. How entertaining.

"Hank?" Emily finally says, just as the final candy domino in the *P* hits the table. "I Know What Boys Like," a song that played on the car radio constantly during George's six weeks in Mexico and Central America, is blasting from the stereo. Saddler doesn't hear Emily.

"Can you *please* set it up again—E, V, P, C, C, S, S, P. *¿Comprendes?*" Then, to the brush squad, wiggling a big toe over the carpet: "Right there—*un poquito más verde.*"

"Hank!" George says, trying and failing to make a shout sound both tentative and friendly.

For a moment, Saddler looks embarrassed.

"I guess we're . . . early?" Emily asks.

Saddler quickly and gently touches his hairpiece with the nipple hand, then, reassured, grins like Bert Parks, or Bert Convy, a big, electric, dead-game-show-host grin and says, "Olly-olly-oxen *free!*" As he steps over an oblivious carpet brusher, up out of the pit, and toward them, buttoning his shirt as he comes, he checks his watch. "Oh, a smidge on the premature side. But what's twenty-four minutes between teammates? We had a little guacamole disaster over in the inglenook."

"The invitation wasn't for *five?*" Emily asks. "I was sure—"

"Six," Saddler says firmly, "but hey, this gives *us* time to talk, doesn't it? Before the *horde* arrives. Welcome to the penthouse. Drinks? Ramón," he says, turning to one of the men in turquoise, *"bebidos para mis amigos."*

Saddler kisses Emily on both cheeks and then, as he shakes George's hand, pets his right forearm. This may be insinuating body language for *Hey, look what I can do with my two hands,* or, more generously, *What a nice, nice arm—such a shame the other one got blown up.*

"We're so pleased you could be here for the event. Is Elizabeth . . ." He pauses, maybe twitching his eyelids just barely in the direction of the missing hand. "Parking your car?"

"She and the kids are on the way home."

"I understand. I do," he says as he squeezes George's forearm again. "I was hoping to speak to Elizabeth this evening. You know, Harold is very grateful for her help on the digital discussions. Extremely. She is a very cutting-edge business lady! Now, you let Ramón know what he can bring you—Ramón? *¿Por favor?*—and I'll be back in a jiff. Make yourselves at home in the Great Room."

George is drinking more than he did in his twenties and thirties, in relative terms—half a bottle of wine every second night, negligible in 1980, verges on problematic by 2000 standards. Writers are supposed to drink, of course, but hangover grogginess makes writing impossible for him. One of the secret perks of being an executive, he's discovered, is that a bit of a hangover doesn't interfere with work at all, not when you're the boss and your job is almost entirely a matter of keeping a big picture in mind and delivering opinions. Generating fresh ideas and paragraphs requires tip-top energy, clarity, and confidence. Reacting to other people's ideas and paragraphs requires . . . consciousness.

Besides, cocktail party abstemiousness only generates an unbecoming sense of superiority, and seems as pointless as decaffeinated coffee or nonfat potato chips or phone sex, a denatured simulation of fun. As Emily takes a tall, frosty Stoli and tonic from Ramon, George thinks of her aphorism, which he had heard perhaps a hundred times over the last two years, and which he paid to have plastered on a billboard on Sunset for her birthday last summer: JUST DO IT. OR JUST SAY NO. BUT DON'T TRY SPLITTING THE DAMN DIFFERENCE.

"Cheers," he says, lifting his goblet.

"Ted Danson," Emily replies, raising her glass.

They begin exploring. "So *Boogie Nights,*" Emily says. There's nothing but rounded corners, rounded edges, thick wall-to-wall carpeting, and spherical light fixtures. There is an oil painting of a whale breaching off Maui at sunset. There is a lot of lime green, a lot of metallicized wallpaper, a lot of Lucite, a lot of high-priced shine.

George was surprised to discover as he grew up, after he left St. Paul, that the fondness for mirrored surfaces, porcelain figurines, clothes bearing words, and gratuitously motorized objects (window shades, TV cabinets, toothbrushes, beds, knives) is distributed more or less randomly among the classes. Rich people just have the means to be flamboyantly, magnificently, memorably vulgar, the wherewithal to own and display, for instance, a collection of tiny, expensive-looking toy weapons—an AK-47 the size of a stapler, a Luger no bigger than a paper clip, a perfect, itsy-bitsy Uzi, and a dozen more that Saddler has mounted on black velvet in a vitrine above his white desk.

On the desk is a computer, the only object in the apartment George covets—and only the monitor, which is flat and huge, three inches thick and a couple of feet across. The computer is on, logged on to a stock brokerage web site called WinWin.com. A line of big green type speeds back and forth, back and forth across the screen: WELCOME BACK, WINWIN WINNER HENRY G. SADDLER IV! YOUR PENDING ORDER WILL BE EXECUTED WHEN THE MARKETS OPEN 12 HOURS AND 43 MINUTES FROM NOW.

WinWin.com is only nine months old, but has received extensive press coverage because it lets its most successful customers trade as much as they want for free, as long as those customers consistently perform better, even a hair better, than the Dow. The company automatically mimics all the trades, for its own account, of its thousand anonymous Main Street geniuses—and also makes money from the tens of thousands of WinWin.com customers who pay standard commissions in the hope of someday getting comped as a WinWin Winner. At first the scheme looked like it must be illegal, but so far all the state attorneys general and federal regulators who've tried to make some kind of case have been stumped. Indeed, the Patent and Trademark Office has just awarded WinWin.com patent number 6,029,497 for its very premise, which the company describes as "selective strategic exploitation of voluntary client nonconfidentiality."

"Gorgeous, aren't they?"

"Hank!" George, turning to face Saddler, feels nabbed. Had he not just drained his glass, Saddler or his computer would be drenched in sauvignon blanc. "Yeah! I loved toy guns as a kid."

"Henry. And they're not toys, George. I'm a collector. They are exacting replicas crafted by Russian craftsmen in Dallas. I've had six-figure offers for this collection."

George nods and stares at the little guns. Saddler, now fully dressed, with his hairpiece and hair-plugged hair artfully merged, is cuddling a spotted cat as big as a one-year-old child, petting it just as he petted George ten minutes ago. For the second time this week, George finds himself thinking he's in a scene from a James Bond movie.

"Beautiful cat," George says, reaching toward its chin.

Saddler jerks away. "Ah! No, no, no. He's not friends with you yet. Mr. Gable is a Bengakl. A direct descendant of the wild Asian leopard."

"Hmmm," George says. These are the sorts of declarations that leave George literally speechless. His mother would have said, *I'll be darned, the wild Asian leopard, now isn't that interesting!* and his dad would have grinned and said, *What do you know?* and shambled off, but George can bring himself neither to walk away nor to fill the silence with recombinant happy talk. *What do you mean by "direct descendant"?* Lizzie would probably say.

"Bathroom?" asks Emily, pointing as she passes George and Saddler.

"Left, just past the media room, before the lanai," Saddler tells her, and then, after her: "Memorable Academy luncheon Friday, wasn't it, Emily?"

"Memorable?" she replies. "I guess seven women all wearing the same Jil Sander suit is memorable. Hank? What's *EVPCCSSP?*"

Saddler's sneer brightens noticeably. "*Henry.* Shoot, you guys saw my little surprise! Well, you're talking to Mose Media Holdings' new executive vice president, corporate communications, synergy, and special projects. The release goes on the wire tomorrow." Saddler has been head of corporate communications just for the TV network, Mose Broadcasting.

"Congratulations, Hank," George says, lifting his empty glass.

"Henry," Saddler says, toasting. Emily touches her tumbler to the cat's nose. Saddler, too hungry for the attention, doesn't back away quickly enough. Mr. Gable hisses like a wild Asian leopard and leaps out of his arm. "Today, corporate communications, synergy, and special projects," Emily says, turning toward the bathroom, "tomorrow, the world."

George, becoming a little desperate for small talk, pretends to gulp from his empty wineglass, then stares at the magenta beanbag chairs and hot tub out on the terrace, which is covered by half a geodesic dome. "So I guess you've lived here quite awhile?" he says, making a decorating inference, groping.

"No," Saddler answers, possibly miffed, "uh-uh. We purchased the property last year." He pushes one remote control button that instantly replaces a Belinda Carlisle song with Pachelbel's *Canon,* and then another that makes two enormous televisions sink pneumatically into the floor. "Everything's brand *spanking* new," he says as he bustles away.

George walks around the conversation pit—the inglenook—to the floor-to-ceiling window facing east, downtown, which is awash in a perfect L.A. evening orange. Could he live here? These days, the only thing New York has that Los Angeles lacks is the Upper West Side and overt meanness, and he's never liked the Upper West Side. He thinks he could live here. He thinks he would if Lizzie would. But she won't. He thinks he probably should.

———

LuLu and Max have finally nodded off, and the Town Car glides down the FDR Drive, almost deserted on a Sunday evening in late winter. Lizzie's favorite cityscape swings into view—the East River (which isn't actually a river, but a strait), the Woolworth Building (which now has nothing to do with Woolworth's), and the Brooklyn Bridge framed by the Manhattan Bridge, across which a line of little automobiles move above two subway trains with rows of tiny lighted windows, all the cars and trains seeming to travel at precisely the same speed in both directions, a little fake-looking, as if a single gear runs it all. It makes her think of George, of his flabbergasted description of Cubby Koplowitz's model city, and she smiles, in love with her excitable forty-four-year-old boy and pleased that after more than a decade in the city, she still feels, nearly every time she returns, this sentimental, Gershwinized, Manhattan-vista rush.

––––––

Twenty-two years, exactly half his life, a New Yorker since 1978. . . . He smells patchouli. . . . Olfactory hallucination? Midlife crisis? He feels light-headed. If this is a stroke, it's not so bad. He doesn't see but rather senses a bright white light. He turns. An impossibly tall, golden Asian woman is suddenly very close, at his side, staring at him, angelically glowing, adoring. (Weasels, pork, beautiful Asian women . . .) He smiles back. How young she is. Is she naked? This is the Los Angeles he dreams and worries about, the abyss of easy pleasure. He thinks: *I'm dying, and the future, my unlived life, is passing before my eyes.*

Then he realizes that the woman is wearing an off-the-shoulder dress. Only her shoulders are naked. George feels like an idiot.

"Hi," he says.

Two hands land hard on his neck. "Captain McTavish," a man whispers in a thick, fake Scottish accent, "we've got to stop meeting like this." It's Featherstone. And his slightly, tastefully pregnant girl-friend, Ng.

"Hi, I'm George Mactier," he says to Ng, putting his hand out.

"My gosh, I *know!*"

"Ng," Featherstone says, no longer Scottish, "is your number one fan."

"*NARCS* is *incredible.* I mean, it's changed the way I think about reality."

"Thank you . . . thanks very much."

"The show on New Year's? Where you arrested the real dealer? I was like, 'This is *so* incredible.' It gave me chills."

"I apologize," he says.

"No! I mean, it was like the most powerful thing I've seen on television. Ever? One of my cultural studies professors told us it was a watershed."

"Really? Thanks." George never receives compliments very gracefully, even when he feels entitled to them, which he usually does. Praise at this new order of magnitude, show business praise, extreme and frothy, with the breathless southern California edge, that enraptured *reverence,* rattles him. He feels like Goofy.

The bright light has not been a near-death vision of the afterlife, he sees now, but a very bright battery-powered light. A video team has just arrived at Saddler's, and one of the two crew members, a guy wearing an E!^{2} baseball cap, is lugging a shotgun microphone and miniature arc light. They're walking slowly backward as they shoot a skinny young redhead in an iridescent blue top, electric green stretch pants, and old-fashioned black plastic eyeglasses. Her facial expression is unsettled, a frown fighting a come-hither smile. She must be famous—famous enough, anyway, for E!^{2}.

E!^{2}, pronounced "E squared," is the E! entertainment channel's new second-string service, a kind of show business C-SPAN. E!^{2} runs nothing but raw coverage of celebrity events twenty-four hours a day—movie premieres, Broadway first nights, cocktail party fundraisers for Los Angeles County supervisors, charity softball games in Westlake, publicists' wedding receptions in East Hampton, magazine cover shoots, Hollywood High reunions, Vancouver film festivals, Actors' Equity meetings in Hell's Kitchen, anything and everything celebrity—anchor-free, unstructured, and unmediated. On E!^{2}, both "celebrity" and "event" are construed generously.

George watches Saddler kiss the young woman on both cheeks. As they exchange small talk, with Saddler holding one of her hands in each of his, their faces are both pivoted about fifteen degrees off axis from each other, toward the camera and light—show biz heliotropism.

"Sarah Michelle Gellar?" Ng says.

"New hair," Featherstone says. "WB talent at an MBC party? Smooth move, Hankster."

George, thankful for the clue, recognizes the name of the star of *Buffy the Vampire Slayer,* on the WB Network. He's never seen the show, but Sarah—Sarah his stepdaughter—has said since she was eleven that it sucks, and Max agrees, so George takes their word for it.

"Fourteen minutes and fifty-six," Featherstone says, watching the actress, "fifty-seven, fifty-eight . . . How long before we stick a fork in *that* chick?"

George has never witnessed Featherstone's casually cruel side. Is it his way of trying to make a visiting New Yorker feel at home? Maybe in L.A. Featherstone just feels freer (or more compulsive) about denigrating the competition. So Los Angeles has straight-ahead public scabrousness after all. It does make George feel more comfortable.

"You know," Featherstone says, still staring, as the video crew and the young woman come closer, "that *isn't* Sarah Michelle. It's— what's her name, Francesca. From MTV News. The *new* new Tabitha Soren." MTV *News*—that explains the eyeglasses. "George!" Feather- stone says suddenly, turning to him, "What the hell are you cooking up with Mr. Milken? His office was calling my office trying to get ahold of you."

"Yeah, I know. I mean, he called me in New York too. I don't know. I hardly know him. I don't know him."

"Harold and Mike are two musketeers, you know. Serious buds."

"Right," George says, now recalling an article, he thinks, that said Mose had Milken's help building the greeting-card business in the eighties. Why should this make him anxious? It's a good thing, not a bad thing, that he and Mose have overlapping social circles, that George isn't some anonymous network grind, "an $80,000-a-year man" (as Ben Gould calls journalists generically), that he's a—you know, a—a player. George actually forms the word mentally, *player,* dis- gusting himself. *Player* is a hateful word, the flip side of *loser,* possibly worse. Lizzie would be appalled.

It's dark and cold and quiet on Water Street as Lizzie signs the charge slip and they all pile out of the Go! Now! dial-car, Max carrying a Kel- logg's Frosted Flakes/World Wildlife Fund bag, Sarah grabbing a suit- case, Lizzie struggling with the duffel bag as well as the sleeping LuLu. The front stoop seems unusually well lit—it's the neighbors' new giant TV screen. By the bluish glow of a five-foot-high close-up of Agent Scully's face, Lizzie picks out the keys to the front door.

Featherstone has folded his arms across his chest, and silently examin- ing Francesca, he furrows his brow and twists his mouth thoughtfully, as if to signal that he isn't about to say *Really excellent booty for an an- chorwoman,* or *You think Kurt Loder gets to do her?* "George," he says, "has she paid enough dues yet to be considered the real thing in your, you know, journalistic community?"

Paid dues? The real thing? His journalistic community? George considers answering, *Timothy, are you aware that Geraldo Rivera is a senior NBC News correspondent and anchor?* But he glances at Featherstone, who shows every sign of being serious, and then back at Francesca. "I think she does have some Washington reporting experience," he says evenly, "but I don't know that she's really on anyone's radar yet, one way or the other," realizing as the words leave his mouth that it's not just ass kissing, this respectful new attitude around Featherstone—it is his old coat-and-tie newsman mode reasserting itself. Half of *Real Time* will be a real news program. Now that the show has a green light, George is reverting, in automatic atavistic anticipation, to the kind of self-serious conventional wisdom that journalism demands of its senior . . . players.

Francesca now stands about ten feet away from George and Ng and Featherstone, talking to a Spic-and-Span Super-Casual who is younger than George but wears oversize glasses with yellow-orange lenses, the kind that shellacked Hollywood big shots from the fifties and sixties wear when they get old. George, Featherstone, and Ng are in the background of Francesca's E!² shot. After several glasses of champagne at his ABC News going-away party a year ago, George remembers joking to Peter Jennings that he should start just referring to himself simply as Peter, like Francesca. Jennings grinned that reticent anchorman grin and patted George on the back. George couldn't decide if the tight smile and the back pat meant he was pissed off or saddened or confused. And at that merry instant, George didn't care. In journalism, he had been the kooky kid, precocious and refreshingly irreverent. Now, in show business, he's the graybeard intellectual, the grownup, seasoned and refreshingly substantial.

"By the way, last night was a *fantastic* episode," Ng tells him as she steps away. "The flashback? Where Jennie remembers her cocaine binge in college? Was completely *incredible.* I was like, 'Is this a feature *film?*'" No wonder Featherstone is so fond of her.

"The most excellent news," Featherstone says, ignoring Ng, "is that you held on to more of the *Freaky Shit!* people last night than you ever did before. Maybe your twenty seconds of hip-hop is working."

Freaky Shit!, on at nine o'clock just before *NARCS,* is MBC's highest-rated show, the one-line concept for which is "Howard Stern meets the Discovery Channel." In print, the name is rendered as *Freaky S★★★!*, and on the air they call it *Freaky Shhh!*

"And next week," George adds, selling, selling, selling as he had never done until he became a boss, selling as he never imagined he would do, "we're bringing back the kid, the handsome drug dealer from New Year's. He's on the cover of next month's *Spin.* And we've written his girlfriend into the show, too."

"The crying girl in the lingerie and the chamois trench?"

George nods. He has only heard shopgirls say the word *lingerie.* He has never heard anyone say *chamois trench,* ever.

"I loved that girl," Featherstone continues. "With the starburst on her belly? *Fantastic.* Great look. Recur her, definitely. With that wardrobe as her signature look."

"And we've got very strong scripts for the rest of the season." Six out of the nine remaining unproduced shows are written. George has read three of those six drafts. Read two and skimmed one. And one of those two is definitely good. Plus, he intends to write at least one more script himself, maybe the final show of the season, if he can find the time. "I sent you the beat sheet for the last show of the season." *The beat sheet.* He could have said *the synopsis.* During his decade as a print journalist he didn't once call a magazine *the book* or talk about *putting it to bed,* and when he was in TV news he'd tried not to refer to *talent* being on *our air.* But the odds are only fifty-fifty that Featherstone would know what synopsis means, and George is still too much a show business newcomer to reject every bit of jargon. He's happy to use the ones that provide real verbal economy, like MOW for movie of the week, or ADR for automatic dialogue replacement—a phrase for retaping lines of actors' dialogue in postproduction that made George laugh out loud the first time he heard it.

"Yeah, Laura gave me her coverage on your final episode. Sounds very mondo." George assumes *mondo* is good. "This joint is filling up," Featherstone says, looking around. For a man of his age and station, he has an exceptionally short attention span, about which he seems exceptionally unembarrassed. "High school with money. You know?"

Featherstone continues scanning the crowd, finally concluding, "Serious M-A-W glut."

"MAW?"

"Model, Actress, Whatever," Featherstone tells him matter-of-factly, with no trace of a smile, eyeing one MAW after another.

George marvels at how thoroughly jokes and no-bones-about-it insincerity have sifted into ordinary discourse. Irony is now embedded in the language, ubiquitous and invisible.

Featherstone remembers something that excites him. "Did I tell you I happened to chitchat the other night with one of Alec Baldwin's William Morris guys? And mentioned Alec guest-starring on the season ender. As Kahuna." Kahuna is the internal *NARCS* nickname for the nameless, faceless, well-connected Washington political figure connected to a heroin-importing conspiracy. George had already called Tom Selleck's agent about Selleck appearing as Kahuna. "Alec's guy says Alec would definitely want the character to be a conservative Republican," Featherstone continues. "But the guy is into it. I'd say we've got Alec semi-attached."

George pauses, preparing to speak carefully and tentatively, doing his best to mask his alarm and anger. He already sees that, in entertainment television, it's never one big concession that makes a show bad—it's the two or three small concessions every week until you've forgotten what you were trying to do in the first place.

"But the back story so far," he says, "has been that Kahuna is more in the Ted Kennedy, Jerry Brown neighborhood. You know? The Black Panther reference a couple of episodes ago?"

"If you've got Alec f-ing Baldwin semi-attached," Timothy says in a friendly tone that suggests he is nevertheless on the verge of brooking no quarter, "I think you can custom-build. I mean, who cares about the character's *political party*. Does making Kahuna a Democrat get us a number? I don't think so."

Does X get us a number? tends to be a trump card in television, even in television news. In fact, when he was a news producer, George himself used a version of the line a couple of times—uttered in a mock-schlock producer's voice to give it an ironic sugarcoating his staff understood, but it was seriously meant, and his staff also understood that. George knows a would-be anchor on a morning show who had his network news career derailed by a single low-Nielsen guest appearance. *Because, Timothy,* he thinks of saying now, *making the villain a liberal burnout is a lot more interesting than making him some obvious right-wing gangster.* But George knows he'll sound like a whiny writer pleading with a producer, and *he's* the producer, paid to be tough-minded, to treat everything as fungible, to trade creative off against commercial. So he does not quibble.

Instead, he says, "Sure, absolutely, if we got Alec Baldwin, we'll take his notes. Of course." He figures on being saved by his careful subjunctive, the *if:* he has heard about Baldwin's enthusiastic semi-attachments and quasi-commitments. George doesn't like dissembling and conniving, but he has to protect the creative autonomy of his show. That's also being a grownup. That's being a boss, a leader.

Dissembling and conniving in order to defend one's cherished freedom to cast Tom fucking *Selleck*? Is that believing one's own bullshit?

———

It feels so fine to be home, *so* fine, such a relief. Even though one of the upstairs radiators broke sometime during the week. And even though dinner will be a buffet of Paul Newman popcorn, a bag of Le Gourmet baby carrots, Michael Jordan cottage cheese one day past its sell-by date, and a pint of Cherry Garcia. At least the carrots aren't a celebrity brand, Lizzie thinks, staring at the microwave as the kernel pops accelerate. Up in the living room, Max and Louisa sit in the dark, watching Nickelodeon, Max flipping through every one of the seventy-six channels during every commercial break.

———

Again, the bright light. This time, he feels the heat. Ng, along with the Spic-and-Span Casual wearing the Lew Wasserman glasses and Francesca and thus the E!² video crew, have enveloped him and Featherstone.

"George, do you know Francesca?" Ng says, impressively. Among people who consort with the powerful and the celebrated, the flattering standard introduction is *Do you know,* never *I'd like you to meet.* We are all members of the international fraternal order of the somewhat famous. We've met before, haven't we, in some green room or at some gala dinner? Or could have, certainly. *George, you know His Holiness the*

Pope, don't you? And to certify celebrity, here is their very own TV crew, live from Los Angeles.

"No, nice to meet you. George Mactier."

As he puts his hand out toward Francesca, the furry E!^{2} mike swings toward his face.

"It's *great* to meet you," she says. "I'm a serious fan."

"Thanks." How quickly praise palls.

"Of *Wars Next Door*," she says.

The Wars Next Door was his PBS series in the eighties about the insurgencies in Central America. Yes! More!

"*NARCS* is great too. But *Wars Next Door* is my *All the President's Men*. Seriously. It's why I'm in this business."

"*George Mactier!* Hello! We meet at last!" says the Spic-and-Span Super-Casual, bringing his glistening, plumpish face and bloody-urine-colored lenses as close as he can to George. His smile is fierce. How do people manage to smile like that at someone they've never met? "It's Sandy Flandy. How *are* you? The grapevine's buzzing about the new show! And I can't get Ms. *Kalman,*" he says loudly enough that Emily glances over and smiles, "to tell me a thing about it. You're the talk of the town." Flandy is the agent for Angela Janeway. Although Emily does almost all the negotiating with actors' agents, thank God, George has had many phone conversations with Flandy. It was Flandy who called George, for instance, to express Angela's discomfort with a line in which she was to call a tobacco executive a "scumbag." (Angela's daughter, George discovered weeks later, is a Brearley first-grade classmate of the daughter of a tobacco company CEO.) And it was Flandy who last month broached the Nelson Mandela guest-star notion on Angela's behalf.

The camera and lights have everyone talking a little louder, smiling a little brighter. A panpipe-and-drum ensemble has started playing. The room is noisy. With the tip of the mike twitching above their heads like some giant Amazonian insect, and the cameraman circling their little group, now joined by Emily and a very sober-looking bearded man who wants to be mistaken for Steven Spielberg, the seven of them squeeze closer together, and their expressions grow bigger, as if they're being directed telepathically: *Stay in the frame! Look like you're chatting!* It's intimate and impersonal, real and stylized, the smells of their eaus and gels and unguents blending and simmering in the tanning-salon glare of the camera's light. Emily, nodding and solemn-faced, looking as if she might be discussing Tuesday's presidential primaries, is listening to the bearded man tell her about the well-known young talent agent who, having been treated for addiction to both cocaine and sex, went to live on a kibbutz, where he fell off the wagon sexually, because he found the women of the Israeli defense forces irresistible.

———————

From the living room, the children are suddenly screaming, loud, shocked, hysterical. "Mom! Mom! Oh, my God! Mom!" And even before Max adds, "Come! Quick!" Lizzie is leaping up the stairs two at a time, adrenaline-powered. What is it? But no flames, no blood, no wounds, no crying, not even a fight. It's the television that's alarmed them, their father on television, live, talking and laughing with an MTV star.

———————

The E!^{2} camera moves in as Francesca brings her mouth close to George's right ear. She's trying to be heard over the din. "So you're developing a prime-time news hybrid. 'Extreme news,' my friend at MBC called it."

"I don't know about that."

"It sounds amazing."

Ng rejoins them. "Timothy told me about the new show, George," she says. "It does sound unbelievable."

"I hope it's not that," George says.

Francesca laughs. Then, pressing hard against his left arm, she says breathily, "I cannot tell you how utterly available I am." George locks his smile. At least a full second passes. Francesca says, "My Viacom contract's up in June." Then, retracting her mouth from his temple and her breasts from his arm, she says to him at normal volume, "You are the man, George Mactier. My hero. I'm serious."

"We should talk," he says, too softly for the E!^{2} mike to pick up. "Back in New York."

"I want this," Francesca growls to George as Hank Saddler pulls her off to meet George Stephanopoulos, who's in Los Angeles promoting the miniseries based on his White House memoir.

———

Sarah has galloped down from her room too, and now all four of them stand in the dark, staring at the TV. "Yes, LuLu, that's really Daddy, and that party is really happening right this second in California, and it's neither good nor bad. But it's time for dinner." A kind of religious hush has overcome Max. His jaw has dropped. "This is so awesome," he says. Sarah, still holding her Princessy yellow cordless phone, glances at her mother. "Yeah, it's awesome," Lizzie says. "Come on, everybody, it's late, chop-chop, it's a school night," she says as she whomps the power button on the set and marches out of the room.

1 0

Lizzie would never dream of saying *I need some space* or *I'd love the chance to get back in touch with myself.* But she has to admit, the first twenty-four hours of Georgelessness are almost always pleasant. It isn't about toilet seats or toothpaste caps, or the mélange of cream and whiskers coating the bathroom sink, or the damp towels on the bed, the tabloids tossed near the recycling bin, the little drifts of sugar and drops of half-and-half left on the counter around the coffee machine. It's the respite, very briefly, from familial complexity. One day, alone in her office, she diagrammed it on a whiteboard—then, blushing, immediately erased the diagram. As a full family, all present, the house hums with emotional permutation. There's the big, twin-star gravity of her relationship with George; her solar relationships with Sarah, Max, and LuLu; George's relationships with each of the kids; and the subtle but distinct vector, a kind of redundant dotted-line relationship, that passes from George to Sarah, through Lizzie, and back again. As a nuclear family with a single nucleus, Mom alone with the kids, the diagram is much, much more than twice as simple. Life on Water Street isn't literally quieter without him (if anything, Lizzie makes more noise than George does), but it feels more peaceful. She'll have had her fill of emotional austerity by tomorrow night, she knows, but this morning, the chill is still fresh and bracing.

"We saw you on television," she said to him on the phone last night.

"What do you mean?"

"You and *Francesca*." She pronounced the name in an exaggerated Chef Boyardee accent, even though Francesca is thoroughly American, native born. She was trying to sound blithe.

"So they aired that live? Jesus, what a zoo."

" 'You're the *man*, George Mactier.' 'I *want* you.' Talk about fucking California caricatures. I'm surprised she didn't start singing 'Happy Birthday, Mr. President.' "

"Actually, she did, later. I guess the E! channel cut away before the humjob out on the terrace. By the way, it was 'I want *this*.' She wants a job."

Lizzie smiled, alone in their bedroom, but she doesn't like it when George makes his jokes about having sex with other women. "I thought you were going to read scripts in the room all afternoon."

"I did." He paused, a half second of mental rewind, which Lizzie mistook as some kind of guilt over attending Saddler's party and flirting with the MTV girl, when in fact it was guilt over snooping around her computer files. "But Emily called and insisted I go with her to this Hank Saddler party, so I went. By the way, I think I'll go to Las Vegas tomorrow night and surprise Ben at the Barbieland grand opening. I've got nothing to do here until Tuesday. Except visit your dad."

"Whatever," she said. "It's Barbie *World*. I'm going to sleep."

But now, awake and alone in daylight, she checks her George feelings: no peevish residue, no grievance. The Francesca spectacle was funny. She's relieved to be back in New York, refreshed, recharged, and rebooted, happy to be on her way to work, happy even to be on the number 3 train. She's late enough this morning (after loading Max and LuLu into the neighborhood gypsy-cab service's '88 Eldorado, watering the orchids, paying bills) that she gets a seat right away. Several seats. She sprawls, in her jeans and black lace-up boots, across a plastic banquette unit for three, both feet up off the floor, reading the *Times*. The paper isn't folded into tidy little rectangles in space-saving subway origami style, but spread out on her lap and legs, the whole broadsheet.

Since the move to Water Street from Sneden's Landing last year, George admitted recently, he has taken the subway exactly four times. Lizzie maintains her subway ritual, especially in the mornings. She has her public reasons (it's usually faster and always safer than a taxi, the number 3 stops close to her office, and, last and least, it saves thousands of dollars a year), but her attachment to the subway is less about utility than private personal symbolism. With money in New York City, it is tempting to ease into a platinum-card arm's-length soft-focus version of urban life, Manhattan observed from behind tinted Town Car windows. ("What are 'tainted limo windows'?" Max, misunderstanding, once asked.) As it is, the family has a city house, a country house, a sixty-thousand-dollar Land Cruiser, three children in private school. Since *NARCS* began, George has complained more than once about union featherbedding rules, and even she has discovered that EEOC and OSHA regulations can be stupid and intrusive and infuriating. Lizzie would feel too Republican if she abandoned the subway, just like she felt too Republican living on their acre in Sneden's Landing.

Her train ride is a little pageant of race and class, each day the same and on many mornings so vivid it seems staged, a site-specific ten-minute avant-pop performance piece. Usually, before she can step into a car, she must stand aside for the hasty, eager exits of the very white lawyers and stock traders and investment bankers coming from their cheap, million- or two-million-dollar Brooklyn brownstones. At the next stop, the criminal lawyers and civil servants from the more Brooklynesque precincts of the borough get off, half of them white and half black, and are replaced by a shuffle of Chinese, each one carrying a cheap plastic shopping bag. At Fourteenth Street, Lizzie disembarks, slipping off the train and onto the platform between a pair of beggars, ready with their props and spiels, and a pack of actors and models, dreaming of theirs. One of the Fourteenth Street bums this morning—a white man about her age in a filthy T-shirt that has HIV! printed in huge letters across the chest—stands directly under a NO SPITTING ON PLATFORM sign and spits as she passes. Maybe antiexpectoration can be the last great crusade of the Giuliani age. Her loathing of Giuliani is visceral. She voted for him in both mayoral elections, first against a nice black man and then against a nice Jewish woman, and both times she spent Election Day giving out a five-dollar bill to everyone who asked for money, as penance.

The MTA seems to have taken down all the AVOID ARREST signs. When she first moved to the city, Lizzie remembers, in 1987, those signs, as ubiquitous underground as graffiti, struck her as strange and funny. An advertising campaign unabashedly targeting a particular New York City demographic—punks, fare beaters, *criminals.* With a message abdicating any assertion of moral authority in favor of simple, direct, cost-benefit advice that sympathetically presumes a desire to break the law—PLEASE DO NOT FORCE US TO APPREHEND YOU. (Lizzie had wondered why the authorities neglected bilingualism here, of all places. She never saw an EVITE SER ARRESTADO sign.) Maybe she is a Republican already. Maybe, it occurs to her, she could buy an AVOID ARREST sign at one of the antique stores on Lafayette Street.

During just the past week, she sees, one of the three streetfront retail spaces in her office building has become a "tea bar and gourmet premium sandwich and ice cream emporium" called Ellipsis . . .—the word *Ellipsis* followed by dots of ellipsis. When Lizzie went home last Monday it was The Best Offense, a shop that sold bulletproof garments ("reinforced fashion," they called their clothes) and never seemed to have customers. She becomes convinced of the new shop's imminent failure, chokes up over this and all the other hopeful, hopeless immigrant dreams with which New York teems, and then, as the tiny old elevator ascends—we've all got businesses to run—turns her attention to Fine Technologies. The nonexistent Microsoft deal. The nonexistent West Coast office. The folly of staking so much on a fucking *game* that works best only with special fucking *hardware.* Wondering if and when she should bring the company public. Wondering why she's consulting for Mose for free. Fretting, calculating, not quite panicking, almost enjoying the return to overload. She has gone from surprise to sadness to self-involvement, all in eleven seconds.

"Mr. Wizard, *hellllp!*"

"Good morning, Alexi."

He follows Lizzie into her office.

"Your hair! You didn't discuss it," he says, circling around her to look, legal pad in hand. On Friday morning she and Sarah went to the Cristophe salon in L.A. Either Tina Louise or Jill St. John was getting her hair done in the next chair. "I'm like, 'Whoa!' It's disorienting, it's . . . nice, it *is,* very, you know . . ."

"Don't say Sigourney Weaver."

"I wasn't about to."

"Don't say Marlo Thomas."

"Natalie Wood."

"Okay." Lizzie, eager to get started, doesn't mention that she thinks she got her haircut three feet away from Natalie Wood's widower's wife, especially since she would also have to mention the Tina Louise possibility, which would take time and surely prompt Alexi to do his Mrs. Thurston Howell impersonation, which would in turn invite a discussion of Buddy (*Li'l Gilligan*) Ramo. "So," she says. "What?"

"Lance isn't getting back until this afternoon, but he called from the airport to tell you he's 'not very encouraged on the Redmond project.' I think 'the Redmond project' may just be Lance's super-top-secret code for *the Microsoft Corporation*."

"He tries. What else?"

"You're being sued."

"For what? Who?"

"The dreaded Vanessa."

"You're joking."

Vanessa Golliver was a receptionist for four months. When she wasn't given a full-time job as a "computer, like, programmer-in-training" last summer, a job that doesn't exist at Fine Technologies, she quit, urinating on the floor of the reception area on her way out.

"Sorry." Alexi pulls out a federal district court filing that he's tucked into his legal pad. " '*Vanessa Golliver* v. *Fine Technologies, Elizabeth Zimbalist, et al.*' You discriminated against her because of her disability."

"Exactly what is Vanessa's disability? Some urinary disease?"

Alexi turns two pages and reads, using a lawyerly lockjaw that sounds not unlike Thurston Howell. " 'A previous medical impairment, namely cocaine addiction, that restricted major life activities of plaintiff on an ongoing basis, namely, plaintiff's ability to reason and to learn.' "

"Her disability is having been a coke addict? Or flakiness and stupidity?"

"All of the above, I guess. And remember when you were like, 'Vanessa, you can't only work three days a week'? Blah-blah-blah-blah, wait, *here:* '. . . including defendant's repeated refusals to entertain plaintiff's requests to restructure plaintiff's work schedule to better accommodate medical treatment.' "

"Hilarious. Fax it to Katherine." A few years ago she would have been apoplectic. But running a business has inured her to annoyances like this. Instead of outraging her they amaze her. She regards them as freakish and a little worrisome, but also inevitable and fascinating, like hailstorms. Her first employee lawsuit was filed by an aggressively sweet pro-life young woman named Meryl Farah Doyle. She was a bookkeeper who one day refused to do any further work related to Fine Technologies' voice-recognition software because it happened to be used by a confederation of abortion clinics. Since at the time the voice-recognition software was Fine Technologies' only product, Lizzie had to fire Meryl Farah. According to her legal brief, she also could not abide that the software was used by "one or more UFO hot lines, which plaintiff regards as furthering the dangerous and unacceptable agenda[s] of Satan and satanism." Lizzie joked to Katherine, the company's lawyer, that they should ask Procter & Gamble to file a friend-of-the-court brief. But after Pat Robertson mentioned *Doyle* v. *Fine Technologies* approvingly on one of his Christian Broadcasting Network news programs, Lizzie received four letters threatening violence against her, one of them addressed only to "Computer Jewess, Fein Technology, Manhattan."

Alexi is looking over his message list. "Henry Saddler's office just called. From Mose Media Holdings." Mose must want the memo about online video. She'll finish it tonight. But she's having dinner with Pollyanna tonight. She'll stay up.

"George called at nine-ten. He said not to tell you that he was calling to smooth things over from last night, but that I should indicate—indicate!—that he misses you. It was six A.M. his time."

She reddens. "Any other calls?"

"Some woman from *Time* magazine. A reporter. She's working on 'a possible cover,' she said."

"About what? Another Microsoft story?"

"Nope. About medical miracles. She wants to talk to you about your father."

"Fuck."

Bruce Helms pops his head in the doorway.

"Welcome back," he says.

"And Bruce wants a couple of minutes with you as soon as you get in," Alexi says, getting up. "Coffee?"

"Please. Hi," she says to Bruce. "How's tricks?"

"I talked to my friend Buster. At U-Dub? The 'mental-modem' guy."

"Right. Did he tell you it's all a load of overhyped bullshit?"

"No. No, he didn't. He says he believes he's actually had direct, wireless, microwave, brain-to-brain communication between mammals. He's grafted chips onto cats' neurons. Wired-up cat A in room X instructs cat B in a separate, soundproof room Y a hundred feet away that there's tons of food available in room X, and wired-up cat B works his way through a maze and a chute to reach room X to eat. When there's no food in room X, nothing happens. But apparently the university is not being entirely supportive of his research. Strictly speaking, the experiments are somewhat outside his grant guidelines."

"What is he supposed to be doing?"

Bruce screws his face into an exaggerated pooh-pooh look. "Oh, some kind of biomechanical alarm, disposable, to stick inside tin cans that gets triggered when food spoils. But his real problem is politics. Cutting open cats' heads and installing microchips strikes certain people in the academic community as cruel and unusual. In Seattle, PETA apparently has its own cable channel and its own city councilman."

"Bruce?"

"What?"

"This is all very interesting. But why are you telling me about it? Why aren't you telling me, for instance, how we're doing on the game?"

Again he assumes his pooh-pooh face. "Because we're basically done."

Lizzie says nothing.

"Done-*ish*," Bruce says. "Way ahead of schedule. A few weeks from done. Really, we're fine, don't worry. It's going great. I got your message about the name. I still like Range Daze better, and I like Matrix even more, but Warps is fine. Boogie's okay with it, and the Germans love it." He leans forward. "I'm telling you about Buster because U-Dub doesn't control his patents, he does, and he wants to work with us."

Bruce has invested much of his inheritance in five tumbledown eighteenth-century houses in rural New York and Connecticut that he keeps empty, and he spends a weekend every month or two at some hang-gliding ashram in Maine, and once a year he goes to Quito, Mississippi, to visit the grave of his hero, Robert Johnson. Three summers ago, after he spent his summer vacation in Uppsala, Sweden, at a conference on "randomness and nonlinearity," he said that a paper called "Continuous Control of Chaos" changed his life. And he does have a knowledge of computer-history trivia that Lizzie considers demented. (When she went to Albuquerque on Microsoft-related business last March, Bruce said to her, "That's funny—Bill Gates addressed the World Altair Computer Convention in Albuquerque in 1976, I'm pretty sure in March.") But he has never seemed prone to wild technomanias. As an employee, he's been responsible and conscientious. Maybe now that the company is successful, more or less, and the ninety-hour weeks have ratcheted back to sixty-hour weeks, his lurking hacker madness has had the space to fester and grow.

"You just don't get it, do you?" Bruce says, shaking his head.

Lizzie feels frightened and sick.

"Cats are a huge consumer market for computing, for wireless, all of it," he tells her, tensing up, talking faster. "Animals in general! It could be our emerging market! It's absolutely wide open. But animals can't use keyboards. And animals can't use styluses. Styli. Can they? *Can* they?"

Lizzie says nothing. Bruce stares at her, taking quick, shallow breaths. Then he grins.

"I'm kidding, Lizzie."

"Very good." She can breathe again. "*Very* good. You fucker."

"But I'm serious about Buster's research. It sounds astounding. I have no idea what the product would be. Or when. But you'll figure out something. PawPilot. This could be gigantic, Lizzie. Edisonian. Orville and Wilburvian."

Lizzie has never heard Bruce talk like this. She has never heard Bruce sound so excited about anything, not even hang gliding or the blues. His enthusiasm is infectious. She tries to resist the infection.

"Don't I recall your telling me that Buster had some kind of breakdown?"

"Wow. Vanessa Golliver is right—you do discriminate against people with psychiatric disabilities, don't you?" Lizzie flips him the bird. "Yes, Buster got overinvested in his code after his fiancée dumped him, but that was short-term. He's been sane for years. Sane-*ish*. He's fine. He says he only needs five hundred K a year to keep going."

Perfect! In a single stroke she can reduce Fine Technologies' earnings to zero. Lizzie knows her MBA superego is wrestling—tangoing? making out?—with her naked entrepreneurial id. The scuffle excites her. "I'm supposed to start spending half a million dollars a year on R and D? Why doesn't Buster just go to another university? Someone would love to fund him. Georgia or Texas or somewhere. I'll bet in the South there's no animal-wacko problem."

"Buster believes in capitalism."

"That's beautiful, Bruce."

"I'm serious."

"There are lots of people who would make him lots richer lots quicker than we could. *If* we could, which is doubtful."

"No, no. He doesn't care about making money *personally*. Last week, he told me, some venture capitalists flew him down to Mountain View for dinner, and when the appetizers were served he threw up, right on the table, all over a platter of steamed dumplings. He says being around too much money lust makes him sick, like taking too many vitamins. But he does believe that capitalism is our human destiny."

"It's Ayn Rand, Scotty—beam me up!"

"No, no, no—not like that. He's not ideological. He just thinks humans are hardwired for capitalism, biochemically, evolutionarily. In the way that ants are natural communists, you know, like E. O. Wilson says. We're capitalists. And spiders are feudal artisans and so on."

"Edward Wilson says that spiders are feudal artisans?"

"I think that's Buster's embellishment. He's decided it's time for him to fall more in line with the human paradigm. 'I'm not an insect, Bruce,' he told me. 'I just don't do well in the hive.' He's also fallen in love with a woman who lives in Queens and plays in an alternative country-western band."

"You think this is the genuine article?" Lizzie asks.

Bruce nods.

"Why don't I meet with Buster in Seattle next week?"

"Cool. You're going to Seattle? Is the deal done?"

"Who knows?" she says, glancing at her computer to position her cursor and log on, which prompts Bruce to stand. "Lance seems to think not. But I can interview people for this stupid West Coast job."

"One thing? When you talk to Buster, I wouldn't necessarily mention the Microsoft deal—"

"I wouldn't. Not until it's real."

"No, that's not what I mean. They tried to hire him last year and *really* pissed him off."

Bruce lopes out of Lizzie's office, and as she performs her first superficial reconnaissance of a week of accumulated budgets and memos and messages—including, she's amused to see, two e-mails from MsTaft@fuckall.net—she wonders exactly what alternative country-western is. A *Wall Street Journal* writer last year called Y2KRx "the so-called alternative Year 2000 software," which pleased her, even though she wasn't sure she understood the compliment. She figured it meant Y2KRx was cheap and unique and a touch perverse, and unhysterical in its marketing. In reviews of Sauce, the new restaurant that just opened in a townhouse down West Sixteenth Street, she noticed that it was called "the alternative Lutèce" in the *Times* and "alterna-French" in *Time Out*. The young Belgian manager of Sauce wore three tiny earrings and a goatee, but his air of maître d' contempt struck Lizzie as unusually complex—*you are almost certainly too poor and too unattractive to get a good table, but I also doubt that you have ever chipped heroin or read Jean Baudrillard.* When she was in college and just after, "postmodern" was the smartness-helper being sprinkled around like this. When somebody she worked with told her she was giving Sarah "a postmodern infancy," she suspected it was an insult disguised as a compliment. And a Guggenheim fellow she dated right before she met George argued for anal sex on the ground that it was "erotic postmodernism." But still, Lizzie finds the idea of alternative country music fetching. Is alternative country less or more self-pitying than regular country music? Or is it just self-conscious about its self-pity?

———

Being the boss, Lizzie finds, consists of two main tasks. The first one is "finding the signal in the noise." It means the same thing as "separating the wheat from the chaff." She used to call it "torching through the bullshit" until Bruce provided her the more apt and felicitous metaphor she now uses. "Really high noise-to-signal ratio" is Bruce's standard remark about certain frenzied days in the office or particularly chattery people. To be the boss also requires making snap decisions and making them confidently, big consequential snap decisions, tiny snap decisions that accrue into significance, dozens of all kinds every day. It is all improvisation.

The two-color packaging for Range Daze is fine; I mean Warps. (As long as it doesn't look too . . . alternative, or like we can't afford four colors. The idea is to look elegant and semi-old-fashioned. Like eighties movies and nineties magazine covers.

Ask Boogie; that's his call.

Ask Bruce, but Softimage is obviously the preference. Because Microsoft owns them.

Yes, this year people can trade in Christmas Day for the day after Ramadan ends.

Tell them we support—say we have nothing against Gore, the company just doesn't make campaign contributions.

Okay, two weeks paid, four unpaid. Because it's a policy for *paternity* leave, Alexi, and they don't have to nurse the fucking kid is why.

We absolutely do too have NEC's permission to use Power VR in advertising and packaging. Then double-check, but try not to let NEC know.

Tell him Tony said a year ago—no, *two* years ago—that he'd pay for fireproofing the I beams.

Yes, we will cross-promote with Diamond for the Monster 3D accelerator board, as long as Madeline says that doesn't conflict contractually with the 3Dfx deal; no, *not* "component-exclusively." And please don't use that phrase again.

Yes, we'll have real-time deformation, but who wants to know how realistic our digital fur will be? (*What* digital fur?)

Please ask Boogie to stop playing that Massive Attack CD all day, every day; I think it's making people stupider.

Yes, we're optimized for MMX and 3Dfx, but we will work fine with the new Macs. I don't know if that means we're "dual-optimized." Tell them yes.

What's with all the inquiries about fucking *fur*? Tell them state-of-the-art digital fur realism.

No, Fox only has an option on the TV rights, nobody has novelization rights; as of this morning, you can safely assure them that they are still available. (Find out what Doom sold for.) A novel based on a video game! Lord. (No, that's different—the novel is called *Chocolate-Chip Cookie-Dough Häagen-Dazs,* but Douglas Coupland didn't *base* it on a brand of ice cream. I'm pretty sure.)

No. Ask Lance.

I don't give a fuck how many of the game designers have voted to add invisibility and healing powers to the Dark Ages—I'm not running a democracy, and I don't care if Boogie is feeling "harshed"—it's a game about reality, remember?

Tell them Warps is to Time Commando as *The Simpsons* is to *The Flintstones,* or as *Men In Black* is to *Independence Day.* More *prestigious?* Okay, as James Joyce is to Gertrude Stein.

Say we'll call back. *No.* Tell them Madeline will call back.

Duh.

How fast? Tell them we're not interested. Not forever. For now . . .

"I'll take it!" It's Hank Saddler calling again. "Hello, Hank, I'm just back; it's kind of nuts here. I haven't had a chance to finish that memo for Harold yet."

"It's Henry. But take your time, Elizabeth! *Not* a problem. Harold's in Brunei until the middle of the week anyway. I'm calling on another matter, concerning one of your products. The Sho 'Nuff system?"

"ShowNet," she says. ShowNet is a Fine Technologies product that she (and George) dreamed up. It's for movie and television casts and crews to use during production, particularly on location. Dozens of special, dumbed-down laptops are connected into a wireless network, so that script and schedule and budget changes can be transmitted instantly to everyone at once.

"Right, Show*Net.* George probably told you that I'm now executive vice president, corporate communications, synergy, and special projects?"

"He didn't. But—"

"*Thank* you! Anyway, part of my mandate is liaising with the Department of Defense, sitting on a very special advisory board they have. We and Disney are the media-slash-entertainment participants. It's really a privilege. Well, one of the colonels down there happened to mention Fine Technologies and your ShowNet software, and how it is exactly the type of thing they've been trying to develop for use in certain Rangers and Special Forces applications, as a tool for our war fighters' needs. She said to me, 'We're always shooting on location.' Very witty, articulate gal, this lady officer. I told Colonel Rodriguez"—he pronounces Rodriguez with an extreme amount of long-vowel emphasizing and *r* rolling—"that I was a little too far above the line to know much about the nuts and bolts of ShowNet, but that you happened to be part of the Mose Media Holdings extended family. I was sure you'd be happy to help them out pro bono any way you could with software and training, et cetera. Can I give you Colonel Rodriguez's number and e-mail?"

"No. I'm afraid not. That's just not something I want to do. No." Yes! A *serious* snap judgment!

She's never felt any special antipathy toward the military. The draft ended when she was nine, the U.S. finished with Vietnam when she was ten; Lizzie knew almost nothing about the war until she saw *Platoon* in college. In the second grade, all the students and teachers at her private school were required to sing "Give Peace a Chance" together every Friday. (At her stepbrother Ronnie's school they sang "There's No Business like Show Business.") She did take part in an anti-Grenada-invasion teach-in organized by the cute graduate student who taught her freshman seminar on Japanese Noh drama, but in 1996 she wanted to vote for Colin Powell for president. And Buddy Ramo was in the Coast Guard reserves when she slept with him. It's just that she doesn't feel like helping some death squad management consultant repurpose *her* software to track the disappearance of Zapatistas, even if the death squad management consultant is a Hispanic woman. And not for free. And certainly not as a favor to Hank Saddler, the patronizing asshole.

"Super! I'll have one of my assistants call with all the DOD info. Who's your go-to guy? Excuse me! Or gal?"

"No. I *don't* want to help the Pentagon use ShowNet, Hank. Henry. I'd be uncomfortable with that."

"What?"

"I just—I'm afraid not. Especially given what's going on in the news, with Mexico. You know?" She doesn't think George will mind.

"But . . . but Colonel Rodriguez is Hispanic herself! *And* she's an African-American!"

Sorry! Fuck you! *Next!* Sometimes Lizzie very much likes being the boss. Not, of course, enduring the parent-and-child-like grousing about salaries and window sightlines and the relative square footage of cubicles, or having to fire incompetent salespeople who happen to be single mothers. Not the irreducible third of the job that is stupid, dull, draining, and thankless. Lizzie likes being boss because at last she's a member of a cool club that she likes, president of the club, a club custom-made by her for her. As a girl, she was just popular enough to harbor high hopes about the redemptive potential of club membership. But club after club failed to satisfy. Campfire Girls, astronomy club (which almost killed her love of science), chess club (which almost killed her incipient interest in boys), ballet, tutoring first graders in East L.A. (fine until one of the tutors was raped by a tutee's stepfather), and Junior Achievement at Palisades High (the worst; what had she been thinking?), then the Signet Society at Harvard (Junior Achievement for the intelligentsia), a women's investment group when she first got to New York—each one started the same, with cheerful anticipation, and each one became dutiful or worse. She still believes in the theoretical virtue of clubs, as she does in the theoretical virtues of piety and small towns and solar power. But she has come to accept her particular catch-22, a variation on the Groucho Marx line: the sorts of people who join clubs are not, by and large, the sorts of people with whom Lizzie wants to be clubmates. So now she has reverse-engineered her way to contentment. She has her own fourteen-thousand-square-foot clubhouse in a loft in Chelsea, where she does her best to keep everyone busy and interested, but she gets to decide who joins, who stays, and what the rules and projects are. The vicissitudes of popularity and democracy have been transcended, the thing has a fucking *point,* she can swear as much as she wants, she can tell Hank Saddler no without asking anyone's permission, and there aren't any mothers or faculty sponsors overlooking, clucking, organizing. Except her. And her despotism is benign; Bruce said so last week. Yet every two weeks comes the one unavoidable, vertiginous reminder that this is real life and that she is in charge. Being a boss is stressful always, immersive and harsh in ways underlings cannot appreciate, but when Lance knocks on the doorframe holding the three-page payroll authorization form, her mood turns a little somber. All larkishness goes.

"Hi," Lance peeps. Lance Haft is her business manager. (She let him say he was the controller for the first three years. After Bruce admitted to him that the reason he always smiled when Lance called himself the controller was because of the Controllers in *Brave New World,* she let him change his title to chief administrative officer.) He is always a little bashful with this ritual, like a shy mistress. For part of the tension of the payroll signing is its public acknowledgment that none of them, not Bruce or Alexi or Lance or any of them, not even Karen, work for Fine Technologies for the love of it.

"It's $188,500," she says, looking at the bottom line. "That's up."

"Yes. From $185,300. Annual cost of living kicks in."

As she signs her name for the period ending March 10, 2000—seignurially dispensing $188,500, *poof,* as she will again when Lance tap-taps on the doorframe in another two weeks, and again just two weeks later, on and on. Every time it alarms her a little, like a wallop of g-force. She's pretty sure she prefers it, however, to the low-grade, chronic, corrosive nausea of being an employee.

And she has never felt better about the two hundred grand than she does today, since Lance, before the signing ceremony, briefed her on his meetings in Redmond. Moorhead, the oily lawyer with the nineteenth-hole-at-Burning-Tree accent? The one who didn't approve of Ms. Zimbalist's . . . *cussing?*

"Did Moorhead wear a bow tie?" Lizzie asked Lance.

"Uh, *yeah,*" Lance said uneasily. "Yeah, he did. Both days." Almost every employee acts nervous around the boss, a caste condition that surprised Lizzie and saddens her, but Lance has always been the extreme case at Fine Technologies. Her bow-tie guess about the Microsoft negotiator made Lance look as if Lizzie, sorceress of West Eighteenth Street, might teasingly decide to turn him into a flying monkey.

Moorhead agreed to pay $5.5 million for fifteen percent of her company, which is less than the minimum Lizzie told Lance she would accept, but only a little less. Taking the investment would mean Fine Technologies is worth $36 million. Which would make her 25 percent worth $9 million. Lizzie does not dream of big cash sums, and finds George's pinch-me-I-must-be-dreaming money obsession silly and disingenuous, but *fuck!* Nine million bucks! Seven something after capital gains! And Microsoft would own only a sixth of the company. She'd be nuts to turn this down. She told Lance she'd think about it overnight and discuss it with George, and told him to tell Microsoft that she has to discuss the offer with her senior advisers (Ben Gould and George), mezzanine-round investors (Ben Gould and her father), and the other members of her board (George, her father, Ben Gould, Bruce). But the moment Lance said five, even before he said point-five, Lizzie decided. No.

When he's away from home, drifting along, and especially when he's in Los Angeles, where the metaphors are as ripe and low hanging as mangoes in spring, George tends to read meaning into almost everything. On the way to dinner last night, after Saddler's, they stopped at Emily's office at Paramount so that she could pick up a couple of scripts and so George could see the studio lot, which was the only one he'd never visited. (Emily has a housekeeping deal to develop independent films for Paramount—that is, she said, unable to let an oxymoron pass, "quote, '*independent* films,' unquote"; that is, she added, screenplays for movies with "no sets, no effects, and no heroes, which the studio will never produce"). What struck George about the Paramount lot, though, was not the famous gate, a cute vestige of prewar Moorish doodadery, but the names. The Lucille Ball Building is bigger than the Marlene Dietrich Building, the Jerry Lewis Building is bigger than the Marx Brothers Building, and among the biggest of all is the building named after Gene Roddenberry, the creator of *Star Trek.* Is there some scissors-cut-paper hierarchy involving celebrity, vulgarity, and modernity? Or a simple algorithm—one square foot for every ten thousand dollars of inflation-adjusted lifetime earnings?

They had dinner at a place off Hollywood Boulevard called Les Deux Cafés. Emily pretended not to be surprised that George had never heard of it. Although she warned him that "it's *very* 1997" (self-mockingly, he thought), as soon as he walked in, through a kind of secret passageway at the back of a Hollywood parking lot into a Shangri-la of Hollywood eugenics and pixilated Provençal splendor,

George felt the particular, autoerotic yap and buzz of certain L.A. restaurants and parties, where the A-list's collective pleasure in simply being in its own critical mass is intense, the near hysteria of horses at a show. At places like Les Deux Cafés, or events like the *Vanity Fair* Oscar party at Mortons restaurant, almost everyone gets in touch with his or her Merry Chatterer side. Les Deux Cafés made George feel young. The secret-door raffishness of the entrance reminded him of being twenty-two and falling in love with Chumley's, the old speakeasy wedged in a West Village block that was ahead of its time, proto-themed before theming existed to make authentically charming old places seem contemptibly olde and hokey. The proximity of multiple big stars at dinner—not Sinbad but Denzel Washington, eating only vegetables; not some girl from the WB but Michelle Pfeiffer, George's fantasy spouse; not David Spade but Jim Carrey, close enough for George to hear a slight hum he makes when he chews—had turned George slightly, quietly giddy. Giddiness feels a lot like youth.

Such a balmy, swirling feast, such a slick, pretty mural of high inconsequence to inhabit for a couple of hours. Except for her story about the recidivist, sex-addicted talent agent, he barely focused on his conversation with Emily. Whatever she said and whatever he said seemed like pretext, the smiling meaningless yabba-yabba-yabba-yabba mouth movements of extras in the background. Extras with lines! George and Emily exchanged gratifying nods and "how-are-you"s with a well-known agent-turned-personal-manager, a well-known lawyer-turned-personal-manager-turned-studio-executive, and Jamie Lee Curtis, who had been their first choice to play Jennie on *NARCS*. The spectacle required most of his mental energy, particularly after they'd finished a bottle of Napa merlot. Careful, surreptitious staring at one's fellow diners is always exhausting, as is the acute self-awareness—the irresistible mental crane shot of oneself sitting among the beautiful and powerful.

George was so insouciant and preening last night, in fact, that he didn't register Emily's relentless fretting about *Real Time*—it will be all-consuming, it could get expensive, we will take so much shit, it's do-and-die time—as anything but reflexive seller's remorse, late-night liquored-up Emily schtick. But this morning, in the bright, bright

Venutian sunlight of Las Vegas, waiting for his car, he is going through the dailies, mentally playing back last night, pausing at each of Emily's caveats and doubts and grouses about the new show.

"Sir, before you sign the blemish waiver I'd like you to spend a few minutes inspecting the body. In detail. Otherwise, you are responsible."

"I'll be responsible," George says, signing.

As he floors the Le Baron away from McCarran International, he smiles: *Las Vegas.* His parents started coming here every spring when he was in junior high, when the city was still uniquely naughty, before big bare breasts and gambling and waitresses in silly costumes were an hour's drive away from every citizen, before a plurality of hometowns allowed themselves to turn from Bedford Fallses into Pottersvilles. Vegas was Perry and Edith Hope's Cold War Cuba. (Momentarily, he figures, Cuba will become his own generation's Cuba.) Their enthusiastic middle-aged embrace of squaresville decadence, back then, embarrassed and slightly shocked him. One day his mother wouldn't say *stink* or *sweat,* the next she's wearing a sleeveless blouse and baggy shorts on a jet to Vegas. But by the time he was sixteen he had read Hunter Thompson and Robert Venturi, so when his mom and dad asked Alice and him to come along for their annual Nevada pilgrimage in 1972, he couldn't wait to go—because it would be so *trippy* and, like, *surreal,* and because he couldn't wait to see strippers.

Right out of the airport, George spots the famous new two-acre billboard, two hundred feet tall and five hundred feet wide, advertising MEGAMILLENNIUM, the yearlong lottery organized by the Las Vegas Chamber of Commerce. The tickets, ten dollars a pop, are only sold here in town, and the holder of the winning numbers, to be drawn at midnight on December 31, will win a jackpot of at least one billion dollars—the biggest jackpot anywhere, ever. Max has written down his 184 numbers in pencil on Beverly Hills Hotel stationery and given George half his life savings, $230, to buy twenty-three MegaMillennium tickets. Lining both sides of the highway into town are thirty-foot-long metallic gold banners formed into graceful swooping pretzels and staked to the ground, printed with big blue letters spelling out the slogan VEGAS 2000®—EVERYBODY WINS. The Vatican has declared 2000 a jubilee year, and so too, evidently, has Las Vegas. The VEGAS 2000s seem to glow; they flash sequentially down the road toward the horizon into infinity, like runway strobes. George realizes after a half mile that it isn't some trick of fluttering phosphorescence or a desert illusion, but fiber-optic stitching. Electrified golden flags! When George was a boy, the twenty-first century was going to be absolutely sleek and white. Starting when he was an adolescent, in the seventies, the future was going to be rubble, random fires, and highwaymen speaking gibberish—a grimy postindustrial ruin. Now the twenty-first century is here, and it's rococo. High-production-value, fiber-optic, evanescent rococo, imagineered Albert Speer gilded and baking in the desert sun.

This past New Year's Eve, George caught glimpses on a monitor in the *NARCS* control room of the big, broad streets of Las Vegas absolutely filled with celebrants—three times as many people as local authorities had dared to predict. Las Vegas, maybe more than Times Square, turned out to be America's millennial ground zero. Now that the newspapers and magazines and TV news shows and web sites no longer have 2000 to anticipate ad infinitum, and the computer problems to explain and reexplain, they're doing their best to fill the sudden post–New Year's void of factoid and zeitgeist infofluff—thus, the putative national sense of millennium anticlimax. This new fog of media chatter about the millennium anticlimax has been mostly "funny" confessions and opinions. But now, inevitably, the tiresome jocularity is turning to tiresome earnestness, from Andy Rooneyism to Bill Moyersism in a matter of weeks. According to a story in this morning's *USA Today* (EXPERTS FEAR WE'RE SUFFERING "THIRD MILLENNIUM MALAISE") this morning, there has been a sudden uptick in suicides, in Blockbuster rentals of certain kinds of videos (early Bergman, middle-period Woody Allen, late Spielberg), and in attendance at "church services of the USA's more 'somber' denominations, such as Presbyterian." The Harvard professor Stephen Jay Gould was on every television channel twenty-four hours a day during the last week of last year, it seemed, trying to induce the national disappointment early by explaining, over and over, that not only is January 1, 2000, not *really* the beginning of a new century, but that January 1, 2001, will be nothing special either, since Jesus was born in 4 or 5 B.C., and so the third millennium therefore *actually* started back in 1996 or 1997. Max, of course, has been making these very same points repeatedly for the past year. This bout of millennium madness, Professor

Gould kept saying as smugly and chuckly as a huge, bearded nine-year-old, is *hype*! It's completely *arbitrary*! he said, as if Americans have something against hype or arbitrariness. Las Vegas, now that George thinks about it, turning left off the Strip toward the campanile of the Piazza San Marco, is the capital of the arbitrary: giant, arbitrary architectural facsimiles (midtown Manhattan, a pirate ship, Lake Como, Myanmar, a statue of Lenin, the Eiffel Tower, a lion, a space needle, and now, right here—Venice) installed on an arbitrary patch of desert in order to fetishize arbitrary numbers (1, 7, 11, 21) and arbitrary combinations of tiny spinning pictures of arbitrary fruits (lemons, cherries, watermelon) and metal objects (ingots, barbells). Vegas 2000, indeed. He turns left onto the six-lane entrance road and drives under the Ponte Rialto.

"Bone-*jaw*-no, sir! Welcome to the Venetian! Will you require your vehicle again this afternoon, seen-*yaw*-ray?" asks the smiling black giant in a red-striped gondolier's shirt to whom he hands his car keys. He's waiting, plastic gondolier-oar-shaped stylus in hand, to note George's response on a little electronic device.

He stares at him, smiling, momentarily speechless.

"Oh my *God*!" screams a man somewhere nearby. "I don't believe it! Hey! You *came*! I love you!" By the time George turns his head to see what kind of Vegas asshole is screeching like a cartoon character, Bennett Gould is upon him, grabbing and shaking him with both hands. The asshole is Ben, George's pal for twenty years, as overexcited as ever. George feels happy for the first time in two days. "This is *monumental*!" Ben shouts. "This is *fantastic*! This is *sublime*! Where's the wife?" The original comic shading of that phrase as used by George and his friends—"the wife"—has grown so dim it's now almost invisible, like a watermark. "I got a Lizzie Zimbalist message! 'Semiurgent,' she said. What's going on?" People who don't know Ben often assume he's on drugs—cocaine or speed or, as a mutual acquaintance speculated seriously to George a few months ago, some sort of Hoffman-LaRoche synthetic adrenaline that won't be available to consumers until 2004. Ben Gould operates at a high torque every waking moment, but he doesn't take drugs, not even coffee. ("I promise you do *not* want to see me on espresso!" he said to George at the end of a long Italian lunch not long after they first met.)

"Lizzie's at home," George tells him. "So you're staying here too?"

"Yeah! Sixteenth floor. Have you had lunch? We'll have lunch if you don't mind eating with a few Wall Street assholes." Then abruptly, without a word or raised finger or even a pause, Ben reaches into his shirt pocket and has his StarTac 9900 out and open—George is reminded of Superman moving at lightning speed. "Yeah," he says into the phone. Ben's a stock trader but has also, over the last few years, invested a few million here and a few million there in new businesses— businesses such as BarbieWorld, the restaurant-hotel-entertainment complex opening tonight on the Strip. When people ask his occupation, he says, matter-of-factly, "Wall Street asshole." For him, it has become the generic term, now almost entirely devoid of opprobrium or even mock opprobrium, something like how hippies started calling themselves *freaks* in the late sixties and homosexuals started calling themselves *queer* in the late eighties. More embedded irony.

"Sorry," Ben says as he snaps his phone shut and grabs George by the arm. "Let's have lunch! Come on up!"

"Great. Let me check in. I'll meet you up there. What's your room number? Sixteen-what?"

Ben grins sheepishly, lowers his voice, and says slowly, "Sixteen." George has never met anyone whose voice modulates so abruptly between extremes of volume and pitch, an octave and a half up and down, thirty decibels louder or softer without warning. "I took a floor. You need a suite?" As George smiles back, lips pursed, not quite shaking his head, Ben says, blasting away again full bore, "What? *Excuse* me! I'm in business with a lot of people who wanted to come to this event. I guess I'm too generous to people, I'm sorry, I guess I like to seize the day and *enjoy* life, *mea culpa, carpe diem, mea culpa,* punish me, you midwestern gentile cocksucker!"

A few feet away, a group of four old women in shorts and tank tops stand in a little semicircle, happily staring. One has raised her camera to shoot a picture. They seem to think the manic man in threadbare blue jeans and dark glasses smiling and shouting obscenities is part of the entertainment. They almost certainly don't imagine he's worth $247 million.

1 1

"**Bill Gates can't** bother himself to pick up the phone personally? What kind of relationship business is that? 'Ms. Zimbalist, I think you've got a fantastic company, welcome to my family.' Wouldn't that be the right thing? It's a thirty-second call. No wonder everyone wants to kill the prick."

"This is a tiny, tiny, *tiny* deal for them."

"It's big for us. For you. Uh-oh, the nice Filipino boy is here with my baby food. I love you, Lizzie, my shaynala."

Uh-oh.

"I do too." She swallows, hard, and twists the phone away from her mouth as she gulps in a big sobby breath. "I love you, too." The Yiddish endearment had undone her. Mike Zimbalist seems like the sort of man who would pepper his speech with Yiddish, but he rarely did, not even middle-American Jay Leno words like *schlep* or *klutz*. Once she overheard him on the phone telling the movie producer Jon Peters he was "an evil, illiterate little gonif motherfucker." But her father had used Yiddish with Lizzie only twice that she recalls—on the phone from Cedars the night Serene Zimbalist finally died of lung cancer ("She's gone, my shaynala"), and in the delivery room at Lenox Hill

Hospital in New York the morning Sarah was born ("Bubbeleh, you're a *mom!*").

She turns, grabs Bruce's folders from Alexi, says "Thanks, bye," and hustles out, down, out, three strides through icy downpour, and into the perfectly shiny blue Go! Now! Lincoln that Alexi had arranged.

Lizzie hates the idea of turning into a limousine liberal, but she isn't neurotic about hiring the occasional car and driver, either. She's a neo-liberal, anyway, and Town Cars aren't really *limousines*—they're neo-limos. Besides, she's headed for a block between Park and Madison in the Sixties, where a car and driver is the equivalent of a Yellow Cab anywhere else in the city. On a slushy, rotten night like this, a few minutes spent cozying into the clean, quiet, plump leather backseat of a late-model Town Car, with a precise puddle of halogen light illuminating her papers (making them a little more lucid and important), she feels like she's having a cocktail or a massage. Every now and then, a platinum-card soft-focus arm's-length version of urban life is fine.

"You have Go! Now! VIP number?" the driver asks.

"I do. Z four seven three."

"Z? Zed?"

"As in Zimbalist."

In the five years she's known him, Bruce has never done anything so businesslike. So seriously Town Car. An actual memo, with *FROM:* and *TO:* and *RE:* at the top and boldfaced subsections. A ten-year P&L projection—*Bruce!* so cute!—and supporting technical documents. Even a draft one-page contract between Buster Grinspoon and Fine Technologies, stipulating the patents they would co-own, already signed by Grinspoon.

Bruce has attached a dozen journal articles, including the unpublished account of Grinspoon's wired-cat experiments. (Eleven animals died, according to a footnote, in the course of the research.) There's also an article on research in England on the neurobiological effects of video-game playing. Lizzie hasn't known the details before. For the study, players' brains were doused with radioactive dye and a drug called raclopride, then monitored by PET scans as they thumped and jerked their joysticks. The researchers found that the brain is flooded with dopamine, according to the article, "to a level commensurate with that produced by injections of amphetamine." In other words, as

Bruce has summarized, "playing video games is the same as mainlining speed." In another experiment, women in particular enjoyed games that induced "serotonin cascades" in their brains. Bruce wants to run the tests on some Warps players as soon as they have a finished prototype.

So much strange, witchy, tinkering science, and all of it described in such willfully flat, anodyne terms. There are the Japanese who attached a computer chip to the head of a live cockroach, then used a joystick to move the roach. There are the university researchers who put individual brain cells from a rat embryo into individual electrode-loaded wells on a silicon chip—like bits of batter in a tiny muffin tin. The rat neurons sprouted dendrites and axons—real, all-meat cerebral wiring—which rose and snaked their way up out of the microchip wells and over to other neurons, to which they spontaneously grafted. In other words, half rat, half computer. *It sounds like the setup for a Microsoft joke,* Lizzie thinks to herself, looking out at all the filthy slush covering the most expensive real estate in America. *Roaches and rats: heroic vermin, the unlovable creatures for whom animal rights activists can't manage to whip up any sympathy.*

"Sixty-fifth Street runs east," she says to Yuri, her driver, a Russian man listening to Schoenberg or Tippett or some other anxiously unlikably mid-twentieth-century piece of music. "You'll have to go up to Sixty-sixth and come around down Fifth." He nods and reaches to nudge the stereo volume up a notch, then pulls the car over, stops, and gets out to squeegee the snow off his windows. Lizzie can't imagine telling any driver to turn off classical music, no matter what it is, especially not an immigrant. She doesn't want to discourage any flickerings of civilization. It is the same logic that inclines her to indulge the squeegee bums—the homeless men who used to try to clean windshields at stoplights until Mayor Giuliani had them eliminated. She always figures it's rude and chaotic and they do a lousy job, but don't we want to encourage the *idea* of work among the underclass? The suppression of the squeegee men, Lizzie remarked with a twinkle to Rupert Murdoch at a News Corporation cocktail party in 1994, was Giuliani's Grenada invasion—his easy, unnecessary triumph over irritating brown-skinned men. "I think Rupert didn't like me even before I said it," she told George that night.

Only two of Bruce's articles concern human beings. In Lizzie's favorite, a neurosurgeon provoked emotion mechanically, by shooting electricity into a particular spot in the brain. The surgeon got a wide-awake sixteen-year-old girl to smile. When the electricity was turned up, she laughed—the doctors performing the experiment on her, the girl said, had become suddenly, inexplicably hilarious. Lizzie smiles as she reads the deadpan academic account of their "intracranial subdural electrode" probing the "supplemental motor area of the left cortex" of the laughing teenage girl. She thinks of Fanny Taft, her giggling fan in St. Paul. She thinks of the time Sarah giggled at George last summer when he was wearing socks with shorts and he asked her, "What? What are you laughing at?" She thinks of herself, years before, laughing when the Harvard policeman asked why she had walked back and forth across Mt. Auburn Street three times at four in the morning with a grin on her face.

The work most similar to Buster Grinspoon's is in Atlanta, where a human brain is in wireless communication with a computer. A tiny glass cone has been implanted in the brain of a paralyzed stroke victim. Surrounding neurons have attached themselves to the device, and with an antenna strapped to the top of his head, the mute patient is able to communicate basic commands to a computer.

Dopamine, raclopride, joysticks, PET. Cerebral probes, electrical laughter, electronic rodent brains, wireless feline telephony, 400-megahertz stroke victims. A man getting a pig's liver. *God,* Lizzie thinks, looking out at the old-fashioned snow drifting down on charming old upper Madison, *maybe George is right—about life imitating* A Clockwork Orange. It's as if the grand, dreamy nineteenth-century research of Dr. Jekyll and Dr. Frankenstein has been spliced directly into the twenty-first. *It's postmodern science,* she thinks, sounding silly to herself. But isn't it?

The research is all interesting, fantastically so. But interesting research is why government grants and Microsoft exist. What is Bruce thinking? Have all these computer boys read too many William Gibson novels? Or is it her fault? She likes telling people to always think *outside* the box, think outside the *box,* but in a small company maybe that's vanity. By pursuing unconnected projects—the speech-recognition code has nothing to do with Y2KRx, Y2KRx has nothing to do with the graphics software or ShowNet, which has almost nothing to do with Warps—maybe Fine Technologies doesn't have any box to think outside of. With each new product her strategy changes, and Fine Technologies turns into a different business. "The lightbulb and the phonograph and the movie projector were unrelated too," she said to George one time last year, trying to reassure herself, and he was kind enough to let the Thomas Edison analogy pass. Is she strategically nimble, ideally evolved for the New Economy? Or is she someone with a short attention span who's made a couple of lucky stumbles? As her youngest child perpetually asks, *Is that a good thing or a bad thing, Mommy?* As the car rounds Fifth and turns down Sixty-fifth, she checks her face in a backseat flip-down mirror. "Obviously," Bruce has written in his memo, "this would be a long-term investment for us, since marketable human applications are probably five years away, at least." *Five years!* Hell, why not ten? Why not fifty?

She pops the mirror shut, shoves Bruce's papers across the seat, and tells the driver as she slides out, "I'll be about two hours."

In the anteroom, there is nothing but yards of gorgeous, rough yellow marble and lighting that gives the impression of candlelight—no art, no bar, no plants, no coat-check window, no podium, nothing. The more they can afford restaurants like this—conversation-piece restaurants, restaurants where couples spend as much for dinner as they pay a nanny in a week—the less George and Lizzie seem to go to them. She's glad Pollyanna made the reservation.

"Welcome to Zero this evening," the meticulous little pig-nosed woman in short black hair and a blue Prada dress whispers enthusiastically, pronouncing Zero, and only Zero, with a French accent. This is no doubt a woman who has described herself as *jolie laide.*

"I'm meeting Pollyanna Chang."

"Excellent," the woman says, stepping aside, sweeping the air. She ushers Lizzie through a short hallway and down three stairs into a dining room, handing her off there to a skinny man with very short silvery brown hair (like George), who's wearing an expensively baggy four-button brown suit (not like George), for the remainder of the journey. He oozes deference too, but his is evidently a nonspeaking role.

The room is circular, sixty feet across, with a circular bed of dark blue delphiniums in the center and a domed ceiling twenty feet high.

The floor and first ten feet of walls are pinkish white stone—antique limestone, she remembers reading out loud to George from the *Times,* imported from Corfu. There's no art, no draperies, no decoration at all (unless you count the mottled silver leaf covering the interior of the hemisphere overhead), only lighting and stone and tables covered in linen—linen, she remembers reading in a different story about the restaurant, with thread counts approaching a thousand per inch. The tables are ten feet apart. The minimalism is breathtaking for such an expensive restaurant, particularly uptown, where, except for a few clothing stores, the public wealth displays are still nearly always old-fashioned and unabashed, luxe of the kind that wows children; conversely, Lizzie has never encountered such insanely high-priced austerity outside a museum. It is a splendid place, as Lizzie had expected, even though she still finds the name embarrassing to say, as she does the name of the new perfume she's wearing, Too Intense.

"Why is that man standing there?" Lizzie asks Pollyanna, moving her lips like a bad ventriloquist and nodding slightly in her friend's direction. A young man with a shaved head and an expensively baggy four-button brown suit stands facing the room a few feet away, between Pollyanna and the wall.

"He's the bartender. There's no actual, physical bar, but he's the bartender, so he stands there. That's because this is the smoking section. Or vice versa, I'm not sure. I ordered you a drink." Pollyanna pulls three different brands of cigarettes from her jacket pocket—More, Now, and her own open pack of Camels. "Want one?"

"You are sick. Yes, thanks," she says, taking one of the Camels. Now that Lizzie is a pack-or-two-a-week connoisseur rather than a pack-or-two-a-day addict, she finds the act of pulling a cigarette from the pack—not the first too-tight couple or the last loosey-goosey ones, but cigarettes three through eleven, more or less—slightly but distinctly sexy. George, who has never smoked, didn't get this at all when she confessed it and called her a fetishist, but said he found her sexy for finding it sexy. He has also been accusing her lately of seeing more and more of Pollyanna because Pollyanna smokes and Lizzie can bum cigarettes. She denies it, feeling hurt on Pollyanna's behalf, and reminds him that Pollyanna Chang has been her friend for seventeen years (a number that makes her feel old). But of course he's a little bit right, just like her mother was right when she'd asked Lizzie in eighth grade if her new set of friends at Oakwood, the cool Hollywood private school, were drug abusers. Because Pollyanna works as a lawyer for R. J. Reynolds, cigarette smoking for her is halfway between a job requirement and a perk.

The bartender is suddenly lighting Lizzie's cigarette with a dull silver metal bar as thick as a finger and twice as long, which shoots a slender, highly concentrated flame—the most beautiful blowtorch ever made. Being lit she also finds a little sexy. "How's Warren?" she asks. Pollyanna's boyfriend is a psychiatrist who sees patients in his home office. George has known Warren slightly for a long time; they met for three fifty-minute sessions in 1984, after the accident in Nicaragua, in fulfillment of the "minimum mandatory posttrauma counseling" that George's medical coverage required.

"Mezzo mezzo. He quit. Smoking."

Lizzie smiles. "And? That's a violation of corporate policy or something?"

"Smoking was healthy for Warren. Mentally. Walking those three blocks to the newsstand and back every day was his connection to normalcy and reality. Now he doesn't buy cigarettes and he has the newspapers delivered. He literally doesn't leave his apartment for days at a time. Except for his two-year-old son and the au pair on weekends, all he sees are his crazy people and the takeout delivery guys."

"And you. Can we get menus?"

"They don't have menus. Last Sunday I was at the office all day working, and I had my stuff in a white plastic bag. The doorman at his building was new, some black guy with an attitude. He went into his little booth to call up to Warren, and came back and said, 'Dr. Holcombe informs me that he already received his Chinese food this evening.' "

"No!"

"Yes. I was so pissed," Pollyanna says, taking a drag and elaborately exhaling, "I turned right around and went home."

"Did you call?" Lizzie is an eager audience for her unmarried friends' relationship stories, even and maybe especially the nightmares. She enjoys the hits of vicarious unhappiness.

"No. And when I called the next day, I was like, 'Why the *fuck* didn't you call my apartment? I could've been *dead!*' And he said, 'Because I fell asleep, and in the morning I figured out what had probably happened.' "

"Yikes. That's not good, Polly. That's bad." A habit of extreme directness is one virtue of spending a lot of time with small children.

Pollyanna says nothing, then, "Yeah, well, it's badder than that. . . . There's a cute new boy at work."

"Uh-oh," Lizzie says, smiling. "The return of *Danger Girl!*" Danger Girl is the third-person alter ego nickname Lizzie and Pollyanna traded back and forth in the eighties, when both of them were single. She is kind of an imaginary super-antiheroine who smoked and drank too much, sometimes used cocaine, had imprudent sex with incorrect men, but always got every bit of work done perfectly. At thirty-five, Pollyanna, with her deceptively lost-little-Chinatown-girl smile and cascade of straight black hair down her back, still communes with Danger Girl occasionally. Another flavor of vicarious emotion Lizzie counts on her friends to provide.

"He's pretty seriously cute. I mean, he's still a *lawyer.* I've hardly talked to him. But he listens to Philip Glass on his Walkman."

"Possible asshole. Liking Philip Glass is one of those things that can really go either way."

"He also Rollerblades. Which, I know, can also go either way. But Philip Glass *plus* Rollerblading . . . Each, like, sort of counteracts the other?"

"Don't you think he's probably more a symptom of things being shitty with Warren than he is, you know, da-dum, a *boy?*" Lizzie and most of her friends have never stopped referring to men, especially single men, as boys. It's simultaneously girlish and mock girlish, and Lizzie has found it to be a generational litmus test—most smart women over fifty don't call men boys, and they disapprove of smart young women who call each other girls. During the only real fight about feminism she's ever had in her life, with her stepmother Rachel, who dined out for decades on the fact that she once played tennis with Betty Friedan in Sagaponack, Lizzie argued that calling men boys was a way of putting men and sex in their proper places.

"Badder how?" Lizzie asks, taking another cigarette.

"Did I tell you how, a couple of weeks ago, he called me an emasculating bitch? No, I'm sorry, it was *'castrating,'* not emasculating. I was like, *What?* And he said, 'Sometimes the literal prefigures the symbolic.' I wanted to kill him for a second. I mean *actually.* I can't stand it when he gets all psychiatric like that. The last time I got that mad was when he tried to make something out of the fact that I played alto sax as opposed to tenor."

"So you did tell him. About the . . . thing in medical school."

"He's a shrink."

Pollyanna started at Harvard Medical School the same September Lizzie started at the Business School. But she dropped out after the third time she accidentally mutilated her male cadaver's genitals, and started over at Harvard Law the next fall. "But it was just so *dumb.* You know? 'Castrating bitch.' It's like an eighteen-year-old's idea of an insult. I mean, I'm a lot of bad things—an addict, prejudiced against Koreans, a lung-cancer profiteer—but I do *not* hate men. That's a stupid cliché."

"George and I were saying last week, about his mother and my father? It turns out the clichés about parents dying are true."

"That's why they become clichés."

"And there's practically nothing to say *except* clichés! Also about having children. About all the important stuff." Lizzie regrets the swerve into childbearing smugness, but Pollyanna is lighting a cigarette, which helps them squeak past the moment. "All these deep, authentic emotions have been turned into fucking greeting cards and little gift books on the checkout counter at Barnes and Noble. Which makes you feel corny and inferior for having the emotions. Which is wrong."

"Ladies," says a blond man in an expensively baggy four-button brown suit, his grand but quiet and sincere manner more that of a clergyman than of a waiter. "Welcome to Zero. What shall we prepare for you this evening?"

———————

Spending $186 for dinner at Zero, just for her own dinner, does not offend her tonight, partly because the meal ("wild baby North Atlantic salmon from the Hebrides" in a "sauce of "*hwaysah* berries handpicked in the Tanzanian highlands") was as excellent as it was pretentious, and partly because George is out of town and, fuck it, she can spoil herself once in a while.

Confessing her professional anxieties to Pollyanna, however, did not diminish them. Rolling down Fifth Avenue (the Russian driver is now playing Charles Ives, a major improvement), she stares at the folder of papers next to her, now straight and neat (nice guy! she'll tip big). "Are you scared of leaving New York?" Pollyanna asked during the second bottle of fifty-five-dollar Chardonnay. "If I were in your business, I think I might be scared of *not* leaving, of becoming like Dixieland after bebop, you know? Cute and eclectic and surviving but way too proud of itself and, like, just . . . out of it." Polly had hit a sore spot. It's easy to feel successful in New York in the software business because no-body expects you to become Amazon.com or Yahoo!: you can't *really* succeed here, so you can't really *fail*. Silicon Alley? Pathetic. New York lets her have it both ways: major-league city, minor-league digital culture. Bruce says they're fish out of water, but she's also a big fish in a small pond—a big mutant fish trying to do too many disparate things. And she's not even so big. She's just a lucky mutant fish without any go-go gene, a complacent, conservative Dixieland jazz fish. She's so proud of being profitable. Three quarters of earnings. So? So? *Are earnings good or bad, Mommy?* The go-go companies don't have earnings at all. Ben Gould wasn't joking when he said he *prefers* some companies not to have earnings. "Don't be a victim of the mom-and-pop fallacy, Zimbalist," he said as the last Fine Technologies board meeting was breaking up. "Manage for growth, not earnings. Maybe it's a girl thing." That was a joke, the "girl thing" remark. Bennett Gould is Mike Zimbalist version 2.0. Her father always managed for growth. Her father was never a victim of any mom-and-pop fallacy, Lord knows. What *is* it with these guys? Everything's on the come, always on the come. The jackpot is there up ahead, right there, we're sure, just up ahead, honest, just ahead. This economy is geared to the Ben Goulds and Mike Zimbalists, and she just doesn't have the balls for it. Maybe it is a girl thing. She hasn't had this much to drink in a long time, since Christmas. Since 1999. Since the previous century.

She phones her office number to leave a message, reminding herself to tell Lance to run the new Microsoft numbers and to ask Katherine about the legal implications of co-owning Buster Grinspoon's software patents.

"You are in softvare business?" the driver suddenly says. "I also. I also vork vith Microsoft before. I am Yuri."

Lizzie smiles. She's dialing again.

"You know grime-spawn?" the driver seems to ask. "I know grime-spawn."

"Hmmm," Lizzie says. But in the middle of waiting the three seconds for her new phone to lock onto a TRW satellite 6,473 miles overhead in geostationary orbit, bounce 6,473 miles back down to an antenna bolted onto the concrete wall of a 1906 warehouse on Peck Slip, then course underground through copper wire the 242 yards to their old brick house, she isn't really inclined to engage Yuri in a discussion of Microsoft and grime-spawn, whatever grime-spawn are. "Hello, Rafaela," she says, speaking as slowly and clearly as a kindergarten teacher. "It's Lizzie. Uh-huh. Bennett Gould called back when? Okay, I'm on my way home. Are the kids in bed? I'll be home in about fifteen minutes. Okeydokey, Rafaela? Bye-bye." *Okeydokey?* She upbraids herself for saying "okeydokey" to a Mayan peasant who knew no English two years ago.

It was weird how the check-in guy had snapped to attention and repeated George's name, *yes* Mr. Mactier, *absolutely* Mr. Mactier, as soon as he'd heard it. Is it possible he knows that George is a TV producer with a hit series? ("Dad, how famous are you, exactly?") No. He *might* recognize the name Steven Bochco or David Kelley or Marcy Carsey, this kid, given that *Entertainment Weekly* and *Entertainment Tonight* have replaced *Time* and *The CBS Evening News* in the hearts and minds of the twenty-two-year-olds who get jobs behind reception desks at expensive hotels. But still: they have not heard of George Mactier. Maybe Ben put him on a VIP list.

Vanity, he thinks, looking closely at his crow's feet. Vanity, vanity, vanity. George seldom uses cologne or mouthwash, but he uses both when he's traveling. Away from home, his fragrance consciousness runs much higher. Hotels encourage a kind of toiletry hyperawareness, with these round magnifying mirrors and wee soap bars and bottles of cleansers and conditioners, the sunlamps, the bathrobe antitheft warnings masquerading as price lists, the wall phones next to the toilets and TVs by the sink, the symbolic paper virginity strip encircling the toilet seat. And when he uses cologne and mouthwash George invariably thinks of early adolescence, and his excited death row primping for church dances. (It was in the darkened basements of Protestant churches, Methodist and Congregational as well as Unitarian, that George experienced all his early foretastes of sex, slow-dancing cheek to cheek, chest to breasts, tightly denimed erection to panty-hosed leg.) Turning to leave the room, tapping off the light, taking one final look in the mirror, pulling down his left shirt cuff, he feels the recurring jolt of gratitude that he didn't lose the hand until he was twenty-eight. He imagines adolescence as an amputee, the Special Olympics kindnesses, the sympathy slow-dances. The thought actually makes him shudder.

When the elevator opens, George recognizes a pair of the Wall Street assholes from Ben's suite earlier today. They're ten, maybe fifteen years younger than George, about his height but harder and tanner than he is, tall and tan and young and lovely. The one speaking nods to George, the other only glances.

". . . because Q1, I hear, will kind of suck is why."

"Suck how bad? Preannounce suck?"

"No. A penny, a couple of cents. No. But if he doesn't have serious Q2 growth, I mean *serious*, he's fucked. He's working on some big net play Q2, I hear."

George has always tended not to like men like this on sight, the big white smirking prosperous know-it-alls. He disliked them in Little League when they were ten and talked about bunts and balks and the strike zone, and when they were thirteen in Protestant church basements playing air guitar along with "Sunshine of Your Love," and on airplanes leaning over seats fondling each other's new laptops. These two probably earn a million apiece, maybe more. George understands that *overpay* is not the form of economic injustice on which he should be squandering outrage, but he can't help it. The Saturday morning last winter that George watched himself, carrying LuLu on his back, ribbing his Sneden's Landing neighbor, a childless professor of medieval art his own age, about how long it was taking him to shovel his driveway was the morning he agreed with Lizzie that they had to move back into the city. There are plenty of jerks living in the city, but not as many of the kind George worries about becoming.

"Big how? Big what? There's no big left to do."

"E-commerce. A sticky video portal. I'm not sure. But my M and A buddy has a boner."

"Acquisition by? Or of?"

"All I know is he's talking to tech people. Don't count Harold out, man. He gets it."

Harold? *Mose.*

"I don't know. The TV shows suck."

"They get some great numbers. Network numbers. That artsy cop show they have, with that bleeding-heart actress. You know, older, but cute, with the tits, Annie . . ."

The elevator opens.

"Angela Janeway," says the other Wall Street asshole, stepping into the air-conditioned interior piazza. "I *hate* that cunt. Won't watch it because of her. Besides," George hears the Angela-hater say as the two men march off, "isn't that show kind of over?"

Wait. No! *No!* According to the most current audience research, eighteen-to-thirty-four-year-old A County male viewers—fellows like *you!*—have 63 percent *positive* feelings about Angela and the Jennie character. And while, yes, ratings have slipped lower for two consecutive episodes, modestly lower, the average rating, even *excluding* the New Year's show (which you guys probably heard about), is still higher for the second half of the season to date than for the first half. And while the producers have certainly experienced their own share of exasperation with Angela over the last year, successful creative people are by their very natures passionate and strong-willed. You arrogant know-nothing frat-boy Wall Street assholes.

"Good *evening,* Mr. Mactier," a concierge says, grinning and bowing slightly as George passes. "So glad to have you here in person." Not bad. "In person?" Maybe the idea is to make everyone feel like a star, someone who exists other than in person. A doorman winks. It's Vegas.

He grabs a leaflet about the new hotel's trained pigeons ("four flock-shifts of two hundred Old World birds, together comprising the most complex animal entertainment production in Las Vegas") and walks off smartly across St. Mark's Square in the direction of the Strip and BarbieWorld, sending a dozen of the current pigeon flock-shift skittering out of his way toward the Doges' Palace.

When George first walked down the Strip one afternoon in 1972 (a date closer to World War II, he obsessively-compulsively calculates, than to the present time), he was alone, just about the only pedestrian on the eight-lane highway between the Desert Inn and Caesars Palace. Back then it didn't seem like a city at all, Vegas along the Strip, but like upper Manhattan in the 1870s, or a twenty-second-century NASA colony—gawky, melancholy stretches of vacant sun-blasted flatland with one odd structure stuck randomly here and another way, way over there. Now the Strip is almost entirely packed with buildings, complete from Sahara to Tropicana, and packed with thousands of people on foot. Isn't the Las Vegas Strip pretty close to the urban planning paragon of the last forty years? Motley (that is, *diverse*) crowds of people strolling in and out of *diverse,* people-friendly architecture! Rich and poor, black and white and brown and yellow, old and young! Very young, tonight. George has passed dozens of happy little girls carrying shiny pink BarbieWorld bags. The Strip is a genuine Main Street that happens to be built at super-jumbo XXXL size. Where is a livelier urban space between Chicago and the Sierras? "George, it's just a giant carnival," Sally Chatham, one of the *Newsweek* snobs, said when he proposed a special issue on Las Vegas. "It's just a shopping mall on steroids, George," one of the ABC News snobs said when he proposed a prime-time documentary on Vegas. Yeah. So? He mounted the same defense in both instances, struggling to seem neither snappish nor pedantic nor arch. Carnivals and shopping malls were just early, slapdash attempts to cook up some urban juice in the middle of the American nowhere, beta versions, and Vegas is the best and latest iteration, a midway that's a real city. *Whatever, George,* their smiles said. He cannot abide dumb snobbery, easy snobbery, snobbery ten or twenty years behind the curve.

BarbieWorld! It's bigger than it looks in the photographs in *GQ* and *Wallpaper* and the *Times Magazine.* The grand opening has been under way all day, but the children are now being ushered out a side door as the invited grownup guests arrive. The complex has three parts. BarbieWorld proper is like a curvilinear Alvar Aalto glass vase enlarged to Claes Oldenburg size. It's pink, a soft pink that glows from within the translucent, undulating cast-glass walls of the building. On the roof, there's a transparent dome with people inside, surrounded by rays of pink and purple and golden laser lights shooting out into the night sky. The BARBIEWORLD sign is classic Vegas semicursive lettering, twenty-five feet high and hot pink. Inside each letter, gallons of viscous pink liquid bubble and flow, sequentially filling and draining the hundred-and-fifty-foot-long word every half minute or so, in a kind of perpetual slow-motion flood surge. Next to the big pink building is a fifties-style casino building, low and rectangular, all glass and white steel. It's brand-new, the synthetic lava nuggets on the ground around the last palm tree even now being tamped down by a skinny man in a dirty pink jumpsuit. The casino is called Swank City, and an old-fashioned flashing yellow-and-silver sign says CASINO AND VIP LOUNGE. Swank City is small and decorous by Vegas 2000 standards. Tucked behind BarbieWorld and Swank City is the third piece of the complex, a black high-rise, a half-size Seagram Building with a shining sign on top, hotel 1960, spelled out in turquoise lowercase letters.

Limousines, all of them white and just long enough to be ridiculous, are lined up around the circular driveway and for a half block down Las Vegas Boulevard. Out of the one now at the entrance steps a very tall, very pretty woman, about twenty-five, with big blond hair and wearing a tight, bright blue sequined gown that's vulgar but oddly demure—very large breasts, relatively little décolletage. Photographers flash, nobodies clap and yell. She must be a TV star, George figures; he has no idea who. Her close-cropped escort, extremely and blandly handsome, follows her out of the limo and onto the serpentine, rainbow-colored people mover that leads to the BarbieWorld entrance. Onlookers applaud more enthusiastically. Photographers pop off frames of the couple, standing still and waving as they're conveyer-belted away. The man is famous too? Maybe he's the star of *Ben-Hur,* the new ABC series. Which could make her, George hypothesizes, one of the Cartright great-granddaughters from *Bonanza: The New Generation,* on NBC. (He read somewhere that the *Ben-Hur* guy and the *Bonanza* girl met and fell in love last Thanksgiving at a pistol range in Hollywood.)

The next white limo pulls up, and another tall, young, bosomy blonde steps out, wearing a dress very much like the first woman, tight and sequined but chartreuse. And her escort looks just like the first man, except he has longer sideburns and military decorations pinned to his dinner jacket. A paparazzo shouts, "GI! Over here, GI! This way, GI! This way, Joe!" Has George also read somewhere that the star of *Ben-Hur* has an identical twin who works as his stunt double? Or is he getting them confused with the identical twin sons of the Gulf War hero who are going to take turns playing the toddler Jesus on the new CBS series *Savior* next fall? Whoever this couple is, photographers shoot and citizens cheer. But now George detects an edge of amusement in the smiling eyes and hoots of the onlookers, something verging on disrespect, not the pure, grateful, shaky awe he sees on the street and in restaurants when he's with Angela or the other *NARCS* stars. Maybe it's some Vegas vein of embedded irony.

Out of the next white limo emerges a young black couple, both very pretty. Flashes, applause, a little less applause. Her dress, kelly green, is tight and sequined, cut just like the last two.

"Yo! Yo!" A fat white photographer in a ratty satin "We Are the World" jacket and an *Us* magazine baseball cap is shouting at the woman. "Black Barbie! Black Barbie! Shooting for *Jet*! Over here! Give us a smile over here! *Without* Ken, please! I need a one-shot, Black Barbie!" The woman obeys, sliding out of her escort's grip and pivoting toward the photographer, who snaps away.

As the line of white limos all pull forward a few feet, each waiting its turn to disgorge more Kens and Barbies, George reaches into his jacket for the pink plastic oval ticket marked VIP in seventy-two-point glitter letters and steps through the crowd, past the security men, onto the rainbow-colored conveyer and into BarbieWorld.

The interior is a three-level shopping center decorated in Camelot mod. The pinks come in even more varying intensities and textures, along with a lot of silvers and golds. Every BarbieWorld employee is under thirty, and both genders have the look of tarted-up Protestant missionaries or very wide-eyed adult film stars. In the Date Zone, one of three restaurants, there's a (pink) telephone on each table from which diners place orders for deep-fried fat-free cheese sandwiches. The gym offers karaoke aerobic dancing, and life-size "As *If* " portraits—live, giant-screen video images distorted by means of a very convincing digital effect to reduce apparent body mass by up to 20 percent. The basement Equestrian Center, which a sign says will feature white ponies exclusively, is still under construction. Barbie Home is a large pseudo-apartment where Barbie ostensibly lives (like Santa in his workshop in Macy's), and where all of the furnishings are for sale. BarbieWorld has what one of the guides describes as four separate "wearables boutiques," or clothing stores, for girls and women—Barbie Baby, BarbieWear, Maximum Cute (for teenagers), and Madame Barbie (sizes up to 24). Doll clothes for Barbie (and for every friend and hanger-on she has ever had) are available at the Totally Perfect Mall, a warren of seventeen separate "fashion miniboutiques" packed into an acre of floor space.

There's a hair salon, two stories high, for adults as well as children, for humans as well as dolls. Up in a second-floor loft area, a male guide sounds like he's leading a tour at Cape Canaveral or the Supreme Court, describing the BarbieStyle Beauty University as "the world's first and only fully equipped hair-play mezzanine." BarbieStyle Beauty University consists largely of several endless counters with scores of Barbies bolted into doll-size leather salon chairs, as well as a dozen real, Barbie- and Stacey-like women, sitting in full-size salon chairs between the counters. Patrons (or "groomer apprentices") may comb, brush, and style—but not cut or permanently color—the hair of both the dolls and the women. Ordinarily, the hair-play mezzanine will be open only to girls fourteen and under (until the class-action suit on behalf of little boys is filed), but tonight, because of Swank City's grand opening, adult men are invited to try their hands at combing, brushing, or styling (but not cutting or permanently coloring). George sees the two Wall Street assholes from the elevator waiting in the human hair-play line. They are joined by a third Wall Street asshole, a young black man who says, "Zig! Shepley! Viva Las Vegas, gentlemen!" Each man is drinking a Cosmopolitan, which is the free pink cocktail du jour at BarbieWorld tonight. *"¡Excellente!"* replies the one who won't watch *NARCS* because Angela Janeway is a liberal. Seeing these three doesn't literally make George ashamed of being a man, a well-to-do heterosexual man who has voted Republican a few times, but it does tip the somewhat delicate balance of George's Vegas-reveling mood in an unhappy direction.

The rooftop restaurant is called Barbie's International After-Hours Penthouse Bistro, but the name aside, it is authentically handsome, actually glamorous.

"Welcome to the Penthouse, sir," says a young man with a Spanish accent. "I'm Klaus."

On the sound system are Miles Davis and John Coltrane playing "Oleo." A Willem de Kooning painting (bought for $12 million, a sign says) is suspended in midair by cables over the bar. Un-pink drinks are being served. George orders a Jack Daniel's, neat, from a European waitress, French or Belgian. He wonders if all the non-American employees are relegated up here, where the theming requires no one to portray Barbie or Ken and so there's no effect for the foreign accents to ruin. This is the one place in BarbieWorld where the lighting is dim and where the sexual subtext of the Barbie ethos is rather less sub. George didn't notice from down on the Strip that the dome itself, a hundred feet wide and fifty feet high, is a slightly greenish glass half globe, etched with longitude and latitude lines and the outlines of the land masses of the Northern Hemisphere. Unanchored by work or family to his middle-aged present, he's sliding once more back to age fifteen, fourteen, thirteen, thrilled speechless, watching Stanley Kubrick (the first-class monochrome serenity of the spaceliner in *2001,* the Korova Milk Bar in *A Clockwork Orange*) and reading *Playboy.*

The spherical tip of a silver Barbie's International After-Hours Penthouse Bistro swizzle stick sticks up from George's drink, pointing at him. On it are little swizzle-ads for the Working Assets Titanium MasterCard—FROM EACH ACCORDING TO HIS/HER ABILITY, TO EACH ACCORDING TO HIS/HER NEED®—are spelled out in black on one side, LIVE WELL, BUT LIVE GOOD® on the other. Every time a cardholder charges something, each of several dozen leftish causes receives a fraction of a cent. Lizzie ordered Working Assets Gold MasterCards for herself and George. George rarely uses his card, as Lizzie reminds him once a month when she pays the bills. He finds the ostentation embarrassing—money ostentation, as with any gold or silver credit card, plus righteousness ostentation, like illness-specific dinner-jacket lapel ribbons. The show of charity is supposed to sanitize the show of venality, but to George it only makes it worse. He finishes his Jack Daniel's just as the waitress brings his second.

Near the spiral staircase tube that leads to the Penthouse from BarbieWorld proper, George notices a small sign that says UNACCOMPANIED CHILDREN ARE WELCOME IN THE PENTHOUSE BEFORE FIVE P.M. THANK YOU! What's the drinking age in Nevada—twelve? Fourteen on school nights? Then he watches a middle-aged black woman clomp slowly up the tube, followed, sure enough, by a child, a white girl of ten wearing a blue leather Ann Demeulemeester dress. And right behind them, also holding the little girl's hand, Ben Gould, wearing a tuxedo.

"Because little kids aren't really supposed to be here now, honey," Ben says. "This is the grownup area of BarbieWorld. And also because it's your bedtime. Watch your step, Sasha! You know, if you were home in New York, it would be nine-forty!"

"My home is in Connecticut, Daddy."

"Look, Sasha! It's Uncle George!"

Sasha points. "That's not Uncle George," she says, happy for the opportunity to contradict her father. "That man is brown-skinned. And Uncle George lives near the docks, in the stinky fish market in New York City. And he's not my actual uncle, anyway."

Sasha, who was a grim, whiny, demanding child even before Ben and her mother divorced, turns away and walks right up to the bar. Her nanny silently follows.

"I want a Shirley Temp—wait, what type of ginger ale do you use?" she asks the bartender.

The bartender glances toward Ben and winks. "Shasta, madam," he says. His accent is Australian.

"Then I'll just have a Pellegrino. But with four cherries in it." She rejoins her father, who is now at George's table. Her nanny remains one pace behind.

"See, Uncle George just has a tan, honey," Ben tells his daughter. "Sorry we're late. Sasha was cleaning out some SKUs downstairs. Can you say hello to Uncle George?"

Sasha, looking out at the lasers, says nothing.

"Hello, Sasha!" George says. "How's school?"

"I'm the second smartest in my class."

"Best little Sasha in the whole world," Ben says.

Ignoring her father's boilerplate compliment, she says to George, "My school is lots nicer than the real Spence." Sasha's mother moved last summer from East Seventy-eighth Street to Connecticut, and enrolled Sasha in Spence/Greenwich, which is a new affiliate of the Manhattan private school—"along the lines of the Guggenheim in Bilbao," the parents and administrators like to say. Like the Guggenheim, the Greenwich parents even paid for a famous architect, Robert A. M. Stern, to design the school. "It has an indoor velodrome," says

the girl, "an art gallery, and a conflict-resolution lab, with a doctor."
George knows about the gallery, since the *Times* just reviewed its Jean-
Michel Basquiat exhibit.

"Do you like BarbieWorld?" Uncle George asks.

She screws up her mouth and sighs. "It's not like I imagined it. *I*
thought it up. It was supposed to be like a *whole city.* This is just a mall.
And the Ken and Barbie people look cheap. Why don't those lasers
move, Daddy? I want them to make pictures in the sky."

"The people who run the airport said no, sweetheart."

"They should be fired."

"That isn't nice, Sasha," Ben says. "You're tired, aren't you, pump-
kin? Kiss Daddy good night. You and I have a very early flight to catch
tomorrow morning."

"But it's our plane," Sasha says. "We don't have to catch it. We can
get on it anytime we want. The pilot works for you."

"Night-night. Etta, we'll have breakfast at about eight-thirty tomorrow. All right? Thanks."

As the little girl leads her handler to the spiral staircase, she says, not
looking back, "The croissants at the hotel suck."

Ben leans toward George with an excited grin. "Sick, isn't it?"
George knows he means BarbieWorld. "Wait until you see the show.
A documentary crew flew in to film it for the *Whitney*! The goddamn
Whitney Museum of American *Art*! How great is that?"

"Sasha didn't make you sign an NDA?" George says. George didn't
know what NDA meant the first time he was handed one, a year ago,
but since then he has signed a nondisclosure agreement every other
month. Journalists are supposed to disclose; grownups, businesspeople—players—are not.

"Hey! No joke, man. Her mother's lawyer called and wanted to negotiate a lifetime royalty from this place for Sasha. A percentage of
gross! I told him, look, asshole, I'm just a limited partner, and it was not
really her idea—her dolls gave me the idea—but I'm not about to negotiate against my kid. She can have my entire interest in the thing,
which is jack, like five million, *today.*" He pauses. "The daily implosion
was her idea." Every evening in the atrium of the hotel 1960, a large-
scale model of the hotel itself will be "demolished" with internal ex-
plosive devices.

"You know, you *look* like a producer! With that tan you could almost pass for a Jew! And without that drink. Your wife says hello, speaking of the tribe. We just got off the phone about this new Microsoft offer. I told her to hold out. If she's bamboozled those pricks into paying five-point-five, she can get them to pay ten. Seven-five, anyway. But she sounded like she's already broken out the champagne."

George smiles and nods with a generic manly meaningfulness, *Que sera, sera,* not wanting to let Ben know that he knows nothing about any new Microsoft offer. He holds up the Working Assets swizzle stick to change the subject. "Now *this* is sick. Your idea?"

"My idea was to give a percentage of the net directly to NOW and NARAL and a bunch of women's groups. Barbie paying feminist reparations. It became this," he says, flicking the swizzle stick with an index finger, "the pussies, because this way the protection money is spread around to so many different groups it's like we're not confessing any specific wrongdoing." He shakes his head and says, unsmiling, "It's a joke."

George watches the three Wall Street assholes trot up the stairs. As they get to the top and head toward the double-wide express elevator down to Swank City, the black Wall Street asshole is holding up a hand for one of his white buddies to sniff.

"So, all these Wall Street assholes—"

"Hey! *You* can't use that phrase," Ben says. "It's like if I said 'nigger.' "

"So, are all these Wall Street assholes you invited actually friends of yours?"

"Are you nuts? They're guys I trade with, guys I do business with, sell-side guys. I knew this would be exactly the sort of thing they'd lap up. No, I've never set eyes on a lot of these guys before. Even though I may talk to them on the phone every week. But 'friends'? I haven't made a new friend in ten years. Besides, most of them probably *are* assholes."

In show business, George thinks, people you deal with a few times a year are, almost by definition, your friends. If you do business with them every week, they would automatically be your very close friends.

"Come on," Ben says, jumping up, "get another drink, we've got a couple of minutes before the show starts. You've got to come see the casino."

Sinatra is singing "Witchcraft" over the speaker in the elevator.

An opening elevator door has never seemed more like curtains parting at the beginning of a play. And given the four steps down into the casino, in the moment before he and Ben make their entrance into the happy, snappy swarm, George has the peculiar mirror-image sensation of being onstage himself.

"Good evening, Mr. Gould!" says a good-looking young man far darker than any of the Kens over in BarbieWorld. He has Pat Riley hair and an iridescent green dinner jacket. "Welcome to Swank City, sirs."

The place is a glamorized dream version of a Vegas casino of forty years ago, not a literal reproduction, which, as Ben says, people today would find cramped and crummy. "That's why the idiots at ITT just spent two hundred million dollars wreck-ovating the old Desert Inn," Ben says. Swank City seems old, but the only genuinely old things in the room, according to Jackie, their guide, are two dozen chrome-and-yellow-enamel slot machines—vintage Bally Money Honeys and Watling Roll-A-Tops. "*Jackie,*" Ben whispers to George, "is his nom de casino."

"How can you afford to have so few slot machines?" George asks Ben. "Isn't that how most casinos make all their money?"

"You haven't been down to the basement!"

"No, the theater, you mean?" George says.

"On the other side of the firewall from the J and B Theater-in-the-Round," Jackie explains, "right underneath the hotel 1960, that's the Rec Room. The Rec Room has distinct period theming elements, a separate entrance, and contains eleven thousand slot machines—"

"Twelve *acres,* nothing but people playing slots," Ben says. "It's a shame Diane Arbus is dead. You should take a look. No, you shouldn't, actually."

"—with *extremely* easy access for the handicapped and semihandicapped," Jackie continues, gesturing by way of counterexample at all the thickly carpeted steps and platforms here in sumptuous Swank City. "And in the Rec Room we offer free cocktails for AARP members and their companions." He winks. In other words, George understands, the dreary RV seniors, all the people old enough actually to remember the era being simulated here, are sluiced away, incentivized with giveaway liquor to stay out of sight to pump quarters into nonvintage video slot machines. Here in "the Swank," as Jackie calls it, the scattered elderly are almost all well dressed or Runyonesque, classy or "classy"—no sweatshirts or New Balances. The idea behind Swank City is not only to evoke the boom-boom Frank and Dean ideal, to be Planet Rat Pack, but also to be the cool superpremium boutique casino, the high-butterfat, high-thread-count casino, the Barneys, the Miramax, the Häagen-Dazs gambling joint. The hotel 1960 has only 720 guest rooms—a quaint, tiny inn by Vegas standards. The lighting in the casino is more variegated than in other places, dramatically unhomogenized, with shadowy zones and hot spots, and the waitresses, dressed in sleeveless, mid-calf satin dresses, are prettier. Because only a tiny fraction of the gamblers who come to the Swank are expected to smoke cigarettes, the designers have equipped the HVAC ducts with devices called cracked-oil foggers that pump in stage smoke near the ceiling to ensure 1960 verisimilitude—"*noir* without the carcinogens," as Ben says. The loudspeakers sweeten the ambient sound of the room with recorded tracks of cocktail-party crowds, laughter, and the occasional winner's shriek or growl, mixed and adjusted continuously to supplement the spontaneous live human sounds.

As George watches a group of rambunctious, crew-cut young men in white shirts, dark suits, and skinny black ties playing craps—"*Give* it to Daddy!" the shooter shouts—two women wearing capri pants, one blond and one redheaded, pass by a few feet in front of George and Ben. The one not wearing dark glasses, who's evidently impersonating Tuesday Weld or Angie Dickinson (as opposed to her partner's Juliet Prowse or Shirley MacLaine), glances hard at George. George, trying to be a good sport, smiles.

"All these actors," George says to Ben. "They're hired just for the grand opening? Or are those *Reservoir Dogs* boys and the babes all part of the entertainment every night?"

"No! *No!* That's what I thought too, like the Kens and Barbies next door, but I asked," Ben says, whispering, but so excited that his voice assumes its hoarse castrato pitch. "These are all just people off the street, people from L.A., from the sticks, from I don't know where. The place was loaded with guys and dolls like this last night too! They're *ordinary people,* George. Theme it and they will come! I said it was fucking sick, didn't I?"

Jackie pokes his head close to Ben. "Mr. Gould? The program in the J and B Theater-in-the-Round is about to begin."

"Holy smokes, come *on!*" As Ben speed-walks off toward an invisible, unmarked exit, George carefully sets his half-finished third bourbon down on a flashing Money Honey and with a slight zero-to-five lurch turns to rush after him.

Inside the former coffee-and-chocolate counting house, 168 years old, nothing is pretending to be old. Three floors down, the thunder of the oil burner stops, and Lizzie hears the sudden quiet. Outside and above her, a little east and a little north, she notices for the first time since she sat down the soft, chronic Doppler purr of traffic speeding up and down the FDR Drive, coming and going across the Brooklyn Bridge. There's a pause in the titter-tatter of her fingers on the keyboard as she stares at the spiral of tea steam rising from her mug and listens to the sounds from the top floor—a scream chopped off before it finishes, a group chant, dogs barking, the same scream repeated in full, Barry Goldwater speaking about extremism and virtue, snatches of the Supremes. Sarah's staying up way too late to edit her civil rights video, another rules violation of which Lizzie approves. She returns to her Harold Mose memo, staring at the screen, writing as fast as she thinks. Rereading the first part of her memo on the advisability of Mose's acquiring TK, Penn McNabb's online video software company ("PROS: high-profile name, Silicon Valley presence, potentially good product; CONS: overpriced shares, product delays, undermanaged company"), she decides it isn't too flip. Now, in the next sections, she's worried she's getting into realms she barely understands, dispensing advice not just about video and content, but about *TV* and *journalism*—subjects in which she is an expert-by-marriage, at best.

4. *Web presence for News.* Disney has spent $100 million on ABCNews.com during the last three years. For what? With AP, Reuters, CNN, MSNBC, and a dozen smaller products already online, it's a practically invisible and completely inessential product. Unless you're willing to spend at least that much or more, you run the

> risk of reinforcing what George says is the
> perception of MBC News as a second-rate

She sips her tea. *No.* Click, slide, delete.

> Unless you're willing to spend at least that
> much or more, I doubt you'll enhance the "brand
> image" of MBC News. In effect, you will have
> overpaid for PR, spending on a vanity web site
> a sum that would, for instance, pay for
> permanent full-page MBC ads in the *Times* and
> the *Journal* every day of the week.

Precisely as George said when he complained to her a couple of years
ago about how much ABC was spending on its web site.

> So yes, in other words: on second thought and
> even on third thought, my earlier advice
> stands.

> 5. *Online video, broadband, and "convergence."*
> As you know, aside from the issue of whether or
> not you ought to buy TK, this is your $64
> zillion convergence question.

Too cute? Too familiar, maybe. What does it matter? He asked for it.
Mose isn't her boss.

> Over cable modems and DSL, you're right, it
> *is* now almost as good as regular TV. But
> penetration is still tiny, 2 million or so
> total after three years. The average person's
> internet connection speed is still slow.
> Online video is still like a parrot: the fact
> that a bird talks is pretty interesting, at
> least when you first get it home, but do you
> really want to listen to it *say* anything? And

```
I can imagine a scenario in which online video
or TV-set web browsing, as they finally do
become widely used, might well increase the
tendency for TV news to
```

Fuck the equivocation, she thinks, deleting words with one hand, hefting her mug with the other.

```
And online video is only going to make TV news
even more of a commodity. If regular people
really are going to grab a minute or two of
digital video news before they run to lunch or
pick up the kids, they'll just want to see the
clip of the guerilla POW camp in Los Platanos,
or the clip of Giuliani shoving the black
minister--no commentary, no analysis, no
"branding." And they will not care one whit
who provides
```

She stops, pulls her bathrobe closed, and reties the belt, gulps the tea, and wonders why she's up at 11:26, after a cranked-up day dealing with her own digital business and drinking too much wine with Polly, advising a man she barely knows about how to conduct his multibillion-dollar business. *Because he's George's boss* would be a plausible answer. But Mose Media Holdings is a big company. *Because he asked me* would be another, *me and not some eager-beaver young Excel asshole in suspenders up on West Fifty-seventh Street.*

```
And news consumers won't really care, or
necessarily know, who's providing them the
video. Yes, make your deals with the portals
to provide them news video and show clips.
Your strategy should be to not get shut out.
Your entertainment programs are a whole
different question, as we talked about, but
online is still going to be a tail your TV dog
wags for a while. As far as that goes, if the
```

```
numbers work for you, I'd recommend doing the
deals with WebTV and with RealNetworks, if
both companies will let you. Use Microsoft
paranoia--their paranoia about everyone else,
and everyone else's paranoia about them--to
your advantage.
```

Print. "It's so much easier to give advice," Mike Zimbalist, world-class dispenser of advice, has always said, "than to take it." It's a ritual self-deprecation, the only one in which he indulges. She looks again at the time on the upper right corner of her computer screen—11:32—and decides it's too late to call him.

In the bedroom closet, way up behind the filched carton of News Corporation stationery she'll never use (like father, not quite like daughter), she feels for the crushproof box, finds it, and flips it open, guiltily as ever. Maybe they're mass murderers, Philip Morris, but at least they still spell it Marlboro Lights, not *Lites.* If they ever do that, Lizzie might quit completely and for good. She fires up the cigarette, the sixth of the day, and tucks the ovoid silver matchbox from Zero into the cigarette pack. *Well,* she thinks, filling her lungs, *at least I'd switch brands.*

"Mommy?"

Lizzie exhales her smoke jet toward the top and back of the closet. "What is it, Sarah?" She drops the lit Marlboro on the floor, grinds it out with her new deerskin slipper, shuts the closet door behind her, and practically leaps the seven steps across the bedroom toward the hallway.

"Can you watch my UAH video?" UAH is short for Unfortunate American History. "It's only eleven minutes. We're supposed to show it to our executive producers this week and get their notes."

Thank heaven for adolescent self-absorption. One of the little kids would have busted her for sure. "Your executive producers?"

"One of the media studies teachers. Each production is assigned to an executive producer. Mine and Penelope's is Ms. Perez-Morrison. What's burning?"

"Penelope's and mine." Lizzie sniffs. "Maybe I left the stove on when I made tea? I'll go down and check." The sniff is over-the-top, Lizzie thinks, absolutely shameless. "I'll watch it, I promise," Lizzie tells Sarah. "With Daddy. I'm really beat, Sarah. I have to go to bed."

"I don't really want George to see it before the premiere." Lizzie is too tired to feel bad about Sarah calling George "George," but she is grateful, retroactively, that Sarah didn't call her biological father "Dad" or "Daddy" when they saw Buddy in L.A. "He'll be too critical. He said using music from 1969 was an anachronism. I told him this is entertainment, not like a documentary. He suggested Joan Baez. Joan Baez is so . . . whiny."

"Whiny, huh? She's not the only one."

"Yuk, yuk. Anyhow, we're not supposed to take notes from parents. Only from the executive producers, the UAH teachers, and the kids in the first test screening. So, whatever." Sarah turns to go back upstairs.

"What's wrong? Did your test screening not go well?"

"No, they liked it. Except they laughed at the close-up of Sir's face when he's beating Penelope with the flashlight. Mom?" Sarah crosses her legs at the ankles and raises her left arm above her head, bends it and grabs a shock of her very short dark hair. It is her Anxious Quizzical Pose. "Do you think I'm a lesbian?"

Lizzie has the urge to retrieve the Marlboro Light from the floor of the closet.

"Well, no, I don't, Sarah. Why? Do you?" She pauses. "It's okay if you do."

"No. Shelly Wheeler says that if you masturbate more frequently than five times a week, the odds are that you're a lesbian. She says there's a scientific study from Harvard that proves it. And she told somebody that, last year when Shelly and I were friends, that I told her I masturbate every day. And I didn't. Tell her that. She's lying. *She's* the one who has all the Indigo Girls' records."

Lizzie smiles and shakes her head, prompting Sarah to come to her senses and smile too.

"Night-night," she says to her daughter, kissing her. She watches Sarah walk down the hall, wearing only panties and a T-shirt with NO MAS spelled in dripping blood-red letters on the back. "By the way? I'm *sure* there's *no* such scientific study. And certainly not from Harvard."

"You're such a snob, Mommy. Good night. Check the stove."

He doesn't feel tired now. A little woozy, but not sleepy. He figures it was stress plus desert heat plus introspection plus air travel plus liquor that made him nod off during the BarbieWorld theatrical gala, *1960,* that Ben commissioned for the grand opening. George was awake when three of the four Monkees first came onstage, their exposed skin thickly covered in gray makeup, to lip-synch "I'm a Believer," but he missed, Ben told him, "the *entire* merengue part of the show with Roger Clinton and Jennifer Jason Leigh." He enjoyed the effect of the clouds of colored gas coalescing into the forms of go-go girls, and he saw William Shatner and Parker Posey leading the parade of Miss America first runners-up from the sixties, which was a little sad, but then he fell asleep again until the very end, when the standing ovation for the writer-director of the piece, Robert Wilson, woke him up. The adrenaline of embarrassment has given him a second wind.

Because hotel 1960 is not yet open, and there are no suites big enough for Ben's after-party anyway, he tells everyone he sees to come back to his floor at the Venetian. Ben is driving a green 1959 Thunderbird from hotel 1960's themed car-rental operation, RetroRent, and George has been supplied with a fresh Jack Daniel's for the road. After Ben told George that Philip Johnson was a consultant on hotel 1960, George started an architecture argument.

"Uh-uh. You're wrong."

"Ben, I promise you, it's *real marble.* They contracted with some ancient quarry in the Veneto. I think I read it in the same *Times Magazine* millennium issue that mentioned your antique jukeboxes—"

"Slot machines. You're shitfaced, George."

"—*slot machines,* fuck you, and this guy at the Venetian is using real Italian stone. I'm positive."

"Bullshit. It's fake." Ben looks in his side mirror, then turns all the way around. "Man! *That* is pretty cool."

George turns to look. Behind them on the Strip is a two-block-long ad hoc caravan—all the white stretch limos with the windblown heads and torsos of various Kens and Barbies sticking up through sunroofs, the real celebrities' black limos, and maybe a half dozen other cars from RetroRent, including a lemon-yellow 1964 Mustang, another vintage Thunderbird, and three huge, black forty-year-old Lincoln Continental convertibles. A pair of motorcycle cops, their head-lights flashing, speed along on either side of the caravan.

"Police escorts?" Ben squeals. "This is extreme."

As the cop on the left pulls up even with their T-bird, Ben cranks his window open—rolling down car windows, another dead twenti-eth-century domestic art, along with shifting gears, dialing rotary phones, using carbon paper, smoking unfiltered cigarettes. Motorcycle cops: very mid-century.

"You're headed up to the Venetian, sir?" the cop shouts. She's a woman, some exquisite Benetton hybrid of Latin America and South Pacific.

"Yes, ma'am!" Bennett shouts back.

She swerves away and signals her partner with a cool cowboy hand gesture, circle and point. (Like a cowboy in a movie, of course, since neither George nor Ben nor either cop has ever seen a real cowboy on horseback giving hand signals to a buddy on the far side of the herd.) The motorcycles converge smoothly directly in front of them and speed up. Ben steps on the gas.

George takes his drink from between his legs and sips it. "Just passed the grassy knoll," he says. "How much farther to Parkland Memorial?"

As they turn off the Strip, riding along the Grand Canal and into the driveway, George feels their mobile microtheme clashing with but then blending into the Venetian's macrotheme. When he sees the pho-tographers and video crews jostling at the hotel entrance, a sponta-neous hybrid minitheme snaps into focus—'59 roadster, Italy, cameras: *La Dolce Vita.* Twist together enough elements and, *kaboom,* sponta-neously, unpredictably, the fake becomes real. Alchemy! He is a little shitfaced.

"Bwo-no *seer*-ah!" says the tanned little dirty-blond valet, whose twangy Gary Gilmore intensity makes his blue-and-white-striped shirt read more as *inmate* than *gondolier.* He sees the limos and vintage cars pulling in behind and grins. "Well! Now! It looks like you gentlemen are anticipating some significant partying this evening. Have a sweet one."

George follows Ben into a small, darkened loggia off the main en-trance. Ben, looking around, reaches into his pants pocket and pulls out a Swiss Army knife. He hands it to George.

"Blood brothers?" George says. "Or are we going to reenact O.J.?"

"That carved area up there is real marble, right?" Ben is pointing to the blocks above the columns.

George looks up, almost stumbling backward. "The frieze? Yeah. I think so. Yes."

"Okay, Mr. Architecture, I'm not tall enough. *Stab* it."

"It'll ruin your knife."

"No, it won't. Go ahead."

George reaches up as high as he can and stabs, hard, into the stone just beneath the frieze. The knife sinks all the way in, squeaking as it goes.

"Case closed," Ben says. "Let's go."

George stands on his tiptoes and, wobbling slightly, stabs again, higher. Again, the knife goes right in.

"Come on, psycho," Ben says, "let's go upstairs."

Then George, leaping toward the wall, grunts like a Marine— "*Yahhhh!*"—and stabs the smooth gray block above the frieze. The knife goes in. On his way down, it cuts a jagged six-inch slice in the wall.

"Polyurethane foam, polyiso foam, and polystyrene," Ben says.

"You prick," says George, breathing a little hard, handing the knife back to Ben. "You *knew.* You hustled me."

"I knew? Of course I knew. Your shirt is untucked, George."

As they step out onto the sixteenth floor, Ben's floor, they encounter two Secret Service agents, both with their hands clasped at crotch level, staring at the elevator. One of the men acknowledges Ben. George raises his glass slightly in their direction as he and Ben walk by, a winky soused-guy toast, as if driven by some atavistic need. He is suddenly reminded of . . . what? He can't quite make it out. How pathetically middle-aged, he thinks—intense but foggy memories, memories both stirred up and then unrecognizably muddied by booze.

"Those guys are part of Bucky Lopez's detail," Ben says. "I guess he's been held up at a rally in L.A." Buckingham Lopez, the former Houston Astro and second-generation Mexican-American businessman, is this election cycle's quixotic, self-financed, ultra-long-shot candidate for president. The pundits call him "the Hispanic Ross Perot" and "a *Forbes* 400 Jesse Ventura." He talks a lot about "wealth creation," and calls himself both "a pro-gun-control conservative" and "the no-bullshit spic," an epithet that *The New York Times* for the first few weeks of the campaign rendered as "the trademark vulgarism Mr. Lopez employs to depict himself as a no-nonsense Hispanic." One of his privatization ideas, auctioning off the right to name individual tropical storms each year, has already been adopted by the current administration; the TV producer Aaron Spelling was the high bidder, at $1.7 million and $1.6 million respectively, for hurricanes beginning with the letters *A* and *C*.

"Bucky Lopez is a pal of yours?" George asks.

"I was the biggest investor in his IPO. And I'm on his finance committee. I love Bucky. Bucky's an honest guy."

At the door of the party suite, the blonde and the redhead George saw at Swank City are thinking about leaving. Tuesday Weld—Tuesday Weld from around 1972, not girlish but still thin, just starting to wrinkle and thicken—smiles at George.

Now, after stifling heat plus liquor plus hotel plus Secret Service plus presidential politics plus high-strung blonde, George recollects the fogged-over memory. The summer of 1988, New Orleans, the sweaty last night of the Republican convention, after Lizzie got on the plane back to New York, after Bush the Elder's read-my-lips acceptance speech, a huge table at the Napoleon House with a dozen people from New York and Washington, journalists and campaign workers, including a brazen young, skinny, blond, right-wing woman. This was a full decade before cable news channels turned brazen young, skinny, blond, right-wing women into a recognizable pundit commodity. She was not *pretty,* really, but she did have many of the standard signifiers of pretty (young, skinny, blond, brazen), which in the course of a night of Pimms cups become *attractive enough* and then became, after everyone else left, sometime after four-thirty, since he was not married or even formally engaged to be married, inevitable. And which, of course, he regretted the next morning—but sincerely regretted, in the bathroom, in the hallway, in the elevator, and in the lobby, even before he was spotted by his mother, who was with her delegation checking out of the Napoleon House at that very gruesome moment. "George!" Edith Hope had said, "you look absolutely overworked, honey. Aren't you *finished*? Haven't you—what do you call it?—put everything to bed?"

Earlier tonight at the hotel 1960, Ben sympathetically mentioned his mother's death and his fourth Jack Daniel's. George, taking a sip, conceded the possibility of a connection. If nothing else, it was a comfortable one-night pretext.

"I thought I recognized you at the casino," the blonde tells George. "It's Sandra. You helped me out when you were here in January?"

George stares stupidly.

"No, I've never been to the Venetian before."

The woman turns up her smile, which now seems potentially insane. "*No!* At NATPE!" she says. "Sandra Bemis? Sandi. Timmy introduced us."

Featherstone's backup girlfriend, the dog aromatherapist to the stars. His disappointment (*She isn't coming on to me*) is transient, entirely washed away by his surge of relief (*She isn't a stalker, or an actress*). "Of course. You have a new look. I didn't recognize you."

"That's cool. No prob whatsoever!" Another adult who talks like a teenager. But maybe doxies always have.

"You're here on . . . vacation?" he says.

She glances at her friend and her smile turns a little wary and wry, as if he's made some subtle private joke. *"Right,"* she says.

And into the party they go. All the Barbies and Kens seem to be here, and each smiling Ken has unbuttoned his tuxedo shirt and loosened his black bow tie. An E!^{2} video crew helps power up the ambient snap and crackle of collective party vainglory, a fever of self-importance that spikes twice, once when Phil Spector arrives accompanied by Nicole Kidman and a pair of seven-foot-tall bodyguards, and then when Bucky Lopez arrives with his full Secret Service detail. Penn and Teller arrive. George sees smiling John McLaughlin stride in and head for Bucky Lopez. Even the celebrities in Las Vegas seem arbitrary.

Ben has personally taken control of the music, George realizes: a Frank Zappa song is playing over the din, "Weasels Ripped My Flesh." Again: *weasels*. Pattern amid the random, signal buried within the noise. Meaningless pattern, pointless signal, but you take what you can get. He should remember to tell Lizzie.

He's suddenly surrounded, and as he whips around to see who's grabbing his arm, he spills a fresh drink on Ben.

"George Mactier, I'd like you to meet Buckingham Lopez."

Are the Secret Service men eyeing George because he's drunk, or because they're Secret Service agents? In fact, every time George is in the presence of a presidential candidate, he imagines assassinating him. It first happened when he was making a home movie of Nixon campaigning in Minneapolis, in 1967, before candidates had Secret Service protection, and he stuck his Super-8 camera right in Nixon's face, inches away. It happened again in 1972 when he was president of Twin Cities Teens for McGovern and met the candidate. It happened again and again at *Newsweek* and ABC. It always occurs, automatically, compulsively—Mondale, Hart, Dukakis, Dole, Jesse Jackson, Steve Forbes, even Lamar Alexander—bang, bang, bang, bang, bang, a dozen or more times by now. He wonders again, hearing the Zappa, if this is a generational neurosis, Mid-Sixties Tourette's Syndrome, Virtual–John Hinckley Disorder—or just his own strange, laughing-in-church tic.

"George used to be a journalist," Ben says, as Lopez, simultaneously shaking George's hand and sticking a little BUCKY? YES, BUCKY! flag in George's jacket pocket. "But now he does real work. The TV show *NARCS,* about the war on drugs? That's his."

"The entertainment business, huh?" Lopez says. "Well, that is one *hell* of a wealth-creation engine. Congratulations!" And then he is off, presumably to tell Sandi Bemis that pet aromatherapy has the potential to become one hell of a wealth-creation engine, and to assure the frenzied busboy in the gondolier costume that stacking greasy, empty wineglasses and half-eaten hors d'oeuvres is also one hell of a wealth-creation engine.

Whenever George becomes fully drunk, he stops drinking. He has stopped drinking. He's sitting on the longest freestanding couch he has ever seen. People are leaving. A woman sits down next to him, right next to him. She's hot—sexy, but also palpably radiating heat. Ah: Sandi Bemis.

"Hi," she says. "Can I make a weird request?"

"About your dog thing? I know, I've been away from New York for a week; I haven't talked to Angela. But I will, Sandi, I promise."

He looks her in the face for the first time since she sat down, and realizes that the woman next to him is wearing pigtails, has brown hair, not blond, and is ten years younger than Sandi Bemis. Her silky synthetic top is loose and low-cut.

"Ah! Oh! Sorry. I thought you were someone else."

"I'm not Sandi, I'm Shawna." She holds out her hand, which George shakes. "I noticed you over at the BarbieWorld? I play one of the Staceys on the hair-play mezzanine. I'm a model." In one of his Manhattan street censuses, she would be an easy *yes,* in all neighborhoods and moods. "I've done a lot of catalogue in L.A. But I'm also an actress."

She wants a job. "Right."

"So, if this freaks you out just tell me, but—can I . . . I'd like to feel your hand, where your hand was? The residual limb? It's really weird, I know, but, I think it's really kind of . . . sexy? You think I'm a pervert, don't you?"

Yes. All the more so since she used the PC phrase for stump. He bends his left arm and holds the forearm straight up. "Feel away."

She puts her hand over his wrist as if it's a stick shift she's gently polishing. This is going nowhere. This is just a gothic Las Vegas moment. He'll tell Lizzie about it in the morning. He suddenly does, however, have a full-bore erection.

"It's *so* smooth," she says. "Gosh! The tip is really hard." *Could* this be more squalid? A girl who plays Barbie's pal Stacey phallicizing his stump in public in an ersatz palazzo in Las Vegas—maybe it wouldn't really be adultery at all, more like a parody of adultery, some kind of permissible performance-art pastiche of adulterous fantasies. He's not serious; he doesn't think he's serious. She makes a little circle around his wrist with her index finger, and stops. Then, looking straight at him very intently, she lifts his arm with one hand and with the other flicks at its tip with one of her pigtails. He smiles. She smiles back, then looks at him hard again, no longer smiling. She leans her head and shoulders toward him a little awkwardly, and with both hands brings the tip of his arm to the tops of her breasts, and slides it slowly all the way down between them. She smiles, and then rearranges herself, twisting her back toward him. Now she is slouching on him like a girlfriend against a boyfriend, holding his arm inside her shirt between her warm breasts, stroking it through her shirt.

"My daddy's was all kind of bony and rough and bumpylike."

Sick? Very sick. "Your father lost a hand?"

"His whole arm, his right one, up almost to the shoulder. And his right leg to the knee. It happened in Vietnam. In Tay Ninh. During the Vietnam War? The country of Vietnam? That's why my middle name is Cindy."

"I know about the war in Vietnam. But I don't get the name."

"Because Daddy's fire-support base was called Cindy. FSB Cindy. He named me after it. He used to say if I'd been a boy he would have named me First Cav." She softly rubs the tip of George's arm through her shirt with two fingers. "Where were you in Nam?"

Exceptionally sick. "I wasn't. I'm a little too young. I lost the hand in Nicaragua."

"Nicaragua? That's in Florida, right?"

Exceptionally sick and exceptionally stupid. "Around there." George's erection surrenders. He feels fortunate. Time to go.

"Is Angela your wife?"

"No. Angela Janeway, the actress on TV?" No sign of recognition. "I produce a television show called *NARCS*?"

"*Oh,* you mean Jennie *O'Donnell*! I love Jennie!" She scoots even closer to George, so close her buttocks rise onto his thigh. "You're a producer? Can I be on *NARCS*?" Her tone is matter-of-fact. "I'd love to be on *NARCS*. Then I could get my SAG card. Which would be so fantastic." George is speechless. Her manner is friendly and forthright but nothing special, as if she's asked to borrow a pen, and it doesn't change as she adds, "I could like come back to your room with you tonight. I know it's bad to brag, but Donny, my manager, says I give the best head in Vegas. Seriously."

"No . . ."

"Or *whatever.*"

"No," George says.

Only now does she lower her voice a little. "You could do me with, you know, your hand. Your arm, I mean. Up my ass, or wherever, I'd be cool with." She's still being disconcertingly casual, no more salacious than a waitress reciting dessert specials.

"Sorry," he says, and with some effort stands. "Bye." To create the illusion of purpose, he walks briskly and starts looking from room to room.

If she hadn't mentioned the father? If she hadn't mentioned "Donny"? If she wasn't such a moron? If she was a nine instead of a seven and a half? If she wasn't *so* transparent, so weird, so Planet of the

Zombie Whores? No, please, God, he hopes not. He has too much invested in his sense of personal virtue. He has too much invested in fidelity—twelve unblemished years but for the asterisk of New Orleans. For New Orleans he forgives himself now as an oafish error, end-of-the-eighties acting-out, premarital cold feet, treacherous learning experience. But this, tonight, *Shawna,* would have reversed Marx—history repeating itself, the first time as farce and the second time as tragedy. Farcical tragedy.

"*George,* you *dog!* You okay? You want to come back to my private lair for a nightcap?"

"Where'd Bucky boy go? Down to create some wealth at the blackjack table?"

"You're still pissed over the real-marble bet, aren't you?"

"What is this wealth-creation-engine bullshit? I thought he was supposed to be smart."

"Hey! *Honest* is what I said he is. Come on. Let's go. Unless you and your little friend on the couch aren't through."

When they finally get to Ben's personal suite at the opposite corner of the floor, the quiet and perfect hotel tidiness is a relief, like slipping into a clean, cool pool. The light is dim. Three open laptops sit on a desk, one of them on, the screen full of numbers. A breeze flicks at the flimsy pages of a stock prospectus. As Ben goes to get drinks, George steps out onto the terrace. Sixteen floors down in the dark, the Grand Canal and its gondolas sparkle, hallucinatory and spectacular, transcending their own kitsch absurdity. *Like the real Venice,* George thinks.

"This is the business we have chosen, Michael."

Ben has stepped out next to George. George doesn't turn around.

"If that's supposed to be Brando, you suck."

"Duvall. Why'd you have such a hard-on for Bucky tonight? He's an okay guy. I thought we were supposed to like mavericks and long shots."

"It's this 'wealth creation' bullshit, Benny," George says, calling Ben by his old nickname. "It's stupid and dangerous."

"Dangerous? *Dangerous?* Are you going left-wing on me, George? You know, we're all free marketeers now. It's required."

"Okay, irresponsible. Undiscriminating. Sloppy. It's Tony Robbins infomercial talk. You know? 'Wealth creation.' Come on."

"Can we talk about something else? Did I tell you about my plan to buy Aqueduct and turn it into the only NASCAR track in the civilized world?"

"No."

"Oh, he's *moping*. Okay, there's a lot of sizzle with the steak out there. Too much. Point taken."

" 'Wealth creation' treats some bogus stock that's, like, *quindoubled* in two weeks as the equivalent of real earnings at General Motors. It's like Tinkerbell, the miracle happens because we clap our hands and"— George puts on a silly *Romper Room* grin—"*believe*."

"Yeah, but Tinkerbell can actually fly. She's actually magic. We're right to believe. By the way, can you tell me how to quindouble some of my positions?"

George stares off at a plane landing, gliding down, out of sight.

"You'll be pleased to know," Ben says, trying to change the subject again, "that we told Pat Buchanan's people they couldn't hold some family-values photo op at BarbieWorld tomorrow."

"I sort of like Pat Buchanan."

Ben looks at him. "You are just determined to be the orneriest asshole you possibly can be tonight, aren't you? Maybe you *should've* fucked that girl. Something."

George shuts his eyes. "Do you have any seltzer?"

"Seltzer?" says Ben, suddenly excited, ducking back in ahead of George through the terrace door, moving like an overwound mechanical doll. "I've got Pellegrino literally on *tap* in here."

As Ben skitters into his kitchen to push the Pellegrino button—hotel room kitchens: the ultimate useless dacha luxury, DIY on an expense account—George flops down on a big, cartoonishly asymmetrical burgundy couch, so soft and oversize it's more an homage to a settee than a settee. The glow of the laptop screen illuminates his face.

"Did you see your pal Buchanan on the news today?" Ben shouts.

"He *disagrees*. He *believes* things. What happened today? Some slur about the Arab League millennium boycott?" Since late last year, the Arab countries have made a great show of being aggrieved about the worldwide hoopla over the two thousandth anniversary of Christ's birth. One of the mainline Moslem groups called the American TV networks' live broadcasts of colorful "millennium celebrations" in Indonesia, Pakistan, Egypt, and Morocco "grotesque and imperialistic anti-Islamic fabrications." And they have a point, George figures, even though it's been hard to argue the case since the suicide bombing of CNN's Cairo bureau in January.

"No. Buchanan claims Panama is funding the Zapatistas. And he stands up in San Diego, right on the border, and says if even a single rebel platoon is spotted within a hundred miles of 'the Canal Zone'—he still calls it that, I guess it's this year's 'Nationalist China'—we should invade. He actually called a retaking of the canal 'America's right of return.' The guy is just *unbelievable*." Ben arrives with the Pellegrinos, which he sets down, and a bucket-size can of macadamias, which he opens with a bass *whoosh*. What a good sound. "Panama has only *had* the canal for two months, and already we're trying to steal it back."

George is stretched out on his back, arms behind his head, eyes closed. "What are we, Ben?"

"Uh-oh. Time for bed."

George opens his eyes. "No, I mean, we're not liberals, are we? But we're not conservatives. Are we?"

His mouth full of macadamias, Ben asks George, "Invade Mexico: pro or con?"

"What, we're playing the *McLaughlin Group* home game now? Against. But I guess I can imagine circumstances where we might have to do something."

The two main guerilla groups in southern Mexico jointly launched their "New Millennium offensive" a little over two months ago, on January first. It was the sixth anniversary of the Zapatistas' first big action, when they seized six towns in Chiapas in 1994. The guerillas' brilliant timing impressed George back then. The North American Free Trade Agreement went into effect that day, New Year's is always a news vacuum, and the first of the year fell on a Saturday, guaranteeing maximum play on the Sunday morning news shows and in the Sunday *Times* and *The Washington Post*. Not that their media savvy generated any enduring interest—the half-life of the story in the States was about two weeks. This year, though, now that the insurrection was starting to get some traction, the guerillas' New Year's timing worked well. The first of January once again fell on Saturday. Coming directly off the interminable syrupy wallow of millennium coverage, the TV news shows and papers and weekly magazines couldn't have been happier: better than Y2K snafus, Mexico was providing unembarrassing, unequivocal, old-fashioned hard *news,* week after week, pitting have-nots against haves right here in our hemisphere. Mortar attacks on hydroelectric facilities, shaky videos inside secret guerilla bases, revolutionaries with American mothers and brothers to interview in East L.A. and Phoenix, army officers smashing video cameras on camera. And plenty of three-hour nonstop flights to Mexico City. Last year's big rebel offensive started during George's final week at ABC, and it made him the most excited he'd been about his job in years. He had to remind the on-air people not to sound *gleeful* when they used phrases like "large Zapatista deployment in the dense Lacandon rain forest" and "the U.S.-supplied Huey gunships based just across the border in Guatemala's Petén jungle."

"Waiting for that trumped-up Gulf of Veracruz incident, are you?" Ben asks George with a smile. "You sound like Al Gore."

"Why do you still give money away to the Democrats, Ben?"

"I don't give money only to candidates."

"I know, I know. You're sending everyone at P.S. 148 to Wharton. You got Def Ex investment-banked." Def Ex is the new, black-owned overnight-delivery company that serves only the twenty largest cities in America.

"Excuse me for caring. Just because you won't give a dime to anybody, don't—"

"Ben, I can't. I couldn't. Journalists can't. But really, Benny, why do you give money to the Democrats qua Democrats? Abortion is not going to be outlawed. Old people are not going to be impoverished."

"It's my religion. I'll always be a Democrat. And I tell you, the more money I make, the stronger I feel that. I know there are Republicans who agree with us on every issue; most of the guys I do business with are like that. But those kinds of Republicans can't be *elected* to anything in a zip code that begins with a number higher than two. I'd rather be in a party where the wingnuts are multiculti union crazies than one with racist anti-Semite antiabortion crazies."

"So it's really just a question of . . . taste, right? It's just *unattractive* when people with money piss on poor people and tell themselves they're acting out of principle."

"I can't stand disingenuous rich people whining about high taxes," Ben says. "Or like when that right-wing ex-junkie on TV, the columnist, what's her name, the heiress who led the demonstration to stop clean-needle exchanges."

"Molly Cramer. I agree: it's *ugly.*"

Ben lifts off his chair for an instant and bellows, "Noooo! No, you've got it backward, George: that is *wrong.* It's *wrong.* It's ugly *because* it's *wrong.*"

George says nothing for a few seconds. He drinks his Pellegrino. "If there's a depression I guess we'll all care about politics again, won't we? Depression or repression. Or real U.S. intervention in Mexico."

"Which you'll be happy to support 'under certain circumstances.' Just like liberals in 1964 with Vietnam. Hey! That's what you are—not a paleoliberal, not a neoliberal. You and I are fucking *retro*liberals. Swank City liberals."

Ben, knowing he's won the round, settles down and leans toward George. "Just because nobody but me and people in the District and a few nuts give a shit about politics right now doesn't mean your beliefs aren't real beliefs. It isn't all 'taste.' You're still more offended by Molly Cramer than you are by, by . . . some ugly zoom shot or something, aren't you? Or polyester?"

"Yes. I am. Absolutely." For the first time all night George smiles and means it. "Although zoom shots are hip again. So's polyester. Get it straight, man."

Ben puts his feet up on the giant wooden coffee table and tips back in his chair, which is a kind of thickly upholstered burgundy throne. "That's why Americans love the market. The rules are clear. And we believe in the rules. And it's exciting, like sports! Everything else is fuzzy. Marriage, sex, religion, art, politics, all that." He glances at the computer screen, where the time, 12:12, is flashing. "Seminar's over. London opens in twenty minutes. A couple of the biotechs are still going crazy from that 'mental modem' horseshit last week."

"It was fun," George says, and gets up to leave.

"Whoa!"

George turns. Ben is scrolling through the Reuters wire. "What?"

"You see what your network did after the close tonight? Announced a new issue. Twenty-five million ME shares! What does Mose need a billion dollars for?" Ben turns from his computer to face George. This seems not to be a rhetorical question.

"Let me go call Harold right now and ask." He puts his hand to his forehead in a salute. "Good night, Benny."

"I smell roll-up!"

"Okay," George says, opening the door, his desire for bed overriding the impulse to ask Ben what he's talking about. "I'll see you."

Getting from the rooms to the elevators in big-deal Las Vegas and Disney World hotels is inevitably depressing, since in the hallways all expense is spared on the theming. The fantasy bubble is burst. It's like seeing a nightclub in the daytime, without even the redeeming stench of ashtrays and perfume and day-old booze.

"*Hey!* Where'd *you* go?"

It's Shawna. He sees she really is sexy, in the thin-lipped, do-a-little-crank fashion of the prettiest checkout girl at the Safeway. Maybe she *is* a stalker. Maybe she's about to pull out a razor blade from between her breasts, and with an unearthly animal cry bare her dripping vampiric fangs. He pushes the down button. She is too close.

"I went to get some air," George says. "With a friend."

"So, like, I've got rubbers." Of course you do, because you have AIDS; the prospective details—*rubbers!*—haven't even occurred to him. "And like I said before, you can do, you know, totally whatever you want to do to me." She smiles her quick, guileless, automatic American smile. "Come *on,* we'll have a blast."

No, not a razor blade, not fangs. She's more android than beast.

"I'll pass," he says.

"Okay. Cool. Hey, one piece of advice?"

Don't stick your arm down a woman's shirt if you don't intend to have sex with her? That's very astute advice, Shawna.

"What?" he says.

"You've *got* to go see the Mandalay Bay. The Sea of Predators has *real* crocodiles and sharks. It's just exactly like a fairy tale my daddy used to tell me."

The elevator door opens and he lets her on first.

"A gentleman!"

George finds himself chuckling uncontrollably.

"*What?*" Shawna says, wanting in on the joke.

"Nothing. It's—I've had a long day."

She reaches between her breasts and pulls out a necklace strung with tiny plastic luggage tags. She snaps one off.

"This is my card."

SHAWNA CINDY SWITZER, ACTRESS is ink-jetted in cursive letters.

"Now," she says as they reach the lobby, "if you ever have any parts you think would be right for me, call. Okay? Or if you just want to, you know, talk." George is now almost entirely sober, but it's impossible for him to tell if by "talk" she means *have the dirtiest sex imaginable,* or *talk.*

"Okay," he says.

"Nighty-night."

As she walks out into the lobby, cheerful as a coed in a Mentos commercial, George, destupefied, presses the button for his floor. *So, like, I've got rubbers!* He has never in his life worn a condom, never even touched one. In this, as he once argued during a *Newsweek* story meeting, he's part of a singular baby-boom subcategory of the condominnocent—heterosexuals whose promiscuous years occurred during the decade and a half after the Pill, before herpes and AIDS. Nonmarital intercourse without condoms, George thinks as he switches off the light and the TV and falls into the crisp and frigid hotel sheets: another dying twentieth-century art, like operating a television manually, and reading (and sniffing!) those damp paper copies with the purplish type they had in grade school. The sixth grade, maybe seventh, was the last time he had been in a conversation about rubbers, using that word. *So, like, I've got rubbers. And you can do, you know, whatever you want to me. Totally whatever.* The *to* in "to me" was, of course, the most acutely pornographic bit of a remarkable pornographic performance—the carte blanche invitation to enter some dark free-fire zone, achieving maximum erotic power in its unconsummated ambiguity.

The phone rings. Christ, maybe she got his room number.

"*Hal*lo. May I help you?" he answers slowly, in a badly faked English accent.

It's Lizzie, speaking softly. "I'm calling George Mactier. Is this room 4063?"

"Hi. It's me, sweetie. I, I—"

"What's wrong, George? Why the funny voice?"

"Nothing. I'm fine. I just thought you might be this insane actress. She wants a part in the show. But, anyway, why are *you* awake? Is everything okay? You weren't home when I called earlier."

"No, I know." She's walking around their bedroom, cordless phone in hand. "I just wanted to hear your voice. I can't sleep."

"Hi."

"Hi." She pauses. "George?" she says a little plaintively.

"Yeah?" He is so happy to be talking to her. He is so happy she's about to admit that she's been advising Mose behind his back. It's cute, in fact, how difficult this is for her. "What is it, sweetie?"

"Microsoft offered five-point-five million for fifteen percent."

"Ben told me. That's good. Isn't it?"

"Yeah. But now they want warrants to buy almost half the company."

"Right." She's not going to mention Mose.

"I don't think I want to do it. I think I want to tell them no. Is that okay?"

"Sure. Why?"

"I don't know. A little because of Virtual Fortress. Five million isn't enough money to make me forget I wanted them all dead three years ago." Virtual Fortress is the company Microsoft crushed shortly after Lizzie signed on to run it. "And if I ever end up joining their fucking cult, or anybody's, I really want to *join* it, not become an auxiliary member with their cult spies looking over my shoulder."

"You think it'll piss them off? Turning them down?"

"Maybe. A little, for a little while. But I'm tiny. And sustained anger is too irrational for those guys. And you always say that when you tell people no, they end up wanting you all the more."

"It's up to you."

"I know," Lizzie says, pacing. "I know it." A mile south of her in the Buttermilk Channel off Governors Island, the foghorn blasts its long, slow, old oboe wail. Hearing that sound is one of the things they like about the Seaport. They also like that their neighborhood isn't much of a neighborhood at all, that living at the Seaport doesn't *mean* much of anything to the world, as living in SoHo or the Upper East Side or Brooklyn does. "Did you hear the foghorn?"

"Uh-uh. Lizzie, why don't you ever touch my, you know, hand? My left arm?"

"What do you mean, George? I do. What do you mean?"

"I mean in an affectionate way. Or when we're making love. It was just a thought I had. Like it's a part of me you consider off-limits or—"

"No. *No.*"

"—or something. I don't know. I miss you. I guess I'm horny."

She sits on the edge of their bed. "Come home."

"I'll get there late, eleven something. I'm going from MBC to the hospital to see your dad and straight to the airport."

"A reporter from *Time* called. About Daddy. I haven't returned the call yet." Johnny hops onto the bed and, arching his back, presses himself against her naked hip, rubbing hard against her. Lizzie pushes the cat away.

"I told *Newsweek* no this afternoon. We can't talk to *Time* if we aren't talking to *Newsweek*. So, tell the *Time* guy we want to keep it private." He thinks. "Tell him your father's condition could be jeopardized if there's too much fuss."

"It's a her. You want me to lie?" The cat returns for more insistent Lizzie-rubbing, and she tosses him off the bed. She thinks of Buster Grinspoon's experiments: she would pay for a device that makes it possible to tell Johnny she likes him and will pet him later, but she finds his pressing and purring creepy now, because it's three in the morning and she is naked. She wonders if there are livestock applications for Grinspoon's technology. Letting milk cows and dairy farmers negotiate optimal milking times. Or linking the jockey and his thoroughbred. Or persuading beef cattle that this dark chute doesn't really lead to stun guns and blood-speckled saws but to a fresh pond and sunny drifts of clover.

"It may not be a lie," George says.

"Maybe. Oh—I talked to your friend Hank Saddler this afternoon."

At last, George thinks. He hates feeling suspicious. Maybe telling him about Mose just slipped her mind, with everything that's going on.

"Saddler," Lizzie says, "asked me to let the Army use ShowNet. To keep track of Mexican rebels or something. He was awful. I told him no."

George says nothing for a couple of seconds. "Okay."

"You're not angry, are you? I don't think Saddler or Mose or anybody will be pissed at you because your crazy wife's not a team player. Will they?"

"No. No. I don't care," George says, leaving just a bit of chilling space between sentences. "Thanks for letting me know about it." Why isn't she telling him about Mose? He thinks, but doesn't believe: *I should've fucked Shawna Cindy Switzer.*

"I can't wait to see you," she says, in the oversincere voice she uses when she's trying hard to reassure him. The effect is nearly always the opposite.

"Me too," George replies. "Bye."

"I *love* you," Lizzie says.

"Okay. Thanks," George says. "Tell the kids I love them." *Mimeographs,* fruity-smelling bruise-colored mimeographs, the grade-school artifacts he couldn't remember earlier.

"Have a safe trip."

As he hangs up, he notices the red light blinking. The message, he learns, is a return call from "the office of Michael Milken." Not Milken, but his *office,* and calling, according to the female assistant with the standard Sunbelt playmate voice, "on Tuesday afternoon, from Pingxiang, in Jiangxi province in the People's Republic." What on earth, George tries not to wonder as he closes his eyes, does Milken want?

1 2

Waking up alone, without a partner's scrutiny, means waking up more slowly. At least for Lizzie it does. It's as if her senses are on a rheostat instead of the regular on-off toggle. Not that George ever tries to make her feel lazy as she lies on her side some mornings for ten or fifteen minutes, watching the three rhombuses of sunlight brighten on the bedroom's one mottled old plaster wall and creep downward, listening to the racket of the last of the fish men tossing their iron tools and empty crates back into their trucks and gassing away. But her awareness of his awareness of her lying there awake makes her feel like a neurasthenic Pacific Palisades housewife, some pretty slug.

Now out of bed, fully awake, going barefoot as usual from bathroom to computer to closet to kitchen, but not needing to wait to let George finish at the sink, not needing to pivot an unconscious inch as he passes by to pee, performing the morning ablutions ballet all by herself, she feels loneliness drifting in. *Yeesh,* she thinks, looking at the pillow creases on one cheek and red filigree in her eyes: at thirty-five she simply no longer has the facial resilience to drink three quarters of a bottle of wine and sleep for only six hours. Does George ever look at his morning-after face, she wonders, and indulge in this kind of penny-ante self-hatred? Vanity will make her drink less, just as vanity, rather than the prospect of lung cancer and emphysema, has made her quit smoking cigarettes. Quit buying cigarettes.

When she returns, topless, to the bedroom, she is surprised to find Max sitting cross-legged on the floor, staring straight ahead as if meditating. He's wearing a small black backpack with some kind of red snorkel sticking out of it, and twisting a knob on a little black box. On the backpack is a stitched-fabric DuPont logo, and on the black control unit a hand-painted label that says ss. Max is not meditating.

"Hi, Mom."

"Hello, Sir," she says. "Contacting your alien friends?" She grabs one of George's dirty T-shirts and pulls it over her nakedness.

"I'm recording indoor-pollution data. For Science and Society. I've got to do it in three different places for three days. We live in a dense fog of dust and skin cells and toxins and smoke, but don't realize."

For an instant, Lizzie actually thinks he has recited a haiku. Max got an A in creative writing last quarter, which was Haiku and Limerick; this quarter it's Imaginary Autobiography. "After you're done recording indoor-pollution data you're going to have about two minutes to eat breakfast."

"I already microwaved Eggos for LuLu and I. The toaster broke."

"LuLu and *me*. Rafaela's not here?"

"No. She's scared of the microwave, anyhow. Oh, Mom, last night I deleted one of your e-mails accidentally. From someone named Fanny at fuck-dot-com or something." Max is delighted with the opportunity to say *fuck* to his mother.

"What were you doing in my e-mail?" It must have been from Fanny Taft, the girl from Minnesota who wants a summer internship.

"It was by accident! You had your password loaded in and I logged on without realizing it was your Fine-Technologies-dot-com account and then I thought the e-mail was some pornographic spam, so I deleted it without reading it. Sorry. I also deleted an e-mail about OSHI Gas Wars or something—"

"Max! *Jesus!*"

"Don't yell! I thought it was spam about some Nintendo 128 game."

The brownnosing this morning at the checkout desk in Las Vegas was extreme. "We're all so glad you had a chance to visit the Venetian *yourself,* Mr. Mactier." But George finds he no longer reviles this kind of American ultrahospitality—he plays along, indifferent to whether it's fake or real, since it's always *nicer.* It's like the permanent sunniness of Los Angeles. He understands in theory how it could get annoying and even slightly scary after a while, like a clown's painted-on smile, as Lizzie says, but George has never felt the oppression. Rather, his emotions correlate with southern California weather in conventional ways: on gray, rainy days, like today, he feels cheated, as if the city has been deglamorized wholesale, its raison d'être washed away.

Aside from the drizzle and colorless sky, he feels nauseated. "Under the weather": hangovers generate cute, sour, cheap little ironies like that. Exacerbating the dark mood, or vice versa, is his anger at Iris. Iris who failed to get any of his *Real Time* files to the hotel before he left. "You didn't *tell* me you changed the name from *Reality* to *Real Time,* George," she blubbered when he woke her up at home in Queens at four-fifteen this morning. "I didn't find any files labeled *Real Time,* so I didn't FedEx any. How was I supposed to know?"

He finds himself cheered a little as he passes into the San Fernando Valley. Because the Valley is inherently dispiriting, the drizzle and the gray improve it in some relativistic way—the lousy weather and the Valley are in synch on a day such as this. Burbank seems less like a failed paradise manqué, and more like Cleveland.

Until late 1998 the MBC complex in Burbank had been a run-down Mose Media Holdings greeting-card printing plant and, next door, the low-slung stucco offices of a bankrupt pornographic-video company. With the two dumpy neighbors now joined together by a brand-new seven-story glass silo with open-air walkways, the MBC West Coast headquarters has been transmogrified. A critic in the *Los Angeles Times* wrote last summer that "the Mose complex looks as if it were built from scratch, not cobbled together from mid-century bits and pieces. It is collage as corporate compound, cleverly mirroring the essence of the feisty 'New Network for the New Century.' " Hank Saddler, as delighted as Mose by the critic's flattering post hoc concept, started spreading the word that feisty-collage-as-corporate-compound was, of course, precisely Harold's intention all along.

EMILY KALMAN, NARCS! Stenciled in yellow on the asphalt! George is new enough to the business that these banal conventions still give him a gol-*ly* tingle. He also feels some envy seeing the empty EMILY KALMAN, NARCS space—stupid envy, since he has spent about ten days here in the past year and can always find a place to park. But of course, visible corporate perks like personal parking spaces and good seats at bad black-tie dinners have a value distinct from any desirability—they are advertising for one's personal brand, George Mactier®, conveying the message of mojo to one's colleagues. Having the perks but preserving (and conveying) a regular-guy indifference to them—that's the trick.

In the bullpen outside Featherstone's office, which occupies half the top floor of the new glass tower, all three of his unsmiling assistants are softly and intently speaking into wireless headsets and watching animated icons and windows of data—the middle-aged black woman with straightened hair in a minidress; the sly young Asian man in a velour shirt; the older horse-faced white guy with close-cropped dark hair and bangs wearing a turtleneck. A woman with a blond Lucy Baines haircut and a tight-fitting blue cashmere pantsuit, evidently the receptionist, suddenly appears out of a sliding pocket door at the back of the reception area. George assumes that the uncanny resemblance of the office to the bridge of the *Enterprise* on the original *Star Trek* is coincidental, or at least unconscious.

"Hello, Mr. Mactier," she says. "Timothy will be just a few more minutes on the phone, but he'd love you to join him. May we get you a Perrier? Konappuccino? Osmanthus tea? A nectar?"

George decides against asking for a complete list of the nectars available, or for a precise explanation of the difference between nectar and juice. "An espresso would be great. A big one."

She pulls her own tiny headset mouthpiece up and says softly, "Hector? *Uno dopio.*" She leads George back through the sliding door into Featherstone's semicircular office. On the wall, to the right of a pristine black granite oval desk, is a very large whiteboard, virginally white except for the word HITS! written in blue marker as if by a professional sign painter. A cable connects the board to the computer, which has a flat monitor, larger than any George has ever seen, as big as a poster—in fact, Featherstone's screen saver is a poster, a solarized Warhol portrait of Featherstone made in 1986. Built into the black plastic frame around the screen is a black glass eye, which George assumes is one of the digital cameras Timothy has raved about. On the side of the desk, by the window facing the foggy Hollywood Hills, is a four-foot-high black steel arch with a curved beige leather pad attached to its summit. The thing might be mistaken for sculpture if Featherstone were not now draped face up on the leather pad, his whole body bent in a backward curve. He holds what looks like a polished silver cannonball in each hand. He notices George, arches his brows, and enthusiastically waves one stockinged foot, apparently an invitation to sit in the plastic egg-shaped easy chair.

A tiny microphone, attached to a miniature black boom, is suspended two feet above Featherstone's mouth. Before the receptionist leaves, she stoops to press the purple rubber earpiece deeper into Featherstone's ear. As George sits down, Featherstone continues his conversation, straight up, into the little mike.

"*Because,* Jiminy Cricket, we don't *have* gross talent. No gross actors. No gross anybody. Period. Yes, Steven *is* a de facto gross producer, but listen to yourself: de facto! De facto! De facto is not de real thing, my man! Bottom line, this is a net, net, net company. But our nets are *real.*" He pauses. "Touché, Jimbo. But we're only eighteen months old. They will be real, down the line. The New Network for the New Century, man, isn't just a *slogan.*" A dark young waiter in a nubbly umber suit and sandals brings George his espresso, and places a glass of pink liquid—nectar?—on the black granite oval. "Don't go there, J! Do not go there! We'll both be unhappy if you go there! This is not a daypart conversation. Okay. Okay. I love you, too, Jamie. *Adiós.*" He waits a moment. "End call," he says in a different, calmer voice toward the microphone, enunciating very clearly.

He drops each silver cannonball, with two muffled thuds, into the fur-lined leather cannonball canisters on the floor. "*Ahhhhhh!*" he moans as he hops off like a gymnast. Then, evidently in a state of rapture, he doesn't speak.

"Hi, Timothy." Having spent twenty minutes the night before last listening to Emily talk about her Pilates machine, George has had his quota of exercise talk this week, and points toward the smaller of the two giant conversation pieces now in front of him. "Impressive whiteboard. Never seen one that fancy."

Featherstone opens his eyes and dives across the desk to grab his nectar. The video lens on the computer's digital camera is programmed to respond to movement, to find the human and focus, but Featherstone is too quick, homing in on George with a little more vim than George is ready for. George stands.

"Mr. Mactier is *in* the *house!* Yeah, my Smart Board." They both stare at the board. "Connected to el PC, which recognizes the different colors of markers. Truly spine-boggling."

"What do you use it for?"

"It's brand-new. Brainstorming, you know, fiddling with the schedule and stuff. Ng wants to use it for an art piece. The monitor is a plasma, BTW." He turns back to George. "Anyway, are you ready to take it to the hole, G-man?"

"What?"

"The presentations! I'm pumped! I want you pumped! You're good to go, right? You got your decks?"

"Absolutely. What's the plan?"

"The worst first. Twelve hundred hours with your friend Barry Stengel. And Jess."

Jess Burnham is the on-air star of MBC News, coanchor of *News-Night 2000,* their thirty-three-year-old Tom Brokaw, their energetic Peter Jennings, their lesbian Dan Rather.

"Timothy! Why is Jess Burnham part of this? Come on. This is no good."

"Jess is here anchoring the convention. Hey, sit. Sit. Caffeinate. Chill."

"It's a primary."

"And she's very interested in this project. You have some baggage with Jess?"

"No, I barely know her. But we can bet that a Canadian who just spent a year in Cambridge as a Nieman fellow is going to think *Real Time* is some horrible, dangerous, Jerry Springer piece of shit. She'll hate it, Timothy. She'll hate the idea. She'll freak."

"Give her your journalist's secret handshake. Better Jess starts representing sooner rather than later. Gives us time to pull her back onto the reservation. George, Harold gets and loves the show. I love the show. The MBC is down with it."

"You know if she makes a big enough stink before we're even up and running—"

"Seduce the lady, Jorge! Hip her to your concept! Take it to the hole! Any*hoo*, after Barry and Jess, we've got lunch with the whole sales and marketing and promotion posse. Get *them* jiggy for it. Where's Emily? Or are you totally DH-ing this today?"

"She'll be here. . . . I talked to Lizzie about your mental-modem idea. I'm really not sure we can use it in *NARCS*. We're a little too married to reality, I think, for it to work."

"So it's, like, totally bogus?" says the fifty-year-old head of the network.

"No, Lizzie thinks it may work. In a few years. The inventor, this guy Grinspoon, wants to come to work for her."

"So maybe using wired-up animals to smuggle dope—hey, *mules*, literally! Or freaking out the DEA dogs at the airport with scary dog thoughts. Work with me. Use it."

"I don't know. Maybe."

"Cool! Lizzie really is our technogoddess, isn't she?"

Our? "I guess she and Harold have had some useful conversations."

"Yeah. He digs her."

Digs? "So what is it Harold wants to do online? Is there some secret MBC internet strategy I should know about?"

"*Should* know about?" Featherstone says. He looks amused. "Those who know don't say, those who say don't know. You know? Harold wants the stock price to keep climbing up the north face. That's his internet strategy."

This is getting nowhere, except giving Featherstone the opportunity to act superior and knowing. "Didn't Jess give you hell last fall for putting on *Freaky Shit!*?"

"SFW, George. And her problem with *Freaky* was that it's low-rent, not that it's, you know, '*wrong.*' Relax, man."

"Speaking of *Freaky*, a doctor I met told me that at some lab in Ukraine they're attaching weasels' heads onto badgers. It sounds like a piece for them."

"Hey, man, we're way ahead of you! They're doing a whole Frankenstein special. There's some old guy right here in town who just got a liver transplant—from a frigging pig! Do you believe it? Barry says we may be able to get the TV exclusive. Oh! I forgot the zowiest part! The old guy is a rabbi or something! It's like, he can't eat pork but he needs it in him to live. Talk about dramedy. Talk about edge. It doesn't get any more edgy and dramedial than that."

"Sorry!" Emily says as she rushes in. "Really sorry. I was on a call I couldn't roll." George is afraid he knows the excuse she's about to give. "With the vice president."

"Hickory dickory dock!" Featherstone says, kissing in Emily's direction as he rushes out in search of an assistant. *"Faith?"*

"So," George says to his partner as soon as they're alone, "I guess the administration is just getting your input on whether they should use incendiaries or regular ordnance against the Zapatistas?"

"Funny."

"I hate being stuck alone with Timothy," George whispers.

"Sorry. Timothy hates being alone with Timothy. So you have that in common."

"Does DH-ing mean being a designated hitter?"

"Uh-huh."

"How about 'taking it to the hole'? " Whenever George fails to understand slang or recognize some obviously celebrated name, he infers the reference is to sports. Lizzie often says she married him because he's "America's only sports-oblivious heterosexual man." Emily, on the other hand, even goes to Rams and Clippers and Ducks games.

"The guy with the ball runs past guards to shoot."

"In basketball."

"You're pathetic, George."

"Timothy just told me to 'take it to the hole' at the meeting with Stengel and Burnham. Did you know we're meeting with Jess Burnham, too? I thought it might have been some sex thing."

"Even more pathetic."

"And SFW? That's short-field . . . something? Baseball?"

"SFW is 'so fucking what.' "

Featherstone bursts back in. "*¡Vamanos, mis amigos!* Our nooner awaits."

———

She mildly disapproved when Sarah wanted to buy the thing last fall. "If you won't let me get a tattoo until I'm eighteen, Mom," her daughter snarled, "then you have to let me get a pager!" Since Lizzie had no real antipager arguments (*Drug dealers and prostitutes use those things, young lady!* wouldn't work) she gave in to the tattoo trade-off. And today she's glad she did. Rafaela called in sick this morning—sick, or something: "Cannot work today, Missus, sorry, goodbye" was the message. Lizzie paged Sarah at school—CAN YOU BABY-SIT KIDS AT 3:30?—and ten minutes later Sarah responded by e-mail, SURE I'LL BABY-SIT. (WHAT'S WRONG WITH RAFAELA?) This is exactly the sort of incident that makes George hum the *Jetsons* theme song or say they're like the happy, efficient animatronic family of the future in the GE ride at Disney World.

And here is the part of that future too boring and odd to depict at any Epcot exhibit: the high-tech executrix, sitting alone, staring at a plastic computer monitor, reading an unreadable internet article about changes in the law covering foreign workers' visas, while eating her ten-minute lunch. Ordinarily, her lunches are standard, spartan, career-girl guiltless—fresh vegetables, shreds of protein, room temperature to cool, no carbohydrates, directly out of a brittle plastic container sold by South Koreans, washed down with some zero-nutrient beverage. (Her one somewhat bathetic concession to gentility is silverware, which she keeps in her desk drawer and which Alexi washes in the bathroom each afternoon.) But today she had Alexi order her a grilled cheese on challah and a giant vanilla shake from downstairs, and already she is reviving.

Bruce has lurked near her office off and on all morning. She knows he wants to talk about going into business with Buster Grinspoon. And now she almost feels up to telling him no. She does find the science thrilling. And maybe she'll be passing up a trillion-dollar jackpot in 2009—*Sorry, Mr. Edison, I just don't see how these electrified tungsten illumination devices of yours can ever be practical*—but so be it. If she agrees to bring in Grinspoon, it would be to please Bruce, and to flatter herself that she is engaged in work more consequential than Y2K gimcrackery and movie-crew messaging and impeccable digital fur. She needs to focus the business, not pick one project from column A, a couple more from column C, no, that's column *D,* and—*whoa!* cool!—a really risky new one from column Q. Brain-to-brain data transfer, indeed. Her conviction is too iffy, the odds too long. Ben Gould agreed with her that for Fine Technologies to invest in Grinspoon's technology would be nuts, the equivalent of the baby-sitter squandering her entire savings on Lotto. (Lizzie was so upset the morning Rafaela matter-of-factly showed her the two hundred losing lottery tickets, she wrote her a check for two hundred dollars that same afternoon, after extracting a promise that she would never play the lottery again.) Still, she'll meet with Buster Grinspoon in Seattle.

"I spoke to your Minnesota girl," Alexi says, standing in Lizzie's doorway, "and she's very excited. She was like, 'I'm like *stoked*.' And this?" He's holding the printout of Lizzie's memo. "Do you want me to messenger it up to MBC or what? *The* MBC, I mean." Before she can swallow her bite of challah and cheddar and tell him to FedEx it to L.A. and e-mail it to hal@mosemedia.com, he adds, "Do you realize you always overindulge when you go out with Pollyanna? The last time was the day in December we split the entire box of Krispy Kremes and you drank the quart of milk straight out of the carton. And the time before *that* with Pollyanna was the day you were like—"

"If you're about to use the word *coenable,* get out. And if this is some kind of an intervention, Alexi, you're fired."

Her telephone is doing its interoffice tweet. It must be Lance Haft. No one else in the office uses the intercom.

"E-mail and overnight it, Alexi." She reaches for the phone. "Please. Hello, Lance." She sighs. "Yes, I have. We are not going to accept the Microsoft proposal. I am not. I am we. Yes. Yes. Of course I'm aware of all my fiduciary obligations, Lance. No, I'm not saying the door is closed, I'm saying that today, five-point-five million for fifteen percent of the company is unacceptable."

———

Barry Stengel and Jess Burnham have two monitors on, simultaneously watching MSNBC's and CNN's coverage of the California primary as Featherstone, Emily, and George sweep into the conference room. Hearing the CNN correspondent say that "our exit polling arguably has some potentially worrisome signs for the Gore camp" reminds George of how deeply uninteresting he finds most TV news, especially the bleating about politics. It never changes. There's something Soviet in its unvarying tedium and one-note self-seriousness. You could take the tapes of the 1996 election coverage, dub in "Gore" instead of "Dole" and "Democrat" instead of "Republican," and rerun them this year. Maybe on *Real Time* in November he'll have them program a computer to write and deliver live election results with voice-synthesis hardware and a digitally animated newsreader: "Based on our exit polling, the MBC is declaring. *Al Gore.* The winner in the state of. *Massachusetts.* By a. *Substantial.* Margin of. *Seven.* Percent. If that result holds up, that will give *Gore* an additional. *Twelve.* Electoral votes." Artificial semi-intelligence. Just to upset the Barry Stengels of the world.

"Hey, Stinger! And my dear Ms. Burnham." George has never before witnessed Featherstone addressing anyone except his own assistants and Harold Mose without a nickname—although, when he thinks about it, "Ms." probably counts as a nickname. Neither stands, but Jess Burnham turns toward them and blasts a smile. Stengel, with a remote control in each hand, presses the mute button for both TVs, and gives a glum nod.

"Jess," Featherstone says, "this is Emily Kalman, and—you must know George Mactier, don't you? Couple of high-end journalistas like yourselves."

George leans in to shake her hand. They have met twice—in 1996 on a tour of the *Titanic* set in Baja California (they were both playing hooky from the Republican convention in San Diego), and last spring under a tent in Central Park during MBC's presentation of its new shows and stars.

"I don't think I do," she says, shaking his hand, "but I'm a big fan of your work."

"Thanks," George says. "This is my partner, Emily Kalman."

"Timothy," Stengel says without looking at George, "you know we need to be out of here by twelve-thirty. We've got a national security briefing at twelve forty-five with Ambassador Holbrooke, and Jess is locked into a one o'clock tape time with Senator Bradley." We are serious. You are goofballs.

"Hey, *I'm mano a mano* with the *boss* at twelve forty-five, post-nap," says Featherstone, chuckling, as he sits down at one end of the table, "so we will definitely wrap on time." Mose famously naps at noon every day, since he also famously sleeps only three and a half hours a night. Last Christmas, Hank Saddler mailed out five thousand copies of the pro-napping bestseller *Always Rested and Rarin' to Go: The Energizing Power of Just-In-Time Sleep Scheduling,* in which Harold is mentioned prominently. "And George and Emily have a few things on their plate, too, Barry—like producing the MBC's megahit."

George and Emily look at each other, each chagrined to be on Timothy Featherstone's side in a shoving match, George thinking Stalin and Hitler, Emily thinking King Kong and Godzilla.

Hank Saddler appears, doing his speed-waddle, palms raised in some nonverbal sign of apology, smiling and nodding to everyone, especially Jess Burnham. George marvels at people in television who never get their appetite for star fucking slaked. Maybe that's why they work in television. Saddler sits at the opposite end of the table from Featherstone, next to Burnham.

"So," Featherstone says, "we know you have some concerns about the *Real Time* concept, Barry, and Harold and I—and George and Emily—want to give you a chance to get them out on the table from the get-go. This is transparency time, okay?"

Stengel turns to face George and Emily, pushing his elbows down hard on the table with a lot of body weight. This is clearly a man climbing onto a very high horse. His body language says, *I'd go over there and knock some goddamn sense into you if I could.*

"This fall, I will proudly celebrate my thirtieth anniversary in broadcast journalism," he says. *Is that Tom Snyder you're impersonating,* George thinks, *or Ted Knight?* "I'm proud of the news division we've created at the MBC, brick by brick, during the last year and a half. I'm proud of what we stand for." *Which makes you prouder—your piece on the East Asian economic crisis where the segment producer had the twelve-year-old Thai prostitute repeat the fellatio three times so his crew could shoot cutaways, or the Golden Gate suicide where you enhanced the jumper's midair scream— to make it, as you said at the time, "real but sweetened"? You were probably proud in a different way of your bulletin about Clinton's nonexistent heart attack, and your two-hour special on the ex-wives and girlfriends of all this year's presidential candidates (which didn't even win its time slot against Moesha).* "George, you've spent time in journalism. You paid a few dues. You used to do some very decent nonfiction work, as I recall." *Fuck you, you patronizing, stupid, sanctimonious, middle-market news director asshole.* "I just don't understand how you think you're going to get away with actors playing broadcast journalists. Or journalists trying to act. Or whatever the hell you have in mind. Maybe it'll get ratings. But it will probably damage American journalism, and it will definitely damage the reputation of MBC News."

Stengel leans back in his chair, proud and spent. Saddler has been taking notes. Everyone looks at George.

"Well, as Timothy said, we do appreciate your concern," George says. "And your confusion." He turns to the anchor. "Jess," he begins in the scrupulously neutral fact-finding tone with which journalists and prosecutors ask tendentious questions. "Do you write what you read on *NewsNight 1999*? On *NewsNight 2000*, I mean."

Stengel rolls his eyes. Burnham half grins. They both know where George is going.

"I tinker," Burnham says. "I polish."

"But you deliver stories and lines other people write for you—you perform scripts drafted by members of the Writers Guild of America East, the same union my *NARCS* writers belong to."

"I didn't know that," Featherstone says.

George is still looking straight at Burnham. "Before commercial, during your bumpers, when you're still on air for that long shot of the studio—"

"The *newsroom*," Stengel corrects.

"—why do you scribble notes, or frown and dial the phone, or collate sheets of paper?"

"Because I'm still on air."

"Right."

"Because if I checked my makeup or stretched or ate pistachios or pulled out my copy of *Martha Stewart* I'd look dopey." She smiles at him.

"So you're doing a performance of seriousness. You are a serious journalist. *And* you play one on TV."

Stengel says to Featherstone, "This is just semantic goddamn BS."

"Let's say you turn to Bill Rossiter for cross talk after a piece about, oh, the president's anal warts, and you feel like laughing—you don't dare smile, right? You fake a very, very sober expression and tone of voice. Right?"

Her grin widens.

"Or when you have a live back-and-forth with a correspondent in the field," George continues. "He knows what you're going to ask, and you know all the answers to the questions you're asking—so you have to *portray* curiosity. Right? That's virtuoso acting. Or when you shoot the subject of a story pretending to talk on the phone or pretending to examine a bullet hole in a doorframe. And at the top of the show every night, that jump-cut black-and-white taped piece of you and Bill and the producers interviewing and opening files and editing—was every bit of that real and spontaneous? And when correspondents do cutaways and ask their tough, probing questions to thin air—"

"Come off it, Mactier!" Stengel snaps. "There's a hell of a big difference between standard packaging and presentational production value items, and a whole goddamn fake-news soap opera!"

"We're not going to be making up news, if that's what you think," George says, staying calm, even smiling a little. "The news we deliver every week on the Friday show, on the news hour, will be one hundred percent bona fide. As straight and accurate and professional and real as anything you put on the air."

Stengel makes a huffy whistling noise, half closes his eyes and shakes his head.

"You're the pioneer in laying music tracks under straight news stories," George says to him. "Didn't you tell *Variety* that's your 'secret weapon' against the major networks?"

" 'The *older* networks' is the phrase we use, George," Saddler corrects. "Not major, *older.*"

"On *Real Time* we won't even go that far—no scoring of news stories. No reenactments, like I've seen Rossiter do on *Point Blank.*" *Point Blank* is the weekly MBC News crime show. "Some of our behind-the-scenes shots will be fictionalized, yes. The two half-hours earlier in the week are going to be scripted dramas—"

"Dramedies," Featherstone interjects. "Dramedies."

"—into which we intercut documentary footage, handheld stuff, cinema verité—shots of interview setups, travel, story meetings, editing sessions. The reporting will all be one hundred percent real. The difference is that we'll shoot a lot more of ourselves doing it, and sometimes actors will be in the shots as well, delivering lines. It'll be like—like two parallel universes that intersect."

"How are viewers going to have any goddamn idea what's real and what's fake?" Stengel says. "They aren't going to be able to keep your little game straight."

George has not wanted to play the populist trump card because he isn't sure he entirely believes it, but what choice does he have? The hangover is emboldening, he realizes, the woozy sleeplessness overriding his usual reluctance to cut and jab. It's triage: defend *Real Time*, destroy Stengel. He even decides to address Stengel by his first name, a Dale Carnegie gesture he loathes, like winking.

"I guess I disagree, Barry. I trust the audience to understand the difference. They aren't thrown when people from CNN and the Sunday morning shows appear as themselves in movies, are they?"

"George," Featherstone says excitedly, "show them those decks from audience research about what happens to anchors' Q scores when they guest on *Leno* and *Letterman*." He turns to Stengel and Burnham. "We've got actual evidence!" He turns back to George. "You have those before and after charts, G?"

"No. No, I don't." Because Iris didn't overnight the files. So that's what "decks" are.

"Our research proves that viewers totally understand the difference between truth and nonfiction," Featherstone says. "Bill Clinton played the president on *NewsRadio*, and nobody was confused. Remember the celebs playing themselves on *Larry Sanders*?"

"That was HBO," Stengel says.

He probably has a point, George thinks. According to the MBC research, the lower a viewer's income and education, the more apt he or she is to confuse entertainment and news, fiction and nonfiction. George isn't about to cut Stengel any slack, however. He decides to take the full cheap shot.

"And we," he says solemnly and slowly, "are the MBC, Barry." Jesus, is he really making this speech? "As Harold says, the major networks—the older networks—were built on underestimating the intelligence of the American viewer. And now those networks are dying for the same reason. We're supposed to be programming for the people out there who *get* it."

"Harold's line," Saddler says, "is 'insulting the intelligence of the North American viewer.'"

"You're on a slippery goddamn slope here," Stengel says. "News is news and entertainment is entertainment, and everyone knows the difference. No matter how you try to spin it."

"Exactly," George says, careful to maintain a friendly, collegial air. "Exactly. And every week Emily and I are going to be producing a little less than one hour of news and a little more than one hour of entertainment. And everyone will know the difference."

"That's just such bullshit, Mactier. Glib, dangerous bullshit."

"No, Barry, I'll tell you what that is: it's *innovation*," says Featherstone, angrier than George has ever seen him, angry in a way—a passionate, appealingly phony way—that seems perfectly calibrated to shut Stengel up. "That's out-of-the-box thinking. That's keeping it real. And that's how we make this the New motherfucking Network for the New motherfucking Century."

George and Emily exchange a glance. Their spokesman and savior is America's oldest living wigger now performing the Act Three soliloquy from *Mr. Doggy Dogg Goes to Washington*.

"And Barry," Featherstone goes on, "I want to make sure you get this straight. From the top. *Real Time* is, sure as shinola, a ten-foot tent pole in this company's new broadcasting . . . new . . . what is it?"

"Paradigm?" Emily says.

"Our new broadcasting *paradigm*. New paradigms take a little courage, Barry, and a little faith. Listen, if Harold didn't believe strongly in George's ability to pull this off with integrity, none of us would be here. And we're here with you as a courtesy, okay? Out of respect. For you and Jess and the journalistic dream. *Not* to give you an opportunity to be the Blah-blah Old Paradigm News Bummer Guy. Entertainment is Mose Broadcasting's core competency. News is your core competency. But George is lucky enough to have entertainment *and* news as his core competencies. He's broadband beta. You're a sea creature, he's an amphibian. You're different species, but you both like water, okay? The four-one-one is: Don't go zero-sum on me. We are not about set-tripping. Play nice, respect others, and everybody wins. You have to make a decision, Barry, a choice: are you down with the program, or not down?"

George has never heard such deeply felt and stirring gibberish.

"Timothy, as the president and editor-in-chief of MBC News, I'm in charge of maintaining the whole network's nonfiction standards and practices. And I think I have an obligation—"

"*Real Time* is a go project. Period. Okay? The light is *green*. You don't have to work with George and Emily—"

"No," Emily says.

"—but working against them is a no way José. Big time. *Capice?*"

No one says a thing. Jess Burnham shifts her weight in her chair, leaning away from Stengel, turning herself into a bystander.

"Barry," George says, feeling suddenly magnanimous, "we're only going to share your *facilities.*"

"*Not* the news *brand,*" Saddler says.

"We're not taking any of your *air* away," Featherstone says.

"Or any of your on-air people or producers," adds George.

"My people? My people? I'm about to be downsized by seventy-eight people, thanks to you. Thanks to your brilliant wife. Who says our online news video is like a bunch of parrots squawking. Is that what you think too, Mactier?"

Not exactly—what George thinks, what he has been saying for years now, is that not just MBC but all video online is like a talking parrot, or as he says in certain situations, like Dr. Johnson's female preacher—a novelty, amazing but not compelling. So Mose *is* dissolving MBCNews.com, as Lizzie suggested. George suffers one of those complicated moments when fresh emotions (curiosity, satisfaction, a kind of emasculated dismay) are at odds with one another and with the expression (triumphant pseudo-empathy) still frozen on his face.

"Barry, Barry, *Barry,*" Featherstone says. "We've been through that. You know we're just trying to put all our wood behind one arrow. And hey, most of those online folks are getting lifeboated over to *Finale.*"

"The new obitutainment show," Saddler whispers in George and Emily's direction.

"Yeah," Stengel says to Featherstone, "last week you told me we'd be staffing up with entertainment-division people, this week it all comes out of my own hide. Thanks so much, Timothy."

"I don't remember saying that. If I did—"

"You sure did," Stengel replies, taking the offensive. "You absolutely promised me staff from *Freaky Shit!*"

George remembers hearing Stengel declare, somewhere, that he would refuse to work with staff from *Freaky Shit!* "But Barry," he says, "I thought you said you'd be a laughingstock if those infotainment banana-brains ever worked on one of your shows."

Stengel, stopped in his tracks, looks at George. He's actually breathing hard.

"Yeah," Featherstone says. "Right. That's right."

George, with a flash of panic, realizes where he'd heard Stengel's "banana brain" remark: eavesdropping from his cell phone in Minnesota. Fortunately, Stengel, cornered, tangled up in his own apoplectic dither, moves on.

"And Emily," he says, red-faced, looking back and forth between Emily and Featherstone, "what about your involvement with Gore? How's it going to look for one of the guy's biggest fund-raisers and major advisers to be producing a quote-unquote 'news' program? How the hell are you going to be able to cover Gore?"

" 'Major adviser' is really an exaggeration," Emily starts, "and certainly, if there's any question of—"

"Fuck Al Gore," George says, pronouncing each word with gusto, shocking his partner. "Emily's not going to be involved in shaping any of the news coverage. And we can't *wait* to be tough on him."

At the center of Emily's forehead, where she had collagen from a human cadaver injected during Christmas vacation in order to smooth out her first deep furrows, the muscles tense and bulge.

"Or Bush Jr.," he continues. "Or Dick Gephardt. Or Dick Holbrooke, or Dick Armey, or—"

"All the Dicks," Jess Burnham says.

Featherstone laughs enthusiastically (real but sweetened), and accompanies himself on conference table with a quick two-handed drummer's rim shot.

"Or Bill Gates," George says, thinking of Lizzie's and MBC's involvements with Microsoft, "or Michael Eisner or Katharine Graham or Rupert Murdoch," he continues, thinking of everybody's former employers, preemptively and gleefully full-disclosing, letting a hundred conflicts of interest bloom. "Or Mike Milken."

Saddler looks at Featherstone, who's still enjoying George's performance.

"Or even," George adds with a small smile, "Ted Turner."

Stengel's previous job was at CNN. When he left for MBC, he took a half dozen senior producers and correspondents with him. Turner, asked about the raid by an *Access Hollywood* reporter a couple of days later at the premiere of Warner Bros.' *Batman 5, Superman 5, Earth 0,* used the opportunity to refer to Harold Mose as "the Ho Chi Minh of broadcasting." When Turner's wife yanked on his arm, he stutteringly amended his dis. "What I mean is, uhhhh, Mr. Mose is the *Saddam Hussein* of broadcasting. The gentleman doesn't play by the same rules we observe in the civilized world."

Jess Burnham sits up and looks at George, then at Emily. "I don't entirely understand how your show is going to function. And it may be a slippery slope," she says, shrugging in Stengel's direction. "But I've got a house in Aspen." She grins again. "I'm afraid I kind of *like* slippery slopes." She checks her watch and stands. "You guys are going to have a gas. Let's go, Barry. Time to go hear about nonmilitary military aid to noncombatant combatants in Chiapas."

On the way back to his office, Featherstone does the talking. He congratulates George ("You literally rocked the house, man!"), and asks Emily if Gore's youngest daughter is interested in a TV career ("She was at some fund-raising gig the other night at the Mondrian— *born* spokesmodel"). As they reach the top floor, they see the blond receptionist squatting in Featherstone's office, evidently explaining a digital device to someone sitting just out of sight. She gestures out the door toward them, smiling a little nervously. The man holding the gadget leans toward her and cranes his neck to look. It's Harold Mose.

"Hello, *chief*!" Timothy says with sudden startling fervor, abandoning in mid-sentence his solemn, sotto voce description of a "proposed multiphase reengineering" of Bill Rossiter's on-air hairstyle. It's as if a bolus of time-released methamphetamine just reached his cerebral cortex.

Mose stands briskly. He is wearing a blue turtleneck darker than navy, plush gray trousers, and black suede loafers. He has no jacket. Harold Mose is the only man whose clothes George regularly envies. ("Two words," Featherstone said last year when Mose was named to the International Best-Dressed List. "Bespoke vicuña.") George seldom wears a tie, but today, as on any weekday that he wakes up feeling wobbly, he's put on the full executive costume, overcompensating, dressing the part of responsible adult. But now, in his unpressed gray suit and stained tie (a fresh dollop of room-service raspberry yogurt camouflaged, more or less, by maroon paisleys), George feels both under- and overdressed.

"Faith was showing me how she's able to track your every move with her GPS gadget here, Timothy." He looks over at George and Emily. "Orwellian, isn't it?"

"Motorola," Featherstone says.

"Do not *ever* tell Gloria about this thing," he says, tapping the screen. Gloria is Mrs. Mose. "She'd have me wired up in five minutes flat." He winks, then turns and heads back into Featherstone's office. It is a silent command, somewhere between rude and informal, that they are to follow him.

George is experiencing not just a Featherstonian wave of alertness, his own automatic teacher's-pet eagerness to please, but a glint of something else, like contempt, or fear. Maybe it's the hangover.

Mose leans against the front of Featherstone's desk, half sitting, his feet touching the floor, arms crossed low over his belly, casual but definitely proprietary. Featherstone leans against his black steel chiropractic arch, also half sitting, mimicking Mose as best he can. George and Emily, thus driven toward the couch, exchange a look. The bodies in the room have suddenly assumed a bad-news fait accompli arrangement, as if Mom and Dad are about to tell the kids about the divorce.

"So, my friends, what do you think of our schemes?" Mose says. "Are you both aghast?"

Neither has any idea what he's talking about, although each has a reliable generic answer to that question, no matter what the subject— *Yes* for Emily, *No, not really* for George. When Mose sees they're both baffled, his default wry smile disappears and he shoots a look at Featherstone—a sharp, hard look. *Thwack!* George's moment of pleasure is not malice, but rather the same kick of relief he feels whenever he watches the man (always a man) at the dinner party knock over the giant goblet of red wine. Nasty luck; thank God it wasn't me.

"I was just about to explain the whole megillah to them. You mean ABS, yes?"

"Correct."

Featherstone is still leaning casually against his exercise rack, but he has unfolded his arms. His bright eyes seem suddenly too bright, his tail not just bushy but painfully horripilated. "You know, George was a hero over there just now, and Emily too, but, Harold, our meeting with Barry and Jess got a little more . . ." He glances at George with a hey-buddy half grin. ". . . complicated than we expected."

Mose stares silently at Featherstone for another instant—*thwack!*— then turns to George and Emily. "*NARCS,* as you both know, is on its way to being a very profitable business for Mose Media," he says.

A very profitable business! What a fine, lustrous, grownup way to describe a cop show, George thinks, and Mose didn't even mean to flatter. *George Mactier, profit center.*

He continues. "You're familiar with the basic idea of securitization? Asset-backed securities?" Before they have time to say no, he starts explaining. "Essentially, any revenue-producing asset can be turned into a security, like a company's stock or a bond. Well, my bankers and I have an idea that we can do the same thing with our library at the MBC. With shows like *NARCS*."

"Like the Bowie Bonds, remember?" Featherstone says. "Backed by all the future royalties from David Bowie's songs?"

George knows they're getting the *Junior Scholastic* explanation, but even as he resents being patronized, he also knows he would be out of his depth if Mose and Featherstone were not talking down. Unlike sports, the minutiae of which he's sure he could understand if he spent the time, certain areas of finance are to George like theoretical physics or musical composition—simply beyond his ability to comprehend. He has had Ben Gould explain puts and calls and short-selling over and over, for instance, but he still can't keep it straight.

George realizes he's been tuning out Featherstone's even more rudimentary recapitulation of Mose's explanation when he registers Emily's skeptical, almost huffy tone.

"Meaning?" she is saying sharply to Featherstone.

"Meaning, my sweet M&M, that Mose Media Holdings and Well-Armed Productions need to snuggle even closer together in bed. You know? Grandfather in our affair before the marriage, so to speak. Make it kosher SEC-wise and all that Howdy Doody."

"In other words," George says, "you need our approval in order to securitize your half of *NARCS*?" He is proud of pulling *securitize* out of the hat. Twenty years as a journalist made George good at simulating authority—cutting to the chase, jumping to a conclusion, summing up glibly. Or is it a knack for glib summary and faked authority that made him a successful journalist?

"Correct," Mose says. "Precisely."

"Ah," says Emily, the hedgehog to George's fox. "I see." She understands one big-business thing: *leverage.* George sees her relax and go a little wide-eyed, as if some stupendous dessert had magically appeared before her.

"I'm sure it'll be no problem," George says, "but we'll have to talk to our lawyers."

His first flash of fear and contempt for Mose has simmered already into a congenial clubby chumminess. As a journalist, the only leverage he ever wielded was a not-unfriendly few columns in a magazine, or a two-minute interview on TV—theoretically wielded, since in journalism, explicitly exercising quid pro quo leverage seemed ignoble. But this is business. The horse-trading and self-interest are undisguised and unembarrassed. Shall we open the cognac? Light up the Cohibas?

"Of course," Mose says. "Although there is *some* urgency here," he adds. "Just for this room, we're planning to float a few new shares. And the underwriters insist we get all the securitizations in line ahead of the offering. You understand. Since it's a little unconventional."

"New Network for the New Century!" Featherstone says in a not quite rapped singsong. He looks at Mose, then, refolding his arms, says, "The other idea we wanted to test your waters on is co-branding. We're very close to a deal partnering with Smucker's for *Reunion*— 'Smucker's Presents *Reunion.*'" *Reunion* is the forthcoming MBC show, an "all-specials series," that has three installments already in the can: *Family Ties* (the Michael J. Fox character's daughter is a pierced Hillary Clinton intern, although Fox himself doesn't appear in the show), a *Hogan's Heroes* V-E Day show (minus Bob Crane and Werner Klemperer), and *Family Affair* (minus Brian Keith, Sebastian Cabot, and the little girl). "You guys wouldn't have any problem with possibly co-branding *NARCS,* would you?"

"Like, 'Seagram Presents *NARCS*'?" Emily asks. " 'Pfizer Presents *NARCS*'?"

"Well, could be, but a packaged goods advertiser probably isn't the ideal fit," Featherstone says.

"I believe Emily is joking, Timothy," Mose says.

"We would have a big problem with that," George says. He pauses and thinks of adding, *It would be bad for the* NARCS *brand,* just to remind Mose and Featherstone that he's a grownup, with commerce on his mind. He's pleased that Emily jumps in before he can.

"Major problem," Emily agrees. "Big time."

George and Emily look at each other, pleased and surprised to be in unrehearsed agreement on the side of virtue.

"You guys don't want to keep it on the table, nibble on it overnight?" Featherstone asks. "Think about it as a return to an old-fashioned tradition—remember *The U.S. Steel Hour* when we were kids? And I mean, you had no problem with the Prada deal? And we're all pretty coolio with the American Spirit gig, aren't we?" Last year, George, Emily, and MBC gave the fashion designer Miuccia Prada the exclusive right to dress the cast of *NARCS* for all their public appearances, and signed another deal selling product placement on the show to American Spirit organic cigarettes. The Kahuna character is a chain-smoker of American Spirits; the network has defended itself against criticism with what Saddler calls "the *X-Files* defense," emphasizing that it's only the show's *evil* character who smokes. "New network, new century, new revenue stream," Featherstone continues. "Co-branding would be money in the bank for all of us."

"Sorry, Timothy," George says. "Especially given the shit we're about to take from the Barry Stengels of the world on *Real Time.*"

Mose smiles and puts his hand on George's shoulder. "No wonder you married your wife. You're both a couple of liberals, and you both love telling Mose Media to stuff it."

George forces a smile.

"Say," Mose says, "I ran into your friend Peter Jennings the other night at some god-awful Canadian consulate event. He said he's very pleased that you've finally found your niche."

"Thank you so much, Peter."

There is a high-pitched *beep-beep* sound. Featherstone turns and says to the ceiling, "What is it, Faith?"

"Laura wanted you to know ASAP that Jason's people have committed to the MOW. And we're getting the life rights."

"*Yes!*" Featherstone says, and slaps himself five. "Awesome!" Then, to the room: "Jason Alexander, helming *and* starring in a reality-driven telepic for us for November sweeps. Total quality management! Eventissimo!"

Does Mose enjoy Featherstone's ridiculous jargon for the same reasons he built the soundstage on Fifty-seventh Street, because it reminds him that he's in show business, makes it palpable, the same way some men enjoy women with preposterous synthetic breasts? Watching Timothy do an ecstatic pirouette because he has persuaded a former sitcom second banana to direct a movie of the week, George marvels at his boundless hair-trigger capacity for excitement over the trivial, his demonstrative enthusiasm—his "passion," as they say out here.

Too much happens too quickly. An hour and a half later, after asking Featherstone if his MOW liver-transplant rabbi happens to be named Mike ("NFI, my friend"); after the quick *Real Time* lunch with the MBC sales staff ("Instead of like having an *actor* play the president on your show," one dim bulb suggests, "you could have him be like just a voice on the phone, like Charlie on *Charlie's Angels*"); after Saddler's confidential suggestion that George hire a communications coach ("I think she could help you evolve a more welcoming speaking style, with friendlier hand gestures, to draw people into the George conversational realm"); after Emily's explanation of NFI ("no fucking idea") and a farewell that is abrupt even for her ("I'm late, we'll talk"); George is weak-kneed with relief and exhaustion, finished for the day with corporate song and dance, overstuffed with undigested raw intelligence (about Mike Zimbalist, MBC News, Mose Media Holdings, Lizzie), and headed out of the Valley, away from the slough. Speeding past a shopping mall called Media City Center and onto the Hollywood Freeway, he mentally rewinds, fast-forwards, cues up, and plays again and again the meetings with Mose and Featherstone, Stengel and Burnham.

Mostly he dwells on the inconsequential moments—such as Mose's reference to "your friend Peter Jennings." What did Mose mean, precisely? His usage was surely not the mocking form used for one's embarrassing acquaintances (*Your little friend on the couch,* as Ben said last night in Vegas, or *Your friend Mike Milken,* as Lizzie would soon start saying). Maybe the irony intended was the softer, specifically intercorporate form of "your friend," which refers to almost any employee of any competitor—the consorting-with-the-enemy connotation. Or did Mose mean to insinuate that Jennings actually slagged George? Or was it, he thought hopefully, definition four, the version used only to refer to famous people and meant to imply, gently, that one is a starfucker?

George used to make a point of referring to celebrities, even when he knew them well, by their full names. Lizzie called it his "Charlie Brown rule." Now that he's in show business, he's become less rigor-ous. A few months ago, after a *Vanity Fair* photo shoot with the *NARCS* cast, he mentioned at dinner that he'd had a nice chat "with Annie, at her studio." "Really?" Lizzie said. "With *Annie?* And were Demi and Lorne and Arnold and Leo also there?"

He is reveling some in the humiliation of Stengel, but even more in the endorsement of *Real Time* by Jess Burnham, the $2.9-million-a-year anchor, the star, the talent. What a surprise! What a fine example of the upside of George's ritual pessimism! Burnham may be a Canadian and a Nieman fellow, but she's also young enough, it turns out, to have been spared the ravages of Edward R. Murrow Disease, that knee-jerk sense of pseudo-regret about the passing of the putative golden age of TV news—of *broadcast journalism*. He has detected sparks of mischief and self-deprecation in her on-air persona all along, he's pretty sure, his mind now collapsing into a kind of fond revisionism as he drives back into L.A. She's not a prig. Hell, she let MBC fictionalize her *name*—how could she object to *Real Time?* On Canadian TV, as their Washington correspondent and then as an anchor, she was Marian J. Burnham. Saddler convinced Mose that Americans would more easily embrace an anchor with a one-syllable nickname, like Dan or Tom or Ted or Jim, and so out of her middle name, Jessica, Jess was invented. Does Burnham know, George wonders, that one of the reasons she was hired over a newsreader named Maureen O'Connor was the luck of syllabication? "*Burnham* is a highly anchor-appropriate surname," one of Saddler's lieutenants wrote in a confidential memo that made its way to George, "both nonethnic and bisyllabic with the accent on the first—like *Rath*-er, *Bro*-kaw, *Kop*-pel, *Jen*-nings, and *Lehr*-er." Also, maybe her sexual orientation makes her more open-minded about unorthodox crossbreeds of news and entertainment. She is definitely open-minded: after Saddler changed her name, she also let him stage-manage her outing—the planted story in the *Star* about a nonexistent affair with Anne Heche, Burnham's good-humored denial a few days later, her semiautobiographical prime-time MBC special a week after that.

He starts feeling a little queasy about stumbling into a de facto alliance based on mutual willingness to play fast and loose in the name of airtime—slippery slope, slippery slope, slippery slope, slippery slope. Then he realizes he's gone too far down La Cienega and missed the turn for George Burns Road. The rain is getting him lost. Making the U-turn, he sees it's five of three, he's late to see Mike Zimbalist, and his plane's at four forty-something. Jesus Christ. He'll have to take a flight tomorrow. That'll be another whole day wiped out. *Jesus Christ!* He's made himself anxious again. He's overreacting. Why is he so perturbed? It isn't the hangover. It isn't the extra night in L.A. *No wonder you married your wife,* Mose had said, squeezing George's shoulder, with that grin.

1 3

There is nothing but a six-inch-high black dollar sign on the door of Bennett Gould's office suite, which occupies a grand space near the top of the Woolworth Building, a suite of offices almost untouched since the building went up in 1913. (Ben moved there a decade ago, after he made his first twenty million and George told him his offices in a new Water Street high-rise were "cheesier than necessary.") Almost everyone calls the company Bennett Gould, like Goldman Sachs or Morgan Stanley, even though Ben's firm officially has an unutterable name—since 1989 it has been $, simply $, on the letterhead and corporate records. "Kind of like Yahweh," Ben tells people, particularly if he thinks it will upset them. Messengers and deliverymen and the security guys downstairs generally call it "the dollar-sign company." He has thought about changing it twice. First in 1993, after the singer Prince changed his name to a typographic symbol and people started teasing Ben that he ran "the hedge fund formerly known as Bennett Gould." He was ready to change again this past November, after a seventies-themed clothing and tchotchke shop called ☺ opened in TriBeCa and the same week the *Times* ran a story about a trademark fight involving a new magazine that called itself ®. Both times George and Lizzie convinced Ben to stick with $.

Early every day from seven-thirty until about nine, and again every afternoon from four-thirty until seven, Ben phones and e-mails and meets with the managers of the businesses he's started or helped start—the BarbieWorlds, the DefExes, the CompuCares, his new NASCAR buddies. From nine-thirty until four, however, he buys and sells stocks and options, mostly for his own account. Technically a hedge fund, Bennett Gould Partners, LP, is still the centerpiece of $. But Ben has made so much for himself that he's now the fund's largest investor by far. Some of his investors have left him for more orthodox money managers, money managers who wear suits and don't buy up acres of New York billboard space in order to keep it blank and who wouldn't think of telling a *Wall Street Journal* reporter, "I'd have personally given Bill Clinton a blowjob to keep Bob Rubin at Treasury." He has also thrown investors out of Bennett Gould Partners when they displeased him, particularly the "goddamn rich weenies (nothing worse than *rich* weenies)" who second-guessed and badgered him in October '87 or August '90 or September '98.

Back at work after his two days off in Vegas, Ben is unusually revved. "Let's ramp!" he announces to the occupants of the Big Room—to his assistant Dianne, whom he brought along from *Newsweek* fifteen years ago, and his two traders and his analyst. It's nine forty-four, and Ben is trading. For most of the seven or eight hours a day that he's trading, Ben sits in his Big Room, rather than his private office, at a horseshoe cluster of desks with the staff, looking and tapping back and forth between his eight computer screens. He has his hinged, two-screen Bloomberg terminal (for bond and commodity prices), his Reuters terminal (for news), his Bridge terminal (for charting stocks), and four ILX screens for stocks—one for the thirty stocks that make up the Dow-Jones average, another for the NASDAQ 100, another for the stocks in which he holds positions right now, and the other for stocks he's considering buying or shorting. He likes using all the screens at once, but the real reason for eight computer screens is redundancy—systems crash, and Ben has no intention of letting the technology ever stop him from trading. For e-mail, he has a PC.

Right beneath one of the ILXs is his turret, the big, gray computerized phone, a state-of-the-art diptych of telephony, with rows and rows of names—Morgan, Goldman, Lehman, Smith Barney, First Boston—displayed in white on little blue screens.

Ben thinks out loud, barking buy and sell orders to his staff and making phone calls that rarely last as long as a minute. Almost every day he's a fountain of adrenaline, like a bureau chief on election night, or a squadron commander during a mission, or a teenage boy who takes his video-gaming way too seriously. Although it is only a slight overstatement to say that Ben Gould lives to trade, he knows he's just about too old for this. He's told himself that the years of sloughing off faithless investors is phase one of the exit strategy; that he will change professions with the century; that he will quit trading stocks when Cal Ripken quits playing baseball. Taped to the top of his Bloomberg terminal is a cheap black plastic sign George Mactier gave him for his thirtieth birthday, now cracked almost in half and held together with Krazy Glue and staples. THE TEST OF A FIRST-RATE MIND, it says, IS THE ABILITY TO HOLD TWO OPPOSED IDEAS IN THE MIND AT THE SAME TIME, AND STILL RETAIN THE ABILITY TO FUNCTION. It's an F. Scott Fitzgerald line—which is why, George explained back in 1984, he had it printed with no attribution, so that Ben could display it without looking like a jerk.

Ben prepares to make his first trade of the day. It will be the first of eighty-seven trades over the next seven hours, in the course of which he will buy and sell stocks and options worth $28 million. This will be a typical day for Ben. Right now, he has decided, he wants to buy puts on General Electric. He sees it's trading at 112⅟₁₆. He happens to believe GE stock will decline in value between now and the middle of May. Puts are a way to sell a stock short, to bet that its price will go down during a specific period of time, the next week, the next month, the next ten months. A put is like the insurance policy that gives a homeowner the right to rebuild his house for its full value, what it's worth today, should it happen to collapse during the term of the policy—a put on 100 shares of stock gives an investor the right to sell those 100 shares at their full value, what they're worth today, if the price of that stock happens to collapse during the term of the put. ("The *fantastic* part," Ben loves saying when he explains this to civilians, "is that with puts, I don't have to own the house—I get the payout when my *neighbor's* house is destroyed!")

Ben lifts his head a few inches, looks over the Bloomberg screen at his derivatives trader Billy Heffernan, and says, "Hit the wire, Billy. Get me a market in the GE May 105 puts."

"The screen market is 1¼ a half." They can buy GE puts for between $1.25 and $1.50 a share.

"What's it good for?" Ben wants to know how many he can buy without pushing the price up.

"It's 500 up market," Heffernan tells him.

"Buy me 500 GE May 105s. *Puts.*" Every put is the tail wagging the dog of 100 shares of common stock. Ben is telling Heffernan to buy 500 puts, a bet on 50,000 shares of GE dropping below $105 a share by the third Friday in May. Derivatives, puts as well as calls, expire on the third Friday of the month.

"You got it," says Heffernan. He punches the button for his options trader on the derivatives desk at First Boston, whose name is Dowd. Until the last decade, almost all the options brokers were Irish or Italian, $450,000-a-year Great Neck men with $42,000-a-year Middle Village fathers and brothers, which is one of the reasons Ben fired his Yale brother-in-law, Kip, in 1987 and hired Heffernan straight out of St. John's. Only in the last decade have the options desks started gentrifying, with fewer street kids, more MBAs, and a very few women.

On his screen, Ben sees that the put-to-call ratio for Mose Media Holdings is high and rising, 324:120, meaning that a large majority of his peers and their Heffernans are voting against the stock. On one of the ILX monitors he sees that Mose Media is already down 1⅞ to 33⅞ this morning. Ben decides to buy.

"I want to get long Mose," he turns and says to his other trader, Frank Melucci, who negotiates all of Ben's orders for common stocks. "I want to get in something big. Get me a floor picture of Mose."

Melucci punches the button on his turret next to the name of his favorite broker on Goldman Sachs's trading desk to buy Mose Media Holdings stock for Bennett Gould Partners, maybe a million dollars' worth. Melucci's conversation with his Goldman broker will be tape-recorded, and so was Heffernan's call to First Boston. Every brokerage house records every trading call these days.

The broker at Goldman calls his floor broker, who goes to the specialist booth—the Goldman employee who actually deals with the stock of Mose Media Holdings. And in less than a minute, back up the human chain the information bubbles, the floor picture that Ben wants.

Melucci describes the market to his boss. "There's 10,000 Mose offered at 33¼. Another twenty-five at 33½. So, we can take 35,000 between here and a half. You want to take them?"

He can buy 35,000 Mose shares for about $1.2 million. "See what he can do for me. Have him go upstairs, see if they have some to go on their desk."

Melucci covers the phone with his hand. "We're looking."

"Is he real, or is he trolling? I want somebody with merchandise."

A minute later Melucci says, "Goldman can stop you at an eighth." Meaning they'll sell the stock at 33⅛.

"Yes. Stop me at an eighth on the 35,000."

Ben hasn't taken his eyes off his screens during his conversation with Melucci. As on the monitors on brokers' and traders' and investors' desks all over Wall Street, all over America, all over the world, the pixels forming the names and prices of the stocks and bonds and options that have appreciated in value since the market opened at nine-thirty appear in green. The names of companies that have lost value during the last half hour are in red. Whenever a thousand shares of any stock are sold by anyone anywhere the name of the company flutters for a second on Ben's screens.

"Why is *Dugger* up?" Ben says, looking at the green letters and digits, not so much asking as thinking out loud. Bennett Gould Partners is a very large holder of the stock of Dugger Broadcasting, which operates TV stations, cable systems, and movie theaters in the Pacific Northwest. "Sinclair and Chris-Craft are red. Viacom's red. Why is Dugger so green?"

"The *market's* up seventy," says Cheryl Berger, his researcher and analyst, whom he employs in part to deliver the conventional wisdom on demand, which she reliably does. "The *screen* is green."

Most of his friends and all of his employees play along with Ben's experiment in extending the binary color-coding to personal correspondence: since 1998, the texts of Ben's e-mail messages containing bad news have been red, and good-news e-mails are green. He got the idea from Sasha. She disapproves of his modification of her system—he sends and receives certain ambiguous news in regular black type. "But, Daddy," she remonstrated, "*all* news is either good news or bad news. You just don't always know it yet."

"Hey! Pete! Hi!" Ben says into his phone to the chief financial officer of Dugger Broadcasting. "How's it going, man? Happy spring."

Ben hasn't talked to Peter Sutherland about business for a week, because it has been against the law to do so. During the last twenty-four days of each financial quarter, the SEC doesn't permit investors like Ben to talk much about company business with corporate officers like Pete. During the first sixty-six days of each financial quarter, however, the Bens are free to call the Petes to pry as much earnings information out of them as they can. Since the quarter still has weeks to go, the no-talk period is on, and Ben, who for the moment owns 351,000 shares of Dugger Broadcasting, is unable to speak plainly with his good pal Peter Sutherland (whom he has met face-to-face only once). But he can still call, just to say hi . . .

"I read about you in the *Journal,* Ben, you naughty fellow."

"I've always said I'm too honest for my own good. Congratulations on your quarter, man."

"Uh-huh."

"You got to love those thirty-two-percent margins, Peter."

"Uh-huh."

"Are things still good?"

"Well, you know . . ."

"I know what? I know every quarter can't hit it out of the park. That, I sure as shit know. But, so, are things feeling good?"

There's a long pause. "I can't say, Ben."

"Hey, I know," Ben replies, finishing with the encoded portion of the conversation. "I know you can't. And I know you won't tell me if Riley is still talking to Mose about swapping your station group for Mose's shitty Canadian theaters." He has double-clicked Sutherland's name on the PC screen and opened a window containing the names of his wife and four children, and the children's ages.

"By the way," the CFO says, unable to resist Ben's feint, "the offer from their side has always been assets *plus cash.* A lot of cash." He pauses. "As you know, Ben, the board and Zane do not exactly see eye to eye on that particular strategic issue."

"Hey! I say if the chairman and largest shareholder wants to become a Hollywood guy, he ought to be able to go for it. Dugger Broadcasting *is* Riley Dugger. In my opinion. So, Marcie is good? The kids?"

"Family's super. Thanks."

"Remind Andrew and, uh, Jason they've got Yankees skybox seats waiting for them if their workaholic old man ever brings them to town."

"Andrew and Jasper. I sure will, Ben. You stay out of the papers."

"I can't guarantee you that," Ben says, changing JASON? to JASPER, then clicking the Sutherland box closed. "I'll talk to you soon, Pete." Before the receiver is back in the cradle, Ben is shouting to Melucci, his common-stock trader. "Shit quarter for Dugger. Start unloading. Sell 150, 200 today. Not too fast. Work it. But I want it *all* off the sheets tomorow."

"What happened?" Berger asks.

"One quarter of so-so growth, everybody explained away okay. But back-to-back quarters of so-so growth, and all these momentum longs who think Riley Dugger is some kind of bumpkin Midas are going to freak fucking out. Frank," he says to Melucci, "you *got* to get out of the 200,000 Dugger today."

"Ben?" Dianne says. "It's George Mactier on three-seven."

He takes the call because it's George, but reluctantly, because the market's just opened. "Hi. What is it? I'm a little jammed."

"MBC told us a month ago they want to securitize their half ownership in *NARCS*. Is there any reason I should say no?"

"I'm not a lawyer. Call your guy, what's his name, at Paul, Weiss."

"Thanks a lot, Ben."

"Hey! It's nine fifty-seven, man!"

"I know, but we're supposed to tell them yes or no right away, they're about to do their stock offering, and I just wanted, you know . . . sometimes the lawyers don't know the big picture."

"Sometimes? Never. So Mose is ABS-ing individual *shows,* is he? Interesting. Let me call you back a little later, okay? I'm really jammed here."

"Okay, but—Ben? You follow the company some, yes?"

"They're way oversold."

"Oversold meaning the price is still dropping?"

"George! *Yes!* I got to go, man."

For five, ten seconds after he hangs up on George, Ben stares into the middle distance. The two traders, sitting eight feet away, know that a period of silence this long means one of them is about to get an order. When Ben's quiet extends to fifteen seconds, both men wonder what's bothering him. Melucci looks over.

"Frank," Ben says, "get me another 10,000 Mose."

1 4

The *sun*! Today's sun break (the local phrase) has lasted a couple of hours already, since before lunch. It's chilly, it's March, but because of the sun break, a dozen people are on the grass, five of them playing Frisbee and all but one wearing at least one garment made of polyester fleece. (Polartec is so ubiquitous for hundreds of miles around that it is now beyond stereotype, like black on Manhattanites and tans on Angelenos, like scales on fish.) The buildings are big but low, made of brownish brick, blandly symmetrical, neither friendly and picturesque nor cruelly lean, vaguely modern but lacking any modernist conviction. This is the newer, classier campus, but the place is as style-free as possible without being ugly (which would amount to a kind of style), *nice* in the prosperous hinterlandish way of people who spend no time thinking about haircuts or tradition or spectacle. On the cement stairs hugging the little fake waterfall—that is, the *water feature*—a young man with lank gray hair sits with a bare foot, using a spoon to clean the treads on the soles of one of his sneakers. He's thinking about Fibonacci numbers and singing along with a Yes song ("I've seen all good people"), a song exactly as old as he is, playing through wireless speakers plugged in his ears. Two men climb the stairs past him, the younger one wearing a

St. Olaf College sweatshirt over shorts, with sandals and dark purple socks, and the other, over fifty, the oldest person in sight by more than a decade, wearing a tie. But the tie is a bow tie, self-conscious and eccentric, so it doesn't quite count as a tie. (It's like the way stylish men in L.A. and New York wearing three-button $3,100 Armani suits buttoned only at the top aren't *really* wearing suits.)

"What does your Russian limousine driver in New York want?"

"Nothing. We happened to call Yuri—his old lead had a question about telepresence he wanted to kick around with him. And Yuri asked him about 'Booster Grime-spawn' and Fine Technologies, and here we are."

"This is a trustworthy guy?" the older man asks. "And he understands what he heard and saw?"

"Definitely. He got his master's under Buster Grinspoon at U-Dub Comp Sci. He helped write some tools that shipped, Japanese Windows 98, and then we used him as a contractor in Research. On user interface and telepresence. His leads say he's a very high-bandwidth guy. They wanted him to stay, but he has a wife and some kind of family business in New York." He opens the door for his colleague. "The leads tell me he was an absolute straight shooter."

"Absolute straight shooter—is that right, Gary?" Moorhead asks, looking at the younger man to see if he catches the irony of a conscientious snitch.

He does not. "Uh-huh. And as far as I'm concerned, what he happened to see were unencrypted objects distributed in an open environment. It was Yuri's vehicle. And no NDAs were signed."

Moorhead, wondering if his colleague may be attempting humor now, referring to papers left on the backseat of a car as "unencrypted objects distributed in an open environment," looks at him again. But there is no trace of a smile, only that look of earnest, untroubled self-confidence that is the default demeanor of executives here.

"Just to get some more data on this, I contacted a friend over at U-Dub this morning, who—"

"You didn't e-mail, Gary, did you? This is definitely one of those no–e-mail subjects."

"Oh, no. I phoned. And he says Grinspoon has been talking about moving back east."

Moorhead, considering this, seems both bewildered and amused, as if by an account of the shenanigans of a bright but willful child. The two men pass a Foosball machine whose playing field is filled by a five-foot-high pyramid of empty Mountain Dew cans, and a video arcade game, Gravitar, circa 1984, flashing its rudimentary, elegant white silhouettes of planets and gently thrusting spacecraft. Moorhead prepares to board a shuttle bus back to One Way, the main campus. (Fifty-two years old, a man of stature and means, taking a plebeian little van from office cluster to office cluster! Only his 243,000 shares and options mitigate the gall.)

"Well, Gary," Moorhead says, "these are very useful data to have. Thank you." And then, as the shuttle heads out for the main campus, he speaks into his wireless phone. "Adam, I'm just leaving Red West? As soon as I'm back I'll need to speak with Elizabeth Zimbalist? At Fine Technologies in New York City?"

1 5

Saying no had not been a negotiating posture. She adored saying no. Her no meant no. She wasn't intending to push the number up.

"You play a very impressive game of hardball, Ms. Zimbalist," Moorhead said. "We'll need your answer tomorrow by noon Pacific time?"

She wasn't meaning to play hardball. When she told Lance Haft the number, he thought she was pulling some kind of sophisticated Harvard joke on him. Then he literally couldn't speak.

"My God, Lizzie," he finally said. "My God. You called their bluff and they blinked. Stock? Vested stock? Not options? My God. What made them blink? My God."

She wasn't trying to call anyone's bluff or make them blink. She wanted them to leave her alone, let her stay doofy and small and amateurish.

"You're acting spooky, Mom," Max said when she came home.

"Did Daddy die?" LuLu asked.

"Sarah," Lizzie said. "Take the kids over to Uno's for pizza. Please? I'm fine. I'm good."

She doesn't want to talk to anyone about it—not Ben, not even the children, not even in bowdlerized kiddie-speak—until she can tell

George. She didn't tell her father when he called from the hospital to announce that he had agreed to let MBC make a TV movie about his operation, starring "the chubby bald superstar jerk from *Seinfeld*." ("Why aren't you pissed at me for this?" he said. "What's wrong?") It doesn't feel like she's hit the jackpot. It feels more like she's been in an accident, but an accident in some other universe, where getting decapitated is not necessarily a bad thing. Being alone hasn't restored her equilibrium, nor has the glass of wine. Doing yoga in the bedroom for twenty minutes, down dog *and* corpse pose, has not helped her realize her eternal nature as pure awareness, which transcends all duality and yearning (and which, as the poster in the dressing room at Yoga Place also says, is the ultimate goal of human existence for which all other labors are merely preparatory), or even diminished her desire for a Marlboro Light. Smoking a cigarette isn't helping, either.

Why *is* she acting so spooky? Why is she sitting cross-legged on the filthy black roof, in the cold and the dark, staring over at the big time-and-temperature sign on the Brooklyn waterfront? So that she can witness the 10° C flash off and—at just the instant she happens to be watching, change to 9° C—so she can entertain the notion that some momentous countdown is under way.

You're acting like a fucking girl, Lizzie Zimbalist, she thinks, *like some L.A. dope.* She stands and stubs out the cigarette on the chimney, making a tiny ash graffito, and then, for no reason she knows, takes cautious tiny steps toward the front of the house, mincing up the incline of the cornice toward the edge, and peeking out and over, four floors down. As her vertigo swells and passes, she sees a black Town Car turn down Water Street and come to a stop in front of the house. George is home. She watches him step out in that get-it-over-with fast motion he has, with a suit bag already draped over his bad arm, then reach back inside for the carry-on bag, then slam the car door with his hip. She has seen him make this series of moves dozens of times, maybe hundreds. But she has never really *watched* him do it. The bird's-eye view is clinical. She is a Georgeographer, a spouseologist. She has never before studied her one-handed husband and thought, *So plucky! Pluck.* Pluck is precisely what she admires in George, she realizes, and in herself when she can muster it.

Honey, guess what? she does not scream down. *Microsoft wants to buy half the company now!* And then she does not leap out over the rotting wooden cornice and, as she descends magically to the cobblestones right in front of George, add, *For thirty-one-point-five million!* Fuck.

———

Five hours later, the bass-laden snatches of a white rap song no longer radiate down to Lizzie and George's bedroom from Sarah's ("Scissors cut paper / Paper wraps rock / Rock smashes scissors"), but George is so tired he can't fall asleep. "It's the jet lag, I guess," he says when he turns the lights back on. And, of course, the electricity of greed, his anticipation of Lizzie's seven million dollars worth of Microsoft stock. She hasn't even tried to sleep. They have talked and talked and talked. Their brains are sore. Both of them are sitting up in bed, naked, both with Grandma Mactier's ripped and faded patchwork quilt pulled up almost to chest level. Both are staring through raised knees at *Badlands,* on the Miramax Channel, which is muted.

"So what in God's name," she says, holding the hand-rolled cigarette off to the side of the bed, toward the cracked-open window and its concealing breezes, "do you suppose that means?"

"It's not a sex thing. I know what it means."

"Yeah?" she says in a choked voice, holding her breath, looking over at him.

"Featherstone uses it. It's like 'do me a favor.' 'Can you do me a prop, George, and lose the greeting-card crack from your first act?' "

She exhales. "Are you making this up?"

"No. *Jesus,* Martin Sheen is *so young.* He is so much cooler-looking than his sons. Was. Don't worry about Sarah. Some boy at school must have done her some kindness. Carried her books to class, given her a ride home." George gingerly takes the burning cigarette from Lizzie's fingers. "Paid for her abortion."

Lizzie grimaces and nods in acknowledgment of the joke. "I've never heard of Felipe. *'Felipe* did me a *prop,'* she said. I felt kind of sick when I heard her say it."

For a couple of seconds, holding his breath, smiling, he says nothing, then exhales smoke between his knees toward Sissy Spacek.

"Is she still married to Sam Shepard?" Lizzie asks, pushing her hair, her entirely natural hair, behind her ears with both hands. She has always worried she looks like Sissy Spacek with a perm and henna.

"It's not her, it's Jessica Lange who's married to Sam Shepard. But they're not *married*."

He holds the joint out toward her, but she shakes her head, and he turns and drops it, barely lit, into a turquoise-encrusted sterling silver cuff-link box that Mike Zimbalist gave him a few birthdays ago. It springs shut with a loud snap.

"Bruce is all bummed out we're not going into business with his friend Grinspoon."

"I have no idea what you're talking about."

"God, we *have* been apart. Bruce's friend, Buster Grinspoon, the user-interface biomimetics genius—the mental-modem guy. Bruce wanted me to buy Grinspoon out and move him to New York and spend half a million bucks a year on his cat-brain experiments. I decided I couldn't afford it. And it's not what we *do*. I guess now I could afford it, with the Microsoft money." She pauses. "That is, Microsoft could afford it." She pauses again. "How weird. How completely fucking weird." And then: "Shall we have a party? A big spring party. With everybody we know? I feel like we need to get back in touch. We never had the housewarming we said we were going to."

"Is this a party to not celebrate Fine Technologies' liquidity event?"

George is curious but also joshing, and he knows Lizzie understands this, and Lizzie knows he knows she understands, so they both stare straight ahead, watching Martin Sheen and Sissy Spacek make out.

"Maybe so," she answers. "I ran into Cynthia on the street yesterday. She quit the agency! Just *quit*. 'To garden for the summer,' she said. I was jealous."

"Like you are of Buddy?"

"I'm jealous of Cynthia and Rich because they're the kind of people who you could imagine just giving up the rat race and moving to, you know—to Portland."

"Which Portland?"

"Either Portland. Any Portland."

"My phone finally died." My *phone*. In his present state of mind this seems freighted with meaning. "I just realized that nobody says 'cell phone' anymore, or 'mobile phone,' or even 'wireless phone.' It's just 'phone.' "

She nods. "You still call e-mail 'e-mail,' though, right? In Seattle I've heard people call e-mail 'mail' since, I don't know, 1997."

"I remember as a little kid," he says, "noticing one day that everybody had stopped saying '*transistor* radio.' Sometime after 'Purple People Eater' and before 'Satisfaction.' "

" 'Purple People Eater'? Was a song?"

He smiles. "Yes. From a few years before the presidential assassination that happened before you were born. You know, this is sort of the same thing that happened with plastics."

"Oh, wow, like . . . *plastic?*" she says, in a mock-stoned idiot's voice, imitating the hippie girl she never pretended to be.

"When I was little, plastic objects were cheap and crummy. Nobody wanted a plastic anything—even plastic toys were kind of suspect and low-rent. Nothing any grownup cared about was made from plastic. (Except telephones.) I may be a member of the last generation to remember when a plastic object was by definition an inferior object."

"You are. I have no plastic stigma whatsoever." She turns to face him. "You know, George, you have a high signal-to-noise ratio, but I even find your noise pretty interesting."

He smiles, at the compliment as well as at the nerdy engineering trope. "And your signal-to-noise ratio is . . . what?"

"Too high, probably."

Their mutual debriefing spirals further into randomness. They have already been through every major ramification of the Microsoft offer (fiduciary duty requires that she do the deal at this price, she needs to go to Seattle soon, he thinks *Real Time* is on track) and of her father's situation (he seems good, and despite his movie-of-the-week deal, no interviews, none) and the children (when Max's nosebleed wouldn't stop this afternoon, Sarah said, LuLu proposed letting Rafaela "come and live in his room after he dies"). They are down to third- and fourth-level agenda items—to automatic file sharing, to filler.

Mentioning Harold Mose's mysterious remark now, George thinks, wouldn't seem paranoid or disproportionate or weak. He turns to look at Lizzie.

"What did Mose mean when he told me you told him to go to hell?"

"What?" she asks, surprised.

"Harold Mose said you're a liberal who told him to get fucked."

"Told him to *get fucked*?" She is smiling in a way that doesn't please George. "I don't know what you're talking about. What did Harold say?"

Harold. "Just that."

"Oh! He must have meant the thing with ShowNet."

"What?"

"I told you. I told Hank Saddler we wouldn't help teach the Pentagon to use ShowNet for free, to keep track of the guerillas in Mexico."

"Right." Of course. She did tell him, he remembers, on the phone. George feels stupid.

"Was Harold pissed?" Lizzie asks. "He hasn't responded to my memo."

"No, he didn't seem to be. You know, he took your advice about MBCNews.com. They're shrinking it down to almost nothing. Getting rid of seventy-eight people."

"Firing them?"

"Moving them to other jobs in the company." Both watch Martin Sheen noiselessly shooting Sissy Spacek's father to death. "That looks exactly like Verve. Around Grandpa and Grandma's farm," George says. And only then: "What memo?"

"The memo about what he should do on the web. My free consultation." She looks at George. "I told you." She's not sure she did.

"No, you didn't. This is the first I've heard about it." A lie, but technically true.

"Yes, I did. You remember. Timothy called in St. Paul, from the plane, and said Harold wanted 'the four-one-one on online video.' Don't look at me like that. We discussed this. How Timothy said I was 'mad flossin',' and I didn't know what he meant?" As soon as she says it, she remembers the "flossin' " conversation was with Sarah and Buddy, in the stable in Mandeville Canyon. George wasn't there. *Oh, right, it wasn't you—it was Buddy Ramo who I told about the work I've been doing for your boss. Sorry! By the way, did I mention Buddy had his shirt off at the time?* No. She turns on her side, toward George, and looks into his eyes, feeling girlish but wise, trying to snuff this before it becomes a fight, trying somehow to transmit the complicated stupid truth without words, the only possible way it won't sting.

George doesn't remember any conversation about her memo or Featherstone. But since he's jet-lagged and stoned, thoroughly beat, he doesn't trust his lack of memory or his mistrust of Lizzie. And she couldn't have made up "mad flossin'." Still, he has the dark, frightened thought: maybe she realized after she got home from L.A. that she left copies of her memo on his laptop, and now she's admitting to it pre-emptively, pseudo-glancingly, pretending she told him, before he can confront her.

"One of us," she says, snuggling toward him, "must have Alzheimer's."

Confront her about what? Explaining video search engines and megabytes-per-second to Harold Mose without George's permission? Repeating his parrot analogy about online video without proper attri-bution? In the frenzy of the last ten days, she probably just forgot to mention the memo. Or maybe she did mention it, and he wasn't listen-ing. Or else, he thinks, he's playing the Ingrid Bergman role in *Gaslight 2000: One of Us Must Have Alzheimer's.* George smiles, and gives his head a tiny shake.

"What?" she says breathily, pushing against him. "What?" she says again.

He is too easy, he thinks.

He is *so* easy, she thinks, gratefully, a little enviously.

The second the tip of her tongue touches his chest, his erection launches, with each heartbeat rising again by half—like a simple but reliable toy, a sweet, homely, mechanical toy, premicrochip—and five, six, seven pumps later, her fingers are making circles on the skin behind and beneath it.

This seems new, George thinks. He then has a jealous thought, ineluctably, neurotically, that he's had before: *Where did she learn this?* But pleasure trumps suspicion. Scissors cut paper, paper wraps rock.

As his arm, the bad arm, moves back and forth across her lower back, stroking lower and harder, and then sawing, she kisses him furi-ously, gulping his tongue. *That's new,* she thinks, feeling his arm pry her, and he's teasing, pushing the arm, not quite, half again harder, then moving under and in, not hurting but goring, nudging in farther. His fingers, his other hand, the good hand, work the flesh, touching her in the usual way. *You never touch it,* he said on the phone last night about the missing hand, his stump, like he was about to cry. Was he punishing her? Is he punishing her?

Twenty-five minutes later, they have not dissolved into a creamy pool of unconsciousness, hand in hand, hip to hip, in the dark. George is uncovered, looking at the TV but simultaneously regarding his own naked body, thinking how gothic penises look, like gargoyles, as opposed to the elegance of women—symmetrical, discreet, spare, classical. Lizzie's light is on, and she's reading *The Aeneid*.

On the TV now is the Millennium Channel, a yearlong "multiplexed, infomercialized edutainment joint venture of Microsoft and The Learning Channel," George remembers reading in *Variety*. The program on now, *Information Ecstasy*, is narrated by Madonna. "Because our whole planet, and each and every one of us on it, is moving together through the universe at six hundred sixty thousand miles per hour," Madonna is saying, "forty times as fast as the space shuttle."

"That fact actually makes me nauseous," George says.

Lizzie lays the book on her stomach. "I guess this is an offer we can't resist, like Lance said—"

"Refuse. 'Can't refuse.' "

"Whatever. But I still don't like Microsoft. I don't. I can't. No matter how many billion shares of stock we own."

"It is the business we have chosen, Elizabeth."

She picks up the book and reads:

> A few succeed
> By Jove's grace or a hero's soaring will.

Just as the sweet Nebraskans are about to electrocute Martin Sheen, George snaps off the TV. "Speaking of the business," he says, looking over at her from his dark side of the bed as he sinks into the pillow. "Asset-backed securities? Mose wants to create asset-backed securities based on *NARCS*. Should we let him? Am I going to wind up in jail?"

Lizzie does not look up from her page. She smiles and says, "Let me send you a memo on that."

PART TWO

March

April

May

June

1 6

They are driving back into winter. Mile by mile as they head north, the signs of spring disappear. The trees are budding in Jacob Riis Park on the Lower East Side. The new sign outside Pepsi/Taco Bell Yankee Stadium lists the times and dates for the season openers. But even in Westchester the green is attenuated, and now in Columbia County the landscape is gray and skeletal and people on the side of the road are wearing down jackets.

Last spring, after they sold the house in Sneden's Landing and moved back into the city, they also bought a country place in the lower Adirondacks on Lake Marten. This is the first trip up since Thanksgiving. George and Lizzie are looking forward to it, but not with the pure, blithe anticipation of brainless submission to nature. Rather, they feel like old allies heading to Camp David for a weekend of confidence-building measures that they hope will lead to a renewal of their historic ties and long-standing confederation. Pollyanna and Warren, who have moved in together instead of breaking up, are in the car right behind them, along with Warren's son and au pair. Emily arrives tomorrow morning by plane with a boyfriend.

It's a four-and-a-half-hour drive from the city. A satellite leased by Toyota has locked in on the Land Cruiser, beaming down data and thirty channels of video as Lizzie speeds north into the twilight middle of nowhere. In the backseat, Max is hunched over the built-in laptop, clicking around the web site of a college in Ohio. (LuLu is asleep, and Sarah is in the city alone; her St. Andrew's fund-raising dance for Zapatista medical supplies is tonight.) On the TV screen that folds out over the glove compartment, George switches back and forth between MBC's *Great Big Nutty Wayne Newton and Robert Goulet Variety Hour* and Jim Lehrer on PBS discussing a guerilla attack on a hydroelectric dam in Chiapas.

Lizzie, driving, spots a black man walking along the shoulder of the parkway in an orange jumpsuit and says, "Escaped convict?"

George looks up from Goulet and Newton, who are impersonating Gore and Clinton in a skit. "Racist," he says, joking but mirthless.

"You're the one who always thinks black guys driving Mercedeses are drug dealers."

"Or UN diplomats," he says, returning to the video screen.

Five minutes later, Lizzie passes a sedan with a long whip antenna on the roof, driven by a smiling young Japanese man. His passenger, a smiling Japanese woman, is holding a big, boxy black telephone or radio, like a military walkie-talkie. A few cars later Lizzie passes another car of smiling young Japanese, with the same antenna and strange phone, and then another. Is this some game? A tourist caravan? George will make another joke about racist paranoia if she mentions it, so she doesn't.

Somewhere in Rensselaer County, the phone rings. George snaps off *Hero,* the NBC hit about regular people who acquire superpowers for twenty-four hours. No one but Alexi, Iris, Emily, and Featherstone has the car-phone number.

"Mobile unit one, this is the MBC HQ!"

"Hey, Timothy. What's up?"

"Nothing major. You rusticating?"

"We're on our way upstate, yeah."

"Where exactly do you cats do your rural brand-extension thing?"

"A place in the Adirondacks."

"Hip."

"Near the Vermont border."

"Convergence! Harold and Gloria have a glorioso lodge-type mansion in Vermont. Robert Frost stayed there. You should shag an invite."

"Right," says George, wondering how long this will go on. A pointless gibbering Hollywood call to a car on Friday evening seems extreme even for Featherstone.

"Hey, bud, I can't spend all night shooting the fat. Is the sophisticated lady available?"

"You want Lizzie? Sure."

"Plant you now, dig you later, Gorgonzola."

George hands the phone to his wife, and turns the TV back on. Under the circumstances, he must pout privately.

"I put a bowl of milk but I only see Buzzy," LuLu tells her parents an hour after they arrive at Lake Marten.

Lizzie glances out at the calico cat and nods.

When they were last here, seven skittish cats and kittens were perpetually outside around the house, living high off weekend scraps of risotto and veal and guacamole. Now, it seems, there is only one. Charlie, the caretaker, was supposed to have fed them over the winter.

Weekends in the country regularly feature some awkward dance of misunderstanding, of course. At the Grand Union outside Albany where they stopped for groceries, they were happy to find endive, radicchio, and fiddlehead ferns, but they went through the usual little duel of mutual embarrassment with the checkout girl (whose name tag George half expected to say SHAWNA) as she asked them to identify not only the endive, radicchio, and fiddleheads for her, but avocados, then zucchini, then parsley, then rhubarb, and then nectarines as well.

George is in the kitchen, opening two more bottles of Chardonnay and staring at the window behind the sink. At eye level, clinging to the wood mullion between two of the panes, is a fly. At first he is surprised that it doesn't buzz away when he blows at it, but now he sees that it's dead, an absolutely perfect, undamaged dead housefly stuck in situ. It's fantastic, he thinks, this tiny accidental museum of natural history. He wonders how he might phrase a note to the local girl who cleans the house that won't make her think he is insane: *Cora—Please don't touch the top panes of the window by the sink. We want to keep the dead fly right where it is.* He could lie and say it's a child's science project.

When he returns to the living room, they're still discussing Lizzie's worries about trying to run a software business in New York, three thousand miles from the mainstream. This line of conversation, with its implicit threat of relocation, never pleases George. Her anxiety breeds his counteranxiety. And in response, she finds herself defending the digital Northwest against easy New York disparagement like some mixed-breed ambassador.

"I guess I should move to L.A., then," George says, smiling as he tops up Pollyanna and Warren, spilling a drop on Warren's corduroys. George has known Warren for fifteen years, but he doesn't know him quite well enough to ask why, no matter the season or the venue, he wears wide-wale brown corduroys and a long-sleeved turtleneck. Here and now, it's a good outfit. But in the summer, Warren always looks hot.

"*George,*" Pollyanna says.

"Sinbad reads *The Economist,*" he says. "And Francesca, the woman from MTV, watches fifteen-year-old documentaries about Central American civil wars."

George and Lizzie exchange friendly, oversize, fuck-you smiles.

"I would rather live in a sunny city of stupid pretty people," George continues, "than a rainy city of smart ugly people like Seattle. I would." He doesn't know if he really would, but he enjoys saying so.

"New York is more like all those other places now, anyway," Warren says.

"How would you know?" Pollyanna says. "You barely go outside, let alone to other cities."

"I read, my dear. And I don't *want* to go out when I read that there are now twenty-eight thousand missionaries of the Church of Jesus Christ of Latter-day Saints in New York City now. *Yes.* Twenty-eight thousand. Almost as many Mormons as there are *cops.* According to the article, there were only four thousand of them twenty years ago. I think they've been drawn to the city by Chelsea Piers and the World Financial Center and Disney and MetroCards and no-smoking laws. Didn't we all come to New York to *escape* Mormons?"

"Have some more to drink, Warren," George says.

Pollyanna and Lizzie have been out running since before Emily and Michael arrived. Emily and Warren are sitting in the sun on the porch with George, along with Suzie, Warren's weekend-custody au pair, who's holding the Holcombe baby. George suddenly realizes there's no polite way to indicate to Emily and her boyfriend that Suzie is not Warren's cute, young, blond wife, but rather his employee with a Texas BA in Caregiving. But since Emily met Michael when he was her employee (he played the DA on *Girlie*), George decides his impulse for caste clarity is priggish and beside the point. Let the ambiguities fly.

Out in the yard, between them and the lake, Max catches his baseball, looks at it, and shouts "Sixty-*eight!*" before throwing it back to Michael. Emily brought the children gifts—a play surgery kit for LuLu and a Rawlings Radar Ball for Max. Packed inside the thread and rubber at the ball's core is a speedometer, wired to a tiny LCD window on the surface that gives a readout for the speed of each pitch.

"Fifty-nine," Michael shouts to Max, then throws back. Sitting on the porch of his country house, holding a mug of coffee as his son plays catch with this pleasant, dumb, handsome, childless, two-handed actor, George feels like a well-satisfied burgher relieved of a child-rearing duty—Michael can be Max's sports wet nurse for the weekend.

Then, as he watches the caretaker drive his muddy Dodge truck up the road, he feels even more like a recreating Knickerbocker. Charlie climbs out of his pickup with his fly-fishing gear and a package in a tight garbage-bag wrapping.

"How are you, Mr. Mactier?"

"Fine, Charlie, how are you?" *My good man.* "How's the winter been up here?"

"Not too bad. I took care of the barn cats, like you asked. Except that one cute little calico."

"Buzzy." George suddenly realizes that his instruction to Charlie as they were driving away last November—"You'll take care of the cats?"—must have been very badly misinterpreted.

"Not much browse all winter, so the deer chewed up your garden some. Nice season for us, though," he says, holding out the neat garbage-bag package to George.

George takes it. It's frozen solid and weighs ten pounds.

"Some venison," Charlie says, nodding at the frosty black plastic.

George feels silly over his momentary horror that he was holding the frozen carcasses of six cats. "The season," of course, is deer-hunting season.

"Thanks very much, Charlie." *I shan't demand the thirty pecks of barley this jubilee year, however, nor the night with your comely eldest daughter.*

"Mr. Mactier, will it be any bother to you if I'm fishing down at your stream today?"

"No, not at all, Charlie, go right ahead."

"Excuse me," Warren says from the porch, "may I ask you a question?"

Charlie, startled and apprehensive, has no choice but to turn. "Yes, sir?"

"You're a fly fisherman, right?"

"That's right."

"Do you buy them," Warren asks earnestly, "or do you farm these flies yourself?"

Charlie apparently thinks this turtlenecked snob from the city is teasing him. George intervenes.

"They aren't *real flies,* Warren. They're made out of feathers and Mylar line and glue." He turns back to smile at Charlie, who looks thrilled by the instant passing of humiliation from himself to the stranger.

But Warren is a psychiatrist from the Upper West Side of Manhattan. He does not humiliate easily, if at all.

"Interesting," he says. "I also have another question. Do you trap martens around here?"

"*What* are you talking about?" George says.

"Lake *Marten.* You know, martens—they're a kind of weasel," he says to Charlie, "aren't they?"

"Sure," the caretaker says. "I took my six last season." He pauses. "You didn't want any pelts, did you, Mr. Mactier?"

———

Dinner is done, the peach and rhubarb pies are heating, the wine is still being poured.

"You don't bring your nanny to the country?" Emily asks. Max and LuLu are upstairs watching the new animated *Lusitania* with Michael, Suzie the au pair, and Warren's baby.

Lizzie shakes her head and George says, "Between Charlie, and the housecleaner, and the contractor, and the pond man, I think—oh, and the kid who mows, *and* the snowplow guy—we've got enough servants up here without throwing Rafaela into the mix." He is smiling and means to be self-mocking. "You must have a big staff, Em."

"Gardener, pool boy, housekeeper. That's it. At the house."

"Plus Michael," George teases. "Did you ever think we would employ so many people?"

"Shall I put on the *Big Chill* soundtrack now or later?" Pollyanna says.

Emily is counting on her fingers as Michael returns to join the grownups. "Lawyer, lawyer, agent, manager, Becky, kid at Paramount, business manager, doctor, doctor, shrink, and Tranh."

"That's about four FTEs," Lizzie says. Everyone looks at her.

"Full-time equivalents," she explains.

"Our liability insurance policy on this place," George says, "actually has a clause saying it covers 'the accidental dismemberment' of 'the occasional servant.' I don't *think* it means the occasional dismemberment."

"Why does this all not embarrass us?" Lizzie asks.

"Why should it?" Emily says. "We're good bosses. In L.A. there's none of that guilt. About help."

"The slave class," George says, "that allows you and Barbra to spend your time raising money for Gore and stopping the war in Mexico."

"There isn't real servant guilt in New York either," Warren says. "Trust me."

"In Seattle there is," Lizzie says. "About private schools, even. They're democrats. Small *d.*"

"Is that a good thing or a bad thing?" Michael asks.

Instead of answering, Lizzie continues. "I think it's because they're not jaded enough yet to live with hypocrisy. You know? They're too rational, in a kind of easy, adolescent way. I feel like Kirk with Spock or Picard with Data whenever I'm out there."

"But that's why you like it," George says. "That's why you want to move there."

"I do not want to move there."

"No, you do; it'd be like Cambridge all over again. Rainy and brainy. You'd like it too, Emily. Very lefty. They've got a municipal department of ecology."

"In Los Angeles," Michael says, "we have a Museum of Tolerance."

"I think I would like Seattle," Emily says, "except for the rain. That innocence, and the missionary spirit. Like writers, but not cynical."

"*Please,*" George says.

"No, Emily's right," Lizzie says, recanting for the moment her recent renunciation of Seattle. "The dream of the big score out there isn't so much about getting rich or getting famous or getting laid or getting invited to fab parties."

"Because they're already rich," George says.

"No, no," his wife says. "They sincerely believe they're bringing the New World into being. It's sort of creepy. And admirable."

"Mormons," Warren says. "Creepy and admirable."

"Do they do drugs?" Pollyanna asks Lizzie.

"I don't think so, much," Lizzie says. "But, you know, that constant tingle out there, even more down in the Valley—the money, IPO, next-big-thing mania—reminds me a lot of cocaine. The cocaine high, I mean. Not just their speediness, but their intoxication with their own brilliance and infallibility. Very coke-y."

"Mormons on coke," Warren says. "*Truly* frightening."

"I thought you always said they were more egoless than people in L.A. and New York?" George says. "What, they're egoless egomaniacs?"

"*No,* what I *said* was that in Seattle, nobody ever puts his own name in his company's name."

"No Warner Bros. or Goldwyn or Mayer in Seattle, huh?" Emily says. "Or Morgan Stanley or Lazard Frères or whatever?"

"That's right. I can't tell you how often people in New York think that my name is Elizabeth *Fine*—*Fine* Technologies."

Michael, evidently operating on a several-minute time delay, asks, "It rains a lot in Seattle?"

There's a pause as everyone registers that he's not joking.

"One hundred and seventy-four days last year," Lizzie finally says.

"I think people in Seattle take the gray weather as some kind of proof they're not superficial," George says. "Cloudiness equals intellectual depth. In some Scandinavian way. Just like New Yorkers secretly need all their man-made unpleasantnesses—noise and real estate prices and co-op boards and no place to park—so they can feel like soulful survivors. Like Berliners used to be."

"That's sad," Michael says.

"You're *such* a bullshitter, George," Emily says.

"Who's articulate who you *don't* think is a bullshitter, Emily?"

George is sitting outside, finishing the Sunday paper. Lizzie steps out onto the porch with LuLu, about to join everyone else down at the lake.

"Is there some reason," she says as they pass him, "you felt the need to be such an asshole last night?" She looks at the shadow of her hands on the side of the house, gesticulating as she searches for her words. "I'm not your enemy, George. And I don't believe Emily is, either."

"Isn't 'asshole' bad?" LuLu asks.

George doesn't reply.

"Are the deer and the squirrels homeless?"

"What do you mean, LuLu?" her father asks.

"They live outside all the time, and nobody feeds them. They act scared and crazy. They're like bums."

Lizzie remembers a book she read in college by a nineteenth-century writer named Cesare Lombroso, who believed that animals were, in fact, criminals by nature, violent and homicidal. She remembers learning in the same course that weasels kill more prey than they can eat. But after George's Cambridge crack last night, she decides not to mention Lombroso or weasels.

"No," Lizzie says, taking LuLu by the hand and walking toward Lake Marten. "Animals can't be bums, honey."

1 7

The phone in the kitchen rings as it does every weekday morning around now. Ordinarily, Lizzie takes the call, but she left for the airport when it was still dark. *"Sarah?"* George yells, getting up from the fiberglass Eames chair to answer it. Your bus!" He picks up the receiver, but doesn't say hello. He sometimes does, and then feels stupid. "Hello!" the machined female voice on the other end of the line announces brightly, almost lovingly. "Today is Tuesday. Your child's transportation will be waiting at the designated location in. Four minutes. And thirty seconds!" Lizzie would hang up now, but George, not yet coffeed up and curious to hear today's non sequitur, stays on the line. "Campbell's soup is m'm-m'm-good!" the ReadyAim lady says. Then, after a pause, her voice suddenly quickens and empties of emotion. "This ReadyAim automated advisory was not reviewed by human staff, and by terminating this call you waive any and all liability claims against ReadyAim, its employees, and agents." He smiles and snorts once as he hangs up.

"Daddy?" LuLu asks between mouthfuls of high-fiber *Star Wars: Episode I—The Phantom Menace* Home Video–themed Eggos, "Why do you laugh so much?"

"I didn't laugh."

"You did that *thing.* Like a laugh."

"You did, Dad," says Max, who is at the counter carefully filling out an order form. Max loves filling out forms, dry-run forms he rips out of magazines (subscription cards, subscriber surveys, NRA postcards to congressmen, credit card applications) and the forms his teachers give him (order forms for Scholastic books, for Disney Books, for Nickelodeon software, for *Time for Kids'* current events activities books, and Cool Candy of the Month Club order forms masquerading as consumer surveys). George glances at Max. *Buying stuff didn't qualify as homework when I was a kid,* he refrains from saying for the tenth time this school year, probably because Lizzie is not around to hear it.

"Oh," George says, "the bus recording was sort of funny."

"You mean the part at the end where she says it's not their fault if your child gets stolen or killed?" LuLu asks. "That makes Mommy sad to hear, so she doesn't listen."

"Uh-huh," George says, turning the pages of the *Post,* scanning and skipping the midsection of disappearing-Queens-hubby and murdered-Bronx-tot articles.

"I don't think it's funny *or* sad," LuLu says. "Daddy, why does Mommy think the men at Microsoft might kill her? Will they kill her?"

"No. It's a figure of speech. She's worried they'll be mean to her. Finish your waffles."

"They're *Egg*os."

Tag-team marriage, he thinks. If he were still working for ABC, he would be ready to suggest a *GMA* second-hour piece with the title already invented. No, *no*—first commission the book, *Tag-Team Marriage: New Relationships for the New Century* (or *A Third Way to Love: Staying Married in the Third Millennium;* test both), get a pleasant Dr. Somebody to be the author, a clinical psychologist or psychiatric social worker, a high-energy female shrink who *then* gets her interview with the Society writer at *Newsweek,* and *off that* her two-minutes-thirty on morning TV, and *then* sell a show to Lifetime. Since he's left journalism, his daydreams have become more vertically integrated.

Sarah appears, her short hair still wet from the shower. Zipping up the loose olive-green jacket, strapping on the overstuffed thirty-pound backpack, unsmiling as ever, she looks like a scared, brave young B-29 crewman suiting up to fly across the Channel.

"This afternoon?" she says to George, beginning her statement in the middle to avoid the intimacy of *Dad* or the snub of *George*. "I'm going with my friend Felipe to see his older brother's web site office. In Chelsea? I'll be home at roughly five. Thirty?"

"*Who* is *Felipe*?" George asks. He knows he has Lizzie's proxy here, although by overstressing the first and last words the question sounds more contemptuous (more Wall Street asshole, more Republican) than he intends.

"A guy in my class. Felipe Williamson."

"It's Philip Williamson, Dad," Max says from the other side of the kitchen. Philip Williamson, Jr.! Philip Jr. is the pale, blond son of a Goldman Sachs partner and a Davis Polk partner. He has been Sarah's classmate off and on since first grade.

George does not smile. "How did Philip become Felipe?" he asks Sarah.

"He was adopted, you know. From Arizona, he found out last year. So he changed his name."

"His biological parents were . . . Mexican?" George asks.

"They could have been," she says. "I have to go."

"Right," George says, straight-faced.

George and the little kids leave a half hour later for the drive to school. Gaping potholes are fine, uneven cobblestones are fine, even the collapsed sawhorse and shards of drywall in the middle of Beekman Street are fine. They all make George feel as if he has a good excuse for wheeling a giant sport-utility vehicle around Manhattan. They'd bought the Land Cruiser (George wanted a Land Rover, but Lizzie vetoed it—her Anglophilia phobia) when they moved to Sneden's Landing. Their single longest off-road experience has been parking at Nancy McNabb and Roger Baird's outdoor wedding in Litchfield County, but George figures that navigating New York City's infrastructure qualifies as *utility*, maybe even *sport*.

"Can we listen to the blues?" LuLu asks, by which she means a Screamin' Jay Hawkins CD they have somewhere in the car.

"I can't find it and stick it in while I'm driving, sweetie. This," he says, nodding toward the radio, "is related to the blues. Probably."

WNYC is playing African music that sounds like a concerto for oboe, very flat string quartet, and the-men-of-the-village-makingcricketlike-sounds. George likes international music because he can't understand it, neither the words nor the music. It's the same reason American graphic designers love Japanese magazines. It's why strangers speaking foreign languages look more attractive and interesting than they would if they were speaking English—we hear their voices without judgment, snobberies deactivated, oblivious to nuances of class and education and geography. Conversely, it's why fashion models become less beautiful the moment they speak. It's why the temptations of a Shawna Cindy Switzer become easier to resist as the night goes on. He has to remember to tell Lizzie about Shawna Cindy Switzer.

"Related to the blues," Max asks, "like apes are related to us?"

"Well. Yeah. Sort of like that," George says. *But my dad told me that African-Americans are like monkeys, Mrs. Bosgang.* George begins constructing his explanation of why an analogy involving apes and the music of black people is inherently tricky and probably unwise. But they are only a block from St. Andrew's. He decides to let it pass.

Max and LuLu are already scrabbling across the seat toward the curbside door by the time he brakes to a stop.

"Have a great day," says their father. The moment the children are out of the car, as he always does when he drives them to school, he switches from NPR to Howard Stern.

"So," Stern is saying as George drives sixty through the empty Brooklyn Battery Tunnel on his way to the *NARCS* location shoot in Staten Island, "if I could say something intelligent to you about, like, the presidential election campaign or the Mexican rebels or something, then you *might* make love to me? You'd consider making love to me? Like, even though you're on MTV and every rock star on the planet wants to get in your pants, the fact that I've got a tiny penis isn't a problem for you, right? Because even though you're very hot and even though you live in L.A., you're an intellectual chick."

"Something like that."

George slows to let the E-ZPass ray gun read the bar code stuck to the inside of his windshield, and then speeds through the open gate. Magic! E-ZPass is one of the great blessings of dehumanized modern life. Online book buying, ATM machines, MovieFone, and E-ZPass.

"Now what's the deal with the name? Did your manager make that up for you to sound sexier?"

"My parents named me Francesca. I'm afraid that's my name."

"Were they like Italians or something?"

"Just pretentious."

The car phone rings. It is, of course, Iris.

"So those are what, C cups?" Howard asks Francesca. George turns off the radio.

"George," Iris says in her *Def-Con 4* whisper, "a producer from MBC News says she needs to talk to you about Mr. Zimbalist *right away*! Shall I patch her through?"

1 8

Of course she doesn't like the name *business class.* But she likes it, the class. Since the airlines have defined discomfort down, flying business class isn't profligacy (she reassures herself), it's playing along with a protection racket—you pay extra, or you just might get roughed up in coach. If it were up to George, they'd be flying first class all the time. His line lately is, "I'm tall, we're rich." She knows he's being deliberately coarse with the "we're rich" part, but it still makes her nervous, reminding her of how her father brought home brand-new his-and-her 1975 Mercedes coupes the week before MGM fired him. "That upper-middle mama-bear thing is very . . . sweet, Lizzie," George said once, making her feel like a frump. "I guess in your family Great Depression anxiety skipped a generation." Last summer, after she drove two hours round-trip to spend $950 on shoes at the secret Manolo Blahnik factory outlet in New Jersey, he said, "Neoluxury. You're the poster girl." Jokes about neoluxury and neolimos she doesn't mind.

The armrest Airfone is ringing. She turns to dig the telephone out of its compartment, and gives an apologetic little smile to the pudgy man in the suit and tie working next to her. He looks like a congressman. Almost everyone in business class looks like a congressman.

"Alexi?"

"How's the flight? Harold Mose called. That boy you interviewed for the Seattle job, Chas Prieve? The dip from Boston? The *I'm-your-guy* guy? He called to follow up, and I told him you were on your way to Seattle, and he was like, 'Well, I just happen to be overnighting in Seattle tomorrow night on my way back from Vietnam to talk to some major VC people.' And he'd love to get together with you."

"Kismet."

"I told him you were fully booked. On the other hand, he did call all the way from Asia. It's gumption."

"I guess I should see him. Tell Chad to meet me for coffee at the Sorrento."

"*Chas.* Also, the invites to your soiree *are* going out today, Karen worked all night and finished them. A hundred thirty-eight! She's a good slave. Go look—it's open."

"What?"

"Bruce. He needs some article he says he left in your office. Speaking of slaves, the girl from St. Paul, Fanny Taft? She gets here May the tenth. I forged your name on some Justice Department affidavit about her."

The man seated next to her, only a little older than she, is now snoring, and his necktie has flopped over the armrest onto Lizzie. As she hangs up, she uses the opportunity to toss the tie back onto his belly and glance at the spreadsheets and yellow legal pad on his lap. On the top sheet he has written only "PURPOSES?" and underlined it twice. The instant she's finished shoving the phone down into its home, it rings again, startling her.

"What is it, Alexi?"

"Ah-*ha,*" the man's voice says, "*Alexi!* The lover with whom you're rendezvousing in Novopolotsk."

"Who is this?"

"It's Harold Mose," he says from his office on the Fifty-ninth Floor in New York, standing alone with the door closed in a room as big and quiet and lush as a pond, looking out over the northern half of Manhattan, the view that makes rich New Yorkers feel richer, wiser, untouchable. As he turns and moves behind the desk and sits, the tiny video lens built into the rim of his computer monitor pivots and rotates, finding him, zooming back as he wheels in closer, focusing. "Don't worry, Lizzie, I won't breathe a word to George."

She smiles. "Hello, Harold." *He makes his own calls,* she thinks, a little impressed, and also a little impressed with herself for getting the call. "Alexi's my assistant. The guy who gave out this number without authorization?"

"Correct."

"What can I do for you?"

"You've done it." Mose's computer is on, and as he speaks he clicks around the screen from window to window, the contemporary equivalent of doodling. His mouse is heavy and black, carved out of Indonesian onyx; the little rubber trackball lodged inside, like a ship in a bottle, is a globe. "I've been meaning to call you for weeks to tell you your memo is absolute genius." Open in one window on Mose's screen is Lizzie's memo.

"Thanks," she says. "It's good to know my six years in this stupid business weren't for naught." ("Looks like our spin control was all for naught," Lizzie said to her father on the phone yesterday after she told him *Newsweek* was threatening to go ahead with a story about his transplant because MBC had announced its plans for the TV movie they're calling *Mr. Piggy.* " 'For *naught,*' " Mike Zimbalist said back. "I can't believe you're my kid, Lizzie, and not some goddamn *Redgrave.*")

"One does tend to forget that the average Joe does not have a T1 line or a cable modem installed in his rumpus room yet. Streaming video isn't exactly mass-market, is it?" Another of the open windows on Mose's computer contains a video image, live television as small as a pack of matches, streaming in crisply across his T1.

"Not quite."

"So I suppose you're not going to tell me about your sudden secret mission to Seattle, are you?"

Did Alexi *tell* Mose where she's headed? Now she can't lie, but she can't tell the truth either. So she creates the illusion of candor. "It's been in the trade press—we've talked to Microsoft about selling a small equity piece. You know that, don't you?"

"Correct. By the way, we didn't even come close to a deal that made sense for the MBC. We're not talking any longer."

"No?"

"Not even close. Elizabeth, I need to take this company to the next level. Quickly. As you say in your memo, convergence really is coming. As you also say, we can't afford to get locked out of the game. Whatever the goddamn game turns out to be." Mose is now looking at another window on his screen, the one he keeps permanently open, under a large red ME, Mose Media Holdings' New York Stock Exchange ticker symbol. The box displays not just the current stock price (39⅙₆, down 1⅞ since this morning's open) and trading volume (a little higher than usual), but the number of Mose shares sold short (much higher than usual); the relevant Wall Street analysts' public guesses about the company's earnings for the quarter that just ended; the company's internal reckonings of its earnings; and the ratings of last night's MBC prime-time programs—an empire of messy facts and squirrelly hunches collected and conflated and then distilled down to the salient digits, and that salience reduced still further and squeezed neatly into a few square inches of pixels. "I found them to be arrogant shits, Gates and his boys," Mose says to Lizzie. "For once somebody's lousy press is correct, eh?"

"Absolutely," she says, pleased. "They can be assholes." Not that she's planning to turn down their $31.5 million tomorrow morning. (*Sixty-three million.* Fine Technologies is worth *sixty-three million dollars!*) But discovering a shared personal loathing is the single quickest way to forge a friendship, Lizzie has found. There's seldom time, like there was in her teens and twenties, to construct relationships a brick at a time, by agreeing on enthusiasms—for the Talking Heads, for big gin martinis straight up, for William Carlos Williams and Saki, for onion rings, for cunnilingus, for Richard Diebenkorn and seventeenth-century Dutch painting, for the woods, for Albert Brooks, for children—all the personal-ad particulars that become embarrassing in synopsis. Besides, Harold Mose probably doesn't know "Psycho Killer" or *Paterson,* and Lizzie doesn't foresee much opportunity to bring them up.

"So who needs the evil empire? Come be my digital czar. Czarina."

"Yeah, right." Lizzie giggles. He isn't serious. "I'm afraid I've got a company of my own to run."

"So you do. And so do I. Did you know that word of your brilliant husband's brilliant new show is leaking out and nudging our stock price down? Evidently the Wall Street herd agrees with Arnold that committing two hours a week and fifty million dollars to his mad, untried concept is bad business." Arnold is Arnold Vlig, the Mose Media Holdings chief operating officer.

"Is that really what happened?" Lizzie says, not knowing how to respond, not wanting to sound alarmed and wifely. Phone calls aboard airplanes are lousy under the best of circumstances. Straining to hear, shouting a little to be heard (and trying not to be overheard), it's telephony as it must have been in Graham Bell's day. Divining nuance is impossible, and Lizzie has no sense now of Mose's intent—frank concern about *Real Time* and Mose Media stock, or just idle fuck-the-Wall-Street-pissants small talk in his Ted Turner manqué mode?

"Ah, well," Mose replies, "George just has to make a hit and show the little bastards. I won't take any more of your time. You have your company to run."

In fact, she has a company to *sell*. Thanks again, my pleasure, great, see you, absolutely, stay in touch, bye. She starts to dial her father in the hospital, but that's a conversation she doesn't want to conduct in a semi-shout aboard an airplane. (*I know they just medicated you, Daddy, but I can't hear you! Your ass feels like what?*) Seattle is two hours away, and she hasn't looked at the pages and pages of financials Lance has prepared. The Newtish man next to her has just awakened with a noisy apneic snort, and returned to his computerized spreadsheet and empty yellow list of underlined "PURPOSES?" It's not business class, she thinks, settling in with her own columns and rows of numbers, it's study hall.

Lizzie stares at her numbers but cannot engage. She is too anxious. She is anxious about the prospect of selling half her company and selling it for $31.5 million and selling it to Microsoft. She is anxious on George's behalf over what Mose said about the Wall Street reaction to *Real Time.* She is anxious about whether she should tell George or not. Even Mose's "digital czarina" line has made her anxious, anxious that her trifling surge of interest is somehow disloyal to . . . her employees? Herself? But Mose wasn't serious about the job, she decides. It was CEO auto-charm, Mose's version of White House M&M's with the presidential seal, a cheap bit of flirty praise that means next to nothing. Even though all well-executed flattery feels good, no matter how insincere, like a drug, or sex.

1 9

George is polite with the MBC News producer, who wants exactly what George assumed she wants: exclusive TV access to the world's first person to survive with a pig liver. "Your father-in-law is in *play*," she says, sounding more terrified than terrifying, like the Wolfman just as the full moon comes over the horizon. *I am a journalist, and I am driven by forces beyond my control!* Her line would make Lizzie hang up immediately. But driving across the Verrazano Narrows one-handed, speaking into the microphone Velcroed to the roof of the car, he cannot easily hang up. Plus, he knows what she means. So he doesn't get snippy, or tell her that *Dateline NBC* and *20/20* are both after Mike, with the implicit "fuck off, you loser" disparagement of MBC News. He doesn't tell the lie he advised Lizzie to tell the reporter from *Time*, about how Mike's condition is too precarious for interviews. He tells the truth, that the family doesn't want any attention. But then he feels bad for the woman, who is desperately wheedling and pleading (just like George used to wheedle and plead with sources and subjects, despising every second of it), and promises her the TV exclusive if they decide to talk to the press. It is some kind of atavistic professional courtesy. It is also, he knows, a thrown bone that might prevent her from telling her executive producer that George is stiffing his own network, which might prevent the executive producer from complaining to Barry Stengel, with whom George does not need another drop of bad blood before *Real Time* gets going. In other words, he's trading Mike Zimbalist's dignity for some hypothetical leverage on behalf of the new show. Or more like a hypothetical option on a small piece of Mike's dignity, a dignity derivative. *Exactly as Mike himself would do,* George tells himself, and then bats the thought away as he pulls the red Land Cruiser up to the yellow POLICE LINE tape that real police from the department's movie and TV unit have strung up to cordon off the fake police and make-believe federal agents in the nonexistent squad that George has invented for *NARCS.*

There are only two autograph scroungers today, both middle-aged men in ratty coats with many zippers, paparazzi without portfolio (or cameras). There is the usual ad hoc crowd of civilian bystanders, but small because the location is way out in Great Kills, which is one of the reasons the location is here. They can get by with fewer production assistants. Two teenagers in extra-huge cargo pants and extra-extra-huge T-shirts, both chewing gum and one feeding her baby daughter granola and bits of celery; a thin, plain woman in a wide-brimmed Gibson girl hat and lace-up boots, displaced Manhattanite or strenuously Manhattanesque; a pair of Hasidic men talking and gesturing with their lit cigarettes toward the Panaflex Platinum cameras; and a dozen dark, chunky neighborhood guys watching the dark, chunky Teamsters standing around doing nothing for forty-six dollars an hour on the other side of the yellow tape. Sometimes, to save money when they're shooting a crime scene, the *NARCS* crew turns a camera around and shoots the crowd of New York pedestrians staring at makeup trailers and craft-services buffets, thus transforming them for a second or two of screen time into actors playing New York pedestrians staring over a police line at corpses and pallets of cocaine. (Whenever anyone questions some niggardly production decision, Emily Kalman says, "It's the MBC, not NBC," or simply, "MBC—M.") Today's bystanders, George thinks, wouldn't cut it—too dressed, too art-directed, and the Hasids would look like some mysterious plot point.

Beyond the makeup RV and the wardrobe RV, he passes the day players' RVs, each with taped-on paper signs indicating the designated actor-occupants—MIDDLE-CLASS BLACK GUY, SHY GUY, MULE/RETARD, and ORIENTAL SLUT with ORIENTAL crossed out and ASIAN scribbled over it.

Outside Angela Janeway's trailer, George sees Gordon Downey and Phoebe Reiss, his director and executive story editor. They are having a furious whispered conversation.

"Good morning," George says. "Why aren't we shooting? It's quarter past nine. Whom do I punish?"

"Angela and Lucas both have 'issues' with the new pages," Gordon tells him. "The end of the bust scene." Lucas Winton is Angela Janeway's costar. Their characters, Jennie O'Donnell and Horace "Cowboy" Quesada, are supposed to be mismatched teammates, the Queens-girl NYPD detective and the rich-boy DEA agent who, according to the show bible that George wrote a year ago, "love and loathe each other in equal measure." The loathing scenes tend to be shot in one take.

"What's Lucas's problem? And why are we getting their notes this *morning?*" If the script changes at this point, and Angela or Lucas isn't going to say some lines that are in the script, the first assistant director or the script supervisor will have to let all the camera people know, and the sound department, and the guy who swings and dips the boom microphone, and so on down the line.

Phoebe sighs. Gordon explains. Both are relieved that Daddy has come to make everything okay. "Lucas says 'looking like a pussy' isn't going to get him film work or win him an Emmy. He wants Cowboy *standing* during that final speech, not sitting on the ground with Angela standing over him. I say fine. Let's get to work."

"He also objects," Phoebe says, "to Jennie winning the argument by ignoring him, *and* getting the button. And Lucas wants to call the smuggler 'the screwy slant-eye' instead of 'the screwy Asian kid.' "

Angela, Jennie, Lucas, Horace, Cowboy—five names for two people used interchangeably by everyone all day long. Sometimes George thinks this is the biggest difference between producing news and entertainment: in the former, the talent always play themselves, Ted Koppel is always called Ted Koppel. Not that the difference is absolute—Jerry Seinfeld played Jerry Seinfeld, and Jess Burnham has been *Jess* Burnham only a little more than a year.

"Oh, Mr. Man can stand up, I guess," George says. "But the line is the line." He pauses and says softly, "*Film* work?"

"On the lines," Gordon says. "I think his note was really a reaction to *her* note." On "her," Gordon nods hard right, toward Angela's trailer.

"What's her problem?" George asks Phoebe.

"The *Hawaii Five-O* joke."

"She doesn't get it?"

"She thinks it's racist."

Phoebe shrugs as George stares at her and then Gordon for an appalled, uncomprehending moment. He breathes through his nose, in and out fully, the way his wife tells him to do. He thinks of his $16,575 a week. "Gordon," he says, "can you go shoot the Hawaiians getting whacked *now,* so we don't get any further behind? Thanks." He knocks on the RV door. He thinks of Lizzie's line about the truth of clichés. The richest child he knows *is* a brat who behaves like a ghastly little adult, his star *is* a capricious diva who considers herself the Simone de Beauvoir of show business (even though she's under the impression that Simone de Beauvoir was Jacqueline Onassis's mother as well as Jean-Paul Sartre's lover).

Her hair is being combed and twisted and teased. *"George,"* she says, glancing back and forth between their reflections as he sits down beside her. On the wall behind them, also reflected in the mirror, are the posters for her best-known feature films from the eighties—*Killer* and *Killer Again.* "Thank you."

He smiles. "You're welcome, Angela." Then, "Well, I guess that settles that. I'm glad we had this chance to talk things through."

"Don't tease. Everything is not a joke, George. But I want you to know I appreciate your collegiality." She pronounces it "college-ality"; because he's wearing a tweed jacket over a cardigan and carrying a spiral notebook, George thinks for an instant, maybe *college-ality* is what she means. "I just don't think I can do it. I can't . . ." As she searches for *le mot juste,* her chin jabs toward the script sitting beneath the platter of sun-dried boysenberries on the counter. (A steady dressing-room supply of sun-dried boysenberries is one of Angela's contractual requirements, along with a production assistant to take care of Peacemaker, whom she likes to bring to the set.) "I cannot . . . *validate* Lucas's racist remark. Do you know? Mary Ann," she says to the stylist calmly, "I can still see that same fucking piece of frizz by my left ear."

"He's not going to say 'slant-eye.' "

"No, the other one. In the script."

George knows what she's talking about. As the scene ends, two pot smugglers from Maui are on the floor, apprehended and bleeding. Cowboy Quesada has a speech that ends with the line, "And your little creep here isn't the gook we want." Jennie O'Donnell, Angela's character, is supposed to ignore Cowboy and say to her black sergeant before she walks off-camera, "Book 'em Dan-o." That's the button of the scene, and the end of the act.

"I don't think you're validating anything with that line," George says. "Except that Lucas is sort of a pussy and a dope." George momentarily worries: is one not supposed to use "pussy" in this sense? "Cowboy, I mean."

"But the *Hawaii Five-O* reference, it's just so—it's Jennie saying, 'These suspects are Pacific Islanders and so I'm going to make a wisecrack referencing their race.' It's just bad form." Although Angela Janeway grew up in Council Bluffs, Iowa, and on *NARCS* plays a character who grew up in Middle Village, Queens, her off-camera speaking manner is from some imaginary place out over the Atlantic due east of New Haven, where classy Americans still have nearly British accents. The verbs she favors—*validate, referencing, empower*—save her from being a straight Hepburn impersonator, the same way that in brand-new old-looking houses the skylights and cathedral ceilings and giant TV screens remind you that it isn't *really* 1903. "*I* wouldn't go there, George. I never even watched that show. That isn't me. That just isn't Jennie."

"That just isn't Jennie" or "Cowboy wouldn't do that" are the euphemisms actors and producers and directors and writers use instead of "I hate the line you wrote" or "Your acting is phony." It's a white-lie etiquette code meant to spare feelings, but not because show business is humane: candor would provoke arguments and name calling, which sends people stomping off sets, which delays shooting schedules, which results in overtime, which is expensive, which is impermissible, particularly in television, and particularly at MBC.

It isn't you, Angela, George thinks, *because* you *have never intentionally said anything funny that wasn't scripted for you by somebody else.* "It isn't you, Angela. I appreciate that. But it is Jennie. Jennie didn't get an MFA from Yale." *You dog, George.* "Jennie doesn't read books—she does watch TV, that's her frame of reference." *You brazen self-loathing dog.* "And as you've put it so perfectly, Jennie keeps the painful parts of life at bay by making jokes." *You pathetic brazen self-loathing corndog whore, George.* "And that's why Angela Janeway is playing her, because she can stretch, and she *can* go there. 'Book 'em, Dan-o' is a witty line. 'Book 'em Dan-o' is the right line. Trust me, Angela." When he's trying to persuade actors (or his children) to do something, George exempts himself from his rule against resorting to first names. Gestures and statements he regards as inexcusably oleaginous come across to actors as menschy. What he considers tasteful adult reticence, Angela Janeway and Lucas Winton consider cold and aloof. Occasionally during the last year, George has forced himself to talk like an asshole Merry Chatterer so that his actors won't consider him an asshole Inscrutable Hardass. "Okay?"

The stylist squirts and brushes the star's hair one final time.

"Mary Ann likes the line," Angela says, glancing toward the stylist. "She said it's 'postmodern,' didn't you, Mary Ann?" The young woman smiles.

"So we're all set?" George asks.

Angela keeps him waiting for an answer, and waiting. In her pouty old-fashioned girlishness, like a lot of actresses (and so entirely unlike his wife), Angela sometimes reminds George more of a female impersonator than of an actual modern woman. For the first time since he's been in the trailer, Angela turns to look directly at George instead of his reflection.

"I suppose."

"I love you," he says with an inflection that puts it somewhere between smarmy and a good-natured parody of smarm. "Let's go to work."

"George?" She doesn't ask the question, she strings it out, waits to be solicited, like in a script. Talent.

"Havel's a no, but I'm still working on getting Mandela. A guy I know ghostwrote his autobiography. If we can't get him for a cameo here, I'll try to book him on *Real Time*—the new show. With you, as yourself, like we talked about. I promise."

"Actually, the new show is what I was going to ask about. About a recurring role."

"You want to be on *Real Time*?" This could be a good idea. It is probably a terrible idea. Good or bad, the idea is now here in the trailer

with them, like a small, panicked animal. George has to deal with it—
pick it up and pet it, or trap it, something. He needs to keep Angela
happy but he can't commit to anything. Enthusiastic but cautionary. Is
this the definition of temporize? "That's a really interesting idea, Angela. But *Real Time* at its core is going to be a news program. Real
news."

"Oh, I *know*, George. I've read your treatment. It's really quite brilliant. That's exactly why I'm so highly motivated. Reality is so much
more exciting to me than"—she waves toward the script—"this. Sandy
Flandy was going to talk to you, but I said, 'No, I need to talk to George
myself, directly, artist to artist.' " George has never in his life thought of
himself as an artist. " 'So he can understand how totally serious I am
about this.' " She tosses a handful of dried boysenberries into her mouth.
"You know about my work internationally. This is not some silly actress
ego trip, George," she says, chewing, her mouth completely full. "It's
about *War and Peace* and Dostoyevsky's selfish steam." She swallows.

War and Peace *and Dostoyevsky's selfish steam?* George doesn't know
the line. He's clueless about all but the most obvious poetry references,
such as "I saw the best minds of my generation destroyed by madness"
and "In the room the women come and go / Talking of Michelan-
gelo." Typical pretentious Angela.

"You know?" she continues. "Not *my* personal self-esteem so much
as American women's, our f-ing self-esteem as a *gender.*"

Ah: *war and peace and just our f-ing self-esteem.*

"You think you could manage the work, on both shows? With all
your outside commitments?"

"I'd resign from the Creative Coalition, and Friends of the Mexican
Citizens Movement for Democracy, and all of them. So that I'd become objective."

"Well, this is a big idea. We haven't even thought about"—he hesitates—"casting. But I'm completely flattered that you're interested. I
mean, as a vote of confidence in the show. Let me talk to Emily about
it."

"Sandy says I'm nuts, but I'll audition. I don't really audition."

"I know. I know." Since he's already faking a placid, interested
smile, he goes ahead and asks, "Angela, where'd you happen to get
hold of the *Real Time* treatment? From Timothy?"

"No, from Aries, your darling assistant. She is so fantastic. So warm and *giving.* Cute name, too. You don't mind that I talked to Sandy about it, do you?"

George shakes his head, and then, trying to move beyond his rage at *motherfucking loose-cannon Iris,* lets Angela's mention of Sandy Flandy remind him of Sandi Bemis, Featherstone's second-string girlfriend, the pet aromatherapist who wants to enlighten and exploit Angela's German shepherd. "Where's the dog?" he says, looking around the trailer. "Out exploring Great Kills?"

Angela looks at George for a long moment and then crumples back into her makeup chair, crying, sobbing, out of her mind. "Head *back!*" Mary Ann says to Angela, and begins placing cotton balls around her eyes, building a pair of tiny dams to hold back the rivulets of tears from the cosmetically perfect facial plains. "Peacemaker passed on," Mary Ann whispers to George as he heads for the door.

She'll perform the line as written, but now she's a soggy, quivering wreck who wants George to make her an anchorwoman. Peacemaker may have died, but now George doesn't have to ask her to enroll her dog in an aromatherapy class. One step forward, one half step back. As George heads to the set to let Phoebe and Gordon know that he has solved the Angela problem, he passes Lucas Winton, who is tugging down on his prop bulletproof vest, apparently trying to expose some chest hair. "George," he says, "we are not rewriting, are we?"

"Nope. Let's go do the scene."

"Hey, George—when do I get my travel expenses?"

"That's a Barbara conversation." Barbara is the *NARCS* production accountant.

"Quote, 'All out-of-pocket expenses incurred by talent for the purpose of promoting the program shall be reimbursed,' unquote." Lucas Winton flew his own plane down to Washington last month to appear at a press conference for Decent Entertainers Against Dope, a new group whose members vow to make citizens' arrests of fellow actors and crew members if they see them using illegal drugs. This is approximately the fifth time he has asked George to reimburse him for the money he spent on aviation fuel. "My PR gal says *Access Hollywood* aired my 'For me, *NARCS* isn't just acting' bite *again* last week. You can't buy this kind of promotion, George," he says as

George gives a big shrug and says again, "It's a Barbara conversation," and keeps walking.

Talent. Such a funny noun, George still thinks, after fifteen years, the way it's used in show business and news. On one level it's thoroughly denatured and pliable, like Silly Putty. Anybody the camera points at is talent, whether singular (*But George, Sylvester is talent*) or plural (*But George, Angela and Lucas are talent*), with the definite article (*He's the talent, George, not you*) or without. But for all the one-size-fits-all, the word is still *talent,* with the distinct implication that everyone except actors (and news anchors and correspondents) are just . . . regular people, mortals, grunts, grips. And conversely, depending on who is using the phrase under what circumstances, *talent* can also be loaded, discreetly turned into code for *pampered dumbbell* or *vainglorious martinet* or *nine-hundred-pound gorilla.*

In front of the cameras, at the center of dozens of motionless people and tons of equipment, the two actors playing the Hawaiian drug dealers are on the ground, the one who's supposed to be shot staring at the dark red syrup drizzled around his shoulder wound. One of the three actors wearing DEA windbreakers, his MAC-10 propped against a lighting stanchion, seems to be practicing tai chi, or impersonating a cat. The silk, a giant stretched square of white fabric to make the sunlight more perfect, hangs overhead like an angel's trampoline.

"Checking the gates!" the first assistant director announces, to everyone and no one.

Each camera's own first assistant (or focus-puller—*focus-puller,* George's favorite of the filmmaking Dickensianisms) crouches down and slides out a tiny metal-framed glass pane from behind each lens to examine it with a magnifying glass. He's looking for a "hair in the gate"—by which is not meant a human hair (as George spent weeks last summer being teased for assuming) but rather any stray sliver of celluloid.

"Moving on?" the first AD asks Gordon and George, who is just back from Angela's RV.

Gordon looks at George and says, "Happy here?"

George raises his right arm and draws a circle in the air, a hand signal meaning *Yup, move on* that he learned last year from watching Emily run the first six episodes of the show. Making the gesture still feels phony to George, but it pleases him too, the wordless macho theatricality. (Last fall Max visited the set when Dennis Rodman was guest-starring as a crack dealer turned born-again Christian congressman. "Dad," his son asked at the end of the day, "did you do the basketball-ref signal for traveling just because Dennis Rodman was in the show?" Since Max always seems a little upset when his father reveals some new depth of sports ignorance, George just smiled and shook his head.)

"Moving on," the first shouts to the group. And a moment later, "Reloading camera!"

"Resetting lights!" the lighting designer announces.

"Resetting props!" the prop master announces. The show's armorer (another delightfully premodern job title) collects his prop Glocks and MAC-10s and AR-15s.

While George was coddling Angela, Featherstone arrived, and he now sits in the canvas chair imprinted with the words GEORGE MAC-TIER in cursive script. He is, of course, talking on one of his two phones. George crouches to look at a video monitor with Gordon, watching the taped replay of the fight scene they had just shot. Behind him he hears a *snap,* and a sound like little rubber snakes slithering away. He turns to see Featherstone fiddling happily with his not-available-in-North-America Ping-Pong-hemisphere phone as if he's giving an in-store demonstration.

"King George! Truly fantabulous work going on here this morning. They were really wailing." He pockets the phone and walks over. "Gordy is making some mega-auteur choices, literally. Truly amazing they *pay* us to do this, isn't it, guys?"

No, George thinks, *they pay me to do this, and I pay Gordon to do this. They do pay you, and that truly is amazing—although I don't believe it's this, precisely, that you get the three million dollars a year to do.*

"So," Featherstone says a little more quietly, "Lady Macbeth has PMS and won't do your *Hawaii Five-O* gag? You *got* to have that. It's such a genius blow for the act break."

"Angela's okay. She'll do the line. She's just upset because her dog is dead."

"*Peacemaker died?* My God! Well. No wonder."

George nods, a little humbled. Until it froze to death he didn't know that his own children's turtle was named Josh, and yet the second in command at the fifth-ranked television network in America knows the name of the dog owned by one of the stars of one of his twenty-seven prime-time shows. That is executive aptitude.

Just then Angela arrives, with Mary Ann the makeup woman trailing her with a handful of dry cotton balls as a contingency.

Featherstone fixes the star with a fraternal gaze and stops her before she steps onto the set, gently grabbing her by both shoulders. "Angela? *Use* it. *Use* the grief." Angela's eyes open wide, as if God has spoken. "It'll be good for the work—and you know what else, Angela? It's what Peacemaker would want you to do." She nods, wiser, warmed, blessed. Again George is humbled. It's a gift Timothy has.

"And when you're up to it?" Featherstone says, now back to his regular Featherstone FM chirp, "Xoloitzcuintili. You are definitely a xoloitzcuintili person, Angela. It's really just the minidisk German shepherd. Better fidelity, smaller size."

"Waiting on prop department!" the first AD says not quite peevishly, as a young woman primps a burst bale of fake marijuana.

Just behind one of the two cameras, George stands with one foot on a big silver film canister, arms folded, lips pursed, his concentration and hopefulness so intense it aches. The sixty people who stand and crouch around all work for him, and they are all (except for the Teamsters) so *wide awake*. George adores the take-one moment, revels in it, time after time. It is just like in the movies—one more cliché that happily turns out to be true. He's been doing this for almost a year, but on the set, as shooting begins, he still feels like a lucky usurper in some exotic province where the people speak a queer English dialect that's all gerunds, a kind of paramilitary town-crier present tense that serves mainly to tauten the mood. The show is scripted, of course, but for all practical purposes so is every bit of ritual that surrounds the shoot.

"Waiting for sound speed," the first AD says.

"Sound speed," the sound man confirms.

"We have sound speed!" the first says, almost shouting. "Very quiet, we're rolling."

George watches the live video image of the actors, not the actors themselves. Doing this, he reminds himself of his father, who would take a big dry-cell-operated Zenith portable to Metropolitan Stadium so he could watch the Twins on TV outdoors at the game—which had the effect of making an extremely boring experience extremely embarrassing as well, a kind of Minnesota childhood apotheosis.

"*A* marker," says the assistant standing in front of one of the cameras as she claps her clapper.

"*B* marker," says the assistant in front of the second camera.

Gordon is about to give the command. He never says "Action!" He has his own little directorial affectation. "And . . ." says Gordon, standing just in front of George, ". . . *acting!*"

Cowboy Quesada springs up off the floor, and comes up behind Jennie O'Donnell, who is turned away, pretending to talk to Dan, her young uniformed sergeant.

"No, Jennie," Cowboy says, "this isn't about budgets, or about the DEA getting credit for the bust. Or about our personal BS. This is about doing the right thing. And your little creep here isn't the gook we want. Not the one you *ought* to want."

Jennie (Angela Janeway) ignores Cowboy (Lucas Winton), and walks stage left, pausing to glance with an insouciant wiseass smile at Dan (Sylvester Wayans).

She says, "Book *him,* Daniel."

As he yells, "Cut," Gordon looks at George, who has closed his eyes, and then at the AD.

"Doing it again!" the AD shouts.

2 0

It is officially Harold Mose's nap time, twelve to twelve-thirty, when he takes no calls and allows no interruptions. Sometimes he naps. Sometimes he thinks. Sometimes, like today, he fiddles around on the computer. As he uses his black stone mouse to grab the corner of the video image and yank it open, he glances at his little ME window: the analysts at Merrill and at Morgan have both lowered their earnings estimates by two cents a share, and in the last ten minutes the share price has fallen to 38⅞. Below 39! Just since noon! He should call down to Grace Carpenter and have her buy back some more shares, he thinks, and he pushes the yellow videocam button—that is, the picture of a yellow video camera that sits permanently on his screen. The picture of the camera pulsates when he clicks on it. No, he decides then, no: poker face, keep the poker face and don't overplay the hand. He smiles, seeing these bets against the company—down again, 38¹³⁄₁₆—because the wise-guy analysts are all guessing, and Harold Mose *knows*. The end of a quarter can be very sweet, the sweetest, when you feel a little godlike (if God were smug), that moment just before you drop the poker face and show your three kings and jack pair. Lowball projections, upside surprise! Sometimes it is so easy. But now the new quarter is starting and there'll be a whole new hand to play. And Mose Media Holdings definitely needs to make its digital move in the second quarter.

This computer fiddling, then, counts as research. Three years ago, even two, Mose was a little embarrassed to use one himself. He was a conscientious upgrader, always state-of-the-art—386 to 486, 486 to Pentium, Pentium to Pentium Pro to Pentium II to Pentium III—and threw out four successive virgin machines in 1995, 1996, 1997, and 1998. But now he is a virtuoso, a proselytizer, a man of the new age. Using a computer is no longer like mucking around with the coffee machine himself or making his own copies; it's like flying his own jet. Seated six hundred feet over Fifty-seventh Street, blue sky at his back, Mose clicks with his little arrow on Lizzie's memo, pricks it, makes it disappear.

Dragging open the video window is itself a pleasure, like pulling back a curtain in a dream, as the live image grows ten times, twenty times bigger in less than a second. The flashing red numerals above the picture, illegibly tiny before, are now an inch high: "$9.95! (1ST 5 MIN-UTES)" And the very pink human figure, tinier than a Cracker Jack trinket an instant ago, is now suddenly as big as a child's doll, a jumbo-size doll with long blond hair, wearing only thigh-high white leather boots and holding her own breasts. "Hi! It's me, Elizabeth!" she says, lisping, "would you like me to—?" before Mose mutes the sound on his computer by clicking on a tiny picture of a speaker with his right hand (his mouse hand, his free hand, the one not now rummaging through folds of charcoal-gray vicuna and white Sea Island cotton). And then with his right index finger he taps the F3 key, which sends a preprogrammed message to the Tenth Avenue loft where "Elizabeth" and two dozen other young women (and men) sit naked in front of two dozen digital cameras. Her mouth is still moving, but now her words appear in print across the bottom of the computer screen, like a stock ticker. OKAY, Elizabeth is saying, according to the live-text crawl, YOU CAN JUST *WATCH* WHILE SOME OF MY OTHER HOT FRIENDS ASK ME TO PUT ON A NASTY SHOW FOR THEM. She continues massaging her breasts as her face—lips slightly parted, eyes half closed—rather abruptly assumes the standard preecstatic expression. OOOH! flies across the screen, and then: YOU WANT ME TO FINGER MY HOT JUICY CUNT?

But Harold Mose misses her response to the "other friends" as it races by, live, because he's looking again at the corner of his screen, where the Mose Media stock price ticks down to 38⅜. *"Yes,"* he says, before returning his attentions to the naked woman.

Now he watches as she moves both hands down across her belly and between her thighs, and fakes a creditable little shiver. SHOULD I DO IT LIKE THIS? says the text running across her shins. Then, a little later, it reads: MMMMMMMMM! YES, SIR!! Then another long space, and whizzing from right to left across the screen all by itself: :) :) :) :) :). She's punctuating, she's punctuating, *she's punctuating.*

On the opposite end of the global village, 9,582 miles away, another computer screen sits atop plastic beer crates stacked in a one-room cinder-block building half the size of Harold Mose's private office. It's late in Tamranti, Negri Sembilan, Malaysia, long after midnight, past everybody's bedtime, but Radin, the local smart boy, has pleaded with his friends and friends' fathers to stay just a little longer at the community center, which Radin is calling his "cyber–*kelab malam,*" his digital nightclub. He swears the call *will* go through this time, that it will be beyond amazing, unimaginably fine. Since Radin got laid off at the Samsung complex down in Seremban and came back to live in Tamranti, he has been the hamlet's self-appointed entertainment mogul. He leases out his two Nintendo 64 machines by the week, rents videos of Madonna and Jean-Claude Van Damme movies for one ringgit a night, and sells Tiger beer on the side. Tonight eighteen teenage boys and men, half the males in town, sit cross-legged, chatting, by now mostly ignoring the computer screen, occasionally insulting Radin as he desperately taps at his keyboard.

Finally! *"Apa kabar!"* Radin shouts. *"Ya!"*

The men of Tamranti fall silent, riveted and dumbfounded by the live picture that has appeared on Radin's computer screen. After one young boy asks earnestly why on earth the American whore is wearing boots, the men laugh and relax. They begin shouting out which acts they want *"Lee-*zee-beet" to perform. Radin is working hard. He pecks at the keyboard, looks up to watch her follow the typed-in orders of her hot friends in Malaysia, simultaneously translates her words, joins in the resulting chorus of hoots and howls, then furiously types the next command. "Okay . . . my other hot friends ask me to put on a nasty show for them . . . Oooh! . . . You want me to finger my hot juicy cunt? . . . Mmmmmmmmmm! Yes, *sir*!!" Radin is happy, happy because of what this will do for his reputation, happy because he'll collect forty ringgit for the computer show, happy because he's recording Elizabeth's performance on his hard drive—it's one-of-a-kind porno, probably worth some money in Kuala Lumpur.

Again the men fall silent, this time aghast. *"Teedak! Teedak!"* two of the older ones shout. "No! No!" Suddenly, appended to the side of Elizabeth's screen is its evil twin, a grainier video image of another American performing an obscene act—a man! A rich white man in a suit and tie with old skyscrapers behind him, handling his penis! *"Teedak, Radin!"* Radin's uncle stands and carefully places two Tiger empties on the crate in front of the masturbating man, obscuring him. Well done. Their Minangkabau virtue and aesthetics no longer threatened, the male population of Tamranti returns to its friendly dialogue with the compliant girl in the loft in lower Manhattan.

2 1

"**Welcome** to SeaTac International," the Continental Airlines greeter says as each passenger, including Lizzie, shuffles past him. "Welcome to SeaTac *International* . . . *Welcome* to SeaTac International." SeaTac is such a terrible name for an airport, so perfect for Seattle (and Tacoma), like U-Dub for the University of Washington, triple-dub for the World Wide Web, Comp Sci, DOS. This is a city where adults get an undergraduate kick out of speaking slangy abbreviations in lieu of real English words, all on the pretext of *quickness*. She wouldn't have been surprised if the guy at the gate had actually said "Welcome to SeaTac *Intl*." But Microsoft might find that objectionable—bundled promotion for Intel Corporation.

A *beeeep* sounds just as she walks past the unmanned metal detector toward the terminal, and her former seatmate looks back at her skeptically, but it's a phone call, not a weapon.

"Lizzie Zimbalist, please. It's Chas Prieve calling. She'll know what it's in reference to."

The kid is officious but persistent. "This is Lizzie. Hi. Where are you?"

"K-L! Sepang International, just about to board! Have I caught you at a bad time?"

"No, I'm at the airport myself. In Seattle." Malaysia to America, mobile phone to mobile phone, airport to airport: how *now*.

"Gosh!" Chas says, excited. "Airport wireless to airport wireless. Are you using Iridium? I am." Lizzie thinks of Max: this is just the kind of thing that deeply pleases him, like when he spots a digital clock at 11:11. In a nine-year-old, the behavior is cute.

"So your guy in New York told me you might have a second, tomorrow, to let me brief you. Although actually it's *already* tomorrow here."

"The Sorrento at four o'clock?"

"I think there are some superexciting opportunities for Fine Technologies over here. And I now have a great relationship with one of the prime game jobbers in the region."

"Great, see you tomorrow."

Seattle is dumpy, despite the mountains and trees, like a gawky guy with a great body who stammers and wears ugly clothes. It's a kind of urban dumpiness she tries not to despise. "You didn't spend eighteen years living in St. Paul," George snapped a few weeks ago after she suggested that if they lived in Seattle he might be able to produce *NARCS* in Vancouver.

But Lizzie realized again, during the weekend at Lake Marten, that the New York (and L.A.) contempt for Seattle (and for Silicon Valley) can't be argued away. In the last few years, it has diminished some, and changed in texture—from dismissive and stupid, to alarmed and baffled, to supercilious and slightly less baffled. Her husband and her friends regard residents of Seattle (and Milpitas and Sunnyvale and all the rest) the way Americans think of Canadians—they *seem* like us, and their lives look clean and civil, but . . . who wants to hang out with earnest grad students full-time? Or as Ben Gould said about the titans of the digital coast at her last board meeting, "For such gigantic winners, they're such losers."

The main line of mutual contempt that used to flow between the coasts—New York versus L.A.—mostly devolved into Woody Allen and Johnny Carson punch lines by the time Lizzie left Brentwood for Cambridge and Manhattan. For all the civilization versus sun-and-sex schtick, and all of Lizzie's own adolescent rants, her two hometowns seem similar. People in New York and L.A. fuss hysterically over nuances of style and status that would be invisible elsewhere. People in both New York and L.A. are happiest in their souks, bartering and wheedling over the current value of houses and art and reputations. They care with equal and dazzling Bessemer passion about the monumentally unimportant—about living on the correct side of the correct street in the correct latitude of the correct neighborhood, about sitting at the best table at the best hour at the best restaurant, about wearing the right shade of indigo, thickness of sole, expression of sangfroid. Lizzie likes to think she has moved beyond automatic scorn or pity for this strain of bicoastal madness. She has begun to see all the Bel Air and Park Avenue *wanting* as a perverse romanticism, vanity and self-advancement pursued so monomaniacally that they turn inside out and become a kind of naïveté, the naïveté of children. And she also knows that to her painter and social worker friends in Williamsburg and Hoboken (and to George's family in Verve and St. Paul) she and George are themselves kooky, dilettantish neo-Tory socialites devoted to the costly and the frivolous and the irrational.

By Seattle's lights too, she figures, she's a kooky, dilettantish neo-Tory socialite devoted to the costly and the frivolous and the irrational. Out here, they mistrust New York precisely the way Americans used to mistrust Europe. And their contempt for Hollywood is the age-old contempt of sensible, hardworking northerners for the slatternly South. But at the moment, each of the three places—New York and L.A. and the Northwest digitalopolis—hungers for an ingredient only the other two can provide. It's the old Fred and Ginger symbiosis (class for sex) extended into a Metternichian three-way alliance. Give us publicity, and you can underwrite our IPO; you give us gravitas, we'll give you sheen; you supply the video, we'll provide the stream; you give us the candy, we'll give you the eyes; you let us meet movie stars, we'll invest in your studio; you advertise us, we'll advertise you; you promote our shows, we'll take you seriously; you take *us* seriously, we'll give you a 600-megahertz set-top box. Deal; deal; deal. And we all go on *Charlie Rose.*

She knows New York is irrevocably in the dustbin of history. She still enjoys living in her particular part of the dustbin, especially now that it's gotten clean and safe. But she knows it's this strip of America, from here down through Portland to the Bay and the Valley, that is the future, knows it in precisely that dumb, scanning-the-coastal-horizon way—yet another cliché that happens to be correct. Driving up Interstate 5 in her rented white Taurus, she wonders if these malls and endless plains of Boeing hangars and runways will be remembered as comprising one of the great renaissance cities of the new century. Way up ahead, rising behind the skyline, she sees the Space Needle, a ridiculous and wonderful old *Jetsons* folly.

Will history, a couple of centuries from now, conflate the details, so that the Space Needle will be a misapprehended artifact—*You know,* her great-great-great-grandchildren will say, *the Space Needle, Epcot, Reagan, Microsoft, TV, all that early renaissance stuff.* Maybe, she thinks, those same great-great-great-grandchildren will gaze on the software she's making now with something like her own wonder looking at the brass levers and springs and painted details on eighteenth-century automatons, or 1914 Bugatti roadsters, pieces of Golden Age technology that look to us both gorgeous and fusty, miraculous despite their primitivism. A *single* video game that *forty* programmers working together in a *factory* for a full *year* crafted *by hand*!

Lizzie would like to believe she's now present at the dawn of a renaissance, as the zealots and flimflammers and wise men of the digital age have been testifying for a decade. Maybe Speak Memory and Y2KRx and ShowNet and Warps are a perfect little Milanese chapel fresco, a de' Medici tomb carving, a school-of-Titian history painting. Maybe. But in her heart of hearts she thinks this is an industrial revolution, not a blossoming of culture, that she's no artist or patron or merchant princess but a factory owner turning out decent cotton aprons and good, painted crockery. Which would make Redmond and Santa Clara more the Leeds and Birmingham of the twenty-first century than its Florence and Venice.

An insanely courteous Leeds and Birmingham, she thinks, as she passes the electronic road signs warning that the highway is about to shrink from four lanes down to one just before her exit. The cars promptly and prudently slow—*every* car, even the one in front of her with the I'D RATHER BE SMASHING IMPERIALISM bumper sticker—and wait to take their place in a slow, mile-long queue. In New York, half the drivers would now be jockeying madly for position in a game of speed and brake and feint, cutting in line, disregarding the fucking five-mile-an-hour single-file line, fuck *you.*

Such nice white people. Lizzie rarely thinks of Jews as her home team, of gentiles versus Jews as salient, but here, now, she can't help it. Still, she doesn't hate this earnest, earnest, eager-beaver city, if only because of REI. She hasn't climbed in years, but as she browses the store, she finds herself wanting to buy gear simply because the objects are so precise and purposeful—accidentally sexy. She fondles the purple anodized aluminum cam units; the fake-stone climbing-wall grips and holds—black and red and marbleized green, abstract shapes as small as netsuke and as big as skulls; the heavy coils of black-and-gray rope, MoMA-gorgeous; a chalk ball, soft but tough, that makes her remember the one that disintegrated on Mount Washington, turning her hand and face Kabuki white. She hefts a Chinese chrome exercise sphere, smaller than a billiard ball but twice as heavy, and touches the tasteful matte helmets, the magnesium bars for starting fires, the thirty-five-square-foot gold emergency blanket vacuum-packed into a two-inch cube. The only time she was in Seattle with George, for a wedding, she brought him here, and he said it was like touring the supply depot of an alien expeditionary force. Which is true, and why she loves it. He also said, standing right here by the ice axes, that this was her "equipment jones," that she reminded him of Roger Baird yammering about his fly rods and antique cars. George resents her climbing, she suspects, because it is such a *two-handed* sport.

Ten minutes and $245 later, she's on her way back downtown to meet the guy who runs a hardware company called Goat Rodeo. The corporate name isn't just a random whimsy in an industry full of companies called Yahoo! and Oracle, it's particularly cocky and ironical—*goat rodeo* is slang for corporate dysfunction and stupidity. Goat Rodeo sells a five-hundred-dollar liquid-crystal video display called PerfectView, tiny monitors that game players strap onto their face like a pair of glasses. Goat Rodeo's next-generation device, its holy grail, is iZ, pronounced "eyes." iZ is a tube the size and shape of a stubby pencil meant to replace computer monitors the way mice have replaced computer keyboards, particularly for people playing games like Warps. It scans video images continuously and directly onto players' retinas.

She finds the Goat Rodeo address just off Pioneer Square. This neighborhood has its quintessential Seattle aspects—a wonderful overstocked map store, a wonderful overstocked toy store, a wonderful overstocked bookstore. (She doesn't mind, as George said when he was here, that "half the store is devoted to Garrison Keillor and *Blue High-ways* and Louise Erdrich novels.") Pioneer Square also has its obligatory man-made water feature, Waterfall Park. But the neighborhood is flat, the buildings are dark and old and close together, and there is a leavening of winos. It's her favorite part of the city. Walking down Occidental Avenue, she sees a white couple in their late teens or twenties, both lavishly pierced—a gold ball on each of her nostrils and a tin girder through the bridge of her nose; on him at least six rings per ear, three in an eyebrow, and one rough yellow crystal on the upper lip—no doubt intended, at least obliquely, to simulate snot. The woman's T-shirt says CALL ME A CUNT AND I'LL CUT OFF YOUR BALLS. As Lizzie passes them, stepping into the street to cross, she turns and stares for a second, not for the reason the boy and girl happily imagine, but because the Doc Martens nihilists are standing on the curb, waiting for the red DON'T WALK sign to change to a green WALK before they'll cross. They'd rather be smashing imperialism, too.

From the reception area, the Goat Rodeo offices look and feel like Fine Technologies', except even more boyish (along one wall a five-foot-high DAWGS is spelled out in fist and hammer gashes through the Sheetrock) and much roomier—not bigger, but probably twice as many square feet per unhealthy-looking-young-man-with-goatee. She scrawls her name in one second and hands it back to the receptionist.

"Before I laminate I'm supposed to ask you to *read* the language above where you signed," says the receptionist, and hands the visitor's name tag back to Lizzie. "It's necessary"—she makes air quotes—" 'legally.' " Lizzie takes the card back and tries to focus on the tick-size lines of type. Watched by this girl wearing overalls, however, she is careful to avoid even a hint of the middle-aged racking move, the incremental positioning of small print—a little closer, a little farther, a *little* closer—to find the optimal depth of field. She sees that what she has signed is the world's tiniest contract, a five-millimeter-by-thirty-millimeter nondisclosure agreement in which she has not only promised to keep confidential everything she sees or hears at Goat Rodeo, but has agreed preemptively to forfeit any new intellectual property rights that may arise out of any conversation she has with any Goat Rodeo employee. In other words, they own anything she says here.

Lizzie hands the tag back. "Do they want my firstborn too?"

"That's okay," the girl says blankly as she encases the tag in plastic and hands it back, still hot, to Lizzie. "Tommy's office is all the way down the end of that hallway, then all the way to the left."

The offices have doors, but all the doors are open, and every cubicle is standard issue—the hazy whiteboards, the fat EXPO colored markers and plastic spray bottles of colored-marker cleaner, the multiple computers and soda cans, the candy wrappers, the harsh fluorescence, the charmless dormitory mess. And as she click-clacks past the offices in her expensive black shoes and black Armani suit, feeling like the visiting adult, she sees and hears that in two of the offices—no, three—arguments are loudly under way, about "T3 pipes," about how many trillion bytes of data are on the web, and about astigmatism. During her years at the foundation, she never heard voices raised, not one time, since even the people who despised each other agreed about everything and didn't care very much about facts. She's used to discussions among computer guys—almost every discussion boiling into a debate—although at her shop, the language barriers put a fetter on the tendency. But whenever she's been out here, every technical and business disagreement is heated and zero-sum, a friendly fight to the death. Someone is smarter, and the smarter person must win. It is a dialect rarely spoken in New York, and so different from Los Angelese as to be essentially untranslatable. Seattle does remind her of college, like George says, but an all-male college where everyone is majoring in the same subject. She doesn't hate it. It is her major too.

As she turns left, she sees Tommy Thayer in profile at the end of the hall, bouncing a basketball once and passing it, hard, to someone she can't see, inside an office. She recognizes him from the TED conference in Monterey a year ago, where he gave a speech to seven hundred businesspeople and scientists and designers about "what totally sucks in this business." She thought he was an asshole, not because he used the word *sucks* sixty-seven times in twenty minutes, or even because he used the phrase *kick some corporate booty,* but because he oozed pride in being the kind of jaunty, crew-cut, chinos-and-Converse alterna-CEO who would give such a speech.

"The princess of Silicon Alley!" he says, his mouth full of something. "Welcome to the Emerald City."

Fuck you. "Hi," she says, reaching out to shake Thayer's hand. "It's good to finally meet."

As they sit down in his office, the Goat Rodeo chief technology officer, a man named Robbie, who's closer to Sarah's age than Lizzie's, sits on a couch dribbling the basketball on the wood floor between his feet. His wandering left eye, which always seems to be looking at his boss, makes Lizzie feel sorry for him. She sees why Thayer's mouth was full: it's always full because he is a chain-eater of giant, two-inch-diameter SweeTarts, which he keeps in a black wire basket on his desk. In the first five minutes, they get their real business out of the way, which mainly entails Thayer nodding, claiming they are now way ahead of Microvision, the more established VRD (virtual retinal display) startup, and using the word *deliverable* as a noun over and over and over again.

"My guy said you're willing to indemnify Fine Technologies on product liability for iZ?" she says.

Donk-donk-donk-donk-donk-donk-donk . . . Robbie the technology boy is still dribbling.

"Limited indemnity as he defined it, sure, that's definitely a deliverable," Tommy says.

Donk-donk-donk-donk-donk-thwap, swoosh, *thwap.* Robbie passes to Tommy. Tommy proceeds to twirl the ball on an index finger, but he doesn't dribble.

"And in your beta testing you haven't come across any medical issues?" Lizzie asks. "Ophthalmological, neurological, whatever?"

Tommy passes the ball back to Robbie. *Donk-donk-donk-donk-donk-donk-donk-donk-donk* . . . Lizzie no longer considers his strabismus extenuating.

"Zero," Tommy says. "Zero on the retina, zero on the iris."

Donk-donk-thwap. "I've personally logged about nine hundred gaming hours with the product since the fall," Robbie says, speaking a full sentence for the first time, "and look at me. I'm cool."

Lizzie nods slowly, wondering if his bad eye prevents him from knowing when she's staring at it with both of her good ones, and using the pause to calculate Robbie's exposure (nine hundred hours, six months—five hours every day). Lizzie has been in this business six years, her bar is high, but the easy slur (*Get a fucking life, kid*) remains apt.

Donk-donk-donk-donk-donk-donk-donk-donk-donk . . .

"We had a year of animal experiments, offshore, tweaking it before we ever tried it on civilians. A few Irish bunny rabbits got zapped early on, but—" Thayer catches himself, and turns suddenly solemn. "That's between us. You signed the NDA," he says, nodding at the tag dangling from her collar over her left breast.

Donk-donk-donk-donk-donk-donk-donk-donk-donk . . .

"Of course, sure," she says, "no problem."

Donk-donk-donk-donk-donk . . . Lizzie gives a game smile to Robbie and puts her hands up, a foot apart, palms in. *Donk-thwap.* As she catches his pass, she leans down and tucks the ball under the chair, between her feet and her Kate Spade bag.

She turns back to Thayer. "Antivivisection isn't my issue. I'd rather have a few of your rabbits go blind than my customers."

"Exactly," Thayer says, popping a yellow SweeTart in his mouth. Lizzie is reminded of the detergent disks her parents' housekeeper used to let her throw into the washing machine. "But a guy over here at U-Dub has been getting just *creamed* for using animals in his work. They're basically riding him out of town on a rail. The town of Kirkland actually passed a law saying they didn't want him to live there."

Lizzie knows he's talking about Buster Grinspoon. Deciding to commit a fib of omission, to let a sleeping lie lie, she changes the subject to smaller talk. She points to their name tags. Each has a blinking green digital display in the center—some pointless boys' club high-tech trick, she figures. "Why do you LED your ID numbers like that? And why is your number seven digits and Robbie's only five?"

Robbie, sulking since his basketball was taken away, now looks like he's about to cry. He stands suddenly, says, "Later," and rushes out of Thayer's office.

Thayer ignores him, so Lizzie does too.

"They look kind of cool," she says.

"Ms. New Yorker! They're not supposed to *look* cool. It's not an ID number, it's how many shares and exercisable options we own." He flips his tag up and looks down at it, then points at a little line of type. "The ID number is printed down here." He glances up. "You just zapped Robbie in his sore spot. He's only got, what, ninety thousand shares, and I've got a million-one. But I've worked for the company *three years,*" he says. Robbie feels like he's gotten to the start-up party too late. You know? Like all these kids out here now. They're jealous of how much easy money they think people our age piled up in the nineties."

Yet another generation gap! This time not between the greedy old and idealistic young, but between supergreed rewarded and supergreed denied. Lizzie felt something similar when she arrived in Manhattan and discovered that in the early eighties people hardly older than she had bought houses in the Village for $255,000 and giant Fifth Avenue duplexes for $324,000. And once again she thinks of the Microsoft numbers (*$31.5 million* for half the company, *$7 million* for her general partner's share), flashy and titillating, like advertising blimps hovering always just overhead.

"Are you guys making money here?" she asks. She knows you're not supposed to ask this of computer entrepreneurs, that it's the equivalent of asking religious people for proof of God's existence. And like a fundamentalist Christian convinced that the rapture is going to occur the week after next, Thayer smiles at Lizzie's childish, benighted, old-paradigm question.

Robbie returns, licking and biting an ice cream bar as big as his foot.

"Are we 'making money'?" Thayer says, slightly mocking, repeating the phrase as if she has asked where she could go poop. "Well, if you subtract our sales and marketing costs, we're profitable *today.* Even if we don't 'make money' until '02, in the sense of bottom-line *earnings,* the market cap will keep moving money into the business. Nongame video applications are what will take us over the top. But unfortunately, there's still an East Coast. People back there still aren't even doing rich e-mail."

By "rich" e-mail he means e-mail messages that contain photos, recorded voices, video clips. "My husband's company in New York has v-mail," Lizzie says.

"Did they do a VCR?" asks Robbie, the corners of his mouth smeary with chocolate.

As Lizzie hesitates, Thayer explains, "Video CIMBLE Retrofit."

"Beats me," she says. "What's a video symbol?"

"C-I-M-B-L-E," Robbie says, practically giggling with pleasure at her ignorance. "CIMBLE stands for CADETT Interactive Multi-User Business Learning Environment."

They all wait, exchanging glances, Thayer and Robbie smiling.

"Okay, you stumped the girl. *Cadet?*"

"Consortium," Robbie says, pausing to catch a melting vanilla stream with his tongue, "for ADvanced Education and Training Technologies. I have a question for you. On your game, with the polygon attribute editor in the Softimage Sega GDE, is the control of the Sega-specific rendering attributes on a per-polygon basis really up to snuff?"

"I'm not that deeply involved in the architecture of the technology." This is a line she delivers often.

Robbie smiles and nods. She knows he thinks she's mortified. She isn't. But in Seattle and down in Silicon Valley all the nonengineers are a little intimidated by the Robbies among them, because only the engineers understand, deeply understand, how the products work.

"I run the company," Lizzie adds. "I don't spend a lot of time debugging lines of code."

"Got you," Thayer says as if charmingly. "It's the you're-from-Venus-we're-from-Mars deal. We program and slay the beasts, and you," he says, pausing, chuckling, "market, or whatever."

Defending the Northeast against the Northwest, now driven to defend her gender; this really does feel like Harvard 1983. "You know, of course," Lizzie says, forcing a smile, standing to go, "that the first computer was programmed entirely by women. To do the calculations of ballistic trajectories. To blow up Nazis."

"You mean ENIAC?" Robbie says, sucking on his spatula-size Popsicle stick.

"Uh-huh." She prays for a pop quiz—she knows it stands for electronic numerical integrator and computer.

"ENIAC wasn't the first computer," Robbie says. "The *first* computer was developed at Iowa State by John Vincent Atanasoff and Clifford Berry. ENIAC was *based* on Atanasoff-Berry."

"He shoots, he *scores* against the lady from New York," says Thayer, giggling.

Lizzie smiles and, shaking their hands, promising to be in touch, wishing them well, looking at both men's skulls, thinks for a purgative couple of seconds about her brand-new, two-pound, two-foot-long Charlet Moser ice ax sitting in an REI shopping bag in the trunk of her rental car.

"Cut!" says Gordon. "Perfect. It's a wrap."

"Wrapping!" the first AD announces.

Featherstone is back talking to Lucas Winton, who didn't appear in the last scene. If employing Timothy Featherstone and building a soundstage in the basement on Fifty-seventh Street are the irrational prices Harold Mose pays to keep his own show business fantasies burning bright, driving his Hummer an hour through a tunnel and over a bridge to a grubby street in Staten Island is Featherstone's.

"God, I do love being on location," he says as George joins him.

"The smell of greasepaint," says George.

Featherstone sniffs. "Hmmm. I don't smell anything. Hey, George, can you give me a lift into the city?"

"You didn't drive your Humvee?" George asks.

"Sergeant Winton of the SAG wants to take command of the Hummer for a test-drive into occupied Manhattan." MBC pays for Featherstone to lease two identical bright blue three-and-a-half-ton turbo-diesel Hummer wagons, this one and another in L.A., even though they cost twice as much as a stretch limo and three times as much as a Town Car. The budgetary rationalization is that he drives himself. ("Lean, mean, and chauffeur-free!" Featherstone says.) George has wondered how he manages parking. But as they drop Lucas off at the Hummer on the way to the Land Cruiser, George sees that Featherstone's car has both NYP license plates, the New York laissez-passer for working journalists to park where regular civilians can't, *and,* in his front window, a location-scouting permit from the Mayor's Office of Film, Theater and Broadcasting. George feels both envious and superior, since he has never used either perk.

"*Extremely* cool device," Featherstone says about the driving prosthesis as George clamps it onto the steering wheel and heads for the Verrazano. "I've never seen you with that on. Is it Italian? Is that magnesium or titanium?"

"Just stainless steel, I think," George says.

"Man, I'm jealous of you. *I* want one." George smiles, but he knows Featherstone well enough to understand that his covetousness is sincere. If only to eat up dead airtime, George calls the office. Iris does not answer, and the machine picks up.

"You don't have your girl do the recording?" Featherstone says as they listen to George's voice on the car speaker. George dials the voice-mail number to retrieve messages—Milken's office again, a science teacher from St. Andrew's (if one of the kids had been killed, wouldn't he have called the set?), and Francesca from MTV, who's in town and desperately wants to hook up. As Featherstone listens, his eyebrows rise and his smile grows more salacious.

"I've been trying to get a hold of you all morning, and your wonderful assistant told me you were on the floor—"

"*Damn* it, Iris." To be "on the floor" means shooting in the studio, down beneath Fifty-seventh Street.

"—and she also said you were going to be meeting an old pal for a drink at Madison Avenue at six, but said you wouldn't mind if I joined you at six-thirty. So I hope that is okay. Great item in *Variety* this morning. I still really want it. Bye."

"You old fuck monkey! I'm getting hard just listening. 'I still really want it'?"

"She wants us to hire her for *Real Time.*"

"That's not a caca concept."

"What *Variety* story?"

"You didn't see it? Yeah, about your show. Saddler was cuckoo for Cocoa Puffs."

"Happy, you mean?"

"Way happy. It called us 'the premium weblet with class *and* controversy,' and quoted somebody calling Harold 'visionary.' And some analyst said he's 'bold' and 'brave.' Even though 'brave' means we're crazy motherfuckers to commit fifty big ones to you for this candy-mint/breath-mint show of yours. But any publicity is good publicity. What you got cooking with the Milken man?"

"Milken and I are buying the network, Timothy. An LBO. It was in *The Hollywood Reporter* today."

George looks straight ahead, not smiling. He has never joked like this with Featherstone, and in the two seconds of silence he can practically hear his mental gyroscope tripping and reversing as it strains to cope.

"Do you think we, I mean, if it happens . . ." Featherstone stops, and provisionally regains his composure. "You're yanking my chain, aren't you, G-boy? Very funny. But what is the deal with Milken?"

"I have no idea."

"Harold says he's got a red herring for this new power-of-positive-thinking company. Maybe he wants to pick your brain about his Good

News cable channel. Loserama if you ask me. I mean, it's like a parrot—the talking is a cute gimmick for the first five minutes, but do you really want to listen to it *say* anything? I don't think so."

"Is that what Lizzie said? The parrot thing?"

"No, that's what Harold said."

So. He's already watched his online-parrot analogy go from Lizzie to Harold to Barry Stengel, and now Timothy has made it his own and is offering it to him, a nice little closed loop—rhetorical incest. Should he be amused? He is not.

George hasn't been looking forward to the ride into the city with Featherstone. He gives emphatic but vague notes ("warm*er* but not *warm*") on Lucas's and Angela's performances ("You know I used to act, right? As a kid I played Taylor and Burton's son in *Who's Afraid of Virginia Woolf?* on Broadway") and says to "keep laying some deck so the audience can read the arc of the whole season." He also suggests to George that Sandi Bemis could be a technical adviser on the ESP-drug-dealers-and-K-9s episode. But then, after he asks what the Land Cruiser's "approach angle" is (George says he doesn't know; Featherstone says "the Hummer does seventy-two degrees without a winch, believe it or not"), and what he thinks of "that *wack* foul against my man Ewing last night" (George says he missed the Rangers game), Featherstone falls asleep. And so all the way up the West Side Highway to Fifty-seventh Street, through two different traffic jams caused by two different convoys of black Chevy Suburbans for two different presidential candidates, George can chew on his sour new wad of suspicion.

———

Shouldn't she be depressed by this place? Is she trying too hard to like it here because she should? In fact, as she drove her generic white Taurus east on I-90 through generic white Taurus land, she finds herself entertained—George-like—more than grossed out by the premium corporate strip in Bellevue, with its nice view of twenty-one traffic lanes; and by the town of Factoria, which consists exclusively of pet supply superstores, Dave's Sugar-Fried Boneless Chicken outlets, and three-hour-old condominiums ripped into the virgin hillsides. It's grotesque, sure, but isn't that always the way on the frontier? San Francisco was raw and ugly in 1850. West L.A. was raw and ugly in 1920. Lizzie Zimbalist was raw and ugly in 1976, when she was twelve.

In fact, Lizzie thinks as she pulls into a parking space at One Microsoft Way, Seattle's problem is that it's not nearly raw enough. One Microsoft Way: is that not the address of a cult? Notwithstanding the soccer field and arcade games, the lack of suits and ties and regular hours, a 1950s corporate DNA showed itself in these boys' blood strongly and immediately. What qualifies Nathan Myhrvold as the most flamboyant character in town? He's an amateur paleontologist with his own jet! He owns *really* expensive kitchen appliances, and he sometimes spends hundreds of dollars on a single bottle of wine! Whoooo-eee! It's the same with their immense bland houses in Hunts Point and Clyde Hill, and the Microsoft flag flying next to the Stars and Stripes, and the lame little fake waterfall trickling through the Red West campus—billionaires spending, not to transcend suburban backyard-patio boyhoods, but to reproduce them. It's not your father's Oldsmobile, but it sure is an Oldsmobile. Just inside one of the boxy buildings, at a reception desk, a young man instructs Lizzie to type her name on a keyboard. *So very DOS,* she thinks, *so autistically efficient, so ostentatiously techno, so "Hey! we're a computer company!" circa about 1993.*

A young woman in green jeans and a linty cotton cardigan leads her to Scott Thernstrom's office. Thernstrom, an assertively tidy young fellow, extends his hand. He is tan, has a decent Republican-boy haircut, and smiles brightly and looks her in the eye, from which Lizzie infers that he is not on the technical side of the business. "Hi, nice to meet you, I'm Scott."

Hi, Scott, I'm Lizzie, what's your major? "Hello. Will Howard Moorhead be joining us . . . ?"

"He sure will, as soon as he's through at Bill's, and so will Gary Dumbrowski, to backstop us on any technical issues. He's a very senior technical guy."

Like the identically cramped and bland offices of everyone at Microsoft, Scott's includes a display of packaging. Next to his whiteboard, propped up on two bookshelves, are boxes of each of the software products he's worked on, like stuffed and mounted trophy animal heads.

"Those are my boxes," Scott says gratuitously, as he and Lizzie both smile and stare at the empty boxes. "The seventeen products I shipped on."

In a corner on the carpet Lizzie notices a pile of unwrapped baby clothes and toys. "Congratulations," she says, nodding toward the corner, "I see you're about to become a father."

"No, no, he's not an alpha. He'll be kid number four."

His telephone tweets, and he picks it up and listens for a couple of seconds. "Okay." He hangs up. "Have a seat," he tells Lizzie as he comes out from behind his desk, "I'll be just a minute," and rushes out. Lizzie realizes she has spent the last ten minutes working herself into a snit—and just because these people want to give her and her investors 250,000 shares of Microsoft stock. As she waits for Scott to return, she inhales deeply; she exhales; she inhales again; and powerfully exhales. The breaths do not enable her to realize her eternal nature as pure awareness that transcends all duality and desire, but she is a little calmer by the time she hears a cluster of men's voices outside. Looking left, through the half-open office door, she sees Thernstrom; a graying thirty-year-old in sandals; an older grownup wearing a bow tie; and in profile, a slouching middle-aged schlub—uncombed hair, huge steel-frame glasses, crewneck, black shoes halfway between sneakers and wing tips. As the schlub turns and disappears, she sees that it is Bill Gates. (She is reminded of her earliest memory, from age two and a half, visiting Disneyland and meeting Walt Disney himself. Beginning about two years later, after her father was fired from Disney Studios, Walt's name in the Zimbalist household was changed to "the ungrateful anti-Semitic bastard.")

Lizzie stands as Thernstrom and the other two men enter. Gary Dumbrowski, the man in sandals who's also wearing a pullover with the *Slate* logo and carrying a fat and ragged manila envelope, apparently considers himself an intellectual; to Lizzie he looks like a Kinko's assistant manager. Howard Moorhead obviously considers himself professorial, but to Lizzie he looks like the sad, pompous senior man behind the formalwear counter at Bergdorf Goodman. Lizzie tries hard not to judge books by their covers, but she never hesitates to judge the covers.

The handshakes and welcomes and small talk put her at ease, though. Faced with the actual human beings, friendly and solicitous, Lizzie relaxes, and feels the hesitance and mistrust melting and then evaporating, drifting off her like mist. *These* aren't the men who put Virtual Fortress out of business—and if they were, so what? It was just business. Here, face to face, she doesn't find Moorhead's improbable gentleman-from-Albemarle courtliness off-putting. Microsoft wants Fine Technologies—her company—not her soul, not her child; they want to own what she's created; she should be flattered . . . she is flattered.

She doesn't even mind so much when Thernstrom and Dumbrowski separately use "random" in the pejorative computer-industry sense, as a general synonym for *bad*.

She steels herself when Dumbrowski asks a question about her programmers "interfacing to the Any Channel core technology library," and she answers, "I'm really not that deeply involved in the architecture of the technology." But all three men seem to regard that answer as defensible and unembarrassing.

She steels herself again when Moorhead frowns and refers to "certain governance issues we need to hash out?" But she calms down when it turns out he only means which of her board members will be replaced by Microsoft people. When she says she needs ironclad guarantees that she'll remain chairwoman, Moorhead tells her, "Lizzie? May I call you Lizzie? That's a motherhood point if ever I've heard one." Which she's pretty sure is Seattle for *yes*.

2 2

George was a writer. He is a writer. So it would make sense for him to prefer the creative jags and passionate give-and-take of *NARCS* story meetings (*Cowboy has this fantasy that he's Jennie, but we play it with Lucas in drag*) to the banal order giving (*Yes, No, louder, broader, Yes, bright blue*) of *NARCS* production meetings. "It's like a jazz group, jamming," Phoebe Reiss has said to George about the long, headachy hours in the writers' room, the Room, flattering him that he's Miles. The meetings in the Room *are* more improvised, more emotional, more democratic than the meetings with the DP and prop woman and sound guy. But they're not so pleasurable for the person in charge, for George. Being the loose menschy general giving reasonable orders to his officers and noncoms is preferable to being the Philistine suit in a room full of beatniks and artists.

The Room is nicked and greasy, like a storefront car service or a bail bondsman's office—but scruffy by choice, since the lowest-paid person in the room makes $245,000 a year. Paul Hodgman, one of the story editors, keeps his amp and Gibson Les Paul in a corner. The deep bottom drawer of the heavily vandalized credenza contains nothing but candy, grosses of suckers and Kit Kats and Twizzlers. Phoebe stands at one of the two big bulletin boards in the room, holding a notecard on which the writers' assistant has written GRANT, D.T.'S (FORMICATION) AT HAZELDEN. She and everyone around the fake-wood–veneer table is looking up at the Magic Markered notecards tacked in columns under ARCS, TEASERS, A-STORIES, B-STORIES, C-STORIES, RUNNERS. Paul and the drama writers complained at first about *NARCS* bulletin board nomenclature being "too sitcom," which was true, since Emily Kalman had only worked on comedies. ("No, Em and Mactier are perfect—sitcoms plus news *equals* fun, topical drama," Featherstone said a year ago when one of his lieutenants, since fired, raised doubts about George and Emily's experience.)

They have been at this for two hours, including lunch. "Then let's just *bag* the teaser for this one, George," Paul says. "I mean it. *Just start the fucking show* for once. Why do we even need to *see* Jennie's brother in rehab, anyway? Just go for the quiet long chick shot of her waking up, with *Scooby-Doo* on TV and the kid already gone to school. Roll the title and cue the music over that. Like a movie. See if it hurts the ratings. We're supposed to be pushing the edge, aren't we?" Hodgman is one of *NARCS'* story editors, but despite the management title he's just another writer, a writer who has written hour-long network TV dramas for nine years, eight years longer than his boss. And so as a practical matter, pushing the edge of the envelope means whining and pleading to see how far they can prod and guilt-trip George into flouting the network's wishes. But George is too new at this to feel like a hack yet.

"*Every* edge does not need pushing in every show," he says, trying to sound more good-natured than peevish. "This is already the leg-shaving episode, remember. And isn't it edge-pushing enough to open the show with Grant writhing on the floor of his cell scratching his skin raw? Jennie comes in, sees him, *boom,* that's the tease."

MBC, like every network, wants every show to begin with a teaser or a cold open—a minute or two of show into which viewers are forcibly plunged as if by surprise, *right now,* the moment the previous show finishes, at 8:29:30 or even 8:28:45, in order to keep them watching. The traditional interruption of opening titles, credits, and theme music breaks the TV trance for too many people, demesmerizes them, dangerously liberates them to see what's on the other seventy-eight channels, or to turn off the set.

"Okay," says Lou Goldstein, one of the writers, just as George is about to say *We'll come back to this, let's move on* (which means *I'll decide later, by myself*). "We do start with the Jennie-waking-up-in-bed scene, dust motes, light, desaturated color, almost black-and-white. She picks up the remote control, okay, she's still sleepy, punches it to turn the cartoon off—but unbeknownst to her, okay, the remote's been wired by the cartel to set off a bomb on the street downstairs, killing—sorry, *seriously injuring*—little Freddy and his dad. Maybe killing Dad. People at home won't dare change the channel. The subtext is, 'You push the remote, your kid dies.' "

People smile.

"Don't tell the network that idea," George says.

People chuckle.

"And the bomb," Paul Hodgman says, "is programmed to explode only if Jennie switches to Channel 41 or 47." Channels 41 and 47 are the Spanish channels.

"I like that, that's cool, but I'm *serious*," says Lou. Lou fancies himself the Quentin Tarantino of New York–based hour-long television drama. "The Kahuna-ites intend the bomb to be a demonstration of their power, okay, a don't-fuck-with-us-bitch warning shot across Jennie's bow."

Everyone is silent, waiting politely for the idea to drift away on its own. Outside, a fire truck races down Seventh Avenue, sirens whanging and honking.

"Maybe," Lou says, "it's *her* car, and the bad guys thought *Freddy* would use the remote and blow his mom up?"

"It's kind of . . . *big*," George says. "More like a finale event. That's like a whole new arc for a season." George worries that the "new arc for a season" comment will encourage Lou in his dreams of directing *NARCS* episodes, the first of which, he told George last fall, he intends to shoot "entirely overcranked, the whole forty-six minutes."

"Let's hang a lantern on that," Phoebe Reiss says, pleasing George. *To hang a lantern* means to put aside an idea and, with luck, forget about it.

"So, what *about* no teaser?" Paul Hodgman proposes again. "Just start the act."

"Look, Paul," George says, "if we don't give them teasers, we're just asking to be one of the Seamlessness guinea pigs. Do you want to write the scenes where Jennie is a talking head on *Freaky Shit!* and Cowboy is at home watching *The Great Big Nutty Wayne Newton and Robert Goulet Variety Hour?*" Next fall, the network has announced, all MBC shows on one designated night of the week will interact and interweave—the characters and fictional worlds of *You Go Girl* at 8:30 P.M. on Wednesday, for instance, would contrive to refer to those of the *Subaru America Presents Mark Twain* series at 9:00 P.M. on Wednesday. And no commercials will air from seven minutes before every hour until seven minutes after. If the experiment works, and the flow of viewers from MBC show to MBC show becomes more hermetic, Featherstone wants to extend the scheme to other nights and to other dayparts. For instance, the star of the afternoon soap opera *The Naked and the Damned* (formerly *Trailer Park*) would appear as a contestant on the game show *Quacks Like a Duck,* which airs right after *Naked,* and then the civilian winner at the end of that day's *Quacks* would appear as a contestant on *American Jackpot!* fifteen seconds later. Hank Saddler's office is calling this the Seamlessness Initiative.

Paul shakes his head, disgusted. George has effectively ended the discussion by seeming to commiserate, turning it into *NARCS* versus the network. In fact, Featherstone has promised George that *NARCS* will be "safe from Seamlessness at least through the end of '01." George hasn't gotten around to giving his staff the good news yet.

"Runners?" Phoebe says to the room. "We're not too brain-dead to come up with a few runners before we break, are we?" Runners are the conversational threads or bits of subsidiary character business that recur during an episode as amusing or humanizing filler. Up on the bulletin board under the RUNNERS heading are three cards—COWBOY ARGUING ABOUT ERIK ESTRADA ON *CHIPS,* DAN EXPLAINING "NICKEL BAG," ETC., TO ROOKIE, and ANTI-DRUG NEWSPAPER COLUMNIST KEPT IN DARK.

"How about Cowboy browsing porno sites on the web with the DEA mainframe," suggests Jared, one of the younger writers, one of the unmarried subset who essentially live at MBC, playing Meat-Eaters Deathmatch and Implosion CTF and Genocide and other video games all night long. "And then their screen freezes with some really disgusting image on it, and Jennie busts them."

"Maybe," George says.

"There's a piece of software," Jared adds, "from I think Sequel Technology, that lets employers monitor employees' internet usage. It's a real thing." Jared has asked George twice if he can be a beta tester on Lizzie's video game.

"So?" Paul says. "This is fiction."

Lou has a new idea. "How about we bring in the mayor, okay, and he's like super–pro-business? And he keeps calling Jennie to convince her to rent out the *NARCS* squad as extras, okay, in some big shitty Michael Bay–type movie one of his campaign contributors is producing."

George smiles, looks down, starts nodding. But then he realizes he is being teased only accidentally. No one here knows about Mose's deal with City Hall for the New Year's show.

"Implausible," Phoebe says. "The mayor wouldn't call her, he'd call the commissioner or the DA, and one of them would call Jennie."

George has an idea. "How about in the show with the disasters and the, the—"

"The May thirteenth show?" Phoebe asks, turning to look at the other big bulletin board in the room. "Show nineteen."

"Yeah," George says, "the runner could be Buxton saying over and over, 'Any publicity is good publicity.' " The District Attorney Buxton character is a shrewd, politically ambitious black conservative married to a white actress.

"And maybe at the end of the show, okay," Lou says, "after the exposé comes out, okay, Jennie herself says the line. 'Any publicity is good publicity.' You know—*ruefully*?"

"Maybe," George replies.

"I was *joking*," Lou says. "I hate those kind of bullshit rueful Bochco buttons."

Maybe George won't renew Lou's contract.

As they leave the Room, the permanently stuffy Room, Lucas Winton is lingering outside, holding two suit bags over his shoulder as he flirts with Iris. (He buys his entire wardrobe back from the production at cost, and much of the prop arsenal.)

"So tell your cheap boss," Lucas suddenly says, still looking at Iris, "that if he doesn't reimburse me pronto for the expense money I'm owed, I might just have to mention it at Elaine's to my old pal from the *Daily News*."

"You want your fucking money for your fucking aviation fuel for your fucking crackpot drug group, Lucas? *Okay!*" The writers, excited by this, continue shuffling past, toward their offices, but very, very

slowly: *overcranked* is precisely the word. George has dropped his yellow
pad on the floor and dug out his wallet, which he now balances against
his stomach. He takes out a personal check with two fingers, and stuffs
the wallet back in his pocket.

"Do you have a pen, Iris?" he says, regretting the outburst but too
far into it to turn back.

Iris is paralyzed, but Jared has an open Pilot V-Ball at George's hand
almost instantly. He scrawls and signs faster than he has ever written a
check before, leaving the payee line blank, and hands it to Lucas.

"Don't worry," Iris says to Lucas, touching his wrist, "I'll get that replaced with a real production company check ASAP." She pronounces
it "ay-sap." Then she turns to George. "I know you're totally stressed
and whatnot, but you don't want to put all your unrelated negative energy onto Lucas. It's—what do you call it?—*undignified,* and also it's
unhealthy and unfair." She looks around, then whispers loud enough
for the story editors and writers to hear, "*Especially* in *public.*"

"Iris?" George says. *When you have a minute I need to—I'm afraid I'm
going to have to—You know when I asked you to—*

Winton moves to leave. "What, George?" Iris says. "Lucas! Here's
your Cocker-Westie argyles! Don't forget your socks." Iris collects the
brushings from her dogs and the dogs of everyone in her apartment
building, and each winter takes bags of dog fur to a woman in rural New
Jersey who cleans, cards, combs, and spins it into yarn, out of which Iris
knits dog-fur baby booties and dog-fur men's socks to give as gifts all
year. "What do you need, George? Fresh coffee? An ibuprofen? *Yes,* I *did*
reconfirm your dentist for four-thirty. The car'll be here at four-fifteen."
Then, to Winton again, "*Your* car stays outside all day long on shooting
days, doesn't it? Maybe we should do that too."

"Iris?" George repeats.

"What?"

"You're fired," he says.

"What?"

"You're fired."

"Calm down, George. One second and I'll get you an ibuprofen. Although I think we're out. Let me send a girl to check."

"No, Iris, I don't need Advil." He does. "You didn't get me the
show files I needed in Las Vegas—"

"But—"

"Without asking, you invite someone I don't even know to join me and my friend for a drink, you slip a goddamn confidential document to an *agent*. You're supposed to make my life easier and better, Iris. And you don't. I'm sorry." He walks past her, hands the pen back to Jared, and takes the left toward his office, not looking back.

"I am not your wife, George," Iris finally says to his back. "Your wife is supposed to make your life easier, not me. Don't blame me." Then, to herself and her rubbernecking coworkers: "I don't believe this. It's like he's coming *unglued* or something. Did that just happen? This can't be happening!"

They are practically wheelbarrowing in the stock certificates. *This is so easy,* Lizzie thinks. *This is really happening.* When Thernstrom mentions that "folks here" aren't crazy about the title Range Daze for the new game, she says no problem, she's already chucked it for Warps, and he says he's thrilled they're all plugged into the same port on this and suggests Real Time as another possible name.

"Just think about it."

"Real Time is not a bad idea," Lizzie says sincerely, thinking the title sounds so right and familiar because she and they *are* plugged into the same port.

"I've heard on the grapevine," Howard Moorhead says, "that y'all are exploring some exciting new user interfaces and AI?"

She assumes he means the iZ device, and the new Yo! Friend! software that will allow players online to talk and shout to each other while they're playing Warps. Or Real Time, or whatever they name it. But in fact, of course, he means Grinspoon's patents.

"Uh-huh," she says. "I was just downtown meeting with one of our partners in that area." Goat Rodeo is in no sense a "partner" of Fine Technologies, but that is the expansive corporate term of art—like "friend" and "creative" in Los Angeles.

"Okay!" Moorhead says. "Great! We'll have a draft deal document for you at the meeting tomorrow, won't we, Scott? Is there anything else we need to know before we start dotting *i*'s and crossing *t*'s?"

"Well," Lizzie admits, "when we started these conversations six months ago, my revenue expectations for our ShowNet system were more bullish than they are right now. And you know our royalty rate on Speak Memory cuts back at the end of the year. And I am still leaning on the game team for the deadline, but, well, you know, it could get pushed into the summer."

"Doesn't sound like anything fundamental," Moorhead says.

Lizzie runs through her standing mental checklist of worries, trying to be scrupulously honest. It's like at Newark this morning, when the Continental woman looked her in the eye and asked if she'd packed her bags herself, and Lizzie felt obliged to say that her six-year-old had packed and repacked the carry-on bag several times. "I've also got an insane former employee suing me. For discrimination against insane people."

Everyone smiles sympathetically. Lizzie feels a little Republican. "If lawsuits by disgruntled staff were deal killers," Moorhead says, "M and A would come to a screeching halt, wouldn't it? Now, you're planning to have an office out here?"

"I've been interviewing. My leading contender is someone who used to work for Microsoft. Charles Prieve?"

"Chas Prieve was my assistant!" Thernstrom says.

"I remember Chas," Moorhead says. "He was that boy who loved the movies and gaming so much? Ambitious."

"Very ambitious," Thernstrom says. "He'd be perfect for you."

Moorhead stands. "Well, I look forward to finishing this up tomorrow morning?" They begin making their way out. "Do you need directions anywhere?" he asks Lizzie. "Or if you don't have dinner plans this evening, why don't you come over to Madison Park and join my wife, Ping, and me for supper?"

"Actually," Lizzie says, "I'm meeting one of your local bad boys for dinner. Buster Grinspoon, from the university? The mental-modem guy?"

"Oh, we know Grinspoon," says Scott, exchanging a look with Moorhead. "Brilliant. And very hard-core."

"Hard-core squared," Gary adds. "The guy's a real six sigma."

"Well, that's just *super!*" Moorhead says, more excited about someone else's dinner, Lizzie thinks, than seems reasonable. "Now as far as Grinspoon or anyone else goes, your discussions with us, of course, are totally confidential? I don't want a loose cannon like that knowing anything about this deal before it's done."

"No, no, don't worry. My CTO told me that Buster has a little . . . history with the company. I don't want him or anyone to know about this until we're ready to announce."

"So Mr. Grinspoon is going to be joining Fine Technologies?" Moorhead asks. "Bringing over his patents?"

Good guess, Lizzie thinks. "He'd like to," she says, smiling.

"Super! It's been just super visiting with you, Lizzie."

"Super," Lizzie says as she shakes his hand. "Talk to you tomorrow."

Super? She cannot quite believe she said "super."

2 3

He has come late to gas. He once vaguely disapproved of it. Those winking baby-boomer endorsements, *Go for the nitrous, man,* put him off, like ponytails on middle-aged record executives. But in his forties, oral surgery has become a regular annual ritual, like getting a new car, and George has started saying yes to his periodontist's offers of nitrous oxide. And so through the back door of middle age, he finds himself in one more way revisiting boyhood, when going to the dentist always had S&M undertones. Now, wallowing in the sweet stupor of nitrous on Central Park South, sprawled on a leather recliner under an arc light, he surrenders to the young woman in a tight, starched white dress pressing and re-pressing herself against him, latexed fingers in his mouth, Kenny G music ("noninvasive jazz, twenty-four-seven") inter-mingling with his own slurping and spitting sounds. Is it some dirty-minded stretch, a fantasy of the kind indulged by forty-four-year-olds who wear ponytails, to feel that he has just spent an hour in a crypto-pornographic *tableau vivant*?

The chilly cocktail-hour air cuts away the last wisps of George's groggy fuzz. Here he is at Madison Avenue, the street as well as the eponymous new bar where Zip Ingram proposed they meet to celebrate

Zip's new job. George has read about the jukebox that plays nothing but advertising jingles, so as he enters the place, which is decorated like an art director's idea of a 1963 first-class airport lounge, he's not surprised to hear a male chorus belting out "Winston tastes good like a cigarette should." And because he knows his friend was just named editor-in-chief of a mail-order "anti-fashion fashion and lifestyle magalogue" called Home Again, which Zip says "is going to pay half a fucking *mil*, George," he's not surprised to see him in a brand-new suit and waistcoat (Anderson & Sheppard, surely), paying for strangers' drinks.

"George!" he says, and "George!" again, dropping a fifty on the bar and rushing over to hug with his personal cloud of Player's smoke and kir royale fumes. It's one hug George always enjoys, in part because of Zip's height—when a five-foot-two-inch person wraps his arms around and squeezes, it feels more like a hug for Daddy from one's child than from a fifty-one-year-old "alleged creative genius," as Zip has always called himself. Zip would not be deterred in any case, and he is also George's one male friend whose greetings and farewells always involve kisses. As his friend's stubble scrapes each cheek in turn, George feels sympathy for women and gay men.

"Jesus Christ, your scalp looks like a hedgehog!" Zip says. "You might as well just shave the sodding thing."

"Ten percent shorter every year, that's the plan. Keep changing the subject, so assholes like you call me a hedgehog instead of making cracks about the gray, or the hairline."

"You should go all the way with that, George. Slough off another body part every so often—left foot when you get fat, right foot when you hit fifty. Elective cosmetic amputation."

"Then I'd be almost your size."

This is the boyo badinage they've always had, George with Zip Ingram. They grew close during their six weeks in a car in Central America, covering insurrections and death squads and civil wars for *Newsweek,* and Zip probably saved George's life after the mortar shell hit by somehow forcing a Sandinista helicopter to fly them back to Managua. But it was the surprise detour on the way home, to Disney World in Orlando, which has been the bonding moment for George. "Why, Zip?" George asked him as they boarded the plane in 1984 in Nicaragua bound for Miami and Orlando instead of Miami and New

York. "Because," Zip replied, "it is Dr. Ingram's opinion that it would be too stressful for a man in your condition to go *directly* from Nicaraguan totalitarianism back to Manhattan freedom. As a transition, you need a chocolaty couple of days of *American* totalitarianism first. To decompress, so you don't get the bends. Also, I've got an assignment shooting migrant lime pickers." Zip arranged for two Scottish au pairs he knew in Miami to fly in for the weekend, the first blind date of George's life, and Zip and the two women took turns pushing George around in a wheelchair through the Magic Kingdom and Epcot. It was a very chocolaty couple of days of American totalitarianism, British sex, and Jamaican marijuana.

Zip leads George back to the bar (ever since Nicaragua, he has been reflexively protective of George), and orders him his Bombay martini. One of Zip's new drinking pals looks like the old MTV veejay Kennedy; George remembers about Francesca.

"We should probably get a table, Zip," he says apologetically. "I'm afraid someone's joining us. A woman. Whom neither of us knows."

"*Don't* be *afraid.*" Zip grabs his cigarette box and both of their drinks and heads toward one of the tiny cocktail tables lining the banquette by the wall opposite the bar, just behind George. "So can I start dating Lizzie?"

"Without asking me, or even telling me, my ridiculous goddamn assistant invited this woman Francesca—you know, Francesca who does the news on MTV?—to come here. She wants a job on this new show."

"No problem. We've already said everything to each other we ever need to say. Sticking a girl celebrity between us might just put the spark back in our tired old relationship."

A waiter places little bowls of bocconcini and breadsticks on their table. At least the bar food isn't themed.

"So," George says, "cheers. When do you start inventing synonyms for *beige* and *taupe*? When do you get rid of the Winnebago?"

"I'm at Home Again beginning next week—as soon as I finish this meat gig. And actually, George, I am seriously thinking about keeping the motor home. Really. I've sort of fallen in love with it. At the end of the day, why do I need an apartment? I never eat at home. I don't 'entertain.' " Since last August, when Zip was fired from his job as creative director of TheMedia.com and TheIndustry.com, after *The New York Observer* revealed that his résumé was spurious (under "Education/Experience" his "Oxxford, etc., 1971–75" turned out to be a reference to his five years as a part-time salesclerk in the English suit department at Barneys), he has been living parked on the streets of Manhattan in a thirty-foot RV he leases by the month. "I've got a beautiful permanent spot now, downtown, at Pier 57, the Hudson right out the windscreen. You've got to come visit."

Zip has, in the seventeen years George has known him, transformed himself from photographer to salesclerk and necktie designer, to music-video producer, to children's newspaper-and-TV executive, to advertising executive, to author, to web-site mogul. As soon as he knows how to do one thing, he always says, he tries to find a new thing to do that he doesn't know how to do yet. The fact that each successive job ends in a spectacular shambles only reinforces Zip's doctrine of what he has taken to calling "adventure careering."

"What 'meat gig'?"

"For the National Lamb Board. It's *fantastic*. The average American eats only a pound and a half of lamb a year. Shocking! And most of the people eating it here are wops and Pakis. I persuaded the lamb people they need a new name. How's Lizzie?"

"A new name for the National Lamb Board?"

"Yes, right, how do *you* think the 'North American Sheep-Meat Commission' sounds? No, shithead! For 'lamb.' For the meat."

"The other red meat."

"*Precisely.* Precisely. It's just a nomenclature problem, right? Beef isn't called 'steer.' A sirloin steak isn't a 'cow chop.' It's 'barbecued ribs,' right? Not 'rack of pig.' You think if the menu word for venison was 'deer' that anyone would order it, ever? They need a new name for lamb that isn't so *beastly*, that doesn't remind Americans they're eating a cute animal."

"How much are they paying you for this insane scheme?"

"A hundred grand." He giggles. "And another hundred if they go with one of my names. No back end, though. Not a dime in royalties. How's Lizzie?"

"What are your names? Like nondairy creamer, or Bac-Os, or what?"

"We did make up some words. Disasters. And we went through every language, every dialect. Anyway, for *lamb,* we got close in German."

"Zip. These fools are not going to pay you a hundred thousand dollars for telling them to call lamb 'l-a-m-m.' Are they?" The only vestige of his *Newsweek* tour in Bonn is menu German, which very seldom comes in handy.

" 'Hammelfleisch.' I put it in as kind of a joke, a control, but it tested really well, surprisingly, and they may use it, right, for some shitty new smoked-lamb lunch meat. The runner-up for regular butcher-shop lamb is *agneau,* which I frankly don't think is, what do you call it, *scalable*—at the end of the day, it's too pseudo and froggy for people in, your, you know . . ."—he waves his hand toward George—". . . Nebraska."

"Minnesota."

"In the fancy vein, *I* liked *mouton,* but the Board thought the Rothschild wine people would sue. Classic and Anglo-American is what you need. Like breakfast cereal—the bestselling cereals, still, are almost all the brands from fifty, a hundred years ago. Cornflakes and raisin bran, Rice Krispies, Cheerios, Grape-Nuts. The classics, right?" Zip sits back. "The first choice, my big idea? It's still a secret, George. Off the record. I'm trusting you. 'Baby mutton.' " Zip grins proudly and evilly.

"Kind of like the young elderly."

"It's classic, 'mutton.' But 'baby mutton' is totally new and just a little sexy, right? Stylish." He finishes the pink dregs of his champagne. "It's a shame they don't give fucking Pulitzers for this work, you know? Or a Nobel." He pops a bocconcino in his mouth. "Did you know," he says, chewing and pointing, "that mozzarella consumption in this country has *quadrupled* since Ronald Reagan was elected president? Quadrupled! A classic cheese for classic times."

"People are *not* suddenly going to start calling lamb 'baby mutton.' They aren't."

"If the Board is clever enough and spends enough, people will, at the end of the day, yes they will. The girl who invited Francesca here, what do you call her?"

"Iris."

"No, she's your . . . what?"

"Assistant? Was—I just fired her."

"And when you first went to ABC, the gorgeous Armenian girl who worked for you, Sabrina, what was she?"

"My assistant."

"Your *secretary*, George. In 1985 you called her your *secretary*. And by 1990 you were calling her your administrative fucking *assistant*. The word 'secretary' doesn't exist anymore! It's been wiped away by marketing. Ninety-nine percent replaced by 'assistant.' What do you call black people?"

"Black people."

"But African-American is halfway there, right? This country went from 'nig-nog' to 'colored' to 'Negro' to 'black' to 'Afro-American' and back to 'black' in, what, ten years?"

"Black people were never called 'nig-nogs' in America, Zip. And how is mozzarella classic? What, compared to Velveeta?"

"Fucking quibbler."

George spots Francesca at the door. She is more blond than she was in Los Angeles, somehow more news, less MTV. He stares at her and cranes his neck an inch or two to get her attention.

"Okay," Zip says. "A thousand dollars. April third, 2010: if 'baby mutton' isn't on menus within, what, three blocks of this joint, you win."

"Hi, is this really okay?" Francesca says, taking off her floor-length white down overcoat, even before George and Zip both nod and murmur 'of course, yes, of course.' She's wearing a serious brown-and-green-striped suit. "Hi," she says, putting out her hand to Zip, who stands. "I'm Francesca."

"Hello. Zip Ingram."

"I know you, don't I?" she says, sitting down next to George on the banquette. "Didn't you publish an autobiography last year that got all kinds of attention?"

"*An* autobiography, nicely put, yeah, that's me." On publication day the *Times* reported that Zip had plagiarized passages in *Conceit: Memoir of a Postmodern Man* from the autobiographies of Winston Churchill, Malcolm X, and Tammy Faye Bakker ("Haven't you ever heard of sampling?" Zip responded at the time), but Zip meant to cause a ruckus anyway. He revealed, for instance, that his marriage to an Anglophilic socialite PBS producer ("You'll forgive the triple re-

dundancy") was purely for green-card purposes; that he has used cocaine with relatives and employees of presidents in the White House
during all of the last five administrations; that at one of the magazines
where he worked the major celebrity profile subjects "literally got
writer, photo, photo-caption, adjective, and adverb approval"; and that
his boss at TVTVTV had wanted to tuck subliminal pro–Christian
and pro-sugar messages into the channel's programming. (TVTVTV
was Zip's idea: beamed onto video monitors mounted in locker
rooms, Cub Scout den meetings, candy stores, and its own fleet of
school buses, it runs nothing but paid promotional clips for TV shows
aimed at children and teenagers.) Zip's memoir was published as a
downloadable computer file as well as a hardcover book, which en-
abled reviewers to scan and savage it with unprecedented effectiveness
for its special tics and inconsistencies. One critic reported that Zip
used the phrases "As I told Andy that night," "wildly entertaining as
well as a creative breakthrough," and "at the end of the day" twenty-
seven, twenty-nine, and sixty-seven times, respectively, and that six of
the twenty-seven "Andy" conversations took place at events during
1988 and 1989, even though Warhol died in 1987. Zip lifts his fresh
goblet of champagne and cassis toward Francesca and says, mock gal-
lantly, "A toast to me, the first digital victim in the last year of the
twentieth century."

After a few minutes of flirty introductions and mutual flattery ("The
scratch-and-sniff patch on your book jacket was excellent"; "I loved
your covering the New Hampshire primary with Marilyn Manson"),
Zip's pack of bar acquaintances move to their banquette and the one
next to them, and after more introductions by Zip—"Clarise, Wendy,
Vespa (sorry, *Vesto*), Trevor; Francesca and George"—the seven of
them become a de facto cocktail party. And Francesca, squeezed between George and Clarise on the narrow blue leather bench, gets
down to business. She uses her résumé like a libretto, turning it into
entertaining light conversation ("During my year at Columbia I got to
be pals with Moynihan's finance committee guy, and Russert used to
work for Moynihan too, so . . ."). She demonstrates her savvy about
news unrelated to Lauryn Hill or the Beastie Boys, first by analyzing
the presidential nominating process ("I know next Tuesday is *supposed*
to be the final slam dunk, but I think Gore may be sort of a Pennsyl-

vanian, psychographically"), then by comparing today's Mexican death squads to the Salvadoran death squads of the eighties (which gives her an opportunity to recite a shot-by-shot rundown of Part Three of George's fifteen-year-old *Wars Next Door*).

Why do women, at least young and youngish women, always become a little prettier when they're holding a big glass of red wine? She is talking, gesticulating with her free hand, occasionally touching his sleeve for emphasis. George has explained the show to her in detail, and now he is listening, nodding, catching Clarise and Vesto and other patrons repeatedly stealing looks at Francesca. Her intelligence and shrewdness impress him—for twenty minutes she lobbies for the *Real Time* job without quite seeming to lobby. "So," Francesca says finally, "shall I send you tape? What do I need to do to convince you to make me one of the *Reality* anchors?" She sips her twelve-dollar glass of merlot, her foreplay finished.

"It's called *Real Time* now." Did Iris slip his original treatment for the show to Francesca's agent too? Christ. "And yes, we'd really like to look at your tape." The "we" is not entirely bogus, since Emily has been meeting with all the candidates too, but it does give him an out later, if they pass. And since he is interested, he uses *like,* which is a more serious verb than *love.* They'd have to make her use her last name. But would that be bad for the brand, her brand, like forcing Madonna to start calling herself Madonna Ciccone? No, he decides, it's more like John Mellencamp dropping the "Cougar." "I have a question."

"Ask."

"What's your last name?"

"Mahoney."

"Francesca Mahoney," George pronounces, thinking: *three-syllable first name, three-syllable last name, no first-syllable emphasis*—if they hire her, Saddler will want to change it to Fran Markey. George might have to use Christiane Amanpour as his counterargument.

"Sucks, doesn't it?"

"Your MTV contract is up soon?"

The bar is crowded now, and noisy, so instead of shouting she leans closer to answer. "June one. Their sixty-day renegotiation period is under way." She pulls back, grins, and rolls her eyes. "Aren't I pushy!"

"No, no. Informative."

She writes down her agent's name on the back of her business card and hands it to George.

"William Morris," he says.

She understands his implication. "I was a starlet my first year in New York, before I went back to J school."

"You must have been a successful starlet if William Morris took you on."

"I lucked into a Wrigley's Spearmint commercial that ran about five million times. Which was my great thespian moment, and all because I could do the 'Wrigley load' so well."

George shakes his head.

"You don't know about the Wrigley load? They have this very specific, market-tested way that actors in their ads have to stick the gum in their mouths. It's like a theological principle." She grabs a bocconcino and strips a mozzarella strand off it. Then, flashing an extreme ad-girl smile, she turns her profile to George, puts her face close to his, tips her chin up, opens her mouth narrowly, and still grinning like a madwoman, quickly tips in the simulated stick of gum. They both laugh. "That," she says, "is the Wrigley load."

"Thanks for the demonstration." It's late; Rafaela leaves at seven-thirty; George gathers his briefcase and coat. "I'm really glad we had a chance to talk. You should definitely meet with my partner, Emily, in L.A."

"I will. And I should leave too." George gives a nice-meeting-you glance to Zip's new pals and consents to a goodbye smooch from Zip.

"I'll see you at your big soiree," Zip says, "if not before."

"Zip? What about chicken? People don't have a problem ordering roast chicken and eating fried chicken, even though it's the name of the animal."

"Not a mammal," Zip says briskly. He has obviously been through this many times. "It's cute-mammal meat people need to call something else. Although I have a theory that 'free-range' was partly an attempt to assuage chicken-eating guilt. Goodbye—*Francesca*," he says. "Night-night, George. Very chocolaty."

"Entertaining guy," Francesca says to George on the sidewalk.

Little asshole is what she probably means. "He is that," George says. He knows that Zip, like Ben Gould, takes up a lot of the air in any room he occupies. He doesn't spend a lot of time making apologies or defenses on their behalf (although with Zip, *He saved my life in Nicaragua* works well). People either get Ben and Zip, or they don't, find them entertaining and full of life, or loud and off-putting. George's loyalty is all the fiercer *because* they are so easy to dislike, as he realized only when Lizzie explained it to him as soon as she met Zip.

2 4

Her father sounded a little tired on the phone, but maybe that was really only in comparison to her, because she's been so wired, full of post-Microsoft fizz. She probably should fly down to L.A. tomorrow night and then go home a day late. George would be cranky, in that passive-aggressive "Fine, Lizzie" way of his. If she ever manages to actually talk to George about it. The increasingly brief and brittle telephone recordings swapped back and forth, back and forth, have been tempered only a little by the faxes from Max and LuLu waiting under her hotel room door. The notes and drawings are so sweet they're sad, the sadness welling up more when she calls and finds nobody home. Where is George? Where are the kids? He must have taken them all out to dinner.

"Zimbalist, for two," she says. Alexi, who at every moment professes to know the hottest restaurant in every North American city that recognizes the concept of hot restaurants, has booked her and Buster Grinspoon for dinner at a place called Captain Bridger's Pacific Markethouse Lounge and Grill. The maître d' is wearing a tight-fitting blue-and-black-striped jacket, which at first she reads as velvet. She now sees it's synthetic fleece. "The reservation is for seven-thirty. I know I'm early."

"Oh! That's *fine*, Ms. Zimbalist!" The fellow seems to crouch in an effort to make himself shorter than Lizzie, and looks at her with a tiny hopeful smile, as if a big welcoming grin might strike her as presumptuous. "Would you like to settle into your table now? Or would you prefer to relax at the bar du vin with a complimentary glass? We have some very surprising Idaho Rieslings." He is the human incarnation of modern customer service, scorched-earth pleasantness made flesh. Ms. Zimbalist elects to sit at the table. She doesn't hate this.

Surrounded suddenly by so much copper and so much pretty old brick, Lizzie feels as if she's stepped back into 1986. The restaurant is like Reagan-era Cambridge, or high-yuppie Columbus Avenue, full of diners in their thirties and forties with gray beards and no ties. Except here, now, they're probably all multimillionaires—digital multimillionaires, at least on paper—who happen to look like $64,000-a-year Smollett scholars or $43,000 senior architects. It's not so bad, Lizzie thinks, feeling twenty-one again, with the husband and children stashed a continent away for forty-eight hours. Looking out from her table at Elliott Bay (to which "*excellent* marine vista" the maître d' commands she pay attention), she remembers being wowed by the view at dusk across New York Harbor from the River Café on her first serious date with George. No, that wasn't George, that was her date with Ben Gould; she hadn't met George yet.

". . . using heirloom grains, and we truck in our own batch every week, *fresh,* from the brewstillery over in Spokane."

She looks up at the greeter, and realizes that for at least half a minute he's been reciting the names and provenances of obscure alcoholic beverages.

"May I tell you about our specialty martinis and premium tequilas?" he asks.

"I'll just have a club soda, thanks." She turns away to look at the bay. But she doesn't hate this.

"I'll bring you the Captain Bridger's private-label brand. It's really not half bad. Our special ragouts today—"

"Someone's joining me."

"*Thank* you, but that's all right, I'll be happy to repeat them. We have our ragout of baby Vietnamese eggplant, our ragout of hacked rabbit saddle (and that's encircled by braised strips of the rabbit's flank—*excellent*); our Olympic Peninsula Sierra Club–certified wild mushroom ragout; and I *think* we may have one more of the Pacific Markethouse ragouts of free-range north Oregon weasel, which is prepared tartare style, with white and cayenne peppers moistened by Burmese mustard; and the ragout of Dungeness crab."

She's starting to hate this. Doesn't he need to get back to his post? The eighties time-warp experience is now total. Lizzie recalls her own intense and stupid excitement about trying exciting new dishes at exciting new restaurants, when going for the first time to Hubert's or Arcadia or Chanterelle was like a combination of Broadway in the thirties (*Let's go see the new Kaufman and Hart . . .*) and sex in the seventies (*. . . at Plato's Retreat*).

"Our Northwest shellfish species of the day are ceviche of Alaska weathervane scallops, and Dungeness crabs. The special vegetarian platter this evening is a salad of sesame-dewed daikon, sprouts of rapini and Walla Walla sweet onions garnished with cilantro aioli and flecks of rock salt accompanied by *either* a blend of squash, sweet potatoes, bean curd, tapioca, and cloud-ear mushrooms; *or* our parsnip and Granny Smith hash with peanuts, basil, lime, and tamarind served in lettuce wraps."

He is not out of breath, probably because he runs and hikes long, kilometer-denominated distances every day. Or maybe because he spent a Seattle boyhood in training, reciting PC specs to his parents until they put him in foster care. He's looking at her, eyes open wide, head tucked down a little, looking as if he wants a pat. "That's quite a choice," Lizzie says. "Thanks."

"Oh! And today's seafood *entrée* special, marinated in a local ale and grilled over applewood, is Dungeness crab. Served with a semi-vinaigrettized double-baked potato-prune gratin. And," he says, evidently saving the best news for last, "I'm afraid we are *out* of the chicken sashimi."

He goes, but thirty seconds later he's back, leading a bearded man in a jumpsuit wearing a fanny pack. He is not fat but his belly is huge, like he's got a Snugli with a two-year-old strapped on and zippered up in there.

"Hi," Buster Grinspoon says.

"Hello," Lizzie says, offering her hand, which he shakes limply.

"You got Corona?" he asks the hovering maître d'.

"No," the man says, almost as if Grinspoon were joking. "The Terminator is very nice."

"You got Budweiser?"

"Hmmm . . . maybe I can get you an icy cold Hammerhead?"

"Water's fine," Grinspoon says, sitting.

"You like all this Pike–Pine Corridor shit?" he asks Lizzie. "I guess you're staying around here."

"Not far. Where do you live?" A single-occupancy room filled with junked Kaypros and *Oui* magazines? On a rusty cot in the lab, arms wrapped around a sawed-off shotgun?

"Over in Issaquah. It's only twenty-eight minutes, door to door."

"From Issaquah to U-Dub?"

"Sieg heil."

"Excuse me?"

"Sieg Hall? The Comp Sci building at U-Dub. My former employers. Issaquah's real nice. My place is too big for me, four thousand square feet, but it's quiet. It's right at the base of the mountains, which trap the weather moving in from over here, so it doesn't get sunny much, which keeps too many assholes from moving in. Used to, anyway."

Lizzie's only friends in Seattle, two women she knew in college, are no doubt exactly the kinds of assholes Grinspoon means: one is a lawyer living in Kirkland, a suburb she understands to be Pelham crossed with Santa Monica, the other a graphic designer in Redmond, which is White Plains crossed with Encino. Unlike New York or Los Angeles, however, little stigma attaches to living in the suburbs. The contempt of the sophisticated takes other forms.

"I used to live in Kirkland," Grinspoon continues, "but they were killing me."

"Who?"

"First I got ticketed by the town for not weatherproofing my house enough. Not energy-saving. Okay. Then it was *so* tight, they made me pay to install fans that totally vented the place six times a day. Okay. Then when I fixed up my lawn and they nailed me for violating the indigenous-shrub protection ordinance, I couldn't take it anymore. That's actually what made my last relationship crash and burn."

"Why don't you live over here somewhere? Downtown? Closer to the university?"

He screws up his face and shakes his head. "Too much clutter. Too random."

A waitress arrives. "Hello! I don't know if you're in a ragout mood, but the hacked saddle of rabbit ragout with rolled strips of rabbit flank really *is* wonderful, and of all our Dungeness crab preparations, my personal favorite—"

"I'll have steak, medium rare," Lizzie says.

"And which of our beef preparations do you prefer?"

"The fillet, with the 'sesame-skilleted cross sections of baby Spokane sweet potatoes,' " Lizzie says, handing her menu over. "Assuming that means fried yams. Nothing to start."

"Vegetarian platter," Grinspoon says.

"Excellent!" the waitress says. "I'll send Mimi, our new vice sommelier, right over."

"None for me," Grinspoon says to Lizzie. "Allergic to nitrites."

Lizzie shakes her head at the waitress, who turns to leave, then pauses and looks back thoughtfully.

"You know," she says, "if you're a yam buff, you should definitely make it to YamFest 2000 over in the Beaux Arts Village this fall."

"Thanks. I'll check my schedule. So," Lizzie says to Grinspoon, "Bruce tells me you despise Microsoft and won't work for them."

"I *did* work for them. As a contractor, years ago. But we'd get to a good alpha stage on some out-there software, and then they'd make us move on. We were just keeping the shit in the bag. And then—well, then the place became a *hive*. And I really don't operate well in hives." He lifts his water and glugs the whole glass without stopping. "So, are we going to joint-venture on bioelectronics and biomimetics?"

"Bruce would certainly love us to. What do you think the business *is,* though? What's our product?"

Grinspoon shrugs. "I thought that's what you were supposed to tell me. I mean, I got these two patents that the telco morons and the networkers want. And the genetic programming, that's a patent too, Microsoft likes that, but it isn't, you know, Quicken or Tomb Raider VI or something. But you mean the new work?" He leans forward. "AI. *Real* AI. Deep AI. Big-bandwidth AI R and D."

Artificial intelligence is not a product, Lizzie thinks. *Artificial intelligence is a theory, a theology, a tenure track, sci-fi semantics, marketing bullshit.* They said

Speak Memory contains AI because it (sort of) understands ungrammatical slang—such as the difference between *doughnut* and *Don't it.* They call it AI when Amazon.com predicts what book you're going to want next. She sold Y2KRx as "AI-enhanced." Her game designers call it AI when, in Warps, they program a Pilgrim to react differently to a player speaking twenty-first-century English than he does to seventeenth- or nineteenth-century English. AI has been defined down to a rudimentary level. *Real AI, deep AI,* she thinks. *What am I supposed to sell?*

"Interesting," she says with a small smile and a cock of her head. "How so? R and D leading to what, exactly?"

"We'll find out. That's the journey. And AI is so much more doable with animals. Especially cats. We have a hundred billion neurons," he says, touching his temple, "so simulating a human brain will take like ten billion lines of code. Hell, these goat rodeos sweat shit to write a hundred *million* lines of code."

"So you're working toward, what, like, a supercomputer simulation of a cat's brain?"

He shakes his head quickly and mumbles an error message: "Supercomputers have shitty user interfaces and buggy compilers. I use multiple workstations, sixty-four different processors working simultaneously, and get where I need to go lots quicker. Genetic programming. It was Bruce who helped me figure out years ago how to use strings of weights as chromosomes in genetic algorithms for the Non-Hamstrung Squadcar Problem. He should actually probably co-own that patent."

Lizzie nods. Her understanding of genetic programming, in which software evolves on its own, changing and improving itself without human intercession, is shallow. Only now does she realize just how shallow.

"When do *you* think the transhumanist moment comes?" he asks her.

These people really are religious. "I'm not sure what you mean."

"Transhumanist, machines beyond us, smarter than us. Around 2020 or 2030, they say, computers get more complex than the human brain. So the machines will be able to start figuring out stuff about the universe, about reality, that we just *can't*—because we're too stupid, because those perceptions simply require more than the hundred billion neurons we're maxed out at. So then, maybe (this is where I'm going out on a limb, so bear with me), *maybe* the computers can figure out ways to explain the mysteries to us, in ways we can understand. Like parents do with children, with concepts like sex and love and loyalty. *That's* the point of AI. To be ready for that time, to be able to learn from the machines."

"Interesting," she says. She means it. Possibly nutty, but possibly brilliant, and interesting in either case. "And I guess that's also the point of wiring up a cat's brain, as far as you're concerned. To learn enough to take advantage of what—what—" She stammers, trying to avoid seeming glib or dismissive, "what the wise mommy computer will be ready to reveal to us in 2030."

"*Exactly.* Do you know," he asks her, "how similar to our REM patterns cats' REM patterns are? Do you have any idea?"

Lizzie can't abide being forced to answer a rhetorical question. Yes or no, it's a demagogue's trick, like when the antiabortion telemarketer asked her one evening a few weeks ago while she was filleting a red snapper, "Do you want your daughter to have an eight-and-a-half-month-old child pulled from her womb and murdered?" Or like Buchanan on the debate last night, asking the candidates, "Do your constituents want southern California and Arizona and Texas to become provinces of Mexico?" So she decides to change the subject.

"I guess that's maybe why the animal nuts all got so upset—"

"There are no data to support the allegation that the micro-electrodes in the anesthetized brain stems of the cats cause any pain," Grinspoon says in an affectless, taking-the-Fifth-Amendment voice. He stares at her.

"I'm sure they don't." She shrugs. "And to be honest, I really don't give that much of a fuck about animals being used in research. I don't use cruelty-free cosmetics. I mean, I'm eating steak. And in fact, my father just had a pig liver transplant, so . . ."

Grinspoon reanimates. "Cats' sleeping patterns are amazingly similar to ours," he says. "So let's say dreams, all dreams, are just meaningless output, gibberish bullshit the brain spits out at night while it's cleaning up its disks, organizing memory."

"Okay." This she's happy to stipulate. Lizzie has never had any luck making sense of dreams.

"And what if we can figure out in a cat exactly which five minutes or two hours of that sleep time every night are when the essential stuff is done—the memory organizing and cleaning? And then we figure out a way to let people get *only those* five minutes a night they need! What have we got *then?*"

Another zealot's rhetorical question. "More chat rooms and lots of four A.M. trips to 7-Eleven?"

"I don't know about you, but I'd pay a lot to be able to get by on two hours of sleep a night. A *lot*. That's a product."

Their food arrives, each dish and side dish elaborately described once again. Lizzie orders a Bombay martini.

She makes one last stab, for Bruce's sake. "What about, you know, the wireless communication part of your work? The cat receiving transmissions of the other cat's thoughts about food?"

"What about it?" Grinspoon says, using his fingers to pick up a baby zucchini by its orange flower.

"Well, near term, couldn't that be a product? You know . . . pets reading pets' minds." As soon as she says it, she realizes how ridiculous the idea sounds.

"Like, so your cat can know when your dog is about to chase it?" Grinspoon says. "I guess. Seems stupid to me, but hey, I thought portals were a lame-o app. I'm just an engineer. You're the blue-smoke-and-mirrors lady." He smiles. "Bruce didn't tell me you were such a *shipper*."

And he didn't tell me you were a crackpot. "What do you mean, 'shipper'?" She wonders if the phrase isn't some anti-Semitic Posse Comitatus mispronunciation and misuse of *schlepper*.

"Being into, you know, shipping product. At my last private-sector job, the company booked no sales whatsoever for eleven years," he says as if she should be impressed. "Look, aside from the patents that we could probably squeeze some cash out of, I'm a long-term play for anybody."

"Long term" in computer businesses is usually a euphemism for long shot. And given the Microsoft deal, her horizon is suddenly very short term—next quarter, next month, next Tuesday.

"I wonder if what you have in mind isn't really too big for Fine Technologies. I have a feeling I'm not visionary enough to be your partner." *It's not anything wrong with you,* she lied when she dumped Buddy Ramo and all three subsequent boyfriends pre-George, *it's really me.*

As they finish dinner and their plates are cleared ("Was there some *problem* with the yams?" the waitress asks, scolding Lizzie for her unfinished meal, waiting to be scolded back), Lizzie and Grinspoon talk no more of joining together, of Microsoft, or of feline telepathy. Instead, she nudges the conversation toward what seem like safer tangents. He explains in detail the genetic-programming software patent he got last year. ("I use a distributed population approach, evolving thousands of populations of programs on different processors, and then migrate the best programs from each population to a neighboring population. It's supercomputer performance but dirt cheap. Most algorithms turn to shit when you distribute them, but mine actually improve, so you can just add more and more machines.") She understands his explanations about as well as she would if he said them in French. She just gets by in French.

The waitress returns. Lizzie asks for the check. "We won't be doing a dessert this evening?" the waitress says in a happy-sad kindergarten teacher's voice. "I can *definitely* recommend the pistachio-kumquat napoleon with anise hyssop ice cream and blackberry and blood-orange coulis, or if you're in a *Continental* mood . . ."

As they leave, and Grinspoon grabs two handfuls of Captain Bridger's Pacific Markethouse Lounge and Grill matchbooks, the maître d' seems absolutely unfazed, as if the boyish doofs who spend a hundred dollars apiece on dinner always haul away as many mint candies and matches as they can stuff into their jumpsuits and Dockers and parkas. Grinspoon's car is parked a long way away ("Over by the Central Gun Exchange—across from Aveda"), and Lizzie offers to give him a lift, but he begs off.

Now, sitting on her hotel twin bed, she feels desperately tired but not sleepy, unsure whether to get undressed or sit here awhile longer, whether to call George back or close her eyes, whether to cry or go blank. She is so beat she remembers the drive from the restaurant only sketchily, feels almost as if she rode in the Taurus rather than drove it. And the moment she stepped into the room and saw the orange light blinking in the dark by the bed, she felt pulled to the phone, too—she could never resist retrieving phone messages or opening e-mail. She played George's message once, and at first, just for a second, she was angry that he left it, since the news wasn't urgent, only terribly unpleasant. But she understands it's a big fact that demands to be told sooner rather than later as a matter of . . . what? Protocol, logistics, hot gossip. And now she regrets the chirpy message she left for him this afternoon, when he must have been driving around God-knows-where in Queens, with the kids. Poor George. As she reconstructs her twittery excitement about the Microsoft meeting ("I actually liked them! A lot! And one of the guys even has a great name for Warps—'Real Time.' "), she despises herself, cannot believe she forgot that *Real Time* is the new name for George's show. But it's too late in New York to call now—one forty-five A.M.—and she'd be blubbery and incoherent. Which she could use to her advantage. But no. She pushes the REPLAY VOICE MAIL button, not for the facts, which were unambiguous the first time, and not to torture herself, but to listen to the nuances in her husband's voice, trying to distinguish angry from grim. She has spent a lot of time lately, she realizes, as she tap-taps the volume button, scrutinizing the emotional gradations at that shadowy end of the George spectrum.

"Hi. You know those two days of work Rafaela mysteriously missed? When I got home tonight LuLu ran outside to tell me that the reason was because her son and daughter died. There was a death squad massacre in their village in Mexico, and Rafaela says both kids were killed. I called it up on the Reuters wire. All nine victims were shot with automatic weapons, M-16s, then hacked with machetes. I asked Rafaela why she didn't tell us; I said she could take some time off, but she doesn't want to. I offered to fly her down there, but she said no, it's too dangerous for her to go, and started crying. I mean really crying. So I drove her home, and then we got lost in Queens or Brooklyn because Sarah recognized the place she goes to see the Golden Gloves fights and claimed she knew how to get us to the Manhattan Bridge. She didn't. So I don't know. Christ. I assume you were joking about *Real Time* as Microsoft's name for your game. I guess I might have found the joke funnier if Featherstone hadn't used my like-a-talking-parrot line to me today. I had a big fight with Lucas and fired Iris this afternoon. Max brought a note home from his Science and Society teacher saying the headmaster wants to talk to us. He, Max, doesn't know what about. I figured we can go after Sarah's screening on Friday. I'm supposed to go on *Charlie Rose* tomorrow night, some whither-reality-TV roundtable. I'm wasted. We don't need to talk tonight. In fact, don't return this. It's already midnight and I've got a seven A.M. call tomorrow at the studio. Bye."

Years ago, when George produced a piece for the news about the kids who use scanners to eavesdrop on strangers' phone calls, he told Lizzie that most of the conversations they pick up are recordings of conversations—the eavesdroppees remotely retrieving their voice-mail and phone-machine messages. Which surprised and depressed her then. And it does again now, as she sits alone in a perfectly tidy hotel room in the dark, unbuttoning her shirt like an automaton low on batteries, trying not to think of Rafaela's murdered family. At least George thought she was joking about Real Time. Let him think that.

2 5

She won't mind coming here once a month. It's pretty pleasant downtown, in the morning, when the sky is blue. In Seattle it's sixty-two and sunny, and Lizzie sits alone on a swivel stool at an outdoor counter eating a scrambled egg sandwich on focaccia. The blue-and-yellow hand-painted sign says THE GOURMET GREASY SPOON (UNCOMPLICATED FINE FOOD 6 TO 6 DAILY). She hasn't smoked a cigarette in four days. She sips her perfect, Equal-sweetened double espresso as *Der Rosenkavalier* blasts over tiny loudspeakers, which makes Lizzie think of the line Richard Strauss uttered shortly before he died, which Mike Zimbalist used as the epigraph of his vanity press memoir: "I may not be a first-rate composer, but I am a first-class second-rate composer!" *Celebrity Name-Droppers I Have Known* is what she nicknamed the book, and now it takes her a second to recall the actual title: *Hubris, Humility, Heroes, Whores: An Insider's Loving Exposé of Hollywood.* She can't remember if there was a fifth *h*-word in there—humbug?—or not.

She's just hung up with Alexi, who told her that two reporters called, from *The Village Voice* and the *Observer*, not about her father, but about the employee lawsuits.

"Law*suits*? Plural?" Lizzie asked.

"I know. I don't know," Alexi said. "I told them to call Katherine at the law firm. Also, FYI, Bruce is clearly working out some . . . issues."

"What do you mean? He's cranky?"

"*Seriously.* And he's wearing *blue jeans* and a *T-shirt*." She doesn't know if her chief technology officer owns two or ten identical gray suits, white button-down shirts, and striped blue ties. But except for the time he came tieless to the Christmas-Hanukkah-Kwanzaa-Ramadan-Solstice party, no one at Fine Technologies has ever seen him dressed any other way. "And he said to me, 'If this is just going to be a widget factory, Alexi, it's time for me to radically rethink.' I was like, 'What?' And he was like, 'Lizzie blew off my friend in Seattle last night.' Do you want to talk to him?"

She already has, at dawn. Bruce called her, in a snit. She has never seen him snitty, not remotely. And he refused to be mollified, even when she said that maybe, with the Microsoft money, they could fund some of Grinspoon's work after all.

She's waiting for a call back from Microsoft, and puts the phone down on her *New York Times.* There is a story about the Cancún bombing and the UN Resolution, with a reference to "the increasingly violent human rights abuses by groups believed to be associated with Mexico's ruling government party"—an oblique reference, Lizzie presumes, to the massacre of her baby-sitter's family. (Should she clip the article for Rafaela?) The national edition of the *Times* always disappoints and disconcerts Lizzie a little. It's too spiffy and concise and bland, like her friend Jill, the left-wing campaign manager who went on Prozac and had her jowls surgically removed and became an image consultant and event planner. What the *Times* editors cut out for readers in Seattle and San Francisco and St. Paul—the Metro section, the stories about deaf subway token-booth clerks, voodoo-scented murder-suicides on Avenue D, Holocaust survivors picketing Philip Johnson tributes—are her favorite parts of the paper.

The phone beeps. One of the reasons she chose this place for breakfast is that it's outside, and she is expecting calls. As soon as she woke up, she left a message at Microsoft to let them know that Real Time would not work as a name for the game; that they were right, Buster Grinspoon is hard-core, too much trouble, and she's definitely not teaming up with him; and to reconfirm her meeting in Redmond at nine-thirty this morning.

"I have Scott Thernstrom calling Lizzie Zimbalist."

"This is she." A moment passes.

"This isn't going to be a pleasant call for either of us, Lizzie. We finished our next phase of due diligence last night, and I'm afraid we're going to need to redraft."

You fucks. "Redraft how?"

"The top line on the ShowNet system is considerably lower than we had been given to understand. We get a reduced royalty stream on the speech-recognition software in year two. You're not going to ship your game until fourth quarter, and we already have real concerns about how late we are in this game-market cycle. And then there's your legal problems, the Golliver suit and so on. It's not any one issue. It's the convergence of all of them." He doesn't mention Buster Grinspoon's patents.

You fucking bastards. Thernstrom is simply recapitulating the boilerplate caveats she gave them yesterday afternoon. Except that they looked up insane Vanessa Golliver's name during the last twelve hours. *You evil fucking bastards.*

"Now," Thernstrom continues, more warmly, "the company still has the highest regard for you, and wants to proceed with an investment in Fine Technology, subject to further due diligence, but more along the lines of our earlier offer."

It's Fine Technologies, asshole. Haircut boy. Golfer. Smug little prick. "Meaning what, exactly?"

"A ten percent stake for two million dollars. And of course we wouldn't expect more than one board seat."

"That's pretty funny," she says, actually chuckling. She's surprised at her calm. Yes, she would like Thernstrom and Moorhead to die now. But the disappearance of the $31.5 million feels correct, like a return to common sense. As soon as she started running toward the stupendous mirage, it disappeared, as mirages do.

"Excuse me?" Thernstrom says.

"You're not only offering a valuation two thirds less than what was on the table yesterday, you're offering less than you talked about a month ago. That is some serious fucking gall."

"The earlier valuations were always subject to further due diligence."

"Are you *reading* that, Scott? Or are you just an animatron?"

"Excuse me?"

"I guess we're done. Bye."

She gave them the bullets to shoot her. She should be furious. She should feel humiliated, and scream about integrity and lawyers. She finishes her coffee. She smiles, and dials George to tell him the excellent news. But there's no answer (right: no more Iris), and this is too large an event for voice mail, so she calls Ben Gould, the only other member of her board whom she loves and who isn't in intensive care. She has to tell somebody.

He used to think that when Lucas didn't know his lines, it was because Lucas was lazy. But George has come to realize that it's a stratagem. In a scene with Angela or Sylvester or one of the other actors, if Lucas throws his line back a second late, it not only screws up the other actor's performance, it means that George will be forced in postproduction to cut back to Lucas. The screwups are devices to give himself more screen time, make himself more of a star. It's only twelve-thirty and Lucas has done his little fake pauses three times, and George would have called him on it if not for the blowup about the expenses yesterday.

"Cut!" Gordon says. "Doris." The wardrobe woman appears from the crowd. "Fix Cowboy, please."

"What?" George asks him.

"His marks from the fight scene are stuck to his ass."

George watches Doris kneeling behind Lucas, peeling two crosses of red tape from Lucas's left buttock, then licking two fingers to wipe the adhesive residue off his pants.

"Shall we go ahead and break for lunch?" George says to Gordon. "And please tell him to deliver the lines on time, will you? Lucas and I evidently aren't speaking today."

"Lunchtime," Gordon says to his first AD.

"Lunch!" the first shouts to the room.

George retreats with his script alone, to the Glass Booth, as Emily Kalman calls the glass-fronted module parked on a plinth in a corner of the soundstage. From there, Featherstone and other MBC executives ("the Men in the Glass Booth," in Emily's phrase) can eat and drink and carp while they're watching shows being shot. George and the writers use it as a conference room during shoots. He dials, and Ben Gould himself answers.

"*George!* Hey! You holding up? Man! I know how it feels to lose seven million dollars in one morning."

"What do you mean, Mose Media stock is still dropping?"

"No, I'm talking about *Microsoft!* Fucking your wife. Brutal, man! I thought of calling Ballmer about it, just for the pleasure of telling him they're pricks."

"What are you talking about? What happened?"

"You don't know? Microsoft lowballed the shit out of Lizzie's deal an hour ago. She told them to forget it."

George says nothing. He's angry that she didn't discuss it with him before doing it, even angrier that she told Ben before she told him. And the mountain of money, what she's called the mirage, has been looming pretty realistically for him.

"She sounds kind of happy about it, actually," Ben tells him. "So what were you calling about?"

"You know, the securitization thing. For *NARCS.*"

"Right, if the lawyers say okay, I'd do it. Worse comes to worse, Mose goes belly up and you're in business with the bondholders."

"Ben, do you think Mose Media's stock's going down because of our new show? Is that possible?"

"That was maybe a half point of it yesterday. But no, George, you aren't personally destroying your company. The dipshit at Paine Webber downgraded this morning, that's what's pulled Mose down two—Jesus, two and an eighth. Which is five percent. One analyst burps and wipes out five hundred million dollars of shareholder value. They're not shitting on you for this, are they? Tell me they're not that stupid."

"No. No, in fact, Mose seems ecstatic about *Real Time,* full speed ahead. I just wondered how all this Wall Street stuff affects me. Or not."

"Let me call you."

They agree to get together soon, before George and Lizzie's party, and George asks, by the way, did Lizzie happen to mention if she's flying home from Seattle early, or what?

"She didn't say. I got a giant position to unload in the next fifteen minutes, George. See you."

Ben wants to liquidate his long position in USA Loves Toys, not because the company manufactures two of its hit products, Rainbow Mega-Mucus and Maggotty Rat Guts, in Chiapas (the market has already discounted for disruptions that the guerilla uprising might cause), but because he thinks the stock has gotten ridiculously expensive. The 1.1 million shares he bought last fall and winter for $9 million are now 2.2 million shares worth $31 million, a value that can't be justified by the company's prospects. In other words, USA Loves Toys has just made Ben *too much money,* so it is time to take his profits, turn them from hypothetical to actual gains, and ditch the company. USA Loves Toys will announce its first-quarter earnings in ten days. Ben is fairly sure the number is worse than Wall Street expects, so the stock price will drop sooner rather than later—sooner, since Ben's belief in the imminent decline of stock will begin to become self-fulfilling in a few minutes, as soon as he unloads his two million shares, which amounts to about 1 percent of the company. He's also selling because he lost trust in USA's management after the company's chief financial officer misguided him badly, maybe deliberately, about the company's current earnings last month. Ben has no financial reason to sell out at one o'clock sharp, as opposed to ten-thirty or three. But he's decided he wants to punish the CFO, and while he's at it embarrass the CEO, whom he's never met but never liked, since his foundation sponsors eugenics research and publishes antiabortion comic books.

Ben looks over at Frank Melucci, who's looking back at him, holding the phone to his belly, ready to push a button on his turret. Ben unmutes the Big Room TV and switches the channel from 24 to 82, CNBC More, the new CNBC sibling channel that broadcasts live feeds of bankers' conventions, Commerce Department press briefings, communications satellite launches, oil and gas conferences, new product announcements, antitrust trials, the raw public domain of capitalism, twenty-four hours a day.

USA Loves Toys' annual shareholders meeting is on CNBC More right now, broadcast live from the Astrodome in Houston. The company declared a stock split yesterday, and the share price today has popped to its all-time high. On the giant digital screen above and behind the Astrodome stage, they've got a moving graph of the stock price over the last twenty-six weeks, a steep blue Everest face, and above the half mountain, a readout of USA Loves Toys' share price at this instant. That magnificent price, 14⅛, is throbbing, and encircled by a penumbra of multicolored video fireworks. The company's CEO is at a podium, talking about how "the lucrative Judeo-Christian toy tradition" is at the heart of "our sacred free-enterprise system itself."

"Frank?" Ben says quietly. "Offer 2.2 million ULUV at 14⅛."

"Just one broker, right?" Melucci confirms.

"Shit, yeah! Ten-b-five, man! I'm no fomenter." Under federal securities rule 10b-5, a stock trader breaks the law if he deliberately foments a market panic by, say, dumping large blocks of stock quickly through multiple brokerage houses.

Ten minutes later, the number on the big Astrodome screen, twice as tall as the proud, dapper, amplified man speaking beneath it, has clicked down a half dozen times to 13¾₆. The CEO, still wading through history, is oblivious. In a mighty peroration he is equating USA Loves Toys with the United States itself, NAFTA with the Declaration of Independence, his factory in Chiapas with the Alamo, himself with Davy Crockett ("a *victorious* Davy Crockett, fighting to maximize shareholder value"), and armed nineteenth-century Mexicans with armed twenty-first-century Mexicans. Now the throbbing number above him is 12⅞. Watching TV from lower Broadway in Manhattan, Ben sees that a few yards to the CEO's left, two young men in suits scuttle to within crouching distance of the CFO, who turns around and looks up at the screen, where the blue graph line is now crawling steeply downward from the summit. A few seconds after the price drops to 12¼, the camera jerkily zooms in tighter on the CEO, but the Everest-descent graph line is still visible behind his head. At 11¹⁵⁄₁₆, the real-time USA Loves Toys stadium-board stock-price spectacle is replaced by the simpler message, GO ASTROS!

Finally, *finally,* Ben Gould brings his laughter under control, from a dog-whistle yip down through fire-alarm whoops to a machine-gun guffaw. "Holy *baloney,*" he says, "is that great entertainment or what? *God.* That was so fantastic." He wipes his eyes and turns back toward his cockpit.

––––––––––

This could be a stage set, Ionesco or Beckett, with a ghastly banality that would make a smart audience chuckle when the curtain rises, or a room in a modern penitentiary where the warden is sincere about running a "correctional facility" rather than a prison. The fluorescent lighting is bright and unmodulated. The several dozen plastic seats, the greenish blue of toothpaste and shaving gels, are bolted to a black steel bar running around three sides of the room. The fourth wall, looking out on the broad corridor at the disused end of a SeaTac concourse, is all glass. Two men are in the room with Lizzie, both at least twenty years her senior, both overweight, both smoking cigarettes. Lizzie just bought her first pack in two months. She is smoking, too. This is the SeaTac smoker's lounge. There is no TV, and no piped-in music. The room is filled with an even thunder from the third of the ceiling that's taken up by the sheet-metal casings and grilles of an air filtration system, so massive and powerful that the smoke from Lizzie's Marlboro Light disappears the moment it leaves her fingers and mouth. The smokers, sealed away together, are fully protected from one another's secondhand smoke. She has finished looking at the papers Chas gave her this afternoon, and sinks happily into her fresh copy of *InStyle* magazine, an impulse buy as delicious and toxic as the Marlboros. She hears muffled little squeals and laughter. She looks up. A half dozen children on identical yellow leashes, kindergartners probably, have stopped at the front window wall to look in at the woman and two men sitting alone, smoking. The children are scratching and knocking on the glass, pointing and giggling, screwing up their little faces and saying "*Oooooh,*" beckoning another squad of kids over to look. She returns to reading *InStyle*'s celebrity liposuction guide (she wonders if George knows that Angela lipo-sucked her ass), and continues smoking on principle, making a special show of Bette Davis imperturbability. Only when she sees that the children's minders have finally pulled them along to the next stop on their field trip does Lizzie snuff out the cigarette and leave. She is reminded of the Atlanta airport, where they've started having children make all flight announcements because, a gate agent told her last time she was there, "it's special, and cute as can be."

On her way through the concourse toward the locker where she stowed her luggage, she thinks about throwing away her brand-new pack, but instead tosses out only Chas's candy-colored half-English brochures touting the "strongly disciplined and semieducated electronics workforcefuls" of Malaysia and Vietnam. Chas Prieve does seem to know his stuff. (His most recent employer was a video-game company before it was sued for copyright infringement by the makers of the guns-and-ammo game Doom, and turned itself into a law-enforcement human-resources-training software company.) She didn't tell him about this morning's disintegration of the Microsoft deal, but he told her that Scott Thernstrom was a terrible boss at Microsoft, technologically in over his head, and on his third marriage. And Chas said he would be willing to work for Fine Technologies half time for the first six months if she'll pay to move him from Boston to Seattle *or* Silicon Valley. He did pressure her some, and annoy her by saying his "MT-BOO is getting very short." (After leaving Chas, she called Alexi and asked him about MT-BOO. "Mean time between other offers," he explained.)

She's having trouble getting locker 324 open. She puts her purse down, and her heavy bag of magazines and newspapers, jams the key in again, and starts jiggling it. A woman depositing her tote bag full of Beanie Babies one locker-bank over, George's age but matronly, offers to help.

"Thanks," Lizzie says as the woman takes her key, sees that it says 224, not 324, and sticks it in the correct lock. Lizzie shakes her head. "Believe it or not, I do have a college degree."

"You know," her earnest Seattle volunteer says, "so many people here in Seattle do."

A flight to Los Angeles, she sees on a DEPARTURES monitor, leaves in half an hour. She could make that one. She could make it.

Waiting at the gate, Lizzie forces herself to scan a front-page article in the paper entitled "Microsoft One Year Later: Rebuilding Trust After Antitrust." All she reads that she doesn't know are details of the company's various new charity offensives, including something called the Virtual Home Project. This is a plan under which the company has offered to scan and digitize all the "two-dimensional possessions of any homeless American at no cost"—letters, snapshots, lists, doodles, food-can labels, filthy clippings, demented screeds, whatever. The homeless person gets a disk (up to a maximum of 100 megabytes) in "a rugged weatherproof plastic container," and Microsoft will also keep an archive of the data "for backup as well as posterity and next-of-kin purposes." The project will be coordinated in each of eighteen big cities by the company's Sidewalk movie-and-restaurant-listing web-site staffs. " 'Since many of the Virtual Home clients actually live on the sidewalk, literally,' says a company spokesperson, 'it seems like a superfortuitous branding opportunity for Microsoft Sidewalk to give something back to the communities.' "

"Is this seat taken?"

A very white man is smiling down at her. He's about her age, and wears a tie and V-neck sweater under his windbreaker. The back of the windbreaker says YOU KNOW THE SECRET ALREADY. She sees that his computer has a label on it: THE GLOBAL SECRET.

After a minute, he says to Lizzie, "I'm glad this airport is getting so much more business these days. It's a real neat facility."

"Mmm," she replies, staring down at her *Post-Intelligencer*. She worries he may be intending to hit on her, or worse, talk to her about Jesus or Dianetics.

"I see you've stocked up on computer mags," he says. "Are you in the field?"

"Uh-huh."

"Good to meet you," he says, putting out his hand. "Rex Dinsmoor! I'm senior evangelist at a software company."

She shakes his hand. Back in 1993, when Lizzie first heard someone who worked for a software company refer to herself as an "evangelist," she thought it was literally a joke. After she got into the business and she encountered "technical evangelists" and "product evangelists" everywhere, she came to think of it first as a charming oddity, later as a tiresome affectation. Now she doesn't even register its oddness.

"ControlQuest—that's my company. We make the Global Secret? Specialized enterprise software for multinationals."

Lizzie nods.

"You are . . . ?"

"Lizzie Zimbalist. I'm a consultant in New York. I consult for entertainment companies, help them figure out how to migrate over to the net." As a child, Lizzie would sometimes spontaneously lie to strangers, about where she lived or what she wanted to be when she grew up, and to her mother. But she had grown out of it, forced herself out of it, really, when she started worrying in seventh grade that she might have inherited the casual, compulsive fibbing habit of her father.

That flight to L.A. leaves in fifteen minutes. But she has to go home.

"I advise TV shows who want to set up web sites, that kind of thing," she continues. It's not untrue.

"I don't watch much television," Rex Dinsmoor confesses. "A little MSNBC and the Chopper Channel is about all. I sometimes don't get home from work until eleven, so I miss most of the entertainment shows."

"My husband's on *Charlie Rose* tonight." This startles her a little too, the bragging and the chattiness. Maybe, she thinks, it is just a convenient excuse to say "my husband."

"Who's Charlie Rose?"

Lizzie explains, feeling like she's in a foreign country.

"I'd love to send you a demo of the Secret. It has a next-generation plain-language translation engine. *Really* powerful. It takes global frictionlessness and transparency to the next stage. To a real tipping point."

She nods. *Frictionless transparency.* Maybe he is trying to pick her up.

"I honestly think," he says, "it's going to change the way humans think about doing business in the twenty-first century."

She nods again and examines a photo spread on the new Mrs. Leonardo DiCaprio. Out here, everyone sincerely does believe his own bullshit, believes it thoroughly. Rex Dinsmoor *knows* he's helping to build some kind of late-capitalist utopia, a wired Cascadia, Oz. A few years ago, they all gushed about "push" technology transforming the web—but then it didn't because it was fake, a hysterically overbilled replica of real bandwidth. Before that, they said ordering movies over cable TV was imminent, any movie you wanted. But the technology was a decade away at a price anybody could afford, so a big cable company faked video-on-demand, too. As the innocent Dorothys at home pushed buttons to order *Pee-wee's Big Adventure* and *The Bonfire of the Vanities,* a kid on roller-skates in a room in Denver cued up each videocassette by hand, grabbing another tape, rolling to the next VCR, grabbing, rolling, madly trying to fulfill twenty-first-century dreams (frictionlessly!) in slapstick twentieth-century fashion. *Pay no attention to that man behind the curtain.* These people out here are the men behind the curtain—Rex Dinsmoor, truculent Buster Grinspoon, the smug Goat Rodeo boys, even Microsoft. But unlike the Wizard of Oz, they believe in their magic! It isn't cynical bluster. These wizards have faith. And Lizzie knows she's an agnostic.

They call her flight.

2 6

George was asleep, almost, when Lizzie got home from Seattle the night before last, and pretended the rest. Before he left at six-thirty yesterday morning to make his *NARCS* call at seven, they exchanged goodbyes—just that, his "Goodbye" from the bedroom doorway and, from under the sheets, her "Bye." Last night, the children were around as buffers and objects of affection, and George was asleep by quarter to ten. This morning, George and Lizzie are alone for the first time in a long while. She is eating her daily $2.49 cup of Old Chatham Sheep-Herding Company yogurt, with pecans and cinnamon, while she reads the *Times.* He is eating his daily strip of bacon and Grape-Nuts with skim milk as he turns the pages of the *Daily News.* The little kids are already at school, and Sarah is staying home her first two periods, rescoring her civil rights video upstairs.

Since Lizzie asked George, "Did LuLu take her umbrella?" and he answered without looking up from *Doonesbury,* "I didn't notice," neither of them has said a word for sixteen, going on seventeen, minutes.

He slides the *News* away and grabs the *Post.*

"You know," he says, "I really hated finding out about Microsoft from Ben."

"I called you. At the office. I even tried your cell."

"It died," he says, looking down at the front-page—WILD-MAN RUDY! "I told you it died last week." He opens the paper. "You could've tried the car."

"I didn't know you'd driven. I'm sorry, George. Okay?"

"Whatever."

"*I'm* the one who got fucked," she says, standing, walking over to the Bose, turning it on. "I apologize that you weren't the very first to find out I got fucked." She pushes the channel button preset for 92.3.

"Sarah's still here," George says.

"I know. I think she's old enough to hear Howard Stern and survive." She sits down. "You still sneak it from the kids in the car?"

George doesn't answer. In the *Post* he reads a story about a bipartisan pack of congressmen who have drafted a bill to outlaw "mind-reading microchips" and "mental modems" as a "threat to every American's privacy and human dignity. 'We stopped cloning and Ebonics,' declared Representative Horace Wolfe (R–South Carolina), 'and we'll stop this.' " The story also quotes a Democratic congresswoman from Oregon on "the frightening animal-privacy-rights implications."

"Hmmm," George says.

"What?"

"Your friend Buster Grinspoon." He holds up the paper.

"How completely stupid. Save that for me, okay? They're not really going to pass a law, are they?"

"Nah. The story doesn't actually mention Grinspoon." He turns the page to "Page Six," one of the four gossip columns in the paper—five, if you include the biweekly publishing column; six, if you include the column of items about TV; seven, if you include the new column summarizing the gossip reported the previous day on TV and in other newspapers. Eight, in fact, if you include the "*Hey,* Sport!" column in the sports section, but George doesn't know that exists.

Like every *Times* reader who buys the *Post*, George subscribes mainly for "Page Six." Yet he reads "Page Six" (which is on page eight) as quickly as he can, scanning the bold-faced names and then pausing over the stories about fashion models and musicians and unalloyed socialites only if they seem to involve grotesquely gothic misbehavior, glancing at the stories contrived simply to promote restaurants and nightclubs, and of course, entirely skipping the stories about professional athletes. After twenty years, his scan-and-skip technique is now so deeply ingrained that when there's a bold-faced name of a person George knows personally, his eye moves to it before he's even registered the name consciously. It's a kind of simulated half-second precognition.

And so he takes a quick hot dilated breath, aware that in a moment he's going to read a "Page Six" item about himself. "Insiders on the hit MBC show *NARCS* say that costar Lucas 'Cowboy' Winton kept his cool the other day when producer George McTeer ripped into the politically conservative hunk in the West 57th Street studios in front of cast and crew. The dispute concerned a minor money matter, and network sources say McTeer 'overreacted like an insane person.' After screaming at Winton and dissing the actor's pro bono anti-drug-abuse work, the producer suddenly pink-slipped his own longtime personal assistant. 'He really lost it,' says a witness to the confrontation. 'But Lucas was a total class act. Everybody worries that George is stretched too thin, with personal problems, and trying to launch a new show and keep *NARCS* running at the same time.' The superexpensive top-secret new show, *Real News,* which one MBC source calls 'a totally fake-news soap opera' and 'a ticking time bomb for the network,' is being coproduced with sexy Al Gore fund-raiser Emily Kalman. *Real News* is expected to premiere this summer on MBC. Stay tuned."

Jesus Christ. Lucas Winton; Barry Stengel; who else has become a lifelong enemy? He rereads the story. They didn't even call him for a comment! Unless he didn't get the message, since he has no assistant. And, of course, he couldn't have denied the story, since their account of the incident is more or less correct. George takes a deep breath.

"Listen to this." He reads the story out loud to his wife.

"What 'personal problems'?"

George looks at her.

"That sucks," Lizzie says, "but you said yourself that the new show will create a shitstorm. I guess this is the beginning of that. These are the shit flurries." She sips her tea. "You changed the name to *Real News?*"

"*No!* And it isn't superexpensive, or a ticking fucking time bomb, either. Jesus! Barry Stengel has to die."

Lizzie cringes. "Don't say that."

"Your career hasn't just been blown apart in the goddamn *New York Post*."

"George, you're overreacting."

"Oh, fuck *you,* Miss Yoga Perfection. I live in a fishbowl, okay? You don't."

Lizzie gets up and walks to the other end of the kitchen, ostensibly rummaging for some half-and-half in the Sub-Zero.

It's eight-thirty. When he gets to the office he'll call Featherstone. He'll call Emily. He'll call Saddler. He'll call Lucas, pretend to apologize, smooth things over, and pretend to believe him when he denies that he had anything to do with the *Post* story. He'll call Stengel, and . . . what? No, he won't; he'll call back his friend at the *Journal* instead.

"I'm sorry I shouted, Lizzie," George says, swigging his coffee, returning to "Page Six" to read the story a third time, and then a fourth, before moving on to the day's blind items.

"WHICH brilliant zillionaire," George reads to himself, "is pressuring business associates to back the latest lamebrain creative project of his arrogant young progeny-about-town?" He thinks: *Which one isn't?* "WHICH erratic, egomaniacal rap superstar drove his $150,000 foreign car up onto a SoHo sidewalk to stop his gamine starlet girlfriend from stalking off?" Still a little generic, but better. "WHICH teen-media tycoon was spotted at a Village gay bar partying heartily with two members of his demographic? WHAT distinguished casino mogul and real estate genius arranged to get which liberal newspaper columnist reprimanded after the writer unfairly attacked him?" Much more interesting, although George wonders how many items Donald Trump must offer to "Page Six" that they *decline* to run. "WHAT married show biz whiz (and former network journalist) was canoodling over cocktails with what rock-and-roll news babe the other night at the new chattering-class boite Madison Avenue?"

He thinks the owners of the bar must have phoned it in, but then decides they wouldn't know who he was. He feels a sickening pang: was it Zip? No; please not. Maybe one of Zip's new best friends who sat down with them . . . Vesto? Or one of the blowsy women accompanying Vesto? George's eye flicks up to the top corner of the newspaper page, as he has another of his instantaneous pseudo-precognitions:

Clarise was the overinterested woman with the insinuating smile sitting on the other side of Francesca, and there it is, Clarise Flannagan, one of the names in the *Post*'s group byline. George is relieved: Zip hasn't betrayed him.

"You won't believe this," he says to Lizzie, grinning. " 'What married' um," but then he pauses, noticing on the next column over a continuation of the item. "(The man's a serial extracurricular canoodler, since he was also spotted engaged in some semi-heavy petting with an actress half his age at a celebrity-studded Las Vegas party last month.)"

"What is it?" Lizzie says.

He reads the Donald Trump item to her.

"So?" she says.

"I wonder who the 'liberal columnist' is?"

"No idea."

George used to think he isn't prone to feelings of guilt. He used to think that guiltiness per se wouldn't be a problem for him if he ever, say, committed adultery. But after Las Vegas and the episode with Shawna Cindy Switzer, he realized that one of the reasons he didn't take her back to his room was his horror at the prospect of self-loathing—a kind of early warning guilt-perimeter trip wire. As a practical matter, he realizes, self-hate is probably indistinguishable from guilt itself, and in the end may be indistinguishable from morality. Now, however, he's feeling anxiety over trespasses he didn't really commit, certainly not with Francesca, and not even with Shawna Cindy Switzer. *Well, honey, she did fondle my arm, and shoved it between her tits, actually—in public, yes, at Ben's BarbieWorld party, and then she did ask me to fuck her, really begged. But I declined! Why didn't I tell you at the time? Because, because, because, because . . .* He shuts the *Post*.

"Hand me that," Lizzie says from across the table, "I want to read the article about Congress outlawing Grinspoon's research."

George thumbs open the *Post* and, holding down the bottom of page seven with his bad hand, tears out the CAPITOL HILL MIND-READING PANIC article rather more carefully than he usually rips newspaper articles, and hands it over to Lizzie.

"Thanks," she says.

Turning the ripped tabloid half-page, George sees the blind items in "Page Six" are still there.

"Georges *Cinq*! You crazy-ass gangsta man of the hour!"

"Hello, Timothy, I didn't know you were in town."

"Here, there, everywhere! I thought you gentlemen of the Fifth Estate were supposed to protect each other. I guess the *Post* isn't a signatory to that deal." He waves George ahead toward the *NARCS* offices. "After you—*tu oficina es mi oficina*."

George goes in ahead of Featherstone, past Daisy's replacement at the reception desk, toward his corner of the floor.

"You saw 'Page Six,' " George says.

"*¡Que será!* As long as they spell your name right."

"They didn't. Or get the name of the show right. Good morning," he says as they get to his office.

"Good morning, George," Daisy says. "Hello, Mr. Featherstone." Featherstone acknowledges Daisy's greeting by putting his left index and middle fingers together in a kind of Boy Scout salute, then kissing the fingertips.

"Buzz is buzz, my G-man. Gross media impressions are gross media impressions. Although Hank Saddler's a little freaked about the 'ticking time bomb' line."

"Me too," George says, tossing his briefcase on his desk and sitting down. "And gee, I wonder what president of News gave them that quote. Hmmm."

Featherstone sits, leans back, and puts his Guccis up on the maple desktop. He's not smiling.

"George, as a friend, level with me if we've got budget problems on *Real Time*. Better to lance the boil now, before it kills us."

"How could we have budget problems? We're still staffing up and commissioning scripts. We're just reading actors for the roles. Everything's fine."

"Cool. Yeah, that's what I told Harold. By the way, he says thanks for rubber-stamping the *NARCS* agreement, for the bonds."

"No problem."

Featherstone and Mose have discussed his "Page Six" humiliation. Featherstone is nodding, looking at George. George wonders if he's here to tell him he's fired, and to clear out of the building by noon. But Featherstone and Mose can't fire him. He's not an employee.

"Really," George says, "we're completely on track." He pauses. "It was the *Post*."

"Hey, I know. Been there, dumbed that." He lowers his feet to the floor and rests his elbows on the desk.

"George?"

"Yeah?"

"The personal problems. This is totally nonjudgmental. But if it's a sabbatical you need, or a medical leave—well, whatever we need to do. I *love* you, man. Like a brother."

George wonders if Featherstone has a brother in addition to the one he accidentally killed crashing his Porsche.

"I'm fine. *Real Time* is fine. Everything's fine."

With his elbow still on the desk Featherstone puts his left hand up, as if he's about to arm-wrestle. "Steady as she goes, bro." As George shakes the hand, Featherstone says, "That's *exactly* what I told Harold."

George is not reassured by his reassurances or, fifteen minutes later, by Hank Saddler's call. "A minor bump," Saddler says, "totally minor, in all likelihood, I'm sure, although this does make me think I want to start keeping a mini–MPI for you, track the little press problems before they become big press problems." Since *NARCS* is almost finished for the season, George has more time to pay attention to this new rising tide of anxiety and dread. The instant he hangs up on Saddler, Daisy says she has Jess Burnham and Emily Kalman both holding, Emily from her car.

"Hello, Ms. Burnham," he says playfully.

"Just one moment," a dour young man says back. Will George never learn to avoid that mistake? (A few years ago, Zip asked George to track down a piece of BBC tape on which he'd been told that a Republican congressman had used the c-word to describe Hillary Clinton on English television. When Zip called back, and George picked up the phone and said brightly, " 'C-U-N-T, *cunt,* absolutely," Zip's female assistant hung up and complained to the TVTVTV human resources department.) It's only a tiny dose of mortification each time when he speaks to an assistant that way, but it is mortifying, not only as a stumble in the status contest, but because it requires George to repeat the cheerful greeting a second time. The Take Two *hello* is always self-conscious, a performance, fake.

"Am I speaking to the serial canoodler himself?"

What are you talking about? will not do. Nor will stunned silence. "Hello, Ms. Burnham!" George says, repeating the line verbatim as he plays for time.

"You're going to hire Francesca to anchor *Real Time,* aren't you? George?"

"She's one of the people we're talking to." If he doesn't say something more, he'll be on the defensive. "So why did your boss call *Real Time* 'a ticking time bomb'?"

"Because he doesn't get it. And because you're smarter than he is, and a traitor to journalism, and you're having fun."

"I'm not having fun today, I swear."

"And because I told him on Friday that I want to anchor *Real Time.*"

George feels hot. Everyone wants to work for him! Except for the people who want to destroy him. Daisy ducks in, points to the phone, and mouths, "Emily," but George puts up his index finger and turns away. He asks Jess why she wants to do this, and she says she wants to invent something new, and he proceeds to give her arguments against it—she may never be able to go back to straight news; she'll have to move up from Washington; it would pay a lot less. She replies that Mike Wallace used to host a game show (not to mention that Ronald Reagan went from *Death Valley Days* to the presidency), she and Marie would kill to live in New York, and the money is the money.

"What about *NewsNight 2000*?" George asks.

"If your show works," she says, "I'm betting they shit-can *News-Night 2000* by Christmas. Maybe Labor Day. Why do you think Barry is so scared of this? Your wife killed dot-com, now he's afraid you're going to sink his flagship. By the way? If acting experience is an issue, I've never done chewing-gum commercials, but I've acted—I was in *The Chicago Seven Conspiracy Trial* and *Inherit the Wind* for a whole summer in Ottawa."

"Incidentally, I was discussing the show with Francesca at that bar. Period. We were not 'canoodling.' "

"Yeah? What's your definition of *canoodle?*"

"I'm serious. She went back to work, and I went home. It was absolutely professional."

"Save the alibi, I'm teasing. I know it was nothing. You're not her type."

Hey, wait a second! We were *flirting. There was definite a sexual edge! She told me I'm her hero!* "What do you mean?" he says with the hint of a chuckle, as if he's amused.

"I don't think Francesca canoodles with boys. Before Marie and I got together, when Marie still worked at the Pentagon, she and Francesca had a thing. Francesca Mahoney is ambitious, but even she's not enough of a whore to pretend to have the hots for you to get a job. I don't *think.*"

George tells Jess he's completely shocked and excited that she's interested, which is true. He's also confused and anxious. Francesca would probably be better than Jess as an anchor, but Jess would probably act the non-news scenes better. Francesca is more fuckable, in the TV-Q sense, but is that what this show needs? (He thinks of the LuLu question: *Is that a good thing or a bad thing, Daddy?*) Hiring Jess, a real journalist, might win him points with the pundits, or it might piss them off even more—the infotainment Beelzebub seducing one of their own.

"Shall I try Emily again in the car?" Daisy asks.

He sighs. "Let's wait until she's on a land line." George is serious (although he started using "land line" humorously last year after a couple of conversations with Mike Ovitz in which Ovitz, worried about eavesdropping, used the phrase repeatedly). Ever since the *Real Time* meetings at MBC in L.A., Emily has been a shade harsh, totally business. The morning after her man came in fourth in the Texas primary, she admitted that she was still upset about George's "Fuck Al Gore" comment during the meeting with Featherstone, Stengel, and Burnham. The phrase she used was "deeply, *deeply* disturbed." George simply cannot understand the arousal of deep political passion, pro or con, by Al Gore. Gore is a placebo. George W. Bush and Elizabeth Dole are placebos as well. They look real enough, and they make Democrats and Republicans feel as if they're taking their prescribed medications. They're nontoxic, but they contain no active ingredients. Any effects produced are entirely in people's minds. George apologized to Emily for his anti-Gore crack, but when she grumbled something about how the vice president "*made* Lizzie's company" and how George was giving aid and comfort to the enemy, he reminded her that they are planning to put on a prime-time *news* show. And she has remained chilly whenever they talk about *Real Time*.

"Messages," Daisy says. "A woman called *Rusty* phoned, she said on behalf of Barry Stengel. She sounded dodgy. She's calling about your, quote, 'freezing MBC News out of the liver-transplant story.' Do you want her?"

George shuts his eyes. He's about to tell Daisy yes, to charge straight up the hill into the enemy fire—be a man, clear the air, earn this week's $16,575—when he stops himself.

"No, first get me Glenn Murkowski."

"Glenn Murkowski." She says unfamiliar American names as if they are self-evidently amusing, like Engelbert Humperdinck or Mortimer Snerd. She's even worse about all the freshly concocted African-American names that contain *sh*. Daisy joked to George the other day that she was considering changing her own name to Dayshara. "Mr. Murkowski is on the Rolodex, I presume?"

"I presume. He's at *The Wall Street Journal*."

2 7

George was yelling at her when she left home, and Sarah was crying about the music in her civil rights video. Now Alexi is crying about the "Worst Downtown Workplaces" story in today's *Voice,* and Bruce is about to come in and yell at her. The *Voice* has declared that it's launching "a tough but fair-minded investigative war" targeting the "so-called 'hip capitalists' and 'alternative entrepreneurs' who abuse the cachet and informality of the so-called 'New Economy' to exploit young and non-native North American workers." Lizzie, described as a "member of a glitzy Wall Street and millionaire media crowd," is accused of brewing $10.95-a-pound Starbucks for herself, but serving $7-a-pound Chock Full o'Nuts to her staff. She is also, apropos of the woman who peed in the reception area, accused of "sadistic callousness" toward "employees seeking help for substance abuse problems and special psychiatric needs." She is accused of contributing money to a "Republican-dominated Washington group lobbying to increase the number of H1-B visas to allow more foreign workers into cyber-sweatshops like Fine Technologies." She is accused of "pressuring non-native-English speakers to speak English" despite an "informational warning letter" from the ACLU Language Rights Project. She is accused of "willfully ignoring" an "off-gassing e-mail alert" from the

Occupational Safety and Health Administration concerning an employee's complaint about fumes the new office carpet was allegedly emitting. And she is accused, finally, of refusing to allow employees' "animal companions to accompany them for any part of the workday."

"Pull yourself together, Alexi. I'm not a fascist because I wouldn't let Reginald bring his fucking ermine into the office last winter." There is a trace of déjà vu. "This is bullshit. And, Alexi? Why don't you start buying Starbucks for *everybody*?"

"I'm so sorry, Lizzie. Shall I send a memo to the staff saying it was my decision? Or a letter to the *Voice*?"

"Neither. Ignore it. Forget it." The thing in the article that bothers her is the toxic carpet business. For one thing, she worries it could make her insurance go up. It is also wrong—she was *delayed* in responding to OSHA because Max accidentally deleted the e-mail, but she has not "ignored" it. All the other charges are factually correct. "Leezy?" asks Markus, one of the German programmers, as she walks to the bathroom this morning, "is it correct that you are aligned with the Republican party?"

Forty-eight hours ago, Lizzie felt charmed. Forty-eight hours ago, Fine Technologies' public relations challenge was whether to give the news of her Microsoft acquisition to the *Times* or to George's friend Greg at the *Journal*. Forty-eight hours ago, her major legal problem was figuring out how best to share some of her Microsoft profits with her employees.

"Forty-eight hours ago," Bruce declares, "you told me you had a completely open mind about doing a deal with Buster Grinspoon. And that evidently wasn't so." His weirdness is all of a piece: Bruce with the door closed, Bruce raising his voice, Bruce in brand-new jeans and T-shirt.

"Come *on*. I did have an open mind. I did. *Sit*." She wants to convince Bruce. So she pushes her luck. "That was also before the Microsoft deal died. I no longer have a few million extra in the bank to pay for five years of AI R and D."

Lizzie knows she's revising the truth, since the Microsoft offer was jerked away the morning *after* her dinner with Buster Grinspoon. She hopes Bruce won't notice the chronology problem.

And Bruce doesn't, because he thinks he's caught her in a larger lie. On Tuesday afternoon, while she was away, he went into her office looking for an *Industry Standard* article about web gaming. Buried under a stack of paper on her desk, he happened to see the furious Post-it note she wrote weeks ago, reminding herself to tell Bennett Gould about the original Microsoft lowball: "2/28/00 BG—NO $!" Bruce, however, believes BG is Buster Grinspoon. He believes that "2/28/00 BG—NO $!" means Lizzie decided against a deal with Buster on February 28, long before Bruce put together his proposal.

"Lizzie, don't lie to me. You were just humoring me about Buster. I know that. And I suppose in some sense I do appreciate that." He doesn't.

"I wasn't humoring you." She was.

"Well, in any event," he says, "the time has come for me to light out for the territories."

"No. *Bruce.* No."

"Buster and I talked on the phone all night after you told him he was crazy. And most of yesterday."

"I didn't tell him he was crazy."

"Well, anyway, we're starting a company, Lizzie. I can fund it for a couple of years. And you won't be able to make fun of me for owning my 'ridiculous empty piece of shit building on the Bowery' anymore. It's going to be the corporate headquarters of Terraplane."

Bruce smiles. She shakes her head.

"You're serious."

"Lizzie!" It's Alexi's voice on the intercom. The intercom! More weirdness. "Molly Cramer is on two, and says she needs to talk with you. On deadline."

Molly Cramer is the weaselly right-wing syndicated columnist and TV commentator; she must be doing an attack on the *Voice* attack on downtown businesses. Lizzie is eager to tell her side of the story to a sympathetic conservative, and she's dismayed by her eagerness. The day is dismaying. (*Weaselly:* it wasn't déjà vu before, Lizzie realizes, it was Reginald's ermine companion and this crazy weasel motif—ermines are weasels. If George wasn't being such a nincompoop, she'd call and tell him.)

Bruce stands. "It's your fault," he says, still smiling, "you're the one who convinced me running a business can be fun. Don't worry. I'll stay until we move Warps to beta."

"I'll take it!" she shouts to Alexi, and then says to Bruce, "See how fun?"

As Bruce opens the door, she notices the tiny oval XL sticker on his new T-shirt. *Terraplane.* The company name, she figures, is a Buster Grinspoon idea, another stupid, made-up sci-fi word like Compaq or Intel or Microsoft. Not only is Bruce leaving her, he's disappointing her, which makes the abandonment a little easier to take. In fact, "Terraplane Blues" was Robert Johnson's first hit recording, his signature tune, but Lizzie has no idea. She doesn't know anything about the blues.

George sits in shirtsleeves on an old warped granite step of the broad front stoop of St. Andrew's School, flipping through a copy of the *Entertainment Weekly for Kids* he picked up from the stack in the lobby. He notices a double-page spread comparing four young blond actresses— Dominique Swain, Melissa Joan Hart, Reese Witherspoon, and Becky Tipton, the actress who plays Little Jo on *Bonanza: The New Generation* (and who, he reads, is about to start shooting a "teen noir" Nancy Drew film). He also wonders if all the stories in the monthly *EW for Kids* are simply repackaged from the regular *EW* for adults. When he and his *Journal* friend Greg Dunn, who is black, were at *Newsweek* in the eighties, they used to joke about proposing to their bosses a brand extension called *Newsweek for Negroes.*

"Hi," Lizzie says. "I'm late."

He stands. They don't kiss.

"Hold on," she says, "I want to smoke a cigarette before we go in."

George looks at her, but not in a charmed or charming *tsk-tsk*-you-rascal way.

"Yes," she says, "I bought a pack. In Seattle. I'm bad."

"I saw the *Voice* piece," he says. "Not so horrible."

She gives a minimal one-shouldered shrug, lighting her Marlboro and squinting down the street toward the bright disk of sun behind the clouds.

In her twenties, Lizzie gave up reading short stories. Right now she remembers why. They all felt just like this moment.

"So," she says, tossing the match into the rhododendron, "what exactly does *canoodling* mean? Alexi showed me 'Page Six.' "

George smiles. "I guess it can cover pretty much anything from a friendly job interview to fucking under the cocktail table." George is glad she's caught him by surprise. Otherwise, if he'd been expecting it, his smile would have that nervous, frozen tilt. "In my case, it was the former."

"What's the thing about Las Vegas? 'Heavy petting'?"

For the record, dear, 'semi-heavy petting' is the phrase the Post *used.* "An actress at Ben's party who wanted a part on the show. Some crazy white-trash girl. She tried to pick me up, and she was kind of all over me—I mentioned it to you on the phone the night it happened. I didn't kiss her or anything."

"Ah." Lizzie takes a last drag on her Marlboro Light. "You didn't tell me about Mike Milken, either. What's that about?"

George rolls his eyes and checks his watch. "We can continue this, but we should get inside. Rafaela's saving seats."

Lizzie flicks her cigarette into the gutter, hefts her tote bag, turns away from George, and heads up the stairs toward the door.

"I have no idea what Milken wants," George says. "But don't I have the right to consult with an attorney? And if I can't afford an attorney, won't one be appointed for me?"

Lizzie doesn't smile.

"Emily is being extremely unpartnerlike," he says.

She looks at him. "Hey, it's *synchronicity!*" she says, her tone for that instant all rancid pseudo-glee, making him wonder if she means their marriage. Fortunately, no. "Bruce is leaving me to start his own company with that jerk from Seattle, the cat telepathy guy."

George holds open the door for Lizzie. He's not even aware that he makes a point of holding open doors for people, men as well as women, since he doesn't do it as a matter of antifeminist chivalry.

"What's Emily's problem?" she asks.

"*Real Time.* She thinks it means she'll have to abdicate as the princess of the Hollywood liberals."

The entrance hall is empty but for the security guard, so they walk faster toward the chapel, which is what the school still calls its auditorium.

"Do you think it has anything to do with the Mose stock price going down? You know, because of the announcement of the show?"

"No," he says. "No." And then, "How'd you know about the stock thing? Ben says it isn't dropping because of *Real Time,* by the way." And then, as they approach the big double mahogany doors, he asks again, "How did you know about the stock price, Lizzie? And about Milken calling me?"

"Iris told me about Milken. She called to tell me"—as he opens the door, she lowers her voice to a whisper—"that she'd try to talk her PETA chapter out of putting me on their Most Wanted list for my crimes against ermines."

They scan the pews full of parents, searching for Rafaela and the children. Lizzie's sudden good humor, as well as the polite twitches required by wholesale acquaintanceship (quick nods, arched eyebrows, little shrugs, a few mouthed "Hi"s), almost make George forget that she never answered his question about Mose's stock price and *Real Time.*

Rafaela went home right after the last Unfortunate American History video. George has chatted briefly with a few parents, including the Williamsons (who referred to their son as Flip, which must be the public compromise between Philip and Felipe), and now stands alone in a corner, sipping ginger ale with Max. Louisa is hanging on to Sarah, who is talking to Ms. Perez-Morrison. Lizzie is somewhere in the crowd.

Noticing all the the dark-skinned baby-sitters standing in their corner as he watches LuLu and Sarah, George remembers the moment, the horrible moment, last summer, when the grinning innkeeper on Martha's Vineyard asked if "your au pair will be occupying her own room." They had no baby-sitter on the Vineyard; the man had assumed Sarah, unsmiling dark-haired olive-skinned teenage Sarah, was paid to look after the two little blond Mactier children.

George found Felipe Williamson's video remarkable and moving. He intercut shots of several Manhattanites and their Upper East Side travel agents discussing fancy Cancún and Puerto Vallarta vacation plans with interviews of Mexican and Salvadoran busboys and waiters at the Viva Zapata Taquería discussing the current Zapatista insurrection. George also praised Sarah and Penelope's video, *1964,* which was about what you'd expect from fourteen-year-olds, although he regretted that he couldn't tell Sarah how much her soundtrack "mistake" pleased him. The old songs they finally used—"I Dreamed I Saw Joe Hill Last Night," "We Shall Overcome," "Amazing Grace"—are instrumental versions by the Ray Conniff Orchestra, saccharine and ridiculous in a way that seems intentionally unsettling.

"That wasn't the kind of movie I really like," Max confides.

"Too . . . newsy?"

Max shakes his head. "No. Too *TV.* You knew everything that was going to happen before it happened. The good people were all *so* good and the bad people were so like *completely* bad."

George cannot, of course, tell Max that his critique is exactly right. "I thought they did a fine job."

"Do you think my movie is good?"

On his computer, Max has downloaded hundreds of video clips from which he's stitched together a ninety-second trailer for a nonexistent feature film in which the running joke is the hero inexplicably vomiting small animals—a kitten, a gopher, and a pigeon—at inopportune times.

"I think your movie is brilliant." The last time Max fished for this compliment, George called it "Buñuelian," and Max stayed up most of the night looking at hundreds of the thousands of pages on the web that mention Luis Buñuel.

"Dad?"

"What?"

"Can I go talk to Griffin B.?" He waits, then says, "Will you be okay?"

May I hug you first, Max, squeeze you and kiss you, and then fall to my knees and sob? That wouldn't embarrass you, would it, son? "Sure, go ahead," George says. "If you see your mom, tell her it's time for us to go talk to Mr. Hoff."

Griffin B. is Griffin Bisette, Penelope's little brother. George has been amazed to discover that there were two Griffins in Max's class this year, who are called Griffin B. and Griffin L., like bacterial strains. But Griffin is precisely the kind of name that's in vogue among parents who send their children to nonreligious private schools called St. Andrew's, who buy forty-dollar-a-gallon Martha Stewart paint and fifty-dollar doll-size American Girl butter churns made of solid chestnut. One of Max's classmates is named Huck—not Huckleberry, Huck—and in LuLu's class there is a Truman, a Chester, a Sawyer, three Benjamins, two Coopers, a Walker, and a Hunter (Hunter Liu), as well as multiple Amandas, Lucys, and Hopes, and even a Gwyneth. In Sarah's class, there is a black kid named Van Blount, short for Vantrel ("which we discovered is also a type of *rayon,*" Vantrel's mother informed George at a parents' night, laughing and unembarrassed). Blissed Henderson (a girl Sarah's age who changed her name to Bee in fourth grade, then back to Blissed in eighth) is the only child in their kids' classes with an over-the-top, movie-star-offspring name. Yet another of George's stories the ABC News brass hated: how show business parents have taken up where hippie parents left off, inventing novelty names for their children—the Dakotas (Don Johnson and Melanie Griffith), the Deni Montanas (Woody Harrelson), the Jetts (John Travolta and Kelly Preston), and the Maya Rays (Uma Thurman and Ethan Hawke). George didn't learn until after the story ran that one of his semi-bosses at Disney had a son named E. (for "Eternal") Frontier and a daughter named Angel Fire.

"Ready?" Lizzie says, and they head into the hallway, passing the three-foot-high Campbell's soup cans into which children are supposed to deposit real cans of Campbell's soup for the poor, and passing the Taco Bell/KFC minicafeteria that provoked a ruckus among the parents before it finally opened in the fall. The ceilings in the anteroom off the headmaster's office are twelve feet high. The portraits on the wall gleam. The oak wainscoting is old, and the plaster is real. Private school headmasters may not be paid well, but they get magnificent CEO offices.

Mr. Hoff will be just a moment. Mr. Hoff's assistant seems a little scared of them, probably because they're clients, Lizzie thinks, $62,000-a-year clients. Lizzie wonders if this meeting is some kind of sidelong fund-raising gambit. Or maybe Mr. Hoff wants to push Max into the new ultragifted program one of the parents has bragged about. In any event, she's ready to receive praise—"*Congratulations, Elizabeth,*" she remembers the principal of Pally High saying such a brief time ago, "*you're second in the class.*" "*Congratulations, Elizabeth, you're a National Merit Finalist.*" "*Congratulations, welcome to Radcliffe.*" "*Welcome to the business school.*" "*Congratulations, it's a girl.*" "*He's a great guy you've*

snagged." "He's *a beautiful little boy."* "She's *a perfect little girl. Congratu-*
lations, Lizzie."

George wonders if Mr. Hoff is going to tell them Max has some
newly invented learning disability, or uses hate language to taunt his
classmates. He's catching the assistant's funny looks too, and reads sadness and possibly disgust folded in with the fear. Maybe Max got
caught with a lit cigarette, like George had. (Although where is the St.
Andrew's equivalent of the alley behind the metal shop?) Maybe Max
has been secretly taking a dump on the floor of the boys' bathroom
every day for a week, like George's friend Tuggy did before his parents
sent him to military school. Maybe Max and his pals spelled out
FUCK with their fingers in a class picture, as George did when he was
a boy. (He had been the *C,* chosen because it had plausible deniability,
although not plausible enough, as things turned out.) Or maybe Max
dismembered the class hamster, as serial killers do when they're boys.

"This is not an easy conversation," Mr. Hoff begins, shocking
Lizzie. "Are you . . . *familiar* with the Science and Society curricu-
lum? The indoor-pollution homework the children have been doing
these last weeks?"

They say they are, yes. Well, Mr. Hoff explains ponderously, when
Max's Science and Society instructor got Max's indoor-pollution
samples back from the lab, he discovered not just the usual—household
poisons, lead paint flecks, tar, nicotine, and peanut dust. In the air and
surface samples Max took from his parents' bedroom—Mr. Hoff actually says *"his parents'* bedroom"—the teacher found "incontrovertible
evidence" of recent marijuana use.

"Now," Mr. Hoff says, leaning forward, "this is not the first time
we've had an . . . *incident* like this."

George and Lizzie both nod, trying to look contrite rather than embarrassed and angry.

"It's the fourth time," Mr. Hoff says.

George's brow is literally sweating. Lizzie feels a little like she did
when the Harvard doctor told her she was pregnant with Sarah.

"After a discussion with our *lawyers,* we've decided to reaffirm the
existing school policy, which is not to notify law-enforcement authorities."

They both relax a little.

"However, I must tell you that in one of the previous cases, we did feel it appropriate to notify the child-welfare authorities."

They both think: *Which lawyer do we call?* George's show business attorney; Lizzie's corporate attorney, Katherine; the trusts and estates guy; or the former assistant Manhattan DA they know? And George thinks of the *Post* headline writing itself (REAL NARCS BUST *NARCS* TV BIG).

"In *that* situation," Mr. Hoff says, "a small trace of *cocaine* was registered as well as marijuana residue."

George and Lizzie both nod, frowning, overacting, gravely affirming—yes, *mm-hmmm*—his distinction between marijuana and cocaine. After a few more minutes of quietly acknowledging the seriousness of the parenting responsibility, and agreeing what fine St. Andrew's students all three children are, they say they will consider his suggestion of substance-abuse counseling.

"I want you to know," Lizzie says as they stand, realizing Mr. Hoff has no threats or ultimatums up his sleeve, "that we very rarely, um, indulge. Once every few months, maybe." Maybe, or maybe every few weeks. "And this is going to sound like an excuse, but we've both been under a tremendous amount of stress lately."

"I understand," he says, "and *that's* why I'm urging you to seek the intervention of a counselor."

Fuck you, Mr. Hoff, George would like to say.

Fuck you, Mr. Hoff, Lizzie would like to say.

As they leave the school, Max asks, "So what did Mr. Hoff want?"

"To tell us what a great student you are," Lizzie answers almost before he finishes the question.

"He wanted to make sure we're happy," George adds. "You know, with St. Andrew's."

Their unspoken precinct-house bond has a half-life about as long as the ride home, however. Their perfect one-two instant dissembling to Max gives George and Lizzie both a little chill. As he unlocks the front door on Water Street, George even has the thought, *She bought the pot,* cravenly imagining his separate defense as he watches Max and LuLu tumble in and upstairs, driving the terrified cat ahead of them.

Sarah has gone out for dinner with Penelope and Felipe and Gwyneth, in order to plan their Saturday junket to a Junior Golden

Gloves boxing match and tabulate the audience response cards rating their docudramas. (Sarah said Ms. Perez-Morrison told them that the videos that "test over 120" will get a minimum grade of B+. George told Sarah to make sure she gets at least 10 percent of first-dollar gross, but she didn't laugh.)

Lizzie is sitting out back in a cheap folding aluminum chair placed in a spot where she can't be seen from the rear living room windows. She's smoking, mentally examining yet again each twist and turn and tunnel of her runaway Microsoft train ride, trying to figure out what happened. She can faintly hear the drone of the upstairs television— "*. . . not only a small miracle, Debi, but hilarious too! Check this out . . .*" The little kids are watching *Small Miracles,* LuLu's favorite program, a "family variety show" that combines magic acts, circus performers, *Believe It or Not* freaks, and reports on UFO abductions, religious visions, and breakthroughs in cosmology and astrophysics. *Small Miracles* is the wholesome CBS rival show to MBC's *Freaky Shit!,* and the promotional line of the people behind *Small Miracles* is that they're "broadcasting America's first and only advertising-free commercial program—a Small Miracle in itself!" *Small Miracles* is sponsored and produced by AgroSnax, however, which manufactures the Small Miracles line of "permanently fresh" chips, cookies, and " 'meat' nubbins." Max will watch anything, but he professes to dislike *Small Miracles* because his favorite television *is* the commercials: when George once mentioned having met the Coen brothers, his son said, "*Whoa!* You mean the guys who directed the Honda ad?" Max liked the Coens' minivan commercial even more than Jean-Luc Godard's new TV campaign for Apple, which is extreme praise for Max.

From his office on the top floor, George is finally talking to Emily, who's in her car.

"Love the finale script. You nailed the arc. What the—*fuck you!* Jesus."

"Emily?"

"Love you too, bitch! *Mwah!*"

"Emily?"

"Sorry. A 500SL cut me off. Thought it was a rapper ambush or something. But it's somebody from Fox 2000 I know."

"So you like the script?"

"Yup."

"Great. Thanks."

"George?"

"Some bad news."

"What?" Her masseur quit. The polls have Gore way behind in Pennsylvania. They *are* over budget on *Real Time*. She's found out she has cancer. She's found out he has cancer.

"We should do this face-to-face."

"Do what?"

"Divorce."

"What are you talking about, Emily?"

"I'm not a journalist. I can't do *Real Time*. It'll give me ulcers. It'll make me nuts."

"You're not; you won't be. Like we said, you'll take over *NARCS* with Phoebe and Paul, and I'll do *Real Time*."

"No, George. What about my Jesse Jackson documentary? What about the NARAL hoedown this summer? What happens if I work in the Gore administration?"

"The Gore administration?" *Good luck,* he thinks. "He's promised you a job if he wins?"

"No. Hypothetically. But I can't put my *deepest convictions* in a blind trust for the sake of some stupid *journalism* rule. If it's journalism versus loyalty and friendship, loyalty wins. I can't split the difference. Some kind of fake, arm's-length relationship won't cut it."

George considers making a joke about *fake arm's length* and *cut it,* pretending to take offense. But if she's going to go earnest, he'll go earnest too.

"So what do you mean? You take *NARCS* and I get *Real Time*? I'd call *that* an asset parity problem, Em." When they negotiated their deal to create Well-Armed Productions two years ago, her lawyer repeatedly used the phrase "asset parity problem" as a euphemism for the fact that George had never produced an entertainment show and Emily had. What George means now is that *NARCS* is a hit that might pump out millions of dollars for years to come; *Real Time* is a kooky idea for a show that doesn't exist yet.

"You produce and own *Real Time*—your dream show. I produce and own *NARCS*. We're both locked forever into passive creator participation on each other's shows. Financially, contractually, everything is still fifty–fifty."

George finds it interesting how loquacious Emily has become now that she is breaking up with him and making complicated financial stipulations.

"So we raise the two children separately," he says, "with visitation rights."

Emily, who is unmarried and childless, doesn't reply.

"Who would I get to do all the business stuff, Emily?"

"Any of a thousand people."

"What about the projects in development?"

"*The Odds* is mine; the other two are yours."

George wonders if she already has *The Odds* set up at a studio or a network. "You know we can't move *NARCS* out to Burbank," he says. "The network won't let us. We're half the reason for the soundstage on Fifty-seventh Street. Not to mention Angela and Lucas and—"

"I'll move. I've got a bid in on a condo on West Sixty-fourth, by the Park."

Decisions have been made. Plans are afoot. George has been clueless. "So I'm supposed to accept this as a fait accompli? Christ, Emily! You've probably cleared this with Featherstone already, too."

She pauses. "Not really."

"What the *fuck* does 'not really' mean?"

"It means he and Saddler called me yesterday after Lucas called him about your fight—"

"Hank *Saddler*? It was not a 'fight.' "

"Timothy called to ask about *NARCS*. But I told him you and I talked about my coming back here to help run things for a while. And he said that sounded like a pretty sensible interim plan."

George is accustomed to being the aggressively calm and reasonable combatant, letting the other person flail.

"Featherstone called it 'a pretty sensible interim plan'? What, did Saddler use ventriloquism on him?"

"Timothy said, quote, 'Himalaya, that is a genius short-term fix.' Unquote. It doesn't matter what he said, George. This isn't a squeeze play against you. We've got two shows. I can't be associated with one. Let's solve the problem. *I'm* the liberal activist scumbag Stengel and company are using to attack *Real Time.* Right? So dump me! We'll say we made a tough choice, did the right thing, bullshit, bullshit, bullshit."

"You can't be 'associated' with *Real Time,* but you're willing to take the money."

"I'd be happy to give you all the dough from *Real Time* and keep everything . . . what you want, George. As a matter of fact, I . . . given Mose's . . . thrilled, although the budget looks closer to one-point-seven. But either we share cash flow, or we don't. And worst case, you . . . better for the budget if I'm off your P and L . . . , to remember, George. It really isn't *you*—it's *me.*"

"You're breaking up, Emily. You're all static-y."

". . . ville Canyon. I'm coming out now. Better?"

"Mmm."

Neither says a thing for many seconds. Finally George, stumbling provisionally toward a no-fault concession speech, says, "Well, shit. This sucks, Emily, this really sucks."

She says nothing.

"So I suppose you've already got lawyers drafting this?"

She says nothing, but George hears a kind of muffled keening.

"Emily? Are you crying? Emily?"

He still hears the electronic whine, which is just noise, not signal. The connection is lost.

He hangs up and joins Lizzie outside. He tells her Emily wants to dissolve the partnership.

"Welcome to the club," she says.

"Bruce isn't your partner."

They talk it through. After George says he half expected it to happen, he wonders if he really did.

"It's going to mean a fuck of a lot more work for me," he says. "Alone." George is still standing. "Did you talk to your dad today?"

"To Tammy. He was asleep. Oh my God! Guess what?"

He shakes his head.

"Tammy," she says, "told me that Buddy is dating Emily."

"Emily? *Emily* Emily? She dumped Michael?"

Lizzie nods enthusiastically. "Tammy thinks there's an Alan Alda or Tony Roberts movie with exactly this plot. It's amazing, isn't it?"

"I guess she's jettisoning everyone."

Neither of them speaks for a while.

"Are we done talking about Emily?" Lizzie asks. "Because you know, the thing I *still* just can't figure out about Microsoft is how they knew about me and Buster Grinspoon. If Bruce is right, and I'm sure he is, about their suddenly getting so hot for the company because they wanted Grinspoon's patents. I remember now, at that meeting on Tuesday, how they really *knew.*" She doesn't remember the deal memo she left in the backseat of her dial-car weeks ago, or the phone call her driver overheard.

"Who knows?" George says. "The grapevine." In fact, he's afraid he knows exactly. He believes he's the vine—by mentioning Lizzie and Grinspoon's research to Featherstone, who, George figures, mentioned it to one of his contacts at Microsoft. "There's a message from Pollyanna for you, by the way. About some Vermont trip. You're going climbing? When did you start climbing again?"

"Polly and I talked about it, yeah."

He says nothing.

"I figured Memorial Day weekend when we go up to the house, we might spend Saturday in Vermont, climbing. Polly and I."

He stops to muse, staring past Lizzie, who's carefully grinding out the cigarette on a giant terra-cotta pot. Buddy and Emily, Lucas Winton and Iris, Stengel and the *Post* reporter, Shawna Cindy Switzer and Sandi Bemis . . . he sees them all over the country, all over the globe— Vermont, the Hollywood Hills, Las Vegas, Madison Avenue, MBC News, Fifty-nine, up in the Bombardier at fifty thousand feet—the enemies of George are all trading glances, grinning, allying, plotting. Not the *enemies,* maybe, but not the friends either—the Switzerlands, the Frances, the Jordans, the nonaligned nations, all the amiable quislings and collaborators-in-waiting. Harold Mose and Lizzie.

"Daddy is sleeping a lot, Tammy said, but the doctors told her his condition is still stable. He might get out of the ICU next week."

George's hazy, frightened little glimmer is stupid, he tells himself, baroque, some stress-related hallucination, paranoid delusion as hokey montage. (*Use it!* Featherstone would say. *Use it in the work!*)

"How long have they been 'dating'?" he says, emphasizing the sanitized word choice. "Emily and Buddy."

George is sitting down now, on the ancient oak stump that has been used as a chair for decades, and before that as a chopping block for fowl. He hasn't forgotten that he's engaged in some sort of domestic cold war, but he has lost track of the real grievances, if there are real grievances, and is relieved that Lizzie seems to have moved past his "Page Six" quasi-infidelities.

"I guess he was a technical adviser on *Mr. Dead.*" *Mr. Dead* is Emily's little supernatural teen comedy for Paramount about the avenging ghosts of dead mustangs. "They ran into each other again at the screening for the crew, and started fucking."

Since it's Buddy's penis she's talking about, the "fucking" stings a little. (For three years in the eighties George avoided seeing Arnold Schwarzenegger movies because his girlfriend at the time had slept with Arnold in the seventies.)

The word *fucking* and the low-budget-movie talk makes Lizzie remember her discovery when she paid the bills.

"You watched porno movies in L.A. last month after I left," she says delightedly. "Three."

He says nothing for a second.

"They're on the hotel bill," she says.

"Yeah? So what is this? Sex interrogation day? Jesus. Are you *trying* to start fights?"

"Oh, Christ, George, *please.* I think it's cute. It's like a cute little secret boy thing."

"Okay, okay, okay. But cut me some slack. My work life pretty much turned to shit this morning."

"*Your* work life turned to shit? Mine isn't so fucking peachy, either, bub."

"I know," he concedes. "I know. But all this dumb, giant corporate stuff I have to deal with, I mean, *Jesus.*"

"Giant and corporate sounds like a vacation right now. At least then it wouldn't be me, me, *me* the *Voice* hates, *me* my employees hate. I was getting pretty used to the Microsoft idea. The buck stopping over *there* somewhere. You know? Maybe I should talk to Harold about his job."

"What?"

"You know, his digital job."

"What do you mean? What are you talking about?"

"He called me on the plane and said I should come and, I don't know, run online for him. Whatever that means. It wasn't like a serious job offer. It was just, you know, flattery, bullshit. I didn't tell you?"

"No."

"I thought I did."

"No."

He wants a *Sorry*. He gets only one of her little single-shouldered shrugs, which makes him want to hit her.

He has always tried to tell the truth, as much as he can, especially to Lizzie. As Lizzie says, clichés are clichés because they're true: sometimes the truth does hurt.

"Well," George says, "I should tell you I'm sorry. If I triggered this whole Microsoft craziness in the first place. It was an accident."

Inside, the phone rings. Up in the windows, he sees a child's shadow fly across the white curtains.

"Huh?" Lizzie says. She wonders if George is making a strange joke she doesn't get, or if he's even farther off some flaky abracadabra deep end than she imagined.

"When I was in L.A. I mentioned your deal with Grinspoon to Timothy. And I guess Timothy probably told one of his Microsoft people about it."

Max opens one of the back windows and shouts, "Dad? The phone."

"Okay," he says back.

Lizzie is standing. "You just can't keep your fucking mouth shut about anything, can you, George?" She is livid. It may have been George's blabbing that made Microsoft double their offer, but she is still livid. The spleen wants what it wants. "No wonder you need Emily to run the business." She turns and marches inside.

He stands in the Seaport gloom, not flinching as the door slams, watching her disappear into the dark end of the kitchen, thinking, *That'll teach you to tell the truth, George Mactier.*

"Dad?" Max shouts again from the window upstairs. "It's Greg Dunn at the *Journal*. He said he heard about Grandpa."

George takes a deep breath and looks at Lizzie inside, opening the refrigerator, coping with some trifle.

"What *about* Grandpa?" Max asks.

"I don't know." But now he knows. When he was at *Newsweek,* George phoned a woman in Brooklyn to ask her about the killing of her Grenadian son by the Army during the U.S. invasion of the island; she hadn't known. It remains his most awful professional moment, worse than getting wounded, which he doesn't remember, worse then firing people.

"Greg Dunn said he loves you and Mom," Max shouts, "and if you're 'grieving,' you can call him back whenever."

2 8

Is Lizzie still grieving? She's hardly noticed the verb before, except passingly to hate it, both because it's one of those words forced into verb drag and because *grieving* seems designed to turn sadness into a hobby. At Edith Hope's funeral, the Unitarian minister talked about "a nurturing, web-connected community of grieving," and gave George and Lizzie a "grieving video" that taught "grieving exercises" and incorporated bootlegged clips from *Terms of Endearment, Ghost, Fried Green Tomatoes,* and *City of Angels.*

But when Mike died last month, Lizzie surprised herself by insisting that they fly to and from the funeral in L.A. on different planes, and astounded herself even more, when they got home, by staying away from the office for three days. "I need to organize my father's stuff," she told Alexi and Bruce and George, but that took only a day. She doesn't understand precisely why she has been spending so much of her time in hiding—lunch hours at work on a bench in Madison Square Park and cigarettes on the roof of the building, avoiding Nancy McNabb's IPO calls, canceling a drink with Pollyanna for no reason. But she has come to believe that grieving is not such a phony notion after all.

Her father's death got her mind off the Microsoft fiasco quickly, and has kept her from obsessing over the Molly Cramer attack, which was worse than the *Voice* attack, because a few people actually saw it. In "America's Side," her *Post* column, and in her Fox News commentary, Cramer accused Lizzie of being "the perfect twenty-first-century limousine liberal hypocrite. This is a woman who once disrespected my friend and employer Mr. Murdoch at a public event and who, Pentagon sources tell me, compromised American national security by refusing to sell one of her computer programs to the armed forces. She cuddles up to bleeding-heart liberal Democrats like Al Gore—all while she *fires* disabled employees because they're disabled! Now that Ms. Cyber-Chic Radical is hoist with her own P.C. petard, *we* get the last laugh. This is Molly Cramer," she had said, grinning into the camera, "on *America's* side."

In the Elisabeth Kübler-Ross five-stage bereavement scheme, which is now a pillar of American popular science (as real to most people as the laws of thermodynamics, more real than theories of relativity and quantum foam), anger is supposed to be stage two. But Lizzie has proceeded directly to anger, passing up denial completely. She spent the flight out to L.A. rereading that morning's Molly Cramer column until she could recite it, which she proceeded to do for George as soon as his flight landed. Dr. Bambang S.H.H. Bob Hardiyanti met them at LAX with two limousines, one for the kids and one for George and her. On the drive into town, Dr. Hardiyanti started congratulating Lizzie fulsomely, saying that Mike and she and the whole family have been "the key actors" in "a historic breakthrough moment in medicine." What made her angry, so angry that she ordered Dr. Hardiyanti to get "*out* of this fucking limo, *now*" on Century Boulevard (George overruled her and let him stay), was the doctor's proud revelation that Mike Zimbalist's swine-liver transplant had never actually taken place. He'd had no surgery! There'd been no pig liver! The doctor explained excitedly that it had been "a fantastic validation of a new placebo protocol, placebo surgery," and that because Mike *believed* he had a new liver, he had lived "much longer with a very much superior quality of life" than if he had simply been told the truth. What kept Lizzie's rage burning, however, like a small fission reaction she could control but not stop, was the fact that George wasn't angry enough about the charade.

Tammy, it turns out, knew about the placebo procedure all along. The hospital had to have her permission. "Who says it didn't work? I had *an extra month* with Mikey, sweetheart," she said to Lizzie, "and we even got to make *love* one last time. What's to be pissed about now? Mikey wouldn't be." Tammy told them she had performed fellatio on Mike in his deathbed not long before he lost consciousness for the last time. " 'I'm so glad I'm in the zone,' " she says he said to her happily, 'I'm in the *center* of the *zone!*' " Mike Zimbalist's cosmic last words were quoted at the Kaddish, and repeated lovingly by Tammy and Lizzie's stepbrother Ronnie as evidence of Mike's next-worldly bliss. George waited a week to tell Lizzie that by "the zone" Mike almost certainly meant not a corridor to the afterlife but the Hollywood production zone the studios established in the old days, back when her father was at Metro. It's a sixty-mile circle, within which producers don't have to pay per diems to actors and crews, and its center is the intersection of Beverly and La Cienega Boulevards—exactly where Mike Zimbalist died. George was charmed by the misunderstanding. Lizzie, monitoring her little isotope of hostility, was not.

To her surprise, she's looking forward to her party tonight, the big, loud, expensive, everybody-we-know party she ordered up that dizzy morning weeks ago to (not) celebrate her Microsoft liquidity event. *Her party.* That's how it seems. Even though this afternoon Alexi folded his arms and gave her the interventionist look, his maternal fret, when she leaves work early to prepare and primp, she feels she's coming out of hiding.

It is such a luxury to be all alone at home (with Rafaela, but alone) in the still of a weekday afternoon. Rafaela's attitude toward Lizzie has changed subtly but unmistakably, as though in Rafaela's eyes Lizzie has finally become corporeal. Lizzie doesn't know if it's Mike Zimbalist's death (*The gringa superhero, she suffers pain!*), or the murder of her own family, but Rafaela looks her in the eye now, as though they share a secret. Lizzie has tried to be kind. She arranged for the FedExing from Mexico of the children's cremated remains. (Lizzie now knows that the mortuarial term of art is *cremains*. And her baby-sitter's full name—Rafaela Ek Canul.) She and George attended the endless Spanish memorial service out in St. Albans, Queens, during which Lizzie got her period suddenly, heavily and tamponless. On the way out of the church, marveling at the cookie-size red spot on the back of Lizzie's white Calvin Klein silk sheath, LuLu asked, of course, "Does everyone here think Mommy was shot?") Lizzie knows it's sentimental and self-flattering, but Rafaela's changed manner has in it the glint of something like solidarity. "Yeah," George teased her the night she finally got up the nerve to mention this to him, "Mutt and *jefe*."

"Rafaela?" she shouts down from the top landing, "your money is on the counter in the kitchen. Before you pick up the kids at school, can you help me carry these boxes downstairs?" Lizzie has let Ronnie and the stepsiblings keep most of her father's glamorous memorabilia—the cream-colored spat bearing Jack Warner's signature and several of Nancy Reagan's crimson lip prints (also autographed), the brittle photo of Mike grabbing Bugsy Siegel's ass with one hand and the nineteen-year-old Marilyn Monroe's with the other, the framed signed contract with Elvis Presley that Elvis pissed on and Special Deliveried back to Mike. What Lizzie wanted, she culled and curated last month, in L.A. and Palm Springs, down to five big boxes (including the one filled with thick, dense, black Tommy Dorsey 78s and thick, dense, white stationery, one mint set from each old hotel).

"Two trips, I think," Lizzie says to Rafaela as both women, the dark one just over five feet and the rich one just under six, pick up a loaded UPS carton and begin stepping carefully down the stairs. The papers in these boxes—telegrams and letters and photos and ticket stubs and ledgers and clippings—have transformed Lizzie's view of her father. Because Mike Zimbalist was such a chronic embellisher and dissembler, Lizzie had left home assuming that nearly all the fabulous stories about his past were just that, cooked-up tales meant to entertain acquaintances and children. But these boxes are a trove of evidence to the contrary. Mike Zimbalist's tallest tales were true, it turns out. He really did sail to Tokyo as an eighteen-year-old tap dancer to perform as part of a secret vaudeville show imported by Emperor Hirohito's courtiers, and he did have an onboard romance with his Japanese language tutor during the *Nitta Maru*'s Pacific crossing. (Imprinted in gay red letters on his NYK Lines ticket folder is the line, SAY GOODBYE TO THE TURMOIL OF "SCARY HEADLINES"!) He did cash in his first-class return ticket and head overland through India and Palestine, ending up in Paris, where he really did buy a Matisse oil for $475 in July 1939. And he really did sell the Matisse privately in Palm Springs in 1961 to finance *Beatniks on Mars,* his disastrous attempt to become a writer-director-producer. Mike Zimbalist's maternal great-grandfather *was* a cofounder in 1868 in St. Louis of a magazine called *The Communist.* (Its name was later changed to *The Altruist,* and it went bankrupt in 1917.) Zayde and Bubbe Zimbalist did emigrate from Berlin in 1924 after their pawnshop was wiped out by Weimar inflation, which really had amounted to 3.45 quintillion percent over a couple of years, and he did go to work for a federal agency actually called the U.S. Bureau of Efficiency. Lizzie never thought Mike was lying about the "quintillion percent" and "the Bureau of Efficiency"—she'd always assumed those parts of the story were purely jokes, like something out of *Willy Wonka.*

After they stack the cartons in the basement and Rafaela leaves, Lizzie has a few minutes for a cup of tea before she goes uptown to get her hair done—to "the beauty shop," as she always calls it, an effort to take some of the curse off her three-hundred-dollar haircuts. Waiting for the water to boil, she notices that on Rafaela's de facto patch of kitchen counter, between the Duolit toaster and the Nuova Simonelli espresso machine (a gift from MBC they never use but, because it's worth twenty-four hundred dollars and looks cool, they keep), there's an envelope addressed to Rafaela in Sarah's handwriting. And sitting under it, a creased color snapshot of Rafaela squatting and smiling near an orchid tree in a forest, with her toddlers Fernando and Jilma. Stuck to the photo is a Post-it on which LuLu has written, "Here your kids piktur back, Rafaela. Louisa Z. Mactier." Lizzie loves her children.

———

He dreads expiration days. He despises the gun to his head. "Billy," Bennett Gould says, half standing, "what are we going to do with those Microsoft May 110 calls? And the USA Loves Toys May 9½ puts?"

In truth, he doesn't care what Billy Heffernan thinks. It is his polite way of announcing that he now intends to decide what to do. It is thinking out loud.

Ben has always been bullish on Microsoft, and his enthusiasm reignited last winter, after he saw a preview of the Mendacita software and the company declared its three-for-two stock split. But Mendacita hasn't taken off yet, the analysts' sales projections for Windows 2000 were so extreme that it's been hard for the company to beat them, and the free Linux system is taking market share. The share price has been stalled between 108 and 112 for months now, which (especially for a stock like Microsoft) turns into a self-propelling stream of anxiety and dither—if *Microsoft* isn't rising smartly, something must be wrong (even if nothing is wrong). His 9,000 Microsoft calls that expire momentarily are bets he made two months ago, in March, that the company would have a killer first quarter. Even their relaunch of the webzine *Slate* as a same-day-delivery home-office-supply site and selective-admission chat room looked auspicious to Ben, since it was evidence the company finally understood it had no business in media. But the Microsoft calls are more or less a wash—the stock price today is 112½. Ben hasn't made or lost money.

After he had such fun unloading his USA Loves Toys stock last month, he decided he wasn't finished hating the company. And so he bought 5,000 USA Loves Toys puts, one-month-long bets that the stock would continue its ugly downward slide. USA Loves Toys is still at 10, so he can just let the puts expire worthlessly. Or, if he's convinced now that the fighting in Mexico will put a crimp in the manufacturing schedules for USA Loves's two big new Christmas toys (a remote-controlled flying saucer called Alien Craft and some stuffed piece of shit called To Hell 'n' Back Booby Babies), he can keep his money on the table, essentially roll his puts over by buying some June puts. If on the other hand he decides to exercise the puts he owns now, Heffernan will do nothing, and next Monday Bennett Gould's account at Goldman Sachs will automatically have 500,000 shares of USA Loves Toys shorted. Ben doesn't like being short common stock, because then he has unlimited liability. The more USA Loves Toys goes up then, the more he loses. If he's short 500,000 shares of USA Loves Toys at 9½ on Monday, and it pops to 20 on Tuesday after some bogus e-commerce announcement by the company, Ben would be liable for $5.25 million. And in his professional lifetime, the market only goes up, always up. Ben likes to think of himself as a contrarian, but shorting common stock feels uncomfortable and dangerous, like some alien sexual practice. On the 5,000 puts, he's out maybe $100,000—$200,000 maximum. His downside is capped.

"Fucking USA Loves Toys. I still think it's going to tank big time before the end of the quarter. Price out some June nine puts."

Heffernan tells him, "They're the same as July."

"Buy the Julys." Ben is extending his bet for another two months that USA Loves Toys will indeed fall below $9 a share.

"People are not going to like this close," Melucci says, checking his unhappy red screens.

Ben asks Heffernan, "You sold all the Micron calls, right?"

"EBay just collapsed," Melucci says.

"Ms. Grundy," Dianne says, "is on three-seven."

"*What?* She calls me at ten minutes till *four?* What is that woman thinking? I don't need to talk to her. Tell her yes to all eight, at her bids, except the Bellow. I'd go up to 800 on the Bellow." Ms. Grundy is the pseudonym of the agent who runs his movie and TV company, which is called Permanent Productions. Ben has committed $25 million to Permanent, which is in turn a shell holding company for other movie and TV production entities he has set up all over the English-speaking world—Chimera Filmed Entertainment; Invisible Media Ltd.; the Over the Rainbow Company; Null & Void Productions; Charade, Incorporated; and a dozen more. In the two years since he set up shop, he has spent $14.4 million purchasing the film and television rights to thirty-two mid- and late-twentieth-century novels, plays, and stories that have never been filmed and that he particularly loves. He started with a wish list of a hundred, and his intention is to buy up, anonymously, the rights to as many as he can. He has no intention of making any of them into motion pictures or TV shows. In fact, his idea is just the opposite: Ben Gould wants to save contemporary literature from Hollywood, the same way conservation groups organize in rural areas to buy up farms to save virginal landscapes from real estate developers. Having fairly compensated the rights' holders—studios and producers, writers and writers' estates— Permanent Productions and all its component entities will simply sit on the rights in perpetuity. The man in Los Angeles who runs Mirage doesn't know he's a corporate sibling of the husband and wife in London who operate Invisible; they all deal individually with Ms. Grundy. Ben tells himself he would prefer to be doing this on the up-and-up. But he knows honesty would distort the market—the press attention would make it look like a stunt and complicate the process. Agents would hold him up, and he knows some writers actually want their books turned into Meryl Streep vehicles and HBO miniseries.

In the Big Room, the flaps are up, the landing gear is down, seat belts are fastened, and tray tables are in their locked and upright positions.

"There's four million Merck for sale," Melucci tells Ben. "Do you care?"

"No. Ugly close," Ben says. "Ugly close. Where is Mose going out?"

"At 45 and a teeny," Berger tells him. A teeny is a sixteenth of a dollar.

It's five minutes after four.

"We're done," Ben says, propelling himself away from his desk with a shove as he does every afternoon at this moment.

Everyone in the Big Room calms down, even Ben, relatively speaking. They have until five-thirty to tell their brokers what to do with their thousands of expiring put and call options, whether to exercise them or sell them. Because it's Friday, he won't be able to trade Tokyo in four hours, as he does some nights. The trading week is over.

Dianne announces, "I've got Cubby Koplowitz holding from Rome."

"Hey! Mr. Koplowitz! *Buòna sera,* partner!"

"Bennett, the Vatican City meetings went unbelievably well. We really have their blessing. I didn't even have to sell them. Father Ludlum—he's our go-to guy, a super guy, grew up in Ventura County too, turns out we rode at the same go-cart track when we were kids!— Father Ludlum says we have a 'blinking green light.' The Holy Father will need to sign off too, since this qualifies technically as a liturgical change, but approval is a done deal, Father Ludlum says."

"Really?" Ben is excited. "That's fabulous! They really get the concept?"

"They not only get it, they'd love us to time-frame the pilot project for a holiday-season premiere. *This* year's holiday season. When I told Father Ludlum that on the rollout we'd help arrange prime-plus-one financing on a diocesan level, he was, well, he was *ecstatic.* They don't like 'location-based entertainment,' though. As a phrase."

"The deal with the rabbis is not an issue for them? And with what's his name, the Orange County guy?"

"Reverend Schuller. No, in fact, Father Ludlum said that solves one of their concerns, that this would look too 'RC-centric.' They love the ecumenical concept. Especially now, in the jubilee year, since they've been taking a little flak on the Christian-themed millennium issue."

"How about the name? Which name did they vote for?"

"Father Ludlum agrees with you about Sacred Visions—he didn't actually say it sounded too Protestant, he said 'low-rent.' But they have no problem whatsoever with the Guild."

"Koplowitz, this is a fucking miracle."

Cubby's notion is simple. The inspirational rituals and artifacts at the heart of all religious services—the organ music, chants, and choruses; the vestments, stained glass, groin-vaulted naves, and bone fragments of saints; the incense, wafers, and wine; the never-ending lamp oil; the gold-leaf kashi-kari mosaics, the calls to prayer from the minarets, and the circling mobs of the faithful; all of these are special effects, but special effects from a thousand years ago, special effects that have not advanced beyond a medieval state of the art. The night Cubby and Alice forced George and Lizzie to go see *Beauty and the Beast* (after that humiliating hansom cab ride down Broadway from Central Park to the Palace Theatre) was the night Cubby had his epiphany: If they could transform the Beast into the Prince onstage, imagine the pseudo-miracles that could be performed on altars and bemas and at mosques! Cubby's specific ideas are still sketchy. He and Ben are recruiting a team of special-effects artists—engineers and designers who have worked on Six Flags Great Adventure attractions, Cirque du Soleil, and arena shows for U2 and Kiss, the computer-animated movie *Toy Story,* and the Broadway productions of both *The Phantom of the Opera* and *The Lion King.* They will collaborate with client denominations and sects to craft religion- and site-specific special effects and stunts. (Ben knows they need to come up with a more apposite proprietary phrase for "special effects and stunts.") As Ben and Cubby envision it, the Guild will work within a wide range of budgets and sensibilities—from inexpensive and simple church retrofits with dramatic lighting, audio, fabrics, smoke, and synthetic scents, to more spectacular productions involving projected digital video images over the altar, blue-screen simulations behind the bema, motorized pew movement, holographic effects, and animatronic figures. In their first, pilot phase, the Guild is offering to create and install one of its shows (another word they need to replace with a solemn proprietary phrase) free of charge at a church or temple or mosque of each major faith in North America, South America, and Europe. Cubby is in Rome to get the Vatican's go-ahead.

"I am very excited, Ben. I feel like we have a genuine winner."

"Aren't you glad I talked you out of the cemetery business?"

"You didn't talk me out of it. You talked me *into* my other location-based entertainment concept, that's all. I'm still committed to Families Together Forever, Ben. Which I do think leverages very nicely off this operation. By the way, the fellow I met with in Fez? He says they are interested in partnering—he called me here with a lead on a mosque in Rio de Janeiro."

"Hey, terrific!" Dianne hands Ben the two stacks of Friday-afternoon reading. There's his trading stack (companies' fresh quarterly and annual reports, clippings from newsletters about metallurgy and cable TV) and his making stack (conceptual designs from his NASCAR track architect, deal memos for the rights to William Gaddis and Vladimir Nabokov books, the April P & L from BarbieWorld). She salutes and mouths "Goodbye" to Ben, who waves.

"Cubby," he says into the phone, "may I ask you a personal question?"

"Sure thing. I enjoy personal questions."

"What's your real name? On the birth certificate."

"What do you mean, Ben?"

"If we're going to be in business together, I would love to be able to call you Andy or Jack or Myron or whatever your real name is. Every time I say Cubby, I think of the Mouseketeers. No offense, but it makes it hard for me to take you as seriously as I want to."

"My real name *is* Cubby, Ben."

———

The walk from the $ office in the Woolworth Building to George and Lizzie's house is easy, particularly on a Friday in May. The dogwoods in City Hall Park, fully leafed, bob and shimmy in the evening breezes. The brokers and traders and bankers and their lawyers are long gone to East Seventy-eighth Street and Garden City and Summit, as are the cops and bureaucrats and the other sorts of downtown lawyers, back home to their boroughs and Nassau County townships. Ben's driver, Melik, creeps along near Ben with the Mercedes, not because he has been asked to, but just in case Mr. Gould decides to cut his constitutional short, or send Melik off on some spontaneous errand.

"Holy cow!" Ben shouts to Lizzie as she opens the front door on

Water Street, making her smile as she leans down to kiss him. "May I have a sexual encounter with you right this second?" Hank Saddler, chatting just inside the foyer, is startled. Lizzie's wearing the Badgley Mischka dress she bought to wear to the Emmys last fall, its scrim of tiny violet beads tight against the indigo silk tight against her body. "I have to stare at your breasts for a second," Ben says, and he does. The Louboutin mules give her an extra couple of inches on Ben, and her hair, pulled up and held in place with a silver tusk (Ted Muehling), makes her seem taller still. He keeps his arm around her waist as he steps into the house. "I mean it, Lizzie, you look amazing. Did you have work done or something?" Because she decided this afternoon to go for makeup (another hundred dollars) along with the hair, she blushes.

"How's work?" Lizzie says as she leads Ben up to the second floor, just behind Hank Saddler, leaving the downstairs to George.

"Good, good—I thought of you the other day. I bought a few June puts on Mister Softee."

She smiles. "Thank you, Benny."

"It wasn't vengeance, darling. I already sold them. It was just a quick buy on the lie—the Microsoft CFO got the shit misquoted out of him in *Barron's* and I knew it'd be a day before it got corrected." Most weeks Ben makes money this way, "buying on the lie," as he calls it. He exploits the routine sloppiness of the press. When negative news about a company is about to come out that he believes is false, Ben will short the stock before the great mass of investors panics, then get rid of the short before the truth comes out and investors are reassured. The idea is to predict who the lynch mob will decide to hang next, get to the victim first, sell members of the mob tickets to the lynching, and then scram before the mob returns to its senses and decides against the lynching.

"Ben, do you know Hank Saddler? Hank is Harold's right-hand man at Mose Media." Lizzie can never keep titles straight, so some flattering generic—right-hand man, top person, secret weapon, marketing genius, creative wizard—is frequently her way of handling introductions.

"It's Hen—" Saddler starts to say, but Ben interrupts.

"*Really?*" Ben says, the pitch of his voice rising a half octave. "Wow, you guys are on a hell of a roll! How many more of these companies is Mose going to buy?"

Standing in the back doorway, one foot on gravel, George half listens to the bebop quartet in the backyard, half listens to Bruce Helms converse in their dialect (computers) with seventeen-year-old Fanny Taft, who is dressed in several layers of black mesh. Earlier he talked to Fanny by himself for five minutes, and liked her. He watches his friend arrive and kiss Lizzie, and eye-poppingly look at her cleavage as she giggles. He watches Ben and Lizzie talk. He watches her introduce him to Hank Saddler. He watches Lizzie drift upstairs, smiling at Hank Saddler, full of herself. He watches and listens to the efflorescence of the party, as people he knows and vaguely knows begin streaming in. He should animate; he's supposed to host; but he sips his seltzer, grudgingly sober, still at work, nibbling at some of the hundred nagging and impending hangnails in *Real Time,* goddamn *Real Time,* which is supposed to go on the air in a month.

Phoebe and Gordon from *NARCS* arrive together, behind them a few of Lizzie's employees (George assumes: very young men, tattooed and stubbly), and just behind them old Daniel Flood (a Kennedy White House intern and the MBC senior vice president for pointless ethical exercises). Stuck in the ad hoc receiving line behind courtly, slo-mo Dan Flood is Roger Baird—Mr. Nancy McNabb—grinning as he slides out a virgin bill for the beggar who has posted himself by the stoop. And there is dark, giant Nancy close behind on the cobblestones, grimly instructing their driver, turning to make an entrance in her empress-wear, a long purplish silk jacket and red silk pants. Nancy and Roger instinctively head upstairs, toward the cushier, quieter hum of voices and music (Bobby Darin singing not just "Mack the Knife" but the whole Brecht-Weill oeuvre) and waiters pouring champagne. Lizzie wanted the champagne.

Guests of a certain stripe head straight back, through the kitchen, past George, and into the garden. As people pass, he only nods as necessary, pretending to engage in Bruce and Fanny's impassioned conversation about the UNIX operating system; he joined them because he thought they were discussing the virtues of eunuchs. The guests filing outside are attracted by the live music, the twilight air, the chance to have a cigarette. Almost no one buys cigarettes anymore, or officially smokes; but this is a party, and half the people in the backyard are smoking bummed Marlboros or Merits or Trues, the same half who in 1979 would have been in the bathroom having a taste of someone else's cocaine. The girl-boy ratio out back is three-to-two.

Both upstairs and down, there are younger, relatively poorer guests—their friends who teach school and write fiction, Lizzie's junior game designers and old underlings from the foundation, George's production assistants—who have the bemused and nonchalantly giddy air, somewhere between grateful and resentful, of local farmers and deacons invited into the great house for a fancy-dress ball. There are other guests—Nancy and Jolly Roger, Hank Saddler, a few of George and Lizzie's law-partner friends, George's agent, the publisher of *Perfectly* magazine—who have the self-satisfied expressions of uptowners on a mad lark down to an out-of-the-way bohemian happening.

Then there are the guests who are in their element, who live to straddle castes and realms, finding everyone and no one exotic. Like Zip, for instance, in his three-piece, creamy white linen suit, with a young date who has an archipelago of small port-wine stains dotting her left temple like the Aleutian Islands, and on her right temple a permanent tattoo simulation (but more abstract and geometrical) of the birthmark. And in a very different way, like Timothy Featherstone. He's heading straight for George, booming.

"Mr. *Real* Time, the buzz monster partying hearty! T minus four weeks, four days, and counting! How is my homey?"

As Bruce and Fanny are blasted by the gale of Featherstone's arrival out the door and into the garden, he makes a little Bob Hope growl toward Fanny's back, then pounces hungrily onto the major MBC event of the week.

"So what'd you think of the *Journal* story?" he asks George.

"Today, about the MotorMind and TK Corporation acquisitions? It was pretty straightforward. The internet skepticism paragraph was pure boilerplate. And calling us a rival to WebTV is good, right?"

"No! I mean the hatchet job on Stengel! Savage!" He is smiling.

A month ago, Glenn Murkowski, George's editor acquaintance at the *Journal,* called about a big story the paper was planning on all the second-tier TV news and quasi-news operations—MSNBC, Fox, MBC, E!², the Chopper Channel, and so on. George told him that MSNBC and Fox were old stories, and E!² and the Chopper Channel were too niche. Why not just focus on MBC News? Murkowski happened to assign the story to George's old *Newsweek* colleague Greg Dunn, who naturally called George for information on MBC News. Greg's initial take on Stengel was predictable and positive—serious broadcast journalist heroically adhering to old-fashioned standards in a screwy new world. Greg apparently knew nothing of George's fight with Stengel over *Real Time.* And George trusted Greg enough to talk to him off the record about MBC News. In the *Journal* article he quoted George twice, one of those times as "a knowledgeable MBC colleague" saying that Barry Stengel "is, in all fairness, too stupid to realize that he's a hypocrite."

"It *was* a dumb thing News did," George says, "but the *Journal* piece actually made me feel sorry for Barry." Which was true, even though it had pleased him as well. The article was much tougher than George expected. And page one! The most damaging item was the "airbrushed news" revelation. On last month's hour-long premiere of *Finale,* the MBC News obitutainment show, they aired a live remote of mourners arriving at the service in Hollywood for a young movie star who died of a heroin overdose. The live shot of the funeral was dominated by a Fox TV billboard next to the mortuary advertising the home-video compilation special *When Celebrities Go Berserk II!* The executive producer of *Finale* used a digital technique to "erase" the Fox billboard from the live broadcast. In Greg's *Journal* story, Stengel claimed he was unaware of the digital airbrushing, and that such techniques are "contrary to MBC News policy." However, "an MBC source familiar with news practices" (George) was quoted as saying, "Tell me why Stengel's guy even had the software available. Either Barry is running a very loose ship, or he's not telling the truth now."

"Hank's still freaking about it big time," Featherstone says. "Do you think Barry's cred is totally toast? I mean, in the news community?"

George shrugs. Featherstone moves closer to him and lowers his voice to a confidential murmur.

"So I understand the lady of the abode is still giving Harold thumbs up–thumbs down on all these other cockamamie internet outfits the strategic planning boys are wet for."

George shrugs again. He doesn't know. Every time they've started talking about the advice she's giving Mose, the conversation has turned into a fight and stopped.

"His lips are sealed! Keep the shit on the low! Strong encryption! Straight up, home," he says, grabbing a cilantro ratatouille tartlet from one waiter's tray and at the same time carefully lifting his martini from another. "But we're counting on you to do everything you can to help the team, George M. Cohan."

George cannot simply shrug a third time. So he says, "Needless to say."

"Thanks. And the show is grooving? I liked the feminist-anchor-chick-breakthrough hokey-pokey in the Sunday *Times*. Terrific counterbuzz to the snarkocity of all those tight-ass fantasy-reality snipes. Oh, and I loved the *People* thing on Francesca's monkeyshines with Brad Pitt. Did Saddler make that up and plant it?"

"No, they've dated."

"What the fox-in-the-henhouse does 'post-gay' *mean*?"

George shakes his head and shrugs once again.

"And the show? No problems production-wise?"

"Nothing major." If you don't count Jess Burnham and Francesca Mahoney each complaining to George once a week that her coanchor can't act her way out of a paper bag, and that both have a point.

"Stupendo. Off to check out some of these babes in toyland," he says, raising his eyebrows and nodding slightly toward the backyard, then following his own nod.

George turns and watches Sarah and Max, who are outside with Fanny Taft and Bruce. Like most fourteen-year-old girls, Sarah radiates excitement and panic about being fourteen, that mixture of embarrassment and sly pride about her astounding bosom. Just before the party started, he overheard Max say to Lizzie upstairs, "I guess you're more famous than Dad now." Are even the children sliding out of his gravitational field? He watches Featherstone, bobbing and shaking his head along with a klezmer solo riff, approach them. He watches him smile and shake hands with Bruce and Fanny and Boogie Boffin, and kiss Sarah on the cheek. Thirty seconds later he sees Featherstone touching Boogie's horn implants covetously. George wonders if he should ask Featherstone for a 7-percent-higher license fee for *Real Time* just before the first shows air, or right afterward?

Grownups are allowed to give either cocktail parties for two hundred people that end by nine o'clock, or six-table sit-down dinner parties.

But they aren't allowed to do what Lizzie would prefer, which is a cocktail party for two hundred that lasts well past midnight, with enough passed canapés to qualify as dinner. What she would prefer, as George said back when they had conversations, is a college beer blast with very high production values and no vomiting. So the dinner is served buffet style (the very phrase makes Lizzie feel old), and forty-year-olds in suits are obliged to sit balancing plates of calamari and baby lettuces between their knees.

Arranging the places at tables has a certain godlike thrill, like brokering blind dates wholesale, but Lizzie gets a deeper satisfaction from seeing people she knows freely converge and settle into semirandom dinner-partner subsets on their own. What on earth is Hank Saddler saying to Fanny and Daisy and two of the Germans? Are Pollyanna and Ben bored explaining themselves to that awful earnest *Newsweek* woman Sally, who came with Greg Dunn? Or are the two of them enjoying her does-not-compute look of contempt and bewilderment as she listens to an Ivy League woman of color defending big tobacco (Pollyanna: "The price of all our personal freedoms is a certain number of extra deaths") and a liberal Democrat explaining his plan to retrofit neighborhoods in London and Paris and Venice as seamless *in situ* urban theme parks? (Ben: "We're doing the opposite of 'destroying' the Left Bank, we're restoring a trashy piece of it, making it more authentic"). She spots George downstairs when she tells the caterers to start serving dinner, intensely chatting away with Warren Holcombe, George looking as worried and pale as Warren. Timothy Featherstone and Zip Ingram are born to be pals, sitting cross-legged and deep in their own fop-to-fop, grifter-to-grifter symposium about certain tiny bottlings of "the really *austere* Mendocino cabs."

And Lizzie is on the floor with Bruce, sharing a corner of the low Corbu table. If she'd ordered him next to her with a place card, it would be like an exit interview with goat cheese and focaccia, her enforced fond farewell, but here they are chatting, as if spontaneously.

"So your friends in Redmond made another pass at Buster this week. They offered to invest in Terraplane."

"And?" Lizzie says, finishing her fourth glass of champagne.

Bruce looks at her, frowning elaborately, saying nothing. Which means: *No, we are not selling out to Microsoft before we've even started—and I'm shocked, in a half-serious, brotherly way, that you'd think otherwise.*

"The day after he told them to fuck off, his office was ransacked, and a bunch of his files and tapes were stolen."

"He doesn't think Microsoft burgled his office?"

Bruce smiles. "He would like to think so. But unfortunately there were Animal Salvation League pamphlets strewn all over the place, and even Buster's not quite paranoid enough to really believe that burglars from Microsoft would leave them as disinformation."

She is going to miss Bruce. "You met our intern from Minnesota?"

"She's a really smart kid. Scarily."

"Scary because she's a juvenile delinquent?" She glances up at the waiter bending over her with Dom Perignon. "Yes, please." People are drinking a lot, it seems to Lizzie. That's because the party is on a Friday. That's why the party is on a Friday.

"No, scarily smart. I mean, she's not just some wanky 'warez dood' teenybopper. She knows her stuff, that kid. You should hear about how she hacked a few of the places that the feds *don't* know about. She made me promise I wouldn't tell you, but ask her sometime about what she and her pals dug out of the Kennedy School server up at Harvard." He smiles, shaking his head. "By the way, you know how George always used to make such a big deal over the fact that you and I have no memory of President Kennedy's death?"

Lizzie, unsmiling, blinks for a long moment and nods.

"Well," Bruce says, "Fanny claims she doesn't remember when when *Jackie* Kennedy died."

"Room for one more?" Nancy McNabb says.

Lizzie scoots over, and Nancy pulls up an ottoman. Lizzie has watched Nancy at dinners, staring in apparent fascination at people (influential business people, so nearly always men) making the most banal statements in the most tedious possible ways. And at a black-tie diabetes fund-raising dinner, she watched Nancy stand up and leave the table just as the doctor sitting between them started to explain to Nancy why his possible breakthrough cure did not have, as she had put it, "any significant private-sector upside." She was the one, however, who introduced Lizzie to George at Ben's loft party twelve years ago, and she was the one who found them Margaret, the godsend baby-sitter Lizzie employed for nine years, and it was at her (and Roger's) dinner party in 1997 that George had met Emily and started talking about *NARCS*. Those favors excuse everything else about Nancy.

"Nancy McNabb, Bruce Helms. Bruce is the brains behind Fine Technologies."

Nancy shows tentative interest.

"Was, I mean," Lizzie says. "He's starting his own company."

Nancy turns instantly to Bruce.

"Yes?" she says. "*Are* you? Software? Or the net? Who's VC-ing you? Tell me, tell me, tell me."

"We're self-financing," Bruce tells her, "and it's really just basic research for now. For quite a while, probably."

"Ah," Nancy says, finished with Bruce, turning back to Lizzie. "When are *we* going to do our transaction? The market is feeling very, very ripe to me again. Exceptionally ripe. Late-1998 ripe. By the way, that is gorgeous, Elizabeth. Badgley Mischka?"

Lizzie nods. Nancy knows everything and, for all practical purposes, everyone. She runs the media and technology practice for the investment bank Cordman, Horton, which as nearly as Lizzie can tell calls itself a "merchant bank" purely as an affectation. Nancy wants Cordman, Horton to take Fine Technologies public. A year ago, just before the internet IPO market had its ugly spell, Cordman, Horton took her brother Penn's TK Corporation public for $230 million ("a valuation equal to approximately infinity times earnings," Lizzie likes saying), and they've just finished negotiating the sale of TK Corp. to Mose Media Holdings for $327 million. ("I see Penn McNabb's P–E is up to one-point-four infinity," she thought of saying to George this week, and said to Bruce instead.)

"At least let me take you to lunch, all right? It'll do you good to get up north of Fourteenth Street."

Lizzie knows that the riposte *But, Nancy, my offices are on Eighteenth Street* isn't worth making. "Sure," she says. "Although we're insanely busy right now."

"Your utensils and beverage, Nan," says Roger Baird—Jolly Roger. He's not trying to be funny. Nancy takes the napkin-and-silverware roll from Roger without looking up, and he sets the glass down by her plate.

"It's just club soda," he says, meaning that the bartender had no name-brand mineral waters. "Tap water *avec* gaz." Now he's trying to be funny.

"I saw the thing in the *Observer* about the TriBeCa show, Roger," Lizzie says. "Congratulations." Roger looks like a commercial banker, or an old-fashioned gentleman publisher, but his business (which involves reselling parcels of telephone bandwidth) is not his passion—his passion is "outsider art," of which he is a major collector. He and Nancy specialize in sculpture and collages created by noninstitutionalized early- and mid-twentieth-century paranoid schizophrenics. Their privately printed catalogue *raisonée,* which Roger wrote himself, consists mainly of quotations from Antonin Artaud. He is sweetly ridiculous, like so many men married to tough, professional women in New York, the Charlie Browns to their Lucys, the Duncans to their Lady Macbeths.

"We just want the work seen," Roger says, and then reminds his wife, "Cameron wanted you to call before bedtime, Nan. Since you'll be on your way to London when she wakes up." Cameron is their younger child. Lizzie can never remember if it's a boy or a girl. Nancy takes the phone from Roger and punches the green button, since he has predialed their home number. That is, he has dialed the number for their live-in baby-sitter, Beth, famous Beth, who not only is white, but also graduated from Barnard and whom everyone in Nancy's circle calls, with envy and awe, "Nancy's Jewish nanny." As she tucks in her daughter by remote control, Nancy holds the itty-bitty Motorola a couple of inches away from her ear, not because she worries about brain cancer (as Bruce imagines) but (as Lizzie and Roger know) to keep her hair perfect. Nancy once told Lizzie that she buys a new phone every four months "just on principle." "What principle?" Lizzie asked. "Bestness," Nancy said in all seriousness.

Downstairs, George says to Ben, "This is all a joke, isn't it? You just got off so much on horrifying Sally Chatham about the Euro Quarter projects that now you're just riffing, right? By making fun of my sister's pathetic husband." The two of them are sitting scrunched together on the old backyard stump. Between his legs, George has a lit votive candle—one of the gross of them Lizzie bought for the party. He's staring at it and dipping his pinky finger into the molten wax. Three of the four musicians are taking a break, but the pianist is playing a minor-key arrangement of "How High the Moon."

"No, I think we might actually make something happen."

George looks up from the candle. "You are going to finance his idiotic cemetery theme parks? With the video gravestones? Ben."

"They'd be regulatory and operational nightmares, but the idea isn't stupid. But no, your brother-in-law and I have been working on something else. An amazing idea."

"It's not the organic sequins and recycled yarn thing? Eco-Krafts?"

"No. This is big. This is a whole new industry. Ten-figure revenues in ten years."

"So?"

"Totally off the record, George?"

"Fuck you."

Ben tells him about the Guild, and the plans to install special-effects packages in five thousand churches and temples and mosques by 2005 at a median price of $300,000, literal smoke and mirrors and subwoofers and lasers, all computer controlled, to make the glory of Jesus (or Jehovah or Allah or Ron Hubbard or . . . whomever) more palpable to the believers.

"And on his own," Ben is saying, "Cubby's already trademarked 'Unbelievably Believable!' 'Too Good to Be Untrue,' 'Making Every Church a Cathedral,' and 'Push-Button Miracles for the New Millennium.' The guy is some kind of weird genius."

Now George is pushing his little finger to within millimeters of the flame itself. Ben's explanation, excited as ever, is making George gloomy and apprehensive. (Gloomier and more apprehensive.) Not because it debases and degrades faith and ritual. Who cares? Not because he's envious of Cubby Koplowitz getting rich or Ben getting richer. Who cares? George isn't sure why it's depressing him. It's depressing him because it feeds this tumor of dread, his sense that beyond the cone of candlelight, inside, upstairs, on Fifty-nine, out in the Valley, everywhere just beyond view, outside his control, alliances and loyalties are shifting by means of whispers and nods, all shifting in a direction unfavorable to George Mactier.

He is slowly shaking his head.

"But, you know," Ben says, "maybe recordings of humpback whales and Martian winds, all synched up with lighting effects. Tasteful. More abstract."

"Unitarians really aren't into spectacle, I don't think," George says. "They're like Baptists and Moslems. Atheistic Baptists and Moslems."

"And 'theotainment' and 'sacredtainment,' " Ben asks him, "those both suck, don't they? I mean, let the journalists invent the stupid catchphrases on their own. Right?"

"I guess." George is staring blankly, past animated clusters of party guests, through the glass doors, into the kitchen filled with waiters and drinkers. He sees the most officious of the caterers suddenly leave her mates, head down the hall toward the front door and out of sight, then after a few seconds he sees Harold Mose, in a dinner jacket, accompanied by Gloria, stepping smartly into his house before they make the zigzag toward the stairs and disappear again. Harold has come. As George stands, he thinks of the LuLu question (*Is that a good thing, Daddy, or a bad thing?*) and rubs his waxy fingers on the tree stump before heading inside. As he makes the landing and sees the fringes of the crowd, he notices the pseudo-casual fuss being made over Mose, like iron filings moving in slow motion toward a magnet. He arrives in his living room just in time to see Harold retract from kissing Lizzie and hold both her hands at a distance, scrutinizing her for a moment like a superb new Milanese highboy.

Kissing Gloria Mose, George grazes his eye on the corner of her dark glasses as he swings over and heads in for the second cheek.

"We've just come from supper at Zero. You're so right. *Brilliant* place."

Every time he encounters Gloria, George feels clueless. "We haven't been to Zero," he says, willing himself to smile.

"Ah. It's Harold's new favorite, and he says Elizabeth introduced him to it. So I assumed."

Struggling to maintain the smile, a smile that feels phonier than any he has ever faked, literally like a Halloween mask, George says, "I understand that your daughter took a job at Miramax." What is her name? Has he been too addled even to remember the name of the girl he wanted (theoretically) to fuck and wouldn't consider hiring? "That's great. She actually—Caroline seemed more interested in making movies than American television, anyway." *"American television"—George, you miserable panderer.*

"She's working for their publishing bit, actually."

A waiter and Nancy McNabb arrive simultaneously, both eager to please a Mose, any Mose, and interrupting George and Gloria's con-

versation about a restaurant he's never been to and her daughter he
didn't hire. He uses the moment to move two furtive steps to his left,
but by the time he's there, Lizzie, jaunty Lizzie, is moving Harold away
into the crowd, off to meet someone new. George is left literally in the
lurch. And then he stands in his lurch, giving a quick nod and a smiled
"Hello" toward the halogen torchère in the back corner of the room,
in case anyone is watching.

Happy-looking nightmares are even scarier, George finds himself thinking, startling himself; he regrets having drunk so much, and then remembers that he's had nothing but plain soda all night. It's Lizzie
who's been drinking like a flapper. *Drinking like a flapper* is a phrase that
hasn't occurred to him for decades; it's something his mother learned
from her mother, he recalls dimly, and used to say about his Aunt Nora
(that is, "Perry's divorced sister Nora") and about his father's blond
strumpet secretary.

Outside, it's gotten chilly, and some of the votives have burned out.
The quartet is playing again (a Raymond Scott medley, its kooky *wah-
wah* 1939 gaiety not so much leavening George's mood as tickling it,
mocking it), and George is smoking somebody's cigarette, his first in
years, down here in the courtyard with all the odd people out, the people with no interest in discussing the new think tank Steven Rattner's
funding and whether he'll hire Clinton, or the outrageous thing
Howard Stringer said about PBS and the BBC, or the thirty-one-page
pundits' roundtable critique of pundit-on-pundit punditry that appeared in the final issue of *Brill's Content.*

The discussion group huddled on the gravel in the corner by the
pink Victorian playhouse, quiet but for the occasional gasp of antic
laughter, consists of the cool-cat geeks, the computer youth—Fanny,
her new German programmer pals, and Bruce, with Max and Sarah
standing nearby as unaccredited observers. Next to them, splayed in
Smith & Hawken teak chairs, are Ben Gould and Hank Saddler drinking port. Each is trying to worm information out of the other—Ben
about Mose Media Holdings' "internet acquisition spree" (as the business reporters are calling it), Saddler about two Vancouver Stock Exchange companies he's interested in short-selling. During their
pseudo-gentlemanly Sandeman-sipping pauses, both men eavesdrop
on the conversation going on next to them.

"It's not a virus," Fanny is saying to Bruce and the Germans, "it's a really nasty *applet*. With a nasty applet I could crash any machine with twenty lines of code."

"A friend at home," says Willibald, the cutest and most stylishly sallow of the sallow German programmers, "says he was informed that the explosion of that big American telecom rocket at Baikonur in Russia? Was a hack that went bad."

"Globalstar," says the other German, Humfried, who's wearing a TELETUBBIES T-shirt. "The Globalstar Corporation," he elaborates, pleased to repeat the company's perfectly sinister name.

"Or maybe a hack that went right," Bruce says, getting into the late-night James Bond spirit. "Globalstar's value went down, I don't know, about half a billion dollars five minutes after those satellites blew up."

"So somebody who, like, hated the company did it?" Fanny asks.

"Well, somebody who wanted the stock of the company to go down, maybe," Bruce says.

Before any of them can ask what he means, Max speaks. "Fanny," he says, "what did you *do,* exactly? Why did they arrest you?"

"Max!" his big sister says.

"That's cool," Fanny says. She enjoys explaining her life in crime. Since her arrival in New York a week ago she has bewitched Willi and Humfried with her hacker creds. As far as they are concerned, working alongside a seventeen-year-old American political prisoner is a job perk. "Two girlfriends and I hacked a federal computer and had it send money to some women's shelters that they'd, like, cut off from funding or whatever? I think they were going to let us go, but the day before they busted us for that, we jacked into the local newspaper system and posted a thing about our principal, saying that he, like, had sex with the star of *Felicity* but then killed himself—just as a joke? But then our thing ran in the paper the next day, and that *really* pissed everyone off. So then they decided to prosecute."

Willibald finishes his Sam Adams and says, "We should purport that Bill Gates is killed, in the same way. Hack the newspaper."

There are chuckles and nods.

"Virtual assassination," says Bruce, feeling like a kid again. "You'd be heroes." He pauses. "Lizzie would certainly enjoy it."

"Finish their anniversary celebrations with a . . . how do you call it," says Humfried to Willibald, "a *wirklicher ein realer Knall?*"

"A real bang," Willi tells him.

They talk about spoofing and pinging and sniffing and hacking for a while longer, about smurfs and smurf amplifiers, driving each other to more abstruse mischief-making extremes, Bruce mentioning November 29 (the day in 1975 when Gates first called his company "Micro-soft"), Willibald describing a new stealth-sniffer program a friend in Berlin told him about, Humfried recalling "*Der verrückte Belgier* who tossed the pie at Gates." After Bruce wanders inside, Fanny and Humfried and Willibald get more raucous and comical, but more serious too, getting high off their own hypothetical power, confirming dates, declaring commitments, making oaths. Fanny mentions a hacker friend who once forced a core dump in a computer system of the "Rooters" news service.

"It's R-e-u-t-e-r-s, but it's pronounced *Roy*-ters," Max says. "And this year November twenty-ninth is a Wednesday."

"He can do that, with days and dates," Sarah explains, slightly embarrassed.

Ben and Saddler have said nothing to each other for ten minutes. They're both staring upward, pretending to be marveling at the unreasonably huge moon, just past full, rising over the house and the nine-story-tall stone anchorage of the Brooklyn Bridge.

"It's like some wonderful black-and-white picture of old New York, isn't it?" Saddler says.

"Sure is," Ben replies, looking at the sky. He shouts over to his friend. "You see the moon, George?"

Standing across the grass and the gravel patch, near the house, George glances up, and then inside his house, where he sees that guests are beginning to leave. Has he ever hated a party more in his life? For some reason, though, its imminent end unsettles him. Everything is unsettling him, thanks to this beast of a television show he's dreaming up, and Lizzie. He should go in and say goodbye to people, since he never said hello to most of them. But instead he starts flirting a little harder with Zip's date, finding that her right-temple tattoo helps him avoid staring at her left-temple birthmark, and wondering if that is the idea. He used to be able to gin up strong momentary interest in almost anyone's profession, but tonight, after two minutes, he has run out of questions about Canada and musical comedy (she is executive director of something called the Canadian Experimental Musical Comedy

Archives). When she mentions that she grew up in Thailand, Pakistan, and Honduras, though, and her father's twenty-six years of service in the CIA, his interest spikes.

"What was Bangkok like in 1975?"

"I don't know. I was three. It smelled. We moved after my brother got addicted to opium."

"When were you in Honduras?"

"In junior high. I'll tell you everything I know about national security, but first you have to give me a cigarette."

"This isn't mine. And all they have over there," George says, nodding toward the computer kids, "are menthols and cloves."

"Blehhh. Zip is out too. I may have to leave."

"My kingdom for a Marlboro. Hold on," he says, ducks inside and turns left, trotting up the back stairs. (He loves excuses to use the back stairs, both because it's the one part of the house that still smells like cocoa, and because it's a secret passage.) Down the hall and into the cool, darkened bedroom, into the back closet, he reaches up and feels for Lizzie's hidden stash, grabs the box, and trots back downstairs and out. A police helicopter is passing low and loud overhead, toward the river, its *thud-thud-thud* crescendo like airborne electronic timpani.

"No luck?" the woman asks.

"Voilà," he says.

She slides out a Marlboro, and with it a tiny silver oval box of matches tucked in the box. She lights up, and hands the cigarettes and matches back to George. As she begins describing the insinuating lizardy men, evidently contra commanders, who would visit her parents' house in Tegucigalpa with gifts of awful cinnamon-flavored chocolates for her, George tunes out. He's looking at the exquisite little matchbox, with its embossed silver-on-silver lettering: ZERO, it says.

He lies on his side, facing away. She is in the bathroom. They've had one exchange in the forty-five minutes since the last guests left. The conversation consisted of "Did you lock the back door?" (Lizzie) and "Yeah" (George).

"Well," she says abruptly from the bathroom, "*I* had a *wonderful* time. I think people did."

George says nothing.

"Are you asleep?"

"No."

"Isn't Fanny Taft a great kid?"

"She is. She is."

"I was surprised to see you spending so much time with Warren. Was he his usual upbeat self?"

"I like the guy. He said he thinks Max could be a candidate for antidepressants."

"What?"

"He says he fits a pediatric predepressive profile."

"Bullshit."

"Warren says they make a minty-flavored liquid Prozac for kids."

She pops her head out of the bathroom. "Max is not a fucking depressive, and Warren is an asshole." She pops it back in.

"Are you drunk?" he says. Soberly.

"A little. Too bad you aren't. Gloria Mose said a very Gloria thing to me tonight. They went to a Lincoln Center tribute to Sophia Loren tonight, where somebody apparently quoted Victorio De Sica. We were talking about Giuliani and Clinton and—"

"Vittorio."

"Sorry, Monsieur Cinéma. Anyhow, she said, 'Elizabeth, as De Sica said, "If you remove adultery from the lives of the bourgeoisie, there's no drama left!" ' Isn't that pure Gloria? And then Bruce said that only ten percent of the animals who supposedly mate for life are actually faithful. Among primates, he said, only marmosets and tamarins don't fuck around. Gloria loved that. Did you know she used to be a stewardess for Laker Airways? Zip told me she picked up the first husband literally on the sidewalk at Gatwick."

George thinks of mentioning the matches from Zero. Zero, the restaurant where Lizzie evidently dined with Harold Mose. He wouldn't mind the fight per se. But if he has caught her at something, he doesn't want to give her the satisfaction of knowing he's upset. And if it's nothing, just some lunch sometime she didn't happen to mention, then he'll seem paranoid, and he certainly doesn't want to give her the satisfaction of thinking he's nuts.

"Did I ever tell you about my sidewalk sex censuses?" he asks, still lying down, facing away, both arms beneath his pillow.

She turns out the bathroom light and sits on the bed.

"What?" she says with a small giggle.

"Every so often when I'm walking down the street, I look at every woman on the sidewalk coming toward me, and decide if I'd like to fuck them or not. Yes or no; boom, boom, boom; half a second to decide each one. (It's difficult in midtown, it's so crowded.) I usually do a hundred, and keep a running tally, sixteen out of a hundred, or whatever it comes out to."

"Huh," she says.

"I guess you think that's some sick, sexist thing."

"No! I think it's funny. Pollyanna and I used to do almost that same thing with all the men at a party, or in a bar, or wherever, and then we'd announce our totals to each other. Polly called it How Many Guys. When I'm traveling by myself, sometimes, or waiting for you at a restaurant, I still do it, just in my head. Like your thing, only not with percentages." She snaps off the black snakelike halogen lamp on her side of the bed, and turns over, believing they've had their first pleasant conversation in weeks. "Night."

───────

Seven hours later, the phone is ringing. George is gone already. He's working weekends now on *Real Time,* every Saturday and some Sundays. Lizzie experiences what is always for her the hangover nadir— that first conscious moment, when she feels so . . . *disappointed,* not in herself but in the mingy, second-rate day that now lies ahead. "Hello? Hello." She's rehearsing, making sure she doesn't surprise herself and the caller with a croaking, phlegmy *hello,* working toward a believable simulation of wakefulness. She picks up the phone. "Hello?"

"Hello! We had such an *interesting* time. You know so *many* interesting people! I wish I'd had a chance to talk to George. Was he feeling all right?"

"Hi, Nancy. It was good seeing you and Roger too." Why the fuck is she phoning at six minutes after nine on Saturday morning? Unless Roger has dropped dead since ten-thirty last night (and even Nancy wouldn't sound so cheerfully widowed so quickly), this call is unnecessary, bordering on inexcusable.

"Didn't want to bother you at home, but I insist for your sake on getting our lunch calendared immediately. And I'm already on my way to London, so."

And if you somehow managed to get hold of a working telephone in England, by the time you called me, it might be as late as four, even five in the afternoon my time. So . . .

"I don't have my book in front of me," Lizzie says.

"Then why don't we say you'll come up to Cordman, Horton around noon the Tuesday after Memorial Day, we'll figure out how rich we want to make you, then grab a bite at Square One? I've already cleared the decks for you. The middle of my day is all *yours.* Let my kids know if that *isn't* doable."

By "kids," Lizzie knows Nancy means her two assistants, rather than Cameron and Sydney, her actual children, but she's never heard anyone outside show business use *kids* in that sense. Square One is the imitation-1945 McNally bistro (Brian McNally, Keith McNally . . . one or both of their ex-wives, she can't remember which) that just opened in the old Times Square Howard Johnson.

"All right? Otherwise, I'll see you the thirtieth. Shall we send a car down?"

"No," Lizzie says, "that's okay. But if you could arrange a nonstop for me on the A train, that would be terrific."

After a beat, Nancy says, "*That's* why you know so many interesting, irreverent people, Lizzie—because *you* are. Here I am—No, driver, *British* Air! You'll have to loop all the way around now. 'Loop'! You don't understand the word *loop?*—I'm sorry, Lizzie. And you're lobbying to let in more immigrants?" This is supposed to be funny. "See you Tuesday, dear."

She'll blame Nancy. It's Nancy who's forcing her to have a cigarette at nine in the morning, she thinks as she gets up and heads toward the closet. She feels. She gropes. She pulls in a chair and stand and squints and hunts some more. Somebody has taken her cigarettes. If it wasn't George, it was a kid; and if it was a kid who took them to smoke (and not to throw in the garbage, which Max and LuLu always threaten to do), she isn't quite sure what posture of disapproval she'll strike.

2 9

Arrogant little fucker, he thinks, hanging up the phone on the high-pitched altar boy of a *Time* reporter and his dumb Feature Writing 101 questions. There always have been reporters who go for that passive-aggressive interview style, contempt disguised as earnestness, but it seems to George that in younger journalists it's more virulent and un-conscious, and certainly more irritating. He glances out the window, not to contemplate Olmstead and Vaux's blooming glory, nor to bring some fleeting inspiration about the show into sharper focus, nor just to catch his breath. He is trying to remember what he is supposed to do next. These cartoon moments of slow, deliberate, banal recollection—*I, um . . . huh?*—make George feel like Ronald Reagan.

What he can't remember is that he's supposed to go watch the recut Mexican war footage, with more of the jerky firefight shots of Francesca taking cover in her Kevlar tank top.

He thinks, when he thinks about it, that he's enduring these ninety-hour weeks and all the time away from the family because he's revel-ing in the very hell of the job. He thinks his mood has brightened because he's back in journalism (half back), because he's an adrenaline addict, and because of all the thumb sucking and chin stroking he's provoking among the thumb-sucking, chin-stroking class. He thinks he's just professionally excited and panicked about *Real Time,* which (much more than with *NARCS*) he feels as if he's squirting from his brain directly onto television, making it from scratch, *inventing.* It's not just another drama set in a newsroom, or a comedy set in a news-room, or a comedy-drama hybrid set in a newsroom, like the twenty-two shows—literally, *twenty-two* of them, on the air right now—set in proscenium newsrooms and proscenium media lofts. Nor is it just an-other newsmagazine show, like the nineteen metastasizing through the networks' and cable's news schedules (the meiotic and mitotic doublings and redoublings of *Dateline NBC, 60 Minutes, 48 Hours, 20/20, CNN Newsstand*). *Real Time* is new. *Real Time* is *new.* Which is why so many thumb suckers and chin strokers are concerned and out-raged and sickened (*"Sickened,"* a *Washington Post* columnist said on CNN over the weekend) by the mere prospect. Yesterday, reading the paper, he thought: It's the same scaredy-cat, constipated caste of offi-cial twits and drudges who couldn't bear listening to *Le Sacre du Prin-temps* when it was first performed eighty-seven years ago. There is only one person to whom he could dare mention this analogy with the correct mixture of seriousness and self-ridicule (*I'm Stravinsky, and Timothy Featherstone is Diaghilev*), so he will mention it to no one. "May 29, 1913" was the first entry in "Today in History" in yester-day's paper: "*The Rite of Spring* melee in Paris—as the debut perfor-mance of Igor Stravinsky's ballet finished, and the Chosen Victim convulsed in the 'Sacrificial Dance,' bewildered and horrified audi-ence members panicked." Maybe *Real Time* is his *destiny,* God forgive him. *Destiny* is a word she would use. Not only was yesterday the twenty-ninth of May (she and the kids were up at the house on Lake Marten all weekend with Pollyanna), his producer pointed out that next Tuesday, the night of the first shakedown episode, happens to fall on June 6. Their D-day is actually D-Day. She would enjoy that. That would be a bolt of synchronicity for Lizzie, some kind of flaming sign in the sky. But they've hardly seen each other in the last month.

The three shows he's producing next week won't go to air. But the idea is to come as close to broadcast ready as possible, with real tape packages, actual second-week-of-June-2000 breaking news. "More than fake, less than real," George said to the staff. He didn't mean it as a joke, just shorthand, but it instantly became a kind of nervous, joshing mantra among the staff. The two half hours, the Tuesday and the Thursday, are mostly in the can, and for the news hour they will go live to tape next Friday, start the cameras at five-thirty and roll the credits at six twenty-nine. Around the office they're calling it "shakedown"—shakedown is a week away, the cast ("the *talent*," George continually corrects) feels good about shakedown, the shakedown overrun has to stay in the low six figures. Saddler officially named it BetaWeek. (He even registered the trademark, so that every reference in all network memos is to *Real Time*® BetaWeek®.) Featherstone calls it their "damp run," as opposed to dry run, which is witty for Featherstone.

"George," Daisy says, "it's the guy from *Time* magazine again. On three-two."

"Fuck him. Call back. I have to go down to editing."

"He says he only has one more quick question."

George picks up. "Hello."

"Mr. Mactier? Hi. Barry Stengel told us that you have—let me find his quote—'an agenda as committed as it's ever been to the destruction of hard-news broadcasting.' Do you have a response to that?"

"And I've stopped beating my wife, too."

"You what? This is Boris Faber, Mr. Mactier, calling from *Time*."

"Look, our Friday program is going to be hard news by any definition. We're not going to run naked interviews with Jim Carrey to promote a movie, like Barry Stengel did on *MBC Week*. We're not going to have service pieces about . . . celebrity *yoga* or, you know . . . the medical benefits of *rock climbing*."

"Mr. Stengel broadcast stories about rock climbing and yoga when he was running the news division?"

Barry Stengel "resigned" last week.

"I don't know. All the shows put on stories like that. Those are hypothetical examples. Here's my quote: our Friday *Real Time* news segments will be the hardest news in prime time. Bar none. Okay?"

"And one more question? How do you feel about ABC moving *Right/Left* to go up directly against you on Fridays at nine?"

How do I feel? I feel personally assaulted on several fronts. I'd like them to fail. Right/Left is the new ABC News show now on Saturday night, hosted by George Stephanopoulos and one of the skinny, blond con-

servative women. It consists of half an hour each week of news-magazine stories produced with an unabashed right-wing bias, interlarded with half an hour of stories produced with an unabashed left-wing bias. At the beginning of the show, the cohosts flip a silver dollar, on air, to see whose team of investigative ideologues gets to go first.

"We welcome it. *That* is soft news. *That* is agenda mongering. So now viewers will have a stark choice. Between the real news on *Real Time*—interspersed with a little entertainment that's honest enough to call itself entertainment—and stories on ABC about . . . video games or something."

"Thanks for your assistance, Mr. Mactier."

Such an earnest little dick, George thinks. *At least this time he didn't go for the existentialist questions.*

Daisy is back. "George?"

"What *is* it?" he snaps as he scrolls through the dozen e-mails that have arrived since that call began, answering one from his codirector ("No music at all on Friday shows"). He's a fast one-handed typist, and the speedy leanness of e-mail—no parsing, loose punctuation, type and shoot—has come just in time for George, but the phone is still easier. He's never said that to a colleague, because then he'd seem doubly pathetic, both gimpy and old-fashioned. He intends to get a speech-recognition setup so that he can dictate his e-mails, but not until it's a little more commonplace so it won't look like some special Americans With Disabilities Act accommodation for him, software as prosthesis. He looks up and sees Daisy in the doorway, smiling and frowning, as simmeringly ironic as ever. "Sorry, Daisy. Yes?" Well, *yes,* he thinks; he'd definitely have sex with Daisy Moore, hypothetically, in the sidewalk census sense. Maybe the sidewalk censuses have been preparatory exercises, a form of contingency planning, and he just hasn't realized it.

Between the one-handed speed typing and the one-second sex fantasy, he remembers: Francesca, the recut and revoiced Mexico package. He's so late.

"Mr. Derek Dreen is calling from England. Mr. Dreen's assistant says that Mr. Dreen would like 'a personal word' with you. Do you want to take it?"

He's never met or spoken to Derek Dreen. He knows who he is, of course. Dreen created *Down With It,* Fox's urban crossover hit with an almost all black cast and a 72 percent white audience (and 100 percent white creator), and he's developing a second show called *Dope Sick* that sounds like a cooler, younger *NARCS,* and another, *The Illionaire,* which is a younger, blacker remake of the old show *The Millionaire. Down With It,* or *Down,* as it's usually called, is filled with gunplay and nakedness but of a highly stylized, almost arty kind, with plots, Dreen says in interviews, "largely adapted from Shakespeare." The show broke three number-one hits in its first season, a fact George used to convince Featherstone to let him use bits of rap on *NARCS.* George has theorized that Derek Dreen's name, which sounds black, helps him get away with being the white producer of such a show. Dreen is now directing a feature film about two chimps taking over a space shuttle mission after all but one of the human astronauts are accidentally ejected into space. The script was written as a comedy for Eddie Murphy and Charlton Heston, but Dreen is filming it as an inspiring millennial drama starring Daniel Day-Lewis. It has been described in the trades as "*2001* meets *Forrest Gump* meets *King Kong.*"

Of course he'll take the call.

"Hi," George says.

"Hello, Mr. Mactier, I'll patch you through to Derek at Pinewood."

No, he thinks about saying, *this isn't Mr. Mactier, this is Mr. Mactier's senior executive assistant—and as soon as you put Mr. Dreen on, I'll patch him through to Mr. Mactier.*

"Hello, George. Great to finally speak with you. Big fan of your work, what you've been able to do over there."

"Thanks." He's supposed to reciprocate, of course. "Coming from you that really means something."

"Tough for Emily to keep that edge, I think."

He's never really enjoyed this kind of sneaky, backhanded praise. *Tough for George to keep that edge,* Dreen would be telling Emily, George assumes, if the partnership dissolution had divvied up *NARCS* and *Real Time* differently.

"New show's causing a tremendous buzz," Dreen says.

"Excessive."

"Listen, George, the segment you're preparing on Sir Farley Lyman, you really ought to reconsider. I'm telling you this as your friend."

As a friend with whom George has never had any contact whatsoever—*that* kind of friend. Farley Lyman is a British hero of the Falklands War who now runs an international entertainment distribution business. One of the *Real Time* producers is working on a story alleging that Sir Farley secretly uses his military contacts in Asian and Middle Eastern countries as a means of getting government-run TV channels to buy his educational children's cartoon shows. He funneled antiaircraft weapons to North Korea, for instance, in return for broadcasting 110 dubbed episodes of his show *Planet of the Kidz*. To George, the story still seems unbelievable, literally unbelievable; the ironies, as Zip would say, just too "chocolaty"—too sweet and rich and dark.

"I don't know what you mean. Reconsider? Why?"

"Sir Farley is a military hero in England, you know. And I'll be honest—yes, we're in business together. He assembled some of the financing for *Giant Leap*." *Giant Leap* (formerly *Monkey Do,* previously *Houston, We Have a Banana*) is the movie Dreen's directing. "But this call isn't about business. I've known Farley for years and years—almost seven. He's the godfather to my wife's stepson. Your story about Farley is going to be totally inaccurate. I'm asking you to walk away from it. As a personal favor to me."

A "personal favor," because he's a "friend." George is speechless. He finally hems and haws something about keeping close tabs, making sure any story that airs is absolutely fair and accurate. He stands, but stops to mow through the three fresh e-mails (Hank Saddler is desperate for MBC News to name the new epoch: "like the seventies were the Me Decade and the eighties were the Greed Decade—but this is a brand we can own and leverage for a hundred years." With Barry Stengel gone, Saddler wants George's help in preemptively branding the entire twenty-first century.)

He's got to go. He's got to go. It's like the invisible quicksand nightmare, where you struggle to run but can't.

Featherstone appears just as George makes it as far as Daisy's desk.

"I know you're crashing twenty-four/seven here, and I'm late for an oh-one up-front brunch, but do you have a second?"

George retreats to his office, and Featherstone closes the door. It's not the slow-motion frustration dream, it's an *I Love Lucy* episode where Lucy and Ethel improvise endless stupid diversions to prevent

Ricky from going into the kitchen. Featherstone is in New York for next year's prime-time schedule announcements and the up-front advertising sales season.

George remembers Daisy telling him that he has sent flowers and blue cashmere pajamas to Timothy—Ng gave birth last week, becoming the third mother of the third Featherstone child. "Hey," George says, sitting back down, "congratulations, Timothy."

"Yeah. Thanks. But it was only for daytime." *The Naked and the Damned,* MBC's handheld, partly black-and-white, two-hour-long afternoon soap opera won three Daytime Emmy Awards last week.

"The baby, I mean. Oliver?"

"Olivier. Oh, *thanks.* George, my sources tell me you're working on a negative story about the National Institutes of Health?"

"It's not really negative. It's funny. About their Offices of Alternative Medicine and Dietary Supplements. Why?"

"Well, this Reality Channel project, the New Age channel? It's fast-tracking, it's sensitive, and Harold got a call from Washington. We need their cooperation on this deal. You know? Planting the Mose Media flag on the anti-alternative-health side of things, right now, would be a drag."

"It's not some tough investigative thing, Timothy."

"Now, you know that if this were a *news* show, for the news *division,* I wouldn't be here at all. I am Mr. Mad Props for the whole Chinese Wall church-and-state deal. But you're state, right? This is an entertainment program. So we're talking state to state. Grownup to grownup. When were you planning to schedule the NIH piece?"

"Maybe the third week."

"Ouch."

"What?"

"*Not* great timing for us, in terms of hoop jumping and deal doing."

"I wouldn't worry too much about it."

"Yeah?"

"No."

Featherstone is acting somber for Featherstone. He has not high-fived, or power-clasped, or fake-boxed, or said "Yessss!" while pumping his arm, or called George by a nickname.

"I trust you on this, George. Be careful." He leans back and crosses his legs. In encounters with subordinates, men never cross their legs. "Keep me looped in. Choppy times right now."

"What?"

"Oh, Sandi is threatening to sue me for palimony in Vegas, and she refuses to give up the suite there. And I think horrid little Hank is poisoning the well with the boss. Just between you and me, okay? I mean, six months later I'm still *acting* president."

He doesn't dislike Featherstone, but he doesn't really like him, either. And as much as he might want to hear someone with power over him confess weakness, he does not have the time right now to play pal and listen to Featherstone open up.

"It's the business we have chosen, Timothy."

"Ain't that the God's honest. By the way, the boss says he had a fab lunch up in the boondocks with Lizzie and her Chinese friend this weekend."

"Right," George says, feigning knowledge, mustering calm. "I guess they took a drive over to his place in Vermont. Great."

They both head for the door.

"Hey, you want to shoot up to Five-Nine with me to screen the short-list pilots? *Give* notes to some poor schmucks instead of just taking them? We got some true shit this season." For a moment George is startled, thinking Timothy has frankly disparaged the entire slate of MBC pilots. But then he realizes it's his rap lingo.

"I really don't have the time, Timothy. But thanks."

Also, watching almost any television show projected in a theater tends to embarrass George. The overeager mediocrity of TV is too apparent at that physical scale. (Movie screens make TV seem worse; watching movies on TV screens makes movies seem worse. This symmetry first occurred to him during lunch with a Cap Cities executive when he was at ABC. When he called it the "first law of degradation conversity," the Cap Cities guy looked at George like he was insane, and asked for the check.)

He starts to follow Featherstone to the elevators.

"George?" Daisy says.

"I really have to get down to editing, Daisy," he says, zooming past her. "What?"

"A big wadge of questions from the lighting girl. She needs to order more lights and filters for the crews, and she wants to know if you've a preference. She thinks Frezzi Mini-Arcs bring out 'eye sparkle' the best. And for the silks, she likes Chimera—"

But George has already turned his back on Daisy and thrown his arms up and out in an exaggerated shrug, walking away. The day is evaporating. He's done nothing. Rushing full-speed downstairs to the editing rooms, going to forge in the smithy of his soul the uncreated conscience of his demographic, George is still pissed at the brat from *Time,* earnest young Boris, even though it's possible, he realizes now, that his question might not have been as adversarial as George took it. "I guess the first thing I want to ask you, Mr. Mactier, is pretty basic: Why are you doing this show?"

3 0

"The explosions, especially the Civil War explosions but also Vietnam, are totally realistic. Hiroshima is awesome, the way you can toggle back and forth between aerial view and street-level, and the way the shock waves and heat ripple out and catch buildings and individual stuff on fire, plus the way you can *see* the people from like a block away. There were almost no bad graphic twitches, even when you force like four really quick time-warp jumps. The sound and the force-feedback effects are like dope sick—especially the meteors hitting the dinosaurs and wooly mammoths, and the guillotine, oh, and the Triangle Shit-waste factory fire. The music was okay, except it'd be cooler if some of the old, like, *waltz* music were more electronic or fast or something. The Paris and Switzerland part with the crazy artists is kind of boring until World War I starts. To me."

For the last two hours, Lizzie, her boy-genius Boogie Boffin, and Bruce have been watching videotaped bits of Warps focus group testimony annotated by the marketing consultant Lizzie hired. Madeline, the Fine Technologies sales-and-marketing vice president, should be here, but she quit last week; Lizzie thinks her politician husband pressured her to get out because of the Brouhaha.

"So that's the plus-or-minus gamut," the consultant says, standing to shut off the VCR, "with both your Typical Typicals and Typical Outliers represented proportionately. FYI, we found a great deal of player interest—like that older fellow in the suit—for *future*-time-travel capability."

Boogie looks at Bruce, and Bruce and Lizzie exchange a look. This had been the major debate from the beginning. Lizzie ruled that they would stick to historical events. "We can do the future in Warps 2: To the End of Time," she tells Bruce and Boogie.

"In all eleven focus groups," the consultant says, "the music negatives are the only issues with any predictably impactful consumer salience. Which I understand you're already dealing with."

"The 'authentic' versus the 'twenty-first-century' player choice for the music track," Boogie reminds Lizzie. "Toggled."

"And after our third retesting," adds the consultant, sotto voce, sounding as dumbstruck as if he were leading the archaeological team unearthing the hull of Noah's ark, "the f-gender scores remain simply unprecedented." In other words, girls and women enjoy playing Warps.

"*Great.* Speaking as a member of the f-gender." She turns to Bruce. " 'Dope sick' means that kid *liked* the Triangle Shirtwaist factory fire, right?"

"Yes, Mom," he replies.

"And the focus groups' reported game-play excitement levels," the consultant says, "correspond beat for beat to your new London dopamine and serotonin data." Lizzie gave Bruce the okay to commission the English neurobiology lab to perform a second battery of tests on people playing the latest version of Warps. Based on those results (the 1348 Black Death excitement level was too intense, the Cuban missile crisis simulation was not frightening enough), Bruce and his people have been tweaking the game, trying to get the balance of simulated fear and actual pleasure just right. Optimized, not maximized.

Lizzie is pleased, so pleased to be finishing with Warps at last. But now that they're nearly done (Friday is Bruce's last day), she is permitting herself to see squarely that she's not ecstatic, she's relieved. She's proud of having done her job, not of being the auteur responsible for "a groundbreaking multiplatform game that for the first time in gaming history straddles and synthesizes four major genres—role playing, action, strategy, and journey/enlightenment," as her web site puts it. True enough, that blather. But it's just a video game. She has happened into a *fun, youthful, exciting, challenging, cutting-edge* business, she realizes, about which she doesn't really give a flying fuck.

Unlike George, who always loves what he's doing at some deeper level than she does, even when it's hellish. Lizzie assumes it's hellish for him now, inferring from the pallor, the tight, frightened look, and the metallic, skunky odor when he gets home after midnight and slips into bed, not quite waking her. Finishing Warps will deprive her of the excuse she's had for putting off the "George, we need to talk" talk. Except for bare-bones logistics—the kids and the car and her father's estate (her stepsister-in-law, Gennifer, wants to turn the Palm Springs house into a day spa)—they haven't had a conversation in weeks. Or sex. On the other hand, they haven't had a fight in weeks. After George's show premieres, she figures, he'll be normal again, and they can try to move from peaceful coexistence toward détente. LuLu asks every few days if "Daddy is going to suicide himself." (The question that follows is "Then will he murder *us*?") But the kids seem otherwise engaged, and oblivious. Lizzie is pleased that Sarah is pleased by her user-support job two afternoons a week at C. Girls, Felipe's brother's hair-and-makeup-information web site. Max is even more eerily self-contained than usual, on the computer all the time. She was both relieved and a little sad when he announced that he doesn't want anyone to call him Sir anymore (too many kids at school thought it was some Knights of the Round Table fantasy, a misconception he found intolerable). She still figures Max is the one who swiped her last pack of cigarettes from the closet, particularly after he announced one night out of the blue that he was "studying" carcinomas, but she replaced the pack, found a new hiding place, and has never mentioned the disappearing Marlboro Lights.

Lance Haft stands in front of her desk holding budget printouts, trembling.

"I was already planning to get rid of Chas," she tells him, "but I certainly did not fucking 'lie' to you." *Lance!* Accusing her of *lying*! The postadolescent anarchosyndicalist spirit of the Fine Technologies staff has finally infected the controller. "I was being *optimistic*," she says. Lizzie has temporarily brought in extra programmers and designers to meet the

June deadline for Warps. And now there is the Chas Prieve debacle. She hired him to set up an office out in Woodside, California ("Two minutes from the old Buck's," he bragged, which meant nothing to her), and he booked $400,000 in revenues the first week, selling ShowNet software and hardware to equip a movie studio in Bombay. But then it turned out the Indians thought the deal was for 400,000 rupees, or $9,457, and Chas has done nothing but spend money and annoy Lizzie in the six weeks since. Fine Technologies' costs, Lance says, are running $420,000 over budget for the quarter, with a month still left to go.

"Okay," he says, pulling nervously at the bottom of the gray cotton crewneck, his spring uniform, which seems newly pinkish. "All right. Okay."

The first act of self-assertiveness in his life, and she's stifled it already, quashed him, cut off his tiny Massapequa balls. He'll probably go home and shave the new goatee. Poor little Lance. "In any case," she says in quasi-conciliation, "if we do the IPO, the market is not going to care that we have negative earnings from operations. In fact they'll probably like it."

"Okay. All right." He disappears.

Lance is discombobulated by the Brouhaha, but the rest of her employees seem to be getting off on the crisis atmosphere. They're young; round-the-clock work and the influx of freelancers are exciting. They even enjoy the press depictions of themselves as dupes and peons and victims. As long as morale isn't souring (and Bruce and Alexi assure her it mostly isn't), she can laugh off the *Voice* series (NOT SO FINE TECHNOLOGIES: THE CHRONICLES OF LATE CAPITALISM PART IV) and the second and third Molly Cramer whacks on the op-ed pages of the *Post*. The best was her use of a quote from a computer magazine, in which Lizzie called Fine Technologies' approach "militantly agnostic." This, Cramer wrote in one column, was evidence of "Zimbalist's liberal antireligion agenda." After Lizzie finally agreed to appear the other night as a guest on *And Another Thing!*, the MBC Entertainment newsmaker Q&A show, the host sandbagged Lizzie. He humiliated her over her involvement with Buster Grinspoon ("Still doing that cat ESP work out there in Area Fifty-one, are you?" and "So, that would be pussy-to-pussy communication?"), called her "very attractive for a cyber-Nazi," and encouraged his studio audience to boo her. As soon as the show ended, he apologized very warmly, and told her that the show had been going nowhere and he needed a villain. Sometime she should remember to tell George she's sorry she wasn't more sympathetic when Molly Cramer attacked him and *NARCS* last fall for "giving aid and comfort to the trendy drug legalizers." At the time, she made fun of him for finally proving her point about people in the media—that no one's skin is thinner than journalists' when they get bopped by other journalists.

Lizzie's Brouhaha acquired critical mass the day the second *Voice* piece and a *Teen Nation* exposé (UNCOOL!) came out. She had gone a little overboard, and called a staff meeting. She intended to celebrate the removal of the off-gassing carpet, demonstrate that she was unfazed, and answer questions (dissemblingly) about the IPO and takeover rumors, to reassure everybody that everything was fine. When one of the game designers asked about the Vanessa Golliver discrimination suit, Lizzie said, deadpan, "You're fired. Any other questions?" When people laughed, she launched into an extemporaneous employee-by-employee culling of each person into their respective "protected classes"—people over forty (the receptionist and Lance), women (most of the nontechnical staff), people of color (nineteen), people whose religious holidays (two Sikhs, five Muslims, and a Wiccan) are not on the official company holiday roster; and the disabled (Bruce, for diabetes, and Karen, because of her stutter). Finally, she asked everyone currently taking antidepressants to raise their hands (about a third of the staff), which by her reckoning ("*psychiatric* disability, like your former colleague Vanessa Golliver") pushed the last two employees into a protected class. Everybody smiled and went back to work. The following week, both the *Voice* and the *Daily News* ran items about this exercise, both neglecting to make clear that it had been a joke.

Ben Gould told her that she's a victim of the presidential primary season winding down, that the clucking about Fine Technologies has become a pretext for filling one Manhattan nook of the late-spring void in political chatter. "You're getting cut up by crossfire," he said to her, "from a Great Asshole Convergence. In a month, with the conventions coming up, it'll all be forgotten." Since the *Times* ran its front-page story on the Pat Buchananites' and the Dick Gephardtites' mutual obsession with reducing the number of foreign high-tech workers, and cited her as the prime New York example ("where roughly half of the programmers are working thanks to H1-B visas"), Lizzie has been turned into a kind of poster girl for the issue: "CEO Elizabeth Zimbalist" and "the little-known Manhattan software company Fine Technologies" have been Nexised from newspaper story to magazine story to TV story, like a contagion.

Lizzie is bored by the cardboard depictions of herself (*what* "flair for the politically incorrect"?) and distracted by all the attention, which she figures is consuming a third of her time. The staff, however, seems to bask and glitter in the reflected ignominy. The various *causes* have all become so muddled that the only part of the Brouhaha remaining in clear focus for her employees is the *célèbre,* which they enjoy—even Reginald, who burned his company ID card as the centerpiece of an ermine-themed, animal-rights media event on the sidewalk in front of the building yesterday. The murderous work schedule to complete Warps is blamed by the staff on the collapse of the Microsoft deal, not on Bruce's leaving or on Lizzie's overoptimistic scheduling. Lizzie has made no effort to disabuse anyone of their grumbled "Microsoft *scheisskopfs*"'s and late-night "motherfucking *Gates*"'s. The company's new intranet that Fanny Taft set up includes a REASONS MICROSOFT WILL FUCKING IMPLODE page. (The old system consisted of a three-year-old swath of corkboard opposite the elevator, crudely labeled INTRANET in Wite-Out and covered with tacked-up layers of staff memos, clippings, snapshots, single mittens, and felt-tipped SANE M/F ROOMMATE WANTED posters.)

"New hat?" Lizzie says to Alexi, who has just arrived wearing a yellow beret.

"You won't believe. Yesterday as I was leaving? One of the animal assholes at Reginald's little demonstration insisted that GO HOMOS was about *Homo sapiens.* I'm serious! She finally called me a 'humanist,' grabbed the hat, and ran away. It was very *Invasion of the Body Snatchers.* At least I didn't get splashed with the fake blood, like Lance. He told them he was the CFO and controller, and they thought that meant he was the boss. By the way, did you really say to somebody at *PC Week* that the protests weren't disrupting the production schedule 'because we're all used to working in goat rodeos of various kinds'?"

"Something like that. Yeah."

"Well, my friend at *New York Press* says the Animal Salvation League was faxing around a communiqué last night saying you've 'admitted to participating in bizarre rodeos involving goats.' "

When she sees a copy of the fax, she gets more upset than she's been since the beginning. Not only does she purportedly discriminate against employees with animal companions, "Zimbalist has personally sanctioned macabre violence against pigs in order to 'harvest' livers for untested, unproved transplantation into humans. And until recently, her company was preparing to hire Buster Grinspoon, 'the Butcher of Seattle,' whose gruesome experiments involving painful brain probes in living cats were halted by authorities last winter. On a chilling tape recording obtained by the ASL, Zimbalist can be heard bragging to Grinspoon, 'To be honest, I really don't give that much of a fuck about animals being used in research. I don't use cruelty-free cosmetics . . . I'm eating steak!' " The president of the Animal Salvation League calls her "the new Dr. Mengele of the animal-cruelty establishment." For further information or interviews, members of the press are invited to contact the group's media liaison, Iris Randall—George's Iris.

The one ethical issue that has given Lizzie real qualms is the neurological game testing in England, measuring the dopamine and serotonin levels in the brains of people playing Warps. She commissioned those tests, in which the brains of a dozen young adults, human brains, were injected with radioactive dye and raclopride. Given the Brouhaha, Katherine, the company's outside lawyer, advised her two weeks ago to put out a preemptive press release describing the London tests in detail. She did, including the possibility that an excess of dopamine may provoke symptoms of schizophrenia. Not even the Animal Salvation League expressed the slightest interest. The *Voice* mentioned the "diversionary press release" in one sentence, accusing "the Fine Technologies PR department" of "attempting to change the subject by pumping out positive news." The Fine Technologies PR department! "Are they still up on the thirty-fourth floor, or do they work out of the midtown building now?" Bruce joked. He had been trying to jolly her out of her rage at Buster Grinspoon, whom she called "your sneaky fucking Linda Tripp partner," for tape-recording their dinner.

Alexi tells her the Cordman, Horton limousine is downstairs. It's kind of like cigarettes, she has decided: if she doesn't pay for the limo, it doesn't count as a sin. Besides, it looks as if it might pour any second. On the way up Sixth Avenue she skims the papers Nancy has faxed over. The Cordman, Horton cover sheet lists "Telecopier" numbers instead of fax numbers, and the exchange for Nancy's private Telecopier line is rendered as "KNickerbocker 3" instead of 563. Lizzie already looked at the interesting fact—"Near-term median valuation range: $70MM"—but now she looks at it again. When Microsoft was telling her in March that her company was worth $36 million, she was virtually offended. Now that Nancy McNabb is predicting that the world in general—"the market"—might be persuaded to value Fine Technologies at $70 million, she finds herself pleased. *But it's not because of the money.* Maybe it's because the Microsoft bait-and-switch humiliation has turned her into a seller. Maybe it's Nancy's draft red herring that makes it more real and thus somehow untroubling. Maybe sentences written by lawyers that drone on unreadably for sixty-five words—"This document contains forward-looking statements that are subject to risks and uncertainties, including, but not limited to, the impact of competitive products and pricing, product demand and market acceptance, new product development, reliance on key strategic alliances, the regulatory and media environments, fluctuations in operating results, and other risks to be detailed from time to time in the company's filings with the Securities and Exchange Commission"—are boring intentionally, word analgesics to numb anxious buyers and sellers. *Maybe it's the limo,* she thinks, as they turn left toward Times Square from Fifty-first Street, swinging down Broadway. For a block, the rows of prices on the looming black Morgan Stanley stock ticker are racing south at exactly the same speed she is.

CORDMAN, HORTON, MERCHANT BANKERS: brushed metal letters on a granite square, a pretty Scrooge and Marley serif typeface but unmistakably *now,* exquisitely subtle silver-gray against silver-gray. The sign does not say EST. 1960, of course. But in another twenty years it will.

The building is new, and looks as if it were built from an Erector set with a few stray Lego and Duplo bits stuck on the roof, but inside, on the thirty-third through thirty-sixth floors, Cordman, Horton's offices are meant to suggest serious rooms from a century or two ago, Colonial Virginia with desktop computers, the State Department with better acoustics. Freshly milled wood paneling covers every visible perpendicular surface, not dark, stained, wood-colored wood (so 1950s by way of the 1980s, so comically "old"), but painted in one of the twenty-two designated Cordman, Horton shades of cream and gray (the 1780s by way of the 1990s, guaranteed tasteful through 2005). If Andrea Palladio or Thomas Jefferson had designed cubicles for M & A executive assistants, wouldn't *their* partitions be trimmed with dentils, and wouldn't the staff vending area have an oculus?

Nancy and another managing director have their own reception lounge, the third Lizzie has encountered since she's entered the building. The young woman sitting inside the wooden half cylinder, (evidently a miniature domeless U.S. Capitol building) is whispering into her phone—no rocket-ship headsets at a *merchant bank*—and she looks rattled, even a little scared.

She is one of Nancy's "kids."

"The cobbler guy *lost* them, that's what I'm *saying*. . . . She won't care it's not my fault, it's a TOT-Q thing, and last time they said she said I *wasn't* 'taking ownership for total quality.' . . . Yes, which is why you *have* to give me your psychic's beeper number. . . . How come? If he has the power to visualize what Peter's doing in California, why *couldn't* he visualize where a pair of Manolo Blahniks are? I can give him like an *exact* description. One sec—Good morning, with whom do you have an appointment?"

"Nancy McNabb. I'm Lizzie Zimbalist."

Another of Nancy's assistants, not obviously quaking, appears momentarily to bring the visitor nearer to Nancy herself. Lizzie has to admit: she could get used to the hush and the fifty-dollars-per-square-foot-per-year plush, the multiple assistants, the mineral water appearing unbidden, the phased labyrinth of reception areas.

"Elizabeth!"

And the effulgent *glow!* The office is drenched in light, resplendent with light, making Nancy shimmer like a goddess. On a bookshelf behind her, the clusters of solid-geometry investment-banker commemoratives—dozens of Lucite cubes, Lucite pyramids, Lucite obelisks, and Lucite spheres and hemispheres in honor of the M & As and IPOs and follow-ons and convertibles for which Nancy has been responsible or taken credit. Lizzie forgets about the overcast outdoors. She is unaware of the PSP system. On the exterior of the thirty-third through thirty-sixth floors, secreted in soffits above the windows of each corner office, banks of theatrical lights allow the workspace of every managing director to remain awash in perfectly angled rays of rich, dramatic "sunlight" from sunrise to dusk, regardless of the weather. PSP stands for Perpetual Sunlight Parity.

The women kiss, twice, and for an instant Nancy extends her arms and holds Lizzie by both hands, *regarding* her a little creepily, just as Mose did at the party.

"Are you excited? I want you to be excited."

"I'm getting there," Lizzie says, glancing at a young man standing in the doorway.

"Sit. You met my Grover? Grover is going to take notes, so that you and I can just dream out loud! Now. First off. We want you to be an internet company. That's valuation maximization. End of story. I mean, you *are* an internet company—the game, which I understand is truly next-generation, 128-bit, and net playable, yes? Yes?"

"Yes."

"So I think our story is: we're platform-agnostic, but web-committed. And Y2KRx and ShowNet, that whole piece of the business, here's our story on that, you're going to love this, Elizabeth: Y2KRx was a huge e-commerce hit, right, so you have a unique e-commerce core competency, *and* Fine Technologies is the first company—this is the genius part—to migrate enterprise resource planning software over to the consumer and small-business side. Yes? How much do you adore it?"

"It sounds . . . plausible."

"The Russell 2000 market cap is running eight times revenues," Nancy says, by which she means the average high-tech company is deemed to be worth eight times as much money as it takes in in a year. The market values of normal companies, real businesses not contingent on some fantastical future, run to one or two or three times their revenues. But it is not unusual for an internet company to be valued at fifty times its revenues, or a hundred times its revenues, or even, at the maddest moments, a thousand times its revenues. "Eight might put us south of seventy-five mil, but with the internet story, I think we can end up north, nicely north. The KillerWare offering Thursday and the BeMyFriend-dot-com IPO tomorrow will tell us a *lot* about the weather we're facing out there, microcap-valuation-wise." She pauses. "You have earnings, yes?" The question is an afterthought.

"We cleared a few hundred thousand last year, but it could be wiped out this year because of development costs on Warps."

"*This* year, *last* year. Lizzie! Silly! We're selling you based on *2002* earnings, 2003."

In 2002 Fine Technologies is supposed to make a profit of $2.7 million. Lizzie regards her earnings projections as realistic, even conservative, but only relatively speaking. How many copies of Warps will she ship in 2001? Not one has been sold. Will ShowNet become standard software in TV and movie production, or moot, replaced the day after tomorrow by some miraculous PalmPilot add-on? She doesn't know. No one knows. Earnings in 2002 are a fantasy, albeit a fantasy she has constructed scrupulously and in good faith. The numbers may turn out to be accurate, but if they do, it will happen by chance.

"You know, Nancy, I haven't definitely decided to do this yet. Everything people tell me about running a public company makes me think I'd hate it. All the outside pressure. Everyone watching you. Everyone knowing everything."

"So, twenty, thirty, thirty-five times earnings two years out. *Very* conservative valuation. I'd love us to file by August one. Shall we go eat?"

3 1

"I took it slow with the actors because there are so many stage directions," Gordon tells George. Gordon will direct the Tuesday and Thursday *Real Time* shows for the summer, while *NARCS* is on hiatus. Oz Delehanty, who worked with George at ABC News, will codirect *Real Time*'s Friday hours with Gordon—Oz in charge of the newscast, Gordon directing the acted, behind-the-scenes segments, most of which will be performed live.

"Gordon," George says, "the *talent*. Not 'the actors.' Okay? They're newspeople. I don't want to have to say this to you every time."

"George?" says Davey, one of the writers. "What did you mean before when you said Gore's not a McGovernite? Is that like McWorld or McJob? Because he is like Mr. McGovernment. You know?"

Where to begin? George is reminded of the time at *Newsweek* in 1984, back when it still teemed with fact checkers (and McGovernites), that a fact checker not much younger than George didn't understand what he meant by the phrase "zany SDS delusions about socialism" in a reference to the twentieth anniversary of the Port Huron Statement. "By SDS," he remembers the fact checker asking earnestly, "do you mean SDS the Norwegian telephone company, Statens Datasentral, or sudden death syndrome, the fungus that kills soybeans?"

"Gore *isn't* a McGovernite," George tells Davey, and leaves it at that. At least he's one of the show writers (one of five, who will work Saturday to Thursday inventing the "off-camera" dialogue for Francesca and Jess and the correspondents), rather than a newswriter. Davey is the writer who fought hardest to write George into the show. But George ruled that as the producer of the fictional parts of *Real Time* as well as of its news hour, it would represent some impermissible blurring or smashing of the fourth wall if he played himself on the Tuesday and Thursday shows. For now, he has agreed to let them refer to an executive producer of the news hour, who will be called George, and exist only as a disembodied voice on phones and intercoms. "You know," he told them, "like Charlie on *Charlie's Angels.*" When he started each of his previous jobs, unsure how to do what he'd been hired to do, he remembers feeling as if he were writing parodies of newspaper stories, then parodies of newsmagazine stories, and finally of TV news stories, deadpan parodies with no jokes. That self-consciousness always withered away after a few months, like training wheels he outgrew. He assumes the same thing will happen with *Real Time.*

"Martha?" he says to the head show writer on his way back to his office for a sandwich. "The Francesca and Cole B-story scene in the opener just sits there."

Cole Granger is one of *Real Time*'s three star correspondents. As an actor, he had a recurring role as a columnist on *Lou Grant,* but from 1990 on he's been working as a TV news reporter in San Diego, where he's won several local Emmys.

"I've been assuming that after Cole gets back from Tennessee with his Al and Tipper interviews," Martha says, "we'll work references to whatever happens there into that scene, and then pay it off on the Friday show when we run the interviews. Also, George—we *are* going to do the Deep Throat story during shakedown?"

"Write for now as though Deep Throat is in," he tells her. "But leave open the possibility that it won't run." George pauses. "In other words, the actual situation."

"Will we know about Deep Throat before the table read of the Friday show on Friday?"

"A table read? Fridays are *news,* Martha. Jess and Francesca can just read the Friday show off the TelePrompTer. We don't want it to look overrehearsed."

The Deep Throat story is based on the revelations of Sylvia Boudreau Shepley, a well-connected Georgetown woman who claims she knows the identity of Deep Throat, from Watergate. Mrs. Shepley, who's sixty-nine, has become a devotee of a new, extreme Quaker sect whose animating idea is its motto—"No secrets, no lies." Her new spiritual devotion to absolute truth, she says, has obliged her to spill the beans about the reporting of Watergate, "even though Bob and Carl will be upset." Mrs. Shepley says Deep Throat was (in whole or in part, she's not sure) George Bush. If Jude McAllister and his producer can corroborate it before the first Friday show, which happens to be the day before the anniversary of the Watergate break-in, it would be the perfect, killer story for the premiere week. So far, Bob Woodward and Carl Bernstein have both refused to confirm or deny to McAllister that Bush was a source. Woodward laughed when George called him, but Bernstein, George thought, sounded a little nervous. "I know Carl," Featherstone told George when he briefed him on the show, "from when I worked with Liz Taylor. Why don't we just drop a hundred thousand or so on him to play along? I'm sure Carl could use the cash." "If Bernstein were going to sell out Deep Throat," George replied, "he could've gotten a couple of million from some book publisher a long time ago."

"Your lunch, Mr. Mactier," Daisy says, handing him a paper bag as he passes by without stopping, and into his office.

"One of the writers said they're all Quaked and Daikatana'd out. Video games? He asked me to ask you," he hears her saying, "if in the interests of writer harmony and productivity you could possibly nick a prerelease copy of Warps for them to play." He knocks the door shut with his foot.

"*No,*" he says.

The only live music she ever hears these days is on sidewalks and subway platforms, thirty seconds of steel drums here, a snatch of cello or a capella gospel there. This guy, sitting right under one of the 14TH STREETs spelled out in tiles, playing bluegrass on a slide guitar, is new to the station. He looks fifty, with the smooth, lightly roasted skin of a drunk (the kind of tan that once made tans unfashionable) but he's probably younger than Lizzie is. He looks alert but stunned, as if he was badly startled months or years ago, like a face in a Mathew Brady photograph. As she passes him, a dozen smiling white teenage girls and boys bound out of the turnstiles toward her, each one wearing a white T-shirt with the logo MISSION 2000! As her train thunders into the station, she glances again at the teenagers (the backs of the T-shirts say KNOXVILLE SAVING NEW YORK!), who now look a little startled themselves by the sight of a white derelict in New York City playing beautiful country music.

What does Harold Mose want now? she thinks, sitting and staring at the cover of her *Business Week* (HELLO: THE GOLDEN AGE OF TELEPHONY) on her way uptown.

Such a shitty day, and not just Monday shitty, either. The fax about Chas Prieve that came in over the weekend from the Malaysian Ministry of Energy, Telecommunications and Posts seemed amusing ("Informing you officially of seizure of pornographs allegedly distributed by your MR. PRIVE, who is under ministerial investigation for violation of national and provincial antipornography statutes"), but then she learned from a wholesaler in Hong Kong that the Southeast Asian distribution deal for Warps that Chas claimed to have closed before she fired him ("A 100 percent done deal, Lizzie") has been undone, partly because of the Malaysian pornography problem. None of the morning's papers mentioned the company or her personally, which is a good thing. But the front-page story in the *Journal* assessing last week's collapse of the market for high-tech IPOs is a bad thing. ("Although the BeMyFriend.com pricing debacle may have no lasting impact on 'blue chip' internet stocks," the article in the *Journal* said, "analysts agree that the 83% plunge in KillerWare's share price within minutes of the open on its second trading day may be a paradigmatic event for the software sector.") Nancy McNabb's phone call to Lizzie at home was meant to be reassuring and upbeat. "Timing! Timing! Timing from hell!" Nancy cackled as soon as Lizzie said hello. "I *won't* say that if we went out three months ago like I wanted, you know what—but, Elizabeth, just sit tight, and by first quarter '01 it'll be like none of this ever happened."

Lizzie's staff, unfortunately, does not read *The Wall Street Journal.* They read the *Post,* which reported last Friday morning that she was about to get very rich at their expense. "Although her employees may be left out in the cold," the *Post* story said, "politically incorrect limousine liberal Lizzy Zimbalist will be laughing all the way to the investment bank after prestigious superfinanciers Cordman, Horton take her Silicon Alley software firm public this summer. A source close to the deal told the *Post* that the flamboyant Zimbalist stands to personally net $70 million." Even Karen, worshipful Karen who defended Lizzie so passionately during the private-coffee-cache scandal in April, has gone over to the other side. "If you want people to stay c-c-c-c-c-committed, Lizzie," Karen said too loudly at Bruce's going-away party on Friday, waving her Dos Equis like a pike, or a villager's torch, "then you need to start running the company open book. I mean, hello? *Transparency?* D-d-d-d-democracy?" In other words, let every employee know how much every other employee is paid. She told Karen and a half dozen bystanders that she'd have to think about going open book (*no fucking way* is what she was thinking), and assured them that she had not even decided whether to take Fine Technologies public, that some of the wealth would be shared if it did happen, and that she would get only a tiny fraction of $70 million in any event. "Kudos, my Mother Courage," said Willibald, one of the German programmers, raising his beer in a toast. Aside from Bruce, who made her sob and laugh at the end of the party (by assuring her that she's not "flamboyant" as he hugged her goodbye), only Alexi, Fanny, Willibald, and his pal Humfried still seem to trust her. She's not sure if it's actually resentment over the putative IPO money, or if the money is the trigger for latent hysteria about animal rights, or if what's going on is some surge of post-Warps spring-fever Parisian-barricade sentiment. But it sucks. She loathes it.

"Excoose me, pliz, mees, one second, pliz?" A slightly lost-looking older man holds his big old-fashioned cellular phone toward Lizzie.

The Metropolitan Tower doorman has already opened the door for Lizzie to enter, and frowns, irritated on Lizzie's behalf.

"Pliz, mees? I cannot be understand," he says, handing her the phone. "You spik, pliz? I must spik to *him*," he says, pointing with his thumb to a name and phone number written on an LOT Polish Airlines ticket folder. "Meester Vallayce Gonshaleez. Pliz?"

She puts the phone to her ear. "I'm afraid I don't understand what you're saying," a recorded female voice says, sounding a little stern, flaunting her own perfect, plummy, prerecorded American. "Please try

again. Speak in a normal voice. Otherwise, I'm afraid I won't understand."

Lizzie gets the problem. To the speech-recognition software at the
other end of the line, this man's Polish-accented English might as well
be gibberish, all noise, no signal.

"Wallace Gonzalez," she says into the phone slowly and firmly, a
normal American voice, but not hers.

"*Thank* you!" the recording replies, now sounding like an old
friend. "One moment and I'll connect you." She hands the phone
back to the man, wondering if lines of Fine Technologies' software
code are buried somewhere inside the huffy computer.

She plunges from the unseasonably hot blare of Fifty-seventh Street
into the quiet air-conditioned dim, wondering if the Golden Age of
Telephony is a good thing or a bad thing. And wasn't 1900 the true
Golden Age of Telephony? Isn't this more a Late Mannerist Age of
Telephony?

The concierge is using three at once, one land line ringing through
to Mose upstairs, another to a car service that has him on hold, and a
third, his own wireless phone, to someone he knows. "*Momentito,*
Cordelia," he says into the wireless, and lays it on one of the stacks of
five different Asian newspapers on his black marble desk.

What does Harold Mose want? It's urgent enough that his assistant,
Dora (actually, Dora's assistant, Lucy), called Daisy to get Lizzie's wireless number after they couldn't get through on any of the regular Fine
Technologies voice and fax lines. Hundreds of friends of animals and
people for the ethical treatment of animals have been calling since Friday as part of their organized "education and lobbying" campaign,
keeping every line permanently busy with their sermons, their photographs of butchered puppies, and their death threats. In their single
real conversation this week, after George reminded Lizzie that Charlie
the caretaker had possibly murdered cats and definitely killed weasels
on their land at Lake Marten, he added with an unfunny grin, "Don't
worry, honey, I won't snitch on you to PETA."

At Mose's door, his Filipino manservant—that is the word—informs her that Mr. Mose will be just a few minutes, then takes Lizzie
to a room that has no obvious function, a rarity in Manhattan. There is
a single huge upholstered chair (or a very small love seat) and no TV
set. Although there are a few shelves of books (*Like, Cold: An Oral His-*

tory of the Canadian Beatnik Movement, The Zen of Curling, Moderation Miracle, CanadaPop: From Anka to Alanis, Hail Salmon! and *101 Rather Unusual Things to See in the New Province of Nunavut*), it is too small to be the library. On a red quilted-bubinga-wood table is an open laptop with a screen saver (a tiny MBC logo grows to fill up the screen, then tastefully disintegrates as NEW NETWORK FOR THE NEW CENTURY scrolls across, the two NEW's alternately throbbing), but the table is too cramped to work as a real desk. Except for a Karsh portrait of Mose himself, and his framed 1997 U.S. citizenship certificate, the walls are hung with a dozen medieval maps of the heavens. Gloria Mose, she decides, calls this the sitting room.

She stands. Examining the computer, a limited edition Intel 1000 (only a thousand 1000-megahertz machines made, given as gifts last Christmas to a thousand "planetary leaders"), she idly taps a key. The screen saver blinks away, revealing the ticker symbol for Mose Media Holdings and the current price, ME 51⅛, and below that a graph charting the stock price since January second. The graph bears an uncanny resemblance to the southern border of Texas, Lizzie notices. (The *Times* has been running a lot of maps lately of the Mexican border). At the beginning of the year, Mose's stock price was 47, around El Paso, then meandered south along the Rio Grande, jagged up some in March, then turned south again, hitting Brownsville, its bottom, in early April, before heading steeply north-northeast as it has done ever since. It snaked through Corpus Christi and then during the last few weeks flattened out and turned east near Houston. The price, Lizzie notices, just has ticked up a teeny to 51³⁄₁₆. A *teeny:* since the Stock Exchange sliced price fractions from eighths of a dollar down to sixteenths a few years ago, Lizzie has enjoyed imagining Ben Gould and the testosteroned louts on Wall Street shouting *teeny* all day long.

"I want that *up.*" Harold Mose has appeared, wearing a gray suit, pink shirt, no tie, and red velvet slippers covered with golden stars and crescent moons. If men still wore ascots, he would have one on. He has new glasses—the round red plastic frames have been replaced by rough black steel ovals.

"Hello!" Lizzie turns her cheek for the kiss.

"I can't tell you grateful I am. For popping up here on such short notice. Your plate is full, I know, overflowing. But I've got to be at Teterboro at two, and we absolutely had to talk before I leave. Did Luis get you whatever you wanted?" He directs her toward the living room, and a bright purple Sottsass couch with, of course, a view of the park.

"L.A., and then Tokyo, your assistant said?"

"Correct. And very quickly downhill from there—Singapore, Moscow, and Kiev, where they're desperate to pay me to buy their television and telephone company. As if I could do anything with their boatloads of hryvnias. It may shock you," he says, sitting down in an old Frank Gehry corrugated-cardboard armchair across from Lizzie, "but the Ukrainian hryvnia is a somewhat illiquid currency." He can't help glancing outside. A cloud shadow is drifting over the Time Warner–CBS construction site on Columbus Circle, about to darken acres of trees and grass on its way toward Fifth Avenue.

"Astounding view," she says. Rich people spend a lot of time contemplating Central Park. Some of them half believe they own it: *my view, my park.* Or is it the unattainability—*someday all this will never be mine*—that makes the view such a luxurious fetish? No matter how many millions may drift into her possession, Lizzie believes, she will never be a rich person.

"Last week was a bit of a bummer for we digital revolutionaries, eh?"

"Well," she says, "MyBestFriend-dot-com was dead from the start, because of the porno piece. I *know* their spin, the sex business is only part of it, it's 'a relationship community,' all that. But 'the market' is still just a bunch of straight guys from Chappaqua and Evanston. Committing the firm's and clients' capital to live video feeds of anal intercourse—we're not there yet. Quite. And the KillerWare pricing was just crazy."

"So we're not seeing the beginning of the end of the web? More of the bubble bursting?"

"Nah. Anyway, it's not *a* bubble. It's more like foam. In foam, individual little bubbles burst all the time, but new ones form, and the foam doesn't go away. Some little bubbles shmoosh together into bigger bubbles. You know?"

He's smiling. *What does Mose want?* Maybe he's delivering a speech in Europe and wants to steal some ideas duty-free from her.

"The novelty of the web isn't wearing off?"

"No, people your age, baby boomers—"

"Thank you." Mose is almost sixty.

"—starting with baby boomers, the big idea is getting whatever you want right this second. *Now.* TV twenty-four hours a day, sex, drugs, all of that. Earnings growth *this* quarter. So the web delivers in spades—books now, CDs now, flowers and groceries now, stocks, data, letters, anything I want I can get *now,* all the time, by tapping a button." She's surprising herself with her conviction. She feels like an evangelist. It's so much easier than running an actual business.

Mose turns his head to let the uniformed manservant address him.

"Mr. Featherstone has arrived," Luis informs his master. "In the sitting room."

Mose nods. If George were here, he would want to hum the opening "Goldfinger" bars. She does miss George.

Mose asks her, "Do we think interactive entertainment is going to make anyone any money?"

"Well. If by interactive entertainment you mean video on demand, ordering up any movie or show when you want it, *right now,* that'll be great. Throw away the VCR. But I guess I don't know how that makes money for anyone but the Intels and the movie studios. And game playing. But if interactive entertainment means most people will do anything but sit on the couch and stare at *Monday Night Football* and *Baywatch*? No."

"The couch potatoes will continue to bake."

"It's the lazy-sex paradigm," Lizzie blurts, regretting it.

Mose tilts his head and squints.

"Oral sex became the easy default mode, just like dishwashers and microwaves. Given a choice, people would rather be performed on than perform. That's why they're going to keep watching TV for a long, long time. Just watching it, not 'interacting' with it."

Happily, Mose does not dwell on her metaphor. "Any film *now,* any TV show *now,*" he says. "What's the tipping point there, do you think? We can't get enough bandwidth to send your husband's program to an individual viewer whenever she wants, but until she sees how that works, she's not going to *demand* the bandwidth. You need to build the pipe to get the business, but you need the business to pay for the pipe. Catch-22. How the Heller do you get around it?"

Pipe, bandwidth, tipping point. The man is a connoisseur. His Joseph Heller pun was lame and labored—but "she," the *she* was slick. "I don't know, you see the predictions. Five years? Maybe. Who knows?"

"But you don't doubt it will happen?"

"It'll happen. I've bored you with my hypoglossal analogy already, haven't I? In one of the memos?"

"If you did, I very carefully paid no attention."

"The hypoglossal canal is the hole in the bottom of your skull where the spine connects to the brain," she says, touching the back of her neck. "It holds all the nerve fibers that run from the brain down to the muscles in your tongue. In chimps and gorillas, the pipe, the hypoglossal, is really small. A million years ago, humans had little chimp-size ones too. But over the next half million years or so, the hypoglossal canal expanded, doubled in size. So more nerve fibers could run up to the tongue. And so then, finally, humans could talk. And here we are."

He's looking at her with his mouth slightly open, as if she may have just told him an elaborate joke.

She blushes. "I wrote my college thesis on this. Biological anthropology."

He takes a deep breath. "I must have you for myself, Elizabeth."

Lord. Her blush spreads, and she tries to look amused.

"I'm serious," he says. "I need you."

She looks away, toward the reservoir and Harlem. Her frozen smile jitters. "Harold? *No.*"

"If Mose Media Holdings is ever to be more than just some pipsqueak poseur—what did the columnist call us last month, 'UPN on steroids, PBS on acid, NBC wannabe, and Fox putting on airs'—I've *got* to get a serious digital strategy. We've bought all these crazy little dot-coms and TK Corporations, but I need someone to stitch it all together. Make convergence *happen.* You've got to come work for us. President of Mose Media Holdings, Digital. And executive vice president of Holdings itself."

"It's completely flattering, really, but—"

"*Stop.*"

"—but we're not going public, not this year anyway. I can't just walk away from the company. I couldn't."

"Correct. I know the IPO's off, and of course you can't cut and run."

"What?"

"Fine Technologies would be the final purchase in my 'digital shopping spree.' The jewel. I'm proposing that you shmoosh your little bubble into my bigger bubble. You and your shareholders get a couple of million shares of Mose Media Holdings, and I get the hottest computer game of next Christmas, plus ShowNet—synergy!—as well as your telephone-robot software, what was it? Speak Memory. Plus the Y2K thingamajig. As a write-down, anyway. And you. Most important, I get you."

A couple of million. Ten minutes ago, two million Mose Media Holdings shares were worth $102 million. One hundred and two million dollars.

She's flattered that he is serious enough to have had someone dig up the name Speak Memory.

She's flattered and disconcerted that he already knows her IPO is off.

She finds the number, the *nine-figure* purchase price, dizzying. And flattering.

She thinks of how she's ridiculed executives with multiple titular incarnations as "corporate Shivas," president of one entity, executive vice president of another, vice chairman of something else.

She remembers what George told her a long time ago, when she almost took a job at a publishing company as "senior change agent and executive vice president at large," about the folly of being a general with no troops. "Everybody salutes you," he said, "but you can't launch an attack. And you get shot at anyway."

"Look, I can probably strategize and deliver opinions as glibly as any other MBA," she says. "And I'm not saying you aren't serious about new media and digital, but I really have no interest in being a glorified consultant. Half my business school class became consultants, and it was the half I didn't like."

"No! Absolutely not! Ask Timothy," he says, nodding toward the front hall, "how often he's briefed or been debriefed by some three-thousand-dollar-a-day MBA fuckwit. *Never.* Consultants are my bane. And my McKinsey and Booz-Allen."

He grins—bane, Bain, *get it?*—expecting a smile back, which she gives, even though she finds all punning slightly repugnant, like an old-fashioned salesman with a loud suit and bad breath. (Mose's breath is sweet, of course, and his suit is perfect.)

"What I *need*," he goes on, "is someone to integrate TK Corporation and MotorMind and TurboSearch and all of the new properties into Mose Media, someone who understands that . . . mind-set, to *run* them for us. If you're worried that you'd be an admiral without a fleet, no: the operating heads would report to you."

She must take this seriously.

"Are the existing managements at the acquired companies," Lizzie asks, "you know, faits accomplis?" She is asking if she can fire people freely—such as Penn McNabb, Nancy's stupider and prettier brother, whose financial success in the software business offends Lizzie.

"Entirely up to you. There are a few employment contracts. But nothing an egregiously large severance check couldn't resolve in about thirty seconds."

She nods, but she refuses to smile. This sort of clubby, callous boardroom talk Lizzie has always found creepy, somewhere between boys frying ants with a magnifying glass and a Judenrat planning session. But at this instant, Mose's hypothetical cruelty on her behalf, with the spectacular green of Central Park below and $102 million in mind, gives her a dirty aristocratic thrill. All that relentless Mose *wit* might get exhausting. But it could also be a refreshing change from George's current autistic despond.

"You sure you would want a greedy vivisectionist working for you? Wouldn't I be terrible for Hank Saddler's popularity quotient?"

"Media Perception Index. Hank is all for you, Elizabeth. When you told him no on the software for the Army, he got scared of you—or, should I say, began to respect your astute public relations judgment and decisive management style. Hank is a bit of an S-and-M'er. As for our MPI, getting these motley web businesses shipshape will drive up the 'visionary-slash-reinvention-slash-cutting-edge scores.' So Hank reckons. And hiring a very senior, very high profile young *woman* also gets us MPI points, for 'progressive-slash-enlightened.' Where I'm shockingly low."

Transparency, Lizzie thinks. This is transparency, not in Karen's young-Maoist *Animal Farm* sense, but true transparency, jolly candor about every mixed motive. She likes Mose. She likes Zip Ingram. She likes amusing scoundrels, as long as they're honest and loyal to her.

"Remember," Mose adds, "*I'm* Commodore Slave Ship." He's referring to his involvement in the Classical Galley Circuit. The CGC is a very rich man's hobby in which a dozen 150-foot-long wooden boats, imaginary replicas of ancient vessels powered by double-decked galleys of 150 oarsmen, compete in weeks-long races six times a year on six different seas and oceans. Mose owns one of the boats, the *Sic Transit Gloria,* and co-owns with the Chopper Channel the TV rights to air the CGC spectacles. Lizzie has never watched a race, but she did see the famous catapult-accident clip, from *The MBC MegaSports,* which occurred during last winter's Mumbai-to-Djibouti run.

"Well," she says, shifting to a more upright, predeparture posture. "This is a pretty astounding offer, Harold. I'll need to think about it."

"Of course. And I apologize, but unfortunately I can only give you the rest of the day. The shareholder meeting's tomorrow in Burbank. If we're going forward, my crack team of investor relations advisers say we need to go forward *now.* At least agree in principle."

Mike Zimbalist's seat on the Fine Technologies board has not been filled, and she has his proxy. If she wants to do this, she requires the agreement of only one other board member, George or Ben or Bruce. She needs to double-check the price. She wants to say, *By 'a couple of million' shares of stock, do you mean* two *million?*

Instead she asks, "You're proposing an all-stock deal?"

Mose nods. "Two million shares. Two million shares, I should point out, at their fifty-two-week high, and which every analyst in America rates a buy or strong buy."

Lizzie nods and says dead seriously, "Well, I'd better get back downtown and begin having some conversations with my board."

On her way out, glancing into the sitting room, she sees Featherstone. Silent, and unsmiling, he looks like a different person. He spots her, smiles weakly, and gives her a thumbs-up. In the lobby, on her way out, she doesn't even notice the FedEx driver dumping a dozen packages on the concierge's desk; buried among them, in a trim envelope the size of a paperback book, is a computer disk from Chas Prieve. As she hits the sidewalks, she feels like walking the two miles back to the office, despite the heat (she likes hot city days, particularly wandering home through Chinatown, pretending she's in Shanghai), but she does need to get back as quickly as possible, right now, and begin having conversations with her board.

"Please. *Talk* to her. The lady just doesn't get it. She needs to understand that Angela Janeway does not want to be in the series business anymore. End of story. Angela Janeway is transitioning to the *news* business, the broadcast journalism business. Plus feature films, of course. You know we're up for the *Driving Miss Daisy* prequel, in the Jessica role?"

"I don't produce *NARCS* anymore, I haven't talked to Emily in weeks." The last time he talked to her, in fact, was when she called about an actress, a day player named Shawna Switzer who said she knows George well. He told Emily to go ahead and hire her, but that he couldn't vouch for her.

"I've got my own show, Sandy, which goes on the air in about ten seconds." It's the beginning of shakedown week. *Real Time* premieres in eight days.

"Please. Call her." Sandy Flandy ostensibly phoned about his new client, Francesca Mahoney (she needs George's permission to go on the road to emcee The Gap Presents the New Lilith Fair this summer), but wheedling on behalf of his other big MBC client is Flandy's real agenda. Barry Stengel's firing removed the only drag on *Real Time,* and the main obstacle to Jess Burnham becoming George's star anchorwoman. Stengel also was deadset against trying out Angela as an MBC news correspondent ("We will not, repeat *not,* put some *actress* on our air!"), so his departure has permitted Angela's real dream to come true—during the *NARCS* summer hiatus, she's coanchoring *NewsNight 2000.* Already the ratings have moved up. And now her agent wants George to persuade his former partner to let his former star out of her *NARCS* contract, so that she can become permanent coanchor of *NewsNight 2000,* and complete her transmutation into Angela R. Murrow.

"Will you do it for me, George?" Flandy says. "For the Flan Man?"

George isn't sure whether losing Angela Janeway would help or hurt *NARCS.* He can imagine the write-out episode: *Cowboy Quesada (Lucas Winton) kills Jennie O'Donnell (Angela Janeway) by mistake as they're storming a crack factory. SEASON PREMIERE.* He ought to want the show to succeed. He created it, and he'll still get a quarter of any profits it throws off. (He is, his new agreement with Emily affirms, "a passive royalty recipient in perpetuity," which makes him feel like he is signing a contract for a slot in a mausoleum.) George used to pride himself on his disinclination to schadenfreude, but now he wants Emily Kalman to fail, a little, with *NARCS*—not cancellation failure, but painful, bad-buzz failure. He wrote the season finale, and it got a 7.9 rating and 15 share. But because Emily changed the depraved Kahuna character from a charming, liberal senator to a thuggish conservative manufacturer (played by Stephen Baldwin) of a mind-reading "mental modem," the show's positive reviews didn't wholly please him.

"Emily's stubborn," George says, "and I know she thinks I'm the cause of the problem, by hiring Jess and opening up the slot for Angela in News. But I'll talk to her."

"George?"

"Yeah?"

"I love you," Sandy Flandy tells him. "I really mean that."

He's going to be late for Featherstone, his first lunch out in weeks, maybe a month, but Daisy stops him as he tries to shoot past her, holding up two fingers, like a peace sign.

"One," she says, "Lizzie phoned again. It's important but nothing bad, she said. Two, your very loud friend, Mr. Gould, is holding, and he also says it's important."

George grabs the receiver off Daisy's desk.

"I'm late, Ben. What?"

"Pat and Mike! What do you think of Lizzie's news?"

"What news?"

"Uh-oh. I'm not going to spoil it by telling you. I wish she hadn't told me."

"Am I going to wish she hadn't told me?"

"No, it's *positive*. It's great for you guys. But it screws up my trading. Call her."

"We did," he says, glancing at Daisy. "It's constantly busy."

"Call the wireless number, dummy. The animal nuts are flooding the phone lines. She's using her cell."

Daisy punches the speed-dial button for George, who's still standing by her desk. He's looking out over the office, over the plain of four-foot-high green partitions and the tops of human heads, with the

folders and papers and books scattered everywhere like mulch. His secretary watches him as he waits for his wife to answer.

"It's me," Daisy hears George say into the phone.

He listens, staring, saying nothing for half a minute. Daisy has never
seen his face do this, tighten and darken, almost change shape. He shuts
his eyes for a moment and takes a deep breath.

"Yes," he says finally in a careful, flat-line bass, like a POW. "No,"
he says, and then with a flicker of rage, "No, as *me*. Not as a member
of your 'board.' " Seconds pass. "Where?" His whole body seems to
deflate. "No," he says after a while. More seconds pass. "No. It's your
life." He flips the receiver away from his mouth as he takes another
deep breath. Then: "Congratulations. I'll see you."

PART THREE

June

July

August

September

October

3 2

She finds evidence every day of George's occupying the house, his residue—wet soap, ripped dry-cleaning stubs, holes in the newspapers, coffee dregs—but she goes days without seeing him in the flesh. "It sounds more like forensics than marriage," Pollyanna said. Lizzie knows couples who live this way all the time. Creating the show, as George says (said, six weeks ago), is "a fucking monster." But since she's taken the Mose job, his absences seem deliberate as well as un-avoidable. The two of them are ships passing in the night, but he is now on an obviously calculated harbor-traffic schedule. He was home by seven the nights she was in San Jose and Burbank, the kids told her, and he stays around to help Rafaela get them off to school the mornings that Lizzie leaves early. ("Daddy wouldn't answer my question," LuLu told Lizzie after one of those mornings. "I asked if him working for you was a good thing or a bad thing.") Lizzie hasn't had dinner with George in a month, including weekends. The weather was still cool when they last ate breakfast together, at the table out back. The last time they had sex wasn't long after the memorial service for Rafaela's children, where Lizzie bled through her dress, in April. It is almost July. The weather is sweltering.

He was gone as usual by the time she got up this morning, and the ReadyAim system went haywire. The kids have been out of school for two weeks, but every minute beginning at seven-fifteen, the phone rang, each time with the same recorded message: "Your child's transportation will be waiting at the designated location in zero minutes, zero seconds! Got milk? Got milk? Got milk? Got milk?" After the fifth call, Lizzie left the phone off the hook.

Because she's been putting in an appearance at Eighteenth Street for a couple of hours each morning before going up to MBC, and because it's gotten hot, she capitulated a week ago and started taking the car service to work. She still calls Go! Now! herself each morning to order the car, though. A standing reservation would be like buying a whole carton of cigarettes. Today, though, since she gave the Fine Technologies staff the day off (it's the beginning of the long Independence Day weekend, Warps is nearly finished), she's heading straight for Fifty-seventh Street.

As she swings around the horn, and the FDR turns into the West Side Highway, Lizzie looks out at the Hudson, trying to catch glimpses of the three- and four-masted schooners, antiques as well as fake antiques, sailing past the buildings of Battery Park City.

"I take you before," the driver says suddenly, glancing at her in the rearview.

"Oh," Lizzie says. "Hmmm."

"You work with Microsoft, yes?"

She doesn't remember the driver. But she can't imagine that she ever discussed the Microsoft deal with him.

"No. Not really," she says, baffled, eager to end the conversation.

"Yes. And a dill to do with booster grime-spawn?"

"Nope. Sorry. It wasn't me." Whatever the fuck you're talking about. She hunkers down into her *Wall Street Journal*. In the month since she agreed to become a corporate executive, she has started reading the boring stories in the *Journal*.

"Booster *grime*-spawn, his brain *cheap*? Yes?"

She doesn't look up. "Nope."

She's forcing herself through a story about American companies buying up Asian companies since the crash in '97, utterly bored ("Although companies like Microsoft have benefited from this anomalous trend in the ringgit-yen exchange rate . . .") until she comes to a paragraph that mentions Mose Media Holdings. "Some U.S. investment banks are scrambling to take advantage of the Asian economic comeback before prices get too high. 'There's still misery and chaos over there, which continues to present fabulous opportunities for client companies,' says Nancy McNabb, senior managing director at Cordman, Horton, which, sources say, is scouring East Asia for acquisition bargains on behalf of Microsoft, Chase-Citigroup, and Mose Media Holdings."

Nancy is amazing. Three weeks ago, after accusing Lizzie of slandering her brother and her brother's company to Harold Mose (true) and thus lowering the price Mose Media paid, she took credit for convincing Harold to offer her two million shares for Fine Technologies (possibly true). At the end of the conversation Lizzie had, in any event, agreed to let Nancy handle the deal, out of which Cordman, Horton will get a fee of one million dollars. And, evidently, new business from Harold Mose.

Coming back to midtown every day reminds her of being young, but now that she's executive vice president, Mose Media Holdings, as well as president, Mose Media Holdings, Digital ("I guess that's like being a wife *and* a mother," Pollyanna said), working in a tower on Fifty-seventh Street makes her feel middle-aged. The giant metal letters on the sidewalk out front, THE MBC, slick and swaggery, are *so* midtown. Because the logo is italic, the letters look like they're tipping over. A smiling tourist dad is framing a digital snapshot of his teenage tourist son cowering just to the right of the C, clowning, as if he's about to be crushed. *"Ein bisschen mehr ängstlich,"* the man commands his son, and the boy puts on a look of terror.

Her office is on the Fifty-ninth Floor. During the only real conversation she had with George about selling her company and taking this job, he went suddenly mute when she said she thought she'd be working on Fifty-nine, and a minute later started yelling.

It's silent here, hermetic and still, unlike any place Lizzie has ever worked. The children's foundation was always quiet, but the space was tight, with people crammed everywhere sharing desks, so that one was always aware of nice, polite, modestly paid people *being* quiet. Here on Fifty-nine the silence seems more religious or royal, less like a busy library than a sanctum where few mortals are permitted entrance. It reminds her of Myst. (She has yet to find a computer game that she loves playing, but Myst and Riven she found actively unpleasant, opaque and pretentious and dull.) Even Featherstone seems to subdue when he's on Fifty-nine. She's seen him just once, and he called her "Beth," the most drab and desultory nickname of the twenty or thirty he's called her in the year she's known him.

The intercom *chimes.* They use intercoms up here whenever possible, and the speakers in the phones on Fifty-nine are so high-end that every time a call comes, it sounds like a cymbal has been gonged by someone hiding under her desk.

"Mr. Saddler is here." It's the voice of William, her secretary, a grave Mrs. Danvers–y man of about fifty. Lizzie has not yet transplanted Alexi north.

"Okay," she says.

She is still thrown by the extended five- or six-second time delay between William's announcement of visitors and their arrival in her office. It makes her self-conscious, the waiting. More of the imperial hush. She's convinced that the physical distances up here reinforce the sense of executive self-seriousness, since everyone has so much time to prepare for each encounter, to put on a face.

"Welcome, *Lizzie,*" Saddler says, a little whispery, pronouncing her nickname like a plaything. "I'm just back from the big island. Pardon my tizzy." His tan is deep and dark. He was on vacation when she started work, although he's sent several video e-mails from Hawaii to tell her "how thrilled Harold and I are about your joining the MMH team."

"Hello, Hank. Are we supposed to speak in rhyme?"

"Funny! Are you in the swing? Anything you need from me? FYI, I've already got an MPI running on you personally, pre- and post-MMH."

"Nope, I'm fine. Already deep into it," she says, waving at her stacks of papers. "I think I've almost finished repurposing and remastering myself."

" 'Repurposing and remastering myself,' " he says as though she were Noël Coward. "Oh! What a genius bite. I'm going to steal it for Harold. If I may?"

"Sure."

"Magnificent haploxylon," he says, looking over her shoulder. "I'm so glad." He must mean the tree. Every Mose senior executive office has a live white pine tree in his or her office, and three framed vintage Eugène Atget photographs. Lizzie's black-and-white photos are of a butcher's window, a broken stone planter, and a grave. "Well, I'm here. And Harold and I feel so blessed that you're here."

Blessed? "Me too, Hank. Thank you."

"Henry," he says, and leaves.

She returns to the profit-and-loss statements for MotorMind, one of the newly acquired internet companies she's overseeing. She is to meet with the CEO today. MotorMind's main product is Raging Id, a plain-speech search engine that is supposed to enable people anywhere in the vicinity of their computers to blurt out desires—*I want a pound of pancetta overnighted from Umbria and a gift certificate for Pilates training in Sherman Oaks! I want to tell that Jess Burnham she's a liberal cunt! I want to see the* Hindenburg *blowing up!*—and have their wishes fulfilled instantly, invisibly. The MotorMind strategic plan calls Raging Id an example of EUI, or "extroverted user interfacing." (It reminds Lizzie of the Clapper.) In its ten months of existence, according to its P&L, MotorMind has all *L* ($16.2 million), no *P*, and a total income, all in the "Interest & Misc." category, of $174,383. Mose Media Holdings paid $137 million in stock for MotorMind—another price-earnings ratio on the high side of infinity, and a multiple-of-revenue valuation somewhere around 800. The MotorMind numbers make her think that the price they're paying (we're paying? he's paying?) for Fine Technologies may be low. She knows a hundred million is absurdly high, but still, she wonders if it's too low.

The *chime.* "Mr. Mose's office called," Mr. Danvers says. "Mr. Mose is on his way."

Extra-early warning! Mose has not been in New York since she's worked for him. She finds herself quietly freezing in place, papers still on her lap, pen clutched in her hand. She is making a point of doing absolutely nothing different from what she was doing, acting unnaturally natural.

It isn't Myst or Riven that Fifty-nine is like, she realizes, staring at her white pine. It's Japanese Noh drama, just as she was taught in her freshman seminar. Scenery consisting of one painted pine tree. Stylized lines of verse spoken by characters in weird makeup or masks (Saddler), the colloquial *kyôgen* farce episodes (Featherstone), the insane characters (Mr. Danvers) and "festive spirit" characters (Mose, Featherstone). She's pleased with herself. George would love this, if George could bear to listen to her talk about work.

Then she remembers the other stock Noh character—the woman with a tragic destiny. But Noh performers are exclusively male, Lizzie tells herself, feeling silly and superstitious.

Chime. "Mr. Mose is here," announces the voice from the hidden sub-woofer.

And so he is, ambling in, wearing a pinkish suit as fine and silky as carpaccio, and a loose white shirt buttoned at the top. He looks like the richest architect on earth.

"And how is my digital president this fine, fetid morning? Christ! We might as well be in Bangkok."

"Hello, Harold."

"I trust you're not already too disillusioned with the rampant incompetence and venality." He comes closer. "Ah, MotorMind. Did we overpay less or more for them than we overpaid for WhamBam-dot-com?" WhamBam.com is a children's web site that lets kids click on the names of toys and videos and other merchandise written into animated stories and games they can watch and play for free. By clicking on the names, the children receive e-mail advertising for the products— or, if their parents have provided a credit card number and a Wham-Bam.com "weekly allowance," actually buy the stuff. "And TK Corporation—certainly we were fleeced more there than on Motor-Mind?" He sits.

"About the same," she says. She does enjoy Mose. In fact, she is enjoying this job for the first time right now.

"But it does work, correct? Raging Id?"

"It does. And I assume internally, in News, it can be useful right away. For clip research."

"Mmm. I wouldn't predicate too much synergy on the MBC News division. MBC News is being . . . rethought."

How she would love to be able to tell that to George! She knows she shouldn't. Given his mood, she knows she won't. "My only question," she says to Mose, "is how ready regular people are to verbalize everything. You know? 'Send my mother tulips, but don't spend more than thirty-five dollars.' Do people want to say things like that, sitting alone in a room, talking to a machine? Or more embarrassing things. Typing and mouse clicking are discreet."

Mose shakes his head. "People will adapt. Modern people don't need much encouragement to spill their guts. Ten years ago, who'd've thought we could put on a circus like *No Offense, But . . .* every morning." *No Offense, But . . .* is an hour-long talk show–game show hybrid on MBC, hosted by Dr. Juanita. Guests compete for prizes by predicting the embarrassing facts that friends and family will reveal about them on the air—and then, in the "Di$ 'Em Back!" round, try to double their money by revealing embarrassing facts about their friends and family. For five minutes at the end of each show, Dr. Juanita counsels the guests.

"But those people get to be on TV for an hour. That's a big incentive to embarrass yourself."

"Correct," he says. Then he twists his permanent wry smile up a notch. "But what about your sexual-revolution paradigm? The same squares who become accustomed to oral sex also get used to talking dirty when the bedroom door is closed, don't they?"

"I suppose." She suddenly feels fastidious, mousy. "Yeah, that is analogous."

Before the bubble of awkwardness drifts away, out of control, Mose says, "For the record, this is not sexual harassment. Or a hostile sexual environment. And I want a notarized affidavit to that effect from you by noon."

She smiles. "Sure thing, boss. I'll have my people negotiate the language with your people."

"You've already earned your salary this month, Elizabeth. That gadget you got Hank to borrow from your friend at Lucent? Impressed the hell out of everybody in L.A."

He's talking about the Bell Labs panel, consisting of several hundred tiny microphones, that was mounted on the stage at the Mose Media shareholders meeting. Whenever a shareholder in the auditorium rose to make a comment or ask a question, it invisibly found the person and homed in from a hundred yards, amplifying the voice as if he or she were speaking directly into a mike a few inches away. The technology is unsuited to real democratic hurly-burly, since it can only pluck out one speaker at a time. In order to function properly, as Lizzie has told her Lucent friend, it requires extreme politeness, everyone waiting their turn to talk—or else a bully ready to take over, since the thing is programmed to zoom in on the loudest voice in the room. It can deal with orderly corporate meetings and legislative deliberations, or Germany in 1932, but nothing in between.

"Half the audience comments were *about* the damn thing," Mose says. "I'm afraid most of the people there thought we invented it. A misapprehension we made no special effort to correct. Timothy," he says, grinning and shaking his head, "Timothy used it, after we adjourned, to eavesdrop on Hank gossiping with that stupid tart from CNBC, Maria what's her name."

"So I heard. May I ask an impolitic question?"

"*Please.* My favorite sort."

"What is the deal with Timothy? I mean, I like him, I enjoy him, but . . . That's one guy with a very high noise-to-signal ratio."

"Meaning he's a jabbering fool? And an embarrassment?"

" 'Merry Chatterers' is what George calls people like Timothy."

"Does he? What does George call me?"

She smiles, and says nothing.

"*Timothy,*" Mose says, "is perfectly suited to this business in many ways. As nearly as I can tell, the only one of the living TV legends who has a mind is Barry Diller. Barry is an intelligent adult. (And even Barry has his tantrums.) No, most of the genius executives seem a little . . . well, *goofy.* Not stupid, but childlike. Michael Eisner is a giant boy. That's why he's worth a billion dollars. Timothy Featherstone loves watching TV! He's like a kid when he talks about inventing a show based on your game . . ."

"Warps."

He shakes his head again softly. "When I hired Timothy two years ago, he knew more about this ridiculous business than almost anyone I'd ever met." Mose puts his hands on his knees, preparing to go. "That was two years ago. And will this company even be in the network entertainment business two years from now?" He raises his eyebrows and cocks his head, a miniature shrug equivalent. "Maybe not, if you're as successful as I know you'll be." He stands. "But enough doctrinal discussion! I'm boring myself. Mr. Mactier killing himself on *Real Time,* is he?"

"Mmm," Lizzie replies, nodding.

She imagines the conversation at home. *Oh, honey? By the way? I think Harold is going to close down News, can Timothy, and maybe get out of entertainment altogether. Just FYI. Pass the hummus?* Ethics forbid her (don't they?) from giving George any inkling of this conversation. If they were on better terms, she knows she would anyway—she'd at least give him "guidance," as Ben calls it. So this breach has a silver lining: his rage makes her scruples easier. Maybe once *Real Time* is finally up and running and he snaps out of this psycho funk, she'll violate the corporate confidences and begin to let George in on the truth.

"Well," Mose says, "I'm back to L.A. tonight. Over to Vietnam for the start of the galley championships, then Hong Kong. I'm back here a week from Tuesday for our Elizabeth Zimbalist celebratory dinner. And—only a month late—mirabile dictu, *Real Time!*"

Lizzie thinks she hears a trace of derisive fake enthusiasm in the way he pronounces the name of the show.

"Say," he says, "we don't want to be in the internet chat-room business in the Chinese 'special economic zones,' do we?"

"I doubt it."

"I thought not. Leave the People's Republic to Rupert. Farewell, my dear."

"So when do you start fucking Harold?" George said in their one screaming fight about her Mose deal. "Or am I behind the curve on that, too?" *Poor, silly, stupid George,* she thinks, contemplating her magnificent haploxylon (and the trees of the park behind it like a painted theatrical scrim). But then Lizzie thinks: she's talking more to Harold Mose these days than to George, and Mose doesn't even live in New York. She thinks: the conversation with her boss just now was more civilized and relaxed, smarter and sexier, than any encounter she's had with her husband in a month. As the next thought begins to form (Would Harold Mose, spotted anonymously at a party or a restaurant, make her How Many Guys list?), she bears down on Penn McNabb's one-sentence mission statement justifying the $327 million Mose Media Holdings paid for his company: "Although the very name of TK Corporation proudly privileges the central wealth-creation fact of the New Economy—that the precise shape of the future as well as its component technologies are perpetually embryonic, perpetually 'TK,' or *to come*—there can be no question that our proprietary technology, Ultra-Streaming Video®, will be a mission-critical feature of that unfolding multimedia future."

3 3

His brain aches. He feels sick. The air and the light are rotten and inescapable. He keeps a bottle of Visine and a green plastic pint of Mylanta in his briefcase. There is not enough time. There is never enough time, of course. But this is worse. This is the worst. The Postshakedown Breakdown, the staff is calling it. They mean it as a cocky, making-their-TV-bones joke, *Postshakedown Breakdown,* a password to snicker in the fluorescent buzz over take-out pizza and Dr Pepper. It's all a crazy multimillion-dollar dorm party for them, a two-month all-nighter to finish the term papers and cram for exams. They're young. It's a job. They're not responsible.

The sixteen-hour days on *Real Time* mostly keep his mind off Lizzie, twenty-one floors above, but this compensation has not occurred to George. He does think, when he arrives alone at six-thirty or seven, before the regular guards are at work, that his elevator bank, for the thirtieth through the fifty-eighth floors, is different from hers. Until the sixth of June, he was oblivious to the Mose Media Holdings elevator-bank hierarchy. Now, even though he's grateful for the lobby separation, for the thick, high, stone-and-wood bundling board between them, the sight each morning of the express elevator to Fifty-nine enrages him, but for just an instant, so quickly he doesn't even register it as a distinct speck of anger.

He's angry at Molly Cramer, who somehow got a dub of the Friday shakedown show. Cramer accused George, "the millionaire pro-heroin producer," of "apparently pulling the plug on his Deep Throat 'exposé' for fear of angering his liberal media buddies." He's angry at *Time* for calling *Real Time,* before the show has aired, before he's even finished inventing it, "a highly worrisome new postmodern milestone in the helter-skelter morphing of fact into fiction and news into entertainment." (If they only knew: he turned down a videotape of Michael Jackson swimming with Joey Heatherton and two dolphins in a pool of water dyed red, and not just because of Jackson's stipulation that the on-air copy contain the words *bizarre* and *kinky.*) "Fucking *Time* magazine," he ranted to Timothy Featherstone, "this from the company that publishes *InStyle* and puts pay-per-view porno on my cable TV and owns professional wrestling." He got angry when Featherstone replied that *InStyle* is his and Ng's favorite magazine. He's angry at Hank Saddler, for telling him "Harold and I found BetaWeek a little buggy," and for coming down to his office on Monday to complain about George's quoted claim in *Time* that "our Friday news segments will be the hardest news in prime time." "I don't need to tell you, George," Saddler said, "that the perception of 'hard news' is ratings poison. And 'hard' can also strike people as meaning difficult to understand, or painful, which I know you don't want. Especially given your own MPI trendline." He's angry at himself for giving Saddler the go-ahead to use "Postmodern milestone!" as a blurb in the newspaper ads for the show. In her e-mail about the *Time* story, Lizzie tried to laugh off his quote denigrating MBC News coverage of yoga and rock climbing and video games, but her ha-ha-ha magnanimity had also made him angry.

It was easier when she was angry too, that first night. "You're acting like a fucking *child,* George," she said to him, "a pathetic, disturbed child. There's no cabal plotting against George Mactier. It's a new job. And it's a business deal that makes sense for me. For *us,* for Christ's sake. *Period.*" Okay, sell the company. Okay, go to work up on Fifty-nine. But why didn't she let him know she was going to Mose's apartment? (George has never been to the apartment. George has never been invited to a golf outing with the guys from Fifty-nine, either, an exclusion for which he's been grateful until now.) What had made her tell Mose about Inscrutable Hardasses and Merry Chatterers? Featherstone claimed he wasn't pissed off at George ("I've been called worse, believe me"), but he seemed upset. Probably what Featherstone overheard in Mose's apartment that morning ("They were talking blowjobs, man, straight up") *was,* as she insisted (with that patronizing chuckle), "a completely metaphorical discussion of bandwidth and interactivity." But who chose the metaphor? And who deleted the files from the laptop? Who sneaked into his desk at home sometime in the last couple of months, dug out the PowerBook, and deleted HAROLD MEMO and BLAH-BLAH-BLAH NOTES? He has no evidence, but the files didn't evaporate. And he never did read them. "You're too honest, Mactier," Ben has always said, and George has always taken it as a backhanded compliment, never as a warning.

George is angry that he's going to be working all weekend, through the Fourth, while Lizzie and the kids are out in East Hampton with Ben. He was angry, at first, about the postponement of the premiere. "One piece of event programming at a time, G-man," Featherstone said. Starting Monday, MBC will be broadcasting the Classical Galley world championship race, live by satellite, across the South China Sea from Ho Chi Minh City to Bandar Seri Begawan. "It'll give you more time for testing and tweaking your baby," he'd said, "supertesting and supertweaking."

But Featherstone is right. The extra month to test *Real Time* has been useful. The test screenings have shown him how blurry the lines are, for most viewers, between fiction and nonfiction. They've shown him that reality and make-believe are more fungible, for most viewers, than he'd dreamed possible. The month has given him time to fight the fights with Fifty-nine *before* the show is on the air rather than after. The scores of the first regular testings of the Tuesday and Thursday shakedown shows, awarded by 337 strangers in the San Fernando Valley, are encouraging. A 100 is average, and the shows got a 120. The Friday news hour, however, tested poorly, as George knew it would. He has done his best for months to lowball Fifty-nine's expectations about the Friday hour. "It's *news,*" George said when the disappointing number came in.

"Real news." But as Featherstone said, "Seventy is still seventy, George, even if you expect seventy. Would you *want* to fuck the ugly ho just because your boy told you beforehand she wasn't yummy?"

In the twenty-two focus groups held around the country (in Tucson, Charlottesville, and Omaha), the responses became more precise, refined. George was surprised to learn that some of the participants were hooked up to polygraphs as they watched the show. "Viewers want more frequent and 'real-seeming' comedy," the research report summarized, "and they want the dramatic 'news' interludes used only occasionally, as a way of providing the anchor and correspondent characters with something to react to, and thus giving them more human dimensionality."

The highest negatives in any of the three shows were for the segment on Kim Jong-Il, the North Korean dictator, and for Francesca Mahoney's spiky hair and dark lipstick.

"I guess it's too bad Kim tested poorly," George told the head of the audience-research firm an hour ago, "but he was displaying his secret biological weapons arsenal. It was news. And he's a bad *guy.*"

"We understand," the woman said, "but it wasn't just the *character* Jong-Il that the audience didn't feel positively about, it was his *country.*"

"So North Korea tested badly?" George asked. It was the first time this month he remembers smiling.

"Exactly. We showed one of the Tucson focus groups a redubbed segment, with 'northern Japan' looped in over all the North Korea mentions? Scored almost ninety percent higher positives. See what I'm saying?"

"I guess you're saying keep the foreign news to a minimum, unless it's Tom Hanks and Bill Clinton at a commemorative ceremony on Omaha Beach."

"That *was* fantastic. And your over-fifties are more interested in international events. The Mexican war, with Francesca under fire, tested pretty well even among eighteen-to-thirty-fours. Mexico is well known."

"A familiar *brand,*" Saddler interjected.

The research woman nodded. "Now, your other foreign story had a different problem, an interesting problem, more along the real-unreal axis."

"The Kurd piece?" George said.

"A majority of our test audiences thought 'the Kurds' were a fictional people, invented by the writers for the program. The end of the story scored pretty high, but only because viewers thought the word *Kurdistan* was, you know, a punch line—they found it funny. Unfortunately, most people today just don't know that Kurdistan is an actual place."

Since George had decided to kill the piece anyway, he didn't bother explaining that the Kurds have no homeland, and that Kurdistan is not currently an actual place. After she left, Saddler told George he had "one more major bee to insert in your bonnet." He said that since the two anchors and two of the three chief *Real Time* correspondents are white, Fifty-nine wants George to assign more stories *about* people of color.

"I know you agree, George, that this is the right thing to do."

"What if the stories turn out to be negative?"

"Why would they be?" Saddler replied. George didn't answer. "Also? Diversity-wise, you might want to task your folks to find African-Americans with darker skin tone, and Asian people who look more, you know, *ethnic*. Forty-three percent of your test groups didn't even realize that Cole Granger is black! On the other hand," Saddler said, checking a printout, "almost twenty-seven percent thought Francesca Mahoney was 'other,' so that's an unanticipated plus. But you don't want to go to the trouble of making a batch of quesadillas and have everyone think it's just grilled cheese, do you?" Saddler also asked if he had considered "preteen leveraging of the *Real Time* brand." He meant a children's version of the show. George said he's absolutely considered it. But not seriously, George failed to add, since children's TV news programs are nonstarters. They seem redundant and unnecessary, not dumbed down so much as made overfriendly and condescending. And George has always understood why. His *Real Time* show next Friday—an entire hour of hard news, in prime time—will consist of approximately five thousand spoken words, or about the same number contained in an issue of *Weekly Reader*. Not one of those words, as a matter of network policy, is supposed to surpass the understanding of an average seventh grader. In a real sense, TV news is already news for children. *Is that a good thing or a bad thing, Daddy?*

George is now alone in his office, fast-forwarding again through the shakedown shows in their so-called "data-rich" form. The screen looks like a financial news channel, with numbers and abbreviations moving across the bright red lower quarter of the screen. Instead of stock prices, though, the numbers and letters are a distillation of all the salient audience-testing research, synchronized to the relevant moments of the shows. In the second-act opener of the Thursday show, 32% NEG 18–49 M (SMILE: POS) scrolls by as Jess Burnham is shown leaving her house and hailing a taxi on Hudson Street, replaced by 13% NEG 18–34 M (HAIR: NEG) as soon as the show cuts to Francesca awakened in bed by a phone call from her field producer in Mexico City. Later, George sees that the research woman was absolutely right about Kim Jong-Il—under the shaky video of him grinning and looking into a vial of anthrax, the screen says 68% NEG AVE ALL DEMOS (HAIR & SMILE: NEG).

Cole Granger's teasing piece about the government's embrace of "alternative health" tested well, particularly among men. The improvised news-staff discussions and arguments about the Deep Throat exposé in the Tuesday and Thursday shows tested extremely well (95% POS >34 M/F), although George pulled the story from the news-hour lineup the afternoon of shakedown Friday—not because of any pressure from his liberal media buddies, but because Sylvia Boudreau Shepley started hedging on whether Deep Throat was in fact George Bush or Bush together with Alexander Haig and Richard Nixon's son-in-law, David Eisenhower.

The shows were tested with commercials plugged in, so that the test audiences would experience the programs, the research woman said, "in a more authentic context." George is a little surprised to see that on the data-rich tape, a stream of test results flows along with the ads as well. The commercials test very positively, generally as well as the shows, and sometimes better. "Slightly apples-and-oranges," she said, "but if it's any consolation, it's extremely common for program material to test lower than adjacent advertising." And now, as a handheld two-shot of Jess and Cole discussing the Republican convention fades to black and is replaced by a jaw-droppingly gorgeous thirty seconds for Coke—an old-fashioned bottle zooming through space, finally turning inside out and becoming the universe—he sees why. It's entirely a function of budgets. Second for second, the budget of that miraculous, inspiring Coke ad was a hundred times his budget for the Friday show, twenty-five times his big-budget Tuesday and Thursday shows. Are the killing hours and the panicky solitude making him cynical? Or has he been naïve? Why has it taken him fifteen years in television to notice that the budget disparity between ads and shows may be the point of television?

He needs to look at something old and plain. George slides in another tape, a compilation of raw archival footage, mostly black-and-white, and mutes the sound. First up are two minutes of slow pans from thirty-five years ago, Bobby Kennedy campaigning for the Senate in Manhattan. George really isn't in the Kennedy thrall, never has been, but both the phenomenon and his own bewilderment fascinate him, as with professional wrestling and opera.

If they don't nail Deep Throat by next week, George plans to run the first "Kennedy World" in week one. "Kennedy World" is a simple idea: every Friday, a minute or less on a Kennedy, newsy if possible, elegiac or enthusiastic or irreverent, depending. He figures the feature will either run out of steam after a couple of months or bloom into its own program—"Hell, dude, its own *channel*," Timothy says. Watching Bobby from the sixties, with Jack and their little brother, it occurs to George that even black-and-white footage shot today looks thirty-five years old. He wonders if he ought to shoot all the contemporary "Kennedy World" segments—John Jr. and Caroline, Bobby Jr. and Patrick and Joe, Maria and Arnold, whomever—in black-and-white, as a signature style of the feature. He doesn't mean to keep thinking about the show.

Bobby's funeral is in color, on videotape. Teddy, in his neck brace on the Vineyard in the summer of 1969, looks hardly more dazed and callow than he did seven years earlier, when everything was fine; maybe demeanor is destiny. A color reenactment shot of the limousines driving through Dealey Plaza in Dallas, from 1963, pans up the School Book Depository and zooms in on the black-and-yellow Hertz billboard on the roof. As the scratchy gray leader comes up, George steps toward the TV to shut it off, but he stops when a 6-5-4-3-2 Academy leader appears, and then an old TV commercial, so familiar from ages ago: the fedora'd gray-flannel man falling from the sky in a sitting position and gliding smartly into the driver's seat of a speeding Hertz convertible. Cut onto the end of the Hertz ad are a series of period movie car crashes, oversaturated long shots of old Barracudas and Mustangs and Cougars leaping off California cliffs and exploding in fireballs. George is reminded of the remarkable video loop Max made earlier this year on the computer from two scenes he'd taped off TV, one from Nick at Nite and the other from an *American Sportsman* rerun. He'd intercut back and forth between the shot from the opening of *The Mary Tyler Moore Show* where she throws her cap in the air, and a clip of Joe Namath firing a shotgun into the sky.

George giggles the way he giggled tripping on LSD twenty-five years ago, gaga about receiving signs from a God in whom he declined to believe even as he was receiving the signs. He remembers what Lizzie said one night, drinking her martini, months ago, about life becoming art. He isn't sure why his eyes are wet and his throat is tight, but it has nothing to do with Camelot. He wipes his shirtsleeve quickly across his face, and remembers to breathe.

"Daisy?" he shouts. "Who put together this Kennedy reel? Was it Davey?"

Daisy appears. "No one. I mean, it came straight from the clip place."

"Can you get me Jude McAllister in Washington? I need to talk to him about the Deep Throat piece."

"Aye-aye, sir."

Daisy never makes him angry. Maybe after he becomes a certified cuckold (and he's thrown out of MBC, and show business, and barred from reentering real journalism), he'll have an affair with ironic, wise, smiling Daisy Moore. The children's resentment of Daddy's girlfriend would abate if she was black, he thinks.

At the threshold, Daisy turns back. "George?" she says. "I know this is the last thing you need to think about. But would it be awful if I took a two-week holiday in August? It looks like Cole and I are getting married. On the sixth."

"Daisy! Congratulations! That's fantastic." *Your wedding is on the fifty-fifth anniversary of Hiroshima,* he thinks. "The first *Real Time* marriage!" he says. George hasn't known she's been serious with Cole Granger. "Take as much time as you need." *But just a thought—you and I should*

probably begin this affair right away. That way, only one of us will be an adul-
terer officially, plus, as I understand it, I'd be grandfathered in. "And tell Cole
that if the result of this is my losing you, he's fired." Her smile is huge.
You wouldn't mind if I fist-fucked you in the ass, would you, Daisy? With the
stump? You're a plucky girl. I don't think you would mind. Would you?

3 4

"Yeah, it sliced," Randy says, "but you hit the hell out of it. Didn't she, Doug?"

"She did. She really did. Real power."

"No wonder Harold is so excited," Randy says. "He knows you can keep us bozos from Fifty-nine on our toes out here on Friday afternoons."

All four chuckle. She hands her club to the caddie. She and Doug and Randy and Steve begin to walk toward the green from the ladies' tee, which is many yards in front of the regular tee. The ladies' tee, golf's gesture of built-in old-line affirmative action, is one of the reasons she's never really liked the game, even when the old-fashioned phrase is politically corrected to "forward tee."

"Where do you mostly play, Elizabeth?" Doug asks.

"I mostly don't," Lizzie says. "As a kid I played a lot. In Los Angeles and Palm Springs."

"Whereabouts in Palm Springs?" Randy asks.

"La Quinta?"

"Super course," says Randy.

"*Super* course," Steve agrees.

"Haven't played it," says Doug. "I like the Gary Player Signature Course out there. I haven't played La Quinta."

"It's super," says Randy. "Next time you're in Burbank, you should try to make it out."

"It's nice," Lizzie agrees. "I love that cheesy old clubhouse. Very Palm Springs '67."

No one says a thing for a while.

"You see there," says Randy to Steve and Doug, gesturing off to the left, "how they've pushed that long grass way back from where it was two summers ago? Easier to get some speed play going."

"They fill up some of the courses so much now," says Doug, "it takes five hours sometimes just to play a round."

"How long did it take us to do eighteen last summer at Piping Rock?" Randy asks Steve. "At that charity tournament with that guy from Disney who went to AOL, Brian . . . Brian . . . ?"

"Brian Gardner," Steve says.

"Right. We were out there six hours."

"Brian Gardner quit Disney for AOL?" Lizzie says. "I didn't know that. He is such a loser. Brian Gardner's perfect for AOL, isn't he?"

Again she has managed to stop the conversation cold. The rest of the hole, she doesn't say a word.

Randy and Doug are colleagues from Fifty-nine. The last time Lizzie played golf was on a foundation staff outing at Maidstone, eleven years ago to the day. She remembers feeling very Jewish then, too. George stayed back at the Goulds' in East Hampton. She remembers walking up Ben's big wooden porch after the round, sweaty in her Lilly Pulitzer culottes and teal shell and pigtails and NOSFERATU baseball cap, and George seeing her and rushing out with his finger to his lips because Sarah was napping inside, then taking her by the hand to the pool house and latching the door. She never got the glove off her left hand. "I'm sorry," he said when they'd finished, "but the Muffy-wear makes me completely horny." That was the day—June 30, 1989—they conceived Max.

She noticed a memo this week from Doug, copied to about a thousand Mose Media Holdings executives, entitled "Quality Circles 2001: A New MBO at MMH." MBO, she knows, stands for management by objective, which has always struck her as a tautologous concept. "So,

Doug," she says, trying again, a few holes later, "you're head of strategic planning?"

"EVP organizational and management effectiveness, competitive intelligence, and continuous improvement," he replies. "Most of the strategic support specialists work under me—eight FTEs. You and I will definitely interface."

"And you report to Harold?"

She notices Randy and Steve smile.

"I report to Arnold," Doug says, referring to Arnold Vlig, the COO, a dour, sleepy-looking lawyer who very seldom leaves his office on Fifty-nine.

Randy, the one who invited her along, is president of sales and marketing. Steve is a senior vice president, and he explained as they teed off what his job is—she heard the phrases "external reporting," "demand planning," and "loss mitigation." She has no idea what Steve does, or what floor he works on.

"I understand you were responsible for that big microphone dish for the stockholders meeting," Randy says. He gives a thumbs-up. "Super device. Folks were impressed. It was very impressive."

"It was," Steve says. He catches Randy's glance. "I mean, people *told* me it really was."

"Did you all hear about that Microsoft analyst presentation yesterday?" Randy asks.

"So-so quarter, I understand," Doug says.

Randy makes his putt.

"— putt," Doug tells him. Whenever they compliment each other, Lizzie has noticed, they swallow the adjectives completely. Except when they're speaking to her, *nice* and *good* are never actually uttered. This must be a piece of boy-golfer protocol her father never told her about.

"No, this wild thing with the phones and pagers," Randy says. "It sounded hilarious."

Randy explains that five minutes into one of Microsoft's end-of-the-fiscal-year Wall Street shows, the phones and pagers of everyone in the room went off at the same time, fifty little devices simultaneously trilling, beeping, dinging, vibrating.

"Five minutes later, they're in the middle of demonstrating Open Windows, and then it happens *again*. Everything's beeping. So then, five minutes after that, everybody's waiting for it to happen a third time. And nothing happens. People are laughing and talking, and it's hard for the Microsoft guys to get the thing back on track. But then, ten minutes after that, all the phones and beepers start going off in *sequence,* one after another, every two seconds, around and around in a loop. They finally had to stop the meeting."

"It was a prank?" Lizzie asks, smiling naturally for the first time this afternoon.

Randy nods. "The *Post* said Gates and Ballmer got e-mails from the practical jokers saying, 'You have been circle-jerked, jerks. Happy 25th anniversary.' Sounded *hilarious.*"

"It sure does," says Steve.

She asks Steve, trying to be friendly, "What losses have you mitigated lately?" He smiles and nods. Now she has run out of small talk. As they prepare to tee off on the fourth hole, a long par three, Randy says, "Is this a great hole, or what?"

"That's for sure," Steve replies. "Two hundred fourteen?"

"Two-fourteen on the card," Randy says. "Pin's back, so call it two-twenty-five."

"So," Doug says to Lizzie, "I hope you're getting on our creatives about interactivity. Have you seen my Convergence Objectives memo? One of the areas we can really leverage, and *use* MBC show ownership, is getting producers to let the viewers interact with advertising. As a form of entertainment. The advertising becomes an entertainment component. And vice versa. You're using the five-wood, Rand?"

Randy swings. His ball lands a few yards from the green.

"His ball lands just short," Doug says, as if he were a TV announcer. "Chip and a putt."

"We call it *fungibility,*" Randy says to Lizzie. "Fungibility is the way we're selling the net to advertisers. So when the character on the show is feeding the cat or in the bathroom, the gal at home will be able to push a button on her remote, and automatically receive literature about Tender Vittles or Oil of Olay or what have you. Instant customer."

"Exactly," Steve says.

"We need to be out in front to extend the advertising surfaces," Doug says. "I want us to take a leadership role in product-based programs."

"Like, what," Lizzie says, smiling, unable to control herself, "a show about elves that Keebler would sponsor?"

"Is that one of the ones Featherstone's got in the pipeline?" Randy asks seriously. "I haven't seen that on the development lists. Very clever."

"*Very* clever," Steve says. He swings. His shot is short, and lands in the pond.

"*Fuck* me!" he says. He glances at Lizzie.

"Steverino gets kettle-holed," Doug says.

Lizzie knows kettle holes from rock climbing. They're ponds formed by glaciers.

"I thought that looked like a kettle hole," she says. "This whole moraine is, what, twenty thousand years old?"

The men shrug and say nothing.

Randy says to Lizzie as she prepares to swing, "I read in the *News* that on *Real Time* they're planning to use that same digital video-insert technology that Barry Stengel got canned for. It said they're going to pretend one of their stars is in California with Charles Manson even though he won't really be."

"Sounds cool," Doug says.

"Not to me it doesn't," Steve says. "It sounds *wrong*."

Lizzie pulls her shot and ends up in the sand trap.

George? Lizzie. The good news is you'll only have to write one scene into Real Time *promoting Tender Vittles. The bad news is—and I'm speaking here as an MMH EVP, to whom you may have dotted-line reporting responsibility—I forbid you to use the live video-insert technology.* At least she won't be obliged to deal with this for another five days, until after the Fourth.

"In the bunker," Steve says.

"Yup," Randy says, smirking slightly. "It's a hard green to hit and hard to hold, this one."

The next three hours are the longest of Lizzie's life, a sun-baked, stifling drone of FTEs and postentertainment scenarios, Output Management and extended advertising surfaces.

As they step off the last green and Randy pulls a bizarre pitching wedge from his bag in the back of his cart, he asks, "So, is Gerald joining you out here for the weekend?"

"George. No, he's stuck in the city, working. On *Real Time*."

Randy's special club is not a real club at all. It has a clear acrylic shaft with a screw-off cap. Inside are six half-foot-long cigars laid end to end.

"Lady? Gentlemen? A post-eighteen Fuente Fuente?"

She takes one. Her father started giving her cigars to smoke when she was eleven, as a kind of novelty act to amuse his friends. Lighting up Randy's Fuente Fuente, she self-consciously tries to look unself-conscious. Before they begin smoking, the rest of her foursome heads for a corner of the clubhouse veranda, where they join five other sweaty men standing at a small circular bar. Above the bar is a circle of Gatorade jugs hanging upside down, each one encased in a fancy silver bracket. Randy, Doug, and Steve grab special double-length drinking straws from a dispenser, plunge a sharpened tip up into a rubber flange in one of the suspended jugs, and begin sucking on the other end. The height of the jugs requires even the tallest men to tip their chins up to drink. Lizzie smokes, watching them. She thinks of Buster Grinspoon's line about working for big companies, "*I really don't operate well in hives.*" Randy, smiling and sucking, glances over and gives her a thumbs-up.

At this time of day, you can almost hear the rumble of the approaching battalions. In the primping and strained smiles of the locals you can sense the excitement and dread. Is being ignored preferable to being abused? Will the provisions be sufficient? This time, will the occupiers be kind? The leading edge of the eastbound invasion force—BMWs and Porsches, Lexuses and Infinitis, thousands of spotless, perfectly machined vehicles—is still some miles distant. By the time the main convoy rolls into town, it will have slowed to twenty miles per hour, the speed of a panzer assault column. It is three thirty-five in Bridgehampton on the Friday before the Fourth of July, 2000.

In the tiny gravel parking lot of a bar and restaurant that opened a month ago with the cute, cute name Peggy's (Formerly Morty's), Ben Gould's driver, Melik, stands by the Mercedes S1000, reading. As a red Land Cruiser speeds past on Montauk Highway, driven by a woman still sneering and smacking her lips from the fulsome, acrid aftertaste of a cigar, Melik does not look up from his *Financial Times*.

Inside Peggy's (Formerly Morty's), Ben sits in ragged blue jeans and logo-free T-shirt at a table in the front, nursing a club soda, reading. He left the city before the market closed—the traffic, this meeting—but his StarTac 9900 sits on the table, the line open to Dianne and his traders back in the Big Room on lower Broadway. Peter Sutherland

and his boss, Riley Dugger—the two men joining him for a drink—
are coming straight from a long lunch, and have called to say they'll be
late.

Ben has finished the Friday research reports from his trading stack,
including the half page on Mose Media Holdings. Mose, as he figured,
is taking a gigantic charge for Fine Technologies, almost the whole purchase price, just like he's doing for TK Corporation and MotorMind
and all the rest of the *exciting* little companies he's bought to jack up his
stock price. He overpaid, but his stock still went back up, as Ben knew
it would, and now he's overstating the write-down to try to give next
quarter's earnings some artificial pump—win, win, win! The report
makes Ben happy all over again that he's sold his shares over the last two
weeks. "Nothing against the company or you, Lizzie," he told her, "but
when the fucking guy pays *a hundred million,* and every analyst from
here to San Francisco is calling Mose a 'strong buy,' I got to get out. I'm
loyal to *you;* I'm not loyal to stock." She seemed to get it, although
civilians never really do. He only wishes he could have started unloading his 49,000 shares of Mose when it was still north of 52, as soon as
she called him about her acquisition. But he's on the Fine Technologies
board; that was material, nonpublic information. He was obliged to wait
to trade until the news became public a few days later. To sell earlier
would have been a violation of the Securities Exchange Act of 1934, a
stupid as well as felonious insider trade; making the extra two or three
dollars a share wasn't worth a slam-dunk indictment. But when that
Friday morning rolled around, Ben sure was prepared to sell, everything
in place, Melucci on the wire to his guy on the turret at the Merrill
trading desk, ready and aimed the second the news hit the Bloomberg
and Reuters and Dow-Jones, *boom!*—a convenient head start, thanks to
the material, nonpublic information in Ben's possession. Now he's
wondering, though, whether he should get back in, go long Mose once
more. If their movie-theater swap for the Dugger Broadcasting stations
really goes through, and Mose doesn't get screwed on the price (or even
if he does), the market will start loving Mose Media Holdings again.
And when Lizzie's sale is completed in a couple of weeks, Ben's 25 percent piece of her company will be automatically transformed into a
new load of Mose stock. He's not sure whether he should keep it or
dump it. He needs some reliable information, even a good sniff of reliable information.

It's three thirty-six. Where are goddamn Sutherland and his boss? Ben pulls the *Post* over. It's a slow news day when OUR $9 MIL BILL BILL fills the front page. (The *Post* says Clinton's trip by vintage PT boat from Georgica Pond to Manhattan on Tuesday, as part of the huge Op-Sail 2000 spectacle, will cost the city, state, and federal governments an extra nine million dollars.) When Ben spots the MICROSOFT POOH-POOHS "KILL BILL G" PRANKSTER CALLS headline in the *Post,* he has an adrenaline rush. He grips the paper and zooms in. "A Microsoft spokesman speculated," he reads, "that the unusual version of yesterday's date in the pranksters' e-mail, '29/6/00,' with the month and day reversed from normal American style, could mean that the elaborate prank call originated in Europe. After predicting the 'virtual deaths' of the multibillionaire geek mogul and his bald pit bull #2, 'like the corporate Tamagotchi Frankensteins they are,' the wacko practical jokers wished Gates and Ballmer 'a very happy 25th birthday on 29/11,' and closed their weird message with the salutation, 'FUD You!' A company spokesman said that November 29, 1975, was the date of the first recorded reference by Gates to the name Microsoft. FUD is a well-known Microsoft slang, which stands for the corporate strategy of sowing 'fear, uncertainty, and doubt' among business rivals." Ben's smile shrinks away. He puts down the paper and takes a sip of his club soda. He looks out at the sunny day, analyzing, calculating, knowing what he knows.

A black limo pulls up directly in front, and its driver scurries out to open the rear door. A couple of local teenagers on the sidewalk stop and stare. For all the billionaires and famous people out here in the summer, stretch Cadillac limousines (as opposed to $75,000 sedans and sports cars and SUVs) are rather rare. A grinning Peter Sutherland, wearing a blue blazer over yellow pants and a pink polo shirt, immediately lurches out, turns, and offers his hand to another, much bigger, fatter man, wearing pink pants and a yellow polo shirt and carrying a blue blazer. It's Riley Dugger, the chairman, CEO, and largest shareholder of Dugger Broadcasting. As he huffs and finally yanks himself up out of the backseat, his glasses fall off his face into the gutter. Sutherland retrieves them as the driver helps the big guy toward the front door of Peggy's (Formerly Morty's).

In his *Forbes* 400 entry this year, Dugger was called "a rough-hewn, plainspoken Coloradan" and "an ebullient self-made man of large appetites." Ben smiles. *It's three-forty in the afternoon and they're shitfaced,* he thinks. *This could be good.* Until three months ago, his 351,000 shares made him the fifth-largest holder of Dugger stock. After Sutherland signaled to Ben on the phone that the second quarter looked bad, Bennett Gould Partners liquidated most of that position. But Ben is an investor, and he can easily buy another half million shares of Dugger next year, or next week, so the chairman and his CFO are happy to hook up for a drink since they're in the neighborhood.

"Pete! Mr. Dugger! Welcome to the Hamptons, gentlemen."

Dugger thunders over to Ben and shakes his hand like a man tearing a drumstick from a turkey. "Great to be with you, Bennett! You know there wasn't a single goddamn movie star anywhere over in . . . where the fuck was that?"

"Southampton," Peter Sutherland says, grinning continuously.

"Where the hell *is* Kate Capshaw?!? Where's Kim Basinger?!? Where's Kathleen Turner?!? How long will it take us to get a couple of great big icy-cold Tanqueray gimlets, straight up? You're a casual little fucker, aren't you?" he says to Ben, guffawing as he slams down into a chair and fishes a Lucky Strike from his battered pack. "Who do I have to bribe to smoke a cigarette in this fucking place?"

Ben grabs a matchbox off the bar and lights Dugger.

Sutherland sits, and continues grinning.

"Happy FY 2001!" Ben says, lifting his glass of beer. The new fiscal year starts tomorrow.

"Says who?" Dugger howls. "It's not fucking happy for my business, I'll tell you. Not a bit fucking happy."

"Come on!" Ben says, jollying him along. "Your top line is exploding, and the bottom line on your stations is still pretty great."

"The fucking *stations.*" A waitress approaches carefully with the two martini glasses filled to the brim with gin. "Thank you, darling. Are you Christie Brinkley? I think you're Christie Brinkley, aren't you? Incognito. I tell you, sweetheart—don't spill!—I'd love to get you for a few minutes in *my* cognito." He guffaws again. "Cheers. No, Benjamin, we have had an outstanding fucking ride on the stations, but the train has reached the terminal. Last stop, everybody off. It ain't 1998 anymore. Dugger Broadcasting has seen $95 a share for the last time. You know that, Ben. That's why you sold out. Smart fucking move, boy, I'll tell you. Hell, our goddamn costs remind me of my first wife—I woke up one day and that girl was fat as a hog! (I'm not blaming you, Peter.) And this digital bullshit and 'convergence' bullshit is not going to make me a fucking dime in my lifetime, I'll tell you that. Not one fucking Roosevelt dime. The easy money is all gone." He's finished half his gimlet already.

The market doesn't close for fifteen minutes. Ben still has time to grab his StarTac and make a bet against Dugger Broadcasting. Or not even grab it. The line's open. *Heffernan,* he thinks of yelling toward the phone, *buy me 200 August 85 puts on Dugger now!*

"But I thought you were going to unload the station group on Mose? He's got to have it for the network, or he's stuck. In my opinion."

"The board," Sutherland says.

Dugger finishes the rest of his drink in one gulp. "Oh, Harold wants my stations. Harold Mose would pay through his prissy Canadian nose. Big time. But my fucking white-shoe, never-run-a-fucking-entertainment-operation, local-broadcasting-is-your-core-competency *board* doesn't want to let go of these fucking third-rate stations. Sure, they minted money for a few years, but that mint is closing, son! That's what the *board* won't see. You don't have a board, do you, Benjamin? You're one fortunate SOB, I'll tell you that right now."

Dugger lights another Lucky, leans back, and roars over to the waitress. "Christie? I'd like to pay you five hundred dollars American for another one of those good cocktails—*if* you'll join us for one yourself?"

"So," Ben says, "your board's a little risk-averse, are they?"

"Hell, I'm risk-averse. They're just pussies, *stupid* pussies, since they don't believe me when I tell them we have to do the Mose deal before the whole goddamn world knows that our margins are shooting south like the fucking Special Forces through Mexico." He does a sloshed little double take. "Benjamin! Why don't *you* become a director of Dugger Broadcasting, Benjamin?" He turns to Sutherland. "Why in Sam Hill didn't we think of this before, Petey?" He leans close to Ben. "I'm five hundred percent serious. I want you to think about it." He pushes himself up and knocks his chair backward, but catches it before it hits the floor. "Urination break," he says, stomping off toward the men's room.

"Work must be fun for you, Pete," Ben says.

"It's never dull."

The waitress brings Dugger's second drink, and Sutherland and Ben both order sparkling water.

"So," Ben says softly to Sutherland, "it sounds like the deal with Mose for the stations is a nonstarter."

Sutherland shrugs. "Unless he can get another two votes to go his way on the board."

"The kids are good?" Ben asks.

"Just great. Jasper's hitting .318."

Ben nods. "Fantastic."

The Perriers arrive. Each man takes a sip, and then another.

"I think your boss is setting a new marathon peeing record."

"Yeah," Sutherland says, smiling a little nervously. He heads back to the bathroom.

Ben has told Lizzie he'll walk on the beach with her and the kids at four-thirty, and it's a fifteen-minute drive back to the house. He checks his watch. It's ten until four. After the holiday, first thing Wednesday morning, he's going to short Dugger Broadcasting.

"*Help!* Emergency! 911! Call 911, *somebody*! There's a man dying! Please!" It's Sutherland screaming from inside the bathroom, where he's kneeling on the floor, holding the door open with one hand.

Ben leaps to the bar and grabs the telephone out of the bartender's hand, then jabs the three numbers.

Poor Riley Dugger, Ben thinks. He can't stop the next thought: very bad news for Dugger Broadcasting shares, between no sale of the stations, probate hell (multiple wives, eight children), estate taxes, and no more Riley Dugger to run the thing. Nor can he stop the thought after that: very bad news for Mose Media Holdings and MBC, since their last chance to acquire the Dugger Broadcasting stations is disappearing in there on the floor. Lose, lose, lose.

He describes the emergency to the 911 dispatcher, gives the address, and rushes back to the bathroom. Dugger has one leg cocked back under his butt, his head in a puddle under the urinal. His yellow shirt is pulled up to his neck. His face is blue. His penis, big and also blue, hangs out of his pink trousers. Peter Sutherland is pumping on his bare, hairless chest.

"My car and driver are right outside," Ben says.

"No," Sutherland says between pumps, "the ambulance"— *hlawwnh!*—"is best"—*hlawwnh, hlawwnh!*—"you go out"—*hlawwnh!*— "wait for them"—*hlawwnh, hlawwnh, hlawwnh, hlawwnh!*

Ben walks back to the front. The bartender asks how Dugger's doing. Ben shrugs. The waitress asks if he's the actor John Goodman, and Ben shakes his head. She asks if it's Brian Dennehy, and the bartender says no, it's that Republican writer guy, William Bennett. He tells them both no, he's just a businessman named Riley Dugger.

Life imitates jokes. How many dozens of times has Ben said that if a CEO ever keeled over in front of him and the market was open, he wouldn't know whether to call 911 or his trading desk? He goes to the table, picks up the StarTac, and says quietly but firmly, "Dianne? I need Heffernan. We have to buy a bunch of puts before the close."

3 5

Rafaela has fed the children. ("Why did Mr. Gribbins treat us so weird today when us and Rafaela ran into him?" Max asked Lizzie as she arrived home. Mr. Gribbins is his Science and Society teacher. Lizzie tensed and asked, "Weirdly how?" "Like we're sick or disadvantaged or something. Like McKinley Saltzman when he got sent to live with his grandparents." "Beats me," she lied. "Ignore it.") Lizzie stands looking at her face in the bedroom mirror now, putting on earrings, smelling her perfumed self. Her mother never went anywhere dressed up at night alone until after Mike divorced her.

Sarah sits on the bed, flipping through the new bimonthly Home Again catalogue, which Zip Ingram has turned into even more of a pseudo-magazine. In one portfolio of news photographs, individual articles of clothing on Tony Blair (a shirt) and Angela Janeway (shorts) and Chris Rock (a leather jacket) are circled and lettered and available to order. "Will you be home in time to see the show?" Sarah asks. *Real Time* premieres tonight at nine-thirty.

"I'm afraid I won't." Lizzie is off to an MBC dinner at Zero with Mose, Featherstone, Penn McNabb, and the men who run the other internet and software firms the company has bought. Spouses are invited. George will be at the studio until ten, even though only a few short bits of the show tonight or Thursday are live. He needs to watch with the staff. "Which is why you need to be sure to tape it for me."

"Sir is. I mean Max. Is that Alexander McQueen?" she asks about her mother's burgundy linen dress and jacket.

"No, it's my old Mizrahi."

Sarah shrugs and shakes her head vaguely.

"A vintage piece," Lizzie says with a smile, giving herself a final once-over.

"Oh my God, *look!*" Sarah says from the bed. "It's us."

Lizzie steps over. Sarah has the Home Again catalogue open to a six-page spread. Two panoramic photographs, one on each side of the gatefold, show an ersatz family split in half. On one side of the gatefold are two girls and their father at an Adirondacks lake house: the blond kindergartner is pretending to shoot her smiling male-model dad with a stick, and the dark teenage daughter is alone at a computer on a dock, teleconferencing with her mother, whose face fills the laptop screen. On the back side of the gatefold is the most desirable loft imaginable, with twenty-foot-high ceilings and views of the East River in TriBeCa, the Pike Place market in Seattle, and in the distance, the golden hills of Tuscany. In front of an open casement window (an interior courtyard with a large vegetable garden is visible behind her, and the Empire State Building beyond), the gorgeous, blond, breeze-cooled mother sits at a red Corbusier table looking at her daughter on an iMac See, the "video-optimized" machine with a "semipliable" screen that Apple says it will introduce in 2001. Her young son is in the kitchen, standing in front of a wood-burning pizza oven, playing some exotic cat's-cradle game with a serenely smiling, expensively dressed young Mongolian or Inuit woman, perhaps the au pair, perhaps the artist–fashion designer who lives downstairs. Every inanimate thing in the picture is for sale through Home Again, including the homes. ("Actual views may differ," the fine print warns.)

"It is us," Lizzie says very evenly. *Zip* . . .

"Are you upset?"

She shakes her head.

"Oh! Oh! *Urrahhh! Urrahhh!! Urrahhh!!!*" The screams, the paroxysms, like someone having a seizure, are from downstairs. Somebody is ululating. "*¡Díos mío! Urrrahhhhhhhh!*" It's Rafaela.

By the time Lizzie and Sarah make it to the ground floor, Rafaela has collected her things (a JAVA! baseball cap, the day's discarded newspapers, a canvas *New Yorker* tote bag filled with meats cheaper than she can find in Queens), and she's running, literally running, for the door.

"Rafaela," Lizzie asks from the bottom step, "what is it? Are you all right? What's the matter?"

She doesn't answer, and leaves.

Back in the kitchen, LuLu and Max both stand motionless, stricken. LuLu starts sobbing, not the everyday selfish boo-hoos that Lizzie practically ignores, but a terrified, sorrowful, half-silent heaving that makes Lizzie feel like crying too.

"I didn't mean to, Mommy, I *didn't,*" LuLu says between breaths, then crumples to the terra-cotta floor, hiding her face, sobbing some more.

"We gave Rafaela a birthday present," Max says.

"What?" Lizzie asks. "It's Rafaela's birthday? Why did that upset her?"

"It was the *dolls,*" LuLu says, shuddering and crying.

"She turned thirty today," Sarah says.

"What in *God's* name *upset* her?" Lizzie asks, crouching down to take LuLu in her arms. "It's okay, sweetie, it's all right."

Sarah shrugs and shakes her head. Louisa, her cries more like squeaks now, buries herself deeper into the dark of Lizzie's Mizrahi jacket.

Max explains. It was LuLu's idea, but he helped. Rafaela had shown them a picture of her two children, and LuLu borrowed it to make a copy. Max and LuLu specified the correct skin tones (light brown for Fernando, olive for Jilma), hair and eyebrow colors (brown-black), hair length (ear length for Fernando and mid-back for Jilma) and style (bone straight), bangs style (slightly curled under for Jilma, none for Fernando), eyebrow shape ("other," which Max carefully drew) and thickness (full), colors for eyelashes (black) and eyes (T30), Jilma's pierced ears and the mole on Fernando's right cheek. They put all their savings together, $299.75, and sent in their order to the My Twinn catalogue.

"They look perfect," Max says, disappointed that a great idea went so badly awry.

In the back, near the door to the garden, are the two two-foot-high dolls, still in their packaging. Johnny is pawing and sniffing at the boy.

Fernando wears blue jeans and a green Lacoste shirt, Jilma (according to her label) a Country Garden dress.

Lizzie doesn't know what to say. LuLu's crying is now more normal.

"They're poseable," Max says. "That was ten dollars extra apiece."

She deputizes Sarah, finally settles LuLu and Max down in front of *Ren & Stimpy* (Nickelodeon is running Nick's Nonstop Nostalgic Nineties Flashback), and says goodbye.

"Can one of you go to a special soccer parents' meeting on Thursday night?" Max asks blankly, staring at the TV. "Some parents want to hire a pro coach for us for the fall."

"Your father's second show is Thursday. I'll try. Did you set the VCR for nine-thirty?"

"Yeah." Max turns to look at her.

"Do you think Dad is ever going to get, you know, normal again?"

"Mommy said Daddy looks dead," Louisa says, not taking her eyes off *Ren & Stimpy*.

"I said he looks 'dead *tired*.' I'll see you both later."

"Isn't it sort of unfair to review the show before the full week's been on? Like reviewing just the first act of a play?"

"Yeah," George says to Lizzie. "I'll file an objection with the fairness police."

The children are excited and well behaved, like they're at a restaurant. Both parents awake, both here, eating together, *speaking*. He still looks waxen and ill. But he brought a cup of tea to the breakfast table for her. Lizzie mentioned her work, and said that Fifty-nine is like Darth Vader's Berchtesgaden designed by Michael Graves on a Crate & Barrel budget. He *giggled*. They had a gentle conversation with LuLu, in which they discussed the definition of crying and her claim that tears by themselves do not count. (She threw the My Twinns away, and when Rafaela discovered the dolls in the garbage she freaked out all over again, and LuLu teared up.) They had a conversation with Max about soccer. (They both disagree with the St. Andrew's parents' vote in favor of an Adidas endorsement deal to pay for a professional coach.) They had a conversation with Sarah about her trip to France in August and the journal she's supposed to keep for her European Past class next fall. "They can't call it European *history*?" George said.

But no one minded. George the old grouch is preferable to absent George.

Now he is having a real conversation with her, about the show, the problems, the surprises, the reviews (no worse than expected), the overnights (not terrible), the high points and many low points of his first days on the air. The children aren't interrupting or grabbing each other's Eggos and bagel chunks.

"May I ask a question, Daddy?" Louisa says, a perfect old-fashioned daughter.

"Shoot."

"Did Ben Gould stop that man from dying at the bar?"

Riley Dugger has survived, but he had a stroke as well as a heart attack. He will not be running his company for some time, if ever. Ben's stock market bets against Dugger Broadcasting are very much in the money.

"He helped."

"I have another question also."

"What, honey?" George says.

"What if they do let the murderer go free this afternoon?"

She's talking about Charles Manson. On the Tuesday program they intercut real taped excerpts from Manson's most recent parole hearing. In one four-second live scene, Cole Granger was shown standing among the members of the California Board of Prison Terms as they filed out of the hearing room. Because state officials would allow only a robot camera in the vestibule, however, George inserted Granger into the shot digitally, even though he was actually at the MBC studios in Burbank. The real magic of the technique (which Barry Stengel, the idiot, hadn't even used at the funeral in *Finale*) is that it permits occlusion. Occlusion means that when Manson shuffled between the camera and the digital illusion of the live correspondent, Granger was realistically obscured for the instant he passed, and the camera could zoom in on the correspondent's face apparently reacting (as Cole said as portentously and frequently as possible) to "California state prisoner number B-33920." The shot looked completely real. It was astonishing. In his quotes in the *Times* yesterday morning (EXPERTS DEBATE "REMOTE PRESENCE" OF "NEWSMAN" AT MANSON HEARING), George pointed out that both the Tuesday and the Thursday shows, despite incorporating actual news clips, are repeatedly labeled as fiction at the beginning and end of the program and after every commercial break. On Tuesday, the announcer's disclaimer was even more aggravatingly explicit: "Viewers should understand that the scene of Cole Granger with Charles Manson following the parole board hearing is a digital modification of a real event. Granger was not physically present in that hallway." Until she read the *Times* story, Lizzie didn't know that George had indeed used the same technique that got Barry Stengel fired. She hadn't dared talk to him about it ahead of time, and there's no point now.

"They're not going to let Charles Manson out of jail, LuLu," her mother says. "Not ever."

"Is that true, Daddy?"

"Uh-huh."

"Then why are they pretending to think about it?"

"Is that a rhetorical question, Louisa?"

"What's that?"

"Your father's joking, honey." She turns to George. "So if Gordon is such a problem, fire him. You don't have to work with him on *NARCS* anymore, so who cares? Get somebody who's directed documentaries or something."

"Is that the official Fifty-nine line?"

"*Stop.* (By the way, I'm working late tonight in some Asia strategy-planning session.) No, about Gordon, I just mean it's like what I need to do with Penn McNabb. The one thing about this company is they don't seem to second-guess you if you need to hire someone or get rid of someone. If you don't think Gordon gets the show, and he isn't going to get it, and he's messing it up, then . . . lance the boil."

———————

She was a little duplicitous at breakfast, or at least incomplete. She said Randy, Doug, Hank Saddler, and almost everyone on Fifty-nine except Featherstone do seem like deacons in the Martian Church of Latter-day Satans. George smiled when she said that. They do have the brainpower of Boston College and the self-importance of Harvard. He smiled again. Fifty-nine is expensively dreary and too quiet, like Beverly Hills. She does hate being there most of the time. It is despicably political, she said after the kids left.

Lizzie has had five real jobs. At Procter & Gamble she was at the lowest executive rung. At the foundation and at News Corporation, she was still nowhere near the top. Virtual Fortress was too small and hippie-hackerish to have a meaningful top or bottom. At Fine Technologies she is the top. But at Mose Media Holdings she is, for the first time, very near a truly corporate apex. As one of six executive vice presidents and four presidents—eight different human beings—Lizzie realizes that her job is simple. Each of the other executives on Fifty-nine has two jobs: pleasing Harold, and also keeping the others from fatally badmouthing himself to Harold. She doesn't need the salary (the ridiculous, $1.1 million base salary) anymore, since on paper she now has serious fuck-you money (fuck-Mose money, in the form of Mose common stock), so all she has to do is please Harold Mose. That is now her job. Reductionist but true. It reminds Lizzie of what her mother said the night in 1973, when she left with Mike to fly to Washington for Nixon's second inaugural, despite her flagrant McGovernism. "Lizzie, when you're older you'll understand that any woman's job, at the end of the day, is to please one man." This is different. For one thing, Serene Zimbalist probably meant *at the end of the day* literally, and for another, Lizzie has the wherewithal to walk away anytime she wants. This is different.

What she didn't tell George at breakfast is that a lot of the time she's enjoying herself too. Is it possible to jerry-build a third-rate TV network together with some software and internet businesses, make a few shrewd alliances, and end up with a sustainable twenty-first-century . . . what? Entertainment platform? Information medium? Infotainment plat du jour, medium well? Maybe or maybe not, but it's her job to scope it out and say the magic words. One month into it, too soon to fail or feel frustrated (she knew coming in that Hank Saddler is a smarmy freak), Lizzie is having fun doing it. She's being paid to think *big*. She's a consultant who runs budgets, a strategist who can hire and fire, a general with troops. And the relief of being on a work release from the cage of her humid, high-strung, downtown clubhouse—

"Right there's fine," she tells her driver, "by that sign, THE MBC."

—is like a sabbatical. For the first time in years, she feels unburdened. "One piece of advice, honey-girl," her father told her when she was starting Fine Technologies. "The downside of being your own

boss and running your own show is being your own goddamn boss
and running your own fucking show. The great thing about a studio
gig is it's twice as much money and half as much work as real work."
She is not Mose New Media. It's a studio gig. She is no longer personally signing a $200,000 biweekly payroll check, or mothering
eighty-four people who are under the impression that they're in graduate school or a commune. What Lizzie did not mention to George is
that while she loathes Fifty-nine qua Fifty-nine, she is happiest on the
days, once or twice a week, when Harold Mose is in the office.

"It's very simple," Mose is saying to her and her fellow senior executives, and the COO, Arnold Vlig, in the conference room on Fifty-
nine. Arnold Vlig, with his tired animal eyes and lips like an optical
illusion (squinted at from one angle he's grimacing, from another always grinning, troll-like), is at Mose's right. But a foot or so back from
the table, as if to suggest a Rasputinesque puppeteer's power. Timothy
Featherstone must be in Burbank. "At the end of the day," Mose says,
"each and every one of you has only one job." He pauses. "What is that
job?"

"Customer service?" Doug says.

"No. Your job is making me happy."

They all snigger. Lizzie's comes with a little gasp. She thinks of
Buster Grinspoon's mental modem. She doesn't believe in ESP, but in
some obscure way she thinks serendipity is not always coincidental.
When she was younger, Lizzie used the word *synchronicity* a lot.

"You laugh. But it is precisely the case. And *I* have only one job. To
make the stock market happy. The Market, capital *M,* is *my* only real
boss. Pleasing him, or her," he adds, smiling at Lizzie, "is my job. Full
stop. End of story."

They all smile.

"A question. Let's imagine our stock price is a dense little disk, sitting in the middle of the ice. It hasn't moved anywhere lately. It's just
sitting there. How should we make it move in the right direction?"

Gnomic sports metaphors and patronizing Socratic dialogues: the
first top-level corporate headquarters meeting of her life, and it's already turning out precisely as she assumed it couldn't really be. She
picks up her sharp new Mose Media Holdings pencil, and scribbles a
reminder on her virginal yellow legal pad, HOCKEY = STOCK, ACAT.

ACAT stands for All Clichés Are True. During the animal-rights insanity, she started keeping a list.

Mr. Sales has got it. "You skate out there fast as the devil," Randy says, "make sure your defensemen are doing their jobs, and you shoot that puck down the ice as hard as you can and skate like hell after it." He radiates self-pleasure even more than usual.

"And then, *Randy,* you are tossed out of the game. This game."

Everyone sniggers except Randy and Lizzie.

"Mose Media Holdings has been playing hockey. Building a new network, just as the network business is crumbling, out of its very rubble— a cross-check, *bam,* the stock shoots up the ice. We score! The crowd roars! Our new internet and digital acquisitions," Mose says, glancing at Lizzie again, "more hockey—whack, whack, *whack,* shoot them down the ice. And the crowd—the Market, my boss, that crowd—loved it. But then the stock price got big, and heavy—like what?"

"A medicine ball?" Doug says.

"On *ice,*" Mose says.

This is the silliest five minutes Lizzie has ever spent in the company of adults not on drugs. But she knows the answer. And when a teacher poses questions, and the rest of the class is silent, Lizzie Zimbalist cannot say nothing.

"Curling," she says. "A curling stone." She knows because George played as a kid in St. Paul.

"The gifted transfer student," Mose says. "I thank you. Canada thanks you."

Everyone smiles.

"When Randy hits his stick as hard as he can against this forty-three-pound piece of granite, he looks like an idiot, he hurts his hands, and the stone just sits there."

Doug, Saddler, and the rest glance at Randy, who pretends to enjoy being the butt of the chairman's joke.

"Now our game must change. If Mr. Dugger had not so inconveniently fallen ill, we might have continued playing hockey for another period or two. But if we do now, we'll hurt our hands, and the stone will just sit there. Let the WB and Fox and the other teams kill each other playing hockey. But we know *our* new game going into 2001 is curling, not hockey. And we make our stones move where we want on the sheet by *strength,* yes, hurling the stone up the ice from the hack, but also by fantastic *focus* and *energy*—sweep-sweep-sweep-sweep-sweep. And by *indirection,* not by pushing or hitting the stone, but by *creating the circumstances*—sweep-sweep-sweep-sweep-sweep—that make the stone move as we wish it to."

Five of the seven men listening to Mose write on their pads, and then so does Lizzie. (Arnold Vlig does not.) The five men are presumably writing *hack, focus, energy, indirection;* Lizzie writes ACAT: CORP. DRONES.

"As players on the Mose Media Holdings curling team, what is your new job?"

Randy and the president of Greetings Media both bark out, "Making you happy!"

"Yes," Mose says, a little exasperated, "but I will become happy, as the skip of this rink, if you get your stones home. Which you do by sweeping away the frost, by making it a little wet just in front of the stone?" Mose nods toward Hank Saddler, who turns to his assistant and raises his eyebrows, who goes to a closet in the back corner of the conference room. The assistant fetches eight white-handled, short-bristled brooms, and passes them out. They are imprinted with the logo of Mose Media Holdings, the slogan A NEW 59 FOR A NEW CENTURY, and each executive's name.

Everyone smiles.

"You'll be pleased to know, Elizabeth," Mose says, "that our brushes have all synthetic bristles." Saddler nods solemnly. "Unless you'd *prefer* hog's hair or horsehair."

Everyone sniggers.

As the meeting breaks up, Mose exchanges a few words with Vlig, then walks over to Lizzie. She enjoys and doesn't enjoy feeling like a pet.

"I'll walk you back to your office if you have a second," he says, sounding more earnest than usual.

"Sure." She folds the ripped top page of her legal pad, and leaves the E. ZIMBALIST broom behind her chair on the tiger-maple credenza that encircles the room. As they walk out, she notices jealous glances from Randy and Doug, and Saddler's knowing smirk.

"You'll forgive my brutal reductionism in there," Mose says.

"Sure." They pass Laura Welles, Featherstone's second-in-command

and the company's second most senior woman. She works in Burbank. "I can tolerate brutal reductionism from a brutal reductionist who admits he's a brutal reductionist."

Mose smiles. "You have to focus people. Same thing with my little curling digression. That's the only way . . ."—he lowers his voice— "the only way the Randys of the world, honestly, are going to get it— to learn to repurpose and remaster themselves."

Lizzie looks at him.

Mose says, "Hank put your phrase in my rotation. The Randys need some entertaining noise in order to receive the signal. Thus the curling nonsense. You are not required to display the brush on your office wall, however."

This is a man who believes his own bullshit, even when he knows it's utter bullshit. "Thank you," she says.

He becomes a little solemn again. "Some people here are *never* going to get it. And some people, good people, are going to be casualties as we rush to transform ourselves into whatever new species of business can survive and prosper. There are always casualties. In evolution. And in revolutions."

"It's true." She feels a little sorry for the clueless Randys and Dougs and Steves.

"I am so glad you understand, Elizabeth. This can be a tough, painful game. Have you spoken to Mr. McNabb yet?"

"No. I haven't." She lowers her voice. "Although Arnold's office sent me the draft termination package. I plan to have that conversation next week."

He nods. They have reached her office suite. William, her stern Mr. Danvers, looks up. "By the way," Mose says, "Charles Prieve was once an employee of yours, correct?"

"Speaking of terminations? Yes. God, what a mistake. Why? He's not trying to get a job here, is he?"

"No, no. He—he actually made some threats. To the company."

"*Chas?* What kind of threats? He's not claiming I owe him money, is he?"

"No, no, nothing—"

"The last I heard of Chas Prieve, the Malaysian government was accusing him of being a pornographer. What a little worm."

"Yeah. Well, my dear, I'm off to Idaho—Saskatchewan south. You make sure your passport is up to date, eh? The glorious Gloria will be joining us in Tokyo for the whole trip, by the way, coming round the other way from London and Calcutta. Just in case that affects your choice of resort-wear."

"See you, Harold."

Odd, she thinks as she avoids William's voodoo stare, that Mose said nothing to her about *Real Time*. But maybe that's a good thing, not a bad thing—his way of trying to build a clean professional wall between an MBC producer and the producer's Mose Media Holdings executive wife.

3 6

George watched every American space program launch, live, from Alan Shepard through *Apollo 11*. (It wasn't post-lunar-landing disloyalty that made him indifferent to the rest of the *Apollo* missions, it was puberty.) He never envied the men crammed into the capsules, who reminded him of the boys who loved Indian Guides and hockey and curling more than he did. He envied the busy men in white shirts and ties fidgeting with Pall Malls at their consoles in that vast James Bond room in Houston. George wanted to be a mission controller, not an astronaut.

"Show me the other bird," says Oz Delehanty, *Real Time*'s codirector for news. A shot of a hallway in Sacramento appears on one of the thirty-six video monitors mounted in front of them. "I have that already."

The assistant director, sitting next to him, says, "The Russian satellite picture isn't live, you know, Oz."

"I *know*, Gretchen, I need Fullerton. I want to see the gun guy." After a few seconds on another monitor, a new picture flickers on, beamed up to a satellite from a gun factory in southern California and back down to West Fifty-seventh Street, of a bearded man in a suit aggressively picking his nose with his right hand while his left hand rests on a pistol on a desk in front of him. "Thank you. Hey! Snot wrangler! Okay, I want to see the first Chyron." On another monitor, still black, the words SIR FARLY LYMAN/*PLANET OF THE KIDS* DISTRIBUTOR pop onto the bottom of the screen.

"Scotty?" the director says, looking forward, eyes always on the monitors, to the lighting director three seats to his right, "I've still got that hot spot that looks like it's blasting right out of Jess's ass." Scotty shoots up and heads out to the studio.

"I heard that, Oz," Jess Burnham's voice booms over the speaker in the control room.

Oz pushes a button, then another, and says, "I'm your ass-blast guardian angel, Jess." He lets the button go. "Can somebody manage the IFB, *please*?" Jess wasn't supposed to have heard him.

"Oz?"

"Yes, boss?" the director says, turning his face a few degrees, a deferential symbolic turn. George sits behind and a little above Oz with Daisy; the *Real Time* supervising producer; the managing editor of the news hour; and Laura Welles, MBC's programming senior vice president.

"It's *Kidz* with a *z*. And *Farley* is spelled wrong. It's *e-y*."

They go live to tape in sixteen minutes. Barring a serious snafu, from six to seven o'clock they will run through the show without stopping. From seven until nine they'll do any repairs and polishing they can. At nine-thirty P.M. Eastern Daylight Time, *Real Time* will be leaving the building.

"George? It's Henry Saddler." Daisy is holding the phone. One of the intra-Mose call lights is blinking. He rolls his eyes.

"Hi, Hank."

"Henry. In case I can't get down there, I just wanted to say, George, that you know I've always admired you, and your risk taking. And despite the reputational problems and negative media coverage, despite, you know, everything, this *Real Time* adventure has been fantastic for MMH and the MBC and a rich learning-curve experience for everyone. I do mean that."

"Thanks. I tape in fifteen minutes. Thanks."

"And I do appreciate your gesture on behalf of the Seamlessness Initiative. I do. That is so sweet."

"Thanks, Hank."

"I want you to promise Henry Saddler you'll avoid giving in to any negative self-talk. All right?"

George rolls his eyes again. "I will. I do." *Whatever the fuck you're talking about.* "Thanks for calling. Bye." He hangs up. "I guess you couldn't tell him I wasn't here." He sees a Styrofoam case in Daisy's lap. "Dinner?"

"A thirty-eight-caliber semiautomatic WiseWeapon. From the gun man," Daisy says, nodding toward the monitor on which the nose picker is now tucking neck flesh down under his collar. "A courier just delivered it. A gift. Programmed personally for you."

"That is *so sweet.*"

Daisy smiles. He was given a gun once before, a .22, the rifle his friend Tuggy deeded to him the night before his exile to military school. "Does MBC payola policy cover handguns, Laura?" he says to Laura Welles, who's on the phone but flashes a thin smile of acknowledgment.

George has studied the show's rundown for days, weeks. He's stared at this sheet, the final sheet, dozens of times today. He looks at it again. Not counting the commercials (a parallel show inhabiting his show, like the alien in *Alien,* George can't stop thinking—a pretty, $12 million, fifteen-minute, thirty-episode show about Volkswagens and Claritin and Big Macs), he has forty-five minutes to fill (on a budget of $398,400).

The opening, which has been in the can since midafternoon, runs a minute thirty-five. The desk reads—Francesca and Jess taking turns summarizing the forty-two most important or entertaining of the week's events, Jennings-Brokaw-Rather style—consume nineteen minutes of the program.

"Who Got Rich This Week?" "America's Favorite," and "Kennedy World," the three Weekly Short Formats (what the staff calls "Weak Shit Farts"), take up two minutes in all.

A total of about three minutes, in fifteen-second chunks, will be given over to what they're calling "real-time actions/reactions," or ax/reax. These are to be spontaneous shots from the five robotic ax/reax cameras—mounted in the control booth, on the studio floor behind the manned cameras, and in the newsroom—of writers and producers watching and reacting to the show as it's being taped.

George sent around a memo yesterday emphasizing that the staff would damage the sense of authenticity if they dressed up for the Friday shoot. Nonetheless, there are a lot of freshly styled heads of hair and impeccably loosened neckties, many brand-new black jeans and pressed flannel shirts. Everyone, of course, is made up, at least lightly powdered, even the stage crew.

There are four long stories, each running between four minutes forty-five and six minutes thirty. These are the "High & Inside" segments. First is the Farley Lyman piece. (It mentions North Korea, unavoidably, but he's killed the Kim Jong-Il biological warfare package.) Then comes the story about the federal government's lugubriously solemn new commitment to herbal nostrums and acupuncture. George figures that Featherstone's main note on the show—"more *fun,* George, funnier, brighter Bob Altman–type stuff"—will trump his concern about pissing off the Offices of Alternative Medicine and Dietary Supplements.

He killed the Gores; it was exclusive, but for the first Friday show it would be just too depressing to air six and a half minutes of Al and Tipper sounding upbeat about the future as they gambol in the Tennessee hills. Which gives George the space to run a better political story. Senator Buckingham Lopez (Governor Bush appointed him in April to serve out Kay Bailey Hutchinson's term) is loudly pushing a federal law to outlaw all handguns except "smart" guns, like the WiseWeapon on Daisy's lap. (A WiseWeapon will fire only if its owner says the phrase "Ready to fire" into a microphone inside the grip.) *Real Time* has learned (George knows it's pompous, but he finds the phrase irresistible) that Bucky Lopez's wife, Kimberly ("kissable Kimberly" he called her when he was campaigning for president), owns a large amount of WiseWeapon's stock. George personally wrote the sentence, "Senator Lopez's broken-record odes to 'wealth creation,' however, now have a new wrinkle—*Real Time* has learned that . . ." As it happens, Francesca is a passionate gun-control advocate. A camera crew filmed two takes of her arguing about the Lopez piece with its producer, a half minute of which opened Tuesday's show. It was great television.

The fourth "High & Inside" segment is about Bohemian Grove, the secretive annual summer gathering of businessmen and politicians in the woods of northern California. George's favorite parts of the piece are the ultrahigh-resolution images of the encampment taken from a new low-Earth-orbit satellite operated by Sovinformsputnik, a branch of the Russian space agency. The best pictures are of Kevin Costner and Mikhail Gorbachev skinny-dipping together, and of Bill Gates and Vernon Jordan firing flamethrowers in a mock-mystical "retirement ceremony" for Jack Welch, the General Electric chairman. (George figures the satellite shots qualify as fun, funny, and bright.) The story was reported with assistance from the Bohemian Grove Action Network, which George had assumed for the last three months was an in-house joke between the correspondent and producer. On Monday, he learned that it's a real organization, the same day the MBC lawyer warned him that the story might violate the new federal statute, sponsored by Dianne Feinstein and Sonny Bono after Princess Diana's death, that outlaws "efforts to capture a physical image by intrusive technical means."

Featherstone gave George the go-ahead to ignore the lawyer's concern. "I did love Sonny," he said, "but this is a matter of national principle, isn't it?" On the other hand, Featherstone badly wants *Real Time* to air Jude McAllister's Deep Throat exposé. "It tested through the roof," he said on the phone from L.A. "It's a very fly segment." "I know," George replied, "and I really want to run it, maybe Week Four"—the twenty-sixth anniversary of Nixon's resignation—"but right now, we don't have it nailed." He felt good telling Timothy no. Spending any more time and money to get the story also worries George, however. He's over budget, even the revised 112 percent budget. All day he's thought about scrapping the location in Sacramento, which would save seven thousand dollars in crew and satellite time, since a Board of Prison Terms ruling against Charles Manson seems like an exceptionally safe bet. But *Real Time* isn't just a news show. As a dramatic matter, having set up the Manson story on location Tuesday, they need to resolve it properly in tonight's show: the arc, the arc, the arc. "And once again," Cole Granger can say very soberly in the studio an hour from now, after the news comes through, "California state prisoner number B-33920 has been denied parole. Jess?"

Gordon Downey has arrived and taken Daisy's seat beside George. He has nothing to do in tonight's show (although he's nominally "directing" the ax/reax shots of the staff and crew).

"George," Daisy says from a phone at the other side of the control room, "it's Michael Milken's office calling."

"We trashing Milken in the show, George?" Oz says, looking at the monitors, always the monitors.

"Uh-uh. *No*, Daisy," George says, "tell him we're shooting."

"I'm still seeing the hickey on Francesca's neck," Oz says, which sends a makeup woman a hundred feet away running onto the set.

"Four minutes," says Gretchen, the assistant director.

"Oz?"

"What is it, George?"

"We never decided what to do about that little gap between the logo and the video wall."

"I don't mind the gap if you don't," Oz replies coolly. "Bernie, you're wobbling," he says in a different voice to a cameraman.

"I'm a complete and utter amateur, needless to say," says a voice from the darkness behind and to the right, "but couldn't you just shmoosh your logo and your video wall together?" George turns to look. It is Harold Mose. He's grinning. As is Hank Saddler, holding the heavy metal door open. Standing just behind them in the dark, her face bathed in red from the exit sign, is Lizzie.

"Hi," George says. "Hi." Should he stand up? Should he go shake Mose's hand? Should he kiss his wife? Gordon offers his chair. For the first time in the last hour, Oz actually turns around. George decides to remain seated. Lizzie gives him a nervous wave.

For a few long seconds, no one moves or speaks. Mose takes a deep breath, in and out. "Everyone breathe!" he commands, still grinning. "My new executive vice president says it's the great tension antidote."

Everyone relaxes. Except George and Lizzie.

"We'll get out of your hair," Mose says, turning more solemn than George has ever seen him, "but I did want to pop in and let everyone here know that all your hard work has been appreciated. I wish—well, I thank you all for having been part of this adventure. The world will little note nor long remember what I say here, but it can never forget what you did."

"Thirty seconds," Gretchen says.

"Are we leaving the building?" Oz asks. He means: is the signal being piped out correctly to Burbank.

"We're leaving the building," she confirms.

"As are we," Mose says. He salutes, and Lizzie waves at George again as Saddler lets the control room door close with a vacuum-sealed *whoosh.*

"Stay where you are, camera two!" Oz shouts. "Roll tape."

"We have speed?" the AD asks.

"Speed!" a voice from the squawk box tells her.

"Everyone's speeding," the AD says. "Twenty seconds."

"Oz," George says, Saddler on his mind, "I don't want this going out on the in-house system."

The director pushes a button and speaks. "Master control, this is TV one, please take us off the router." He lets the button up. "You're running silent and running deep, George," and to his AD, "Put camera one online." After a pause he says, "Up in ten. Nine—

The AD takes over the countdown: "Eight, seven, six, five, four, three, two . . ."

And Oz *snaps* his fingers on the unspoken one.

Up comes the *Real Time* theme music, which the composer calls "a Radiohead–Aaron Copland hybrid," playing over a quick-cut montage of the week's events—Hurricane Candy's devastation of Miami Beach, Hillary hugging Al Gore, an oil refinery exploding in Venezuela, Prince William's last home video of the Queen Mother, the Aspen forest fires, the oar's-length victory moment of Paul Allen's galley ship in the Brunei harbor, Quentin Tarantino's acquittal, a swarm of Black Hawk helicopters firing into the Mexican rain forest, Senator Paul Wellstone on his barefoot "Venceremos" walk through southern Mexico, on and on, sixty-two separate shots, each an average of a half second long. (This cold open is George's bow of obeisance to Saddler's Seamlessness Initiative, although it's the way he wanted to start the show anyway. "I want it like a trailer for a Jerry Bruckheimer movie," he told his producer. Thus the explosions.) Then the fast sequence of aerial shots of eight skylines (New York, L.A., San Francisco, Seattle, Washington, D.C., London, Moscow, and Beijing, shrinking and morphing into the letters *R, E, A, L, T, I, M,* and *E,* followed by the fiction/nonfiction boilerplate and then highlights from the Tuesday and Thursday shows—Francesca with an editor at a computer pointing at an explosion on the monitor, Jess arguing with a cop, Francesca watching a grenade explode in Chiapas, correspondents and nameless staff talking, writing, laughing, hefting video cameras, catching taxis, yelling into phones, running in backward media stampedes down courthouse steps. It is by far the most expensive forty seconds of the show.

Then the picture freezes.

"What the *fuck!*" George screams.

"Stop tape," Oz and Gordon both say.

"That's a bust," Oz says. "Stop all tape. Stop everything."

"What happened?" George asks.

No one says a thing. Then—*whoosh*—a skinny older man, one of the videotape operators, pokes his head in and says, "Tape machine broke down. We'll be switched over in thirty seconds." *Whoosh.*

"Restarting at 7:02," Oz says.

George pushes his IFB button and leans into his gooseneck microphone. "Jess and Francesca, tape problem. It'll be a couple of minutes. And have a great show."

Whoosh. One of the associate producers rushes in, thrilled and panicky.

"George!" she shouts. "They're letting Manson *out!* I'm on the phone with Sacramento! They gave him a parole date!"

Oz pushes a button and says over loudspeakers, "Hold on, everybody. Change of plans."

"Holy shit," George says.

"My Lord," Gordon says.

"So we'll put Manson at the top," George says. "Kill Farley Lyman. Holy Christ." He turns to the associate producer as she whips back toward the door. "Are you *sure?*"

"Yeah," she turns to tell him and *whooshes* out.

"Get Cole over to the correspondent position," Oz says. "Well. I guess hell froze over."

Television control rooms exist to contain bursts of pandemonium like this. Oz and his technical directors shout into microphones to change lights, change the 'Prompter, ready tape, wire up Cole Granger. George *whooshes* out and onto the set to tell Jess, Francesca, and Cole what's going on.

"Get the bird from Sacramento up," Oz says. "I need it *now.*"

"Open's ready."

"Tape is rolling?" the AD asks. "We have speed?"

"Speed!" a voice from the squawk box tells her.

"All tape is rolling; we're speeding."

"Everyone's speeding," the AD says. "We have velocity. Thirty seconds."

George feels lucky, blessed: he has a camera in Sacramento, he has an uplink, and he has the satellite. *Thank God,* George thinks, *thank God for the demands of the almighty dramatic arc.*

"Put one online. Up in ten again," Oz says. "Nine—

"Eight," says the AD, "seven, six, five, four, three, two . . ." And the opening bars of Radiohead-meets-Copland swell again, followed by the opening montage and title sequence. This time, through, all the hokey prepackaged urgency is honestly thrilling.

"Make your move, Bobby," Oz says, "and . . . cut back to two!" he says, snapping his fingers each time he says a number, on the cuts from camera to camera. The music and title animation end. "And, take"—*snap!*—"three. And, take"—*snap!*—"one, take two, ready three . . . and"—*snap!*—"take two."

Gordon, overcome with excitement, is pantomiming camera numbers and finger snaps in unison with Oz.

"And . . ." Gordon says too loudly, "*acting.*"

"Cue them," Oz tells his stage manager over the IFB.

In the studio, the stage manager, standing in Jess's and Francesca's lines of sight, has formed his right hand into a pistol, like a child, and squeezes off an imaginary shot at the camera next to him.

"Good evening, I'm Francesca Mahoney."

"And I'm Jess Burnham. It's July fourteenth, 2000. And this is *Real Time.*"

3 7

At last. Saturday morning he woke up thinking he was in a dream, a dream about waking up, because he felt fine. Sunday morning, after another eleven hours of sleep, it was the same—*is* this *real? is this* real?—and he wanted to yelp and skip like a man released from some underground cell, like a quadriplegic who can suddenly walk. He kissed Lizzie on Sunday afternoon before she left for the airport. He really kissed her, even though she's heading for California, and then ten days in Asia with Harold Mose and the goblins from Fifty-nine. And today he feels fine again, the third morning in a row. It's Monday; he's slept late, and he feels just *fine*.

The first week of shows was imperfect, like the first of anything. He has a notebook full of notes. There were a hundred blemishes and glitches and clunky patches. Gordon Downey has to go. His instinct for schmaltz and act-break cliff-hanging made the pure documentary scenes seem bogus. The digital video trick with Manson on Tuesday was a mistake, George will now admit, despite his public apologias last week. The writing in the Tuesday and Thursday shows wasn't great, but what's clear is how much less writing they'll need. Instead of half documentary and half script, as he was guessing, they'll be able to get away with more like seventy-five–twenty-five. Simply dropping the camera crews into Jess's and Francesca's and the correspondents' lives—crawling out of bed, badgering a producer on the phone, cutting a story, snapping at each other over at dinner, chartering a plane, watching *NewsNight 2000* from the makeup chair—is generating some of the best scenes. Francesca needs practice at live interviewing. (Her unscripted question to the WiseWeapon guy, "But *why* are you in the business of making *any* kinds of guns?" provoked an entire Molly Cramer column yesterday.) Jess is superb, especially in her Tuesday-Thursday acting scenes, though she has to work on the ad-libbed profanity; one of the reviewers thought her bleeps were a scriptwriter's running gag.

But the show will get there. It can become great. "Innovation and boundary pushing are always to be encouraged in the TV wasteland," the *Washington Post* critic wrote, "and it is certainly true that there is nothing else like *Real Time* on television. The troubling question remains, however, whether all innovation, like human cloning or last spring's 'mental-modem' scare, is necessarily a good thing. Just because we have the ability to do something doesn't always mean we should." *Is it a good thing or a bad thing, Daddy?* George reminds himself to have Daisy dig out the 1913 reviews of *The Rite of Spring.*

And Manson! *Manson!* Such orgasmic fortuity, such a once-in-a-lifetime bull's-eye! The Board of Prison Terms vote is in dispute now that a majority of the nine commissioners claim it was all some terrible procedural mix-up—but who cares? Manson has been the story on every network and cable-news channel all weekend—he's on the cover of all the newsweeklies today—and George was there, with a live camera, exclusively! *Real Time* in real time! Talk about launching a brand.

When the phone rings he jumps out of bed, *jumps,* making himself smile. It's eight-sixteen. He wonders if it's the ReadyAim school-bus system screwing up again, or another reporter with more awestruck questions about his Charles Manson prescience.

"Hello?"

"*God.*"

"*Emily?*" She must be calling to congratulate him, mend fences, act nice. Fine! "Thank you. Pretty cool, huh?"

There's a pause. "You didn't hear."

He kicks open the trapdoor and peers down into his worst-case netherworld. Mose Media is being sold. Jess Burnham quit. They canceled *Real Time.* Then he imagines Emily's worst cases. Her boyfriend Buddy Ramo was trampled to death by a stallion he was Rolfing. A right-to-life Democratic vice-presidential nominee. MBC canceled *NARCS.*

"No," he says, "what?"

"Timothy killed himself."

"Oh, my God."

"Yes."

"Oh, my God. . . . Jesus, Emily."

"Weird, huh?"

Timothy Featherstone? "If I had to rank everyone I know according to probability of suicide," George says, "Timothy would have been at the absolute bottom. Way below me."

"Mmm."

"When?"

"Last night."

"How?"

"Gun. In the Hummer. In Burbank."

"Jesus. That's *so* depressing."

"Burbank?"

"Well, yeah, and the Hummer too, but I meant, you know, killing himself. I talked to Timothy Friday night. He called and was all 'Supercalifuckingfragilistic show, homeboy.' Completely normal. He asked about little business things, in his normal, stupid, excited way, like why Ben Gould owns the rights to some Robertson Davies novels Mose wants Timothy to turn into a miniseries. Wanted. Is there a note?"

"Nope. And they say he wasn't sick."

"My God." He sighs. "My God." He pauses. "You and I should get together sometime, Emily."

"Yes? All right. *I* liked it, George. The show. It's what you wanted. Right?"

"Yeah, it was. Thanks." *And fuck you, you backhanded harpy, with the stressed "I"—as opposed to everyone else, you mean, who hated the show?*

"So. We'll connect."

Nothing like a suicide to harsh a mellow. On their third date, Lizzie had actually said to him, "You're sort of harshing my mellow." It made him wonder if she might be stupid, and not just young. The only other person he has ever heard use *harsh* as a verb or *mellow* as a noun is Featherstone, in Las Vegas last January, when George was trying to decline to put Sandi Bemis's room and rental car on the *NARCS* expense account.

The phone rings again.

"Emily?"

"No, George, this is Dora, in Mr. Mose's office. There's a meeting at nine-thirty this morning in the small conference room on Fifty-nine. Can you make it?"

"Sure. Of course."

After moving one mile in twenty-five minutes ("FDR is *crippled* from the Twenties on, northbound, use alternate routes, Shadow Traffic, 1010 WINS!"), George has the driver get off at Thirty-fourth Street. He doesn't stop the guy from turning up Third Avenue, even though the extreme east side in the Thirties and low Forties is to George the saddest piece of Manhattan, sadder than the scroungiest blocks of Harlem or the Lower East Side, sad in some permanently modern Diane Arbus way instead of a Jacob Riis way—not poor, but bright and blasted and hopeless. The few old stores and buildings aren't old enough to be charming, and the new "luxury" apartment towers are not just undistinguished but grotesque, freakishly tall stacks of cheap diarrhea-colored brick with views of the First Avenue hospitals and each other (and for the fortunate few, Queens). The streets are peopled by lonely menopausal flight attendants, cut-rate Donald and Ivana Trumps, unusually crabby Korean shopkeepers, single mothers clinging to the first or last rung of respectability, contagiously unhappy people. Poor Timothy Featherstone.

There's a meeting, Dora said. The vagueness, the passive voice, and the fixed time all sound to George like a post-Timothy briefing. Not *Does ten work for you?* Or *Harold would like to see you.* Mose will say how shocked and saddened he is by Timothy's demise; that Laura Welles will fill in as interim acting president of the Entertainment Group; that Timothy would have wanted us to persevere because there's no business like show business. Of course, George's particular obsessive-compulsive disorder requires that he repeat to himself, between sensible speculations, *They're going to fire me,* even though he doesn't really believe that. Mose can't "fire" him, anyway, since George is an employee of Well-Armed Productions. And they don't cancel shows after one week on the air. Tuesday and Thursday did not get spectacular numbers, but 5.4 and 5.9 are higher than the average MBC rating. The newspaper opinion pieces were nearly all antagonistic, but who didn't expect that? Even the damning reviews, which ranged from querulous to curious to bewildered, called the show dangerous, not lousy. Maybe Mose has notes. Mose might have smart notes. Or maybe, he thinks, they're going to ask him who should run MBC News now that Stengel's gone. Maybe they're going to ask him to run News. And he'll say, "That's very, very flattering, but . . ." *Or else they're going to fire me.* Maybe they want him to pitch in on the search for Timothy's replacement.

His new phone is on its third ring before he recognizes the straight beep. Ben is calling.

"You really hold a grudge, George, don't you?"

"I have no idea what you mean."

"Hey! Bucky Lopez! You gutted the guy! The show was good, by the way—but George, the thing on Bucky was brutal."

"It's the business we have chosen. That's what you taught me to say. What grudge?"

"Remember how you got it into your head that Bucky dissed you somehow at my party in Vegas?"

"That isn't a grudge." *Perhaps you sensed a fleeting desire on my part to assassinate him, but that's merely a private quirk of mine, nothing serious.* "I thought the guy was a honking asshole, but I wasn't angry at him. Our piece isn't going to destroy him."

"So, are you the conquering hero over there now? Did they love the show?"

"I guess. I hope. I'm on my way to a meeting with the big boss."

"Hey! You reported high, right?"

George looks outside, and smiles. When Ben uses Wall Street–speak in real life, he isn't trying to be funny. Ben forgets that not everyone talks that way all the time. The car has just passed the mammoth Niketown store and the mammoth Warner Bros. store and dead ahead, across Fifth, is the new James Bond Casino Royale (which is a restaurant, bar, shops, and mammoth video arcade, not a casino).

"I guess," George replies.

"Definitely! The smart-money trade for the last month was to be short George Mactier, right? With all the stories and columns saying you're Moloch. You beat expectations. You reported decently, so now you'll soar. Watch."

"Ben, you're not trying to produce a movie or TV show based on a Robertson Davies novel, are you?"

He doesn't answer at first. "No."

"This guy at the network said he heard you were."

"I'm not making any movies, or any TV shows. That I promise. The open's in ten minutes. Got to go."

"Okay. I'm at MBC, anyway."

It's nine-twenty, so he'll go straight up. He walks past his regular elevator bank and hooks around to the hidden opening for Fifty-nine. The guard finds his name on the computer list, touches the screen with his pinky to make GEORGE MACTIER disappear, and waves him into the elevator. Its interior, the only one like it in the building, consists of alternating strips of cherrywood and sandblasted glass. (The insides of the regular elevators in the Mose building are striped green-and-gold laminate with two-inch-by-two-inch cherrywood veneer "accents.") *It's possible they're going to fire me.* Now that George has successfully launched two prime-time shows in one year, he wonders if maybe they want to extend and enrich his deal. His market price is rising. Mose must have seen last week's story in the trades about Time Warner giving the executive producer of *Hero* a new, ten-year, $55 million contract with Warner Bros. TV, and letting him develop a Time Inc. monthly magazine that *Variety* described as "true-life stories of good triumphing over evil."

The security man on Fifty-nine gives George the usual hard, blank stare, but the woman at the reception desk recognizes him and smiles. As she says hello, she pushes two different buttons, one to unlock the glass door and the other to notify the next gatekeeper down the line, but does it so subtly that George doesn't notice.

Dora's assistant, Lucy, meets him at the next turn, and leads him to the conference room.

Hank Saddler and Laura Welles, Featherstone's deputy, are already here. Fifty-nine-style greetings are exchanged, even more self-serious than usual. George carefully lays his briefcase on a counter near the window, next to Hank's and Laura's things. It's clear this is going to be an executive-suicide trauma-coping exercise, one of those harmless events that the profession of human resources was invented to stage. He wonders who else is coming. Laura is looking back and forth between her hands, and out the window, toward downtown. She seems nervous, unaccustomed to life here in Mose Media elysium, inside the abode of the blessed on Fifty-nine. The mood in the room is funereal. Poor Timothy.

"Harold so much wanted to be here personally, George," Saddler says, "but he had to leave Teterboro at nine for Sun Valley. The Herbert Allen event. Then we're off to Asia!"

"Ah." Mose isn't coming. So they're definitely not going to talk to him about taking Stengel's or Featherstone's job, not that he expected that, or wants either one.

"Also, George, before the meeting gets started? I don't want you to feel *any* culpability whatsoever over Timothy's death. Like they say, guns don't kill people."

Welles looks at him.

"I'm sorry, Hank," George says to Saddler, "what do you mean?"

"The gun. The suicide weapon? I thought you knew. It was the smart gun the gentleman in your story sent to Timothy on Friday."

"My God. Really? *Jesus.*"

Saddler gives one of his pastoral nods. "It almost makes you think certain shows are, you know, *cursed,* doesn't it?"

George thinks of Timothy alone in his military vehicle, turning the WiseWeapon to his head, and then having to utter his scripted, obligatory last words, "Ready to fire."

Arnold Vlig walks in with another, younger man carrying a brown accordion file. George has met Vlig only a few times before. The permanent pained expression and thin black hair combed straight back from his sloping forehead remind George of a Slavic Richard Nixon, Nixon homelier and physically fit. Maybe they are going to offer him some big job after all. But no: Laura Welles wouldn't be here.

"George," Vlig says, and shakes his hand. "You probably don't know Stan Snyder. He's one of our outside counsels." Snyder nods as he sits.

"We're all so sad about the show," Saddler says. "I guess the whole *Larry Sanders, Truman Show, EDtv, Lateline* zeitgeist is just . . . well, like Laura says, 'very two years ago.' "

In the floor beneath him, he hears wood creak and the clatter of a latch opening.

"I don't know what you mean, sad?" George asks.

Saddler is suddenly upset. He looks at Laura Welles and back to George. "No one sent you a hard copy of the new testing? You were supposed to be faxed overnight."

Now Laura Welles is upset. "Timothy's office was handling it," she says to Saddler, "but yesterday . . . I guess it slipped through the cracks. Here's an extra," she says, glancing as briefly as possible at George as she slides an inch-thick report across the table.

It's called "The MBC *Real Time* Post-Premiere Testing," and it's dated today, July 17, 2000.

"What is this?" George says. "What post-premiere testing?"

"Well, of course we tested," Saddler says. "In fact, we used a new outfit, the best. Very intensive focus grouping last week, in real time (no pun intended), and then all day Saturday in Tucson, Charlottesville, and, and . . ."

"Omaha," Laura Welles says.

"*Omaha,* as well as New York and Burbank. And—well, I'll let Laura summarize. She speaks the language."

"Do I? I mean . . ." She looks from Saddler to Vlig.

Vlig nods once.

"George," she says, "the bottom line is, I've never seen such negative test results. Across the board. And it's not just indifference. It's deep confusion and active dislike. The viewers who didn't mind the Friday show (and that was very CBS, very over-fifty) absolutely despised the Tuesday and Thursday shows. The viewers least unfavorably disposed to Tuesday and Thursday were very uncomfortable with the half-hour drama form. And they were generally unable to distinguish between the fictional and nonfictional components. And they *despised* the news program. In two of the focus groups, leaders had to pay participants bonuses just to stay and watch the Friday show all the way through."

Saddler is doing a slow, continuous nod. Vlig stares at George. Stan Snyder is riffling through his own stack of multiply tabbed papers.

The drop is a shock, and he sees the trapdoor dangling as he rushes past, down, down into the murk.

Welles flips to a tabbed page on the report. "Women and men over thirty-four can't stand Francesca." She flips again. "Men don't like Jess at all, especially over-thirty-fours, blue collar and white collar. As soon as the gay thing was brought up on the Thursday show, we saw *tremendous* viewer turnaway in the testing. On Friday, North Korea was a big turnoff." She looks up at George. "As we knew it would be, from the advance research."

Rather than falling, the sense is now of midair suspension, pitching and yawing upside down and sideways in the dark, nauseated and half dead but almost gloating about it—I told you so, I knew it, I told you so.

Welles doesn't look up as she continues. "Viewers didn't understand the point of the gun-control story."

"The point?"

"Whether it was pro or con."

"It was neither. It was about a conflict of interest. It was about politics."

She looks up. "Exactly. As we knew from all our pre-air testing, politics is death among the under-fifties, especially women, which was your only major audience segment still showing signs of life after Tuesday-Thursday." She returns to her tabbed pages. "Viewers found Bohemian Grove 'elitist,' and they don't want to hear another thing about Bill Gates or Sexgate. Big turnoff."

"There was nothing about Clinton," George says.

"Vernon Jordan," Vlig explains. His bass croak is startling.

"Manson?" Saddler says.

"Right, the Manson problem," Welles says. She turns to George. "A majority of people in the Friday night and Saturday morning focus groups thought the Manson story was fictional. Of course, you were warned about that issue in your pre-air BetaWeek testing. Then as the news, and then the confusion over the news, spread during the day Saturday, our groups became angry when they viewed the shows. They blamed your *Real Time* story for *causing* the Manson parole decision."

Saddler, his lips pursed, is still nodding.

"The highest scores, and they were uniformly low highs, were on the alternative medicine story"—Vlig and Saddler exchange a quick glance—"and two of your short features, 'Who Got Rich This Week?' and 'America's Favorite.' "

Welles looks back down and flips to a page near the end of her report. "We even tested your completed non-run stories, your bank, and . . ." She shakes her head. "Test subjects were disappointed by the Farley Lyman story—they assumed that an exposé about a British 'sir' would involve Princess Diana. Plus the attack on children's television was a big turnoff."

"It is not an 'attack on children's television,' " George says.

Welles closes the report. Vlig continues to stare at George, as does the lawyer.

"The research firm," Saddler says, "hasn't had scores to match these since 1973, they told us, for some *Gilligan's Island* remake that didn't even have Gilligan *or* the Skipper!"

"Li'l Gilligan," Welles says.

Deep in the bottomless dark, he kicks his feet and waves his arms wildly, which would probably be hilarious if it were a cartoon.

"Every single demo," says Saddler, shaking his head again but sounding almost boastful, " . . . *ix*-nay."

"Not quite," Welles corrects. "You didn't do badly in A- and B-county college-grad eighteen–to–thirty-fours. But that's a tiny slice of a slice."

"And we're not MTV," says Vlig. Vlig leans forward. "George, I want to ask you something. Why did you charge ahead and violate the celebrity-image and paparazzi laws? Didn't the lawyer warn you specifically about that?"

"She did. But she said it was our call with the satellite imagery. And Timothy gave me a go-ahead." Welles looks a little disgusted. "Who complained? Gates? Kevin Costner?"

"Bohemian Grove isn't the problem, George," Saddler says, glancing at Stan Snyder.

"Not the *legal* problem," Vlig says, taking his eyes off George for the first time in the last five minutes.

"It's that darned Manson," Saddler says. "His lawyers say we violated his right to control his image. He *is* a celebrity."

It is a cartoon. But not Bugs Bunny or Wile E. Coyote; one of the new cartoons, surreal and scary as well as funny.

"That's crazy," George says, "it's *news*."

"You're entertainment," Snyder the lawyer says. "And California has a statute against commercial appropriation of a celebrity name and/or image. There are no exemptions for celebrity felons. And speaking of what Mr. Featherstone did or did not authorize you to do, we have his contemporaneous notes dated May thirty in which he describes requesting that you delay the broadcast of the alternative medicine story. Are you challenging the accuracy of those notes?"

"Timothy said he would rather we held off. But so? So what?"

"According to the Content Arbitration provision in your contract," Snyder explains, "when Mose Media Holdings requests a 'cooling-off' period on a story—as you stipulated just now that Timothy Featherstone in fact did—you are obliged to submit the story in question, unless it has a 'deadline news urgency,' to the ombudsman's office. As you know." George agreed to the provision, but never thought much about it, because of the "deadline news" loophole and because he assumed if Content Arbitration ever came up, the ombudsman, Dan Flood, would be on his side. It never came up. "Was there any deadline urgency to your story on the National Institutes of Health and its Offices of Alternative Medicine and Dietary Supplements?"

George folds his arms, breathes deeply, and does not answer. He feels himself reddening.

"Speaking of medicine, George, and as long as we're clearing the air *totally*," Saddler says, "no one here was exactly thrilled when you refused to give MBC News the exclusive on your late father-in-law's liver transplant."

"He didn't have a transplant," George says. "It was fake. It was a placebo procedure."

Laura Welles looks shocked. At George. "I'm shooting our major MOW for November sweeps as we speak, and you're telling me that the animal theme is out, the scenes on the pig farm with the rabbis are garbage?" She shakes her head, openmouthed. "When were you planning to tell us about this?"

Snyder makes a note.

"Calm!" Saddler says. "Calmness. And let's stay on point."

"George, I don't know if this helps in your spinning of all this later," Vlig says, waving a hand, "but we aren't canceling *Real Time* in a vac-

uum. We're reevaluating the network's non-comedy nonfiction programming commitments across the board. Including News. Frankly?
I'm not entirely comfortable with this company *getting* too much press,
and I'm even less comfortable *being* the press. And audience and costs
aside, on both counts, your program would just keep . . ." He waves
again.

"*Festering,*" Saddler says. "Your MPI, George . . ." He shakes his
head.

Vlig nods. "We just have to lance the boil. Sooner rather than later.
Before it gets bigger. Before it becomes infected."

*Still in midair, still sick and disoriented, but the wild pitching and yawing
has stopped. He can make out shapes and shadow. How quickly one adjusts to
terrifying new physics.*

"Canceling?" George says. "As a matter of fact, I'm afraid you cannot cancel. We have a contract. The contract obliges you to buy at least
two shows a week from me for thirty-nine weeks, or through next
April, whichever comes first." He looks at Snyder. "As you know."

Vlig puts an index finger to his lips and leans back.

Snyder speaks. "Section nine, subsection *B,* Roman numeral four,
paragraph *a,*" he says from memory, looking straight at George. " 'The
Company shall be released from all such obligations to the Producer,
however, at any time that the Production Budget of the Show, under
the definitions in section six, subsection *D,* above, shall exceed by more
than ten percent the Production Budget authorized by the Company,
for more than half of the Shows broadcast in the current season.' You
were nineteen percent over budget in preproduction."

"Which was authorized," George says.

"And you were twelve percent over your *revised* budget for last
week's three shows. Three out of three for this season is, by any definition, 'more than half.' "

Saddler is nodding again, slowly and sadly.

George vaguely recalls the provision. The lawyering and negotiating
part of the business was Emily's, not his. And he can't believe they're
trying to fuck him on the basis of a one-week budget overrun.
("Whenever you say '*I can't believe* nightmare X or violation Y' about
this business," Emily has told him more than once, "I feel like shaking
you, George.")

"Well," he says. "I guess I should go talk to my lawyer."

"Lawyer, lawyer, lawyer," Saddler says. "Don't go there. Do not go there, my friend. You are part of our MMH family—we're—we'll be in business forever, you and us, with our *NARCS* bonds! And Elizabeth is our family. Why, just the other day on this very floor, someone said, 'You know, George Mactier's only problem is that he has *too* high a signal-to-noise ratio.' Which is a compliment! We need you at the MBC, George. You are the future."

George stares at Saddler, unable to speak.

"As Arnold alluded, we may downsize News significantly, but that doesn't mean every News *program* will go poof. I know Laura agrees that *Finale* is a definite keeper. And we're depending on you to produce *Finale* for us, Mr. Show-Runner. Wait! Wait! We also want you to launch *The Supreme Court* for us this fall. You attended law school, didn't you?"

"Architecture school," he says, forced into a humiliating moment of civility by the demands of accuracy, "for a month."

George only knows about *The Supreme Court* because of a dispute between MBC and the federal judiciary over the name of the show. The government has apparently failed to prevent Mose Media Holdings from registering The Supreme Court® as a trademark for entertainment programming and products in all media, including toys. *The Supreme Court* will be the first network fake-trial show in which celebrity lawyers will try celebrities' "cases." Sometimes the celebrity plaintiffs and defendants will appear in person (Wayne Newton has agreed to retry his overturned libel case), and sometimes (Mrs. Phil Hartman, President Clinton) the celebrities will be tried in absentia. There is already a 9,700-person waiting list for jurors. Robert Bork has agreed to play the judge.

"Do we have an understanding, Mr. Mactier?" Snyder says, pushing a document across the table. Scanning the first page, George sees they want him to forfeit all *Real Time* claims in return for a one-year contract as producer of two embarrassing infotainment pieces of shit. On the second page, he sees they want him also specifically to disclaim any right to sue under the Americans With Disabilities Act.

Is this a solid surface? Is he upright? Has he landed? He is alive.

George says, "No, we don't have an understanding. What we have is a deal to produce thirty-eight more weeks of *Real Time.* If you don't want to air those shows, I guess you won't. But I expect to be paid for them."

Saddler stands and shakes his head more energetically. He touches Welles's shoulder, who jumps out of her chair. Both of them leave the room.

"Mr. Mactier," Snyder says, "in addition to your other contractual breaches that I've outlined, there is in your contract a standard 'termination for cause' clause. Conviction of a crime, moral turpitude, gross violation of MBC policy, et cetera." He pulls out a document, points it in George's direction and recites it. "Intermittently from January seventeenth to June third of this year, a Ms. Sandra Cushman Bemis, variously doing business as Wow-Wow Partners, Heavy Petting Seminars, and Sniff! Incorporated, occupied a suite at the Venetian Hotel in Las Vegas. That suite, as well as a rented Mazda Miata, were charged to the travel and entertainment budget of *NARCS,* a program in which Mose Media Holdings owns fifty percent and of which you were then executive producer."

"Sandi Bemis is Timothy Featherstone's girlfriend! She was. I didn't know she'd kept on staying in that room on our dime." He pulls over the photocopied hotel bills. "Timothy asked me to put that first January weekend on our T-and-E, it was NATPE, but—this is his problem. This is the network's problem. I had no idea."

"You signed the original credit authorization, Mr. Mactier, not Mr. Featherstone. We have an affidavit from your former assistant stating that you instructed her to persuade Angela Janeway to accept a Wow-Wow animal therapy class worth eleven hundred dollars. And we have a copy of your e-mail to Barry Stengel strongly suggesting that he, quote, 'somehow plug Sandi Bemis's pet-therapy bullshit,' unquote, on one or more MBC News programs. I assume you're aware of the MBC's regulations governing so-called plugola? And I assume you would agree with me that promoting a commercial venture on the news in exchange for an eleven-hundred-dollar gift, even if that eleven hundred dollars is 'laundered' through two separate network divisions, would violate the spirit and possibly the letter of those regulations? Not to mention the *appearance* issues."

"What?" George says.

"Your appearance of impropriety. You improperly paid twenty-seven thousand dollars for a Las Vegas hotel suite for a woman whose . . . services you improperly sought to promote on MBC News."

Plummeting once more, terrified all over again, trapdoors within trapdoors, vicious new g-forces at each depth.

"She was Featherstone's girlfriend! This is such bullshit, do you know that? I find it very hard to believe that Harold Mose is aware of what you're trying to pull here."

Snyder picks up a remote control.

"In fact, George," Vlig says, "you're right; Harold is not aware of most of these details. He accepted Laura's decision to cancel *Real Time*, of course. But these other matters are between us. As I expect you'll wish them to remain."

Snyder punches a button. To George's left, a monitor in the wall flashes on with the vertical rainbow and electronic monotone whistle—bars and tone, the five or fifteen seconds at the top of every tape in television. Beneath the bars it says E!² MAR 6 2000. The picture appears, mid-pan, with ambient crowd chatter. It's a party scene, handheld but professionally shot. Find a pair of young blond women in ball gowns limbo-ing, cut to Bucky Lopez shaking hands with a busboy. It's Ben Gould's BarbieWorld after-party in Las Vegas. Cut to William Shatner standing with the magician Penn Jillette. Cut to a close-up of a giggling young woman with brown pigtails leaning forward on a white leather couch, pull back to reveal a disheveled, middle-aged man grinning stupidly as the pigtailed giggler inserts his whole arm down into her low-cut top, between her breasts.

Snyder pushes the freeze-frame button. "In April," he says, "while you were still technically executive producer of *NARCS*, Shawna Switzer worked for three days as an extra on the show."

George has his mouth clenched tight. He's shaking his head.

"Frankly?" Vlig says. "It's not any single one of these unfortunate incidents that disturbs us. It's the overall *pattern*."

Snyder punches his remote. The tape rolls. Cut to Penn Jillette doing chin-ups for a small audience on the balcony, cut to blank leader, cut to a very slow wide-angle panning shot of the side of a building, a column and a door from up high, in color but so fuzzy it looks almost black-and-white. No audio. It's from a surveillance camera. Find two human figures on a sidewalk, their backs to the camera, just as the taller figure takes three long-jump strides toward the building, leaping at it, attacking it, leaving a barely visible mark on the wall about eight feet above the ground.

All falling objects are the same: they stop accelerating, and eventually they stop. He clings to his simple Newtonian faith, surrenders to it, waits for the bottom, knows there must be some final thud.

"There are more of those scenes," Snyder says. "As you may recall." He stops the tape. "This came from the Treasury Department, by the way. The Secret Service reviewed all of that night's surveillance videos from the hotel, because of the candidate's presence. We informed them that you do not, as far as we are concerned, represent any threat to any of their protectees. And you'll be glad to know the monetary damages claimed by the Venetian are negligible, four figures." He almost smiles.

Snyder has returned to his accordion file. Vlig sits and stares.

This must be the bottom, then.

George thinks of the villain's ritual speech halfway through the third act of James Bond movies: *Before I kill you, Mr. Bond, you must take a tour of my installation as I explain every detail of my mad scheme.* He thinks of what Lizzie says: All clichés turn out to be true.

Saddler opens the door, sticks his smiling face in. "Do we have closure?"

No one replies. George stands, and turns to retrieve his briefcase. His *Journal* and *Post* have slid out of the side pocket.

"Well," Saddler says, "just promise you'll think about the Judge Bork show. We see it as a very prestigious-type program."

George, looking down at the counter, stuffing the newspapers back in one-handed, has his back to Saddler. *"A signal-to-noise ratio that's too high,"* he said. *"Lance the boil,"* Vlig said.

"Also," Saddler says, "tiny, tiny FYI? We would be grateful if you *would* take Mr. Milken's calls. But in any event, George—and I know this reflects Harold's feelings as well—just keep on being a *neat guy.*"

George is holding his briefcase, but he's still looking down. He's staring at a white curling brush wedged back between the edge of the wooden counter and the window. A NEW 59 FOR A NEW CENTURY it says in red on the white handle, and E. ZIMBALIST, TEAM 59.

This is the bottom. This is the *thud.*

He leaves, and on the way out, he spots Laura Welles in the instant before she ducks into an office, practically leaping away, out of sight.

At least Vlig's lawyer didn't pull out a copy of the St. Andrew's Science and Society indoor-pollution study, the smoke-speck-per-billion evidence from his bedroom.

But maybe they do have it. Maybe they're keeping that secret. If that became public, it would incriminate Lizzie as well. And Lizzie is a member of Team Fifty-nine.

———

Daisy is busy as George wafts past her desk toward his door. "Good news," she says, bent down, holding a plug into the back of the printer as it prints, "I *think* it's good news: we're on hiatus this week." Daisy sits up, but George is already hovering in his office near the window overlooking the park, disintegrating into a blackish mist that will momentarily disappear up into the HVAC vents. "Laura Welles's office called," she says, raising her voice. "Tomorrow through Friday in our slot they're running an encore presentation of a miniseries called *Roots 2063*. So I guess we have an extra week to do the next shows.

"Does 'encore presentation' mean rerun?" Daisy says as she steps into his office. "*Crikey,* George, what spooked *you?*"

———

She went to sleep after a call from Hank Saddler, and she was awakened around six San Francisco time by another call from Hank Saddler. She assumed he was phoning again about Timothy Featherstone. But no, this morning he has *good* news to deliver—the most recent Media Perception Index results for Harold, the MBC, and Mose Media Holdings are all "trending *very* positive." Buying the internet companies and Fine Technologies, and hiring Lizzie, he tells her, have already increased the instances of "shrewd-slash-savvy" and "bold-slash-visionary" by half. "And we're getting a few pops on both the 'stabilizing-slash-proactive' and 'enlightened-slash-progressive' axes," he says, "which we've *never* had. If the stock price follows, Lizzie, you'll pay for yourself in no time!" She can't get back to sleep, so she checks her messages at both offices, and her e-mail. And the stock price, which she finds she can't resist doing anytime she checks her e-mail, since every point up or down is equivalent to $500,000 of her personal wealth. *Paper wealth,* she reminds herself at each peek, *paper pretax wealth,* which isn't hers even on paper until the deal closes. The Dow had been down 44 points in the first ten minutes of trading, but ticker symbol ME, Mose Media Holdings, opened up 1¾. The six-month graph of the stock price still looks uncannily like an Etch-A-Sketch tracing of America's southern border, ending as of this morning east of Panama City and Destin, where the Gulf cuts north toward Tallahassee. Maybe Saddler's Media Perception Index does work, she thinks. A million dollars richer (on paper, pretax), she lets the room service boy bring in her grapefruit and currant-studded Irish oatmeal. "Are you enjoying your stay at Coppola Square?" he asks. So far, she has been asleep for eight of her nine-hours stay. "Yes," she answers.

No one who should call does call. Not Mose, not Saddler, not George. She is walking out the door, headed for her nine o'clock with Penn McNabb in Milpitas, when the phone rings. It is a reporter named Jack something from *Variety,* an apparently young man who seems to be both channeling Walter Winchell and faking Walter Winchell's idea of an Ivy League vocabulary.

"Sorry, I've got to go."

"So you're hypothesizing it was more creative diffs with the big boys than it was just a cost-benefit Ax City kind of decision?"

"Since until two minutes ago I didn't know about this, I have no idea what the reasons are," she says. "I didn't even know it *was* canceled. I've got to go."

"Ms. Zimbalist, off the record, when the rubber meets the road on the Fifty-ninth Floor, has Harold Mose just bitten off a chewier chunk of metanews nouvelle cuisine than he can eat? And when the suits squeezed, he had no choice but to go FIFO on *Real Time* because it was a downside twofer—pricey and provocative?"

"Listen, I love my husband's show. I think it's brilliant. But I've only worked for MBC for a few weeks. I am not a television programmer. What those guys think an audience will or won't like is not necessarily what I like or don't like. I've got to go, I need to make some calls and I'm late for a meeting, okay?"

"So you're positing a kind of execu-lady difference, feminism as regards mass and niche on the tube, is that it?"

She hangs up.

Oh, God. Oh, God. Oh, *shit.* She feels horrible for George. Feeling someone else's pain has become a cheap joke, thanks to the president (like so much else), but Lizzie's heart aches. She knows how it feels to fail quickly and spectacularly (Murdoch online), and she knows how much of himself he has poured into this show. Oh, *George*.

She calls George at work, but there's no answer, and there's no answer on his portable or at home either.

She's crying.

She knows the real torture for him will be the pity. The calls and chance encounters brimming with kindly, soothing, there-there strokes for the poor, poor victim.

And her. His rage will curdle and harden, become a tumor of hatred. He won't believe she's known nothing about this. She will be a collaborator. She will be his enemy. (And maybe she is to blame: she never told him not to use the digital video-insert trick, because she couldn't bear that conversation.) He will construe her as a beneficiary of his misfortune, she knows, the Krupp factory manager exceeding production quotas thanks to the slave labor, a Swiss banker shrugging off the vaultful of unclaimed ingots. Then she remembers the stock price: the reason it's moving up this morning is *because the show was canceled*. Even if that isn't true, he'll be convinced it is. Should she go back home, display her tears, testify to her vicarious agony, hold him, explain? But if she cancels the trip, he will feel monumentally pitied. It may be best that she disappear for these couple of weeks, a stretch of pain that might prevent some deeper, longer, crippling set of wounds. If she's out of his way, he can seethe and rail alone, without her trotting off to Fifty-seventh Street every morning, swearing her innocence and pitying him every night.

She phones him again, and still gets no answer anywhere. She calls Mose in Sun Valley, and leaves a message. She doesn't know what else to do, and she needs to get going. It would be bad form to arrive late to fire her investment banker's brother from the company he started.

The meeting with the staff lasts an hour. Some of them cry. Afterward, he takes fourteen of them to lunch. After lunch, he returns six calls from newspaper and magazine reporters and tries hard to sound sane and blithe. He has never before, as either journalist or subject, engaged in such a recondite discussion of ground rules as he does with the reporter from *Variety,* spending five full minutes specifying and negotiating the meanings of "not for attribution," "off the record," "background" and "deep background." To all the reporters, on the record, he says only, "This is the business we have chosen" and "It's just *television,*" but on background he encourages them to check out the network's plans for a New Age cable channel. (He considers saying that the New Age channel was his and Emily Kalman's idea that the network swiped, but decides it would muddy the issue and might strike the reporters as deranged.) Two of the reporters ask whether there is any connection between the cancellation of *Real Time* and Featherstone's suicide, and to each he pauses meaningfully and says, "Off the record? I have no idea." Three of them bring up Lizzie. George says, for the first time in his life, "I have no comment," after first extracting from each of them a promise not to quote him saying "I have no comment." He makes a few calls. He phones his lawyer. He phones Emily Kalman, who says she will put him in touch with her friend Bert Fields, the Hollywood lawyer. He phones Ben Gould. He phones Zip Ingram. And then he goes home.

On East Forty-second Street near the United Nations, as his car waits for the light, a yellow taxi bumps them lightly from behind. His driver, a young Russian or Eastern European, is out of his car and screaming, it seems to George, almost before the accident happened. And then the taxi accidentally bumps the parked Town Car again.

"You fucking *stupidity* Oriental!" his driver shouts. "You cock-fucking *stupidity!*"

Now the cabdriver, an older Asian man wearing boxer shorts and plastic flip-flops, is out on First Avenue as well.

"Dummy! You fucking stop for small! Fucking stop in roadway! Dummy! Dummy cunt!"

"*I? I?* No, *you* cock-fucking stupidity son of a bitch, Oriental, *you* criminal!"

"*Arrest* you! *Arrest* you! Dummy! Cunt!"

George gets out of the car. It isn't rush hour yet. A taxi stops right away.

"Dad? Why are you home?" Max says from the landing as he comes up the stairs.

LuLu, hearing her brother, scampers out of the playroom, away from Rafaela, to the top landing.

"Daddy?" she yells down.

He tells them both what happened.

They think it's a joke. They think it's like when he claims he's withdrawn them from school and they're all moving to a houseboat in International Falls, Minnesota, where he's going to become a professional bear hunter, or like when he says their mother is an alien from the Crab Nebula who abducted and hypnotized him in 1988. Once last year, he went a whole hour insisting that LuLu was a robot he'd bought from the Sharper Image catalogue.

"I'm really not kidding you. The men who run the company hated the show. They killed it."

"How do you *kill* a TV show?" LuLu asks, smiling and wide-eyed.

But Max is finally persuaded he's telling the truth.

"Can I still go to camp?"

"Of course."

"Dad?" he asks.

"What is it?"

"Why didn't Mom stop them from killing your show?"

"I guess she couldn't," George says.

3 8

Lizzie is right. Lizzie happens to have been right. It is better for him to be here alone awhile and think about what he's going to do. She was heading off, and she just kept on going. Perfect. But he is glad. He didn't want to have to recapitulate the details of the meeting with Vlig and the lawyer, the fraudulent hotel-suite charge sheets and the tapes. The tapes. *The tapes.* It's always tapes nowadays, isn't it? He could explain to her about Sandi Bemis and the knife attack on the Venetian and even his arm tucked for a few minutes between Shawna Cindy Switzer's breasts. But he could not bear to put himself on the defensive, not on Monday and not now. He does not want to have to make the weenie denials and self-deprecating explanations of his Las Vegas behavior. And if she were here, her own denials and explanations—she had no idea, she was out of the loop—would kill him, and make him want to kill her. "It isn't you," she said on the phone from San Francisco, "it's not your fault, and it's not my fault either, it's just fucking television," which reminded him of what all her old boyfriends must have heard her say, gently, wide-eyed, sincerely, as she tossed them over, *It's not you, it's me.* "I do think we need some space anyway," she also said. *Some space.* He deliberately didn't ridicule her phrase, *some space,* didn't even snort, and he was glad he didn't, since his stone-sober silence made her apologize preemptively for using it, forced her to fill the silence with a real apology, an embarrassed apology piled onto her steamy heap of automatic, blameless apology, all that merciless pity. Some emotions can make their way down a copper wire intact, but even when it's sincere, apology turns inert and anodyne over the phone. And the apologizer, if she's really listening, can't help but hear it too, her words transmuted to crap in the nanosecond between mouthpiece and earphone. She started apologizing harder but to no effect, powerless to make the *sorry*s and *awful*s sound genuine no matter how she stretched and sweetened her voice. He could hear her frustration. He enjoyed it. "It's not even two weeks," she finally said. "And then we'll sit down and deal with everything."

He is putting on a good show of Dad buoyancy for the children, whose pity makes him sad (for them) rather than angry (at her). But they'll be gone soon—Max and LuLu to camp on Saturday, Sarah to Provence with the Williamsons on Sunday—and he'll be able to relax. On Sunday he can stop smiling. He can walk around naked and unwashed, figuratively, and do nothing, literally. What George really wants to do is nothing. Although he's decided he will go to L.A. for a couple of days, on Emily's advice. "Take advantage of your moment in the trades," she said. "You're notorious." There's also a memorial service for Timothy Featherstone next Monday afternoon in L.A., at Mortons Restaurant.

Practically every phone call brings another twinge of pain, not salt rubbed into the wound but sodium chloride instilled in it with a surgical instrument, applied precisely to the bleeding nerve ends. A reporter from the *Journal* called yesterday looking for dirt on Mose Digital, for anything George knows about the rumors that the division would be spun off or sold to Microsoft. He evidently had no idea (and George didn't tell him) that George Mactier, presumptively disgruntled former MBC executive producer, is married to the starry, splashy corporate up-and-comer Elizabeth Zimbalist, the new president of Mose Digital. "She's a very sexy story," the reporter said, meaning sexy, George believes, in the nonsexual sense.

Then there was the call from Ben, not the first, wonderful, screaming one at the office Monday afternoon (nobody is better at loyal apoplexy than Ben Gould), but the second one, early Tuesday morning here at home. At first George listened, a good audience as usual, amused but unsure where Ben was going with his line about Calvin Klein ("Who would have thought you could double the price of Jockey shorts by printing the name of some silly guy from the Bronx on the elastic?") or his calculation that the two of them personally know one in every five hundred regular buyers of Häagen-Dazs and Ben & Jerry's ice cream. "Two words, George," Ben said. *"Black Dog."* George is familiar with his claims to being the first person to take Bill Clinton to the Black Dog restaurant on Martha's Vineyard, before he was president. Now Ben wanted to confect chic, eccentric businesses like the Black Dog from scratch. "These are truffle businesses," he said, "but I want to figure out how to *cultivate* truffles." The trick, he said, is to go into towns like Sag Harbor and Aspen and Malibu, invent the right bar or ice cream parlor or bait-and-sporting-goods store (or bar-and-bait-and-ice-cream shop) that reeks of quirky local authenticity, then roll each one out to a few other resort towns ("five physical locations, tops"), and finally launch them into direct-mail and web-commerce brands. Black Dog had turned into a retailing phenomenon unintentionally, even reluctantly, and that took them a decade. Ben said that, with the right ideas, and capital, and *focus,* they could accomplish the same alchemy by 2003. "If RJR and Philip Morris and AT&T can go fake-funky and sell Red Kamel cigarettes and Red Dog beer and Lucky Dog phone service, why can't we do it for leisure retail, pardon the expression? You know? And let's move beyond dogs, and the color red. Hey, what do you say? Ben and George's. (I'm not serious about the name.)" George did not reply, "I'm a journalist, Ben," or "I'm a television producer, Ben," or "I want to write and direct films, Ben," or "I've never heard such a depressing proposal in my life, Ben." It's one thing to enjoy his friend's sick, splendid business ideas from afar. But it shocked George that Ben would try to enlist him in one of his schemes. He said, "I don't want to start a chain of yuppie ice cream saloons." Which pissed off Ben. "You're part of the natural aristocracy, I guess? You want to live like a prince, but actually *making money* is just too tawdry for the refined sensibilities of George Mactier?" "Maybe my brother-in-law would like to do it," George said. "He sure would," Ben replied, pushing the salt grains deeper into the exploded tissue, "but I wanted to offer it to you first."

This morning, Sarah breezed off to work at her web site in a T-shirt that says PUSSY POWER in pink letters. What would Lizzie have done? What would he have done a week ago? But he didn't have the strength to discuss it. (*What exactly do you mean by* PUSSY POWER, *honey? And when did you stop wearing a bra?*) At least the letters are small. At least it doesn't have an exclamation point, or an illustration.

The rich get richer; the bleak get bleaker. It depresses him to bump and scoot past Rafaela during the day, as if they're both intruding. At lunch it depresses him when Max and LuLu insist that he fry up the precut carpaccio he buys from Balducci's. It depresses him to see the half-used bottle of Rose's lime juice in the refrigerator—the Harold Mose mixer. Ordinarily, it pleased him to pound meat thin with the huge cartoony wooden mallet, his single favorite kitchen task. But beating the chicken breasts tonight makes him recall the Sunday he and Tuggy Masterson used two stolen Butterball turkeys for .22 target practice, which depressed him in 1967, and does again now.

Before dinner, lying on the Biedermeier couch in the living room (their first joint Christmas present to themselves; doubly depressing), he's reading the biography of Jean Cocteau that he asked Daisy to get for him during one of his misunderstood-genius rants a few weeks back. He's in the middle of a passage describing the May midnight in 1913 when Cocteau watched Diaghilev, Stravinsky, and Nijinsky sobbing and keening together in the Bois de Boulogne, disconsolate over the spectacular failure of their ballet. George is just forming the thought, *Is it too ridiculous to imagine that a century from now* . . . , when LuLu leaps onto his lap suddenly and says, "That man on your book looks like you, Daddy. Is he dead?" Then, looking at the cover, realizing that he's trying to use a child's random observation to talk himself into a link between *Le Sacre du Printemps* and *Real Time,* he is overcome by a sense of his own spuriousness.

Of course, today, July 20, is also their tenth wedding anniversary, which would be depressing enough, but it turned excruciatingly so when her gift, a photo of the whole family floating and grinning in Lake Marten last year, arrived by UPS. "Have a good evening, Mr. Zimbalist," the UPS guy said. He hasn't opened the note that came with it.

And now, sitting outside on a rich, cool July evening with all three real live children, finishing a dinner of fried chicken salad by candle-light, his sadness is so exquisite it's breathtaking.

"I talked to Francesca today," Sarah tells him, apropos of nothing but the standard family dinner-table download.

"Really?" George says. "Why'd you call her?"

"We talked at you guys' party about *1964,* and I sent the tape to her last week, and she said she thought it was awesome. She says there's some new, like, teen documentary series this fall on MTV, *The Good Fight?* That it would be perfect for. Francesca thinks." Sarah smiles, proud of herself. She shrugs hopefully.

"That's terrific, honey." Now he feels professionally envious of his fourteen-year-old daughter. How depressing. Max catches his eye. George assumes the boy is thinking, *Dad, you think her video is as corny and confused as I do, don't you?*

"She said she thought we should give it a new soundtrack. You remember it, right? What do you think would go best—ska, rap, electro-acoustic, ambient, garage, gothic, psychedelic, noise, or twee-pop?" Except for rap, ambient, and psychedelic, and (maybe) ska, George doesn't know what any of those sound like. That's depressing.

"Ambient might be cool," he says, depressing himself by sounding like some ponytailed, middle-aged asshole.

"Is it okay with you if I go up and work on the computer?" Max asks.

Requesting special permission to leave the table, to abandon his poor old man: how unbearably sweet. "Sure it is, Max. You're not up there spending a jillion bucks on ten-dollar-an-hour web gaming, are you?" His anti-video-game crack reminds George of Lizzie.

"Nope," the boy says as he heads inside.

George asks Sarah if she's packed for her trip to France, and she says yes, mostly, and asks him if he's ever been to Nice, and he says yes, remember, a year ago last spring when he went to sell *NARCS* to foreign TV buyers (with your mother, he doesn't say), and she asks if she can borrow Lizzie's Japanese shawl, and he nods, barely. LuLu asks about the single firefly flitting around the backyard ("Is he lonely, Daddy?" she says, as if a midsummer's line has been written for her), and then about what kind of music they play in hell, and what kind in heaven.

Sarah, of course, professes her disbelief in heaven and hell.

"Ambient, maybe," he says, "in heaven," to which Sarah gives a tiny sympathy smile. No smile at all would have been less depressing.

"Maybe," LuLu says with a pixie preperformance smile as she dips her index finger into the dregs of her father's sauvignon blanc, "it's this." She begins running the wet fingertip around the rim of his glass, three circles every two seconds as he's taught her. He's always pleased that she's enchanted by such a sad, serious, beautiful noise. It's dark enough now, he hopes, that his daughters can't see his eyes. "Just *tears*," he remembers LuLu insisting a few weeks ago (only a few weeks), "do *not* count as crying. They don't."

3 9

She's struggling to keep in mind the distinction between guilt and
sorrow. The plane makes it harder, since flying on private jets always
gives a vestigial frisson of guilt, about ten stretch-limo-rides' worth. Exchanging small talk with Harold and Hank and Randy just now as they
all boarded, the mere fact of chat, has also provoked a guiltlike sensation.

But she has not betrayed George. She is not betraying him. They canceled his show because it was expensive and the test audiences hated it.
She didn't cancel his show. She didn't have any idea they were going to
cancel it.

What if the show were still on the air, and they'd fired her? Would
George resign from *Real Time* in some grand act of solidarity?
Exactly.

She considered quitting. She didn't consider it very seriously. (A
trickle of true guilt, but only a trickle.) If she quit, it would contractually permit Mose Media Holdings to cancel the acquisition of Fine
Technologies, which they may do if she leaves the company voluntar-
ily during the next six months. Then she wouldn't be rich, not even on
paper. Her only out is the change-of-control provision in her contract,
which would allow her to quit in the event of a sale or takeover of her

division. But otherwise, if she told Mose "Fuck you," she (*they,* George and she) would forfeit the hoard of fuck-you money. And then she would go back to running Fine Technologies alone, a prospect that, to her surprise, she finds almost unbearable to contemplate. She has moved on. For better or for worse. For richer or . . . whatever.

Anxiety is keeping her awake (despite a virtually real bed, sheets fancier than the ones at home, a down pillow), but it's not because she feels *guilty* in the sense of deserving blame. She feels rotten, not culpable, slightly heartless for flying off to Asia with Harold Mose and missing their anniversary, but definitely not treacherous.

Her husband may abominate her, and she can sense on the phone that the children blame her for some of his misfortune. But her other family members, the eighty-odd child-men and -women at Fine Technologies, seem to have accommodated themselves to corporatization and her semiabandonment. She wonders if her employees' antipathy is related inversely to her physical presence. The animal-rights protesters declared victory and withdrew after she sold to Mose and decamped uptown, which has allowed life on West Eighteenth Street to tranquilize. The newspaper boors of the left and right have climbed back onto their more familiar hobbyhorses. (She saw in yesterday's *San Francisco Chronicle,* however, that Molly Cramer couldn't resist using the *Real Time* cancellation as a pretext for rehashing all her previous columns about George and Lizzie. The self-composting obsessiveness of hack ideologues like Cramer makes Lizzie wonder: do they finally write one last column that weaves together every previous column, but even more shrilly, and then drop dead?) The mania on Eighteenth Street also subsided, of course, after Warps was finally done. Alexi said on the phone yesterday that it feels like summer for the first time in his three years there: half the staff gone (Bruce in the new Terraplane office on the Bowery, Fanny and her two Germans at the annual Def Con hackers' convention, Karen off selling WiccanWare disks at Renaissance festivals), those still around working at half speed, and Lance Haft acting as if he's *in charge,* like a summer-school teacher. Lizzie assumes that the stock deal she cut for the staff as part of the acquisition helped mellow the mood, too. And with that peaceful moment of George-free thought, enveloped in the white noise roar of the BMW–Rolls-Royce turbines at fifty-one thousand feet, she finally sleeps.

Of course he's flying first class. He has no income, no job, and no show. Fuck it, why not go all the way? He's wearing dark glasses. He's drinking a bullshot. He's listening to a CD (Cowboy Junkies), and he's reading *Variety*.

Jack Delancey's piece on the cancellation is all right. He uses George's "It's only television" quote. He connects (sloppily, without real evidence) the *Real Time* alternative-medicine story to the transformation of Mose's Winter Channel into Reality Channel, and he connects the Farley Lyman story, even though it wasn't broadcast, to MBC's possible deal with Derek Dreen for *The Illionaire*. He quotes George saying, "I'm not in the series business anymore," and mentions "a frenzied flurry of studio interest in the prod's pitch for a retro comedy pic about teen antiwar assassins that Mactier would pen and possibly helm." For a long time, George has had an idea for a screenplay set in the sixties about college students plotting a political murder. Now, given this frenzied (albeit entirely fictional) flurry of interest in letting him direct it as a feature film, he plans on fleshing out the idea, and pitching it to people other than a *Variety* reporter. The worst quote is from an anonymous MBC executive who alludes to the network's "very real and longstanding philosophical qualms" about what *Variety* calls the "edgy journo-entertainment crossbreed concept" of *Real Time*.

But not bad, all in all, he thinks, reading the story again, and again, and skimming it a fourth time before turning the page, where his eye is yanked directly (if not extrasensory perception, what?) to a story headlined IS A WALL STREET WHIZ CORNERING THE LIT BIZ? The article reports that "Bennett Gould, head of the boutique financial firm Bennett Gould Partners, also known as '$,' is said by sources to have quietly bought a studio's worth of pic and TV rights to 'multiple' big-name contemporary fiction and legit works. Authors purchased are said to include A-list biggies Bellow, Updike, Roth, Salinger, Brit bad boy Martin Amis, movie-legit scribe Tom Stoppard, and *Doonesbury* creator Garry Trudeau, as well as lesser-knowns William Gaddis, Walker Percy, Don DeLillo, Laurie Colwin, David Foster Wallace, Lorrie Moore, Robertson Davies, GOP speechwriter Mark Helprin, and porn-lit scribbler Nicholson Baker. From his Long Island summer home in literati-laden East Hampton, Gould declined to comment on his alleged buying spree."

Ben lied to me, George thinks. *He lied.* And then he remembers Ben's friendship with Bucky Lopez, and the *Real Time* story about Lopez's handgun conflict of interest.

As long as he's known him, Ben Gould has said, "Mactier, you are so naïve." And George has always teased Ben that he's Exhibit A in the case for cynicism and romanticism as black-and-white flip sides of the same wrong idea. Staring out at the clear blue sky over America, George realizes that naïveté and paranoia have just the same sort of consanguinity.

It's George who made a doctrine out of befriending cheerful rapscallions, the Zip Ingrams and Ben Goulds, "as long as they're smart and loyal rapscallions." It's George who told her how smart Harold is. And she's not even his friend, besides—she's his employee (and shareholder). How deep does any vein of loyalty run between employer and employee, or vice versa? Canceling *Real Time* was not an act of disloyalty, but rather one of those gut-wrenching executive decisions, those tough calls, those hard choices for which bosses are gravely celebrated and paid their magnificent salaries.

"May I give you more jackfruit marmalade, sir?" asks the Cindy Crawfordesque flight attendant.

"No thanks, my dear, but another Rose's and Pellegrino would be superb, when you have a chance. Elizabeth, anything else for you? Another brioche?"

She shakes her head.

Hank Saddler has retreated to the other side of the plane to call people who've left him messages—"This is Henry Saddler returning," he says into the phone again and again, performing the executive-secretarial trick of making the transitive verb grandly intransitive. Back in the media area, Randy has booted up the DVD golf simulator, and has conscripted the black Pamela Anderson flight attendant to play eighteen holes of Augusta with him.

"Harold," Lizzie says across the breakfast dishes, "this is uncomfortable, but we've got to get it on the table. It's the monster in the room. We need to have a conversation."

"Absolutely correct," he says, pursing his lips, removing his napkin from his collar, taking off his glasses (new ones yet again—tiny brushed-brass circles that look eighteenth century) and sighing heavily. "*Real Time.*"

"Was it honestly just the test results that made you decide to cancel it? I mean, after one week of shows . . . ?"

"Elizabeth, it was the toughest decision I think I've ever had to make as an executive. I know that's a cliché, and I know it doesn't make it one whit easier on George, but it's true. Now, as to the audience testing," he says, shaking his head and turning his palms up, "I know it was the most extensive we've ever performed, but I frankly am not aware of the details, or any of the rest of it. At the end of the day, it was Laura Welles's decision to cancel *Real Time*. And it was a decision I reluctantly accepted."

Push. *Push.* "George said Arnold Vlig used the budget overruns as a pretext—"

"We knew the program was going to cost a fortune going in, Elizabeth—quite frankly, more than we could rationally justify. 'New Network for the New Century' is something I've genuinely believed in, as you know, and I jawboned Arnold and the rest of them into taking a leap of faith on *Real Time*. But one-point-six million a week was already stretching it, and one-point-eight, one-point-nine . . . we were looking at a hemorrhage, quite frankly. A hemorrhage that was not getting good critical and editorial reaction, and a hemorrhage with essentially no back-end revenue."

Lizzie nearly nods along. Harold Mose does believe his own bullshit, and makes the people around him want to believe it too.

"Which we can particularly ill afford," he adds, tipping his head down a little, "given the internet losses we're projecting through '02. If I had insisted, for the sake of my vanity, on overruling Arnold and Laura and letting the show run for nine difficult months, what then? Do you think George would have been happier seeing the thing canceled after he poured in nine more months of his heart and soul? Isn't the more humane act to quit the game after a single end rather than play all ten and never get a stone anywhere near the center of the house?"

She's grateful for the curling analogy. It makes it easier to resist any show of assent.

"I have another question," she says. *Do I personally bear any blame at all?* "What about—well—I know it was under my purview, and—"

"Charles Prieve," Mose says. "I know the Fifty-nine scuttlebutt you must've heard about Charles Prieve's blackmail gambit . . ."

"I, no, I—"

"And in fact, yes, one of his letters did mention you and George and *Real Time* in extremely ugly terms. But that threat, I assure you, had no bearing whatsoever on the cancellation. None."

"I was actually wondering about the Manson digital-insert trick—did that play a big part in the decision about the show? In the end?"

Mose sits back, relaxing visibly.

"Oh, good heavens, no. *No.* Quite the contrary. In fact, I meant to tell you how pleased I was to discover you'd given George the go-ahead on that. Laura was astonished at how beautifully the effect worked! After we got burned on using it in News, she and Timothy were a little nervous about trying it out on the entertainment side. But George proved it can be a *fantastic* weapon in our arsenal." He pauses. "If there's ever the opportunity, please thank him for me."

The flight attendant has reappeared.

"May I clear the table?"

Anxiety drains from Lizzie. The cancellation was not her fault, not even a little. *Quite the contrary.* She finds herself not guilty.

"Are we finished?" Mose says. "Can we get back to *our* businesses?"

She asks him if what she read in *Variety* was true, about the Winter Channel becoming some kind of New Age channel, and he looks at her a little oddly and says yes, possibly, what does she think of the idea? She says she thinks it could be huge, that she's in the lunatic demo herself, that literally half the people in America now inhabit shiatsu, herbal, acupuncture, yoga households, and he asks if "Reality Channel" is better than "The Healing Channel."

"Reality Channel," she says.

"And you know this fellow Edward Ingram, correct?"

"*Sure.* I adore Zip. He's one of our closest friends. Why?"

"Timothy and I talked with Zip about running News after Barry Stengel. But now it looks as if there'll be no more News to run. So we're talking with him about Reality Channel. He's going to be in Sydney next week, as it happens. We'll have a bite."

Since the other job is moot, and she adores Zip, she does not say that Zip Ingram running a network news division, even MBC's, would have been ludicrous, dangerous, an outrage. Mose asks what is finally to be done with "our FCC boondoggle," the new free digital channels. They discuss the pros and cons of acceding to the wishes of the Microsoft lobby and turning the channels into twenty-megabit PC connections, versus Timothy Featherstone's "extreme entertainment" plan—Feathervision, Timothy had called it, in which each channel would become a serially obsessive, hypermarketed, microniche medium—nothing but old Burt Reynolds movies and TV shows for a month, then all *Flipper,* then all Monkees, then Jacqueline Onassis for a couple of months, and so on and on. Mose wonders if there's "some way to play around digitally with our existing brands," and Lizzie laughingly mentions two of her son's fevered and repulsive ideas—R-rated versions of regular TV series distributed in DVD format (*Ally McBeal* with nude scenes, *Homicide* with viscera) and 3D celebrity-transformation software, with which a computer user could do anything imaginable with a famous person, living or dead, on screen—have sex with them, assassinate them, surgically transform them. "This is a *ten*-year-old?" Mose says. "Maybe your son should run the entertainment division." He frets about his backward local stations that aren't broadcasting digital pictures, but she says it doesn't matter, since only one in a hundred homes has a digital TV. He reminds Lizzie of her hypoglossal canal analogy. She replies that MBC may not have the capital resources to become the *first* ape to turn himself into a talking human. Smile, sip, smile, smile, and sip.

"Time for the seat belts, Mr. Mose, Ms. Zimbalist. We're starting our descent into Haneda."

"Well, in fact," he says to Lizzie, finishing up, "before too very long we may be climbing up a different limb of the evolutionary tree altogether. Did you know the broadcast networks' share of the TV audience, all seven of us combined, just dipped below fifty?" He looks down at Japan. "I enjoy being a contrarian, but only when it *works.* The network television business may be Neanderthal after all. A dead end." He turns back to her. "They are the ones who died off, correct?"

"Uh-huh," she says, waiting for Mose to follow up. He doesn't. "What business *are* we in?" she finally asks.

"Ah, I wish I knew," he says. "Ask me tomorrow." He smiles. "No business strategy lasts forever. In fact, you're lucky if it lasts four *quarters.* Welcome to the twenty-first century."

Hank Saddler takes the seat next to Lizzie for the landing at Haneda Airport in Tokyo. He looks for a full, simpy second at her, then at Mose.

"Did you discuss?" he asks, looking back and forth between them again.

He means *Real Time* and George.

"Everything's fine," Mose says.

4 0

He has opened the big front door for her, which in L.A. never triggers any trace of late-feminist awkwardness. "You're George Mactier?" repeats the stylish woman in pencil-leg khaki pants, silk T-shirt, and Gucci loafers as soon as he's introduced himself and asks if she knows where he can find Ned Wisdom. "I think your screenplay *grooves!*"

She is the first Hollywood executive with whom he's had a professional encounter as a would-be filmmaker, and she has complimented him on sight, preemptively, gratuitously. He wonders if she's Ned Wisdom's number two. Emily has said he has a brilliant woman who does all his development. (Emily also said that every big producer has a brilliant woman who does all his development.)

"Thank you. Thanks very much." He knows he should leave it there. "It's—unfortunately, it's not written yet."

"That's cool," she says as he follows her in.

She steps smartly into the cavernous main space, slate gray but California bright, swings left just past the unmanned receptionist's desk, then stops abruptly, standing to look at a fax that tallies, hour by hour, from Friday afternoon through last night, the weekend grosses of every movie in release in North America. "Whoa," she says, "the Adam Sandler *Koyaanisqatsi* remake really *did* open."

"Can you tell me where Ned Wisdom's office is?"

"Sure!" she says, "just a sec." She walks around the yellow metal reception cube and pulls a translucent yellow circle over her head like a halo. It's a telephone headset. "Let me tell them you're here."

She is the receptionist. George can practically hear the quick farting sound of deflation as her compliment shrinks to a useless, flaccid scrap. The receptionist at Ned Wisdom Productions thinks George's unwritten screenplay *grooves*.

"He'll be one sec," she says, "but you can go right on back to his zone. Around those river pebbles over there, left over the bridge thing, then left again. His reception zone is a patio. You can't miss it."

He gets lost somewhere between the industrial-medieval bridge-breezeway and the patio. He runs into a guy wearing Converse high-tops and an ANTICHRIST! baseball cap coming out of a digital-editing bay. The exquisitely lit and furnished room looks like the main cabin of the Space Shuttle *TriBeCa*. The kid looks like a very clean messenger. George figures he's probably a $170,000-a-year film editor.

"Can you tell me where Ned Wisdom's office is?" George asks him.

"I can," he says. "I'll take you to him."

George sees that his left turn after the bridge was more of a veer. Wisdom's office, set just beyond the red sandstone patio, is a separate white building (the adobe smells fresh) apparently built as a scale model of the Guggenheim Museum in New York.

"Come on in," the kid says. "You're George, right?" He puts out his hand and smirks. "I'm him." The kid, of course, is Ned Wisdom, the producer of three surprise hits in a row during the last two years—the violent animated comedy *Ammo Blammo,* the Dennis Quaid/Kurt Russell/Patrick Swayze buddy picture *Comeback,* and last spring's *Who's a Pussy?,* the so-called "MTV *Candide*" that starred Bruce Willis as a present-day L.A. detective and, at seventy-three minutes, was said to be the shortest major motion picture ever released. Wisdom's action-adventure new-millennium comedy *Antichrist!* will be released at Christmas on sixty-five hundred screens. George sees now that Wisdom has some gray hair. He is not technically a kid.

Inside his office—which has a Guggenheimian ramp winding along

the inside walls, all the way up to what looks like a bungee-jump platform near the ceiling—Wisdom sits on a stainless-steel stool. His desk is
an antique Bauhaus drafting table. George sits in a BarcaLounger covered in lush, ocher leather—an ironic BarcaLounger, no doubt, although
the impeccable upholstery muddles the irony.

"You don't really want to become a screenwriter, do you?" he says
to George. He's not smiling.

"Well, yeah, I do, among other things."

"But you're a producer."

"But TV is—"

"Yeah, I know. I *know*."

George has no idea what critique of television Wisdom has just affirmed.

"Emily said you have an idea for a picture about hippie murderers?
Emily is good people."

"Well, not exactly hippie murderers."

"Wait, aren't you the Charlie Manson guy?"

"That was just a story we happened to break on my show." George
leans forward. "This movie is about three boys and a girl, normal suburban kids in Westchester. In the first act, it's 1962 and 1963, they're
thirteen—"

"What's Westchester?"

"It's a suburb. Of New York?"

Wisdom shakes his head and gives an unembarrassed shrug.

"Anyhow," George continues, "the boys are totally into 007; they
play these outlandish, elaborate secret-agent games all the time, and—"

Wisdom is shaking his head more emphatically now. "I don't know
1962. I don't really *feel* 1962. I mean, are we talking *Happy Days*?"

"No, no, not like that at all. These kids sneak into Manhattan for
weekends and pretend they're James Bond, they go all over the city,
wearing suits and ties. It's funny and poignant, but with an edge.
They sneak into strip clubs, they take taxis, they have toy guns,
and so—"

"You know, if Sony can't get their Bond picture made, how the Bob
Evans am I going to get MGM to let me rip off the franchise? Just a
note."

"No, these boys are just Bond *fans*, fanatics, you know?"

"What thirteen-year-old is a James Bond fanatic? Is this like *Austin Powers* with kids?"

"No, no, not *now*, maybe, but in the early sixties—"

"So these are like my *parents* as *teenagers*?"

"I suppose. Sure. Anyhow, the second and third acts are set in 1967 and 1968, during the Vietnam War, and two of these three boys and their other friend, a girl, are at college together. One of them is a serious radical—"

Wisdom puts up his hand. "Pause. Rewind. 'Serious radical' meaning he what, like, eats some mushrooms and skateboards through his father's stuffy law firm and ends up becoming a U.S. senator? Because we're doing that. Sandler. Summer 2001. But that's good, because it means we're in the same sensibility domain, which is rare out here. It's special." He leans forward. "You do crime, noir kinds of pieces, right? *NARCS*? Let me try one of my indie-type stories out, see if it resonates for you. This movie star finishes a picture, goes home to his beautiful ranch in Montana, ten million acres with buffalo and eagles and all that, to fight the mining company that's about to destroy his environment. And when he walks in— beautiful log-cabin mansion, like Eisner's in Aspen—when he gets there, somebody grabs him, and he sees they have his girlfriend, or wife, whatever. And she's about to be fucked up the ass by seven giant black dudes."

Ned Wisdom pauses. He smiles like Bill Clinton smiles when he's proud of something. Then George realizes that it's not a pause, but a full stop.

"What do you think?" Wisdom asks.

"Did you mean the hero is a movie star in the movie—that the *character* is an actor? Or that it's a big-star role?"

"Whichever. Both. But does the *story* work for you?"

"It's not, it's—what happens then?"

"Hey, I'm producing. That's just the *story*. I let storytellers tell their stories. I don't prescribe to writers. I'm known for not doing that."

George shakes his head. "That doesn't actually sound like my kind of thing."

"Okay," says Wisdom, "cool." He leans farther forward, so only the very edge of his little behind is still touching steel. "Another project.

Indie style, but a Michelle/Julia-type vehicle, prestige thriller. She's a doctor, or an executive, whatever, a single mother going to visit her mom and dad in her hometown for Christmas. Maybe the father's a professor, like a computer genius who made a billion, and the mother's an old but beautiful former chorus girl. Christmas morning, Michelle comes downstairs. Dad's dead. Red Christmas stockings stuffed in his mouth. And two guys dressed like Santa's elves, maybe actual dwarves, depends how edgy we want to go, have Mom tied up with tinsel in front of the fireplace. And like five huge black guys are about to fuck her up the ass. *Mom,*" he adds quickly, as if to head off some horrible misunderstanding, "*not* Michelle, or Julia." Then he oozes back into his contented Clintonesque smirk. "Yes? Thumbs-up?"

After the meeting, George has promptly gotten lost again, on his way from Santa Monica to Timothy Featherstone's memorial service at Mortons. To get his mind off Ned Wisdom, he tried to remember every funeral he's ever attended, to see if he has ever been to three in one six-month period before, and ended up driving all the way into Hollywood. At the service, the canapé platters ("A warm Tunisian-style mussel? Or endive hash with soy-milk crème fraîche?") are rimmed with black satin. He knows he won't run into Mose or Saddler (their Asia trip), and Daisy found out for him that Arnold Vlig wasn't going (the cold prick), but he wants to run into Laura Welles. He knows his presence will make her squirm. And it does, although his pleasure in her discomfort is exceeded, he realizes the instant he spots her, by the sting.

Ng is treated as the primary widow, although they were not actually married, with the legal Mrs. Featherstone relegated to her own small, ancillary circle of grief near the bar. (The first Mrs. Featherstone is taking photographs.)

It has not occurred to George that he might run into the virtual Mrs. Featherstone once removed. He watches her, especially her tight, tight chignon, not recognizing her when she approaches him. (He always finds that mourning outfits make attractive women more attractive. He wonders if Louisa gets her morbidity from him.)

"Hello, George. It's Sandra Bemis."

Hi! Hey, funny story—true *story*—*it was your fraudulent expense-account*

living that helped get me canceled! Yours and Timothy's, God rest his soul.
"Hello, Sandi," he says.

"Thank you so much for your quote in the paper. Timmy would have been so pleased." When the obituary writer phoned Monday morning, before the meeting on Fifty-nine, George told him, "Timothy Featherstone was a singular human being and, for me, the embodiment of everything amazing about the entertainment business."

"It was really a shock to me. Horrible."

"You know, the sad thing is, I blame Harold Mose. And all of them there. I do."

Yes, yes . . . that is very sad . . . but interesting! "Why?"

"I think he made Timmy work too hard, for one thing. And I think Harold never really understood Timmy, what he was saying. You know?"

Yes, I do, since I literally didn't understand what Timothy was saying half the time. "Mmm," George says, nodding. "Sandi," he finally says, "were you aware that Timothy was charging off your suite in Las Vegas to my show?"

She has a faraway, innocent look, sincerely stupid. "Within my consciousness, I've *heard* about it, but, like, I don't *know* about it. Was it a lot of money? Did you have to pay for it personally? Because I could pay it back out of the money Timmy left for me in his will."

George feels like he's stepped into *The Maltese Falcon* or *Chinatown*—or, more precisely, *Who's a Pussy?* He shakes his head but doesn't say no.

"Because he left fifty-seven thousand dollars for me to go to grad school, but I only need like about thirty-five for that."

She tells him it has been her dream for a decade to get a master's degree in the history of consciousness from the University of California at Santa Cruz. He says no, keep Timothy's bequest for herself, but if she wouldn't mind, his lawyer did say he'd love to have an affidavit in the file affirming that George Mactier was not part of your, the Vegas, you know, scheme to bilk MBC. And she said thanks so much, since she needs the cash "to grow" the Wow-Wow Partners animal-healing business and ante up capital along with her two new partners.

"You know them. Emily Kalman? And Jeremy?"

"Emily Kalman is going into the pet-therapy business with you?"

"She's sort of a silent partner. I'm chairman and CEO, and my COO is this magic, magic man. He used to act? I think on *Petticoat Estates,* where one of the *Petticoat Junction* daughters has triplets and moves to a snobby suburb? Jeremy Ramo? He used to be *Buddy* Ramo?"

"I didn't know Buddy's name was Jeremy." He doesn't bother telling her it was *Li'l Gilligan,* not *Petticoat Estates.*

4 1

After four days in Tokyo, Lizzie is more than ever convinced of what she has always suspected: the higher you go, the more you make, the easier the job gets. Sure, there are those tough, hard, gut-wrenching moments every so often (firing, downsizing, closing, canceling), but mainly it's easy—listening, lunching, taking planes, giving opinions, forcing babblers to get to the point.

Mose doesn't drink, so Lizzie spends her time after dinner alone in her room. The first night, examining the label of a forty-five-dollar half-pint of bad Australian Riesling, she was startled by a recorded announcement from the refrigerator informing her that because she removed a minibar item for longer than six seconds, she would be charged for it. It was more comical than *Mission: Impossible,* more sinister than *Get Smart.* Each night after midnight, looking out over the little park, Chinzan-so Garden, smoking her dollar-apiece cigarettes, she feels a little like a spy. (Languor is so rare at home.) During the days, she mostly goes off to her own appointments in the Shinjuku neighborhood with computer and video-game businessmen, who all seem to find her obscurely amusing. (She discovered at her first meeting that there is no word in Japanese for *millennium.*) Mose and Saddler go to their appointments with bankers, politicians, and chairmen of media and entertainment companies. Mose may be negotiating deals, but Lizzie certainly is not, unless the agreements she's striking are too subtle for her to register. Randy goes golfing with Japanese TV executives. And Gloria Mose, who has arrived from India, spends her days talking to printers about the lavish children's book she's privately publishing about the angels of aborted fetuses, and shopping for a particular kind of gray, acid-etched, iron-free glass that's unavailable in the United States and Europe because the fabrication process makes the workers who manufacture it sick.

At night, the Moses, Saddler, and Lizzie dine together. (Randy goes out drinking with Japanese TV executives.)

"The quite wonderful thing," Gloria is saying, "is how restorative Calcutta always is. It feeds my soul. Especially seeing the work my people are doing." She sponsors a convent of European nuns who persuade pregnant low-caste Indian women they'll go to hell if they submit to abortions. ("Gloria's nuns," Harold said to Lizzie during the flight over, "are Mother Teresas without the clinics, and every one as angry as a ferret.")

"Did you know," Gloria says to Lizzie and Harold, pointedly ignoring Saddler, "that the little tattoos and colored bits Indian women wear all have *meanings*? I never realized. Isn't that clever?"

Lizzie is pleased the subject has changed from abortion. "What do they mean?" she asks.

Gloria looks at her as if Lizzie had asked why she wears dark glasses indoors or why she keeps herself so hideously skinny. "I haven't a clue, Elizabeth. Now my daughter, Caroline, in 1992, was the very first person in London to get one of those tattoos, with all the little straight black lines, like they have on packages in shops . . ."

"UPC," Saddler says, wedging into the conversation. "Universal Product Code."

Gloria, never turning her face his way, continues. "Caroline had this thing tattooed on her bum when she was seventeen. At first I was appalled. But then *Tatler* called it chic. And she was the *first*."

"What product was her bar code *for*?" Lizzie asks.

"I haven't a clue. But by 1995—dear, what year was Blair?"

"Ninety-seven," Mose says.

"By 1997, that little magazine *Wallpaper* was calling it a *cliché.*"

"What?" Lizzie asks.

"My stepdaughter had the thing lasered off her ass," Mose says. "Needless to say. At great expense. To me. Although you can still make it out—like a fuzzy dalmatian's spot."

This is evidently an established routine. Gloria turns to Lizzie and says, "Harold says I love my dalmatians more than I do him. And he knows Clement and Neville do *not* have a single fuzzy spot on them."

"You have dalmatians?" Lizzie says.

"Two *perfect* boys. Harold gave me a pair of puppies right after we were married, but they did have"—she shakes her head as if she's tasted something bitter—"extremely irregular spots. Poorly spaced. Oddly shaped. Mottling around the edges. And some pink around the eyes. Those two went away, and I ran through three more dogs before we got Clement and Neville from the Goldsmiths. The graphics are glorious, that's why we love the breed. But it's terribly difficult to get them just right. Harold," she says, "did I tell you I went to old man Goldsmith's retirement affair at the Connaught the day before I left? Extraordinary! It was like some big Jewish bar mitzvah."

In one sense, women like Gloria make socializing a breeze. They do all the active work. But as Gloria chatters on during the main course and through dessert about Jews and abortion ("Fifty *million* abortions every year around the world, and I don't hear the Jews caterwauling about *that*"), and wonders aloud if Tokyo is more "urban bricolage or urban *pasticcio,*" Lizzie sees night after night of this looming ahead like a sentence. She realizes she has too hastily understated the rigors of just showing up and smiling.

Outside it is already miserably hot, and Kuala Lumpur is awash in a dank brown miasma of car exhaust, industrial fumes, and smoke from distant forest fires that their VIP handler at the airport said have been burning since New Year's. "Malaysia *boleh,*" the limo driver said when Mose asked how business has been since the economic crash three years ago. When Lizzie asked the concierge if he thought the forest fires would be put out soon, first he blamed Indonesia, but then he said, "Malaysia *boleh,* Malaysia *boleh.*" Lizzie wonders if it's a pidginized "Bully for Malaysia!" or "Boola-boola!"

It's five-thirty in the morning. Hank, Randy, Harold, and Lizzie are seated around a table in the living room of the Moses' hotel suite, staring at a speakerphone. They're listening in on the Mose Media Holdings quarterly conference call, which is originating from the Fifty-ninth Floor, where it's five-thirty in the afternoon. Three executives—Arnold Vlig; the chief financial officer; and the vice president for investor relations—are attempting to persuade several hundred stock analysts, mutual fund managers, hedge fund operators, and large individual investors to please, *please* hold on to their shares of the company's stock. The price at the close today was 45½, down a point.

Lizzie has never listened to one of these conferences before. She's surprised at how scripted it seems. The executives read opening statements, like at a congressional hearing or a trial—but a really convivial congressional hearing, a happy trial. The only downbeat passages are the legal boilerplates. When the investor relations woman says, "If you have a question, press one," Lizzie smiles. (No one else does.) The third time the CFO says "actual results may vary," like a fast-talking small-print announcer at the end of a TV ad for a prescription drug, she smiles again, alone. Even the putatively extemporaneous answers sound cobbled together from pre-scripted modules. Someone asks if there is any chance the company will abandon the network television business. "Giving guidance now," says Brad, the CFO, as if he's about to reveal a fascinating secret, "the network is off to a super, super, flying start this quarter." In Kuala Lumpur, Randy smiles and nods. "Last quarter, as you know," Brad says, "we did encourage sobriety overall. This fall, our key drivers of revenue growth will be internet products . . ." Randy, Hank, and Harold all turn to look at her.

————————

She hasn't left the hotel all day. It's 112 degrees outside, and the smoke and the gases only get soupier toward evening. However, because "it's *Malaysia*," Mose said, rather than Japan, they can force people to come to them for meetings.

"Jimmy!" Mose says as the Malaysian man approaches them in the bar. J. K. "Jimmy" Wong is a deputy at the Ministry of Energy, Telecommunications and Posts. He apparently also has some nebulous ex officio position in a semiprivate television channel. Wong and Mose embrace in a manly fashion, hands on elbows, hands on forearms, hands on shoulders. The two of them are going off to dinner with some Malaysian government and military people. Lizzie will eat in the hotel with Hank Saddler. Gloria has the vapors, and Randy is having his driver take him "straight from the links over to meet Harold at General Rahmat's compound."

The small talk concerns the forest fires, which Jimmy Wong tells them have destroyed 110,000 homes and killed 9,000 Malaysians in the last three months.

"Bad news, but less than the flood and the typhoon," says Jimmy Wong.

"One man's bad is another's good, Minister Wong," Mose says. "Floods and typhoons are a key driver of our Asian business, Jimmy."

Mose says to Lizzie, "*Cards.* Most of Jimmy's citizens can't afford fancy flowers and funerals, but they spend big on condolence cards, great condolence posters."

"People like the big, colorful picture-cards," Wong says.

Harold raises an index finger. "You know what I say . . ."

Lizzie wonders if even a Malaysian government official with a British accent will appreciate a curling analogy.

". . . there's always a bull market *somewhere*—the trick is finding it."

Wong smiles and sips his Scotch.

"We ferry in with the relief workers," Mose explains to Lizzie, "and our guys go hamlet to hamlet, selling."

"You've never seen such a customer-focused business," Saddler says. "It's very moving."

"It's like your American slogan in Vietnam," Mose says to Lizzie and Hank, "you get their hearts and minds, and their money follows."

"True," Saddler says.

"Jimmy," Mose says to his pal, "Lizzie and Hank would get a tremendous kick out of that fantastic bar you took me to last time over toward Petronas Towers." He turns to Lizzie. "It's called Wall Street. Huge bank of video monitors, Bloombergs. The prices of the damn cocktails change all the time, according to global currency fluctuations—your martini's 14.68 ringgit one minute, the second one's 14.82. It's very amusing."

Jimmy Wong suddenly looks unhappy. "Wall Street is closed. Since 1998."

"Ah," Mose says. "I was over in '97 working up some schemes with Jimmy and his friends for the prime minister's Vision 2020 project. The prime minister had such plans, didn't he, Jimmy? Multimedia super-corridor, cybermart, cyberjaya, the Multimedia University . . . Rough timing for poor Dr. M., eh?"

"Malaysia *boleh,*" Wong says.

"What does that mean?" Lizzie asks.

" 'Malaysia can do it.' A Malay phrase. Malaysia *boleh.*"

"Malaysia *boleh,*" Hank Saddler repeats, and puts his little fist in the air. "Yay!"

So Lizzie was right about the meaning, even if her imperialist etymology was mistaken.

"Malaysia *boleh!*" Wong says. "Unless the Jewish speculators attack us again, like in '97 and '98."

"Yes, well, you won't have *that* to worry about with us."

Should she say something? She doesn't even know what angle Mose is working here, what his J. K. Wong deal is all about. But it's not *Mission: Impossible;* it's closer to *Z.* Should she? Gloria is English, and you're supposed to cut them some slack for anti-Semitism, the way you're supposed to accept chronic dissembling in Morocco or smile when Kazakhs fart at the end of a meal. But Harold is Canadian. Would George say something? George would want her to say something. She must.

"What Harold means, Mr. Wong, is that, as a Jewess, the next time I exchange secret messages with my superiors in Jerusalem, I'll make them promise to remove Malaysia from the hit list whenever they're planning on destroying some Asian economies." She smiles as warmly as she knows how.

Saddler looks as if he's going to vomit or cry. Wong is baffled, maybe alarmed. Mose forces a chuckle and says, "The lady is yanking your chain, Jimmy. She's joking." He gives her a look. "And all I meant, of course, is that Mose Media Holdings is in the communications business, not the currency speculation game."

Lizzie shuts up for the rest of drinks. Wong tells them how his government is adapting one-ounce American model airplanes and flying saucer toys as MAVs—micro–air vehicles—for military and intelligence-gathering purposes. Mose tells Wong that Malaysia should imitate the

U.S. Army, and establish an advisory group of private businessmen with whom they can trade ideas and technologies.

"Our company just joined the Army board in the States, and it's a remarkable partnership—Disney got to use some of the Army's top-secret bulletproof glass on their new studio in Times Square, and the Army is using high-tech new Disney microphones to listen for sniper fire."

"It is a super, public-private, win–win–type program," Saddler pipes in. "I liaise with them almost every month. You know, Disney sent one of their TV directors from ABC down to Washington to teach the generals how to *direct* a *war*! Isn't that fantastic? Because you know, with all the tons of video pictures the commanders have rushing at them now, from their smart bombs and wingtip cameras and so forth, the guys just weren't dealing, not in a twenty-first-century way."

"Warteurs," Mose says for Lizzie's benefit. He glances at her. The muscles around her mouth form a smile.

"Harold," says Wong, reminded by Saddler's testimonial of his own cutting-edge public-private video project, "the Malaysian boy, the little entertainment mogul in Negri Sembilan, has been taken care of. His unauthorized disks and videos have been eliminated. The American salesman's as well—jazz privé."

"*Thank* you, Mr. Wong," Harold says. "We appreciate that."

"Is that the visionary Canadian media mogul Harold Mose?" says a British voice from the shadows.

"Good *sir*!" Harold bellows. He stands and hugs the tall, handsome, smiling man who has arrived at their table. Wong stands and shakes the Englishman's hand.

He turns to Lizzie. "Farley Lyman," he says.

"Elizabeth Zimbalist." She's never heard of Farley Lyman.

"*Sir* Farley Lyman," Harold says. And to his friend: "Elizabeth is our new cyberpresident, dragging us into the twenty-first century to save us from the fate of predigital dinosaurs like you."

"A pleasure," Lyman says. "And tragic that you won't be dining with us tonight. Gentlemen," he announces to Mose and Wong, "I'm afraid we'll be late for General Rahmat and his friend if we don't get going."

The men leave. *Only six more months,* she thinks, *and I can cash out.* As Saddler pays, she keeps thinking about Wong's assurances to Mose about "jazz privé." Private jazz? Is it the Asian VH1 concept Harold has been discussing? Or some internet music scheme? And then she realizes: not *jazz privé,* Chas Prieve, the conniving and disgruntled Chas Prieve, corporate blackmailer, alleged pornographer, failed Fine Technologies West Coast vice president.

"He's a great war hero, you know," Saddler says, "Sir Farley. And such a gentleman too. Ah, the English."

But Lizzie's not listening. She's thinking about Harold Mose's weird interest in Chas Prieve. And about the six months.

––––––

"Hi," she says into her phone.

"Where are you?"

"Sydney. Driving from Darling Harbour to Homebush Bay. How *are* you, sweetheart?"

"Asleep. What time is it?"

He's still in bed at nine o'clock? "It's almost six here," she says. "P.M. It's already dark. How was L.A.?"

"Horrible."

This is the second time she's called him. She's decided the morning, his time, would be best, before his mood has all day to become ingrown and nasty.

"I'm sorry."

"Yeah."

"Guess who I'm having dinner with?"

"Mel Gibson."

"Zip Ingram! He's doing some big Home Again shoot down here. Harold wants him to help set up this cable channel they're trying to put together. Isn't that wild?"

When I striate this raw, pus-filled area here, Mr. Mactier, before I apply the hot saline, does that sting a little?

"Yeah. Say hi. Have fun."

"George."

"Oh, that's just *fantastic* news, honey! It sounds like a *really* exciting opportunity for Zip, and for the *company,* too! *Congratulations!*" He stops. "There. Is that better?"

"I'll talk to you later, George."

This conversation is no worse than the others.

In Australia as elsewhere, Lizzie hasn't had much to do, except to demonstrate by her presence in meetings that Mose Media Holdings is a forward-looking, twenty-first-century enterprise. The main business here seems to involve the summer Olympics, which are two months away. Because Mose didn't establish MBC until most of the Olympics marketing deals had already been struck, the company is left with the dregs, although Hank Saddler is doing his best, as they arrive at the restaurant, to keep spirits up; he's auto-spinning.

"The torch relay is so old-fashioned, really," he says when the talk turns enviously to Murdoch and Fox.

"What about the cultural events," Gloria Mose asks, "couldn't you sponsor those?"

"Fairfax has them," Randy tells her, pretending that Gloria might acknowledge his existence. "I think it sounds like we have a shot at that webcast opportunity, though."

At a meeting this afternoon, it was suggested that MBC might be able to buy the "semiexclusive internet advertising rights" to badminton, synchronized swimming, race-walking, and certain Paralympics events.

"Yes," Hank Saddler says. "and that wheelchair rugby star they mentioned, the fellow who got paralyzed playing normal rugby—that sounds lovely. Real *Chariots of Fire*."

Zip is already inside at the table. The moment he spots the Mose group arriving, he stands and upends an empty wineglass, holding it with both hands. And then he begins singing into the glass, shouting, " 'G-L-O-R-I-A, *Glo-o-o-o-o-o-ri-a*, I'm gonna shout all night . . .' "

Since Gloria Mose's facial expression is always contemptuous, Lizzie has wondered how she'd manage to express exceptional contempt. Her face grows more taut than usual. She raises her chin a centimeter. Her dark glasses, shields before, transform somehow into offensive weapons, like one of the kids' robot action figures.

"Hello, Edward," she says to Zip. Zip met her thirty years ago. He was a third-tier rock-and-roll photographer. She was a tobacconist's daughter who enjoyed posing nude for tiny, third-tier rock-and-roll photographers, and later giving free Laker Airways tickets and in-flight bathroom blowjobs to tiny, second-tier freelance newsweekly photographers.

"Hello, darling," he says, standing on tiptoe to kiss each cheek. "The sun's terribly bright in here, huh?" It's dark. "Or—oh, *no,* I'm so *sorry,* Gloria—I didn't know you've gone blind! That's it, isn't it?" He laughs and then hugs Lizzie, who's teary, she's so happy to see him. Then he offers his hand to Harold. "Hello," he says, "Zip Ingram, sir, and it's a privilege finally to meet the man with the largest testicles in television!"

Mose shakes his hand, chortling softly, smiling sheepishly.

"I mean it, Mr. Mose. Canceling *the* most interesting new program in years after just a week on the air—*that* takes *balls!*"

4 2

Tuna is healthy. Fresh white tuna packed in water, eaten straight out of the can. Doesn't tuna prevent all kinds of cancers? He doesn't even mind it twice a day sometimes, lunch and dinner, with a side dish of walnut halves at night for fiber, each nut swirled individually in the butter tub. The sameness has a kind of monastic purity. Fish! Nuts! He's *eating* healthily. Pink lemonade isn't unhealthy. The Krispy Kremes every morning are an indulgence.

Is he supposed to call Ned Wisdom back to tell him he doesn't want to write a screenplay involving black psychopaths and anal rape? Or was Ned Wisdom going to call him? Maybe he should call the Ned Wisdom Productions receptionist. She was a fan.

Lizzie has called him three times in the last ten days. Is that a good thing or a bad thing?

Thank goodness Lizzie will be back before LuLu and Max come home from camp. LuLu and Max alone might be too much to bear. For LuLu and Max.

Dear Harold, he thinks. *I just wanted to let you know that Timothy sent me a letter explaining everything before he killed himself. I guess I should be angry about what he revealed, but learning the whole truth has actually been*

good for me. And your own guilt, I'm sure, is punishment enough for you.
George Mactier. But what if there actually is some plot against George?
What if Mose really did cause Timothy to kill himself? And then, be-
cause of a hoax letter, dispatches a hitman to rub out George? Ho *ho!*
Wouldn't *that* be ironic? *Dear Harold Mose, We know everything you told
Timothy Featherstone, and exactly why he killed himself. Beware. Beware.*
That would work. It would seem to be a letter from an anonymous
creep—either a delusional creep, or a creep who somehow possesses
dangerous information. No downside. Nice upside. Win, win!

But it would make George, who has neither delusions nor dangerous information, the creep. And anonymous creeps are the worst kind.
There are limits.

The phone rings, for the first time since sometime before lunch.
(This morning it was a real estate broker, asking if George wanted to
put their house on the market. He said yes, just to see how much the
woman thought it would be worth.) He turns over in bed and answers
the phone. He listens. "No, I'm afraid Ms. Zimbalist won't be able to
take advantage of your no-obligation gift of parabolic skis to switch for
two years to MCI long distance. She died. . . . Yes. A skiing accident,
in fact, just last weekend in Vermont. In fact, I think she was on old-
fashioned, nonparabolic skis. You have a pleasant afternoon too."

The tuna cans and empty half-gallon pink lemonade jug on the bedside table are . . . what, depressing? Perfect? The cleaning lady comes
tomorrow anyway, or the day after.

This is how rich people live. Rich people probably put on pants
during the day. But maybe not. This is how lottery winners live. Except they have powerboats.

Each of his good friends has called once. Some (Emily, Ben) have
called twice. His lawyer has called several times, once to tell George he
really shouldn't have signed a contract that gave MBC the out if he
went over budget. He has persuaded George that litigation would be
long and expensive and probably unsuccessful, but he thinks he can
negotiate "a quick seven-figure settlement, low seven." ("How low?"
George asked. "One million," the lawyer replied.) He thought there
would be more phone calls. He doesn't know from whom, but he
thought there would be more. That's why he bought the Caller ID
contraption that plugs into the television, so he could screen calls

while he was watching TV. Convergence, right here, right now. He saw the thing demonstrated on those two new fat women's syndicated talk show, he called right then, and the FedEx man delivered it the next morning, twenty-four hours from impulse to satisfaction. And right after he hooked it up, the personal calls mostly stopped. It wasn't cause and effect, but it seems like it.

Now that he's not making television anymore, he has time to watch it. That *is* cause and effect. This afternoon he watched the Cubs beat the Astros, their eighty-third win of the season. It is the first baseball game he's watched since he was a kid. In the sixties, he forced himself to watch some games all the way through with his father, three or four, in order to make Perry Mactier happy. Staring at baseball for three hours made him feel stoned.

Tonight, *Freaky Shit!* runs a story about a Swiss victim of a terrible train crash whom they call "the most bionic man on the planet." He has an artificial heart, an artificial voice box, an artificial eye, artificial skin on one side of his face, a colostomy, false teeth, a hairpiece, two plastic hipbones, a prosthetic right leg below the knee, a below-the-elbow right arm (it looks to George like an Otto Bock model), and pins holding the left arm to his shoulder. The man happily tells the *Freaky Shit!* interviewer that he takes Viagra and Prozac, his wife has had silicon breast implants, and he communicates with the world almost exclusively via e-mail. The other main story on *Freaky Shit!* is about a hillbilly farmer in southern Missouri whose college-educated son has turned the family's 160 acres into a tourist attraction called American Farm 2000. They're growing potatoes that have been genetically manipulated to increase antibodies against *E. coli* bacteria; an antibacterial French-fry stand in the barn has done a booming business all summer. They're also growing cotton from genetically manipulated seeds; it comes out of the ground dark pink and yellow and blue, and they're feeding their sheep a protein called BioClip that makes the animals shed their fleece—sheep shearer, another doomed occupation. George wonders if they'll stick with the name American Farm 2000 after this year, like Sergio Mendes and Brasil '66 did after 1966.

As soon as *NARCS* comes on (it is a rerun of the Russian mafia money-laundering show), George switches over to the NBC special on the upcoming Miss America 2001 pageant. They're running profiles of five of the contestants. Miss Mississippi is blind, and will use her seeing-eye dog during the pageant. *That will be good television,* George thinks. Miss Oregon has one leg, and her talent is modern dance. Miss Nebraska has no apparent handicap herself, but says her "dream is to use ventriloquism to aid the deaf." Miss California is the national student coordinator for Decent Entertainers Against Dope, Lucas Winton's group. Her talent is "popera," which she describes as "opera for regular Americans, Celine Dion–type singing that tells stories about the Lord Jesus or drug addiction."

At eleven, NewsChannel4 goes live to a shot of Savion Glover tap-dancing in the Temple of Dendur at the Metropolitan Museum for hundreds of smiling white people in gowns and dinner jackets. George is happy he didn't go. The event is Cordman, Horton's fortieth-anniversary celebration, which is also a fund-raiser for Martha's Vineyard. (That's all the NewsChannel4 reporter says—"a fund-raiser for Martha's Vineyard, Massachusetts.") George wonders if Martha's Vineyard is the only place on earth where the presence of blacks has actually increased white property values. He misses Daisy.

Just as he's falling asleep, he hears five notes on the piano downstairs, a very low register, bum, *bummm*-bum-bum, *bummm*. He is fully awake. He hears nothing. He hears nothing, and closes his eyes again. But then, even lower, growly notes that practically aren't music: bum-*bummm*. He gets out of bed warily, grabs Lizzie's new ice ax and goes quietly downstairs toward the room with the piano, the room without a name, off the living room. *Bummm*-bum-ding-*clink*—Johnny, the cat, leaps off the piano and makes a panicky run past him up the stairs. *Of course it's the cat,* George thinks, *just like the scene in every bad scary movie.* On the way back up to the bedroom, he accidentally corners Johnny in the hallway. That is, Johnny corners himself. George wonders if the cat is actually frightened of him at moments like this. Or is it frightening itself for fun, like Max and LuLu do when George pretends he's a monster?

Everybody says difficult experiences can produce positive personal outcomes. Embrace the new. Revel in change. "Make lemonade out of life's lemons," Cubby Koplowitz told him. Cubby sent him a book called *Transitions: From Good to Bad to Better Than Ever!* George took it out of the envelope and dropped it in the recycling bin in a single motion. But he is embracing change. He's catching up with the rest of the world. He's surfing the web. Until the last two weeks, he has surfed the web just enough to confirm that life is too short to surf the web. But here he is, surfing the web.

Zip Ingram was the first to tell him, years ago, about all the video cameras that feed their live images to web pages. George has glanced at newspaper articles about the pathetic people who set up cams in their own bathrooms. Now, he finds himself uninterested in those individual nut-cams, where one loser tries to force the world's gaze onto *him* or *her*. George doesn't want to look at anyone who wants him to look.

And he doesn't want to watch women who are paid to pretend they don't know he's watching them.

```
Watch our HIDDEN HI-RESOLUTION CAMERAS, in
GIRLS' Locker Rooms, Sororities, Showers,
Toilets in the BEST Colleges & Universities in
America and Asia!
JOIN FOR FREE!!!
These are snapshots from REAL hidden cameras.
No fakes or setups. This is the real
thing . . . we PROMISE, or your money back!
And you can see it all for FREE!!!
These girls are totally unaware that you're
watching them getting changed, showering, or
peeing.
```

© CHELSEA GIRLS, it says in six-point type at the bottom of the web page. George notices one night that Chelsea Girls is also the name of a web site that charges $9.95 an hour for its "hot hot hot college girls and doctors of PHILOSOPHY, the sluttiest, horniest eggheads locked in the Ivory Tower waiting for YOU to get inside their minds AND their dripping-wet fancy pants!"

He isn't interested.

It's the public cameras on ordinary street corners he finds entrancing. It's sitting at home and watching the fully clothed world at large, the whole world unaware and unpaid, that feels like a breakthrough in human experience. We can each and all be the Wicked Witch of the West, looking down through our crystal balls into Munchkinland and the Emerald City. Although surely Glinda the Good had an all-seeing crystal ball too.

Now he understands why Zip was so bewitched. Now he *sees*. This *is* chocolaty. He clicks to a web site connected to a camera mounted on top of one of the World Trade towers, and watches the sky over the Statue of Liberty for twenty minutes. He spends an hour watching traffic on Interstates 94, 494, and 694 around St. Paul and Minneapolis. The I-494 cam happens to be pointed at the spot where his mother was killed.

He finds nine cameras mounted along Forty-second Street. He discovers that by timing his clicks from web site to web site, cutting from camera to camera like a director, he can follow the same person or the same car for blocks. He clicks to a camera pointed at Main Street in Disney World. He remembers the worst forty-five minutes of his life, the morning five-year-old Sarah disappeared during the Disney World twentieth-anniversary celebrations; the security men led George and Lizzie through secret doors into a big room with dozens of monitors to search through all the closed-circuit Epcot and Magic Kingdom surveillance images for her. "Don't look for particular clothes or hair," one of the Disney men told them. "They might have changed her clothes or cut her hair already. Look for your child's *shape*." (They found her alone and unharmed wandering around Frontierland.) He watches the Las Vegas Strip, and tries to pick out the hookers. He goes to a cam trained on the Managua cityscape and can just make out the hospital where they stitched his arm up.

He thinks, *My life is flashing before my eyes. Literally.* The fuzziness and dumb angles give the images an extra spectral power—as if they are ad hoc and unmediated glimpses into a supernatural world, banality live from the beyond.

First thing the next day, he can hardly wait to get back on the computer, going from cam to cam to cam to cam to cam. There are thousands. Almost all of them are deeply tedious. George finds every one of them interesting.

He feels like he's working again.

He watches lions eating a large hoofed animal live from a water hole in a Kenyan game reserve. He watches a culvert outside Budapest:

every ten or twenty minutes, someone appears and urinates; one out of every six or seven men, George calculates, salutes the camera after he finishes. He watches a cemetery near Polho, in Mexico, where twice or three times a day, it seems, they bury victims of the war. ZAPATISTA MARTYR-CAM, it says on the web page. He's noticed they dig the graves between five-thirty and eight in the morning.

Aside from telemarketers, there are two calls today. Ben calls, and denies he lied to George about buying up the rights to novels. He says he wasn't going to make movies or TV shows, and he's not. He didn't tell George the full truth because it was still a secret, but he did not lie.

That is Ben's loophole.

George asks if Bucky Lopez was involved somehow in getting *Real Time* canceled, and Ben tells him he's crazy, crazy about Bucky just like he was crazy about Cubby. The last time Ben called, he said that he was underwriting the R & D for Cubby's next big idea—turning any PC into an at-home ATM machine, by means of a device attached to a printer port like they do for postage metering. CubbyCash! Ben said then, "There's no conspiracy against you, pal." Until that moment, the word hadn't occurred to George.

And Lizzie calls. It is early again, eight-thirty. He's beginning to think that she intends to catch him groggy and off guard, and maybe even intends to upset him by calling just when she's about to run off to some grand dinner with Harold and Gloria, her voice full of impatience and precocktail cheer. She tells him they're returning to New York a day late. "We can't leave until Friday," she says. *We.* "I cannot wait to be in my home, George." *My.* "But I mean, I can't very well just say *sayonara* and hop on a commercial flight. It's Harold's jet."

It's Harold's jet.

That is Lizzie's loophole.

He thinks about moving to Paris. But Lizzie speaks French, not him. And she's the one with all the money, not him. And the kids. She would presumably get the children. He couldn't bear to leave the children. Which puts her in control.

He doesn't look forward to the kids blaming him for Johnny's death. It happened on his watch. Lizzie always said, "One of those stupid tourist buses is going to run over him someday, out on the cobblestones." She was exactly right. She'll have that consolation. He thinks about burying him in the backyard. But they don't own a spade, and after thirty seconds of digging up dirt by hand like a dog with its paws, he calls the ASPCA. A woman with a slight Spanish accent gives him another number to call.

At the second number, a man with a much thicker Spanish accent asks, "Where do you live?" George tells him the Seaport. "You sure?" the man says, "people don't live down there." *Yes, exactly! And that's the irresistible, idiosyncratic charm of our lifestyle!* "I'm sure," George tells him. The man says, "Well, let's see . . . okay, put the dead pet on the southwest corner of Fulton and Water streets. Somebody'll be there." Two hours ago, right before lunch (tuna from the can: tribute to Johnny), he puts the cat in a shopping bag. He seals it with gaffer's tape, scribbles over PRADA and writes, DEAD CAT. He puts it out on the corner. When he goes out to check two hours later, the bag is already gone.

The pharmacy calls and says they have some photos developed from film that was dropped off a year ago, and that they'll be destroyed if he doesn't pick them up. It is an excuse to leave the house. But now, walking back down Water Street, he finds in among the snapshots from last summer at Lake Marten and the ninth-wedding-anniversary barbecue the kids cooked, a picture of a man he's never seen before. The man is a youngish, good-looking Asian in a sharp suit, blowing a kiss toward the camera. It looks like he's in Madison Square Park. George stops. The pharmacy must have given him somebody else's photo accidentally. No, there he is on the negative strip between a frame of Sarah and one of the Land Cruiser. It's from their roll. Lizzie took the picture.

Late one night, after the first trucks have already pulled in to start unloading huge, whole, dead fish across South Street, he has a strong hunch that Lizzie is going to call him in a few hours, after he is asleep. He decides to call her for the first time, in Jakarta. There is no answer in her room. It is the middle of the afternoon in Indonesia. He awakes at noon. He waits until three and then dials again. He knows what's going to happen. He knows. The phone in her room rings and rings. It's three A.M. in Jakarta, and Lizzie isn't in her room. He knew it. He sits, staring at *Al & Monica* with the sound off, for a full half hour. (She's surprisingly good as a talk-show host. George wonders if they cast Al

Roker in order to make her look slim by comparison.) He calls back at three-thirty—three-thirty in the morning, Jakarta time—and there's still no answer. He knew it. Then he calls right back and asks the operator to leave a message for Miss Zimbalist. *"Ahhh,"* the operator says. He wonders what *Ahhh* means.

She laughs. She says they drove directly from the U.S. embassy to stay overnight at the ambassador's beach house. She says, "Honey, that's absurd, I can't tell you how absurd. You are being paranoid. But I guess it means you still love me." She brought up 1988, and said that maybe he's just working out "old, impacted guilt" over New Orleans. "You've got enough to worry about without being paranoid too," she says. What does that mean—"enough to worry about"? "I am not having an affair with Harold Mose. Or Gloria Mose or Hank Saddler." She is emphatic and extreme, volunteering unsolicited denials. It reminds George of Bill Clinton. It reminds George, now that he thinks about it, now that he's thought about it for most of the night, of the ad for the Chelsea Girls' ersatz-peephole web site. *No fakes or setups. This is the real thing. We promise. And you can see it all for free. These girls are totally unaware that you're watching them.*

The technology would work great right now for terrorists who want to remain safe at home—for bombers of abortion clinics and federal buildings and Israeli buses who want to watch their car bombs go off, to see the survivors stumble out dazed and bloody, to count the ambulances screaming in. For remote-control postattack reconnaissance, command and control for the insane, it would more than suffice.

And soon it will empower everyone. The internet will have fulfilled its revolutionary potential. Then each of us will be omniscient, everyone a Big Brother, and all barriers transparent. For now, however, it's like trying to race a Model A across the continent in a week—possible, but only very theoretically. The odds against Lindbergh were long, too. Such an undertaking has its own old-fashioned American mechanic's nobility, doesn't it? The failed attempt is preferable to the gnaw of passivity. Even the accursed victim can redeem his victimhood.

But alas, developing nations are developing nations. The sharpest pictures, where detail can be made out, are not the sorts that get transmitted from the streets and squares of Third World cities. These on the screen now seem especially hazy, cities in the mists. And nearly all the images are panoramas or close-ups, postcard views or individual rooms and corridors, neither of which are ideal for his purposes.

At first he is brimming with beginner's-luck hopefulness, ready for eureka. The U.S. embassy in Jakarta is on a street called Merdeka Selatan, and then right away he finds two cams operating on Merdeka Selatan. One of them is even pointed in the right direction, with a color image clear enough to apprehend the gender of passersby. After watching sixty real-time images over four and a half hours last night (midday in Jakarta), he thought he lucked out. There was a shot of two women and three men stepping from a Mercedes in front of the embassy. He stored the image and looked closely, but it was impossible to tell.

If she happens to step into information sciences classroom 112A at the University of Jakarta, he will have a stunningly clear picture. But he's not mad; he knows the odds are long. Still, there are at least fourteen cams in the city, including four at the university, two at a giant shopping center called Block M, one on Merdeka Square near her hotel, and one, called the Mikrolet-Mikrolet-cam, mounted next to the driver inside a public bus. The bus image is George's favorite, aesthetically and sociologically. (It's possible she'll get on a bus. She takes them in New York.) Given the rate at which fresh pictures arrive from each camera, it is easy to make the circuit among the fourteen Jakarta-cams, one after another, and never miss an image. There is a surprising comfort and solace in that. Casting into the pond is still fishing, even if you never hook a bass. He is watching her, even if he can't see her.

4 3

Lizzie hasn't had a cigarette since Tokyo. All the smoke in the air makes it easier to quit, aversion therapy on a massive, inescapable scale— the *smokes,* plural, as she has learned here. In Indonesia, seams of coal as well as trees and brush are on fire, so the smoke in Jakarta is more sulfurous than the smoke in Kuala Lumpur. On the other hand, the Jakarta smoke has a slightly sweet top note of burning peat. During dinner at the ambassador's beach house last night, Mr. Hatta, the Indonesian deputy information minister (who's also an army lieutenant general) portrayed "our zone of fire" as a kind of fascinating adventure-travel destination, since the coal started burning when lightning struck "at a time before your Christ." Mr. Hatta also mentioned "some very eye-*row*-neek advantages of the fire," such as endangered orangutans being driven from the forests into villages, where they're slaughtered and eaten "by the starving peasant folk." He agreed to put in a good word with both his cousin, who runs the national TV channel, and his wife's brother, who runs the private HTI, Happy Televisi Indonesia, about buying MBC's programs, including *NARCS.*

They have arrived at Soekarno-Hatta International Airport. She is heading home. Whisking in self-important Mercedeses through unmarked back gates, passing armed men who stiffen and quake a little instead of scowl, Lizzie finds the VIP routine tolerable for occasional, brief, playacting stretches. It isn't the Mose *lifestyle* she finds unbearable (unless Gloria Mose is defined as a lifestyle feature), it's this business itself, big business, business that is only *deal making*—the deals transacted with smug, hard, murky men. She is a shopkeeper at heart, as Ben Gould says. Fine Technologies is a gemütlich $102-million shop selling notions.

"There she is," Saddler says as they drive onto the runway toward the Mose jet.

"It is a lovely machine, isn't it?" Harold says.

The idea that she's sleeping with Harold Mose is so off, so farfetched, that it makes her wonder about George's judgment. Even paranoid fears ought to be in the ballpark. If she were going to have an affair, hell, she'd sooner have it with . . .

She looks around the limo . . . at Hank Saddler reading his DHL-ed copy of *Teen People* . . . Randy, bobbing his head in time to the Garth Brooks DAT piped into his ears . . .

No one here, including Harold Mose. Harold, she realizes, has become less attractive by the day. He seems a little older and homelier after his explanation of the Malaysian condolence-card business, and homelier still after he pandered to Jimmy Wong's Jew-baiting, and tittered about the orangutans.

During the trip, he's revealed a dozen of his habitual fudges to her, microcrimes like "the little accounting time-travel hocus-pocus" he said they've pulled for years. A shell corporation in Tonga straddling the 180-degree meridian, the international date line, allows Mose Media Holdings to get away with booking big sales from the next fiscal quarter in the current quarter, in order to make current revenues look larger. And he told her about how MMH pushes hundreds of millions of dollars in "marketing costs," especially the MBC's, off their income statements and onto the books of various friendly Asian telephone and television companies. ("Partners," Mose called them, and "strategic allies," not "accomplices.") For their trouble, the executives of the Asian companies are awarded cheap below-market Mose Media stock warrants, which they can sell for a profit. "It's half the reason Arnold let me start an American network," he told Lizzie. "It turns out *everything* in TV is a 'marketing cost.' " Hearing Mose's tangled, whispered confidences aboard the jet gives them, in Lizzie's mind, an extra patina of darkness and slime. When she e-mailed Ben from Jakarta to get a reading on whether this cost-shuffling scheme is criminal, he replied, "It's a fucking rig. But legal, probably."

Mose is confiding in Lizzie more and more, and she is afraid she understands why. When she didn't put up a fuss over *Real Time,* she made her bones, proving to Mose that she is a grownup, steeped in realpolitik and focused on the main chance. She still doesn't feel (very) guilty about not standing by her man and quitting. But she detests its implications. She hates that it makes Mose believe she's like him.

"Captain Sam tells me it'll be a fifteen-hour flight to Los Angeles today," the Cindy Crawford flight attendant says, "and I'll be presenting some dinner ideas as soon as we're in the air, including a fantastic fresh pork satay."

They are already high, rocketing northeast. Saddler has stuck in earplugs, and he's wearing a huge, silky black sleeping mask.

"Captain Sam wanted me to tell you that if you look out, you'll be able to see the equator. If the equator were real. Another glazed carambola nugget, Ms. Zimbalist?" the woman says, holding a Josef Hoffmann silver tray in front of her.

"Thank you." No, it is not the interludes of profligate living that Lizzie minds so much.

"I got a fax from Arnold this morning," Mose says. "Your friends in Redmond are apparently interested in our digital portfolio. Part of a 'strategic alliance' with WebTV, maybe something more." He sips his virgin gimlet. "What do you think, Elizabeth?"

She thinks: *It's August now.* She thinks: *Change of control.*

44

Alone on Water Street these last weeks, George has been extrapolating. He sees the time, not at all distant, when traffic has been reduced to nothing but these friendly motorized logos. The streets will be devoted entirely to clean, efficient trucks—UPS, DefEx, DHL, FedEx. The delivery drivers will be people's only direct contact with strangers. Life is migrating indoors quickly, so quickly, to computers and cables and phone lines. And this new economy, prosperity itself, now requires that the transformation proceed. Ten years from now, maybe twenty, the only people on the streets in any numbers will be the smokers, the homeless, and the uniformed drivers of tidy, squarish trucks. And the human drivers' days are undoubtedly numbered.

George signs the man's electronic clipboard, his imaginary paper, with his imaginary FedEx pen. The package, a small one, is from C. PRIEVE in Woodside, California, and addressed by hand. He doesn't know C. Prieve. It's a computer disk, one of the new fat gray ones that can contain the Library of Alexandria in half the size of a Pop-Tart. A purple Post-it is stuck to the front. In very neat handwriting it says, "An outreach from your friends at Mose Media's unofficial 'human resources' dept. . . . Your personal real-time recording of *That's No Lady,*

That's My Wife! Enjoy." He looks inside the little cardboard packet, but there's no letter.

Upstairs in their bedroom, he turns on her computer, slides the empty Krispy Kreme box off the Jaz drive, and inserts the mystery disk. An icon pops onto the screen, but not the regular, factory-installed picture. It is a red letter *M* over a bleeding heart.

A video image appears, looking like one of the nut-cams on the web. Except the room it shows is spare and handsome. And the person on camera is Harold Mose. He's staring at a point just below the lens. His lips are slightly parted. He's squinting, and has a dreamy, faraway look.

Fucking weird, George thinks. *But kind of cool.* He wonders who C. Prieve is.

Then the image shakes and blurs, and for three seconds becomes unreadable, empty.

And then Harold Mose is back on screen. The closeup has changed to a medium shot—a two-shot, in a sense, now that Mose's penis is out of his trousers, erect, and he is masturbating. The penis is uncircumcised.

Who is C. Prieve? And what on earth is George Mactier supposed to do with a video of Harold Mose jerking off?

It looks like Mose is whispering, "Yes." And he has started an involuntary sort of Bob Fosse hip thrust that George finds extremely embarrassing to watch. He can't not watch, of course.

A line of type appears, moving from right to left across the bottom of the screen. HI! IT'S ME, ELIZABETH, it says.

He is hallucinating. He's been inside his own sweaty, malignant head too long.

But then he sees Mose whisper, *"Hello, Elizabeth."*

He is not hallucinating. Or if he is, George knows, it's some kind of full-on psychotic break, and he'd better call 911. He keeps watching.

More type speeds across the screen. OKAY, YOU CAN JUST *WATCH* WHILE SOME OF MY OTHER HOT FRIENDS ASK ME TO PUT ON A NASTY SHOW FOR THEM . . . YOU WANT ME TO FINGER MY HOT JUICY CUNT? . . . SHOULD I DO IT LIKE THIS?

There's a pause in the type. But Mose continues. George can now hear Mose's shallow, accelerating little intakes of breath, and, he thinks, a few grunted *yeahs.*

Mose disappears. MMMMMMMMMM! YES, SIR!! Then the recording goes black.

C. Prieve must be one scurvy creep.

George is disgusted and appalled.

But he's also grateful. Because now there isn't any question. This is what he was after, wasn't it, with the Jakarta cams?

C. Prieve may be a scurvy creep, he thinks, *but he's* my *scurvy creep.*

He clicks on the bar beneath the image, and slides the little button almost back to the beginning. He finds the frame with the words, HI! IT'S ME, ELIZABETH! and clicks to start playing it again.

He's been up all night, but he feels fantastic, entirely calm and clear-headed for the first time in weeks. He feels light and clean, revived, purged of doubt. The last time he stayed up all night like this was at *Newsweek,* crashing a cover story on . . . well, he doesn't recall the story now, probably Reagan and SDI, "Star Wars." It was exciting like this is exciting, the same missionary sense of digging, reporting, analyzing, making sense of a sprawl of facts—piecing together the truth—all by himself on a tight deadline.

It's interesting, he thinks, how he loathed reporting, the phoning of wary strangers to intrude on their dinners or their business or their grief, play on their vanities or anger or righteousness or whatever it took to get in and get over. Back in the eighties, none of this technology existed.

Lizzie said, whenever that was, days ago, that she's returning home on Saturday. But is she flying straight to New York? She didn't say. What time exactly, and which airport? She didn't say.

But George knows. George knows because he's been on a reporting bender since yesterday afternoon, nonstop. He dug out those snapshots Max took last winter of the jet, when the whole family flew to Minnesota for Edith Hope's funeral. *Bingo:* Mose Media Holdings' green Bombardier with its tail number visible, precisely the datum he needed to type into his favorite new web site. Now he knows what the FAA knows: it took off from Soekarno-Hatta International Airport at four fifty-one P.M., Jakarta time, eleven minutes late. He knows it's scheduled to land in Los Angeles tonight at eight P.M. He knows it's scheduled to land tomorrow afternoon in Teterboro at four P.M. sharp.

He knows how many pounds of aviation fuel they're carrying. He knows the names of the pilots, Sam and Jerry. He knows the names of the passengers. (Who is Randy McCarthy? What does the *G* in Henry G. Saddler stand for?) He knows everything.

He stares at Max's snapshot of the jet, imagining Mose and Lizzie naked inside. Maybe Randy pairs off with Gloria. What about Saddler? *Okay, you can just watch while some of my other hot friends ask me to put on a nasty show for them.* He remembers Saddler droning on about the avionics when they flew to Minneapolis, explaining how flight plans are digitized and loaded onto an onboard computer. *It can even be done wirelessly,* Hank said, *from a remote location.* George stares at the photo. He wonders if somebody like Fanny Taft could hack into the jet's system and force it to land. Remote-controlled hijacking! Or force it to crash.

Fanny Taft's number isn't on Lizzie's computer address database. He calls Jodie Taft in Edina, and asks if she has Fanny's number for the summer in Brooklyn. Jodie sounds flummoxed by the call at first. But then she is so pleased that George is going to invite Fanny over for dinner and make sure she's doing okay, and then, Jodie-ishly, so Jodie-ishly, wants to chat, and asks him if *Real Time* has been moved to a new time slot, and says she thinks Jess, the gay one, seems sharp as a tack, and he tells her thanks, but he has to get back to work, even though it's Saturday.

He gets Fanny, who just this minute walked in, back from Def Con. "What's Def Con?"

"It's this gathering of hackers from all over," she says. "I mean, *wizards.* They were like, 'Let me show you how to do this, and this, and this.' It happens once a year. It's insane. Really awesome."

"Well," George tells her, "that's perfect, because the reason I called is that I need to pick your brain, if I can. I'm working on a project about computer security and things like that. Big Brother kinds of stuff."

"Like for a new show or something?"

"It could become a show."

"Cool. I should bring Willi, one of the German guys from Fine Tech. He is an awesome hacker."

And so Fanny and Willibald will be over for dinner tonight.

George spends most of the rest of the afternoon cleaning up, although he wonders if the havoc and trash might be a good thing, Daddy, to a goateed German hacker and a seventeen-year-old computer criminal. Fanny and Willi might think a sleepless, unshaven man alone in a house strewn with two weeks of old magazines and newspapers and piles of empty tuna cans and pink-lemonade jugs and celery ends and cookie-dough wrappers and Krispy Kreme boxes is, you know, *cool*.

But he takes a shower, goes grocery shopping for the first time in calendar year 2000, buys wine, and prepares a real dinner.

Willibald was completely uninterested in George's time as a reporter in Bonn in the eighties. As soon as he tells him that he lost his hand in a contra mortar attack on his Sandinista jeep in Nicaragua during the counterrevolution, however, Willi becomes his comrade, and calls the cancellation of *Real Time* "a *Kulturkampf*."

"You know," Fanny says, "information does want to be free. No joke. What do you want to know?"

They tell him how they can read anything on almost anybody's computer anywhere on earth from anywhere else on earth. If a target (Willi's word) visits a web site that they've hacked or control, they can read the target's cookies.

" 'Cookies'?" George asks.

"Such a newbie," Fanny says. "It's kind of amazing you're married to Lizzie."

And so they explain how the cookies on somebody's web browser are a record of what he does in cyberspace, what he buys, which computer he uses at his company, who he is.

"Do the cookies keep records of e-mail?"

"No."

"Well," George says, "let's say I want to read all the e-mails that an executive of some software company is writing and getting at home—a guy at Microsoft, let's say."

George doesn't notice that Fanny and Willi both smile at his hypothetical.

"Simple," Willi tells him.

He half understands their patois, translating on the fly from the context about as well, he thinks, as he can translate Spanish, or Elizabethan

English. They tell him about trojan programs (as in Trojan horse) like Back Orifice, and the plug-ins for Back Orifice, like Buttsniffer, which lets them "sniff" everything (e-mail, passwords, whatever) that a target computer sends or receives.

"Wouldn't the executive encrypt his messages?" George asks. It's like when he was a reporter, dropping just enough jargon about subjects he doesn't really understand (*But Secretary Weinberger, how would SDI reduce the risks inherent in launch-on-warning?*) to stay in the conversation.

"Buttsniffer logs keystrokes," Willi says.

Which George understands to mean that even if the encryption program turns a message into "9kz%ii&2 3#3xd3#fhd7u +/54R $*gny=p92$ id2sytq<8^," the keystroke logger will see through the gibberish, and tell the hackers that the message actually typed was HAROLD, MY DARLING: CANCEL REAL TIME ASAP--LIZZIE.

They tell him how, with something called an emulation terminal, they can go into a target's computer and look through every file on its hard drive. And during the third bottle of wine, they tell him lots of things he doesn't even register, the Chaucerian English equivalents— getting port 139 open on an NT box, hijacking Kerberos tickets instead of swiping passwords, running nbstat commands and Red Button against the target computer . . .

"Or," Willi says, "if the guy is using a cable modem, it would be completely easy to sniff everything going in and out. To sniff every computer in the neighborhood."

"Bullshit!" George says, chuckling, standing to clear dishes. He figures they're indulging in cyberhyperbole with the middle-aged newbie.

"*True* shit."

"Willi is pretty good," Fanny says. Following him into the kitchen, she asks, "George? Can I ask *you* some questions? About journalism?"

She wants to know how reporters in the field use computers, and wire services, and the jargon of that world she's heard about, *stringers* and *bureau chiefs, running the rim* and *doing the sked,* how they decide which stories will move on the wire, and on and on. She's full of curiosity. He feels like a dad.

"How'd you get so interested in journalism?" George asks.

She and Willi look at each other. They can't suppress little wine-fueled grins.

"What?" George says, smiling.

"You know that prank on Microsoft that was in the newspapers?" Willi says. "The phreaking, with the pagers and phones going crazy at their big meeting?"

"Sure. In fact, we talked about doing something about that on the show, on *Real Time*." One reason George passed on the story was because he'd heard Fifty-nine was in new discussions with Microsoft about a big deal. He thinks: *How apt and how just that my one little act of weaselly play-ball self-censorship was for shit.*

"Well," Willi tells him, "that was us. We're the 'wacko practical jokers.' "

George raises his glass. "Kudos."

"So that got us interested," Fanny says, "in how the media, you know, like *works.*" She doesn't like lying, but she adores Lizzie and George. She needs to protect him.

"You hate Microsoft too?" Willi asks George.

"They fucked over my wife pretty badly." And if Microsoft hadn't reneged on the deal to buy Fine Technologies, she would not be with Harold Mose now. "Yeah, I do hate Microsoft."

Willibald refills his glass and raises it. "Death to the Microsofties!" he says.

"Death to the Microsofties," Fanny says a little meekly, blushing.

"Skoal," George says.

In the end, he doesn't ask about hacking into a Bombardier Global Express's onboard computer to make it crash. He's decided it would harsh everyone's mellow.

4 5

Lizzie and Sarah and Max and LuLu have all arrived home during the same twenty-four hours, which has reinforced the household's apparent mood of normalcy and sanity. George has kissed Lizzie and thought he smelled Rose's lime juice on her breath, but then decided that was his imagination. His skepticism of his own suspicions reassures him that he has not gone entirely around the bend. Lizzie thought George looked tired but pretty good, considering.

She asked him what he ate while she was gone, and he said "summery stuff—tuna, lots of tuna, and citrus."

"So you probably don't want takeout from Hiroshima Boy tonight? I really don't feel like cooking."

"That's fine," he said. "Good date for it too." It's August 6, the fifty-fifth anniversary of the bomb. Daisy Moore married Cole Granger in California today.

Later, as she drops the Sunday-night recycling box of papers and magazines by the stoop, she sees a book wedged in among *Post*s and *Times*es and all the redundant Home Again catalogues. She digs it out, and sees it's *Transitions: From Good to Bad to Better Than Ever!* It makes her want to cry to think he bought a book like this, and makes her choke up more to see that it hasn't even been cracked. Poor George. Tucked inside the back cover there's a discarded FedEx envelope. From C. PRIEVE in Woodside, California.

Chas Prieve is corresponding with George!

Lizzie finally forces herself to take a breath. She feels cold. It's over eighty degrees.

George has really gone off the deep end. He's involved in Chas Prieve's blackmail scheme against Mose Media, whatever Chas's scheme is.

Oh, Lord, what is George doing?

I can't confront him now, tonight. Tomorrow, maybe, she thinks. *And I can't tell Harold.*

It might be something innocent.

How can it be innocent? George never even met Chas when he was working for me.

Lord God, what is George thinking?

"Mommy?" LuLu has opened the front door. "Have you seen Johnny?"

It could be worse, she thinks. He waves off all her attempts to talk about *Real Time,* but he's not picking fights with her, or shouting. He was great with LuLu about Johnny, and Lizzie was careful not to betray any blame in voice or mannerism. (She does blame him.) He was almost sociable at Zip's six-person cocktail party to commemorate both his refusal of the Reality Channel presidency ("the first million-dollar job Zip Ingram ever turned down, and by God I hope the last") and his imminent move from the Winnebago. On the other hand, when she told George the day after she got home that she didn't like working for Mose Media and was trying to figure out how to quit without messing up the Fine Technologies acquisition and forfeiting their Mose stock, he didn't act pleased or even interested. From that reaction, Lizzie decided he couldn't yet bear to talk about anything Mose-related. In the fall, she decides hopefully, after Labor Day, he'll start his descent back to earth. She'll talk him down.

He wanders for miles around Manhattan during the day, most days, and comes home drenched in sweat. "Rediscovering the city," he says to the family when they ask why. "Getting some exercise." *Avoiding the children and Rafaela,* he does not say. When he's home, he stays in his office on the top floor, starting to go through the unopened boxes and boxes of *NARCS* and *Real Time* files. And using the computer.

On a web site that keeps track of urban legends, he discovers a reference to "the Harold Mose masturbation tape." It's a fresh legend to which the web site gives a veracity rating of two Walt Cubes out of five—a Walt Cube being a doodled icon of Walt Disney's cryogenically frozen head.

The web-cam images in New York are of such a superior quality to the ones from Jakarta. And there are dozens—inside restaurants, on roofs, on sidewalks, everywhere. Once, George is fairly sure, he actually spots her on one of the two cams mounted at the entrance to the James Bond Casino Royale, walking east down Fifty-seventh Street. But of course, when the next image comes up, she is gone.

One day he wonders what Lizzie does on the web, and goes down to her computer. He launches her browser, and does something Willibald mentioned, opening the record of her browsing history, and follows the trail of her web-site visits since she's been home. For all her claims of web indifference, she is on it a lot, it seems to George. Yet after spending almost three hours examining the last three hundred pages she's visited, he has found nothing very revealing—an Adirondacks rock-climbing site, HelmutLang.com (she bought a $550 shirt), MoseMedia.com, a story about the Microsoft-buying-Mose-Digital rumor on TheStreet.com, MapsOnUs.com directions to Zip's RV on the Hudson.

He made Lizzie his America Online Buddy. The AOL Buddy system is intended to allow people to exchange instant e-mail messages with friends on AOL. But George has never used it for its intended purpose. Because she's his Buddy now, he knows when she's logged on. His computer makes a sound, the creak of a door, when she logs on and when she logs off. He's discovered she logs on and off to get her e-mail seven or eight times a day. Whenever she logs off, he clicks his browser over to each of the West Fifty-seventh Street cams, and the two on Seventh Avenue, to see if he might catch her coming out of the MBC building. So far he hasn't.

This morning, he went online right after she left for work. Usually he goes out walking by noon, but it's now almost three, and he hasn't heard the creaking door all day or seen her screen name, LizzieZim, pop up on his Buddy list. Which must mean she hasn't gone to the office.

She must be at Mose's apartment. She's on his bed, naked, in some yoga position, saying to him, You want me to finger my hot juicy cunt? Should I do it like this? Or do you want to finger Lizzie's hot juicy cunt now, Harold?

He goes downstairs and turns on her computer. It comes on, but then a message he's never seen before fills the screen. PLACE YOUR INDEX FINGER ON THE FINGERPRINT PAD FOR USER VERIFICATION, it says. He tries to click the message box closed. It won't go away. PLACE YOUR INDEX FINGER ON THE FINGERPRINT PAD FOR USER VERIFICATION. Then he sees a tiny black pad between the keyboard and monitor. It has a logo, Veridicom Open Touch, and a cable leads to the back of the computer, where it's not just plugged but bolted and wired into the machine. He can't get into her computer. She's hooked up this fingerprint device to lock him out.

———

"LuLu," Lizzie shouts, "if you keep the bug in there any longer, he *will* die." She turns to Sarah, who's reading the *Teen Nation* special issue on Mexico. "Will you go punch some holes in that thing for your sister, please?"

They're finishing dinner outside. Max has already retired to his computer.

"I notice you have a new gadget," George says. "The fingerprint thing."

"Kind of stupid and Big Brothery, isn't it? The company that makes it wouldn't stop badgering me, so I let them install it."

They watch Sarah and LuLu playing at the end of the yard.

"Speaking of computers," he says, "do you ever use instant messaging on AOL? The Buddy system?"

She shakes her head and says, "You know, that's funny, I had it on, but I never used it, and I found it annoying to see when everybody I knew was logging on and off. To me it wasn't a friendly 'community' at all, it was like some oppressive little small town where everybody knows what everybody else is doing all the time. I turned it off yesterday anyway, since I'm mostly on the MMH system now, instead of using AOL. Why?"

"I don't know. I just discovered it."

Since she's been at Mose, Lizzie has assumed that any conversations between them about computers or software or the web are dangerous, tacitly off-limits. This is a friendly tangent. She decides it's the opportunity.

"Chas Prieve used to instant-message me all the time. It gave me the willies. I'd log on to get my e-mail, and there he'd be, 'Hi, Lizzie, FYI, the Singapore deals look very close, high six figures! What's new?' You never met Chas Prieve, did you?"

C. Prieve. Chas Prieve. What ugly game is she playing?

"No, I didn't. Who is he?"

He's pretending he doesn't know Chas. This is sick.

"The weird guy who ran the office in the Valley for two months until I fired him after I found out he was incompetent. And a pathological liar."

"The cricket is already dead, Mom," Sarah shouts from the back fence. George and Lizzie watch LuLu open the empty pink-lemonade jug and shake the bug out.

4 6

He badly wants to buy a convertible sports car. *All clichés turn out to be true, Lizzie says, so why not this one?* If anyone deserves to experience a midlife crisis in caricature, he does. And as long as she's paying the bills (with Mose's money, he never forgets), he'll keep spending. It's perfect, in fact. This really is how lottery winners live.

He needs a car. "You probably need a car," Lizzie herself said the last time they spoke. He liked the Plymouth Pronto. The body is made entirely of plastic, which the salesman said is "a breakthrough automotive achievement." He liked the idea of buying an American car, too. (It was Lizzie who vetoed the Ford and Jeep SUVs.) But he just couldn't get past the name—he didn't want to have to say, *That's mine over there, the Plymouth—the purple Plymouth Pronto Spyder.* But the car made of *plastic* gave him his next idea: a red 1966 Alfa Romeo Spider 1600 Duetto, the car Dustin Hoffman drove in *The Graduate.* In ten minutes on the web he finds a dozen of them for sale, including one on Long Island, but then he decides he's delusional—he just doesn't have the patience or mechanical skill to keep a thirty-four-year-old sports car repaired and tuned. But the movie-car notion led to the winning idea, which struck him with the force of one of his big, magnificent once-a-year inspirations. He's going to New Jersey tomorrow to buy a new, five-speed Aston Martin convertible. He's not going all the way—it's not a vintage DB5, it's the 2001 model DB7, brand-new, but it is the car Bond drove before the movie producers struck their product placement deal with BMW. It costs $154,000. But Lizzie is rich.

"Is that Water Street address your home address, Mr. Mactier?" the excited, solicitous salesman from Jersey asked on the phone.

"It's my mailing address, yes."

George thought he would queer the deal if he said, *I don't have a home address, but I guess if you wrote The Winnebago Parked on Pier 58, just south of the golf driving range, New York, New York, 10011, it would probably get to me.* It's reassuring that even though he's a disgraced, unemployed bum who hasn't had a job since July 17 . . . for eleven weeks . . . more than eleven weeks . . . fifty-nine weekdays—*Fifty-nine!*—the world is still very eager to sell him a $154,000 sports car on credit.

He moved into Zip's motor home a week after Labor Day. It was empty, since Zip has moved to a rented triplex loft on Franklin Street. "Home Again says I have to buff my 'profile' in the design and retail communities," he said, "and throw all these bloody parties!" Zip invited George to stay with him in the loft, but George declined. He thought it would raise his-friends-versus-her-friends ugliness unfairly. Or at least prematurely, before he was ready to enjoy it.

He left, although he still feels tossed out. It was the first day the kids were back at St. Andrew's. She came home early to change on her way to a black-tie extravaganza at the Custom House. By the time she got upstairs, he had sprinted from their bedroom up to his office. An hour later, she knocked on his door.

"You're watching an awful lot of TV during the day," she said.

"Is that an accusation? And I'm not."

"You were just now."

"No."

"I felt the set. It was hot."

"You're the one who lies about smoking cigarettes. To your own children."

And then there was no stopping. They shouted. They cursed. She reminded him that his paranoia about her Mose files erased from his PowerBook turned out to be nothing—Max had confessed to deleting them accidentally. And she said Sarah told her she saw him dialing ★69 one night after Lizzie got off a phone call. She said she found one of their monthly E-ZPass records, which lists every date and time (and the direction and the *lane*) that the Land Cruiser crossed the Triborough Bridge or the Henry Hudson Bridge or drove through the Holland Tunnel. It was covered with mutlicolored circles and arrows and checks and question marks. All three kids and Rafaela told her the marks weren't theirs.

"And what the *fuck* were you thinking when you asked Erika Sperakis about renting out a fucking surveillance satellite? Huh, George?" She dropped a piece of MBC stationery onto his desk.

It was then that George decided to abandon his denials. Erika was the producer at *Real Time* in charge of the logistics for the Bohemian Grove story, including the Sovinformsputnik satellite pictures. George had called her to ask about resolutions, advance booking, and costs. Erika gave Lizzie the information to bring home to George.

"It's Exhibit A time, is it? Okay," he said, opening his desk drawer, and rummaging to find her mysterious snapshot of the Asian man blowing a kiss. "Who's *this*?" he asked triumphantly.

"Kenny Chang. Pollyanna's little brother. This was supposed to be part of the scrapbook I made for her birthday last year." She looks at George. "Why, am I being accused of sleeping with Ken Chang, too? He's gay. And you are fucking nuts, George. I cannot stand this anymore. You act like a zombie all the time, and now I'm stalked! By my own husband! I feel like I did when I was five, after the Tate killings."

Sharon Tate and her friends were murdered in 1969, not far from where the Zimbalists were then living. For days, the neighborhood was in a horror-movie panic.

"Oh, I get it," George said, grabbing at a new opportunity to go on the offensive. "You're one of these nuts who holds me responsible for paroling Manson, except you think I did it all just to get back at you by recovering your poor little childhood bogeyman memories. Who's the fucking paranoid, Lizzie?"

"And you're committing felonies. If the SEC knew what you've been doing, they'd indict you tomorrow."

"What? You *are* fucking insane. And the SEC doesn't indict. Get your facts straight." He had no idea what she was talking about.

"Two days ago I found a whole printout of stocks in the wastebasket—Mose, TK Corporation, all of my companies, bid prices on certain dates, sales prices—three thousand shares here, four thousand there. You've got a goddamn inside-trading portfolio, George! Do you want us both to go to jail? Are you trying to destroy this family every way you know how?"

On the one hand, this accusation restored some of George's composure, because it was entirely untrue. On the other hand, it made him nervous: what had she found?

"Show me this list," he said.

"I burned it and flushed it down the toilet."

He stared at her. That very morning, he had called Warren Holcombe, Pollyanna's Warren, the only shrink he knows, and asked if he could come by sometime. He remembers staring at Lizzie and at that moment thinking, *You are crazier than I am.*

"I destroyed it as soon as I found it. To protect you, George. It scared me."

"I have no idea what you are talking about. I have never bought or sold a share of stock in my life."

She just shook her head. Then she said quietly, "George, listen to me: I have never slept with Harold Mose. I am not sleeping with Harold Mose."

"Yes, you are. Don't lie to me, Lizzie."

And that had been that.

Every weekday since September fourteenth he has gone to the house at three-thirty to be with the kids. And every day by six-thirty he leaves, back to the Winnebago for the night, to avoid seeing Lizzie.

That is, to avoid being in Lizzie's physical presence. Back in the RV at the little table, he's got his PowerBook. There's a web-cam on lower Second Avenue not far from the Yoga Place. He looks for her there. There's a web-cam over in the tourist blocks of the Seaport, and he checks in there. But except for that one time on Fifty-seventh Street, he hasn't had a sighting.

Zip has no TV in the Winnebago ("TV without cable, man, is the most depressing spectacle I can imagine"), and the newspapers aren't delivered, so George has come to rely on the computer for his news. He's been following the rumored Microsoft–Mose Digital deal. The latest wrinkle, according to a report today on TheIndustry.com, is that

Microsoft will buy all the MBC shows that Mose owns or controls, to run exclusively on WebTV. Including, the story says, "the sophomore-slumping noir police series *NARCS*." So if Mose and Lizzie have their way, he thinks, his successful creation will be shrunk into some pathetic internet novelty. And his only real asset, a half share in the syndication revenue that Emily might someday derive from her half ownership of *NARCS,* will wither away to nothing.

―――――――

If George happened to cross the highway right now, to walk three blocks east and two blocks south, he would pass a parked Mercedes S1000. If he happened to look inside the front window of Hirst Sensation, the new bar on Ninth Avenue with the artfully charred interior, he would have a whole month of fresh suspicions to sort out. He would see his best friend with his wife, sitting at a table drinking and talking. He would assume they were talking about him, and he'd be right.

"Thanks for meeting me down here," she says.

"Hey! *Up* here! It's practically my neighborhood! I thought you were working on Fifty-seventh Street full-time now."

"I am, but with all this talk about a Microsoft deal for Mose Digital―"

"Is that more Henry Saddler bullshit or is that real?"

She gives him a look.

"Hey!" he protests. "I don't own a single share of your dog company anymore!"

"Yeah. You got out right at the top during the summer, didn't you?"

"Not quite," he says, smiling. "Close."

In the last month, Mose stock has dropped from $45 to $34 a share―a graph line now tracing the Gulf Coast of Florida, currently around Tampa and still heading south.

"How'd you know, Ben?"

"It's been obvious since last winter that Mose was doing a roll-up. Kind of a clumsy one, frankly."

"You mean by buying my companies?"

"Yours to get Wall Street excited. (Which worked for a quarter.) And the weird, boring ones nobody cares about―that Indonesian printing company, the Canadian free weeklies, all those―to fake some earnings growth."

"Why didn't you tell me?"

"I assumed you knew. I guess I thought you were privy to the plan. So, is he selling you to Gates?"

She shrugs. "Anyhow, because of the rumors, my people down on Eighteenth Street need some hand-holding. The prospect of becoming Microsoft employees has them a little unnerved."

"It wouldn't affect their lives."

"They really hate Microsoft, Ben. I mean, it's almost religious." She looks around, then leans toward him. "You know that hack on *Slate* a couple of weeks ago? The fake sweepstakes about the presidential election and encryption law or whatever the fuck it was that stayed up for a whole day?"

Ben nods, and listens very closely. He has wondered about that. He noticed a particular line in the *Slate* hack—"Grand prize: two perfectly dead Tamagotchi Frankensteins! Contest ends 11/29/00!"

"Three of the kids who work for me did that," she whispers. "They're the Wacko Practical Jokerz. That's what they called themselves in the communiqué the next day."

"So I read. Are you going to turn them in?"

She shakes her head. "One of them is a very sweet, very smart girl— George grew up with her parents. You might have met her at our party last spring." Lizzie whispers again. "She was already prosecuted for a hack last year out there, in Minneapolis. She's a *kid*. She'd go to prison, Ben."

"She told you about the *Slate* thing?"

"No, a German boy who works for me, one of her gang."

A waitress brings their drinks.

"So tell Uncle Ben, Lizzie. I am not going to trade on it, I promise. I'm just interested. Mose Digital going to become Micromose?"

She waits a couple of seconds to answer. "A couple of weeks ago in Aspen, at the Forstman Little thing, Harold told me probably yes. They're certainly doing due diligence like they're serious."

"You want to run it? Are you going to stay?"

She finds herself smiling, a huge ungovernable smile, as she shakes her head no. " 'Change of control' is my loophole," she says.

"Hey! This must make our boy George happy, right? His lost princess about to wrestle free from the clutches of *both* evil trolls? And take their chests of jewels with her!"

Her smile disappears. "I haven't talked to him in two weeks, Ben. I haven't seen George since the night he left."

Fanny Taft has come east for a few days to interview at NYU, Cooper Union, Rensselaer, and MIT. When Lizzie tells her George moved out of Water Street, Fanny asks if it would be okay if she visits him on the pier. Lizzie tells her yes, of course, and gives her his cell-phone number.

She knocks on the sheet-metal door. It sounds to George like the knock on the door of a poor person's house. In his three weeks here, it is the first knock he's expected. It's the first one not from a cop, a tourist, a homeless person, or a delivery-truck driver. Fanny is wearing a professionally produced T-shirt with the silhouetted life-size heads of Bill Gates and his number two, Steve Ballmer. A red X, simulating paintbrush strokes, is imprinted over their faces. George smiles at the shirt, reminded once again of the glory of late capitalism, in which there is no consumer urge, not even an anticapitalist fashion urge, too odd or small-bore for the marketplace to satisfy.

"Who's the bald guy?" he asks.

"Ballmer. He's like Gates's chief henchman."

After the briefest of small talk, George rather too emphatically poses a hypothetical question to her about a way he's imagined to "hack into a certain company's phone system" to keep precise tabs on one of its employees all day long as he—"he"—walks from office to office.

Fanny says she doesn't know much about phone phreaking.

"Ah. Doesn't matter. It's just a brainstorm I had. For the same project I was working on over the summer. I was curious. I have another idea, for pagers, sort of like the prank you and Willi did. I just don't know what to do with it yet."

"For your TV show?"

"You know person X is going to be with person Y at a particular time, right? In some very intimate circumstance. You send a message to person X's pager—either an actual message, with words, or a callback number that person Y would know. The idea would be to send a message to person X in the hope that person Y would see it and freak out, be angry at person X, conclude that person X has somehow betrayed him. You don't understand, do you? I wasn't clear. Okay, instead of person X, call her Mary. Mary is in bed with her coconspirator, literally in bed—"

"George?"

"What?"

"Lizzie loves you. She wants to be married to you."

He does not say anything.

"She loves you."

"Yeah, yeah. Yeah."

"She does. And she's not having an affair with anyone. *Trust* me. She's *not*. Trust her. We talked for a long time, and she was like, 'If you can make him believe that, I'll be in your debt forever.' So, believe it."

"Fanny. I'm afraid you don't understand."

"I know you think I'm just some punk kid, and I don't mean to be mean, but you're sitting in this fucking Winnebago, like disconnecting from reality and going loony."

They finish talking. She finishes her Snapple. He thanks her for stopping by and encourages her to apply to Wesleyan. He hugs her goodbye and tells her to stay out of trouble.

"Say hi to Mom," he tells her as she steps down and out.

"My mom? I will. You mean *my* mom?"

He meant Lizzie. He isn't certain what he meant. After Fanny leaves, he sits on the metal step, and stays there very quietly for an hour, looking at the rubble out on the pier, the twisted steel tie-rods and chunks of concrete, pretty in the light of the low evening sun. A few yards to his left, he sees a monarch butterfly flitting in and out of the open Cyclone gate, flying in circles, up and down, a spiral. Between George and the gate, a breeze off the Hudson catches a few dried leaves and carries them off the ground in a tiny whirlwind. For five seconds, the swirling leaves and the butterfly are perfect simulations of one another, side by side. He goes back inside, shuts down the Power-Book, picks up the phone, and calls Warren Holcombe again.

4 7

"You don't mind if I smoke, do you? Because I smoke." Warren holds the edge of his apartment door in one hand and a burning True in the other.

"I see. I don't mind."

"I quit on New Year's, but I started again. Increased, actually."

George's obligatory three sessions with Warren in the eighties, about his hand, took place in a regular medical office building. Warren smoked Trues then, too. You could smoke inside office buildings then.

"Follow me."

Warren is not fat, but Warren lumbers. He's lumbering down a long hallway toward the amplified sound of dinging and high-pitched plink-ing. George has not realized until right now how huge Warren's bald spot has gotten, probably big enough to exceed the strict definition of "spot." He's wearing slippers. Otherwise, he is dressed exactly as al-ways—wide-wale brown corduroys, long-sleeved turtleneck.

"You won't mind the cage, will you?"

George wonders if he should leave.

"What? What cage?"

"The music," he says as they step into his office. "John Cage. It always seems like an insult to the randomness idea to turn off a Cage recording in the middle."

"I do mind, Warren. I hate music like that."

"Fine." He flicks at the power button on the CD player like he's shooting a marble. "Shall I assume we are not here this morning to pick up where we left off on December fourteenth, 1984, when you were telling me you thought the woman you were dating didn't have any problem with the hand?" He directs George to an armchair, then sits down across from him, pulling an old-fashioned ashtray, a three-foot-by-ten-inch metal cylinder, closer to his own chair.

No couch! Nor any cage or unpleasant recordings. George is relieved.

"So I don't know what the protocol is, in a case like this," he says as Warren lights another cigarette.

"What is this case?"

"Because Pollyanna and Lizzie are such close friends. And I'm here to talk about Lizzie. About our relationship. God, I hate that word."

"Why do you hate the word *relationship?*"

"Warren, I didn't come here for that kind of thing. You know," he says, " 'What were you feeling when you said just now, "Do you understand what I'm feeling?" ' "

"What did you come here for?"

"To find out if you think I'm cracking up, having some kind of breakdown."

"What are your symptoms?"

Symptoms? He's pissed off at his wife, who he thinks is having an affair with her boss, who canceled his TV show three months ago after one week on the air. "Well, for a week or so in August, my thoughts seemed to occur like non sequiturs."

"Give me an example."

"Oh, I was watching some Miss America preview show, and then for a half hour I couldn't stop thinking about *Play Misty for Me,* then I thought about this old Mickey Mouse cartoon where Mickey gets whipped. And then about how the ice cream in our freezer gets all soupy after a week and the repair guy said there's no mechanical explanation, and then I couldn't stop thinking about Superman. Each one was sort of obsessive. And none of them had anything to do with the other."

"It's so interesting that they gave it to the blind girl, isn't it? Miss America? When she stood up there with the dog and said to the guy, 'I can see the new century and the new millennium as clear as anything, Bob, and they're so beautiful it's almost frightening.' I got goose bumps watching her say that. Watching *Miss Mississippi* in the *personality* competition! I've got goose bumps again now." He takes out a fresh True. "I apologize for the digression, George. I'm sorry. So, you're worried you've got the clang."

"What's 'the clang'?"

"Clang associations are when you move from one thought to another randomly. Or apparently randomly, based on the *sounds* of words more than the meanings. (In school, I wrote a paper on it called 'The Modernist Disorder.') See—*Miss* America, Play *Misty, Mickey* Mouse *cartoon, carton* of soupy ice cream in the *freezer,* freezer *repairman, soupy, Superman.* So this stopped? After August?"

"Yeah. Yes, it did."

"Probably nothing. In fact, I'm probably the crazy one for making those links. Any other symptoms?"

"I'm sort of depressed. I don't know if clinically I'm depressed. But . . ." He sits up. "Warren, has Pollyanna told you about Lizzie and me? We're separated." It's the first time he's said the word. "Not *'separated'* separated, but I haven't lived at home in a month almost." He blows some of Warren's smoke away. "I think she's having an affair with her boss, and she says I'm an insane stalker."

"Are you stalking her?"

"No. Not physically. Not following her around or anything. But sort of. Yeah. I suppose. Yes."

"And the only reason you feel depressed, aside from your show getting canceled—I was so sorry about that, George; I *loved* it; it may have been my favorite show, network show, *ever*—but the single source of your depressed feelings and the focus of all your neurotic behaviors, as nearly as you can tell, is the fact that you believe your wife is sleeping with this other man?"

George breathes in deeply, and out. "Yes. That's right. Yes. And that she was complicit in killing the show."

Warren stares at him for a long time . . . three seconds, four, five, six. He stubs out his cigarette, stands, and lumbers toward the doorway. "Follow me," he says.

They walk back down the long corridor, but take a left before they reach the front hall. Warren flips on an overhead light with his thumb, marble-shot style, and punches the start button on a computer the same way. They are in an office, smaller than the one they were just in. The shelves are filled with loose-leaf binders and bound trial transcripts and legal books.

"This is Pollyanna's office?"

Warren turns to him and nods as the computer boots up. Standing over the keyboard, Warren types and taps, clicks the mouse, then clicks some more. Documents bloom open. He stands aside, puts one hand in his pocket, and does a parody of a maître d', grandly waving George into the desk chair.

George starts reading. He turns and looks up at Warren, who frowns and nods and makes four little circles in the air with his hand. George continues reading. He clicks documents closed, reads, clicks, reads, clicks, reads, and then opens more. He reads for half an hour, and continues reading.

They are e-mails, dozens of them, short and long, sent by Lizzie to Pollyanna beginning last spring. Lizzie thanking Polly for introducing her to Zero, then Lizzie describing George working so hard on *Real Time* he doesn't have any idea what hell she's going through with Microsoft, or with the animal rights nuts, or with the "left-wing assholes AND right-wing assholes." Lizzie explaining in the longest e-mail George has ever read her acute ambivalence about whether to sell Fine Technologies and take the job with Mose. Lizzie saying how much she misses George, even though they haven't made love in weeks, and with the *Real Time* premiere postponed, "chances for improvement are approximately zero." Lizzie worrying about poor George's health. Lizzie hoping desperately that the show works. Lizzie in a state of shock when the show is canceled, and asking Pollyanna whether she should quit. Lizzie starting to worry seriously about the mental health of "PG" (poor George), and his repeated, "savage" accusations of infidelity with Harold Mose, even though she has "never even seriously THOUGHT about being unfaithful, although I'm frankly just about horny enough now." Lizzie full of deepening dread in hotel rooms all over Asia, despising Gloria and Hank Saddler and finally even Harold, feeling in over her head, feeling like she's "in two rotting marriages at once, one with a psycho husband who hates me and the other with a slightly pathetic semicriminal who thinks I've got blue smoke and mirrors that are going to save his stupid company." Lizzie plotting her escape from Mose Media Holdings before the end of the year. Lizzie frightened about "these crazy things George is involved in, criminal things, that you don't even want to know about." And Lizzie, in the weeks since he moved into "Zip Ingram's fucking *trailer,*" growing even darker, fitfully resigning herself to the fact that "life can just suddenly derail for no reason," and on October first, just a few days ago, that "PG may be really and truly mad" and "just lost to me forever. Which I cannot stand. Even though I may have to."

"George?"

He turns. Warren hands him a box of Kleenex. George has been sniffing and making whimpery throat sounds for ten minutes, but has only just now started bawling, bellowing, weeping like a child. He cries for a long time. Warren pads in and out three times and smokes a fresh cigarette before George is finished.

"There's also Polly's diary on there," Warren says when he stops, nodding toward the computer, "which includes synopses of some phone calls and a couple of lunch conversations about you. If you're not convinced." He arches his eyebrows and twists his mouth. "Although frankly, showing you that material would carry this to a whole new level of ethical dubiousness that I'd just as soon avoid."

"No. No. That's okay."

"Well, you're cured." He looks at his big digital watch. "And your fifty minutes are up."

PART FOUR

November

December

January

4 8

Monday, November 27

"The screen market's 1¾," Billy Heffernan says, looking at the options scroll on one of his two screens. He has one phone in his lap, another pressed to his temple. He's on the wire, on one of his permanently open lines, waiting for his favorite broker on the options desk at Smith Barney.

"What's the *price,* Billy?" Ben Gould asks.

"Can I show my guy the whole picture?"

"If it helps, sure. Same as the others."

"I want you to work it, but I want to get this trade on."

Ben is impatient, even more of a flibbertigibbet than usual, and Heffernan doesn't know why. Bennett Gould Partners is 19 percent up for the year, with a month left to go; 6 percent ahead of the Dow, 8 percent ahead of Standard & Poor's 500. Maybe it's personal. Ben has been having more arguments than usual with the ex-wife, simultaneously whispered and shouted in Big Room style, the latest just this morning, about their daughter. (Her fourth-grade teacher at Spence/Greenwich declined to dismiss the class early on Thanksgiving eve—even though Sasha informed him clearly at half past two that "the driver" would be there in fifteen minutes to drive her and three friends to "the secret underground tunnel under Rockefeller Center for a private showing of the giant Christmas tree by one of the Rockefellers and a professional elf." She "fired" the teacher for keeping the class until three, and walked out.)

Heffernan holds up an index finger in Ben's direction and snaps the phone back to his ear. "Bennett doesn't like Microsoft," he says to Smith Barney. "What can you show me, size, in the Microsoft 120s? We want 5,000."

"That's a lot of puts," his Smith Barney pal says. "What's going on? What should I know? You hedging a long position? Or is Microsoft in trouble? Are they preannouncing?" Companies are required to announce any major financial bad news in advance, before it would ordinarily become public at the end of the quarter, if the number looks to be a lot worse than everyone expects. Of course, the motor of the market up and down, these days more than ever, is surprises—surprising profits, a surprising deal, a surprising change in top management—but the government has decided that the world needs to be warned in advance about surprises, especially unpleasant ones, beyond a certain size.

Bennett Gould owns no shares of Microsoft common stock. "We're not hedging," Heffernan says to the broker, glancing at Ben, who is looking from screen to screen to screen in front of him. "We're just not liking tech. Give me a menu." Heffernan pivots the phone from his mouth to his forehead while he waits.

"Keep him on the *line!*" Ben shouts, still staring at his screens. "Keep him on the *line!* Don't let him go short it himself!"

This is how Ben Gould always behaves when one of his guys is in the middle of a big trade, in the moments of flux before a deal is done. Heffernan knows that Ben knows that Microsoft will drop a couple of dollars as soon as this trade hits the tape, as it ticked down a dollar or two for a few hours after each of the other Microsoft buys they've made this month. The put sellers, Billy Heffernan's broker friends (friends of a sort), will only lose money on the trades with Bennett Gould Partners if Microsoft drops twenty points in the next three weeks. This is an easy trade for them to make, a candy trade.

"Keep him on the *line!*" Ben says again. "Come back with something! Fuck, Billy, come *on!*" Ben stands, twists his neck violently, with seven quick loud cracks, then performs a tae kwan do move and slams back down in his chair. And stands up again, shoving his face close to his Bloomberg screen. This is manic behavior even for him.

"Dianne," he shouts, "did San Jose ever call back? The analyst?"

Ben had phoned a famously skeptical analyst specializing in Silicon Valley stocks. In addition to the extra edginess, Ben's employees have noticed, the boss has been having a lot of phone conversations with people who think computer stocks are overpriced. He's been talking to technology bears, and lately he sounds like one himself. His tech strategy is evidently shifting. "Asia's going back in the tank, Intel isn't shipping the new chip, Micron's the canary in this mine shaft, everybody's fourth quarter looks ugly," he's been chanting, in various permutations, for weeks. Ben has had Heffernan and Melucci place a million dollars in stock market bets against Dell and Cisco, Micron and eBay. "Ben's in the den," Heffernan, Melucci, Berger, and Dianne whisper to one another. "Ben's in the den again." Even Heffernan and Dianne, who have been around forever, haven't seen Ben this bearish since 1990, right before Iraq invaded Kuwait, when he insisted Dianne come as his guest to George Mactier and Lizzie Zimbalist's wedding, so that she could stay on the pay phone with the traders back at the office.

And he's been laying down his biggest bets against Microsoft. Microsoft!

"Yeah?" Billy Heffernan says into the phone.

"I'll offer you 4,000 at $2, subject," the Smith Barney guys says. *Subject* to final confirmation, the broker means.

Billy flashes hand signals to Ben: right four fingers, left two fingers, right four fingers, left two fingers. Ben waves to himself, his palm low, as if he's gesturing to a child to come closer.

"Bennett wants to get something done," Heffernan says to Smith Barney. "He'll take the Microsoft December 120s for 2 and a teeny, but 5,000, and now."

"Done," the broker tells him.

"Done," Billy confirms. "Put me up." He pushes a button on his TradeNet telephone, his turret, and turns to Ben. "You're short 500,000 more shares of Microsoft."

One share of Microsoft stock is selling at this moment for $134 a share. Billy Heffernan's options broker at Smith Barney has offered to

sell Bennett Gould Partners puts on Microsoft stock for $2¹⁄₁₆ per share—
2 and a teeny. These December 120 puts are a bet by Ben Gould that on
the third Friday in December, eighteen days from today, a share of Microsoft will be worth less than $120. If on the third Friday in December
the price is, say, $100, Bennett Gould would pick up $20 a share, less the
2 and a teeny he paid. His December 120 puts will expire on Friday, December 15—although Ben's been buying 130s, 125s, 115s, 110s, and
105s as well, some of them dated to expire in January and February. But
it's mostly December puts, a whole lot of December puts, that he has
been having Heffernan buy for the last couple of weeks, a few thousand
at a pop from Morgan, a few thousand from Lehman, a few thousand
from Merrill. Of course, Ben isn't required to wait until the third Friday
in December to cash out—he can sell the puts anytime he wants during
the next three weeks. Depending on the market. Depending on what
happens to nudge the price of Microsoft stock up or down in the mean-
time. Or what Ben strongly believes will happen.

"Do it 5,000 times at 2 and a teeny," he tells Heffernan. He means:
buy the 5,000 puts. In other words, Ben just gave Heffernan the go-
ahead to spend $1 million and change for puts on 500,000 shares of
Microsoft.

"You got it," Heffernan says.

Ben turns to his assistant, whose desk in the Big Room is a few
yards away from Ben and his traders. "Dianne? Where are we at on
Mister Softee?"

"With that 5,000 . . ." she says, running her finger down a column
on one of her screens, "all the December and January puts (oh, and
your Februarys), from par to 125 . . . 24,200." In other words, he's
paid three million dollars for puts on 2.42 million shares, or more than
a quarter billion dollars' worth of Microsoft Corporation. No one in
the Big Room is very surprised to hear Dianne's total. This is a big bet
for Ben, to be sure, but not such a weird one, not an outlier like the
mad week at the end of the summer of 1998, when his divorce became
final and he bought 40,000 December calls on Amazon.com for
$250,000, for a teeny apiece. On that trade, after the calls paid off three
months later, Bennett Gould Partners cleared $153 million.

Ben nods, and returns to his screens. He regrets the playacting. But
he has no choice. He doesn't really want to own the Januarys and Feb-

ruarys, of course. He doesn't really believe that technology stocks are all going to disintegrate this quarter. He has always been straight with his traders and analysts, or at least never actively deceitful. But this could be the Perfect Trade. The Perfect Trade demands discipline and secrecy. Only he knows. Only he can know. *Hey!* Don't commanders tell white lies to their troops, and don't presidents keep secrets from the people, even from cabinet members, when it's for their own good? *Hey!* Don't all parents perpetrate elaborate fantasies, Santa Claus and the Tooth Fairy and the Easter Bunny—or, in the case of his only child, the best little Sasha in the whole world?

Billy Heffernan is standing at Ben's side. "Can we talk?" he says quietly.

Ben shoots out of his chair and walks the ten steps back to the Mess, where the chef is already setting out the bottles of Perrier and cans of Coke, her platters of perfect maguro sushi and fresh Caesar salad.

"Am I going to hurt somebody?" Billy asks. "With these Microsoft puts? I mean, I can't bag my guys at Lehman and Smith Barney and Morgan."

Billy Heffernan knows the answer. He has worked here thirteen years. How many more times will Ben have to say the plain zero-sum truth of this business? Why do they force him to put the fine point on it? Because he's the grownup.

"Somebody always gets hurt on the other side, Billy. That's how options work. That's how we make money. I told you, on these Microsoft trades just be sure your guys aren't going to principal it." In other words, the brokers selling Bennett Gould Partners the puts on Microsoft should be warned to lay off the bets a few hundred here and there, spread around their risk, to insurance companies and the other great bovine financial institutions too big and stupid to feel the pain.

"You know, all these guys think you're smoking something," Heffernan says.

"Hey! I got conviction. Like I said, all you can do is be honest with your guys, and warn them not to be the losers."

Heffernan, whose salary is approximately thirty times that of his brother the police sergeant, does not go the next step. His Navy machinist father and Roman Catholic mother raised him to stick with the chain of command and to accept the mysteries of faith. He nods and heads back into the Big Room. He assumes his boss is operating in some gray zone. Maybe he knows that an analyst or two are about to announce radically negative new opinions of Microsoft's prospects, and Ben is front-running those research downgrades. Maybe his friend Lizzie Zimbalist discovered some problem on the inside before she quit. Who knows? Heffernan would never ask Ben on any trade, ever, to explain exactly why his faith is so strong.

Heffernan is back at his station, talking to his Smith Barney man again, who has rung back, now eager to feed Bennett Gould Partners' hunger.

"I'm in good shape on the Microsoft puts," the broker says. "I'll do another 2,000."

"Where?" Heffernan asks.

"At two dollars."

"Done."

It is ten degrees below zero, a little chilly even in Minnesota for a sunny afternoon at the end of November. Before she left for work down at LoveMart, next to the new Cubby's SuperHole crafts store out by the Mall of America (she's manager now, and needs to leave by eight), Jodie Eliason Taft carried down a big Vikings thermos full of hot cocoa to Fanny and the German boys. Humfried and Willibald arrived last week, stopping over on their cross-country vacation, and Jodie encouraged them to stay as long as they want in the basement guest bedroom. Fanny really seems to get along great with them. Jodie smiles and shakes her head whenever she hears her daughter down there, talking and laughing with the boys and tap-tap-tapping away all night long, way after a normal person's bedtime. Jodie doesn't know if it was the learning experience of the legal trouble, or the summer in New York City on her own, or turning eighteen and flushing some hormones out of her system, or what. But she's been getting good grades all fall at Adlai Stevenson, and she even dragged Humfried and Willibald to the last Stevenson *football* game over the weekend (the Liberals beat the Cheetahs!). Fanny is enthusiastic about life again. If she stays up a little late surfing the web and playing games on her computers, well, *fine*.

Fanny's at home this morning. She's sitting at one of the four computers in her basement headquarters. Three of them, two boxes installed with Microsoft NT and the other with Slackware Linux, are up and running. One, the Virgin, will remain turned off until some-time Wednesday. Humfried is standing, looking over her shoulder. She sips her mug of chamomile tea, a taste she acquired in New York from Lizzie Zimbalist, and puts it down on one of the lami-nated WACKO PRACTICAL JOKERZ badges she and the Germans printed up. She and Humfried are both eating chunks of cold, leftover turkey stuffing with their fingers, straight out of a pink Tupperware bowl. The little Sony in the corner is tuned to ZDTV, the cable channel devoted to shows about computers. It has been muted since a lamer infomercial came on, something about using the web to buy stocks.

"Willi," Fanny says, staring at the screen. "I still don't get how IP spoofing works. The sequence-number prediction thing."

"RTFM, Miss Taft." She keeps looking at the screen, smiles, and flips Willi the bird across the room. RTFM stands for "read the fuck-ing manual."

Willibald is sitting on a high rattan stool at the terminal on the for-mer wet bar, downloading yet another "amazing, *fantastische* sniffer" from his friend Big Bob back home in Karlshorst. Big Bob, the son of an old Stasi spook, whose real name is Hermann, has sent them several pieces of amazing, fantastic, industrial-strength, KGB-tested software. They used his stealth-scanner programs, which Bob/Hermann calls Grosser Bruder 2000, to connect with the virtual ports in the com-puter system of the Reuters news service.

Over the summer, when they were first planning Project 11/29 in earnest, they made their way into the Reuters system somewhat more straightforwardly, by sending pseudonymous e-mails to several likely reporters. They offered to tell Willibald's stories of hacking the East German secret police computers when he was in junior high, and Fanny's account of what she has discovered in the Kennedy School computers about Henry Kissinger, Al Gore, a Harvard professor friend of Gore's, and three other current and former high government officials. After they led the reporters to a web site run by Big Bob in Karlshorst, Willibald not only dug out passwords contained in the cookies on their web browsers, but planted trojan sniffer programs on their computers. One of those reporters was Carlos Petersen, whose laptop and office computers now also contain copies of software that notifies Willi and Hummer and Fanny in their Minnesota basement anytime he goes online, and another piece of software that lets them read all of Petersen's internet communications.

And so, during the last few days, they've used scanning software on the NT boxes at Reuters, run a password-guessing program against the administrators' accounts at Reuters headquarters, and installed trojans inside those computers. Each time any of the computer system administrators logged on, a *thweeep-thweeep* alarm went off in Fanny's basement—sending one of the hackers lunging for a terminal to log on right behind, piggybacking, copying every password and protocol the administrator typed in.

Late on Thanksgiving night, hours after they came home from a movie with Jodie and her friend Alice Koplowitz, Willibald announced their breakthrough. "I have root!" he said. "We've rooted them!" To have root is to control a target computer. After that, they piggybacked from one machine to the next and the next, installing root kits on each one, until they owned all the machines they needed on the Reuters system. For four days they've had unfettered access, quietly romping among Carlos Petersen's laptop in the Mexican bush, a PC on a desk in the Mexico City bureau, and the big servers at headquarters.

Right now on the black screen of their VT100 terminal emulator, Fanny and Humfried are watching some keystroke logging in real time. From two thousand miles away they're reading the words of Carlos Petersen, the Reuters war correspondent in the Mexican village of Unión y Progreso, as he composes an e-mail to his bureau chief about a disputed expense account. They are way inside.

"It's funny, but it seems like almost an easier hack than the system at my school. I mean, I was young then, but this system," Fanny says, nodding toward the screen, meaning all the interconnected Reuters computers, "is *so* powerful, and has so many servers and scripting languages and everything, it's like, *whoa,* there are ways in all over the place."

"The bigger they are, the harder they fall," Willibald says.

"Like *Emmentaler,*" says Humfried.

"Swiss cheese," Willi says automatically for Fanny's benefit.

Humfried shakes his head and points at the screen. "Look at this poor dummy. All the passwords are *so* stupid! 'Joseph Beirn II' is 'JoeB2.' This guy Petersen in Mexico—'Viva'! It makes me feel bad almost. It's like, you know, grabbing chocolate from *ein Kind* . . . ?"

"Stealing candy from a baby," Willi says, watching Big Bob's latest software download from Karlshorst. "Stealing candy with Kalashnikovs." He looks over at Fanny and grins. "With our partner, Bonnie. Who's Clyde, me or Humfried?"

"We're not 'stealing' anything, okay?" Fanny says, unamused. "We're not hurting anybody. It's just a pie in their faces."

"Okay," says Willi, chastened. Trying to be comradely, he asks, "Fanny, how come you think we're not getting precisely the same keystrokes from Buttsniffer as we were from Big Bob's sniffer? Those small variations when you hacked the DNS servers?"

"RTFM, Nazi boy."

————————

Is this perfect? *This is perfect,* Lizzie thinks. She's watching a very pink sunset, in the backyard, where she just checked her e-mail with one of the wireless ShowNet PowerBooks. Rafaela is doing the dishes from lunch. Max and LuLu are just home from school, watching their snack-linked, prehomework half hour of television. Sixty-seven degrees and sunny on the twenty-seventh of November—Los Angeles imported to New York for forty-eight hours. In the real L.A., people can't help but take the balmy good fortune for granted, or else allow their heads to fill with blissed-out nature joy every waking hour—smug or dopey, their choice. But here she is, unemployed, at her two-million-dollar home on a warm weekday afternoon. Sitting outdoors, barefoot and happy, on a handsomely rotting chaise lounge. Thinking, but not very hard, about money and a video that her unemployed husband has gone upstairs to find. Everything about this moment is L.A., she thinks, and she's enjoying it only because she knows it is an evanescent blessing (like all blessings) that will last barely long enough to appreciate.

One of the e-mails was from MsTaft@fuckall.net. Lizzie misses Fanny and Alexi and Bruce and, collectively, the eighty other employees of Fine Technologies. "Dear Boss," her e-mail begins.

```
Edina is exactly the same boring happy happy
white white shithole it ever was, and the pres.
election makes my Groundhog Day grade-school
deja vu TOO intense. (Although I don't hate
Bush--he reminds me of my principal a lot less
```

> than the other guy did.) The ankle bracelet
> finally came off 10/31 (yay!) & I am semi
> getting along with Moms. Guess what? Willi
> (yes!) and Humfried are staying at our house
> for a few days on route to Las Vegas and L.A. &
> SF--their Byder-Minehof [???] 2000 North
> American Tour they call it. (They say they want
> to spend all their Mose stock money "before it
> turns us into yuppie pigs." And they say to
> tell you THANKS for the stock.) Speaking of
> Mose, btw, a nice guy named Henry Saddler from
> the company (sez he's your friend?) e-mailed me
> for an "informal how-ya-doin' online exit
> interview." Anyhow, we're having a total BLAST.
> Sometime I'll have to show you some AMAZING
> code a friend of Willi's in Germany wrote. SO
> HAPPY when I read about ya quitting after
> Microsloth bought out Mose Digital. (IMHO:
> Yes!) Anyhow, we're all thinking of you a lot
> and miss the good old dayz at Fine
> Technologies. Think of me Wed! Filfre to write
> if you have time. Peace & Love, Fanny

Lizzie knows about Fanny's crush on the German, but "think of me *wed?*" Fanny marrying Willibald might be a fruitful idea for a low-budget dark comedy, but would be a travesty and a tragedy in real life. ("If you marry Willi or anyone else before you're 21 I will have to personally *kill you*," Lizzie e-mailed back. "And Hank Saddler is probably a pedophile, and definitely a weirdo, so watch yourself.")

Lizzie feels a moment of envy for Willibald and Humfried. Unlike her ex-employees, who (thanks to Lizzie) got stock in the Mose takeover, she is still contractually forbidden from selling any of her shares in Mose Media Holdings until the six-month anniversary of the acquisition. That date is December 29, the last weekday of 2000. The accountant has told her she is insane if she doesn't wait to sell at least until after the New Year's weekend, but Lizzie fully intends to cash out on the twenty-ninth, tax consequences be damned. Max mentioned on Friday that Mose was down to 26⅜. She didn't know the market was open the day after Thanksgiving. (Just as she didn't know until two months ago that Max has made a hypothetical fortune this year in a web-site "rotisserie league" stock-picking game. It was a printout of Max's imaginary purchases of Mose Media stock that made her accuse George, the day he walked out, of committing inside-trading felonies.) So her 498,000 shares are now worth only $13 million (on paper, pre-tax) instead of $24 million (ditto). But she's with her husband at nightfall in their house on the Seaport.

"Daddy?" LuLu shouts from an upstairs window suddenly.

"He's somewhere up there," Lizzie shouts back.

"Miss America, the blind girl, just mentioned Daddy's TV show on *And Another Thing!* She was talking about Charles Manson going free!"

"Okay, sweetie, thanks," Lizzie says. "I'll tell him."

The foghorn in the Buttermilk Channel groans its sad but never saddening sound just as George comes outside with a big, goofy, embarrassed smile. He's holding a Jaz disk between his thumb and index finger as he walks back toward her.

"You *found* it," Lizzie says.

"It was in a Baggie wrapped in gaffer's tape up in the crawl space. The scary thing is, I literally can't remember hiding it. I really thought I must have thrown it away. It's like whole days are erased from my memory."

"Good," she says.

He hands the disk to her and sits down beside her. She sticks it into the drive. An icon, a red letter *M* over a bleeding heart, pops onto the screen. She gives George a look.

"I know. Your Chas is a high-production-value kind of guy."

She clicks on the skull and crossbones. A video image appears.

"It's just his face," Lizzie says, sounding confused, surprised, disappointed.

"Wait," George tells her.

"That's funny," she says, touching the screen, "you can see the tip of his white pine right there, behind him."

For a moment, the image becomes jerky and confusing. Then it resolves, a wider shot.

"Yowza," she says.

"Ta-dahhh."

"He does it standing up?"

"I know. I guess that's why the camera on the computer zoomed back, to try to capture more image. He confused it."

At the bottom of the screen, just above the burned-in video date, Helvetica text gushes in, scrolling across the lower edge of the image—HI! IT'S ME, ELIZABETH!—from right to left, whorish imprecation after whorish imprecation—YOU CAN JUST WATCH—as the man on the screen opens his mouth and juts his pelvis every couple of seconds, almost dancing.

"You see," George says.

The image is surprisingly sharp and fluid, given that it is a second-generation copy of a picture transmitted by cable from a computer on West Fifty-seventh Street down to a loft in Chelsea and then by copper telephone wire across America and the Pacific to Malaysia. And although Lizzie is blushing, and George is no longer smiling, their moods are blithe. They're watching a video recording of Harold Mose masturbating in his office on the Fifty-ninth Floor of the Mose Media Holdings tower.

At the end, the little camera tried desperately to follow him as he stumbled over to his wastebasket, then out of the frame, presumably to his bathroom. Lizzie clicks the image away. They look at each other for a few seconds.

"I guess this is a rueful smile," George says, smiling ruefully. "You realize, it wasn't *just* this. I was hating you pretty good before this arrived."

The cartridge is ejected with that brief, pleasingly lubricious electromechanical hum.

"I guess we can put this in a safe-deposit box with the rest of the family cyberporn cache," Lizzie says. "A legacy for the grandchildren."

George smiles, stands, and shakes his head again. Lizzie is referring to Sarah's pornography adventure. After George's dinner with Fanny and Willibald in August, Willi decided to prove to George that he could indeed install a sniffer on the cable modem at Water Street. He did, and recorded all the internet traffic going in and out of their house (and random neighbors in the financial district) for the next month. He sniffed George's Manhattan web-cam stalking, and he sniffed a dozen of Lizzie's e-mails to Pollyanna—which had been the bedrock for Fanny's faith in Lizzie's fidelity.

Willi also sniffed some of Sarah's telecommuting work for Felipe Williamson's brother's web site. Although C. Girls is indeed a "free, advertiser-supported hair-and-makeup database," as Sarah told them, most of the company's revenues derive from ChelseaGirls.com, the live online pornography web site. Chelsea Girls' key selling point is that its naked women are "100 percent Ivy League college girls and grad students," and that they are "the sluttiest, horniest eggheads locked in the Ivory Tower!" Most Chelsea Girls wear prop glasses while they're working, Sarah explained to her parents that terrifying October afternoon when George and Lizzie confronted her with the sniffer evidence, but too few of them can convincingly simulate even the dirty talk of a grad student egghead. Sarah's job was to serve as one of their Cyranos, as Philip Williamson's brother calls them, and sit at a keyboard typing out the faux-educated online responses of the faux-orgasmic women probing and clutching their own bodies according to the whims of their $9.95 wankers downstream.

"Did you ever do that?" Lizzie asked, feigning cool. "Take your clothes off for the camera?"

"*Mo*-ther! Are you joking? *No-o!*"

Then George asked Sarah when she started the Cyrano work at Chelsea Girls.

"May," she told them, "right around the time of that big party you guys had." It was probably stupid to care, George knew, even as he was hearing the answer and feeling deep relief. But the recording of Mose, according to the date at the bottom of the video image, was made April 3. And when Sarah told them she gave most of her fourteen-dollars-an-hour earnings to Rafaela "for her people down there," George and Lizzie felt prouder than they let on.

What Sarah hasn't told them is that the money she funneled through Rafaela, $4,663 in all, went to buy thirty thousand rounds of AK-47 ammunition for the Zapatista guerillas. She hasn't told her parents because she doesn't know. Nor do any of them know that Felipe Williamson's brother, Josh, buys his thousands of hours a month of phone service for Chelsea Girls from a reseller principally owned by Roger Baird, Nancy McNabb's husband. And Roger Baird has no idea that one of his largest customers, Chelsea Entertainment, is a pornographer.

Hanukkah is still three weeks away, but the menorah is already up in the $ offices, filled as it is each year with candles cast in the shapes of Santas. "We don't have a menorah in Greenwich, Daddy," Sasha said yesterday, not meaning to gloat, Ben doesn't think, about her mother's return to Methodism. Cast on the plain Sheetrock back wall of the Big Room, the long pink rectangles of light at sunset remind Ben of the Malevich his ex-wife took to Greenwich and then sold. The problem with this time of year, when it gets dark by four-thirty, is that Ben's twilight tendency to moodiness sometimes kicks in before the market closes.

"So, do you want any more?" Billy Heffernan asks. "He's got 3,000 December 115 puts for 1¼."

Ben thinks: *Don't get too greedy.* He thinks: *Resist the candy trades.* The options desks at Goldman Sachs and First Boston have been on the wire with Heffernan all afternoon, pressing more loads of Microsoft puts on him. It's against the law to own more than 10,000 options, either puts or calls, on most stocks. But for Microsoft and a few other big, heavily traded companies, the limit is 50,000. Ben owns 24,200 Microsoft puts. He could legally double his position.

"No," Ben says, "uh-uh, that's it."

The brokers might turn out to be right, of course, and Ben Gould will wind up on the wrong side of a monstrous $3 million candy trade. Everyone who trades options, he knows and they know, are piranhas (the guys in the pit, massed and frenzied) or sharks. Ben prefers to think of himself as sharklike, discriminating and even dignified, striking at a few great big flailing, sanguinary trades. He's a killer, but he is not a scummer, one of the rock people. He isn't doing anything wrong here; that is, he isn't doing anything illegal. He didn't ask; they didn't tell. He happens to know. He just happens to know. It's a Perfect Trade.

How perfect will it be? Ben remembers writing the story in 1980 about Arrow Electronics, and how the stock price shriveled by half five minutes after those thirteen executives burned to death in Westchester. On the other hand, when Frank Gaudette died in 1993, the stock of his company wasn't badly hit. Even though he was one of the top guys, he'd been sick for so long the market had discounted it—the death was de facto preannounced. Gaudette was head of worldwide operations at Microsoft, second only to Gates. But then again, that was seven years ago, a long time back. These days, on any given Friday afternoon, people bring down Microsoft two or three points on a whisper about something minor, like slow Asian shipments of Windows 2000. Ben knows what he knows. But in the end, who knows?

Tuesday, November 28

According to the big Vikings digital thermometer outside Jodie Taft's kitchen window, it's warmer this morning than it was yesterday, up to six degrees below zero. She hears the TV on downstairs. And she hears Fanny and the boys chattering as usual, up and at 'em already, at seven-ten! What is it with these kids and the computers? It's a different world, that's for darned sure. She steps carefully down the wooden stairs to the basement, balancing the three giant mugs of hot cocoa on a LoveMart bedside sex-toy tray.

"Cocoa time!" Jodie says.

"Thank you, Mrs. Tahhhft!" Willibald and Humfried say in unison, entirely earnest and grateful, not meaning to sound like Arnold Schwarzenegger playing Eddie Haskell. They think Fanny's mom is cute and nice and American. Jodie Taft thinks they're cute and nice and, in their red fleece tops and with Willibald's little blond goat's beard, so *Christmassy*.

The kids have been awake most of the night, of course. Empty ultra-venti Starbucks cups as big as megaphones sit in a neat row at the back of one of the PCs, just beneath a homemade poster, printed in the inch-high letters of a funny-papers Microsoft typeface called Comic Sans Serif: REMEMBER WHERE YOU WERE ON NOVEMBER 29, 2000? WACKO PRACTICAL JOKERZ RULE! On the Sony in the corner, E!^{2} is showing a tour group of movie stars, live, trying to talk to a pair of tou-cans at the grand opening of Salvation, the swank rain-forest Eco-resort thirty miles from Selvapesta, Costa Rica.

"I want you to get some breakfast in you before you leave for school, young lady!"

"I'm taking two independent-study days, Mom. Today and tomor-row."

Jodie Taft smiles as she climbs the basement stairs. She remembers the day thirty years ago—*Goodness,* she thinks, *thirty years!*—when she stayed up all night and skipped classes helping George Mactier set up the Henry Wallace High School Vietnam Moratorium demonstrations.

"Susan and Tim," says the spiky-haired young TV correspondent to two of the movie stars in Costa Rica, *"I know how nice it must be for you guys to kick back for a while here, after your week in the Zapatista territories. Tell me about the fighting—did you see combat?"* *"We did hear shooting one day,"* the female movie star says, *"when we were near Chabajebal with Barbra and her crew, but you know how difficult it is to tell what's going on in that situation . . ."*

Willibald, typing away, nods toward the TV. "See?" he says, "everything is the war in Mexico. I still think a bomb, an accidental bombing by the security forces, is the best. I do. It's more amusing."

Fanny, watching her terminal screen, shakes her head. "It might be. But I told you, I don't want to do anything that involves government stuff." She turns to Willi. "I can't afford to do anything that gets the feds pissed off, okay?"

"Look! Look!" Humfried suddenly shouts. "On the TV!"

The on-air correspondent, who's wearing a sleeveless khaki minidress, is now talking to a hulking bald man in a pink polo shirt.

"God," Fanny says, "he looks like a *Star Trek* alien, with the evil grin and the slitty eyes and the big bulge on the top of his head."

"Maybe they *are* aliens," Willibald says.

"Wacko Practical Jokerz, heroes of the solar system!" Humfried says.

"So," the woman on TV says, pointing her MTV and E!^{2} microphones up toward the man's face, *"is there a place for computers in the Costa Rican rain forest?"*

"Francesca, coming down here makes you realize that there are still so many parts of the world, even in our own hemisphere, that need the solutions technology can provide."

"Tell our viewers what you were saying before to Michael Stipe, the thing your boss said about the rain forest?"

The bald giant smiles. *"Oh, Bill was just saying how being in the jungle here, and deep diving out there, makes him feel like we're actually inside planet Earth's operating system."*

"Interesting way of thinking about this important ecosystem, Steve Ballmer of Microsoft," the correspondent says, stepping away, *"here on a scuba vacation with his boss—the richest man* on planet Earth.*"* The camera follows

her, then pans down to find a pretty blond woman squatting, trying to feed a giant longhaired weasel. *"The tayra want to eat lizard, señora,"* a man from the resort is saying quietly to her, *"he not like banana."* The correspondent squats down beside them. *"Kim Basinger, it's Francesca Mahoney, for MTV/E-squared* Real Time News, *who's your friend here?"*

"The operating system of planet Earth," Willibald says, unsmiling. "That lamer deserves to die simply for that."

From his office on the east side of the Fifty-ninth Floor, Henry Saddler could, if he wanted, see the world's largest electric snowflake suspended above Fifth Avenue. But he's busy. Between the thumb and index finger of his left hand he's pinching the shirt fabric over his right nipple. With his right hand, he's moving his mouse around the WinWin.com web page, calling up the account of WINWIN WINNER HENRY G. SADDLER IV. And he's talking on the speakerphone, to Jack Delancey from *Variety.*

"Well, Jack, those may *be* 'the scoops du jour in the M-and-A chattering caste,' but I think you're going to look silly if you go with that. In all honesty."

"Which? Are you telling me that Mose is *not* off-loading the stations to Diller? Or that you *aren't* going to do a megadeal with WebTV for MBC programming lock, stock, and barrel full of monkeys?"

"At any nimble multimedia entertainment company, all sorts of options are kicked around, Jack, you know that. That's the nature of nimble management." *Nimble* is one of the words on Harold's MPI that needs goosing. "Like our 2001 reinvention strategies as regards the Winter Channel evolving into Reality Channel, which you yourself reported. Exclusively."

"And you already have my sincerest for dropping the dime on that bit of intelligence, Hank."

"Henry. Well, this is no different."

"Which? The station sale or the programming sale?"

" 'Although one top source says the investment in the MBC by Microsoft could be "in the low ten-figure range," the source denied in the strongest possible terms that the Mose O and Os are for sale.' Please do *not* call us a weblet. Please. It drives Harold up the wall."

"I guess if you really were migrating toward the network exit door, Hank, you wouldn't give a hoot about the nomenclature."

"Good point."

"Is this the right number to grab you at, later in the week when I need to Cuisinart your quotes into deadline configuration?"

"Actually, I'll be in Burbank late tonight through the rest of the week."

"Roger wilco, Hank, I'll 818 you Wednesday, Thursday."

"It's Henry."

Saddler clicks a WinWin.com button to check his account. Most of his Mose Media Holdings shares are in accounts managed by the company and its brokerage house. But on WinWin.com he buys and sells a bit of Mose on his own now and then, just for the kick of it, really, when he has . . . hunches. Right now he has a hunch that *Variety* is going to confirm that Mose is not abandoning network television and may get a huge infusion of cash from Microsoft. He has a hunch that the stock of Mose Media Holdings will rise on that news, and keep rising when the WebTV deal does go through. He clicks the WinWin. com EXPRESS TRADE button, and purchases 3,000 Mose Media Holdings shares. TRADE CONFIRMED, HENRY G. SADDLER IV.

He presses the special platinum PHONE ME NOW button that's operative only on the screens of WinWin *Winners,* and waits. He is feeling very clever. He has never shorted a stock before, but he's read and reread *Stock-Shorting for Dummies,* and he knows the material cold. The broker borrows the shares from the vault and lends them to you. You sell the shares today for $100 apiece. Then, after the stock price drops to $50 next week, you pay the broker $50 for the share and pocket the difference. You double your money in a week, just like that. You're a winner!

The phone rings. It's Henry's WinWin.com Personal Privileges Representative, full of "Mr. Saddler" solicitousness. The asking price right now for Microsoft is $131⅞. Henry—Mr. Saddler—tells the broker he wants to short 5,000 shares of common stock. Just one moment, she says . . . and then she's back, telling him *of course,* Mr. Saddler, you have a preapproved margin account. Hank tells the woman he wants to do 5,000 shares short at $131⅞ for $660,000. And no commission at all, Henry asks her to confirm, just like with all his other trades, since he's a WinWin Winner? "Of course not, Mr. Saddler!" And just like that, on Tuesday the twenty-eighth of November, Henry Saddler has shorted 5,000 shares of Microsoft. If the stock should drop (tomorrow, for instance) by $20 a share, Henry Saddler will be $100,000 richer. If it drops by $40 a share, he'll be $200,000 richer. This is what the vice president elect means when he says America is one heck of a wealth-creation engine. This is outstanding! This is sexy! Henry Saddler gleams.

Wednesday, November 29

"Wie sagen Sie 'sicher'?" Humfried asks Willi.

"How can you be certain?"

"How can you be *certain*," Humfried says directly to Fanny, "that this stranger is still in the jungle in Mexico with the Zapatistas? Maybe he's returned now to Costa Rica. Maybe he's right by the phone in the office. *Boom!* He tells them right away, 'This is not true.' "

"*Stringer*, not *stranger*," she says absentmindedly to Humfried. Fanny is at her computer, editing their two stories one last time, plugging in a couple of final facts plucked from a web site about Costa Rican scuba diving. She turns to face him. "Well, yesterday Carlos Petersen e-mailed his boss that he'd be filing another story tomorrow from the Mexican guerillas' camp. Which means today. And last night he e-mailed somebody named Claudia that he wouldn't get home until the weekend. So, no, we're not *certain*. But you've got to figure he's still out in the jungle."

"We've got good mission probability," Willibald says. "Worst case, we're up for one half minute. But even up for one half minute, there will be FUD, right? Thirty seconds of fear, uncertainty, and doubt. And so this will be covered in the media. Because it's a *fantastischer* hack. Because it's him. Like with the phones in their meeting. Everyone knew that was a prank, right? But it still was the big story." He gestures toward their wall poster. " 'Wacko Practical Jokerz.' The Microsoft guys pretended to laugh, but they were embarrassed."

"Humfried," Fanny says, "it's your turn in the kitchen. We're probably getting close."

Humfried bounds upstairs with his Domino's pepperoni, and hops up onto the counter to stare at Jodie Taft's giant digital thermometer.

"One degree under, still," he shouts toward the basement door.

They have decided that since they have no way of knowing the Costa Rican dive times, it doesn't matter exactly when during the day they push the button. Willibald picked up the thermometer trick as a boy, a Thaelmann Pioneer, at his kommunist kinder kamp in East Germany. The idea is to ensure that one's apparently random actions are actually random, to preclude any inferences of logic or motive afterward. Fanny and Humfried and Willibald have done their best to cover their tracks technologically—the phony internet aliases they've spoofed, the root kit they planted inside the Reuters system, the Stasi stealth tricks Big Bob showed them. Willi said, "We will wait for God to tell us when the time is right to launch." The countdown from five below zero to one below has taken all morning.

In the basement, Fanny and Willi are finishing their large mushroom pizza. The fourth computer, the Virgin, is booted up and online. It will be their observation post.

"I guess it's like some form of really high-priced push," Fanny says. "I guess five hundred thousand business guys really need to have, like, every piece of information at their fingertips immediately, all the time."

"But isn't Reuters' news free on the web site?" Willi says. "And even on Yahoo!?"

"Not all of it. Not as fast. And some people would just rather pay for stuff. It's America."

Humfried is coming downstairs. He's got a big smile.

"Yes?" Willibald asks his friend.

"Zero," Humfried says. "Zero degrees."

It's 1:22 Central Standard Time.

"Do it?" Fanny asks.

"Just do it," Willi tells her. "Assassination time."

Fanny clicks her mouse once.

"Awesome," she says in a little voice.

This interlude of temperatures in the sixties and seventies, three days running, gives everything an unreal, antic cast. It's the twenty-ninth of November, and the windows are open. The regular south-side pigeon, the fat, dirty, yellowish one they call Steinbrenner, is hopping in and out over the sill, a little crazily, pecking at bits of soy-soaked sushi rice from Dianne's lunch, going momentarily airborne every time he hits wasabi. Frank Melucci is wearing his $ softball T-shirt. Ben figures the disorienting weather will help camouflage any odd behavior on his part. He's made two dozen trades today, routine stuff, and no one in the Big Room has any clue. He's wound up tight as a crackhead about to stick up a 7-Eleven, but that's normal. He hasn't taken his eyes off the screens all day, but that's not abnormal either. They can't tell he's paying exceptionally close attention to the news-wire feeds stacked above the rows of green and red stock prices on one of the ILX screens, the three inches of one-liners from Bloomberg and Dow-Jones and First Call and Reuters. A new bead of information distillate drips onto the screen two or three times a minute.

```
2:20 = BN Berkshire Hathaway <BRK.A> announces
       unprecedented 100x1 split
2:21 = FC One week after Animal Kingdom
       tragedy, Disney <DIS.0> preannounces Q4
       earnings shortfall
2:21 = DJ Quebec secession schedule hits
       Canadian debt futures
2:22 = RT Clinton and Bush join to "beg" Rubin
       to return to Treasury
```

Ordinarily, Ben finds none of it tedious, these dribs of information appearing one by one on his screens. The picture Ben tries to see is vast, the whole sprawling pointillist mural of the world, changing relentlessly and endlessly, sometimes in a shocking splash of dots but mostly speck by speck by speck. His job is to recognize the new image as it's forming, first, faster, before every dot of color falls into place. Today, though, he's indifferent to the itsy bits of the picture accreting here and there, the weakening euro, the strengthening ruble, the fiscal paralysis caused by the bloating federal budget surplus, the names being bruited for the new cabinet. Today Ben feels like a civilian, a yokel waiting for one big, dumb, dramatic piece of news. He's staring.

It's 2:22 Eastern Standard Time. Microsoft is 131½ bid, 132⁄₁₆ asked.

"Look," Frank Melucci says, "Steinbrenner is actually all the way inside." Frank stands and creeps toward the pigeon.

Ben glances over at the window for an instant.

"St. Francis the sissy," says Heffernan, watching Frank Melucci tiptoeing as Billy waits for his Morgan guy to come back on the wire with a price for Yahoo! January 280 calls.

And then Ben looks back at the ILX screen.

```
2:22 = RT Clinton and Bush join to "beg" Rubin
       to return to Treasury
2:22 = RT Microsoft <MSFT.0> chmn Gates and
       president Ballmer missing in scuba
       mishap
```

"Holy *fuck*! Holy mother fuck. This is huge."

Before anyone can ask Ben what has happened, before the second "Holy," his hands are at the Reuters keyboard, tapping—

```
***GLANCE-Reuters top business news***
11/29 2:22 P (RT)
Rtr 14:22 11-29-00
2:22 RT 8378 > Microsoft <MSFT.0> chmn Bill
Gates and CEO Steve Ballmer missing in scuba
mishap off Costa Rica
2:22 = RT 8374 > Clinton and Bush join to "beg"
Rubin to return
```

—and before the second "fuck!" the full story is up on his Reuters screen.

"Billy!" Ben says as he reads, "start selling the Microsoft puts. Blow out of the puts. *Now!* Gates and Ballmer may have croaked. Reuters."

Heffernan thinks the panic has made his boss misspeak. "Sell puts, Ben? You mean *buy* more puts, right? This is *bad* news."

"No, *sell*. Sell as many of the fucking puts as you can. The company is going to be okay. Do it, Billy. *Now.*"

```
(Reuters) By Carlos Petersen
   Microsoft Corporation chairman Bill Gates and
his number two, president and CEO Steve Ballmer,
are missing in the waters of the Pacific Ocean
off Costa Rica, according to local officials in
the isolated Costa Rican town of Selvapesta, on
the Bahía Fea de la Roca. The two men arrived in
```

> the remote area Monday for a scuba-diving
> vacation, and a Second Quarter Century Microsoft
> corporate brainstorming session next week at a
> nearby resort.
>
> It isn't known whether Gates or Ballmer are
> experienced divers.
>
> "The currents and reefs and volcanic tunnels
> can be treacherous out there," said Homfredo
> Göring, a longtime local dive-master. According
> to Göring, the local marine life includes
> white-tip sharks, whale sharks, bull sharks,
> barracuda, and giant manta rays.

Missing. Only *missing*? That makes Ben nervous.

"Billy," Ben says, looking up from his screen, then back to the green blinking line of Microsoft BID and ASKED prices, "get me a size-ola market in the Microsoft puts, the Decembers first, as many as we can, all of them, as fast as you can. The programs are going to take it down fast. Go, go, *go.*"

"Nothing on Bloomberg or Dow-Jones," Berger says, tapping furiously. "AP says Ballmer and Gates are down there, though, diving."

Ben hears Heffernan saying "*Sold . . . sold . . . sold . . . sold,*" hitting every sane bid, selling the Microsoft puts as quickly as he can to anybody who'll buy.

Not a month has passed in the last decade that Ben Gould hasn't thought of himself as John Henry, muscling ahead on instinct to make trades against the giant, rapacious steam engines of the mutual funds that buy and sell giant tranches of stock automatically, blindly, stupidly, at any price they can get, blasting through transactions recklessly, faster and harder than any normal human trader can or would. This is his ultimate John Henry moment, the apotheosis. He will triumph in the next hour, or he will die.

"Screen price is 129½," Melucci says, "but the screen may not be updating. Might be a bad quote."

That's down two points since two twenty-one P.M. Eastern. In the last minute, the value of Microsoft Corporation has been reduced by $14 billion.

"*Sold . . . sold . . . sold,*" Billy Heffernan is saying.

It's now 2:27 P.M., and Microsoft is trading at $109, down 22 points a share, or around $60 billion in market value. Billy Heffernan has sold 19,000 of the 24,200 Microsoft puts Bennett Gould Partners owned seven minutes ago. The profit on the 19,000 is $21 million.

"Ben," Billy says, "they've declared it a fast market."

A fast market is an official options-exchange designation meaning that prices for a particular company's puts or calls are moving up or down so quickly that the prices listed on computer screens are unreliable, essentially irrelevant. It's every trader for himself. There are no trustworthy prices for Microsoft puts, so if Ben wants Heffernan to keep selling, he will have to let him give a market order—that is, an offer to sell with no minimum sales price. Other traders would be able to buy the remainder of Ben Gould's Microsoft puts for a pittance. "They'll pick us off," Heffernan says. "We'll be fucked."

"Christ, when are they going to halt trading?" Frank Melucci says. "It's five minutes already."

When *are* the men who run NASDAQ, Microsoft's stock exchange, going to certify the chaos, declare a time-out, and halt trading? This is the great do-or-die timing variable in the Perfect Trade. How many minutes will Ben have to buy and sell? Only a few. Certainly a very few. He needs to start buying Microsoft stock at these prices, and fast, because he knows that the bargains will be fleeting, finished the instant Gates and Ballmer are resurrected.

"Frank!" he says to Melucci, his other trader, his common-stock guy, "let's cover ourselves, I want to do the common. Billy, double-check me—how much are we short?"

"The stock's looking 95. You're still short 500,000," by which he means that Microsoft is down to $95 a share, and that Heffernan managed to sell three quarters of the puts before the fast-market declaration.

"Frank?" Ben says, waving toward himself as a signal to his trader, but with both hands, like a loading-dock foreman guiding a truck into the bay. "Take Microsoft until I tell you to stop."

This is the first order Ben has given so far that surprises everyone. This is rare. This is balls-out.

"Any limit at all?" Melucci asks, his voice almost cracking.

"Don't pay north of 95. Let it run. Buy Microsoft common until I tell you to stop."

Frank Melucci has already picked up his phone and hit the wire for Sam Zyberk at Morgan Stanley.

———

"No, I think that's true, Willi," Humfried says, already unplugging and pulling the hard drives out of the dirty computers. "Even for a few minutes, this might affect the cost of the stock, you know? Make it go lower."

Willibald, stroking his goatee as he rereads their first dispatch on the Reuters Moneynet web site, shakes his head. *"No,"* he says to Humfried with absolute Thaelmann Pioneer confidence. "At this stage of advanced capitalism, the business of a giant corporation is not so dependent on the living or dying of individual managers. That's why they're corporations."

"How long's it been?" Fanny asks.

"Almost two minutes," Willi says, pointing at the screen of the Virgin machine. "And SCUBA, I swear, should be all big letters, I don't care what your spellcheck says. It is an acronym."

"I'm not going to change it now. That'd look lame." She clicks. "Boom," she says. *"Adiós,* dudes."

———

His Burbank assistants, Cissy and Hector, were surprised to find Saddler already at his desk when they arrived at 8:30. "Hold *all* my calls, Cissy," he said. "I'll be working flat out all day on an important online project." He loved saying that, and really meaning it. His favorite television show in high school was *The Name of the Game,* Gene Barry and Tony Franciosa his favorite stars, and "Hold all my calls" is just the sort of Gene Barry or Tony Franciosa line he'd gone into the media hoping one day to say. He finally feels like a man in charge, a real insider, a top, *top* executive, now that his office is up here on the seventh floor. Even with the internal connecting staircase, it has always rankled him a little to be down on six, below Harold and Timothy. After Timothy's death, it made a lot of sense for him to move up right next to Harold, and to give his office down on six to Laura Welles.

Henry Saddler has contrived today to be where the boss is not (Mose is Global Expressing from Toronto to Washington for a sit-down with the vice president elect), and Cissy has cleared his schedule through dinner. All morning he's been clicking back and forth between his open web-browser windows. At WinWin.com, he's ready to cover his Microsoft shorts as soon as the stock plunges. At the Reuters web site, Moneynet (*cute*), he's watching the pot that just *has* to boil.

What if the hackers were joking around? What if this is all just some punk kids' Dungeons & Dragons game? It's almost eleven-thirty—two-thirty in New York, and the stock market closes in an hour and a half. What if . . . heavens to Betsy, *there it is.* Oh, goodness—*there it is!* Henry Saddler is fantastically, dazzlingly *clued-in.*

```
    . . . both died today in the waters of the
Pacific Ocean off Costa Rica, according to
local officials in the isolated Costa Rican
town of Selvapesta, on the Bahía Fea de la
Roca. The two men arrived in the area Monday
for a scuba-diving vacation.
    Details of the fatal accident are not yet
known.
    The waters off Selvapesta run to depths of
more than 200 feet.
    Homfredo Göring, a longtime local dive-master
who watched the two men head out for the dive
this morning, says the Microsoft executives
were apparently using state-of-the art
"integrated" scuba gear, in which the oxygen
supply is literally built into the wet suit.
```

Henry Saddler isn't just tingling and breathless, he feels changed, redeemed, rapturous, initiated into the ranks of the chosen. For once! For once, he is a true mover and shaker, a member of the elect. "Thank you, God," he says sincerely. "Thank you."

He has never really *won* before. The grand prizes in life were always withheld, like a treasure room from which Henry Saddler was waved away by the graceful and smart-alecky and popular ones. *I'm a believer,* he thinks. *We really do inhabit a wonderful, wired new world where every one of God's children has a chance for success.* And when a once-in-a-lifetimer like this is suddenly knocking like a crazy fool on Henry Saddler's door, you think he's not going to open up, let that golden goose in, and hug it to death right there in the foyer?

He punches up a Microsoft quote—still high, $129½, there's still time. He pushes the platinum WinWin.com EXPRESS TRADE button. He goes to HENRY G. SADDLER IV SHORT POSITION and after INCREASE? types in 14,000. He punches EXECUTE! As a line of type designed to look like an old-fashioned ticker tape flows past, reassuring him, JUST ONE MOMENT WHILE WE EXECUTE YOUR TRADE, HENRY G. SADDLER IV! the little WinWin.com animation of a cash tornado spins and spins to pass the time. He clicks over to his third open browser window, to see if his online pals at the stock market chat room are crazed.

Talk about out of the loop! He can't resist being the first in with the news. He types in, GATES AND BALLMER OF MSFT ARE DEAD! GET SHORTY! and sends the message, then clicks quickly back to WinWin. com. TRADE CONFIRMED, HENRY G. SADDLER IV! WE EXECUTED YOUR TRADE AT 11:27 PST. YOU SHORT-SOLD 14,000 SHARES OF MICROSOFT CORP. AT $87⅝ A SHARE—FOR A TOTAL COMMISSION-FREE PRICE OF $1,226,750!

He is dumbfounded, incensed. At 87⅝?! He pushed the button when the price was $129, and now they say he's made the deal when the price was down to $87! *"Real-time quotes,"* WinWin.com promises, right on their home page. They've taken advantage of him, he thinks, the old tease and terrorize Henry Saddler routine. This golden goose bit him on the ass, took a dump on his loafers, and then ran away. This is no fair! *No fair!*

––––––––––

It's such a warm, dazzling, improbable day (and the last of them, according to the forecasts) that as soon as the kids were at school, George and Lizzie decided to set out for a stroll, a long one, without any destination in mind. It has been years since they wandered for miles like this together.

Since that last walk, in fact, the city has transfigured itself, changed so profoundly for the better that it might as well be an act of God or a magic spell. As the new century dawns, the streets of New York teem with people who should be dead, who were scheduled to have been shot or strangled or crushed or stabbed had homicides proceeded at the rates that seemed hopeless and uncontrollable, like earthquakes. Two thousand New Yorkers were murdered in 1993; five hundred were murdered this year. Is that not a miracle? Those thousands of fortunate people, the anonymous horde of the reprieved, are right now hailing taxis, buying Yoo-Hoos, eyeing Lizzie's ass, barking random words at George, running, parking, cursing, reading, smiling, spitting, living instead of lying dead. And those ten thousand New Yorkers have not left behind their hundred thousand wives and children and parents and friends to mourn—a small city spared from grief. And another city almost as large has been saved from its self-made nightmares—the thousands of hooligans and punks and psychopaths who were bound to kill someone but did not, thanks to this metamorphosis, this great wonder of the age. How many millions more New Yorkers—*millions*—were not robbed or raped or ripped off or beaten? Luck turned. The better history played out instead of the worse. *It's a wonderful life,* George and Lizzie each think, more or less, as they reach Forty-first Street, the broad steps of the library jammed with people lolling in the winter sun.

They stop in Bryant Park (and consider its transformation, from comatose to staggeringly suave and glistening) for sandwiches on a bench. Afterward, Lizzie smokes a cigarette and they discuss whether to go to Vermont (no) or Nevis (yes) over Christmas, and whether or not to tell Mr. Hoff at St. Andrew's that Max has just received a two-year associate bachelor of arts degree from a junior college in Ohio, online. Max is proud—it took him six months, and he kept it secret from everyone except Sarah (who paid the tuition out of her Chelsea Girls earnings) until his online commencement ceremony a couple of weeks ago. But George and Lizzie worry that Mr. Hoff may consider a ten-year-old's unsupervised, unauthorized college degree a reason to turn them in to the child-welfare authorities after all.

As Lizzie finishes her cigarette in the park, a beautiful old lady in a Chanel suit approaches them and says, holding out a dollar bill, "May I buy one of those from you?" Lizzie gives her one, and the lady insists that Lizzie really take the dollar. "As my penalty," she explains. Then, after inhaling her first drag deeply, she hands the Marlboro to her old-lady companion for a puff and says, "*Delicious,* isn't it?"

George and Lizzie stroll up into Infotainment Zone, intending to take the subway from Times Square and, if they're very lucky, to make love before the kids get home. It's after two already.

"I guess I was hearing all noise and no signal."

George is once again picking over his Lost Time, as they call the period from July 17 to October 4. She accepts his obsessiveness as a kind of apology loop, repetitive elliptical contrition.

This afternoon she tosses him a new refinement, if only to keep herself interested. "You know what you were like? You were like the first, old, eight-bit cell phones. They fluttered and warbled because their primitive chips interpreted every little click and whistle as speech. The phone didn't know any better. It tried to make sense out of meaningless static."

As Lizzie stops to light another cigarette (the last of the pack; her last, period, she swears), George turns to stare up at the quarter-acre TV screen on the new Condé Nast building. He can't resist looking at it, as he couldn't resist the Panasonic and Sony JumboTron screens that preceded it. It is his obligatory gawk, and it makes people think he's a tourist every time he's in Times Square. Yet having spent his first eighteen years in Minnesota, he will always be a tourist in New York; having spent most of the last twenty-six years here, he doesn't care anymore what passersby think. In fact, what he has always enjoyed about the giant TVs is the feeling of being a visitor in some outlandish foreign city of the future—particularly with the English subtitles scrolling across the screen. On the live CNBC feed, now, is a story about the Boston Red Sox lawsuit against the Chicago Cubs, who won the World Series last month with a home run in the bottom of the ninth inning of the seventh game—a homer that the Red Sox now claim, based on an MIT digital enhancement of the video image, was actually a foul ball. There's a pause as the anchor moves on to the next story, and then in the three-second delay before the text of his words begins scrolling, George can see that the man on TV has turned suddenly excited and serious.

"My God," George says as he reads. "My God. Look."

The two of them stand, stuck in place by the breaking news, staring up for the next twenty minutes.

———

Humfried has all but the last dirty computer unplugged and packed up. "You know," he says, "this action now is unnecessary, I think. It's unnecessarily . . . *sagen Sie 'ungünstig'?*"

"Wasteful?" Willibald can't believe his friend is getting sentimental about chips and motherboards and drives. "The machines are evidence, man," he says. "It *is* the evidence. We can afford to buy new hardware."

"No," Humfried says, waving toward Fanny and the last of the live machines, "I mean the smurfing. It seems a little . . . *falsch gezielt,* to the journalists instead of Gates."

"We're not targeting Reuters as an enemy," Willi says. "It's, you know, collateral damage. They won't be down long. But the longer they're out of action, the longer they can't say Gates is alive. And the longer Gates stays dead, the bigger wizards we are." He shrugs.

Fanny's right hand is arched over her mouse for the last big click of the day, her index finger hovering, trembling slightly. "We got the A," Fanny says, "and this gets us an A+." She looks at Willi. "Shall I?"

The network administrators at Reuters have the ability to "ping" any of the hundreds of computers in news bureaus and reporters' hotel rooms that are networked into the system, sending a signal to a machine, which bounces it back. It's a way of monitoring the colonial garrisons, an automated exchange of "Okay?" for "Okay!" Fanny is about to ping scores of Reuters computers around North America simultaneously, by way of a computer on a T1 line in Berlin, which will cause each of those desktops and laptops to respond all at once to their headquarters' computers. Too many *okays* will gush into too few machines. The communication lines will be overwhelmed. The system will be disabled. Reuters will be smurfed.

"Ping," Willibald says, his voice all high-pitched cartoon onomatopoeia.

With one finger, she clicks.

After less than a minute on the Virgin machine, Willibald reports that the Reuters web site is frozen, and then gone, crashed. Fanny clicks quickly around her screen four more times, breaking for good those precious connections between the rec room in Edina, Minnesota, and Berlin, and Reuters outposts all over the Western Hemisphere.

And in less than an hour from now, only the Virgin will remain up and running in the Taft basement, an innocent window on the ruckus. The dirty machines will have had their brains popped out and taken away. The hard drives, nails hammered through each of them, along with a dozen Jaz cartridges and Zip disks nailed together and packed in a Baggie with a brick, will be way on the other side of Minnetonka Boulevard, somewhere in Elm Creek Park, heaved aloft, hurtling through the icy air, one after another, into the Mississippi River.

───────────

The woman from CNBC is standing in Times Square. Like all her colleagues, she is forcing a frown, repeating the words "tragic" and "tragedy" as frequently as possible, doing her best to conceal her extreme excitement over the news they're reporting live and continuously. *"The best guess here right now, Mark Franklin, is that so many concerned investors and traders and ordinary citizens were trying to log into the Reuters system that it simply crashed from the overload. And Reuters executives say that so far they remain unable to reach their reporter Carlos Petersen by phone. Mark?"*

CNBC cuts back to the studio in New Jersey. Off-camera shouts are audible. *"Thank you, Cordelia Jessup, outside the headquarters of the Reuters news service, which is still the only journalistic organization reporting, once again, that Bill Gates and his top lieutenant, Steve Ballmer, have both died in a scuba-diving mishap in the Pacific Ocean off a remote stretch of Costa Rica, where the men were vacationing. At Microsoft headquarters in Redmond, Washington, outside Seattle, company spokesmen say they have no confirmation of the tragic deaths of their top management team, although they do confirm that Gates and Ballmer are on a so-called 'adventure' scuba-diving trip together near the Costa Rican town of Selvapesta."*

The CNBC camera moves back to a two-shot of Mark Franklin and an older man, who has a dazed, close-encounter expression. *"Felix Cooper of Merrill Lynch, we've seen Microsoft fall thirty-eight dollars in fourteen minutes on the basis of this unconfirmed report. Won't NASDAQ have to halt trading?"*

Felix Cooper, looking at a computer screen, nods but doesn't speak.

"Felix Cooper, doesn't NASDAQ have to act quickly to stabilize this market? And what were you telling me a moment ago about the tremendous market implications of two estate sales of how many hundreds of millions of shares of Microsoft stock . . . ?"

Felix Cooper continues scrolling through his computer screen and only nods.

"We've got Daniel Wesselman standing by now, by satellite, from Microsoft headquarters in Redmond, Washington. Dan Wesselman, can you hear me?" The picture switches to a young man standing in a gray mist in front of flagpole and a squat building.

"Mark, as you see, the Microsoft flag is not yet at half-staff here at the Redmond headquarters of the software giant, and I don't think we can repeat enough, Mark, that Gates is a devoted father and husband as well as the leader of thirty thousand employees and the richest man on earth . . ."

No one in the Big Room is paying enough attention to the television to notice that Felix Cooper went AWOL live on CNBC, or the news from Redmond that Bill Gates is a human being who bleeds if he is pricked.

Cheryl Berger is trolling from wire service to wire service, looking for someone else to confirm the deaths, reporting what she fails to find in a kind of monotonic chant as she fails to find it. "Nothing but Reuters reports on Bloomberg . . . same with Dow-Jones . . . AP expects to have its reporter in the area within the half hour . . . UPI's treating it like it's been confirmed, but totally based on Reuters . . . Bloomberg not confirming . . ."

Microsoft is down to $87 a share. The company has lost $130 billion of its value since 2:22 P.M. It is now 2:36. And Ben has told the Big Room that he does not believe the Reuters story. He thinks it's a mistake. There will be a retraction. Gates and Ballmer are alive. And even if they are dead, those guys aren't the company. The Windows and Word monopolies are the company. The stock's going to rebound like a motherfucker.

Frank Melucci is on the wire to Sam Zyberk at Morgan (and only Sam Zyberk at Morgan), buying every share of Microsoft common stock he can get.

Ben seems weirdly calm, facing Melucci, waving toward himself again as the signal to Melucci to keep bidding, keep bidding, keep bidding, take the offerings. He wants more Microsoft. It's going to come back up.

Melucci puts his hand over the mouthpiece. "You want to talk to Zyberk yourself? He wants to talk to you."

Ben seldom makes trades personally these days. He pops forward as if he's spring-operated, and bams a button on his turret. "Hey! Sam, no time, where can you show me a million shares of Microsoft?"

"Are you fucking crazy, Ben, what? It's for fucking sale everywhere!"

"I don't want a discussion, Sam, it's the fucking buying opportunity of my lifetime. I don't care if Gates and Ballmer are dead."

"You know this market'll bury you," says Zyberk, obliged to warn, like the downside boilerplate on every prospectus, but desperate to do the trade. "You're nuts."

"Maybe," Ben says, "but I want the merchandise, bid wanted *now,* every share you got."

"You fucking know something."

"Microsoft is going to come back strong, that's what I think I know." He pauses and adds confidentially, verging on a whisper, "Don't short this to me, Sam. Go long."

"All right," Sam Zyberk says, "the stock's at 87, I got guys willing to sell as low as 81."

Fifteen minutes ago, no one in the world was shorter Microsoft than Bennett Gould Partners. But Heffernan had gotten rid of most of the puts in the eight minutes between 2:22 and 2:30, and now Ben is on his way to being longer Microsoft than any trader on earth. Ben Gould is a wild man, and his world expects him to swim extravagantly upstream, but this is *beyond.* He is way off by himself on this one.

"Make an 80⅝ bid for 400,000 Microsoft," he says into his phone. "I want to do it on the line, right now." He pauses for an instant. "Is this customers, or you, Sam? Because if it's you, I don't want to hurt—"

"It's all customers."

"Done," Ben tells him.

"Size to go, Microsoft, you're good on your 400,000. Done. And I'm working another 400,000, because I think it goes lower."

Ben Gould just paid $32 million for 400,000 shares at $80⅝ a share.

Fifteen seconds later, the Morgan button on Ben's turret display is blinking again. Sam Zyberk is back, offering the 400,000, and still more. Ben takes the offer, buying 550,000 at $79½.

Ben waits twenty seconds. Sam returns with another offer. Ben takes it.

"Done," Sam Zyberk says.

Ben has bought another 320,000 shares of Microsoft for $78.

Sam Zyberk comes back with a parcel of stock "from a multiple seven-figure seller. Big guy up north, Ben." No broker will ever tell a buyer who the seller is, but up north means Boston, and the big guy is the gargantuan mutual fund company Fidelity.

"What's he got?" Ben asks, playing along with the personal pronoun.
"Ten million."

"I don't have *that* much appetite, but I could use a million."

"Where could you take down a million shares, Ben?"

"Seventy-five."

"Done." Sam Zyberk thinks he is killing Ben Gould, knows it, but this is business. Of course, the way he's buying this stock, with this fucking *binge,* Gould may be out of business day after tomorrow. But everyone here's a grownup. Everybody's got free will. "You're wearing 'em," Zyberk says.

Over at Merrill and Goldman Sachs and Smith Barney, the traders are saying, *"Morgan's got a buyer,"* awestruck, as if some mad Arab billionaire were buying a mansion at the San Andreas epicenter during a 7.1 Richter quake. *"Morgan's working a piece of Microsoft as big as a battleship,"* they're sputtering, one to the next, over their hundreds of perpetually open lines to other traders and other clients, *"There's a blowout bid-wanted situation at Morgan, and they're getting a chunk of it unloaded."* Minutes ago there were only sellers, but Ben Gould has single-handedly corrected the order imbalance in the market, going long Microsoft, longer, longest.

Sam Zyberk comes back one last time, offering 300,000 more shares. Ben bids 73.

"Done," Zyberk tells him.

It has been nineteen minutes since the Reuters story appeared. The laissez-faire macho pride of the men who run the NASDAQ stock exchange make them loath to halt trading in any stock. They're not the fuddy-duddy New York Stock Exchange, they're *NASDAQ,* man, and they live for the fast, mad brawl and bloodiness; this is how people get rich nowadays. Besides, even when they stop trading, Instinet and the other unofficial online exchanges will let people go on buying and selling. The ambiguity of this moment has kept the market open for at least ten extra minutes. Right now, the deaths are unconfirmed, and at NASDAQ that's being argued both ways—*"Let the trading go on until we know they're dead,"* and *"Let the trading go on in case they're alive."* But Redmond is screaming and screaming that they've got to halt trading now. And so they do, at 2:40 P.M. Eastern Time.

"They've halted," Cheryl Berger announces to the Big Room. People shift their weight, or kick away from their desks a foot, or take a deep breath; but no one relaxes.

Two minutes later, Reuters announces on the Associated Press that their computer system has been the victim of a deep and vast trespass, a hack, and the stories filed on the Reuters wire at 2:22 and 2:24 reporting the deaths of Bill Gates and Steve Ballmer were false. (Their stringer, Carlos Petersen, however, is still unaccounted for, and has not disavowed the bylined report personally.)

At 2:46, after the brief trading halt—a halt that will forever gall the roughest and readiest cowboys at NASDAQ—the market in Microsoft stock is declared open again.

Now everyone is a buyer of Microsoft, as panicky about getting back in as they were six minutes ago about getting out. Instantly, the price climbs to $138, $6 higher than it was before the hackers' fake Reuters story hit the wire.

And Bennett Gould Partners owns 2.77 million shares, accumulated in the last fifteen minutes for a total price of $214 million and change.

No one in the Big Room has ever seen Ben so quiet and still. No one has ever seen him so *content.*

Melucci's phone display is blinking like mad, every one of his big common stock brokers, his *old pals,* trying to get his attention, desperate to buy back pieces of Microsoft.

"Whoa, Frankie," Ben says, nodding at Melucci's turret, "I think you've got some motivated bidders there."

"You want to take Zyberk?" Melucci asks Ben.

Ben picks up. "Hey! Z-man!"

"*Ben.* Ben, I—that last 300,000 of 'Soft, the one that you bought at 73? I—I'm afraid that one I don't have in hand."

Ben wants to taste this delectable moment, to breathe the sweet aroma, to let it roll around his tongue. "You said 'Done,' Sam. 'Done' means done."

"But, Ben, that's—it's—I'm out nineteen million dollars with that, the customer's not selling the merchandise. The customer says the trade wasn't fair."

"Fair, Sam? Fair? Fair? *Fair?* Since when is anything we do fucking fair, Sam?"

Sam Zyberk says nothing for a long time. "You're going to make me eat nineteen million dollars, aren't you, Gould?"

Ben prepares to delivers his aria.

"The *whole way down here,* Sam, from 130 to 73, did you have that picture the whole way? You were *fucking* me, weren't you, Sam?"

"Well, you know, I had to protect the other—"

"You fucking guy, you're willing to bury Ben Gould for Fidelity—"

"No names, no names," Zyberk says. Then he takes a breath; Ben can hear him exhale. "You're not going to cut me an adjustment, are you? I'm going to eat the fucking nineteen million, aren't I?"

"You know what, Sam? It's the holiday season. And we've had a good day together. So, no. Take an out on that last 300,000, Z-man. Nothing done on the $73 stock." And with that stroke of magnanimity, crazy Ben Gould is about to become a legend, the ultimate Wall Street good guy, the unbelievably great guy, the guy who shared the wealth when he had Morgan by the balls, the guy who doesn't just talk the talk but he walked the fucking walk, $19 million worth.

––––––––

"Henry," Cissy says on the intercom, "Mr. Mose is calling from the plane, shall I put him through?"

"*Not right now,* tell him I'm at a mission-critical moment."

All right. Okay. They may think they've made a fool of Henry Saddler. First the WinWin.com report flashed back that he'd shorted the 14,000 shares at $87, and then his Personal Privileges Representative pulled some condescending mumbo jumbo about "a fast market." All Henry Saddler knows is that he couldn't cover *any* of his short positions where he wanted to, at the bottom, at $79. If they'd let him get out at $79, why, he'd have made $700,000 or something! *"Fast market!"* . . .

––––––––

On another placid, sunny day out in the Bahía Fea de la Roca, with waves hardly big enough to qualify as waves slapping at the sides of *Tiburón II,* Jaime's twenty-one-foot Kevlacat, the *beep . . . beep . . . beep* of someone else's portable phone is not the sound of urgency. It is irritating, but it doesn't suggest alarm. Thunder in the mountains, or the wind picking up, or certain sickening metal sounds in the engine—those would be calls to action. When the phone of the big, bald one beeped and beeped the first time, twenty minutes earlier, Jaime, who owns the boat, wanted to answer. But Pepe is in charge of the dive; Pepe contracted to arrange everything, and Pepe is not about to answer the rich American computer man's phone without permission. It is a private call, he says. Who knows what trouble will come down on him if he answers? And how urgent can it be, after all? Urgent enough to dive down and bring up the Americans? A phone call? No. They'll be up in less than an hour anyway. But then the phone started ringing again, and Pedrito radioed that the men's company was calling Pepe's office in Selvapesta as well, so Pepe answers. On the other end of the line is a woman from the men's office, calling to make sure they are not dead. Dead!? Why would they be dead? (The woman speaks the most perfect Spanish with the most awful American accent Pepe has ever heard in his life.) Pepe explains to her that both her men are carrying special radio alarms with them underwater, that if there is any trouble the other man will signal, and he, Pepe Berrondo, will be in the water personally, eighty feet down in one minute, guaranteed. But the American woman is frantic, hysterical, crazy, and she says she needs Pepe not just to make sure that the men are alive, but to bring them up to the surface as quickly as possible so she can speak to them on the phone herself. Has there been a fire at one of their factories? Pepe wonders. Are their children sick? *"I need to speak to them now,"* the woman says, *"right this second."*

So Pepe throws on his tanks and jumps in. And five minutes later, he is back with both Americans. As soon as he breaks the surface, Pepe tells Jaime both men are just fine, of course, completely fine. But then, as they grip the side of the boat, and Jaime reaches out to help the Americans aboard, the littler one is suddenly ill. Pepe has brought them up too quickly. Jaime pulls, and Pepe lifts and shoves, and gets them aboard, but the pale man with the glasses is dazed, and then he loses consciousness. Jaime has had training to treat decompression illness, and with oxygen, Mr. Gates finally revives, but then he passes out again, and Jaime and Pepe fear they will be blamed. As he climbs onto the deck, the other American, the giant angry one, grabs the phone from Jaime as if he is going to strike him, and then shouts at the woman, his colleague, "I'm fine, but Bill's unconscious, we've got to get him to a real hospital fast. Call D.C. and see if they can help." And now, both big Yamaha outboards are roaring at full throttle, and *Tiburón II* is racing at twenty knots back to Selvapesta. With the American computer genius Gates, the richest man in the world, on his hands and knees on Jaime's deck, groggy and vomiting.

People are sprinting through the blank, beige halls in Redmond, then stopping suddenly, causing a new round of gasps, then sprinting again, spreading the news on foot, in person, face-to-face, *too panicked to e-mail.* "Bill really did have a diving accident," they're shouting to each other. "He's unconscious, it's *true.* Ballmer was on the phone from the boat."

As the news spreads around the Redmond campuses, a few people cry. Most people shake their heads, shocked all over again, unsure what's true and what's rumor. Dozens of people sing the opening bars of *The Twilight Zone* theme song. And a few people begin responding quietly and constructively to the news of their supreme leader's incapacitation. They go to their screens. They click over to Datek or DLJdirect or E★Trade or WinWin. Howard Moorhead is among the rational camp, on the phone in his office, talking to his broker, his bow tie slightly askew.

"I know they aren't dead," Moorhead says, "but I want you to sell. I want you to sell." He waits on hold, listening to an instrumental version of "God Rest Ye Merry, Gentlemen," staring out his window at the dozen of news vans, the cameramen, the correspondents, and satellite dishes.

Ben is staring at the TV. He fights off the thought that this is a delusion.

"How many shares of the common do we still own, Frank?"

"Two million one-fifty," Melucci says, holding two phones against his belly. "Do we keep offering?"

"No. Wait. Hold off." *God is punishing me,* Ben Gould thinks, unsure whether he deserves it. *I am being punished now.*

The CNBC camera is not mounted on a tripod. The picture is a little shaky. And Daniel Wesselman is a little shaky as he looks hard into the lens, making up his words as he delivers them. *"Again, Mark Franklin, that was Microsoft spokesperson Tina Obermeyer, informing us that she has been in contact with CEO Steve Ballmer in Costa Rica, who told her, Mark, that Bill Gates has suffered a scuba-diving-related injury. He is alive, she reports, but is or was unconscious. She says a medevac helicopter from the*

U.S. Southern Command in Panama is rushing as we speak to southwestern Costa Rica with emergency medical help, including a hyperbaric chamber for re-compressing victims of the bends. And in answer to your question, Mark, it is not known at this time if Gates's injuries are life-threatening."

"Thank you, Dan Wesselman, stay right there, of course." Mark Franklin turns to the CNBC studio camera, looking as grave as he knows how. A graphic of the current Microsoft bid price, as big as his head—$109½—consumes the lower half of the screen, along with the flashing words TRADING HALTED 2ND TIME. As the anchorman takes a breath and counts to himself, one-one-thousand, he's thinking, *Walter Cronkite, November 22, 1963,* and says, *"As this extraordinary and dramatic breaking story continues to unfold, CNBC will stay on the air to bring you special live, uninterrupted coverage. When we come back, we'll be joined by a medical expert who will discuss the neurological damage that accidents like this can cause. This is Mark Franklin, and you're watching CNBC."*

There's nothing to do until trading resumes, which probably won't happen before the close at four, an hour from now. Ben was intending to sell his 2.8 million shares over the next hour, even into tomorrow morning, working it, no rush, keeping the price up. Melucci has gotten rid of 400,000 at $137 and $138 a share, for a total of $55 million. Ben still owns 2.4 million shares that he bought for an average price of $78, and which he may now wind up selling for closer to $78 than $137.

In the forty minutes since the first story appeared, Ben has not dis-cussed the big question with anyone. "Frank?" he asks Melucci, "if Gates does croak, or he's a vegetable, where do you think the stock opens tomorrow?"

"Well, we know now it doesn't go south of 75, right? And Ballmer's fine. The next eighteen hours gets everyone past the shock. But if he dies, there's the estate problem. I don't know, Ben. . . . 110? 115?"

"Yeah, I figured par, maybe 110," Ben says. It would be callous, Ben decides, to do the math out loud: if Gates dies and Ben can sell the rest of the shares he bought for $78 at $100, it would cut his net gain in half, to around $75 million. But $75 million is not bad, and that doesn't even count his profit on the puts, or the fact that he still owns 5,000 95 puts, which protect him if, God forbid, the stock really goes in the tank.

Then he wonders, *Maybe this is another part of the hack, maybe one of those kids convinced somebody in Redmond that he was Ballmer?*

No. Not possible, he decides.

Then, finally, a full minute after the CNBC report, Ben arrives at the nightmare scenario, the horrific panicky thought, *What if Gates dies, or has brain damage, and blame falls on him for not snitching on the hackers in the first place?* Ben Gould becomes the new century's Terry Nichols, its Dr. Samuel Mudd, its Marina Oswald (at best).

Do not die, Ben thinks. *Be all right.*

––––––––

The CNBC report is Henry Saddler's final glimmer of hope. By his arithmetic, he has shorted a total of 19,000 shares of Microsoft at an average price of $99½ a share. For $1,886,000! Almost every penny he has is now tied up in this awful, awful mess! If the stock shoots back up to $138, he'll lose $731,000! Three quarters of a *million dollars,* and it's *not his fault!* He was misled by this online *mirage,* quite frankly conned, ripped off. When he calls his Personal Privileges Representative, she just repeats what she said before about the "fast market," even after he threatens an MBC News exposé on WinWin.com. He knows now that there's only one way he's going to come out of this with a nickel. For his shorts to be worth anything, Gates must die. He's just got to! Sitting at his desk, Henry Saddler mutes the TV, removes his other hand from his mouse, and bows his head in prayer.

4 9

Hank Saddler is spending Christmas Eve with Mrs. Saddler in the penthouse at The Wellingtons on Wilshire. He's showing her all his clips, print and video, from the last four weeks. "Hanky," his mother says as she turns a scrapbook page, "your father and I never got near as much attention in '62. Not near." Hank is inconsolable about the three quarters of a million (although it's tax-deductible), and terrified by the possibility of prison, of course, but every time he sees his name correctly rendered in one of the stories—*Henry* Saddler, Executive Vice President *Henry* Saddler, a hundred times over—he does get a kick out of it. "Now of course," his mother continues, "that was a state charge, not federal, so maybe that's the difference. Plus, now, this is your *job*, I guess, isn't it, Hanky? Public relations."

Hank is a PR professional, so how fitting that it's his quote from the second-day story in the *Times* that everybody remembers. Hank's unfortunate line has been reprinted again and again. "I lost almost a million bucks," he said to the reporter the day after, "and you're trying to make some *federal case* out of it. I'm the *victim* here."

Mose would have put him on leave as soon as it leaked out that Hank was an official target of the federal investigations. But he was ready to kill him before the press, the FBI, the SEC, or the Justice Department had any idea about Henry G. Saddler's involvement in the episode. Harold was flying with his friend Mike Milken on the Global Express that Wednesday afternoon. He phoned Hank from the plane to remind him to let George Mactier know that Milken is still waiting for that call back, after all these months. Hank's refusal to take Harold's call was thus fresh insubordination on top of old insubordination, and intolerable. Mose fired him that night.

Saddler's prayers for Gates weren't answered, either. Gates was fine, out of the Costa Rican hospital the next morning and aboard a Gulfstream headed back to Redmond. In fact, Ballmer and other Microsoft employees were quoted in the *Time* and *Newsweek* cover stories saying that, if anything, Gates seems clearer, quicker, smarter than before—and, they added anonymously, "sweeter," "wiser," "almost a *mensch.*" When Ballmer groused angrily at a Microsoft meeting that the stock hadn't dropped *more* than 44 percent on the news of his and Gates's death, Gates reportedly smiled, leaned close to his lieutenant, put his palms on Ballmer's cheeks, and, as *Newsweek* reported, "stared deeply into his eyes for a full minute in what was apparently some kind of 'healing' gesture." *Time* quoted a neurologist expert in hyperbaric medicine who said that a mild decompression illness like the one Gates suffered could cause personality changes, "including, at least hypothetically, personality improvements."

The New York *Post* has devoted a majority of its front pages for the last four weeks to the story—including GATES UNDEAD the day after and HACKER HOAX $182 MILLION MAN the day after that, then WACKO PRACTICAL JOKERZ! (over a photo of Willi and Humfried holding up the *Post* story from June about their endlessly ringing corporate-meeting phone prank), FED DEAD END ON HACKER HOAX, and GOLDEN GOULD "SCOT FREE."

Hank Saddler and Ben have been questioned for days by investigators for the U.S. Attorney for the Southern District of New York. Two major-case units of the office, one for the computer crimes and the other looking into securities crimes, have been handling the case. (The U.S. Attorney in Minnesota made a stink to Washington about wanting to prosecute the hackers, and the U.S. Attorney in Los Angeles begged to have Hank Saddler for himself, but New York owns the whole case.) Ben is proving to be a monumental frustration to the prosecutors—as he is to the confused, appalled editorialists who describe Ben's profits and the hack alternately as a "recurrence of the cancer of eighties greed" and the defining event of the new century.

The problem for the prosecutors is that Ben Gould seems to have committed no federal securities crime. He learned about the hack fortuitously, by overhearing the hackers at George and Lizzie's party ("the May 19 Zimbalist-Mactier event" is the FBI term of art), and had in no way conspired with the perpetrators, or met them, or spoken to them. It looks as if he simply did not violate the 1934 Securities Exchange Act, the federal law against insider trading. For a day or so, the *Post* exclusive about the Saturday cliché tally prank at *Newsweek* (GOLDEN GOULD HACKED MAG IN '83) looked to his lawyers like a problem. It appeared the same day that the *Journal* quoted Ben gushing to a friend that he'd "bagged two hundo, man"—traderese for $200 million. The U.S. Attorney in New York would love to indict him—if not for securities fraud then at least for wire fraud (the phone calls buying and selling Microsoft stock), or for violating the laws against the manipulation of the stock market. "Hey!" Ben said to his lawyers about those two crimes, "that's practically the stock trader's job description right there!" But the consensus among the federal bar (as well as the guests, night after night, on Geraldo Rivera's TV program) is that it would be a stretch for the government to indict Gould, that a conviction might make new law but the case would probably be thrown out. And Washington, buying into that consensus, has overruled the U.S. Attorney for the Southern District. GORE GOT GOULD GOLD, the *Post* headlined its page-one story about Ben's "lame duck Xmas gift from the administration" the other day, which suggested that Ben's years of contributions to Democratic campaigns had put the fix in at Justice. A class-action suit has been filed against Bennett Gould Partners on behalf of Microsoft shareholders (erstwhile shareholders, in fact, the ones who sold in the frenzy of November 29 during the hoax), which Ben knows will cause several million of his new two hundo to disappear in legal bills. But on Wall Street, as a result of his spur-of-the-moment, end-of-the-day, $19 million magnanimity to Sam Zyberk, Ben Gould is God.

Hank Saddler may yet be indicted. Unlike Ben, he tried to contact the hackers after overhearing their scheme at the May 19 Zimbalist-

Mactier event. Even stupider, he posted his chat room message right in the middle of the hoax, GATES AND BALLMER OF MSFT ARE DEAD! which NASDAQ caught with the surveillance software it uses to monitor internet chat rooms and bulletin boards for disinformation intended to push stock prices up or down. The government is worried they won't be able to prosecute anyone successfully. But somebody must be prosecuted. Hank Saddler is the most indictable, so he will probably be indicted. As far as Hank is concerned, he's already suffered enough. On the thirtieth of November, the day after the hoax, before he knew he was in trouble with the law, WinWin.com sent him an automatic e-mail message informing him that he was being dropped from the WinWin.com Winners' Circle, as of the end of the month, because of his "November trading reversals," but that he would be welcome to continue making WinWin.com electronic trades "on a regular low-cost commission basis."

George and Lizzie have been investigated too. "You're a business associate and/or personal friend of Michael Milken, Mr. Mactier, isn't that correct?" a twenty-seven-year-old assistant U.S. Attorney asked George during one of his afternoons in the stifling, fluorescent room down on Foley Square. The prosecutors became particularly interested in Lizzie after they discovered that Mike Zimbalist ("aka Meshuggah Mike the Manipulator," according to an old FBI file) was involved in a faked seaplane accident in British Honduras in 1951; that her stepbrother, Ronnie, was a former cocaine dealer and DEA informant; and that her signature on the federal probation affidavit concerning Fanny Taft's employment was forged by her assistant. (On *Inside Edition,* Alexi volunteered to "go to the electric chair to prove Lizzie's innocence if that's what's necessary.") But yesterday the prosecutors conceded to George and Lizzie's lawyers that, no, they haven't developed any evidence at all that either of their clients had been aware of the hackers' plans, or profited from the hoax. (George and Lizzie hired separate lawyers—"just like JonBenét's parents," Zip Ingram said.) The same assistant U.S. Attorney who pressed George on his close friendship with Milken also questioned Sarah and Max about their participation in the May-19-event discussions, but the derisive press coverage (KIDDIES GRILLED IN HACKER HOAX) actually hastened the prosecutors' decision to leave George and Lizzie alone. "The children do not have a problem," the family's lawyers assured them. Both George and Lizzie have been struck over the last month by the comforting vagueness of that lawyer's locution—"We need to determine if you have a problem," "You may have a problem," "We think you don't have a big problem." As it turns out, no one in the family has a problem.

Everybody in the world knows that Fanny, Humfried, and Willibald are the hackers. Everybody knows they violated various federal and Minnesota statutes. Fanny has tried to stay out of the limelight. But the Germans have consented to be interviewed by any newspaper (the *Post:* GERMAN HACKER'S COMMIE YOUTH) or magazine (*Time:* ANTI-HEROES) or TV program (Diane Sawyer: "Willi and Humfried—was it your intention to hurt America?") that calls. Because they're young and skinny and bright and have little beards and cute accents, America is treating Hummer and Willi as mischievous, magical, lovable imps. They've appeared on Jay Leno's and David Letterman's shows. On Letterman, Humfried used Dave's desk telephone to set off the burglar alarm system at the home of a CBS executive, live on the air. They are careful, of course, never to admit explicitly to the Reuters hack, but the giggles and the coy, convoluted questions and answers are all part of their particular form of celebrity, a kind of feel-good O.J. lite. "Now, Willi— may I call you Willi?—if I assume that a guy *like* you, but *not* you, would feel pretty darned great after he'd tricked the entire free world into believing that Bill Gates kicked the bucket, would you agree with me?"

Everyone knows they committed crimes punishable by years in prison. But the public seems not to care at all, a new death-of-outrage which William Bennett has been following the Germans from TV studio to TV studio decrying. The hackers didn't intend to hurt anyone, neither Gates and Ballmer nor the panicky shareholders. The news service computer system was back up and running by four o'clock the same day, and now that Reuters has proposed hiring Willibald and Humfried, according to the *Times,* "as security consultants, on a short-term basis," popular opinion has exculpated them entirely. The other victims of the crime (or "victims," as the word is routinely styled in news stories) are not exactly sympathetic figures. No one feels very sorry for Gates or Ballmer, or for the greedy stock speculators who rushed to abandon the company instead of grieving over the deaths of two flesh-and-blood human beings.

The FBI has been unable to find any hard evidence of their crime: no disks and no hard drives, no incriminating e-mails or printed documents or telephone records. And the government lacks any real leverage with which to split Willibald from Humfried or turn either one against their American friend. When an FBI agent told Willi he might be deported, he asked her cheerfully and more or less in earnest, "Does that mean you pay for the plane ticket?" And after three weeks of conversations with Fanny Taft, the prosecutors were unable to persuade her to sign a cooperation agreement. She would not flip. In one of their discussions with the U.S. Attorney, her lawyers had sketched pretty clearly the secret information concerning certain senior federal officials that Fanny hacked out of the Kennedy School computer at Harvard in 1998. But whether that influenced the government's decision not to prosecute, her lawyers just don't know.

Lizzie looks up from *The Way We Live Now,* the Trollope novel. "Oh, God."

George looks up from the thick, perfect-bound Home Again holiday catalogue, which he's been reading for the last half hour instead of *The Death of Artemio Cruz,* the Carlos Fuentes novel he's been trying to read for a month. "What?"

"We never ordered the present for Zip. The plum pudding globe."

"Yes, I did."

"Good boy."

And they return to their reading. George and Lizzie's lawyers have said it would be a mistake for them both to go to the Caribbean for Christmas. And they are exhausted by the prospect of driving all the way up to Lake Marten. So they are at home on Christmas Eve, the children all snug in their beds, George and Lizzie sprawled leg over leg on the old couch in their bedroom in their converted cocoa-and-coffee warehouse at the Seaport.

She slaps the Trollope down on her chest. "What was that?"

"I didn't hear anything," he says, not looking up. "Johnny, probably."

Then he lifts his head and meets her look. Although it is an event from the depths of his Lost Time, George does remember leaving Johnny's corpse duct-taped in the Prada shopping bag on the street.

"There were two light thuds, one right after another. All the way downstairs."

"Did you do the alarm?"

She shakes her head. They both look at the clock, and listen. At midnight the alarm system switches on automatically. It's only half past ten.

George says, "If it was a burglar, he'd—"

"*Shhh.*"

They hear nothing.

"Santa," he whispers.

"*Shhh!*"

They hear nothing.

Lizzie whispers, "You know I've always worried about break-ins on holidays because they think you're gone."

"Doesn't that mean we should talk in normal voices, so he'll know we're here?"

"Go downstairs and check."

George rolls his eyes, waits two seconds, and then swings his legs off her and the couch. Scanning the room, he sees her fancy new ice-climbing ax behind the TV, grabs it, and creeps out to the landing.

Lizzie hops up and heads to the closet. She needs a cigarette. The trouble is, she hasn't smoked at home since the summer, and she's forgotten her last hiding place. Standing on tiptoe, she reaches back on the stationery shelf, then steps left and tiptoes higher to feel around George's old-vinyl-LP shelf. She knows what she's touched the instant she touches it, but doesn't know for sure it isn't a toy until she slides it forward and brings it down.

George has a pistol. He must have bought it while she was in Asia. It disgusts her, like vermin, like a snake. She is scared, frightened retroactively, to imagine he was ever nutty enough to buy a gun. She stands in the closet, holding it by the trigger guard with two fingers, staring at it, wondering what George's addled plan was. Shoot Mose? Shoot her? Shoot himself? Shoot her and then himself, like some tragic, stupid, drunken off-duty cop in the Bronx?

"I'll get it for you," she hears George say. "But I'm honestly not sure where it is."

George is talking to someone in the hallway. He is talking to the burglar.

Lizzie peeks out. Across the bedroom and out the door she sees George. He's still holding the ice ax, stepping slowly, cautiously sideways and backward down the hall toward the stairs to the fourth floor. He disappears, and then she hears the burglar—

"I need the cartridge. It's my key asset."

—before she sees him step into view. It's Chas Prieve. He's holding a hunting knife.

"That's the only one left now," she watches him say, "and I really need it. It's my key asset." He steps out of view, following George. And she hears him say, "I *deserve* to hurt her. You probably don't know she sent Malaysian thugs after me? She did."

"Listen," Lizzie hears George say, his voice fading as he moves down the hall, "we're going to find your disk in my office, and you'll be fine. Okay?"

"No, she actually *did*. She had them threaten me and take all the things from my hotel room."

"I doubt that."

They've moved too far down the hall for Lizzie to make out Chas's reply clearly, but she can tell that he's getting more distraught. She hears "King Harold" and either "Wong" or "wrong," followed by the heaving creak of the first step up to the top floor.

Chas Prieve is deranged, and he's broken into the house, Lizzie repeats to herself disbelievingly as she steps out of the closet, across her bedroom, and toward the doorway, quiet as she can be. ("Walk like a Mohican, in the movies," her father used to tell her when they went hiking in the mountains behind Malibu.) *Chas is deranged, and he has a knife,* she repeats to herself now as she presses against the wall by the door and inches her face out to look down the hallway. *He has a long, ugly knife, and he's heading up to the children's floor.*

No.

"Chas, stop right now, Chas. I mean it." She is in the hallway, pointing the .38-caliber WiseWeapon at her former West Coast marketing and sales vice president.

She has startled him. He points the knife at her and with his free hand grips the bannister like a railing on a ship in rough seas. His expression has turned from missionary zeal to rage and fear, as though Satan herself has appeared. George worries that Chas might lunge past him toward Lizzie, and steps up onto the first tread to block his way back down.

"Just let me go get the disk, Chas," George says. "It's yours, and you can have it."

But Chas is staring at Lizzie. "You will not triumph, Lizzie Zimbalist. You and the Mose forces."

The weirdness of his language makes her pause.

"Chas?" she says. "This is not some fucking video game. I don't know what Mose did to you, or what the Malaysians did, or anybody else. But I didn't have anything to do with it, whatever it was. I didn't even know about that disk until a few weeks ago."

"The cartridge is my only remaining asset."

"You come down here, Chas. George will go get the disk, and come back and give it to you. You come down *here*."

Chas shakes his head—quick, tiny, frightened shakes. "I trusted you before, Lizzie." He starts climbing again slowly, glancing back and forth behind him at George with the ice ax and Lizzie with the gun.

"Chas!" she says, sidling toward the stairs and holding the pistol with both hands, like she's seen in the movies, "I'm serious. You *stop*." She takes a step toward the stairs, raising the gun a couple of inches as she gets closer to keep it aimed on him, stops, then takes another step, raises the gun, stops, then another.

George sees that she's feeding the dementia by threatening him. He knows Lizzie has never fired any kind of gun, and won't be able to shoot Chas. George continues his creep up the stairs right behind him, Chas taking a step and pausing, George taking a step and pausing.

The three of them could be performing a postmodern dance piece.

"George, get back out of the way," she says. "Chas, I'm about to shoot you."

Chas turns away from her and starts up the stairs faster.

Lizzie tries to aim low, and pulls the trigger. Nothing happens. She pulls the trigger again, and again. Nothing happens.

Chas is up on the dark top landing now, even more agitated, looking for George's office, heading toward LuLu's and Max's doors.

"Come on, *stop*," George says, right behind him.

Chas doesn't, and George swings the two-pound, two-and-a-half-foot-long climbing ax at Chas's back, grazing his butt. Chas turns and crouches, grunting and stabbing underhanded at the air between him and George (like he's seen in the movies). George swings the ice ax like a tennis racket as hard as he can, backhanded, toward Chas's right hand, the knife hand.

The knife drops and Chas screams. Whimpering and cursing, holding his hand and splattering blood, he rushes past George, past Lizzie, and down the stairs.

"Give me the gun," George says to his wife.

They slowly follow Chas down two flights, but stop when they hear the front door open. They don't hear it close. Upstairs, they hear floors creaking, doors opening, a "Mommy?" and a *"Dad?"*

"You go call 911 and be with the kids," George tells Lizzie, "I'll stay here in case he's still downstairs."

"It's not loaded," she says.

"No, it *is* loaded. But it's a smart gun—only I can shoot it. It's programmed for me to say 'Ready to fire' into the chip on the handle to make it work."

In fact, before George finishes his sentence, he hears and feels a little servomotor *whirr* and *click* inside the WiseWeapon. They both stare at the gun, as if it were alive, as if it had hissed. "I guess it's ready to fire now," George says. The quarter-second *whirr* repeats, but not the *click*.

5 0

Between Christmas and New Year's, the news wants either to be freakishly happy or freakishly grim; either glorious acts of good Samaritanism involving people of different races and children surviving an avalanche by creating bubblegum-bubble air pockets, or else a doped-up bus driver mowing down a dozen carolers and the accidental execution of a rural family by federal agents with the wrong address; either Frank Capra or Oliver Stone.

The news this jubilee season has inclined toward the former. Even the biggest bad news story is not really very terrible. On December 26, Mose Media Holdings announced it was selling all its TV stations to Barry Diller, laying off fourteen hundred employees, and declaring Chapter 11 bankruptcy. "Although the MBC as a broadcasting network will sign off permanently at midnight December 31," the Mose press release said, "it will be reborn immediately as Reality Channel, an extraordinary new tripartite concept in cable programming. . . . During the day, Reality Channel's 'Sunlight Daypart' will feature New Age and holistic lifestyle and entertainment programs; followed by a four-hour prime-time block (the 'Wake! Daypart'), which will feature in-depth coverage of the passings of the celebrated, based on the hit MBC series *Finale;* followed in late night by the 'Camelot Daypart,' featuring documentary nostalgia from the Sixties and Seventies about bygone and beloved American newsmakers, such as the Kennedys." The cable channel reincarnation strategy looks dicey to most analysts quoted in the newspapers, although they variously agree that because Harold Mose is a bold, shrewd visionary whose buccaneering contrarianism has succeeded in the past, his reinvention of Mose Broadcasting cannot be dismissed out of hand. One example of his visionary shrewdness, *The Wall Street Journal* story said, was "his creation of asset-backed securities based on television programs such as the MBC series *NARCS,* which was still a top-rated show last spring—allowing Mose, in effect, to count his chickens before they hatched and sell them before they died." Still, the price of Mose Media Holdings' stock dropped more than 80 percent in one day, from $22⅟₁₆ to $4⅜. (At Key West, Lizzie's startlingly accurate, yearlong stock-price graph line lost its bead and kept heading south-southeast; it is now in the Lesser Antilles.)

And the good news has been spectacularly fine, a holiday media dream, as if orchestrated, exactly the sorts of stories Americans adore hearing and seeing at this season, exactly what producers and editors love giving them. On the twenty-second of December, the first day of Hanukkah, a dozen struggling charitable enterprises around the country received anonymous million-dollar donations, each check drawn on the same account, a mysterious nonprofit New York City corporation called Hey! Free Money! The next day another dozen Hey! Free Money! checks arrived at other charities, and the day after Christmas a dozen more—by yesterday, a million dollars apiece to a hundred methadone clinics, soup kitchens, and literacy groups, to law firms that defend indigent death row inmates and micro–credit agencies that write small loans to impoverished entrepreneurs.

The network news shows gave extensive coverage to one of the first day's recipients, a battered-women's shelter (and "animal rights outreach agency") operated by a church in St. Paul, Minnesota, that lost its funding and was going to close on the thirty-first. "This money will endow our work in perpetuity," the church's large, red-faced minister told her TV interviewers. "We have no idea who the donor is—and as Unitarians we each have our own comfort level with the idea of divine intercession—but right now, I believe in miracles. As our sisters and brothers in Mexico would say, '¡Viva milagros!' "

LA PAZ? is the *Daily News*'s front-page headline this morning about the war in Mexico. (At first, George thought the delivery kid had left them a copy of *El Diario* by mistake.) Subcomandante Marcos, the leader of the Zapatista rebellion, had made a startling announcement during an interview yesterday with MTV News. Ever since his rebellion began in 1994, Subcomandante Marcos, a former graphic design professor, has been a self-consciously postmodern revolutionary. Sometimes his official communiqués are written in the ancient Aztec language Nahuatl, sometimes they quote Hamlet, and they often include the salutation, *"¡Andale, ándale! ¡Arriba, arriba!"* For a time, he even called himself Speedy Gonzalez, after the cartoon character. When the war heated up last spring and he received a stern letter at his secret mountain headquarters from the Warner Bros. legal department, reminding him that Speedy Gonzalez is a trademarked Looney Tunes character owned by Time Warner, he called in a CNN crew and a *Time* magazine reporter. He said into the CNN camera, "Trademark? Trademark? We don't need no steenkin' trademark!" then laughed and announced that "as a gesture of reasonableness" he was changing his nickname to Roadrunner. Yesterday, on the eve of the seventh anniversary of the beginning of his uprising, he held another press conference, outside the town of Polho, Mexico. He thanked the youth of North America for their financial and moral support of the rights of Mexico's oppressed people ("in particular, one noble teenage girl who has been so very generous to our struggle"). And he announced that the Zapatista Front of National Liberation was declaring a unilateral sixty-day cease-fire. Furthermore, Subcomandante Marcos said, his group is now ready to begin good-faith negotiations with the Mexican government (which C-SPAN has agreed to broadcast live, twenty-four hours a day), leading toward what he called "the territorial autonomy we require, our 2001 space odyssey." He said the new spirit of reconciliation was prompted by a hundred-million-dollar donation his group received last week from an anonymous "enlightened Wall Street capitalist" in New York City.

Lying on his stomach in front of the fireplace, George sees in the Sunday *Times* that both Subcomandante Marcos and the Global Computer Generation Y—symbolized by Willibald, Humfried, and Fanny—were runners-up for *Time*'s Man of the Year. He is pleased (and, at the same time, the tiniest bit disappointed) to see that neither in the paper's extensive year-in-review coverage of the Microsoft hoax nor of the Manson parole debacle is George Mactier mentioned at all, just as Lizzie wasn't mentioned in the Business section story about Intel's acquisition of Terraplane, which she had helped broker. Hank Saddler's plea in federal court last week is, of course, the kicker to the *Times*'s Microsoft-hacker story—the paper says that Henry Saddler may be the first white-collar criminal defendant in history to plead not guilty by reason of temporary insanity.

Lizzie, closer to the fire and sitting with her arms wrapped around her knees, is staring, her thoughts roaming in a post-lunch, long-holiday-weekend, absolute-last-day-of-the-millennium drift. LuLu has carefully propped up around the living room every Christmas card they received, as she did last year, but to have enough space this year, she required the Corbu coffee table and both Shaker end tables as well as the mantelpiece. So many are family portraits, Lizzie notices—but black-and-white, as maximum tastefulness now requires. They received several what-the-family-has-been-doing-all-year holiday form letters, like the corny ones Edith Hope used to send out every year, except that all of their friends' versions wink at themselves, in one way or another apologizing for indulging in the custom—neo-corn.

She remarks on the unusual number of cards. George nods and keeps reading.

"What I mean is, doesn't it make you feel good?" she says. "That with all the crap about us in the papers, people are using the opportunity to reach out and say, 'We're thinking of you'?"

George looks up and smiles skeptically at his wife. He says, " 'We're thinking of you, because now you're infamous, and we want to feel like friends of celebrities, even though you're celebrated for being suspected criminal coconspirators, because the crime is so sexy.' That doesn't make me feel *bad*. But I wouldn't attribute all the cards entirely to an outpouring of spirituality and good will, no."

"I hadn't thought of that at all," she says, looking at the fire, not quite smiling. "What an unsentimental prick you are."

"That's why you love me," he says, throwing the A section aside and belly-crawling the four feet across the rug to put his head in her lap, "that's part of my pluckiness."

She puts a hand on his temple and stares into the fireplace. The fire is hot on his face. "So, Señor Plucky," she says, "how long would the film take you to do, do you really think?"

"A month? Two? I don't know. Maybe longer. Depends what it turns out to be." George is leaving Tuesday for a week in Mexico, laying the groundwork for a documentary he plans to make about Zapatista teenagers as an MTV-PBS coproduction, to be partially underwritten by Benetton. He's taking Sarah with him, since she's on winter break.

"I need to get a real job, you know. We don't exactly have fuck-you money."

Her 498,000 shares of Mose Media Holdings stock vested on the twenty-ninth, the day before yesterday, and she promptly sold them all, as she has always planned to do. She planned, however, to cash out for $24 million (the value of her shares in June, when the deal was done), or for $11 million (the value on Christmas Day, before the Chapter 11 announcement), not for only $2.181 million.

"I guess the money said 'Fuck you,' " George says. He turns over on his back and looks up at his wife's face. "Hey, I canceled the lease on the Aston Martin. That's twenty-three hundred dollars a month right there. Seriously, won't the interest on your two million cover the nut for a while? The house, food, the car, tuition? There's also my *Real Time* settlement and your consulting money from Bruce and Buster, plus we have the *NARCS* royalty. If it lasts."

She looks down at him. "I gave the St. Andrew's fund two thousand dollars this year, by the way."

"Protection money," George says. "Good thinking."

"We'll get by. I should clean up the lunch mess so we're out of the caterers' way when they get here. When're your sister and Cubby coming over? Get off, my leg's falling asleep."

"Kiss me first. Not until three. He had a run-through at St. Patrick's."

Cubby and Ben's religious light-and-magic business, the Guild, is having its American debut tonight at St. Patrick's Cathedral. ("Spectacle of the Spirit" is being cosponsored by Lincoln-Mercury and Versace.) George and Lizzie will go to the early show, then come home for the traditional New Year's Eve dinner party.

Lizzie leans down, yogilike, and smooches him quick and sloppy, then bobs up, slides his head to the floor, and stands. "You should put out the thing, their gift," Lizzie says. Alice and Cubby's Christmas present to George and Lizzie is a Home Again reproduction of a red-white-and-yellow turn-of-the-century carnival ring-toss game that looks like a Jasper Johns painting. Unbeknownst to Alice and Cubby, Zip copied it from an antique carnival ring-toss game that George and Lizzie have hanging in the house on Lake Marten.

"Alice actually thanked me yesterday," George tells her, sitting up, "for connecting Cubby to Ben. I almost cried. I think it's the first time she's ever thanked me for anything in her life."

"What did she ever have to thank you for before?" Lizzie says on her way down to the kitchen.

"*I'm* the unsentimental prick?" he replies, trailing after her.

"George, what are those boxes in the closet under the stoop? Are those presents you forgot to give?"

"No." He shouldn't lie. Even the small lies can be trouble. "It's some sporting goods I bought during, you know, in August. I'm returning them."

She turns to look at him. She is stunned. *"Sporting goods?"*

"And other stuff. You don't want to know."

In the boxes are: a Maptrek, a GPS device for skiers that records their paths and speed, but which George planned to hide somehow on Lizzie's person in order to track her movements; a GPS "vehicle locator" that attaches to the car phone, which was to have been a redundant backup system to the Maptrek; and something called Walker's Game Ear, which hunters use to amplify the sounds of deer flanks rustling bush boughs and hooves crackling dried leaves from a hundred yards away. George never developed a specific plan for using the Game Ear, but it only cost $179.99.

"George Mactier purchases sporting goods. *There's* a clinical definition of insanity. You're sure you didn't also buy the pistol?"

He puts his arms around her and grinds himself into her. "Ready to fire."

The phone rings.

"That's probably the kids," Lizzie says. "*Antichrist!* lets out at two-something and you're supposed to pick them up."

"Hello? . . . This is he." He gives Lizzie a funny look, opening his mouth and popping his eyes. Then, "Hello! This must be the longest game of phone tag in history."

Lizzie stares at him, trying to guess the identity of the caller by interpolation.

"Sure," he says into the phone. "No, that's okay. . . . I do remember. . . . No, Harold never did. Uh-huh . . . Uh-huh . . . No, I know you do. . . . Well, I'm afraid I've got bad news. . . . It's real. I don't wear a toupee. . . . Well, whatever you call them. . . . Nope. . . . Right. . . . I understand. No problem. . . . No . . . Really? . . . I hope we can. . . . You have a happy New Year too. Bye-bye." He hangs up. He looks at her, grinning and dismayed. "Guess."

"I have no fucking idea."

"Michael Milken. He said he admired my hairpiece 'tremendously' when we met at that party a year ago, and hasn't stopped thinking about how 'authentic' it looked. He said ever since, he's wanted to know who my 'vendor' is."

Lizzie shakes her head.

"He also said, 'I hope you can come to my little party for Nancy McNabb and Harold.' Apparently *Nancy's* left *Roger* for *Mose*."

––––––––

"When the two angels flew in at the end and landed on the altar," Daisy Moore Granger is saying to Cubby Koplowitz and Lizzie, "I thought, 'Clever. Very nice.' But then when they started *glowing,* and then sort of became that blue light that filled the whole nave, and then the thunder and whirling noise—I tell you, I actually felt like kneeling. And I'm not Catholic."

Lizzie wonders for a second, almost unconsciously, like a fragrance on a stray breeze: *Did my husband sleep with you?*

"And that's not even state-of-the-art, holography-wise," Cubby tells Daisy. "At the mosque in Chicago next month, as a surprise to everyone at the conclusion of the service, we're going to have the prophet mingle among the congregation."

"So," Lizzie asks her brother-in-law, "you and Ben really have a shot at getting Bill Clinton to be your cemetery anchorman?"

At the other end of the table, Bruce Helms's girlfriend, a university-press book editor named Agnes who has annoyed everyone all night long, is talking past Warren Holcombe (whose book, *The Modernist Madnesses,* she once declined to publish) to Ben Gould's date, a young Englishwoman named Caroline Osborne—the prettiest person in the room by far and, as it happens, Gloria Mose's daughter.

"What is the official term for the kinds of articles your magazine prints," Agnes says to Caroline, "is it gossip, or celebrity confession, what?"

"Journalism is the official term," Caroline says. "But I suppose you could call it 'cultural studies primary texts,' couldn't you?"

Bruce's girlfriend aside, the dinner is going well. The standard gaiety is bound up tonight with a complicated sense of gravity. Almost everyone at the table feels it, as they eat and drink and flirt and chatter, this sense of some new hybrid sentiment seeping over them. It's not fear, or giddiness. Is it cheerful rue? Is it wonder? Imminence or immanence or both? What they're feeling, one of them thinks (or maybe several of them), is a mood of respite rather than of completion, pausing here in the middle of the expedition to trade stories and collect thoughts. They've learned the queer new truth that the best way to move between two points isn't always a short, straight line (FedEx and satellites carry urgent messages thousands of miles to move them ten), that any of the zigs or zags may be important. Most of the men and women here have been out on the trail long enough now to understand that the wild beasts do bite and the quicksand kills—that every special effect in life is real—but also that their good luck so far impels them to go back out for more, together and apart, after tonight. Where to? Nobody knows. The road ahead isn't necessarily a road, as everyone in this room should realize by now.

" 'All clichés turn out to be true,' that's what Lizzie's always said." George is reassuring Jess Burnham about her plans to adopt a Korean infant. Jess joked that she would be committing two clichés in one—adoptive lesbian mother and transracial adoptee. "Anyhow, you're now a gay CBS News anchor—that's a total non-cliché, I think."

"If you keep repeating 'All clichés are true' at every *whipstitch,* Mactier," Zip Ingram leans over to say, "*that's* going to turn into a cliché as well."

"Which would be perfect, right?" says Pollyanna Chang from Zip's other side. "Then it can become the final cliché, the ultimate cliché."

"We don't have an English word for *cliché,* do we?" George says. "I mean, with *cliché,* shouldn't Americans be like the Eskimos, with their twenty words for snow and ice?"

"Actually," says Bruce's date, Agnes, who specializes in books with titles that contain colons, "that's a kind of racist myth—this idea that there are so many different words among the Arctic indigenous peoples for ice and snow. And so, right there you have an example of a cliché that is *not* true." She smiles just enough to indicate how pleased she is with her cavil.

Lizzie, three people away, cannot resist coming to George's defense.

"Actually," says George Mactier's anthropology-major wife, leaning in front of both Warren Holcombe and Emily Kalman, "in the language spoken by Greenland's Eskimos (who are the only Eskimos I know anything about) there really *are* a huge number of different words for ice and snow." When Agnes reacts with a doubtful little smile, Lizzie adds, "At least according to Fortescue, in *West Greenlandic,"* and then returns to her conversation with Francesca Mahoney.

"So," Lizzie says, "you really think MTV might want to help out with Sarah's new project?"

"I do," Francesca says. "I'm going to talk to them about it on Tuesday." Sarah and her friend Felipe are organizing a thematically driven, site-specific multimedia performance piece (their phrase) to be performed simultaneously by a hundred cyberpornographic "actors" around the world. Sarah and Felipe would write dozens of simple commands in advance—"Stroke your left breast," "Suck your thumb," "Shake your hair," "Bend forward," "Frown," and so on—which would be delivered electronically in a random sequence for ten minutes to all hundred performers at once. The idea is for the hundred naked men and women, sitting in front of a hundred video cameras in a hundred different grotty cubicles all over the world, to obey each instruction in unison. All hundred images would be shown together on a giant patchwork of monitors—ideally, Sarah and Felipe think, on the video-wall skin of the Viacom building in Times Square.

"I think it's so cool that you support her on this," Francesca says, "since she's only, like, what . . . ?"

"Fifteen next month," says Lizzie, rolling her eyes, "and believe me, I really wish she had something else she was this passionate about. I'm prepared to be completely embarrassed if this happens. Probably even disgusted. But it is an interesting project, isn't it?"

Zip stands and dings his glass. "Since everyone else here is too bloody cool to properly salute the beginning of the new millennium—"

"Hey!" Ben Gould shouts, "enough with the two-thousandth-birthday crap, you anti-Semite. You're making Zimbalist and me feel bad."

George looks at Lizzie smiling at Ben and wonders, in some theoretical microscopic sense: *Did she ever sleep with him?*

Rehoisting his glass, Zip resumes, "A toast, then, Mr. *Gould,* to the conclusion of the fin de siècle—"

"Rerun! Rerun!" Ben says.

"Zip," George agrees, "that *is* exactly the same thing you said, standing right there, a year ago tonight."

"All right, then," Zip says, suddenly more pleased with himself than ever, "a toast: to this fin de *sequel.*" People groan. "May we all continue to have the strength to live in these interesting times."

Glasses are raised, cheers mumbled. George stands.

"I have two toasts," he says. "No, three."

"No need, George," Emily Kalman says.

"Don't worry, Emily," he replies, getting a laugh. "First, to Elizabeth Zimbalist, who allowed me this year to discover all by myself the differences between fact and fiction." No one but Lizzie (and Warren) is quite sure what he means, but there is a sentimental hum of *awwwwwws* around the table, as there is for any modern husband's sincere public display of uxoriousness. "And also to my brother-in-law, Cubby Koplowitz," he says, "who showed me one afternoon last winter that it's possible to construct a world in a room no bigger than this, a strange and perfect little world that doesn't need to be test-marketed or sold. In a garage, in St. Paul, Minnesota. Thank you, Cubby." No one but Lizzie and Cubby and Alice (who is choking up) has any idea at all what this means, but it sounds eloquent, so they smile and say cheers. "And to Ben Gould, for finally giving my brother-in-law the wherewithal to test-market and sell all of his other nutty, appalling ideas."

The teasing relaxes the room. Ben stands.

"And to Zip Ingram," George continues, "for providing me with a lovely padded cell on wheels, for a month this fall."

"Hey!" Ben says, "that's *four,* toast hog. Sit down. Tonight, I want to salute all the weasels in the world"—as Lizzie's eyes lock onto George's, he shrugs—"to forgive them their trespasses against us. Because there but for the grace of God go I. And sometimes there *go* I."

Before the laughter subsides, Ben's heartbreakingly gorgeous date stands. Turning to stare at her in her astonishing Versace dress, the men at the table lock their smiles from a second ago in order to disguise their plain pig yearning, every one of them, for Caroline Osborne.

"I want to thank you all so much for letting me crash your dinner. And in particular, our hosts. George and Lizzie," she says, smiling warmly, "at the risk of being . . . well, risky, let me say, as someone with long personal experience being both expensively provided for *and* rather brutally manhandled by the charming Mr. Harold Mose, I feel as though you and I have something very much in common. To George and Lizzie."

Racy metaphor? Literal fact? Too much champagne? In any event, the other guests now have something to discuss among themselves for the remainder of the millennium.

5 1

Just after midnight on New Year's Eve, Max came running down to announce breathlessly that one of his twenty-three tickets in the MegaMillennium drawing was only a single digit away from the billion-dollar winning number that was drawn in Las Vegas on TV. Max was excited and pleased by his proximity to fortune, even though his luck won him absolutely nothing. "Close, and a cigar," Zip Ingram said to him, stuffing a Carrington Robusto into Max's shirt pocket. But the MegaMillennium moment, as a reminder of real life's long-odds all-or-nothing disappointments, its black-or-white disparities, took some of the fizz out of the grownups' mood.

A day and a half later, Max is still looking at his almost-winning ticket, touching it, deciding how he'll mount and frame it. George left with Sarah for the airport two hours ago to catch the nine-thirty flight to Mexico City (*2001,* he thought as he stepped into the Saarinen terminal at JFK), but he's calling home from the plane just after takeoff.

"I can see you!" George says excitedly as soon as Lizzie picks up. "We're circling sort of low around the tip of the island, and I really think I can actually make out the house. I'm serious! I wish you guys had time to run up to the roof, and, *what—*"

On the phone, Lizzie hears a popping noise, not loud to her but loud, it sounds like, on the plane.

"George? What was that? *George?*" She hears a woman talking, loud and frantic, in the background.

"Jesus, sweetie," George says, his voice worried as it starts to dwindle into static, "we just *dropped,* I guess it was an air pocket, but— whoa, *fuck*! There's another one. It's all right, Sarah. Lizzie, I love you, you know I—"

The connection is broken. On the plane, George hangs up the phone and holds his daughter's hand, and remembers what Zip said to him as he was passing out in the helicopter flying over northern Nicaragua, thinking he was about to die: *Can you still hear me, George, because you're alive if you can hear me—hearing's the last to go, after sight and taste and smell and touch . . .*

On the ground, inside her home, Lizzie hears nothing. She hears nothing. Does she want to look? Can she bear to watch? She puts the phone down and walks away quickly, LuLu at her heels.

"What is it, Mommy? Where are you going?"

"Daddy and Sarah's plane." She opens the front door. "I need to go see if I can see."

"Mommy? You know what?" LuLu says with absolute conviction as they step outside into the shocking January cold.

"What?" Lizzie says, hurrying onto the cobblestones, looking up into the southern sky.

"They're not dying."

ACKNOWLEDGMENTS

David Remnick and Tina Brown, who gave me time off from my work for *The New Yorker,* were models of benevolence.

Bruce Birenboim, Bob Brienza, Carolyn Meinel, Tom Phillips, and David Owen were unstinting with their advice, although the expertise and chance comments of many people (among them Andy Aaron, Katherine Andersen, Lucy Andersen, David Black, Tom Brokaw, Holly Brubach, Graydon Carter, Eric Ellenbogen, Bruce Feirstein, Kim France, Jeff Frank, Deb Futter, Rob Glaser, Bruce Handy, Lynn Hirschberg, Michael Hirschorn, Tibor Kalman, Peter Kaminsky, Michael Kinsley, Gerry Laybourne, Kit Laybourne, Guy Martin, Patty Marx, Susanna Moore, Susan Morrison, Susan Mulcahy, Patrick Naughton, Lawrence O'Donnell, George Rohr, Ilene Saul, Strat Sherman, Ozzie Stiffelman, and Kit White) helped make these fictions ring truer.

Henry Finder, Beth Pearson, and Diana Donovan provided essential editorial guidance.

Four friends—Jim Cramer, Leslee Dart, Joanne Gruber, and Paul Simms—shared their knowledge with a generosity that bordered on excess. And the faith and enthusiasm of Suzanne Gluck and Ann Godoff, from beginning to end, were simply indispensable.

ABOUT THE AUTHOR

KURT ANDERSEN writes for *The New Yorker*. He was co-founder and editor of *Spy* magazine, and editor in chief of *New York* magazine. At *Time,* he was a writer on crime and politics, and for eight years the magazine's architecture and design critic. He has also created and produced several network television programs, and co-wrote *Loose Lips,* a satirical stage revue. *Turn of the Century* is his first novel. Andersen lives with his wife and daughters in New York City.

ABOUT THE TYPE

This book was set in Bembo, a typeface based on an old-style Roman face that was used for Cardinal Bembo's tract *De Aetna* in 1495. Bembo was cut by Francisco Griffo in the early sixteenth century. The Lanston Monotype Machine Company of Philadelphia brought the well-proportioned letter forms of Bembo to the United States in the 1930s.